Yours "for life"

Marty Salotto

The Last Generation

by
Marty Galotto

DORRANCE PUBLISHING CO., INC.
PITTSBURGH, PENNSYLVANIA 15222

ISBN # 0-8059-4635-7
Printed in the United States of America

First Printing

For information or to order additional books, please write:
Dorrance Publishing Co., Inc.
643 Smithfield Street
Pittsburgh, Pennsylvania 15222
U.S.A.
1-800-788-7654

"The adversaries of the Lord shall be broken to pieces; out of heaven shall he thunder upon them; the Lord shall judge the ends of the earth; and he shall give strength unto his king, and exalt the horn of his anointed." 1 SAMUEL 2:10

"Thou shalt be visited of the Lord of hosts with thunder, and with earthquake, and great noise, with storm and tempest, and the flame of devouring fire." ISAIAH 29:6

"This is an age of the world when nations are trembling and convulsed. A mighty influence is abroad, surging and heaving the world, as with earthquake. And is America safe? Every nation that carries in its bosom great and unredressed injustice has in it the elements of this last convulsion.

"For what is this mighty influence thus rousing in all nations and languages those groanings that cannot be uttered . . . is not this power the spirit of Him whose kingdom is yet to come, and whose will be done on earth as it is in heaven . . . and he shall break in pieces the oppressor . . . for, not surer is the eternal law by which the millstone sinks in the ocean, than the stronger law, by which injustice and cruelty shall bring on nations the wrath of Almighty God!"

Harriet Beecher Stowe, from *Uncle Tom's Cabin*

"Woe to you if you do not succeed in defending life." Pope John Paul II, August 15, 1993, Denver, Colorado.

To my children and to yours.

Marty Galotto

Contents

Prologue

Driving toward the hospital, her heart was breaking. She never thought anything could hurt so bad. He had always seemed invincible to her, since he had first started to develop his own personality when she held him in her arms as a baby, and all the way through his childhood as he grew in determination and strength.

What kind of horror must have tormented him as he raced toward the hospital at breakneck speeds to try and save the life of his child?

If he dies, I don't think I'll be able to take it, she thought. Why couldn't he be as plain and ordinary as every other young man from Indian Springs, Connecticut? Why did he have to be so intense in everything he did, put himself on the line all the time for everybody else, so far out on every limb that nobody else could ever save him?

His bedroom at home had that air about it. The screw was always tightened. The stakes were always so high. Martin Luther King and Bobby Sands in pictures on his walls, and Jesus Christ staring over Jerusalem the night before His entry. Boxing gloves hanging over pictures of his father, his grandfather, and his great-grandfather, all in the middle of fights. The unnamed Indian staring stoically over the valley. And that single picture of a candle burning at both ends, the only picture he hung that she never understood.

Turning into the driveway of the hospital, she shuddered as she thought of the times he'd disappear for days on end when he was a boy smaller than her, in his pre-teens when other boys still needed babysitters. It was many years later that they solved that mystery quite by accident. Some investigative reporter spotted his picture sitting at ringside of one of Homer Jones' fights, and looking back over the tapes of all of his fights, he had spotted him again, at ringside of every one of Jones' fights, whether they were in New Orleans, Miami, Philadelphia, or anywhere else in the country.

He had never told anyone where he had gone, not her, not the police, the school psychologist, or anybody. He'd just go off on his own and end up at ringside, staring at Homer Jones with that same indomitable stare, the same one he looked out of his hospital bed with, at the God-awful red building next door to his room, as though he were trying to force his will on the mortar and bricks.

Why, Kevin, why?

Even reaching for the stick shift to put her Mustang in park was an effort for her, as she thought about the emotion she knew would soon start sweeping over her as she made her way through the crowds to his door. It twisted her heart a little more as she thought of what it was that she would say to him today. Nothing else had worked. There had to be some magic words, she thought, even though she knew in her heart of hearts that there were none.

Oh, God, it was Bobby Kennedy whom he had admired the most, she suddenly remembered, and the reason why made her shudder. Plain as day she remembered the day Kevin had run up to her and shown her Bobby's picture laying in the grass, that big loving smile spread across his face, hugging one of his children.

"Look, Ma. Look at this, and listen to what they say here about him. He has ten children, and one on the way, and despite all his other duties, he gives no less than fifteen minutes of prime time every day to each one of his kids. You think that's true, Ma? You think we can believe that? I believe it anyway."

She saw him then, in her mind's eye, bounding away to put the picture in the scrapbook he kept of Bobby. She thought it would crush him when they killed him, but all it did was make him angry. The deaths of JFK and Martin Luther King had hurt him, as it had hurt his father, the two of them sitting together somberly on the sofa, watching the funerals on TV. But the death of Bobby just made him mad.

He never cried during Teddy's eulogy of his brother, even though his father used up two handkerchiefs during that part of the funeral alone. He never cried at all, just glued himself to the TV and shut the world out, especially when they showed the sea of people that came out to meet the train carrying Bobby's body to his rest.

It was the eleven kids that Kevin was most amazed about and the individual time that Bobby had given to each of them. *He wanted eleven kids himself,* she thought, and that was the first time that day that she reached up to wipe her eyes.

She knew, even then, that Kevin was going to be a big man physically. He had huge hands, bigger than his father's, which had always made Sean proud. When he boxed away at the punching bags, you could feel the concussions. *Ring* magazine noted the size of his hands.

She was getting closer to the hospital now, and her mind raced to the Democratic convention, and all the key players lining up behind Bill Clinton and his pro-choice political posturing. They were all pro-choice now, Bill Clinton, Al Gore, Jesse Jackson, Ted Kennedy, Richard Gephardt, every single one that had ever had any presidential ambitions. And every single one of them had at one time been pro-life.

Kevin had stood right up during the convention and laughed sarcastically at the hypocrisy.

"Where is the one Democrat, male or female, with enough political courage to be pro-life?" he said. "The first one who emerges will win the Kennedy Profiles in Courage Award and get into the White House as well. Honest to God, Dad must be rolling over in his grave, the way these Democrats are abandoning their consciences for votes."

Kevin had always listened to his father intently, Colleen thought, and tried so hard to learn how he thought so he could be just like him.

But it was too late for any of that now.

She was reminded of what he had said to her a few days before, and it scared her. *If he dies, the link breaks between past and future. As long as he is still alive, there is still a bridge to the future, but that is precisely what he is being so stubborn about. Millions of people have died already in this country in the years since January 22, 1973. And because of the terrible turn of events, that is what his life has become all about.*

She shook her head in anger as she remembered the media coverage on the night of his arrest:

"Shots were fired in Indian Springs, Connecticut, today, when police arrested an enraged man who had assaulted a doctor and a nurse inside an abortion clinic in that small New England town. A pro-life rally erupted in violence, triggering the arrest of several people as protesters fought with state police."

It was so far away from the truth of what had happened that day that she could not believe the news reporters could legally get away with it. They didn't tell the whole story, only the sensational parts, coloring it with their own liberal interpretations of what had actually happened.

If they only knew the Kevin O'Hara I know, Colleen thought, *and the history of the men he was descended from, men who had fought for and built the country he is now dying for.*

Her heart tightened a little as she opened the door to her car. *This time I won't cry when I walk through them,* she vowed.

She got out of the car and several men rushed to help her.

"It's okay," she said, waving them off. "I'm fine."

People raised their fists in solidarity as she made her way through them to the door. Signs and placards supporting him greeted her as the crowd parted quietly and respectfully to let her through.

His family built this hospital, she thought angrily. *The events that led up to his imprisonment should never have happened. Not in the United States of America. Not to this boy.*

He has the strength of all of the boxers and soldiers in his remarkable ancestry, and he is not the character they're making him out to be. He has his own indomitable spirit, and the way he is prepared to die for his country should be earning him praise, not derision.

Maybe his decision is not yet cast in concrete, she hoped against hope, and she shuddered as she thought of the ramifications for the country if it was.

President Bush had called him America's best and said how proud he was of him. How America had gone through such a glorious era and degenerated to such a pitiful state saddened and scared her. How could it have all come unraveled in such a short time frame? she asked herself. *From the birth of the nation, to the great melting pot, leading to the promised land so many men and women of character had helped to shape, to this?*

And why, of all the people in America, did this cup have to be passed to him. Hadn't he had enough sorrow and tragedy in his life already?

He's at the mercy of weak men and thoughtless women, she thought to herself angrily, *and he's the strongest and most caring person I've ever known.*

If he dies, I don't think I'll be able to take it, Colleen thought to herself as the crowd parted to let her through to him. *I have to try again to reason with him,* she thought. *I have to. There are so many bloodlines that will die with him if he goes, bloodlines that go back forever to Italy and to Ireland; and to way back before his ancestors, John and Priscilla Alden, set foot on the shores of the new world, to several generations before the Indians knew about the strange white men out of the sea, when the only people in the valley he lay dying in were the Indians.*

Part 1

The Birth of a Nation

In the clear open field that led up the hill to the forest from the river, the grass waved and rippled like a great green flag stretched out along the ground. Where the grass met the forest, paths led in and out, and the people trickled out in small groups, dressed in brightly colored furs and feathers and draped in hand-woven blankets.

From every direction they drifted in onto the flatlands by the riverbed where two Algonquians eyed one another tentatively across the clearing. The Massacoes were there, along with the Siwanogs, the Paugussetts, the Quinnipiacs, the Wangunks, the Menunkatucks, the Hammonassets, the Nehantics, the Uncas, the Sicaogs, the Mohegans, the Nipmucks, the Podunks, the Agawams, the Poquonocks, the Tunxis, and the Pequots.

With the crowds growing behind each warrior, their stalking, bobbing and posturing became more and more aggressive as chants broke out concurrently behind each combatant at the powwow.

The chant started out high-pitched and wailing and lowered in tone until it ended on a low, even monotone. Several people on both sides joined in as lone drummers pounded on deerskin drums behind the bobbing, dancing combatants.

"Ay-yah, ay-e-yah, hey-ya, ay-yah, ay-e-ya, hey-ya, ay-yah, ay-e-yah, hey-ya, ay-yah, ay-e-yaaah. . . ."

The battle chant spread through the crowd in rounds as one by one individuals or small groups would start chanting at the top of their lungs and continue on until the end of the chant, the chorus calling more and more spectators out of the forest.

For three days the warriors from the many tribes of the Algonquian nation had been drinking the iron and sulfur mineral water from the natural springs in the valley, and their red skin glistened with the sweat their lively dancing had brought out of their primed and muscular bodies.

Suddenly the Agawam charged the Poquonock across the gap, and the Poquonock met his charge headlong across the clearing. When the two men crashed together in the center of the clearing, the drums and the chanting stopped and they became entangled in a dusty mass of flesh and sinews, and the chanting sounds were replaced by grunting and yipping from the combatants, who battled furiously in front of their people.

In a few moments the Poquonock lifted the Agawam up and drove him into the ground, pinning him on his back. An older red man shouted out a command and pointed at the Poquonock, and the young warrior stood and looked skyward, yipping and yelling out victoriously and flexing his glistening muscles in the afternoon sunlight.

The Agawam gathered himself together and slowly made his way back up the hill on the northwest side of the river and back through his people into the forest. No one spoke to him or made eye contact with him as he walked through them toward his wigwam. There he would be left alone with one squaw who would tend to his wounds quietly as he began the long healing process that would lead ultimately to the next challenge.

On the northernmost point of the wrestling arena the old Mohegan sachem sat quietly and mentally recorded the score as the ritual was repeated with points piling up for every tribe leading up to the grand finale match between the top warriors of the two most successful tribes.

At that moment, in the seaport of Genoa, Italy, a weaver named Colombo sat combing out wool and praying for his son who had been out to sea for over two weeks. He wondered somberly about his son's fate, while out in the middle of the great heaving ocean, young Christoforo manned the helm of the largest of the three small ships that drifted along toward India.

At 2 A.M. on the morning of October 12, 1492, while the red man slept, a lookout on the *Pinta* yelled "Land ho!" Christoforo arose and set his eyes on the moonlit Bahama island he named San Salvador.

Thousands of men that Colombo called *Indians* lived all across the wide expanses of the land he believed to be the East Indies, but no Indian nation lived in a more breathtakingly beautiful forest land than the great Algonquian nation of the area the white man called New England over a hundred years later.

Because of its distance from the equator, there was a marked difference between the four seasons each year, and each season had its own very particular beauty. Perhaps the most satisfying of the four seasons in the land the Algonquians called home was autumn, when the brilliant colored leaves painted the land in remarkable beauty, and no Indian alive that year could be expected to know that autumn was approaching in the life span of the Indian, as well.

Before they even knew the white man existed, their days of dominance in this last frontier of the world were numbered. Had they known that, they probably would have appreciated all the more that forest land a hundred miles inland from the ocean, where two crystal clear mountain streams bubbled down through the valley to join and form the river the Indians called the *We-Am-An-Tuck*.

For centuries the friendly and peaceful fresh water fishermen who lived there, the Nip-A-Maugs, shortened later to "Nipmucks" by the colonists, had roamed the hills of this, their homeland, hunting the abundant wildlife that filled the forests, and fishing the We-Am-An-Tuck for the plentiful salmon and shad.

The abundance of wildlife and the hospitable nature of the Nipmucks brought several tribes together there on the banks of the We-Am-An-Tuck every spring and fall. Their springtime caucus was necessary for self-preservation, because the sheer numbers congregated there when they met saved them when they were invariably attacked each spring by the confederacy consisting of the Cayuga, the Cherokee, the Erie, the Mohawk, the Oneida, the Onondaga, the Seneca, and the Tuscarora Sachemdoms of the great Iroquois nation which lived west of the big river.

Autumn's gathering was for a much more enjoyable reason, for that was when the great wrestling matches were held. Tribal representatives were designated to wrestle with braves of equal size to build their endurance for real war with the Iroquois.

Each autumn the strongest Indians of each tribe who had won representative rights through intertribal victories carried their tribe's colors into the wrestling tournaments of the Nipmuck land which, because of the remarkable medicinal quality of the spring waters there, the Indian called *Medicine Springs*.

As far back as the Indian could remember, the host tribe, the Nipmucks, seemed to dominate the wrestling matches, and the other tribes reasoned that it was because the Nipmucks drank the lively water all year round.

One spring, in the year 1618, the Nipmucks were very puzzled when no coastal tribe appeared for over two weeks into the season. Every evening the Nipmuck tribal leaders would gather their people together for talks with the great spirit to ask him where their brothers had gone, and every setting sun, when the Nipmucks retired for the night, one ear was kept cocked for any sound of their arrival out of the great forest.

Dawn broke quietly every morning over the great forest. Before the Nipmucks stirred, the small birds would awaken the land with their singing and the great eagle would soar high above the Nipmuck camp, silently scanning the horizon for his prey. In the meadow, the rabbit nibbled on wild herbs and gave no thought to the giant predator that soared silently, high above the land. No noise distracted the hunter or the hunted. Guns did not exist, nor did factories, nor machinery of any type, and the only other sound besides the singing of the birds was that of the river that rushed over the boulders where the two smaller rivers met to form the We-Am-An-Tuck in the valley.

Suddenly and silently, the giant predator swept down, and at the last moment the rabbit sensed great fear and started to bolt toward the forest, digging his feet into the ground and dashing back and forth in a random pattern toward the safety of the forest.

But the rabbit was no match for the eagle, and when the predator's claws dug deeply into the rabbit's flesh, the rabbit screamed. The eagle carried him high above the meadow and into his nest in the high stone mountains. Then, when the sun began to warm the land, the Nipmucks emerged from their wigwams and headed for the clean, fresh river for an early morning swim.

On the first morning of the third week after the other tribes were overdue, when the spring flowers were in full bloom, a lone Pequot walked into the Nipmuck camp with a mournful tale of a great plague that had killed one of every three Pequots over the winter.

The Nipmucks were shocked and saddened, as well as puzzled, and the Pequot stayed only one day to refresh himself before returning to his shoreline home. For the next week the Nipmucks wandered about their camp in great bewilderment, wondering what had caused such an unheralded plague to strike their brothers.

A week later they got their answer. White Fox, a messenger of the great Wampanoag sachem, Massasoit, arrived at the Nipmuck camp and requested a meeting with the tribal elders. That night, with a great feast spread before them, the Nipmucks lay their blankets around the campfire and listened frightfully as White Fox described the horrible rashes, high fevers, and thrashing deaths that strange white-skinned traders had brought to the Indian on their strange boats out of the sea.

None of the Indians had ever heard of smallpox, or measles, or any of the other European diseases to which they lacked immunity, and many died before even hearing about the strange white-skinned messengers of death that wandered into Indian camps smiling, only to leave their calling card of disease and death.

That night the Nipmucks slept restlessly, and the next morning when their sachem awoke, he emerged from his wigwam and watched the morning ritual of the eagle and the rabbit.

The only difference between this morning and every other was that this time the chief paid closer attention to the rabbit than ever before. He had always watched the eagle before.

▲   ▼   ▲

Many miles to the east of Medicine Springs, in the area of Plymouth, Massachusetts, the Wampanoags already knew about the white man because they had seen him before. In fact, well before the first pilgrims landed in Provincetown Harbor and went on to settle in Plymouth in 1620, the great Wampanoag sachem, Massasoit, was already prepared for his coming.

Massasoit was forty years old in 1620, and he had already realized that the only way for him to save his tribe from the English was to befriend them. The realization had not come easily to the sage warrior, counter of many coups, or victories, in tribal warfare, nor had it been an overnight decision, but Massasoit had ruled the Wampanoags with wisdom more than might, and he was very much afraid of the threat to his people presented by the strange white man out of the sea.

Massasoit already had a very formidable enemy to the west in the Iroquois, and the last thing he needed now was a new enemy out of the eastern sea. His fears of the white man were not unfounded. In the six years that had passed between 1614 when Captain John Smith had explored the land of New England and the 1620 landing of the pilgrims, over eight thousand Indians between the Penobscot River and Narraganset Bay had died of the same plague that had kept the Pequots out of Medicine Springs in 1618.

While the Nipmucks seemed surprised that plagues of that magnitude could have happened, Massasoit had seen them, and he was very concerned. He knew that the plague had been brought to the Indians by the white coastal explorers whose reports of this beautiful new world had led the Mayflower pilgrims to emigrate from England to escape the religious intolerance of the old world.

He also knew that if the white men could survive these plagues, then they must have the medicines to cure them, and he knew that he had to have those medicines because the Indians' very existence was at stake. It did not take much thought to realize that if only a handful of white men had started these massive plagues, the Indians would be in serious trouble when the masses came. And he knew full well that the masses were coming. He knew this because of reports brought back to him from England by a remarkable brave named Tisquantum. In an ominous warning, Tisquantum told Massasoit that many thousands more were on their way.

Tisquantum had been kidnaped by an English sea captain many years earlier and taken to England where he had served as a slave and learned to speak English. Later, when he was returned to his native country, he had immediately sought Massasoit out, and sitting for one chilling evening around the great tribal campfire, educated Massasoit about the wave of English settlers due to arrive any year for the purpose of settling what was, for the white man, a vast new uninhabited world. Already the white man seemed to think that the Indian did not count as an inhabitant. Where the Indian was going to go to make room for the white man, Tisquantum surely did not know. All that was apparent to him was that the white man very disturbingly discounted any possible claim that the Indian had to the land the Indian called home. The Indian was already being sloughed off in every conversation Tisquantum had heard the white man engaged in, as though the white man believed he could just move into an area and claim it as his own, despite centuries of habitation by the Indian.

Massasoit had many moons to ponder the ominous threat posed by the white incursion, and the first Pilgrims simply never knew the depth of his comprehension of the ramifications of their arrival. And so, well before the Pilgrims realized it, Massasoit had already reasoned that warfare against the first settlers would spell disaster for his people when the armies of settlers, more numerous than the leaves in the great forest, followed.

So, as the Pilgrims lived their first harsh winter of 1620-21 in constant fear of attack, Massasoit was planning to befriend them, come springtime.

In March of 1621, as the long winter was coming to an end, William Bradford, Miles Standish, John Alden, and the other Pilgrim fathers were standing in a group in their Plymouth settlement when they were surprised by a lone Indian who walked right into their midst and started to speak to them in English!

This Indian was Samoset, from the coast of Maine, who had picked up the white man's language from fur traders. All afternoon and well into the evening the pilgrims talked to this friendly ambassador who lauded the great tribal chief, Massasoit, informing the pilgrims of his bravery and honesty.

Governor William Bradford asked Samoset if it would be possible for him to arrange a meeting for them with Massasoit, and four days later three Indians returned. One was Samoset. The second was Tisquantum, whom the Pilgrims called Squanto, and the third was the grand sachem himself, Massasoit!

Thus, in the spring of 1621, on a great green carpet laid out on the ground for the comfort of the seated negotiators, Squanto, who spoke even better English than Samoset, arranged a remarkable treaty between Massasoit and the Pilgrims.

The most important thing they agreed upon was a pact of mutual respect and mutual aid in repelling attacks by outside enemies. The Pilgrims felt that they had engineered a remarkable agreement, blessed by God and designed to ensure their safety as they struggled to adapt to their new environment.

But no one was more relieved that night than Massasoit. Already fearful of his massively diminished numbers losing a war to his Iroquois enemies to the west, he had taken care of the dangers threatened by the impending invasion of countless white men from across the great water. He now had these white men as an ally against any others to come, and also against his Indian enemies to the west.

If anything can be said for the makers of this first Indian-white treaty, it is that they were all shrewd but honest men, eager to uphold the treaty they had agreed to, and determined to carry out each provision faithfully.

It did not take long for the first Indian challenge to arise. The powerful Narraganset tribe sent to the colony a bundle of arrows tied in a rattlesnake skin. When Governor Bradford looked to Squanto, puzzled by the message, Squanto grew pale and frowned.

"It is an old Indian custom," he said. "It is a challenge to fight to the death."

Emboldened by the belief in the integrity of Massasoit, Governor Bradford broke the arrows in half and filled the snakeskin with gunpowder and shot, returning it to the Narragansets.

The Narragansets declined to carry the threat any further. Strength had met strength, and the confrontation was delayed.

For two years the whites avoided a challenge, and an uneasy peace prevailed. Then, in 1623, the Indians got their first taste of Pilgrim resolve.

A new colony of white settlers, different from the original Pilgrims was having trouble with the nearby Massachusetts Indians. No such treaties had been sealed between the English and the Massachusetts, and misunderstandings abounded between the two groups. The whites looked down on the Indians to whom they sold liquor when the Indians got roaring drunk, and the Indians laughed at the hard-working farmers who tended their fields faithfully because the Indians thought they were doing woman's work.

When the whites became abusive to the drunken Indians, pushing them off their land when they sought more liquor, the Indians began to argue with one another as to what right the whites had to land the Indians had always held in common. When large stores of corn were stolen from the Massachusetts Indians, they blamed the whites, and soon Governor Bradford got word that the Massachusetts sachem was planning an attack on the colony of whites that had injured them.

Here Captain Miles Standish got his first chance to show the Indians that the English were not to be fooled with. When Standish got to the settlement, he waited for the Massachusetts, and when they were out in the open, Standish and his men shot and killed all of them but one. This last one they took back with them to Plymouth, where they hanged him. Hearing of the ancient tribal custom of beheading their enemy, Standish took his head and mounted it in plain sight in their Plymouth colony.

The Indians had received their first harsh spanking from the white man. Massasoit filed the lesson away in the back of his mind and worried very deeply, in the privacy of his own thoughts, about the future of his sons and daughters.

It is worse than I first believed, Massasoit thought ominously. *Someday the Indian may have to take a much stronger stand against the white man than we are able to enforce. When that day comes, treaties will not matter.*

▲   ▼   ▲

For the next decade, Massasoit continued to honor his treaty with the Pilgrims, and they with him, and the people living in the region took their best shot at coexistence. The word went out across the land that to confront the white man was to confront the Wampanoag, so Pilgrim safety was secure.

Meanwhile Massasoit's ambassadors showed the Pilgrims their best hunting and fishing areas and taught them how to plant corn. Ancient tribal warfare continued among the great Indian nations, but the new equation in the volatile region of the world was the frequent misunderstandings that arose between white men and Indians. Neither understood the other, and both were fearful and distrusting of the other as the white migration continued.

Trickles of new settlers continued to filter into the new world, and then in 1630 the dam burst. The great migration from Europe that began that year sent more than eight thousand people into the Massachusetts Bay, and all of them settled in lands that had been cleared by the great plagues.

After that year there were as many stories of misunderstandings and skirmishes as there were people, and the inevitability of armed conflict between white man and Indian grew closer and closer with each isolated incident.

Fearful of the types of atrocities the Indians were said to perpetrate on their enemies, settlers would arm themselves heavily and travel in groups, avoiding the forests whenever possible. The Indians were just as afraid of the whites, whom they eyed with suspicion every time they ventured out of the forests into which they had retreated to avoid the white man as much as they could.

Still interaction was inevitable, and isolated incidents of violence were met by retaliation and counter-retaliation so that soon it became impossible to tell who was at fault in any given skirmish. Add to the confusion the difficulty many Indians had in telling settlers apart, and vice versa, as well as the language barriers that divided the two cultures, and you had a powder keg waiting to go off.

Throughout this entire turbulent time, the Nipmucks managed to stay away from the white man, and they were able to resume their biannual ritual of gathering every spring and autumn to host the Algonquian nation at the Medicine Springs powwows.

In the spring of 1634, a handsome young warrior named Lone Eagle carried the colors of the Pequots into the grand finale match, and in one of the most brutal matches ever recorded he was defeated by a strong young Nipmuck named Stone Deer, who fractured several of Lone Eagle's ribs in a savage take down, leaving him exhausted, beaten, and breathing painfully from his injuries.

As Lone Eagle lay there suffering too greatly to move, he overheard a heartbroken young boy from the Pequot tribe whisper to one of his friends, "Lone Eagle looks like a broken eagle," to which his friend replied, "Every warrior gets broken. Lone Eagle will heal this winter and come back next year stronger than ever, and the Nipmucks will wish they never broke him."

As fate would have it, Lone Eagle's wife went into labor in their wigwam that evening, and the following dawn, as the great eagle took to the sky, Lone Eagle's son was born.

In the early morning light, on the banks of the We-Am-An-Tuck, that autumn of 1634, Lone Eagle announced to his wife Little Bird and the women in attendance at their son's birth, "His name will be Broken Eagle, and he will be a mighty warrior feared by friend and foe alike."

That autumn the talk among the tribes was the same that was heard anywhere in New England. Arguments arose about the merits of friendship with the white man. Some in the tribe were persuaded to adopt the white man's religion, while others insisted on holding to their own tribal methods of coming before the great spirit in the traditional ways.

A few days after the powwow was over, as the various tribes prepared to return to their sachemdoms, a tragic event occurred which served to heighten the debate about interaction with the white man. Two young Indian lovers, who were not permitted to marry due to a dispute involving the white man's religion, plummeted to their deaths in a double suicide off a high cliff overlooking the main path that ran parallel to the river south of Medicine Springs.

The young woman's family had adopted the white man's religion, but the man's family had not, and according to the white man's religion, savages or heathens could not intermarry with converts. The cliff became known as Lover's Leap, and it was the first suicide the Algonquian nation had ever recorded. For many of the shocked and saddened Indians, it reeked of the white man's corruption.

Until the incident at Lover's Leap, the Indians had at least stood up and fought when their customs were attacked, but with the double suicide, the robbing of the Indian spirit was underway.

It was becoming more and more apparent to the Indian that whenever he dealt with the white man, he came out on the short end, and so, for as much as possible, the Indian tried to avoid interaction with the white man on as many fronts as he could.

In 1634, the same year that Broken Eagle was born, a tragic incident set in motion a chain of events that led to Broken Eagle's hatred of whites. In an effort to extort as much money as he could from the Indians on what was to be his final voyage to the colonies, a white coastal trader kidnapped the Pequot sachem and held him for ransom. After the ransom had been paid, the ruthless trader, not wishing to be identified, killed the chief and the ransom bearer and sailed back to England with his booty.

Shortly thereafter another coastal trader dropped anchor at the mouth of the Connecticut River where he was greeted by a band of Indians who swarmed aboard and killed him and his entire crew. Colonial authorities demanded that the Pequots surrender the murderers to English justice. Heavy arguments ensued in the Pequot camp, with half the Indians insisting that justice had already been done with the avenging of their chief's death, and the other half insisting that the wars they were already engaged in with the Narragansets and the Dutch traders made conciliation with the English necessary.

The second group won out, and a treaty was agreed to that allowed the Pequots to avoid a third war with enemies they feared more than the Narragansets or the Dutch. The Pequots agreed to turn over the murderers and pay a large reimbursement for the white man's murder.

While part of the reimbursement was paid, the Pequots had to tell the English that the killers had escaped to the north, so the English anger simmered. Two years later, another trader was killed in Narraganset country off of Block Island.

This time the Indians would accept no treaties. English authorities assigned an army of ninety colonists to sail to Block Island where they were to put to death all the male Indians and take all the women and children captive to be sold into slavery. When that was finished, they were to sail up the Connecticut River, past Saybrook to the north of the Thames

River into Pequot territory. There they were to settle the old murder case once and for all.

However, when they arrived on Block Island, they found nothing but empty camps as the Indians hid in underground caves until the colonists left. The frustrated band of colonists set out after the Pequots, and when they arrived they found that the main force of Pequot braves was out on a hunt. Eager to make up for their failure on Block Island, the English spent the entire day burning the Pequot camp.

A terrified little Broken Eagle was carried by his mother out of the camp and into the hills beyond, where the little two-year-old watched, crying in sadness, as his home went up in flames. He could understand very little, only that his mother was crying, his home was burning, and the attack had happened when his father was not there to defend them.

By the time the Pequot males returned home, they were furious, and they made straight for Saybrook. They retaliated on the nearest available colonists, killing three men with arrows, roasting one alive, and floating one downriver on a raft with an arrow in his eye.

Pequot ambassadors next sought to set aside their differences with the Narragansets to concentrate on the sure war that was brewing against the English. All winter the situation simmered, and in March of 1637 the Narragansets finally chose their side. They aligned themselves with the English and sealed their deal by sending the English the severed hand of the Pequot ambassador. This they did for self-preservation so that the English ire would be directed at the Pequots and away from them.

Realizing that they were now alone, the Pequots banded together and in April of 1637 descended on what the locals called the most ancient town of the colonies, Wethersfield, Connecticut, killing nine settlers and sailing past the fort at Saybrook with the clothing of the murdered settlers blowing like flags in the breeze.

English retribution was swift and merciless. In May a small army of colonists left Hartford with a contingent of Mohegan Indians led by Chief Uncas. Their goal was to exterminate the Pequots so as to strike fear in any other tribe, thus ending their problems with the Indians for good. Their concerns about Mohegan loyalty were soon answered when Uncas and his Indian warriors attacked a small party of Pequots, beheading four of them and taking one prisoner, who was tortured before he too was killed.

The cruel manner in which they tortured him before they killed him shocked and angered the Indians when his body was found. They tied one of his legs to a post and the other to a long rope, which six men jerked on until they tore him apart, screaming in agony. Maimed beyond comprehension, he was shot in the head by a white man who took pity on the screaming man.

Somehow the Pequots got word that the English were coming, and almost two hundred warriors from outlying camps made their way to the Pequot stronghold to join forces there while the English managed to recruit over six hundred Narragansets and Niantic warriors to aid them in their assault on the Pequots.

War was imminent, and on the morning of May 25, 1637, when Broken Eagle was almost three years old, it came. English authorities told the Narragansets to surround the Pequot camp and not let anyone escape. At dawn the English stormed the camp. Although the Pequots fought valiantly, they were totally unprepared for the ferocity of the heavily armed English, who mowed down hundreds of Pequots with swords and muskets.

Broken Eagle awoke to see his father, Lone Eagle, scrambling for his hunting knife before dashing out of the entrance to their hut. The loud noises of musket fire terrified little Broken Eagle, but not as much as the next sight which caught his wide eyes. As Lone Eagle dashed back into his hut under a heavy barrage of gunfire, he was shot in the back and sprawled across the room where he fell dead at Broken Eagle's feet.

Outside the English were making short order of their assignment and killing every Pequot male in sight. The huts were then set on fire, and hundreds of women, screaming children, and old people were burned to death. People who tried to run from the camp were killed by the Narragansets who had the camp surrounded and who were themselves terrified of the brutality displayed by the English. Many of the Narragansets just stood and watched in shock, vowing never to induce the English wrath, for fear of a similar fate falling upon themselves.

The massacre lasted only about a half an hour, but when it was over, eight hundred Pequots were dead. When Broken Eagle's hut was set afire, his mother, Little Bird, covered his body and lay just outside their door on top of him, frantically whispering to him that he must be as quiet as possible and play dead or they were sure to be run through by white men's swords. In anger and fear, Broken Eagle obeyed, and by the time the smoke cleared and the English had gone an hour later, Broken Eagle, Little Bird, and four other people walked tentatively out into the center of camp where they discovered amidst the bodies of their murdered friends and relatives that they were the only six survivors of the massacre.

The six fled their smoldering campsite in terror and made their way through the forest to the remaining Pequot fort south on the Mystic River. There they told their sachem about the massacre, and he roused the remaining Pequots for their escape from the ethnic cleansing, certain that the English would next launch an assault on them. They fled westward, aware that they could only go as far as Iroquois country, where they would be in just as much danger. But there were women, children, and old people along with the young men, so their escape was not a rapid one and they were tracked down and trapped in a swamp near New Haven. Old men, women, and children were allowed to come out of the swamp unmolested, but eighty Pequot warriors refused to surrender. There they braced themselves for an English assault, and when it came about three quarters of them were killed. The rest escaped.

When word spread to all Indian nations about the destruction of the Pequots, one of the saddest chapters in Indian history unfolded. Deciding to make points with the English to stave off a similar fate, the vast majority of other Indian tribes sought the condemned Pequots who had survived with the purpose of killing them and beheading them for the English.

The Pequot sachem was one who had escaped, but when he sought asylum with the Mohawks in August, he too was killed and beheaded and his head was sent back to the English in Connecticut.

The few Pequots who were left after the sachem's head arrived begged for a treaty, which they were granted. This "Treaty of Hartford," as it was called in 1638, divided the remaining Pequots among the tribes that had supported the English in their raids. Broken Eagle, who had just turned four years old when the treaty was signed, became a slave of Chief Uncas of the Mohegans, former Pequot friends who had aided in the massacre of his people. Little Bird went to the Narragansets as a slave, and when they tore Broken Eagle from his mother's arms and took her away, reaching for him desperately, the last thing he remembered of her was the horror in her eyes and her outstretched arms as they dragged her away. He never saw her again.

All of this had happened before Broken Eagle was five years old, but it left a searing hatred of the white man and a mistrust of all Indians who were their friends.

No one alive at the time was aware of how vividly the small boy remembered each and every incident that happened as the destruction of his family and his tribe took place. But Broken Eagle filed the horror away in the recesses of his tormented mind, where he nurtured the heartbreaking murder of his father, the terrible massacre of his people, and the abduction and separation of his mother throughout his childhood years.

As he grew in knowledge and strength, so did his quiet resolve to come to the day of reckoning with enemies around him.

▲　▼　▲

Jonathan Hale was only three days into his first year at school in London, England, when, at age six, he realized the ordeal that lay ahead of him. The son of a well-bred university professor and his elegant high- society wife, Jonathan had already been taught his letters and his numbers, and before he started the first grade, he had been reading bedtime stories to his nanny with regularity.

While his mates played games outside in the streets, Jonathan was forced by his disciplinarian father to spend one hour each on reading and piano, and one half hour each on elocution and cursive writing, twice every day. Consequently when he started formal schooling, the word for the day, every day, was boredom.

He skated through his primary school subjects with ease, and lit away from the estate every chance he could throughout all of his early years, all the while dreaming of far off places, pirates, seafarers, and adventurers. On more than one occasion he became lost while roaming the streets of London as a very young boy, prompting search parties that would inevitably find him standing outside of some pub, peering in, or standing on some street corner engrossed in stories told by whatever street commoner with whom he could align himself.

Each time he was severely reprimanded by his mother, so many times that he had shut her out of consideration before he had reached age seven. Thrashing from his father did little more good, and Jonathan Hale grew up champing at the bit for his freedom. When he reached age fourteen, he met Ruth Palmer, age fifteen, and three days after they made their acquaintance, they committed the unspeakable crime of lying down together on the sofa of her parlor where they fondled each other's bodies and kissed so long and hard, and in so many different positions on the couch that it was a wonder to her that they didn't leave any telltale signs of their passion for her mother to discover.

Sneaking out of her home through the flower garden that night, he was certain that a great scandal would rock both of their families if any of this continued because he was sure from Ruth Palmer's demeanor that, while she had drawn lines on him that day, the day was near when she would not do anything to stop him. Although he was not quite certain what consequences that day would bring, he was willing and eager to do whatever groping and exploring was necessary to find out.

One week later, in the heat of sexual passion and confusion, the two young people went past the point of no return, and lying there naked and spent, her mind raced through a myriad of questions.

"What happens now?" she asked him nervously, still breathing heavily from their encounter.

"I guess now you have a baby," he answered, not really knowing for sure if that's how it worked.

They dressed quickly and escaped into the night to huddle together and try to figure out the best way to avoid the impending scandal. They ran through several options, and decided on the one they thought would protect their families the best.

On the morrow, Jonathan would steal from his parents the money they needed for fare on the next ship out of England headed for the colonies, where the two would be married and seek their freedom in the world that matched their wildness.

When they were only two days out at sea, she realized that he had grown much more somber and contemplative than she had ever seen him before, and she was puzzled by his changing mood.

"What's wrong?" she asked him nervously, leaning up against him and staring into his eyes.

"I don't know," he said, staring out over the ocean. "I'm just wondering if maybe we're going a little too fast with everything."

"You mean acting like we're already married?" she said, whispering as though she didn't think they ought to be talking about the subject.

"Yes."

"What do you think?" she asked him.

"I know it's too late for us to turn back to England, that's for sure, but if we have a baby so soon, it could be really difficult for us at this point."

"So you think we ought not to go so far just yet?"

"Not that I don't want to," he answered. "But maybe not just yet."

"Well I'm glad you feel that way, because I didn't want to bring the matter up myself, but I've felt the same way."

"Maybe we'll get lucky and you won't be pregnant this time," Jonathan said. "But we'll ask the ship's captain to marry us just in case."

"But we're too young," she said.

"We'll lie about our ages," he said. "He doesn't know."

After the ship's captain married them, and with their new understanding to slow down their torrid pace, the two young people relaxed and fell into a quite proper relationship as friends, settling in the Massachusetts Bay colonies along with so many other adventurers, and they enjoyed just about every aspect of their exciting new life. With the considerable stash of currency that he had taken as what he termed "an advance on his inheritance," Jonathan bought he and Ruth a quaint farm in Brookfield, Massachusetts, where Ruth set up their home and Jonathan planted their fields, and they prepared to live happily ever after.

For four years they built their farm and their home, and in their fifth year in the colonies, while both of them were still in their teens, they had their first child, a boy they named Matthew. Two years later their daughter Miriam arrived, and they enjoyed several years of satisfaction and happiness, as Jonathan continued along in his quiet way, tilling his fields and tending his farm animals, and Ruth kept house and educated the children.

The family of Jonathan Hale occasionally attended church and community affairs, but unlike the majority of townspeople, they were a private lot, and for the most part isolated themselves from the rest of the settlers, staying on the farm for most of their time.

Logistically, as well as by personal choice, this was so because they lived in the farm farthest away from the town meetinghouse where some of the church gatherings and all of the town meetings were held. On most days it was too late by the time Jonathan was finished with his daily chores to clean up and get to town in time, so they usually only attended events that were scheduled for Sundays, and then they didn't attend all of those.

Throughout all of those years, though, one thing was certain. Jonathan was not permitted to leave Ruth alone on the farm. When he went into town, she went into town, and when he went to church, she went to church, for while their life and times in the colonies were far better than anything they could have hoped for in England, there was the one recurring nightmare that plagued Ruth Hale throughout her life in the colonies.

In it an Indian, like one of the ones she would see on occasion through cracks in their log cabin wall when the moon was full, stealing one of their farm animals or raiding their storage barn, would walk slowly and eerily up to her front door, and even though it was bolted shut, he would walk right through it as though he were some kind of dark, evil spirit. He would then lift up a tomahawk and start to bring it down upon her, at which time she would once again wake up with a start, shaking and sweating in fear, and it would take her several minutes to stop breathing heavily. Whenever this would happen, and it seemed to occur every full moon, Jonathan would console her and try to rock away her fears, and she would cry nervously and ashamedly on his shoulder while her daughter Miriam lay fully awake in the next room, listening to the monthly ritual quietly, with no one to lay her own dark fears before.

Long after Ruth had gone back to sleep Miriam would lay there alone, and scared, harboring her own fears of the unknown part of the equation their life in the colonies presented them with. What would be done about the Indians?

▲　　▼　　▲

The year 1654 was a significant one in Mohegan Indian lore. This was the year that they finally broke into the win column at the Medicine Springs wrestling tournament after more than twenty years of falling short to the other Indian tribes, most specifically the Nipmucks, who had won an unprecedented twelve years in a row, and seventeen of the last twenty years.

Their victory was only slightly marred in their own eyes by the fact that the winning warrior had not been born a Mohegan, but had come into the tribe many years before when the Pequot tribe had been disbanded.

This fearless warrior turned many heads at the wrestling tournament that year, but he did not have to wait for the festivities to prove his valor because of what happened on the Mohegans' way to Medicine Springs.

The warrior's name was Broken Eagle, and although he had grown up as a slave of the Mohegans, his physical strength and his prowess as a wrestler had caused the Mohegan sachem to pick him out early in his teen years as a potential champion. Offering Broken Eagle the opportunity to join the tribe so that he could compete in the tournament at Medicine Springs, the tribal leaders were well pleased when the slave accepted and endured the harshest of initiations into the tribe. He was forced to enter the wilderness naked and without weapons and live off the land for forty moons. When he returned, he had to defeat the top three warriors in hand-to-hand combat, using only his bare hands against the first warrior, who had a club; the second, who had a spear; and the third, who had a tomahawk. Broken Eagle disarmed and defeated each of the three warriors in succession, all in one day, and that night, before the entire tribal assembly, he was officially named a Mohegan and draped with a loincloth and the headdress of his new tribe.

Thus Broken Eagle grew up as a Mohegan, but he never trusted them. In 1654, when he was twenty years old, he was filled with excitement when his tribe began the trek to the place where he had been born.

The place the Indians had always called Medicine Springs had a new name, Indian Springs, given by the English explorers who mapped out the areas west of Plymouth in 1645. That autumn of 1654 brought two great coups to Broken Eagle. They happened about twenty miles south of Indian Springs when the band of Mohegans, numbering about one hundred-twenty was attacked by a superior force of Mohawks, down on a belated raid of the Algonquians.

Before the attack was over, three women and two children had been taken, the children to be used as slaves and the women as concubines. But the woman Broken Eagle was traveling with, a beautiful Mohegan squaw named Morning Star, was saved when Broken Eagle slit the throat of one of the Mohawks who descended upon her and broke the neck of the other one.

Both of their scalps he wore on his belt as he entered Indian Springs. The Mohawk raid lasted for only a few short minutes, and eight Mohegans and four Mohawks were killed, with the lost women and children adding to a total loss to the tribe of thirteen people.

The Mohegans could have sustained far greater losses, and would have if they pursued their attackers, but they let them go and considered themselves lucky only to have lost thirteen.

Disgusted, Broken Eagle looked upon his Mohegan leaders as cowardly for not at least attempting a rescue mission, but he was granted his coups nevertheless, and the Mohegans proceeded onward to the annual wrestling tournament at Indian Springs.

There Broken Eagle was the clear winner of the grand finale match, and when a Nipmuck asked who his father was, he stunned the Mohegan leadership with his answer.

"Lone Eagle, Pequot," he answered proudly, which made him an instant celebrity among the Nipmucks, who had thought for many years that all Pequots were dead.

"But Broken Eagle is now a Mohegan," the Mohegan sachem cried out loudly, and when he did, Broken Eagle smiled and turned away, spitting on the ground as he did.

Many of the young Pequots who had remained Mohegan slaves saw this, while the Mohegan sachem did not, and the Pequots smiled at one another as Broken Eagle continued to rise to his leadership position among them. All of the victories Broken Eagle achieved that autumn pleased him, but none more than his wedding to Morning Star, who bore him three children in the next three years.

Through all of those years, the Mohegans continued to brag about their top warrior, Broken Eagle, while Broken Eagle continued to meet secretly with his brother Pequots, whom he told to bide their time and stay alert for the time when he deemed it best to make their break from the Mohegan dogs who had enslaved them.

"The world has yet to hear from Broken Eagle," he told them somberly, and each of them identified themselves by how well Broken Eagle treated them and how loyal they could be to him.

Peaceful coexistence was the best situation both the white man and the Indian could hope for in the year 1661. The hostilities between the two opposing cultures that shared the land had toned down considerably as they learned to coexist. As long as the ancient men who had engineered the treaties that had kept war from coming to the people survived, the threat of war was constantly kept at arm's length. But then, in 1661, the die was cast for the first and final full-scale Indian war the region would experience by the passing of the elder statesman of the Indian nation that year.

Word of Massasoit's death spread through the region like wildfire, and everyone on both sides immediately set to talking and speculating about the consequences of the death of the old man of wisdom and reason. At eighty-one years of age, the great Wampanoag sachem could not be expected to live forever, but his death nevertheless came as a shock to everyone in positions of leadership, for no one knew what the world would come to once the old peacekeeper passed away to his happy hunting ground.

It had long been understood that his successor would be his eldest son, Alexander, who was immediately summoned to the governor's office in Plymouth Colony to acknowledge his loyalty. There Alexander became sick, and on his way home, he died.

Leadership of the nation now passed to the son of Massasoit's old age, his youngest son, Metacomet, whom the English called King Philip. Philip had been born when Massasoit was fifty-seven years old, and Massasoit had always held both great hopes and great fears for his impetuous young son.

Throughout his upbringing, Massasoit had educated Philip, as he had Alexander, about everything he would need to know when the time came for him to be sachem. Massasoit told Philip about the life the Indian enjoyed before the great white invasion had taken place. He told him about the treaties he had made to protect the Wampanoag from extinction suffered by some of the other unfortunate tribes who had chosen to act impulsively instead of intelligently with the invader. Massasoit taught Philip about inter-tribal and international Indian warfare, and about traditions and customs that must be observed to preserve the order and tranquility that would best serve all of the Indian people. He taught him also about the reluctance a sachem must choose to enter war with, but about the ironclad resolve he must also display once the decision to war was made.

He taught his son about the honesty of the first Pilgrims, but also about their ruthlessness and their willingness to use force to bring the Indian in line. And in his most painful lesson to his son, he taught him about the sad legacy the white man had left to the Indian. Honest men had made treaties, dishonest ones had broken them, and because of the white man's firepower and sheer force of numbers, the Indian had always lost in the end.

All the stories Massasoit told Philip the young boy learned well, but when the time came for him to assume tribal leadership, he did so with much less diplomacy and much more aggressiveness than Massasoit ever had.

His suspicions of the white man began immediately. He honestly believed that his brother Alexander had been poisoned by the white man on his journey to Plymouth. He made the Plymouth authorities aware at once that he would not make treaties with anyone but the King of England, for he considered all others to be subjects of the king, and he considered himself to be the equal of the king.

Although the first fourteen years of King Philip's rule saw no major outbreaks of violence, suspicions about each other's plans for war grew deeper with each passing year. Then in January of 1675, a Harvard-educated Indian was found dead beneath the ice of a pond near Plymouth.

The coroner ruled that he had been murdered and the English set out to find the murderers, suspecting immediately that the crime had been committed by Indians jealous or angry at the conversion of one of their own to the white man's ways. A short time later, three Wampanoag braves were arrested and convicted of the crime and sentenced by English courts to death by hanging. Two of them were hanged, but when the rope broke on the third one's neck, he blurted out that King Philip had done the murder, hoping he could save his own neck by implicating someone more important to his executioners than himself.

He was hanged anyway, but word reached Philip that he was being sought by English authorities to defend himself, and as he awaited their arrival, debates raged in the Indian nation about what they would do if he was convicted and hanged.

Some wanted to hide their head in the sand and ignore the English threat. Others wanted to go along with peaceful coexistence even though it meant compromising the only way of life they'd ever known. Most wanted to complain, with no suggestions short of war. For the next few days, while Phillip awaited his arrest, incidents of violence were met with counterattacks, and tensions grew in the region with each successive incident.

Murders and revenge murders were more, not less, graphic and cruel. White settlers were burned at the stake, Indians were shot and beheaded, their skulls mounted on poles in villages and their bodies left to rot. Rapes were committed by both sides, and young Indians were captured and sold into slavery abroad.

While whites armed themselves and drilled in defense techniques at local meetinghouses, Indians held war counsels in villages in the woods. Young braves formed groups demanding retaliation for every incident, and many insisted on all-out war.

The powder keg was finally ignited when King Philip was arrested and dragged before English authorities to defend himself against the accusations leveled against him.

The treatment he received there set the stage for the bloodiest and most tragic war in the history of the New England area. Philip was outraged that he would be treated so disrespectfully by English authorities, the very descendants of the men to whom his father had been so helpful. He stood before them and lambasted them for their treatment of him, reminding them that when their fathers had first landed, it had been his father who had protected them from other Indians by treaty and by aid of all types, from how to plant corn to where to hunt and fish most prosperously. Massasoit had even given them land, Philip reminded them, squeezing his own people in the process.

The longer he yelled, the more enraged he became, and after listening to both barrels of Philip's wrathful outburst, the authorities realized that everything he had said was true. Thus, devoid of any evidence on which to convict him, they were forced to set him free, but the insults had been deeply felt and he stormed out of the white man's sight aroused to the point of fury.

Philip was convinced now that the English had already set upon an irreversible course of total destruction of the Indian, and he was one sachem who was determined never to let that happen to his people.

In the summer of 1675, King Philip prepared his nation for war. Rumors of Philip's anger spread among the settlers, and tensions were stretched to the breaking point. When an Indian was fired upon and killed in the village of Swansea, the Indians took revenge by killing the murderer, his father, and five other settlers.

English soldiers mounted an assault against King Philip's home, Mount Hope in Narraganset Bay. After a furious battle in which several men on both sides were killed, the English retreated and Philip's men escaped. The great King Philip's War had begun. In what would prove to be the bloodiest war ever fought on the North American continent in terms of the percentage of people lost, more than half of New England's settlements were subjected to attack, with massacres hitting Taunton, Middleborough, Sudbury, Lancaster, Groton, Marlborough, and countless other communities, and no isolated settlement or village was safe from mass murder. Three thousand whites lost their lives, as did over six thousand Indians.

Ambushes would be over in a matter of minutes, and small groups of soldiers were helpless against King Philip's mighty army of Indians fighting for what they viewed as survival of their race.

When survivors would show up babbling incoherently, weakened from wounds, or in shock from witnessing the atrocities that were commonplace, the settlers would cringe and realize more and more that all-out war against the Indians was upon them. Throughout that fateful and terrible summer, New England clergymen of all denominations called for fasting and repentance as military men gathered up their arms for the war to the death between two clashing cultures.

In the Mohegan camp, Broken Eagle heard of the war from the tribal elders who had decided to remain neutral while King Philip's forces waged their war.

This is our land, not theirs, Broken Eagle thought to himself, lying awake in the Mohegan camp. *And the Mohegans are no better than the whites. It's the Mohegans who have kept my brothers in slavery. They do not believe that the whites want to kill all Indians. And I will not trust any Indian who does not understand that both of us cannot live here together. The white man must die, and so too all the*

Indians who align themselves with him. It is the only chance for the Indian to regain his former life and remain free.

On a warm night in late May of 1675, Broken Eagle crept silently through the Mohegan camp, arousing the Pequot slaves who were his followers. He led them to the outskirts of the Mohegan encampment where he gathered them around him.

"Come with me, my brothers, and we will be free," Broken Eagle told them. "Stick with the Mohegans and you will stay enslaved. They do not care about you. They have kept you in slavery after the white men raped your mothers and your sisters and killed your fathers and your brothers. They only call me part of their tribe because I am stronger than any of them. But I do not want their tribe. I am a Pequot. And so are you. Tonight we rise up against these dogs and kill them. And we take our freedom back. We may not live long lives, but we will live free ones. And even if you die with me, you will die with the words of Broken Eagle burned into your spirits. The Pequot Indian nation will rise again. Come with me, my brothers, or die like animals in slavery."

In July of 1676, the hostilities of Philip and his followers exploded in a predawn raid on a settlement in Brookfield, Massachusetts. Before it was over forty-eight hours later, every family had suffered the wrath of King Philip's rampage, but none more than that of the quiet farmer who lived in the cabin farthest out from the settlement's meetinghouse.

That hot summer night, the Hale family paid a horrible price for living in a bad corner of the world to live in in 1676. When the Indians attacked, Jonathan and Ruth Hale, their son Matthew, age sixteen, and their daughter Miriam, age fourteen, found suffering that was far worse than anything civilized or uncivilized people anywhere in the world should be asked to endure.

Ruth Hale was in that hazy state of consciousness that occurs just before sleep comes when she heard a commotion outside of her window. Her heart quickened a beat as she crept across the floor to see what had bothered the farm animals. She never had a chance to focus her eyes on the source of the commotion, because a long red arm reached through the window, grabbed her by the hair, and pulled her out screaming through the window.

Her eyes wide with fear, she looked up into the cold dark eyes of her Indian assailant, who lifted a tomahawk up and threatened to fulfill her most terrible nightmare. Unsure whether it was real or just another nightmare, she never had time to sort it all out because the tomahawk fell once, twice, again and again, until her head was hacked off by several blows of the horrible weapon.

Upon hearing the screams of his mother, young Matthew ran into the darkness screaming gutturally and began chasing two fleeing Indians into the woods. The Hales's loud screams awoke the rest of the settlement and sent them converging on their blockhouse. Armed with nothing but clenched fists, Matthew Hale barreled into the Indians, but before he got to the edge of the clearing, which led into the woods where a mixed group of

Nipmucks, Wampanoags, and renegades from various other tribes were planning their destruction of the town, he took four arrows in his chest, and he was dead before he hit the ground.

As the other settlers rushed to fortify the blockhouse, Matthew's sister, Miriam, boldly and foolishly ran out yelling at her brother to try and convince him to come back, and Jonathan instinctively followed to grab her.

Heeding the hand signal of a large, powerful-looking red man, the other Indians held their arrows back from these two, deciding instead to save them for more enduring tortures later on that would have more of an effect on the white men who would eventually find them when the destruction of the town was complete.

The Indians were involved in a war that they knew was their last stand. They had endured broken treaties, murders, unjust hangings, rapes, massacres, raids by the slave traders, and the slow but definite encroachment upon their homeland and their way of life. In their minds they had to end it now or be exterminated. Any method which would accomplish this goal was considered, even the slow torturous atrocities that would chill the bones of a man who witnessed what was left of one of their cruel and merciless raids.

Add to this a cult hero, a leader finally venting all the pent-up rage within him, and you have a chilling and terrifying condemnation to torture of his hapless random victims. As a handful of strong Indians grabbed Miriam Hale and her father, Jonathan, and dragged them off into the woods, a tall, powerfully built warrior motioned toward a large tree that stood alone in a clearing. There they tied Miriam Hale, who was wide-eyed in horror as the tall Indian walked slowly over to Jonathan Hale, who was being held firmly by two strong Indians. The Indian stared into his eyes with total contempt, spitting into his face.

Jonathan winced but did not react otherwise, and the Indian gestured in sign language to a group who immediately rushed to gather wood for a bonfire that they prepared around a seven-foot- tall pole they had planted in the center of the clearing.

As the tall Indian strode away momentarily, Jonathan looked up and suddenly became aware of the massive number of Indians assembled there. There were hundreds of them, and he felt a sick feeling coming over him as he realized that he and his young daughter had been captured by the main force of King Philip's army of over fifteen hundred warriors that was rampaging throughout the southern New England region that explosive summer.

Standing there, held tightly by two strong Indians, he could not know that by the time the season was over hundreds of settlers would be tortured, murdered, scalped, or dismembered, their bodies mutilated beyond the capacity for civilized minds to comprehend.

It was the inevitability brought on by two clashing cultures, neither of which understood the other, battling over the same grounds. The many tribes of southern New England had finally been pushed farther than they could go. Beyond the Hudson River lived the vast, powerful, and hostile Iroquois nation and the New England Indian nations had no choice but to push the white man back into the ocean from which he had come. To defeat the white man now was the only option the Indian saw left, and his pride, his family, his homeland, and his way of life was at stake.

Of all the individual allies King Philip had found, none was better prepared to serve those goals than the tall brave Jonathan Hale had just met. His entire life had been one marred by one tragedy after another brought on by the relentless encroachments of the whites.

This Jonathan Hale could not have known. All he knew was that fifteen minutes ago he had been asleep on the front porch of his home. And now his wife and son were dead, his daughter was screaming ten feet from him, and he was being held by two of the hundreds of Indians who were there to destroy his town and all of his people.

It was three o'clock in the morning, the moon was full and darting in and out of what appeared to be approaching rain clouds. In a chilling warning, the young brave who spoke the white man's tongue walked up to Jonathan and spoke to him quietly.

"The man who holds your fate in his hands is standing right there." He nodded to the big Indian who had just spit in Jonathan's face. "His name is Broken Eagle, leader of the band of Pequots assembled here. All Pequots are not here, but all who are follow Broken Eagle. Many years ago, the Pequot tribe was massacred, and those of us who were children were divided among the other tribes. Two months ago, Broken Eagle led a revolt. We rose up against our Indian captors, killing many of them, and then we escaped and formed our own group. When we are gone, the last free Pequots are gone forever."

Jonathan's attention was divided between watching his terrified daughter, who was staring wide-eyed at the many Indians who were eyeing her, and this quiet Indian who was talking to him.

"Two nights ago, we met up with Metacomet, who the white man calls King Philip. Broken Eagle offered the loyalty of the Pequots to Metacomet, and Metacomet accepted us. Broken Eagle has no more family. His wife and two sons were sold into slavery. His daughter was raped and killed in our camp last week while we were out of camp. In all the years I have known Broken Eagle, I have never known him to be more determined than he is tonight to make the white man pay for what they have done to him. We have just joined the Wampanoags tonight, and yours is the first town we have chosen and marked for destruction."

Jonathan's legs weakened underneath him, and he felt his knees start to give.

"We are all under the leadership of Metacomet," the Indian continued, nodding in the direction of a makeshift camp from which the Indians had planned to launch their attack on Brookfield. "But Metacomet has let the word go out that this night belongs to Broken Eagle."

Jonathan Hale felt the blood draining out of his face as the chilling words sunk in.

"Will he torture us first?" he asked the young brave quietly.

The young brave looked at Jonathan Hale somberly. "The night belongs to Broken Eagle!" he repeated. And then he walked away.

Jonathan was too terrified to move or to respond in any way. His horror was intensified by the next sight he witnessed as a young brave calmly walked over to the pole to which they were now lashing Jonathan, swinging a human head back and forth by the hair. Jonathan gagged and nearly vomited when he saw that the head was that of his son Matthew, and he felt a sweat breaking out all over his body as his knees began to shake. The brave calmly impaled the head atop the pole to which Jonathan was tied, and when Matthew's blood started dripping onto Jonathan's shoulder, Jonathan heard his own voice crying out as his heart broke.

"A-ah-ar-gh!" Jonathan cried out, straining against the ropes that bound him as tears welled up in his eyes.

Next, they dragged Miriam out in front of Jonathan and ripped all of her clothing off, not ten feet from where he stood tied to the pole atop which his son's head sat.

When Broken Eagle walked slowly over to Miriam, who sat on the ground crying as she tried to cover her nakedness, Jonathan cried out.

"No-o-oooooo! Tell him to do what he will with me, but leave my daughter alone!" he screamed at the English-speaking Indian.

The Indian just turned his head and looked away as Broken Eagle lunged at Jonathan, slashing him across the chest with his long hunting knife. Jonathan felt the warm rush of blood gushing out of the gash on his chest, and he saw in the eyes of Broken Eagle a lifetime of hatred that terrified him more than anything his eyes had ever beheld.

Unable to move from the ropes that bound him to the stake, he did the only thing he could at the moment. He yelled "Nooooooo, noooooooooo!" as loud as he could as though the force of his will could turn the cold determination of Broken Eagle around.

But Broken Eagle turned away from Jonathan, unmoved by his protests, and resolved to torment his terrified daughter. As other Indians watched, Broken Eagle dropped his loincloth and walked toward the helpless girl.

She screamed in horror and revulsion as he descended upon her, and Jonathan continued to cry out to no avail, as Broken Eagle wrestled her to the ground and brutally raped her in front of her father's eyes, slapping and punching her around the face as he drove her into the ground. Her face was frozen in wide-eyed horror and she grew silent as all of his pent-up frustrations and hostilities he unleashed on the helpless young girl, who having just turned fourteen, had left her rag doll dressed in clothes she had made herself, laying in her bed when she ran out to save her brother.

When Broken Eagle was finished humiliating the girl, he turned to her father, whom the rape was designed to hurt the most, and stared at him defiantly, as two Indians held her up and made her take her turn watching what they did to her father.

Broken Eagle pulled a burning torch from the hands of one of his men and set afire a woodpile that had been placed near the feet of Jonathan Hale.

Next, Broken Eagle offered the handle of his tomahawk to Jonathan, and when Jonathan reached for it with his right hand, Broken Eagle snapped it back, and as another Indian held Jonathan's right arm outstretched, Broken Eagle hacked off Jonathan's hand, drawing a scream of agony from the helpless victim and causing Miriam to faint. He tossed the hand to a third Indian, who impaled it on a stick which Broken Eagle held over the fire.

Jonathan was wincing in agony as Broken Eagle grotesquely held the hand out for Jonathan to see. When he turned his head away, Broken Eagle tossed the burning hand into the fire, and gestured to some of the Indians standing around the perimeter, speaking to them in their native tongue.

A dozen or more of them broke out into a wild dance around the stake to which Jonathan had been tied, and every so often one of them would dance over to Jonathan and slash his arm, leg, torso, or head, and before long his entire body was covered with bloody gashes.

With one slash across the tops of both of his legs, Jonathan vomited, and with another slash to the same area, he passed out.

Broken Eagle then let out with a long blood-curdling war-whoop and knelt at Jonathan's feet with a flaming torch. With this he lit Jonathan's pants afire at the ankles, and as the flames leaped up devouring the flesh of her father, who was revived and screaming in agony, something inside of Miriam Hale's mind snapped reality shut, and she just slumped to the ground, where she curled up in a fetal position and closed her eyes against the world.

Back at the blockhouse, a relentless attack kept the residents of Brookfield pinned inside as wave after wave of flaming arrows were sent in on the fortress. Once or twice during the night, the Indians succeeded in setting the house on fire but the inhabitants were able to put each fire out. When the Indians sent a flaming wagon careening into the house, a predawn cloudburst doused the flames and they were forced to wait until the next day's sunlight dried the area.

In the excitement and confusion of the predawn raid, a young scout sneaked through the Indian lines and ran on foot for an astonishing thirty miles to Marlborough, where he collapsed, totally exhausted.

Fortunately for the survivors at Brookfield, a large cavalry force was on its way to Lancaster when the scout's message reached them, and they set off at a gallop toward Brookfield, where the siege was into its forty-eighth hour when they arrived.

After a furious fight, the Indians retreated and several men, women, and children who survived knelt and thanked God for their deliverance, but their joy soon turned to horror as they found the decapitated body of Matthew Hale and a trail of blood that led them into the clearing where they winced and drew back in horror at the sight that met their eyes.

There, tied to a stake, was the charred skeleton that was all that remained of Jonathan Hale. The torture he had gone through first had been totally unnecessary, because nothing remained of the flesh the Indians cut open before burning him at the stake. Atop the stake was the head belonging to the body in the field.

As the men stood back from the grotesque sight, they heard a whimper from the edge of the clearing, and when they went over there, they discovered Miriam, naked and shivering, and curled up in a fetal position, moaning incoherently and severely bruised from the savage beating she had taken, which was designed to maim her but not to kill her.

For many weeks thereafter, she lay in a state of semiconscious shock that nothing or no one could shake her out of. She was cared for faithfully by the people in the community, who took turns taking her into their homes, but no one had the ability or the knowledge to help her out of her shocked stupor.

Three months later, a visiting doctor stunned the congregation to whom he spoke at their Wednesday night prayer meeting.

"Miriam Hale is pregnant," he said, and the silence that followed betrayed the group's quandary over what in the world they were to do with her now.

▲　▼　▲

Although the tribes that joined King Philip's War were many, not all of the Indians joined in Philip's last stand against the white man. Several tribes were not convinced that the hour to make a last stand had yet arrived, and in the winter of 1675-76, after many savage battles throughout southern New England, King Philip had moved a majority of his forces to an area northeast of Albany, New York.

There his ancient enemies, the Mohawks, who used to raid his allies every spring, wreaked their final havoc on his forces, attacking them in New York and driving them back into New England where the white men were waiting for them en masse. That following July, the most painful loss of his valiant campaign to save the land for his Indians was dealt him when a mixed band of Indians and English took several prisoners from among the Indians encamped away from the war parties, and among the prisoners was Philip's wife and nine-year-old son.

The whites debated furiously over what to do with the pair, with a majority calling for their executions for the atrocities of Philip. The Plymouth authorities were at a loss because so many people were calling for their executions, but they knew they could not order the murders of two innocent people, so after many days of argument, they decided to consult the clergy.

It was the Godly ministers' advice which the authorities settled on, and the solution broke Philip's heart.

Metacomet, son of Massasoit, and great young chief of the Wampanoags, never saw his wife and son again, because they were separated and sold into slavery abroad. When Philip was told the crushing truth he fell to his knees and wailed in the Algonquian language, "My heart is breaking. Now I am ready to die."

On August 11, 1676, an Indian traitor gave up Philip's position to English authorities, saying that Philip had just killed his brother for suggesting that the small number of savage warriors left in Philip's ravaged army surrender and make the best of what the white man's treaty would give them.

At midnight a vastly superior number of heavily armed Englishmen stormed Philip's Mount Hope camp. The Indians scattered and ran as the white forces advanced, and none of the advancing whites could believe the next sight they all saw. There, standing alone at the edge of the camp, was a tall, muscular savage, armed only with two tomahawks, staring hatefully at the masses of white men who advanced upon him relentlessly.

Walks at Night, who had aligned himself with the English, grew pale as he reached out and touched the arm of the white leader.

"I will go no further," Walks at Night said. "I will not fight against Broken Eagle. He has a spirit which cannot be defeated."

The Englishman looked up as the tall Indian screamed a blood-curdling war-whoop and ran directly into the masses of white men, swinging his tomahawks wildly and slashing away at white soldiers anywhere within his reach. One soldier he killed, and then two, and he was lifting his tomahawk against a third when a musket blast ripped into his right arm, and Broken Eagle winced but kept on coming. With his left, he slashed the throat of a third white man, as another musket blast tore through the side of his face, severing an ear. Still the Indian advanced, and now the white men scattered. A third musket blast tore into Broken Eagle's thigh, and he doubled over but did not fall, and when he took several more steps forward, the whites stepped back, fully expecting him to fall. He did not.

Instead, wracked with pain and wincing under the terrible burden of his injuries, he somehow managed to regroup for one final charge. He stood, looked around, and zeroed in on the man he took to be the leader of the white men.

Walks at Night, who had spoken to the white leader, stood aside and watched the charge of the great Indian warrior, and suddenly he felt ashamed of himself for lining up against this Indian hero. As the white leader stood and prepared himself for Broken Eagle's last charge, the proud Indian warrior gathered up every last ounce of strength within him and ran headlong at the white leader.

Walks at Night turned away from the sight that everyone else saw. All he heard was the final blast of a musket. He did not see the musket ball rip into the face of Broken Eagle, but he did hear the giant man's body hitting the ground with a loud thud as a cloud of dust rose around his fallen body.

As several of the whites stood around the dead body of Broken Eagle, the chase continued in the forest for the other Indians who had run off. There another Indian was felled by the blast of a gun fired by an Indian who was loyal to the English. In the morning light, when they went out to retrieve the bodies, the white men discovered that this was the body of King Philip himself.

Philip died at thirty-nine years of age, and when English authorities ordered his body to be butchered, the Indian who shot him beamed broadly as he lifted Philip's head and hand high in the sky.

"He believes he has the greatest trophies ever received since David took the head of Goliath," an English major laughed.

The rest of Philip's body was quartered and hung from four different trees.

This final victory totally demoralized the remaining Indians who saw any hope of defeating the English die with Metacomet. Most of the remaining Wampanoags and other warring captives were sold into slavery in the West Indies or Spain.

With the death of Metacomet, King Philip's War was all but over. Scattered skirmishes lasted for two more years, but with no real leadership or general battle plan, the fractured Indians were fighting a losing battle. All this had happened in two Indian generations—from Massasoit to Metacomet—since the white man had come to shore on a land he was determined to make his own.

▲   ▼   ▲

While Miriam Hale sat and stared out the window, devoid of all expression and unable to converse or to care for herself, an entire town rallied to her support. As she grew closer and closer to the time when her child would be delivered, she was given every consideration by each and every townsperson. The families of Brookfield took turns caring for her, and no one ever spoke of the tragedy that had befallen her, only of the scheduling of her care.

The child, a beautiful baby girl, was born at dawn on a warm day in April of 1677. Miriam delivered easily but rejected the child shortly thereafter. When the child was offered to her she turned her head away and stared into space, totally unwilling and unable to care for the infant. The women in the village were in a quandary over what to do, but one woman, Jane Porter, whose own child had been stillborn two days earlier, regarded the event as a Godsend, taking the baby in to nurse as her own.

Daniel and Jane Porter had a son, David, age one, and the child of their good fortune they named Dawn. Not Dawn Porter, just Dawn.

When Miriam Hale wandered out of camp six days later, Jane Porter took it upon herself to raise the child, having grown very attached to her as the days had gone by. Search parties were sent out to find Miriam Hale, but she could not be found. A week later, a small contingent of settlers, including the Porter family, moved from Brookfield to Hadley, Massachusetts, where they hoped the memories of the Brookfield attacks would not haunt them.

Two years later, the badly decomposed body of a young woman, believed to be Miriam Hale, was found lying in the woods by a hunting party about eight miles outside of Brookfield. The cause of her death was never determined.

For twenty years Dawn lived in Hadley as a member of the Porter family, which now numbered twelve children: five Porter sons, six Porter daughters, and Dawn.

Few people ever questioned why she carried no surname. The story that was given is that her parents had died when she was an infant and that Daniel and Jane Porter, out of the kindness of their hearts, had raised her as their own.

The story was only half true. While Jane really did love Dawn, Daniel had always treated her coolly, attending to her needs but withholding from her any of the affection which he lavished on all of his natural children.

Dawn herself rarely asked questions. When she was six, Jane explained to her that her mother had died shortly after Dawn's birth and that they never knew her father. She was never told anything else. The rest of the children were told simply that Dawn was not their real sister, although they always treated her as though she were. She was darker than any of the Porter sisters, and markedly more beautiful, with smooth dark skin and long, straight, black hair. Her teeth were very white and her eyes big and sparkling.

One day, in the summer of 1696, young David Porter approached his father, Daniel, while Daniel was loading the horses into their stalls in the evening.

"I have to talk to you, Father," David said shyly.

"I'm listening," Daniel replied, not turning his head away from his chores.

"You know, of course, that Dawn is not my real sister," David said.

Daniel looked at David expressionlessly.

"I told you that twenty years ago."

"Well that's good," David said hesitantly, "because I'm going to marry her."

Daniel dropped the harness he was holding in his arms and stared sternly at his eldest son.

"That is absolutely out of the question," he said. "And I don't want to hear anything so preposterous from you ever again."

David grew just as stern as his father at that moment, and stood his ground firmly.

"I don't think you heard what I said, Father. I didn't ask you, I told you, I'm going to marry Dawn."

Daniel Porter grabbed his son by the shirt with both hands and shoved his back up against the wall.

"You'll do no such thing," he sneered, his face only inches away from his son's.

David grabbed his father's arms and looked down at his hands. "Father, please," he said, and Daniel dropped his hands and backed off. "It's not a question of whether I can or whether I can't. I have to marry her."

"You don't have to do anything," Daniel yelled.

"I have to marry Dawn," David said quietly, looking down at his father's feet. "She's pregnant."

Daniel Porter felt a rage rising up inside of him unlike any emotion he had ever before felt. He lifted his large right hand up and swatted his son a solid backhand that tumbled him down on the ground and rolled him over and up against the wall. With his voice trembling and tears of rage filling his eyes, Daniel started pacing back and forth before his son, who knelt dabbing the blood from the corner of his mouth.

"David, boy. You can't marry that girl. There's something I've never told you about her."

David looked up at his father, and he knew that nothing his father could say could possibly make any difference.

"She's . . . she's . . . ," Daniel could not get the words out as he paced. "Her father was an Indian."

David stood and stared sternly at his father, an anger of his own now building up within him. "No wonder she has such beautiful eyes," he said coldly.

Daniel gritted his teeth, clenched his fist, and reached up to hit his son again, but David stopped him in his tracks.

"You hit me one more time, and I'll give you a fight you'll never forget," David Porter said firmly.

Daniel stood with his hand cocked, and as his son's words sunk in he felt his hand lowering. "How in God's name could something like this have happened?" he said, shaking his head and trembling.

"She never had a father," David said passionately. "You rejected her from the start. The only man who ever loved her is me. It's not that hard to understand."

Daniel was pacing back and forth. It was true. David had always treated Dawn tenderly and taken her side all his life against anyone who would confront her.

"It will destroy your brothers and sisters," Daniel said, still pacing, " . . . and your mother."

"I doubt it," David said. "The only one it will bother is you."

"Does anyone else know?" Daniel asked.

"Just Dawn and me," David answered.

"Then go back to the house, and I'll think about what's to be done."

"What's there to think about?" David asked.

"Only one thing, really," Daniel said in words that froze David in his tracks. "What's the best way to dispose of the girl so the reputation of your family will be intact."

David winced in disbelief at the words his father had just spoken, and he had no doubt that his father had been serious.

"I'll go back to the house, and wait for your word."

For several seconds, David stood looking at his father. There were so many things he wanted to tell him, that he loved him and respected him, and that he knew his father could forget his prejudices in due time if he tried hard enough, and other things.

"I'll be going back to the house then," David said finally, and when he got outside of the barn, he broke into a full-speed run.

Dawn was waiting for him at the front door of the farmhouse, and he kissed her with his hands on her shoulders.

"Get ready quickly. We have to go away at once."

A look of sadness crossed her face as she darted off to her room to grab a few personal belongings. David threw together a change of clothes and met Dawn in the kitchen, where they took David's mother to the back door and both of them put their arms around her.

David spoke as Dawn buried her head in Jane Porter's shoulder. "Mother, this may be the hardest thing I've ever had to say to you, because there's a possibility we'll never see you again."

Jane immediately felt herself growing faint as David continued.

"It should be a happy moment for all of us, but Father will explain to you later why it can't be. Dawn and I are going to have a baby, and Father can't accept it, so we'll be leaving now, and God only knows if we'll ever be back."

"Oh, dear Lord," Jane gasped as she lost the color in her face.

"This much I promise you," her son said. "We'll love each other. We'll stay together, and we'll never stop praying that someday we'll be able to return to you with a beautiful grandchild, or two."

David smiled at his mother as Jane embraced Dawn and then him.

"Where are you going?" Jane asked him frantically.

"Wherever God leads us," was the first thing Dawn said, and Jane Porter pulled the both of them close and hugged them.

"My prayers will be with you hourly, and you'll never leave my thoughts," Jane managed to say through her tears. "I love you both."

"I love you too, Mother," David said, embracing her.

"I'll be the best wife any of your sons have," Dawn promised, embracing Jane. "And I'll never forget the love you have given to me all of my life."

With that the two young people walked out the back door, and they were gone.

The night they made their escape, they had no idea where to go. They decided to head south where the winters would be warmer and walked for only about ten miles the first night, where they pitched camp under the full moon of July. There they lamented having to leave, but renewed their vows of love to one another under the summer stars and dreamed aloud together about the life they would have together and the happy children they would raise.

The next day they covered about twenty miles and began to follow a river downstream. It took them only one more day to reach a beautiful land they had never seen before, where two rivers met to form one, and they were stunned by the beauty of the area.

They set up camp on the banks of this new river and found evidence all around that Indians used to live there. There were cleared areas and hills behind the clearings where rock formations jutted out from caves, and upon exploring these hills, which were only a few hundred yards each direction from the river, they found arrowheads, fishing poles, bows, and other Indian artifacts.

They did not know where they were, but that evening when they bathed in the river they felt so good about the place that they decided two things. First, they would be hard pressed to find any land even remotely as beautiful as this area, no matter how far they traveled, and second, they were far enough away from Hadley so that Daniel Porter would never find them, but close enough to visit Jane Porter when the time came.

The thing that amazed them was that no other settlers were anywhere to be seen. For over twenty glorious years, they had the area virtually to themselves. Only occasionally would they see anyone, a few scattered travelers passing through. From their vantage point on a cliff high above the river, they watched, out of sight of the visitors. Once or twice while they explored the outlying areas they saw the sod huts or log cabins of isolated settlers, but here in this marvelous land they lived like Adam and Eve in a paradise, locked away in a pocket far removed from the clustered villages that were growing up all around them.

There, in their wilderness paradise, David and Dawn raised three daughters, each one as beautiful as her mother, and David hunted the forest and fished the streams, as their diet consisted of salmon, shad, venison, rabbit, squirrel, and whatever vegetables Dawn and her daughters raised in their garden.

The topic of visiting home came up on occasion, but each time they weighed the consequences, David postponed it, not willing to do anything to risk the paradise they had found. Soon the months led into years, until twenty-three years had passed, and their eldest daughter was twenty-two years old.

It was in that year, 1719, that twelve settlers moved into the area with permission from the Connecticut Colonial Assembly for the purpose of establishing a town. They decided not to change the name of the town that had been called Indian Springs on all of the local maps.

The twelve settlers had found a little paradise, and their town became the most famous of all the mineral springs in America, due to the curative qualities of its springs and its beautiful layout along the rivers.

When David and Dawn met two of the original founders, Benjamin and Lon Werner from Hadley, Massachusetts, they looked at one another and thought the same thing simultaneously.

"How long ago did you move to Hadley, Mr. Werner?" David asked Lon Werner on the day they met.

"Oh, by God. it was a long time ago. Over forty years."

"You moved there from Brookfield, Massachusetts," David said, surprising the man.

Lon Werner stared at David and squinted, but he did not recognize him.

"A couple by the name of Daniel and Jane Porter moved there at the same time," David said.

"Yes," Werner answered incredulously.

"Do they still live there?"

"Why, Daniel Porter died about ten years ago," Lon Werner said, and David felt a rush of sadness course through his veins.

"But Jane, yes, Jane Porter still lives there."

"In the same dwelling?"

"Who are you?" Werner asked.

"I'm David, her son. And this is my wife, Dawn."

A smile broke out and spread across Lon Werner's face as he began to recognize them. "The long-lost David Porter! And Dawn! None of us had any idea where you went, but I'm glad you're finally found. Do you have any children?"

"Yes. Three daughters."

"Then tonight the five of you will dine with me, and I'll tell you all about your family in Hadley."

That evening Lon Werner sat and cordially filled the Porters in on twenty-three years of Porter family history, and after two hours he capped the evening off with a story that moistened the eyes of all five Porters, and his own.

"Throughout all the years, I attended church services every Sunday I could. Every Sunday that I was there, she was there. For twenty-three years, she never missed. And every Sunday when the pastor asked for prayers from the congregation, it was understood that the first prayer would come from Jane Porter. Each and every Sunday she would stand and repeat the same prayer, yet each time it sounded like a new prayer because of its sincerity, though it was identical for over twelve-hundred Sundays. She said, 'Lord God Almighty, if it is Your will, let today be the day that I turn from my seat and see my children, David and Dawn, behind me. This is my will. Your will be done. In Your son Jesus' name. Amen.'"

David was deeply moved as Dawn put her head on David's shoulder and cried.

"I personally never stopped believing that one day her prayer would be answered," Werner said. "There's got to be a reason why we were brought together in this place today."

"God sent you," Dawn said softly, wiping the tears from her eyes.

David held Dawn close and lifted her face up with two fingers under her chin. The moon was full and the breeze airy and light. The stars shined brightly in the deep clear skies over the Willimantic River and the only sounds besides the river were the crickets and frogs, or the occasional hoot of an owl, which added peace to the night.

"I think it's about time our daughters met their grandmother," David said to Dawn.

She smiled up at David, and then at their new friend, Lon Werner.

"Will you accompany us, Mr. Werner?"

"A-yup. I reckon I will," he answered with a broad beaming smile across his face. "T'will be a fine day in Hadley."

▲　▼　▲

The next Sunday Lon Werner told the pastor what was happening, and after the service had started, David, Dawn, Leah, Sarah, and June Porter slid into the seat behind Jane Porter. She did not turn around.

All through the service, the pastor kept referring to the power of prayer. At the part of the service when prayers from the congregation were requested, the many people in the congregation turned their attention to Jane Porter, who stood, as she had for twenty-three years, and directed her eyes forward as she spoke.

A beam of light from the long glass window that stood ten feet high on the side of the church illuminated the woman who stood there with her hands and her voice raised to her God. The church was silent as half the church closed their eyes and bowed their heads, while the other half gazed at the woman in the beam of light. Behind her her children and grandchildren stood waiting to close the twenty-three year gap that had separated them.

"Lord God Almighty, if it is Your will, let today be the day that I turn from my seat and see my children, David and Dawn, behind me. This is my will. Your will be done . . . in Your son Jesus' name. Amen."

Behind her Dawn was unable to hold back her tears, and the congregation started buzzing as Jane Porter turned and fixed her eyes on the girl she had raised from infancy who had left so urgently over two decades before.

Just as David reached for her, she collapsed into his arms in tears and the handkerchiefs started popping out all across the chapel. For once in his life, the pastor stood speechless, and the three girls stood smiling as Jane Porter reached for them one by one. From across the aisle, one of the Porter sons and two of the daughters who had remained in Hadley came across the aisle and David firmly shook the hand of his brother Benjamin and embraced his sisters Rebecca and Christina.

There was joyous celebration in Hadley that day as everyone caught up on old times at the church picnic, and the biggest hit of the day was made by the three beautiful Porter girls, who divided the attentions of the young men of the congregation who gathered around them.

Two romances started that day, and before the year was finished, the oldest daughter, Leah, and the youngest daughter, June, had fallen in love with two Hadley men, and the next time the family visited there in May of 1720 it was for a double wedding.

Both daughters married fine Christian men, but David and Dawn felt very empty as they rode back to Indian Springs by horse and buggy with their remaining daughter, Sarah. All the way back, Sarah was very quiet and Dawn asked her why.

"It's all over for me now. I'll end up an old maid for sure," she said dolefully, and David looked at his twenty-one- year-old lovingly as he held the reins lightly in his hands.

"You don't think that God would let me lose all three of my daughters at once, do you, child? You mark my words, you'll meet a fine young man from Indian Springs and live close to your mother and me."

The rest of the way home, the three Porters spoke very little, enjoying the beauty of the landscape, and Sarah had not been home two weeks when a tall boy with sandy hair and a handsome, ready smile strolled up to the house. He had visited occasionally and could always be found laughing and talking with Leah, and when he spotted Sarah, his big smile crossed his face.

"Where's Leah?" he asked her younger sister.

"Why, I'd kind of hoped you'd come to see me, Thomas Bradford!"

Thomas smiled nervously and scratched his head behind his ear.

"Leah's married, Thomas," Sarah said smiling.

"Married?" he repeated, more surprised than disappointed.

"And so is June. So unless you want to talk about the spring planting with my mother and father, I'm what's left."

Sarah smiled up at Thomas Bradford, and the young man thought very fast for an answer.

"Shoot, you were always the prettiest sister anyway," he said, biting on a long weed he snapped up out of the ground.

That afternoon, Thomas Bradford and Sarah Porter walked for many miles through the farmlands of Indian Springs. By the time they got home that evening, they both knew all they had to know about each other to make the kind of decision some people agonize over for years.

David Porter was coming in out of the woods with a buck draped over his shoulders as Thomas and Sarah strolled up to the front of their log cabin. Dawn was inside, baking cornbread. The sun was big and yellow as it dipped low in the western sky and a red tint colored the clouds above the farmlands.

"Hi, Thomas," David yelled from the back of the house. "Done with the plowing already?"

"Go into the house with your mother, Sarah. I'll ask him by myself," Thomas whispered.

He walked around the house to meet Sarah's father and called out to him as he rounded the corner. "I'm done with my father's plowing. It's my own I'll be starting next."

"Your father give you a parcel of land to till, son?"

"No, sir. But I heard in town this morning about a public land drawing they're holding on June twenty-ninth. All you have to do is register, and you can draw lots for the meadowlands around Stafford Street."

"Have you registered?"

"Of course. I've always wanted my own farm that I can work hard and fill with fat, happy children."

"You're not married yet, are you, Thomas?"

Thomas Bradford smiled his big engaging smile at David Porter.

"No, sir, but I think your daughter Sarah is the prize of the county."

David threw the buck down off of his shoulders and stared at Thomas Bradford quizzically. "Exactly what's that supposed to mean?" he asked him seriously.

"Means if you and Mrs. Porter don't mind, I have a lot of work to do on the farm and not much time for courtship."

If Thomas hadn't been so friendly and sincere looking, David Porter might have been upset by the bluntness and quickness of his decision, but the boy had always had the ability to charm the frown off an ornery bull, and David fell easily under his spell.

"Have you even spoken to Sarah about this yet?" David asked him.

"Spent the better part of an afternoon with her, walking in the fields. That ought to be enough time for a woman to make up her mind," Thomas smiled.

The whole scene seemed too unbelievable to be real, and something in the warmth of Thomas Bradford's smile and the sincerity in his demeanor, added to the naivete with which he had made his last statement, got David Porter laughing. For a good two minutes he laughed and laughed, and when Thomas caught sight of Dawn and Sarah staring at them out the back window, he started laughing too, because they both looked as somber as though they'd just seen a ghost.

They couldn't hear a word the men had said to one another, and their immediate reaction was that David had found the idea so preposterous that it had rendered him hysterical.

Sarah had told her mother what Thomas was up to, and Dawn's only fear was that David would not take the young man seriously. Instead, David Porter and Thomas Bradford just stood there and laughed, so hard that the cabin seemed to shake, as Dawn and Sarah looked on somberly.

When they finally stopped laughing, David stood Thomas straight up with his only demand. "I'll ask you one question, Tom. And if you answer correctly I'll give you my blessings, but if you answer wrong, I'd better never see you near my daughter again."

The laughter stopped instantly, and Sarah and Dawn clanked heads together trying at the same time to get their ears closer to the window.

"Will you promise to do your level best to stay in Indian Springs, so I'll have at least one daughter near me in my old age?"

The broad Bradford smile covered the young man's face as he reached out his hand to his future father-in-law. In the kitchen, pots and pans clattered and clanged all over the floor, as the eavesdropping women backing away from the window toppled them on their way to the cabin door.

Sarah ran into Thomas Bradford's arms and he laughed as he lifted her up high into the red summer evening sky, and when he put her down, he reached out for Dawn as she walked slowly into his strong arms, where he hugged her naturally and smiled deeply into her beautiful dark eyes.

"Hi, Mom!" he smiled, and Dawn knew that this was a boy she was going to like.

▲　▼　▲

Two weeks before the July 29, 1720, land drawing, Thomas Bradford and Sarah Porter were married atop a beautiful high cliff overlooking the Willimantic River, where Sarah's parents, David and Dawn, had built their first home in the paradise known as Indian Springs. The place was known as Lover's Leap, named after an old Indian legend the origin of which they were not sure about.

Two weeks later, Thomas Bradford was one of thirty-seven participants in the drawing of lots for the meadowlands around Stafford Street. The plots were parceled out for homesteads, and Thomas drew a fertile flatland where corn would grow tall and firm, where cattle and oxen could graze freely, and where Sarah could tend to the hogs and chickens while Thomas hunted and worked the fields.

The Bradfords had seven children in the next seven years, six girls and one boy. The boy, Cornelius, who was born in 1727, was named as heir to the farm, and when Thomas was found dead in the cornfield late one autumn, at the age of forty-five, Cornelius took the farm over at age seventeen.

For six years, Cornelius worked the farm alone, and one by one his sisters married and moved out. In 1749, Cornelius married Lottie Vinton, and the couple wasted no time having children to help out on the farm. They had three consecutive sons the first three years, and seven consecutive daughters over the next twelve, and friends of Cornelius used to kid him that he'd lost his touch after the third boy.

In 1757, when Cornelius and Lottie's third son, Joshua, was five years old, a man who rode into town changed his life at that early age.

On a large white horse, this stately gentleman dressed regally in fine tailored clothing happened to stop at the Bradford farm where Joshua was tending the hogs, and when he pulled in his reins, he looked, to the young boy, to be at least ten feet tall in his saddle.

"Good day, lad," the gentleman said, tipping his hat to the boy, who bowed to the man politely. "Can you direct me to the mineral springs?"

Joshua pointed south through the meadowlands toward the downtown area where the furnaces had risen up like popcorn once a high grade of bog iron had been discovered near the springs.

"What's your name, son?" the stately gentleman asked, smiling broadly.

"Joshua Bradford, sir," the boy answered.

"You look like a fine young American."

The gentleman tipped his hat and turned his horse around, and as Joshua watched his big white horse trotting through the meadowlands, he knew that he had met someone important.

That evening at supper, Cornelius Bradford announced to the family that a statesman had appeared in town who was going to be staying awhile until his health got better. He was going to be recuperating by his doctor's orders, at the springs.

"What's his name, Father?" little Joshua asked.

"John Adams," Cornelius answered his son. "He's a very important colonial representative."

"He told me I looked like a fine young American."

"You met him?" Joshua's brother Caleb asked, deeply impressed.

"He rode through the farm this afternoon," Joshua answered.

"How do you know it was him?" Elijah asked his younger brother.

"It was him," Joshua answered. "I recognized him the same time he recognized me."

This brought a hail of laughter from Joshua's brothers and sisters, and even from his mother, but when Cornelius looked up at his family, the only one who wasn't laughing was Joshua.

"Enough!" Cornelius boomed angrily, slamming his large clenched fist down hard on the kitchen table, and the laughter ceased immediately. "I want the person in my family who does not believe that Mr. Adams can recognize a fine young American to stand and step forward to face me immediately and explain himself."

For a tense and quiet moment, no one budged, and even his mother realized the mistake she had made while Joshua was filled with a sense of pride that in one day both John Adams and Cornelius Bradford had recognized the same thing about him. The incident was filed away deeply and securely in his subconscious mind, where one day, many years later, it would surface again.

With ingenuity and hard work, Cornelius Bradford, his wife, Lottie, and his ten children built a large, prosperous farm with cattle, oxen, horses, hogs, and chickens in the barn area, and over two hundred acres of farmland sprawled out across the northern border of Indian Springs. A good deal of the work on the farm was done by Joshua Bradford, age twenty-three, who at 6' 2" and 225 pounds, had spent the better part of ten years working his body over eighty hours a week into the mass of solid muscle that it was.

Joshua was good on the farm, but better with a musket, having spent the majority of his leisure time in the woods hunting the abundant wildlife that the forestlands of Indian Springs provided.

A common joke among the Bradfords was that Joshua had received the identical looks of his grandfather, Thomas, with one glaring exception. He had the same sandy hair, receding a little bit, even at age twenty-three. He was tall and handsome with the same even disposition. The exception was that Thomas's face seemed to be frozen in a smile, while Joshua's seemed to be frozen in a frown. It was not a real frown, but more of a serious stare, with the corners of both sides of his mouth dipped downward, giving him the appearance of sober contemplation.

The Bradfords were devout Christians. They worked six days a week and rested on the seventh, and it was not only on a Sunday that the family would be led in prayer, for never would a night go by when Cornelius Bradford would not call his sons and daughters together, and with all assembled, hold family devotions offering thanks to God for the increase of their land and the protection of his family.

Joshua Bradford knew that the day would come for him to marry and own his own farm, but for now he was content to help his father and mother, at least until his younger sisters married and moved out on their own.

On a warm and sunny April afternoon in 1775, Joshua was out in the fields driving a plowhorse. At the sound of thundering hoofbeats approaching out of the northeast, he reined in the plowhorse and squinted his eyes against the horizon. Out of the northeast acreage there appeared a man named Israel Bessel, who was covered with dust, his horse lathered in a deep sweat.

"To arms!" he cried. "The war's begun. The British are here, and they've fired on the colonists in Lexington."

"Where are the British now?" Joshua called out to him.

"On their way to Concord," Bessel yelled, and without another word he was off.

Joshua's face, already locked in a frown, deepened in contemplation, and he hurried to tie up the days work.

Back at the farmhouse he met with his brothers, Caleb and Elijah, and there the three discussed enlisting in the colonial forces.

"It's a six-month enlistment period," Caleb said, scoffing at the length of time.

"We can't leave the farm for six months," Elijah answered.

"If everybody felt the same way there would be no more farms," Joshua said.

Caleb and Elijah laughed.

"The farms will still be here, and the taxes will still be paid to the crown," Elijah said.

"While Americans spill their blood for freedom," Joshua observed, not judgementally, but matter-of-factly.

"There'll be plenty of men to enlist, Joshua. Factory workers with nothing to lose."

"And a fair share of married men whose sons and daughters need them alive and well," Joshua countered.

"Well you go then, Josh. I'm staying on the farm," Caleb said.

"Me too," said Elijah.

At dinner that evening Joshua ate very quickly and left the table to go outside, where he strolled down the lawn and gazed out over the land his parents had raised him on. He was deep in thought as the big orange sun hung low in the western sky.

"I'll be talking to my son, and I'll have no interruptions." Cornelius said to his family as he left to follow Joshua out to the back pasture.

When Joshua heard Cornelius behind him he turned, and the serious way he gazed into his father's eyes was the giveaway that he would be gone on the morrow. Joshua reached down and pulled a weed out of the ground, and putting the stem into his mouth, he turned away from his father and looked out across the fields toward the setting sun.

"The colonials are fighting the British in Lexington and Concord, Massachusetts," Joshua said, scanning the sunset, which had now turned a brilliant red.

"Yes," Cornelius said softly.

"You have my brothers and sisters to help you on the farm. Caleb and Elijah have said they'll not be going, and it shouldn't be necessary for you to send more than one son anyway."

"Men have been marching off to war for as long as mankind has existed," Cornelius told his son. "Many of them never come back."

Joshua looked somberly at his father. "I'll be back," he said. "But if I go, I'll stay until the job is finished. There'll be no six-month enlistment for me."

"Why do you want to go, son?"

"Because I'm young and I'm strong and a good hand with a musket," he said softly. "And because my country needs me."

"Is that the way you truly feel?"

Joshua knew that his father was testing him, which he had often done before in his life. He wanted to know the depth of his convictions and he wanted to be sure that Joshua knew the consequences of volunteering before he did it.

The cool evening breezes waved the branches of the tall trees that lined the grassy field behind the farmhouse as the father and his son talked.

"I was born here, Father." the son said. "You were born here. Grandpa Thomas was born here. The British soldiers that killed the men at Lexington killed men like you and me who live here. They tax us. They hand us all sorts of laws. They want us to adopt their church. That's not the kind of country I want for my grandchildren."

The father gazed into the son's eyes with love.

"What kind of country do you want, Josh?"

"I want a country where I can pray in whatever fashion I desire, where I can serve my Lord in freedom and seek His will for my life unhampered by foreign powers and excessive laws, where I can own the land I work, and vote for the men and the policies I want to govern me. I want a voice in my government and I want my tax money to be spent to better the lives of my children. Great Britain is the land our ancestor's left. America is the land they found. It will be what we make it. Nothing more, nothing less. But it will not be what someone else tells us it will be, not now, not ever."

The father broke off a long weed and put it into his mouth to chew. He stood closer to the son, and the father's arm found its way around the son's shoulder.

"Well spoken, son. I've always known you to be mature beyond your years. I've known that from the time you were five years old when you met John Adams."

"I remember," Joshua smiled.

"But war is serious business, Josh. When you choose to enter it, there can be only two ways out."

"Victory or death," Joshua said before his father could continue.

"You're sure you want to go?"

"I have to go, Father. For our future generations, and for all the men who want to go but can't, for various reasons."

"Then I'll not send you into battle unarmed," the father said.

And with that, Cornelius Bradford, age forty-eight, 6' 2" tall, and 245 pounds of solid muscle, dropped to his knees on the ground outside his farmhouse and under the deep red sky he voiced a prayer for his son to his God.

"Almighty Father, God of our refuge and our strength, send Your mighty hoards of angels down to encircle Your son Joshua, as he marches off to do Your will. Be with him every moment and keep him ever mindful that Your eyes are always upon him. Give him courage, and strength, and grant him the victory in Your son Jesus' name. Amen."

▲   ▼   ▲

The next morning, Joshua was up before anyone else in the family and his mother found him cleaning his musket by the dawn's early light. She cooked him an ample breakfast of bacon, eggs, cornbread, hotcakes and maple syrup, biscuits, gravy, and ham. He drank two quarts of milk, and before he left, each of his brothers and sisters embraced him and wished him God's blessings.

The last to bid him farewell was his father, Cornelius, who gave him a big bear hug, patting him on the back and smiling at him with pride.

"I'll probably be home in time to harvest the fall crops," Joshua said.

"You can't be sure about that," Cornelius said. "It might take longer than you think."

"Shouldn't," Joshua answered. "With so many men answering the call from all over the colonies, how long can it take?"

"We'll pray for you, Josh," Cornelius said seriously. "You're free to use your own judgement. If you want to, you come home after six months."

Cornelius did not want Joshua to feel bound by the vow he had made in conversation to him the previous day to stay until the job was done.

"I'll be leaving for Indian Springs when the British are leaving for England," Joshua said.

With that he turned and left.

"Godspeed," Cornelius said again, but an aching entered his heart as he watched his son depart.

"Fathers should never have to send their sons to war," Cornelius said to his wife, Lottie, ashen-faced and shaken.

"God will bring him home," Lottie answered, and the day on the farm began.

As Joshua entered the churchyard on Stafford Street, men were saying good-bye to their families all over the yard, and at ten in the morning Captain Robert Moulton gave the order to march. As one man played a fife and another a drum, sixty-five sons of Indian Springs left the security of their hometown for the uncertainty of battle against the world's number one fighting force. Only forty-three of them would return.

The men who left that day were proud young men. Confident and anxious to fight, they went into the American Revolution willingly. For too long they had had drummed into them the injustices of the taxation system the British were imposing on the colonists, and now that the British had fired on the colonists at Lexington, here was a chance to rid themselves of the menacing curse once and for all.

By the middle of June, these sixty-five and almost three thousand others were preparing themselves to defend the southern projection of Bunker Hill known as Breed's Hill, on the Charleston Peninsula across the Charles River from Boston.

The British were excited about the opportunity to meet the loose-knit colonial rebels on their terms, European-style. They readied their eighteen-inch bayonets onto the ends of their muskets and prepared to teach the Yankees a lesson the colonials would do well never to forget.

At two o'clock in the afternoon, the British intensified the cannon fire from their ships in the harbor, and long columns of redcoats launched their small boats. The colonials continued to dig themselves in, as they had all night, and prepared to meet the enemy face to face.

Front and center in the American lines, a sandy-haired American with a stern expression scanned the horizon and tried to determine what course the action would take. Behind him a church bell struck three bells, and the British started coming. Three lines of them formed, and they looked like a giant red tidal wave as Joshua Bradford leveled his musket and waited for the command to fire.

The American commanding officer was William Prescott, who patiently waited until the British were within range before he gave the order to fire. When he did, eight out of ten British soldiers fell and they were quickly replaced by men in the column behind. Stepping over their dead countrymen, the British kept on coming as Breed's Hill turned red with blood.

When they were thirty yards away, Prescott yelled, "Fire!" again, and again almost the entire British front rank was destroyed. Now the exchange was deafening, with hundreds of men dying on both sides, but before they advanced any further, the British broke and ran down the hill to their boats.

There they were rallied again, and this time the colonists were low on gunpowder. When the Yankees fired their next volley, it was their last, and when the British saw that their powder had run out, they started storming the hill.

As the Yankees stood to meet the charging British, whose bayonets were leveled as they stormed up the hill, Joshua took a musket shot across the cheek. He felt a hot searing pain, and the warm blood that ran down his face filled his mouth and covered his shirt. When the first line of British soldiers reached the Yankee trench, Joshua swung his musket like a club, knocking the first British soldier he came in contact with to the ground and wrestling his bayonet away from him.

He ran the soldier through with his own bayonet, and as he pulled it out, he saw another British soldier out of the corner of his eye barreling down on him. He moved just in time to save his life, as the bayonet cut a slice of flesh across his chest, but when he moved, the soldier's momentum carried him past Joshua, who kicked him to the ground on the way by and ran him through as well.

The man screamed as Joshua's bayonet became lodged in his ribs, and as the battle raged, the colonists heard the order to retreat. Joshua was the last man to leave, standing his ground and yelling at the British as he pointed this way and that with yet another bayonet that he had retrieved from a dead British soldier.

Standing there menacingly, covered with his own blood, the young American waited until all of his fellow Americans were behind him before he, too, turned and ran.

So the British took Bunker Hill that day, but the cost had not been cheap. Over one thousand British soldiers lost their lives that day, as did over four hundred Americans. But that day a soldier was born whose bravery and resolve has been matched countless times down through the history of American warfare ever since.

Holding the stripe on his chest with one hand, and dabbing the blood from the wound on his face with the other, Joshua Bradford walked somberly on to Cambridge to await the next confrontation.

"We lost a lot of good men out there today," a young man walking next to Joshua said to him.

"A-yeah," Joshua answered, looking at the blood that covered his hands. "You see that?" Joshua said to the man who was walking beside him. "That's American blood, spilled on American soil. They ain't gonna get by with it."

▲　▼　▲

At that moment in Philadelphia, Pennsylvania, a man Joshua had met eighteen years previously was preparing himself to present to the Continental Congress the name of a modest, mature, and God-fearing man to become commander in chief of the new Continental Army.

Although he did not want the job for which John Adams formally nominated him, the Continental Congress voted and George Washington was unanimously chosen. When he accepted the position, and declared that he would serve without pay, Washington also said, "I beg it to be remembered by every gentleman in this room, that I, this day declare, with the utmost sincerity, that I do not consider myself equal to the command I am honored with."

When the tall, firm-jawed Virginian with the deep blue eyes mounted his horse and rode off toward Cambridge, Massachusetts, to assume command of the Continental Army, he had no idea what awaited him.

The men at Cambridge had already seen military action against the British, but they were not an army, and they were definitely not disciplined.

Loosely led, in many cases by men with whom they had grown up, they were a rough conglomeration of hometown units unprepared to fight, but given to drinking and rowdy behavior and most undisciplined in their manners.

Seeing this as he rode in and observed the appearance of the men of whom he was about to assume command, General Washington's first command given the day after he formally took command perked up everyone's ears. The word went out to the various units that the general required and expected a due observance of those articles of war established for the government of the army which forbid profane cursing, swearing, and drunkenness. In a like manner, he required and expected all officers and soldiers not engaged in actual duty to punctually attend Divine services to implore the blessings of heaven upon the means used for their safety and defense.

George Washington was a man after Joshua Bradford's own heart. Upon hearing his orders, Joshua was the first man at worship service that next morning, and he studied carefully the eyes and countenance of the commander in chief, who humbled himself to pray for the men he was about to lead. The quiet, unassuming way that the tall, blue-eyed Virginian placed everything in the hands of God left a deep and lasting impression on Joshua Bradford.

For several minutes after the service had broken up, Joshua followed George Washington with his eyes, and as he watched him he made a firm decision within himself. *This is a man I can follow,* Joshua said to himself, and once the decision was locked in, the bond of loyalty was sealed.

All that summer, as the officers Washington had chosen to whip the Continental Army into shape drilled them, Joshua and the rest of the patriots in the army grew in confidence as together they watched a group of unorganized men become an army under the guidance of their tall, quiet leader.

By the time they were ready to engage the British in full military action, Joshua would realize what a Godsend this general was. But for now, that time was a long time coming. None of the veterans of the battle of Bunker Hill knew this, of course. And many of the critics that General Washington counted as the months went by could not understand why he would not just dig in and fight instead of retreating, retreating, retreating.

But if Washington knew the strengths of his fledgling army, he also knew their weaknesses. Numbers were his main problem. As enlistment periods would come to an end, men would begin to pine for their homes and their families, and by the end of their short stints, they would be gone. The Continental Congress would not give him a full regular army or allow long term enlistments, so it was men like Joshua Bradford re-enlisting which kept the army alive. The rapport they were able to build with their field commander kept them coming back. Because General Washington personally rode among the troops, rallying and encouraging them, they talked of the respect they all had for him and their mutual desire not to let him down.

Each man grew in confidence as their general would talk to them personally and refer to the Divine plan and the providential manner with which they always fared after each encounter with the enemy. Because their leader believed, they believed.

On and on they marched through the colonial wilderness, retreating from the powerful British when chased, but then turning to follow them and harass them when they, in turn, withdrew. The revolutionary war dragged on this way, with the Americans winning a great military victory at Saratoga, while losing badly at Brandywine as they tried in vain to stop the British from taking Philadelphia.

When the British set up an armed camp in America's chief city, things began to look bad for the Americans as thousands more British troops poured into the colonies.

With no supplies, little ammunition, and winter approaching, the remnants of Washington's troops limped into an area fifteen miles outside of Philadelphia in the fork of Valley Creek and the Skylkill River. This lonely outpost is where the turning point in the war took place, and it was not a military encounter that did it.

While the British enjoyed warm beds and good meals in Philadelphia, the Americans were freezing and barely surviving in the desolate winter camp which became their proving ground. Fifteen miles from Philadelphia, crowded into hastily built log cabins where all were bitterly cold and one in four were in grave danger of freezing to death, a new determination slowly grew within the minds of each of the individual patriots at Valley Forge.

Many of them were nearly naked, as articles of clothing had been stripped away to create makeshift footgear when their shoes had worn down the previous fall. Their main food consisted of cornmeal mixed with water. It was baked on a big stone in the middle of an open fire. They were called firecakes, and they barely kept the men alive. Many men lost limbs to amputation, as fingers, toes, and even arms and legs would freeze and then turn black.

Eleven thousand men came to Valley Forge that winter. Only eight thousand, two hundred and fifty were still alive when spring came. The rest died of flu, smallpox, typhus, or sheer exposure. The biggest problem was that they could not allow their true condition to be known to anyone, lest the British find out and destroy them in their weakened condition.

But incredibly a strange peace settled in over the army that winter as their stolid general moved among them, encouraging them, and leading them by his own rock-solid determination, the absoluteness of his belief in their cause, and his willingness to endure along with them. The men who came into the army had been a group of individual patriots banded together by a love for freedom and a hatred of oppression. In Cambridge, Massachusetts, in what seemed like ages ago, this group of men had been molded into a united army. Now, under the leadership of this most incredible man, the army was being harshly but effectively molded into a nation.

Joshua and the men who were with him listened as George Washington encouraged them, warning them to fear only God and to turn away from every sin and base thought that it would be easy to turn to under the existing circumstances in favor of virtues that Godly men ought to practice. Personal discipline and fear of God became their individual creeds.

Washington was humble. He was gentle. He cared for each and every man under his command and for the cause they had taken up. He believed in God, and he believed that all of them were engaged in an exercise of God's will. He translated that belief to his men. For this reason, they believed in him and followed him. And when Joshua limped out to the edge of his camp to watch the general walk apart, for Joshua was one among many who had always been drawn to this inspiring leader, he stopped and watched from a respectful distance away as Washington fell to his knees, alone in a wooded area, and prayed silently, binding his will to that of his God.

At times like these, Joshua Bradford was reminded that he was involved in something that was much bigger than either the general or his army.

The following spring, Joshua and the other followers of George Washington emerged with a new spirit that the British would never succeed in subduing. After battling the British to a standstill at Monmouth, the Americans wore the British down. Never again would the two main bodies of the opposing armies meet in combat, and for two years indecisive skirmishes became the rule, until slowly the British began to realize that the Americans would simply never give up.

The major American victory came at Yorktown in the fall of 1781 when Earl Cornwallis and six thousand British troops were forced to surrender to the Americans. For two more years the war dragged on. Then late in 1783, the peace treaty with the British was finally signed.

December 4, 1783, was the last day Lieutenant Colonel Joshua Bradford would ever wear a uniform. He stood at Fraunce's Tavern in lower Manhattan, ten days after the British had left the city for good. There Joshua and all of the senior officers of the Continental Army stood and waited for the farewell luncheon which would be their last chance to say good-bye to their commander in chief.

George Washington arrived promptly and was greeted by a roomfull of men who had grown to love and respect this man with a depth of feeling that only men who have fought together in combat can understand. One by one, the men approached General Washington, and very few words were spoken as each man stood in front of their leader and either shook his hand or embraced him.

When it was Joshua's turn, he was unable to stop his tears from falling as he stood face to face with America's leader.

"General," Joshua said as his voice quavered. "You are the father of our country."

There, in the warmth of the lower Manhattan tavern, General George Washington and Lieutenant Colonel Joshua Bradford embraced, and it was a moment that Joshua would cherish for the remainder of his life.

A reporter on the scene recorded Joshua's words to General Washington, and the following day's local newspaper greeted the people with the headline, "Father of Our Country."

Increasingly the title caught on and it was one of the many titles the great leader was remembered by in the decades which followed.

After each man had had the opportunity to bid his own private farewell to America's leader, the general offered his final farewell to the lot of them. "Gentlemen, I have prayed that your latter days will be as prosperous and happy as your former ones have been glorious and honorable."

With that the tall American turned and started to leave the room. Characteristically Joshua followed, once again, as always, keeping a respectful distance between them, as others surrounded him on his way out of the room. Outside, Joshua watched him until he was out of sight, and only then did he start to think about his long journey home. He had been a boy of twenty-three years of age when he had last seen anyone in his family. Now he was a man of thirty-one, and as he started for home, he remembered for the first time in many years the vow he had made to his father not to return until his job had been finished. It was finished.

Two men retired in opposite directions that evening. Washington went south to his home in Virginia and Bradford went north to his home in Connecticut. Both left with the humble realization that each of them had played an important role in the birth of a nation. For every soldier then, as it is now, the trip home was exhilarating. Not for a very long time could Joshua remember craving a tall pitcher of ice cold milk and a home-baked apple pie.

▲　▼　▲

The Christmas of 1783 was one of the most memorable ones ever spent on the Bradford farm. When Joshua had left, the world had been a different place. But despite the many changes that had taken place in the world, the Bradford farm had remained very much the same.

At the Christmas party held in his honor, Joshua met a girl that had grown up in Laurel Hill, Connecticut, the next town east of Indian Springs. Her name was Julie Alden, and she was a descendant of John and Priscilla Alden. Joshua began to court her, and at the same time fell in love with the sprawling town that stood high in the hills overlooking Indian Springs.

The following summer the couple was married, and Joshua obtained a 200-acre plot of land where he started a sawmill which he ran for the remainder of his life. By the turn of the century, in 1800, lumbering had become one of Laurel Hill's leading industries, and many of the town's 500 residents made their living working at Joshua Bradford's sawmill.

Joshua and Julie had three children, George, Martha, and Milo, named after America's first president and his wife, and Joshua's superior officer who had been killed at Yorktown while fighting alongside Joshua. It was after Milo Ives had died that Joshua had received his battlefield commission from General Washington.

All three of the children of Joshua and Julie Bradford worked hard at the sawmill, but when Joshua died in 1816 at the age of sixty-four, George inherited the business, and as much as Milo loved and respected his older brother, he did not want to work for him, so he started to look around for other opportunities.

It did not take him long to be led back to Indian Springs, where the farm his grandfather had owned desperately needed a man to take over. Still a large, sprawling farm in the northeast corner of Indian Springs, high above the factories that had sprung up all around the center of town, the farm had fallen into disrepair as one after another of Cornelius Bradford's children had left to seek careers elsewhere.

When Milo came to the farm in 1816 with his wife Edna and two children, his grandmother Lottie was eighty-seven years old. For the next five years, Milo devoted himself to bringing the farm back, and when Lottie died at age ninety-two, he was stunned when he found that she had named him as sole owner of the large farm.

Milo was twenty-five years old when he inherited the farm and never had he felt so wealthy in all his life.

"George can have the sawmill in Laurel Hill," Milo said to his sister Martha, "Farming is what I want to do, and now I own this magnificent farm."

Within the next twenty years, Milo and Edna's family was completed. They had nine daughters and seven sons. In the summer of 1839 an event took place in the farmlands and rolling hills in the northeast corner of Indian Springs which sent positive repercussions into the lives of hundreds of future immigrants to whom the United States of America was still only a dream.

The event was significant because it was a kind of photograph of the mind set of the Bradford family in 1839. They were people of great faith and full prayer lives. The Bradfords had always believed that it was absolutely essential to keep faith with God and with one another. They were sure that if they kept faith with God, God would keep faith with them. It was the reason they believed they had come through every war, storm, and family challenge in early New England days and the very same reason so many others who had not kept faith had fallen through the cracks.

They believed in God's mercy in the form of Divine providence, and they believed that one Bradford son, Cyril, had been marked out for great blessings by the incident that befell him that memorable summer of 1839. It is a story that has been passed down in great detail and with much celebration throughout all the generations of Bradford family history, and it happened like this.

In the early summer of 1839, when Milo Bradford's eldest son, Earl, was twenty-five years old and already farming the expansive acreage on the south side of the farm, near Indian Springs, Milo's son Cyril was five-and-one-half years old. At that time a visitor came riding up the dirt trail that led through Bradford land to the central area of the farm. The main house sat overlooking the vast barnyard that was full of oxen, cattle, pigs, and chickens. The man was a real estate salesman looking for interested buyers of large plots of farmland in the southern part of the state.

Hearing that the Bradfords had sixteen children, he thought them to be prime candidates for a land deal, and it was no secret to the sons of Milo Bradford that they could not all inherit the farm. The family of Milo and Edna Bradford was beginning to feel the pinch of a population that was exploding.

From a few families in the 1600s to a few hundred in the 1700s, there were now thousands of settlers that were hunting the woods and farming the lands of southern New England. The way had long ago been cleared for the settlement of the area by the disappearance of the Indians after King Philip's War, and now, except for the few Indians who were left on isolated reservations, almost all of the Indians were gone.

With sixteen children to watch out for, Milo Bradford was quietly concerned with how his children would divide the holdings he had acquired and how many of them he would be able to keep on the farm. With so many young people moving westward, Milo, who loved each of his sixteen children equally, wanted to keep as many as he could down on the farm. Of course he knew that this would be impossible, so it was with keen interest that he listened to the salesman who sat with him that evening.

"I represent the Hammonassets of Southern Connecticut, who are selling large parcels of land for farming to a selected group of people. The Indians need money, and they don't want to sell the land to developers but to farmers who will preserve the rural character of the acreage that surrounds the reservation. The farmland is not so far away that you will be unable to visit back and forth, and it beats sending some of your children westward, where you may never see them again."

Milo's second son, Elwin, was intrigued by this salesman, and asked his father if he couldn't leave for a few days to inspect the farmland in question.

"How far away is it?" Milo asked the young man.

"Twenty, maybe thirty miles south of here," the young man answered, honestly not realizing that the land in question was nearly fifty miles away near the Connecticut shoreline.

"If I like the land, I'll buy it in a heartbeat," Elwin said, and Milo gave his son permission to take the produce cart with tents and enough supplies to last for over a week.

As soon as Milo's son Cyril heard the conversation, he bolted across the room and jumped into his father's lap.

"Can I go with Elwin, Dad? Please?" Cyril begged.

"Oh Cyril, you're much too young to take a trip that long." Milo answered, but when the boy persisted, Elwin looked to their father and shrugged.

"It's okay with me, Dad. It'll probably be fun having Cyril along to ease the monotony."

"Will you obey your brother and do everything he tells you to do?" Milo asked Cyril.

"Oh, yes. And I'll take Lady along to keep me company," Cyril said of his pet collie, Lady.

Edna looked sternly at Elwin. "Can I trust you to watch over him?" she said.

"I'll protect him with my life," Elwin answered, smiling.

So Milo consented, which sent Cyril leaping into the air with joy. Except for an occasional trip into town with his father, young Cyril had never been anywhere, and the prospect of a week-long trip fascinated him as though he were traveling abroad.

The next day, Elwin, Cyril, the dog Lady, and the young salesman set out to look at the farmland, and after traveling about thirty miles they stopped to rest. For hours Cyril talked, and talked, and talked to the point where Elwin smiled broadly in amazement that so small a boy could have so much to talk about.

"We gonna' see real Indians, Elwin?"

"A-yeah."

"With bows and arrows, and headdresses?"

"Maybe."

"You gonna buy their land?"

"A-yeah."

"I bet you can get it cheap."

"Why?"

"Because Indians are stupid."

"Who told you that?"

"They lost the land we live on didn't they?"

"A-yeah."

"If they were smart, they'd have kept it."

"That's not fair, Cyril. You don't know how they lost it."

"I know they lost it and we have it. They must be stupid."

"Cyril, you may know it, but we're part Indian ourselves. I don't know exactly how many generations ago, but somewhere in our ancestry there was a great Pequot warrior. Daddy can tell you what he knows about it when we get home. Besides it's not right to judge people until you have all the facts, Cyril. And you can never judge an Indian until you have walked a mile in his moccasins."

From that point, Cyril took his brother down many other avenues of discussion, and forgot for a time that he had called the Indians stupid. After many miles were behind them, the sun started setting in the western sky and Elwin began to get annoyed at the young salesman who had told him it was only a twenty or thirty-mile trek.

"It's farther than I recollect," the salesman explained, and when they had traveled another five or six miles, they set up camp for the night. Elwin was only mildly upset, but midway through the second day, when they had traveled almost fifty miles, he was angry.

Without speaking his mind to the salesman, he had already decided that if the man would lie about the distance to the land in question, he would also lie about its desirability, and Elwin had quietly resolved that unless the land was of exceptional quality for farming, he would write off the entire experience, chalk it up to education, and return home.

The next day the salesman showed Elwin and Cyril Bradford the large area of shoreline that makes up what would become known in future years as Hammonasset Beach, and when Elwin saw how sandy the land was and heard the price, $100 an acre, he was angry and insulted.

"How much land are we talking about?" Elwin asked quietly, trying to mask his anger.

"Almost a half mile of oceanfront property, guaranteed to double in value in only a short time," the young salesman answered.

"Prime farmland, you told me," Elwin said rapidly losing confidence in the validity of anything the salesman said.

"Oh yes," the salesman said enthusiastically.

"A hundred dollars an acre?" Elwin asked.

"A good price, don't you agree?"

"What do you grow, seaweed?"

The man laughed, but Elwin was not amused. *Probably a couple hundred feet of ocean sand, if this guy's estimate of distance is anything like his description of the property lines,* Elwin thought to himself.

"It's been nice knowing you," Elwin said, offering his hand to the salesman, who looked perplexed that Elwin had been so unimpressed.

When Elwin took Cyril's hand and walked back to the wagon, Cyril was stunned upon discovering that Lady was missing, her collar still hanging from the wagon.

"Elwin, where's Lady?" the boy cried out in horror, already starting to feel his eyes fill up with tears.

"I don't know, Cyril. Let's look around."

Cyril was in a panic, so Elwin drove the wagon up and down the shoreline, asking everyone they saw if they had spotted a beautiful collie dog and getting the same "No," each time.

One man laughed and said, "The Indians around here steal everything that isn't tied down, and a lot of what is."

Cyril immediately reasoned that it had been his bad-mouthing of the Indians that had reaped this tragic result, and the remorse he felt was overwhelming. All day the two brothers rode up and down the shoreline, tracing and retracing each of their steps and leaving their address and offers of a reward wherever they went. After describing the dog to local police officials and posting a reward sign on the town hall bulletin board, the two Bradfords pointed the wagon northward and began the long trip home, without Cyril's dog.

All the way home the boy sobbed, and no amount of consoling could do any good as they made their long voyage back. The first night Cyril slept fitfully and awoke crying several times during the night.

When they finally returned home on the evening of the second day away from the shore, Elwin went straight to their father with the story. "The land's no good, and Lady's been stolen. Cyril's been crying for two days, and I can't get him to stop, no matter what I say or do. He was probably too young to have taken along. I'm afraid his first venture away has been a very hard experience for him. I'm sorry."

"Come here, my son," Milo said, extending his long, strong arms to his little son.

Without looking up, the young lad walked over to his father and climbed into his lap, and when his head hit his father's shoulder, the tears flowed freely as though a faucet had been turned on.

"We are all asked to accept a little bit of heartache in our lives, son. This one, I guess, is yours."

"The . . . Indians . . . stole . . . Lady," Cyril sobbed, as Milo hugged him with his big strong arms.

"So many times in our lives we lose the things we love. It's a mystery that only God knows the answer to," Milo said, but Cyril would not be comforted.

"Do . . . you . . . think . . . God . . . could bring her back?" Cyril pleaded with his father.

"God can do anything He wants to, Cyril, but most probably He has some other reason for taking the dog away. No man knows the ways of the Lord. Maybe another boy poorer than you really needed a dog," Milo suggested. "Or maybe the dog was sick, and God didn't want you to have to watch her die. Or maybe God has a better dog for you someplace else, just waiting for you to find her."

"There's no better dog than Lady," Cyril said, "anywhere in the world. She's the greatest dog God ever made, and now she's gone."

Cyril again collapsed in tears, and for the first time in over twenty years, Edna Bradford saw tears in her husband's eyes as he hugged and rocked his boy.

Turning away in embarrassment, Milo Bradford thought to himself, *There've been sixteen children born to our marriage, and never have I seen such heartache in any one of them. There has to be an answer for it somewhere.*

For several moments there were no sounds, save the runners of Milo Bradford's rocking chair going back and forth on the floor as Cyril lay in his lap, his little heart breaking. An occasional sniffle was all that broke the silence in the room until Cyril became strangely quiet and stared into the floor, concentrating on a revelation that was coming to him.

"It's because I called the Indians stupid. I just can't believe I did it," Cyril said, too ashamed to raise his eyes to his father's.

"When did you call the Indians stupid?"

"When I was talking to Elwin in the wagon on our way to see the land."

"What made you do that, son?"

"I don't know, but I'm paying for it now."

"It's not really nice to call anyone stupid, but I'm just wondering what made you say that about the Indians."

"They're different than us."

"Cyril, there are many, many kinds of people in the world who are different than us. Just because they're different doesn't make us better or them stupid."

"I know that now," Cyril said glancing up at his father before lowering his eyes again very quickly. "But I'll tell you one thing. I know that God didn't like it because I'm paying a heavy price for it now."

This from a five-and-a-half-year-old boy.

"You know now that it was wrong."

"Yes," Cyril answered meekly.

"You know that if you ask God to forgive you, He has said that He would."

"I know."

"Well."

On his father's lap, in the living room of their old farmhouse, Cyril Bradford buried his head into his father's shoulder and started sobbing.

"I'm too ashamed," the boy said.

"Cyril, none of us is perfect. We all make mistakes. But God knows our heart. And He forgives us all of our wrongdoings if we tell Him we're sorry and that we won't do it again.

"Come on," Milo said, taking his son by the hand and walking him out into the back yard. "Now it's only you, me, and God. Go ahead and ask Him to forgive you."

Cyril took a deep breath and closed his eyes and the agony in his face told his father of the sincerity of his remorse.

"God, I'm sorry I said what I did about Your Indians, and I'll never say anything bad about them or about anybody else, ever again. And now could You please bring back Lady? And God, I love you. And God, Amen."

Cyril opened his eyes and looked at his father, and Milo beckoned to him, and when Cyril hugged his father, Milo said, "Good prayer, Cyril."

"Could I go and wait for Lady now, Dad? After I do my chores?"

"As long as you're within sight of the farmhouse, it'll be all right with me," Milo answered, caught off guard by the boy's request.

"Thanks, Dad," Cyril said hugging his father.

"Dad?"

"Yes, son?"

"God is going to bring Lady back, isn't He?"

Milo looked at his son who wanted more than anything to believe it was true. "God doesn't always answer our prayers the way we want Him to, but He always answers the right way," Milo told his son, certain within himself that the dog was lost.

"God is going to bring Lady back, Dad. I know He is."

If Cyril Bradford knew it, he was the only one who did, because neither his parents nor any of his siblings could believe the miracle he was hoping for, but the glimmer of hope in the small boy's heart was enough to finally give him the night's sleep he had long needed, and he slept overtime the next morning, arising a full hour and a half past his normal time of six o'clock.

After laying him in his bed the night before, Edna turned to her husband and asked him pointedly, "What are the odds of the dog returning?"

"None," Milo answered. "The Indians who have stolen her have either eaten her or tied her down for certain, and we will never see her again. Even if she escaped, it's over fifty miles through rough terrain, and no animal of God could possibly remember the way."

"We'll have to get the boy another dog soon then," she said with pleading eyes she knew her husband could not resist.

"A-yeah. Soon as we can."

Meanwhile the boy slept soundly and rested himself for his vigil. The next day, after a full breakfast of pancakes with maple syrup, cornbread and butter, bacon, eggs, and milk, Cyril ran out into the barnyard to do his morning chores. He cleaned the chicken coop and gathered the eggs before slopping the hogs and carrying the milk buckets from the barn to the house. After emptying the trash out of the wastebaskets in the house and carrying it out to the fireplace outdoors and dutifully burning the trash, he lit out for the edge of the cornfield to sit and wait for his dog to return.

For several hours he sat there anxiously, his heart aching and breaking a little more as each hour went slowly by. Finally, close to dark, Milo walked the half mile down to the edge of the field where his son was seated on an old stump, staring off into the empty horizon.

"If the dog comes home tonight, she won't stop here, son," Milo said, picking his little son up into his arms. "She'll come all the way back to the farmhouse and there you'll be awaiting her."

"Probably it'll be tomorrow, Dad," were the only words the boy spoke as Milo hefted him onto his back and ambled up the long hill, carrying his boy piggyback.

Cyril's routine was the same for the next several days, and Milo's was as well, and as each day went by the boy grew more and more silent and more and more withdrawn. Finally, at the end of the ninth day, Cyril surprised his father as he managed the first smile, however slight, that his father had seen in over a week.

"Tomorrow's gonna' be the day, Dad. I know it is."

"Why do you say that, son?"

"Because I said my best prayer today, and I know now that tomorrow's going to be the day."

Milo said nothing, just carried his boy on his back and wondered silently how in the world he was ever going to explain to him that God loved him anyway, despite the loss of his dog.

The next day, Cyril Bradford ran to the edge of the field and every time his father's plowing took him within sight of the boy, Milo glanced over at his little son standing on his tiptoes on the stump until finally Milo could stand the agony no more.

He reined in his team, left it standing in the field, and walked boldly into the house.

"Make him the feast of his life, Edna, with all the trimmings he most enjoys, because I'll not let him go down there ever again."

The boy's mother busied herself about the kitchen as Milo walked once again the long half-mile down to where the boy stood searching against hope at the unyielding horizon. When he got to within ten yards of his little son, he stood for over a minute and tried to gather his thoughts as the boy, Cyril, stood droop-shouldered and stared into the empty ground before him.

Finally the boy turned around to his father and the look on the boy's face nearly broke the man's heart, and just when the agony had reached its greatest point, a miracle occurred, the likes of which no one in the entire Bradford family history had ever witnessed, much less heard about, and one which was talked about for many generations to come.

Far off in the distance, the boy heard a sound that his father did not hear, which at first froze him in his tracks and then spun him around squinting at the horizon.

Thinking it was just the young boy's fantasy, Milo at first patronized him, turning his head away to wait another minute, but when the boy leaped up onto the large old stump and cocked his ear, the second time the boy heard the sound his father heard it too.

Far off in the distance, on the farthest edge of the great green pasture, was the faint, but very distinct barking of a dog!

"Lady!" The boy yelled as his feet sprung off the stump and propelled him through the field toward the hills beyond.

Now the man ran to the stump and jumped atop it himself, as a look of stunned amazement spread across his weathered old face. When the dog broke through the woods and appeared at the far edge of the open field, Milo Bradford felt a rush course threw his body and goose bumps covered his arms and back.

"Lady!" The boy yelled again, and the triumphant sound of his voice carried back to the farmhouse with the breeze long before any of Cyril's family heard the barking of the dog.

The second time the boy yelled, the worn and tired dog leaped with a joy of her own and started barking louder, and with her last measure of strength leftover after a fifty-mile trek through the Connecticut wilderness, the dog, Lady, bounded across the field toward the source of her salvation, the boy, Cyril.

The scene which next met Milo Bradford's eyes was one which he carried with him to his death as the happiest, most thrilling moment of his entire life.

The boy and the dog met one another in the middle of the grassy field and leaped at one another in a joy that few people experience in a lifetime.

Milo cocked his head sideways and bellowed at the top of his lungs, "Ednaaa!" not wanting to turn his head away for fear of missing even one frame of the almost surrealistic drama being played out before his eyes.

A sudden breeze rippled the grasses in the field, and as Milo Bradford memorized the miraculous reunion of the boy and his dog he whispered, "Praise the Lord God Almighty."

Out in the field, in the warmth of the yellow summer sun, under the deep blue skies colored only lightly with the wisps of a few scattered clouds, Cyril Bradford, age five-and-a-half, with the collie dog that was bigger than him licking his face and neck, lifted his hand skyward in a clenched little fist and offered thanks to his God.

"You are a great God!" Cyril yelled loudly through a broad, beaming smile. "And I will always love You and serve You, and I will never treat any of Your children with disrespect. And as long as I live, I will never forget that today You have answered my prayer!"

With that Cyril Bradford dropped his hand and ran smiling up the hill toward home, his dog, Lady, barking at his heels and leaping around him, and his father close behind. When Milo's son Earl and his wife Edna saw them coming, Earl said, "I don't believe it!" over and over again, and Edna laughed and cried while clapping her hands and wiping away her tears.

Back at the farmhouse, Milo rang the dinner bell a dozen times, calling his family in out of the fields, and when his four oldest boys were assembled he turned to them beaming. "Slaughter the fatted hog!" he instructed them. "Tomorrow we feast and give thanks to the Lord our God for the answer to a young boy's prayer!"

Many years later, the man, Cyril Bradford, would be responsible for hiring hundreds of immigrant workers in the textile mills he would own, and the memory of the day God answered his prayer would serve to make him the kindest, fairest employer the immigrants could possibly hope to have, despite the fact that the workers in his factory were from Ireland and the religion they practiced was Roman Catholic, a denomination that many of the Connecticut valley Protestants could neither stomach nor understand.

▲　▼　▲

About the same time as these events were happening in the farmlands of the northeastern section of town, the downtown area of Indian Springs was growing into a thriving factory zone. When the bog ore beds that had given rise to the first casting and foundry plants began to approach exhaustion, it became necessary for the people who had made their living in the blast furnaces that lined Furnace Avenue to adapt to the disappearance of the bog iron industry.

With enterprising genius that was characteristic of the men of the day, new industries were started that gave the iron workers their new lease on life. As the town changed and grew, small factories emerged along the Willimantic River. By the mid-nineteenth century, Indian Springs had two cotton factories, a clock manufacturer, three clothier works, two carding machines, two tanneries, six grain mills, and twelve sawmills. The women of the town became well known for the manufacture of straw braid and bonnets, which they produced in their homes.

The natural progression of the smaller factories soon led to expansion and bigger risks, and by the time 1845 arrived, the woolen mills began to arrive. The first mills made the machinery for the manufacture of woolen goods, and once the machinery had been produced, the production of woolen clothing followed.

Only a short period of time after the woolen mills moved into the production and manufacture of fine men's and women's woolen wear, the Indian Springs woolen mills began to become well known in the major fashion centers of America. With the arrival of the woolen mills, machine shops and printing presses soon followed, and by 1845 Indian Springs was a full-fledged factory town.

While the original factory workers had been family members of mill owners, expansion led to the creation of more jobs, and the work forces at each of the factories grew. For several years, the owners made do with what they could afford to produce, and as factory after factory cropped up along the river, the population continued to increase.

Then in 1845 a natural disaster of monumental proportions began to occur across the Atlantic Ocean. One of mankind's worst tragedies hit the beautiful green country of Ireland and changed the course of history for millions of people in the brief period of 1845-1850. It was known as the potato famine. Perhaps it would not have been so devastating had the history of the Irish Catholics not had them in such a precarious position when it began.

The Irish Catholic problems may have all started with the arrogance of one man. When England's King Henry VIII became disappointed when his first wife Catherine did not bear him a son, he asked Pope Clement VII to annul his marriage so he could marry Anne Boleyn. When the pope refused, Henry persuaded Parliament to pass laws separating the English church from the Roman Catholic church. Parliament agreed and the Act of Supremacy established the Church of England, with King Henry as its head. In 1533 Henry married Anne, whom he later beheaded for being unfaithful.

Although the foremost leader of the Reformation was Martin Luther, a friar of the Catholic Church whose sincere reservations about certain church teachings fueled the movement which ultimately led to the creation of the many Protestant denominations, King Henry's church was founded for political and personal reasons rather than the agonizing conscientious objections to church teachings through which Luther had gone.

When King Henry declared himself King of Ireland and Protestant leader of the Irish church, the Irish people simply said no. With stubborn persistence, they remained steadfastly Catholic and rebelled immediately against King Henry.

A series of uprisings by the Irish against the English over the next sixty-five years were met with superior English military power which won out in the end every time. The last straw came in 1602 when the British massacred the Irish at Kinsale. As a reward for their service to the crown, the Anglo-Protestants were given large parcels of land in Ireland where they took ownership of banks, factories, farms, and businesses.

To secure their interests in the land they claimed as their own, the British imported a solid block of 150,000 loyal Scottish Protestants whom they placed in northern Ireland to replace the Irish Catholics they had massacred or driven out. This land they sold off at low prices to men who pledged their loyalty to Britain.

The displaced Irish Catholics inevitably came back to regain the land that had been stolen from them by British interference, and the civil war of the 1640s raged on for a decade, killing half the people involved.

Thousands of Scottish Protestant colonizers were killed, as were thousands of returning Irish Catholics, and then came Oliver Cromwell. With far superior military might, the British army under Cromwell destroyed tens of thousands of Irishmen, and when his carnage was complete, he had stolen over two and a half million acres of land.

This land he divided among his soldiers as back pay for their massacre of the Irish people, and to make matters worse for the conquered people, the penal laws drove them into debasement. Under the punishing penal laws, Catholics were not allowed to own land, receive an education, vote or hold public office, practice law or their Catholic religion, or avail themselves of the court system. To add insult to injury, they were required to tithe the Anglican Church.

These laws lasted for over a hundred years, and under them the Irish went underground with their pride, their religion, and their nationalism. Home rule became the great Irish dream, and when the penal laws began to be relaxed, the idea of Irish self-determination began to become more and more popular. As the voices in the Irish parliament became more and more bold, the people became more and more restless.

Finally, an Irish freedom fighter named Theobold Wolfe Tone led an armed rebellion in 1798, but his forces ran into a British general who was hungry for vindication. This general had been driven out of the last British colony he had tried to preserve, and he was not about to be driven out again. His name was Lord Cornwallis, prominent British general of the American Revolution, and now he was the British viceroy.

In many ways, the Irish dreams for self-determination were the same as the Americans' had been. Both were passionately committed to home rule and disgusted by British intervention. But there were major differences in the situations of the Americans and the Irish. America was many times larger than Britain and separated by a large ocean. Ireland, on the other hand, was smaller than the state of Maine and just across the Irish sea.

Both faced the most powerful army in the world, but the Americans under George Washington had time and territory on their side, while the Irish, under Theobold Wolfe Tone, had only pride and passion, but little chance against far superior military power.

While Cornwallis had been defeated by Washington, his face-saving campaign led him to crush Wolfe Tone. After Wolfe Tone was killed, the Irish were forced to dissolve their own parliament and unite with England. No Catholic served in Parliament until thirty years had gone by, and again the Irish were caught on the short end of the stick.

Even though Catholics still made up over 95 percent of the Irish population, new laws were passed that were severely discriminatory against them. Catholic farms were required to be divided among all the sons when a father died, and in this manner, land was divided and divided and divided until soon barely enough land remained in one Irish Catholic's possession to survive on.

Then came 1845 and the potato famine. It started out inconspicuously enough when a handful of potato farmers noticed that a blight had struck their crops. The blight began to spread, however, and while it affected only potatoes, the potato had long since become the staple of the Irishman's diet. Many families who lived on small farms relied solely on their potato crops for their very existence, and when they lost their crops, they lost their ability to survive.

The potato blight continued for six torturous years between 1845 and 1850. All across the country, people were starving to death. In all about a million people starved. Another million fled the country, with thousands dying at sea before reaching their destination of America or Canada.

The final death blow to many Irish came when England passed a law making it illegal to divide the land any further. One son would inherit the land; the others were forced to emigrate. The people were afraid to marry too young for fear of having families too large to support, and the emigration of all sons after the first destroyed the Irish family forever. Unlike the American colonists who drove the British out in the American Revolution, the Irish were unable to do so in a country that could not even support its own people. So instead they came to America. Farsighted factory owners looking for cheap labor would send representatives to the dock cities with promises of housing and jobs, and soon the face of America changed as hundreds of thousands of Irishmen moved in.

By the time the potato famine had hit, Indian Springs, Connecticut, had over thirty factories, from textile mills to iron foundries, and hundreds of these Irish made their way into Indian Springs during those years.

The factory owners set up the workers in crowded tenements in the downtown area, and before long Irish taverns and pubs sprang up all across the town. With the large number of Irish in town, a Catholic church became the local Irish dream. When Reverend Luke Daly said the first mass in the home of John and Margaret Hanley on Church Street, the prayer of the handful of Irish assembled there was for the means to accomplish their dream. Mission priests from Willimantic said the earliest masses every other weekend, but as the Catholic population continued to grow, the coffers began to rise, and the dream of the Irish Catholics grew closer to becoming a reality.

One consequence of the large influx of Irish Catholics into town was the intentional segregation of the two groups from one another. The Protestant descendants of Englishmen and the Catholic immigrant Irishmen were instinctively distrustful of one another and not interested at all in each other's religious beliefs or practices. Soon two very separate and very different cultures began to coexist in the town.

While never openly hostile to one another, the two groups remained skeptical and suspicious and instinctively shied away from one another. At first the economic reality of the situation was the same in America as it had been in Ireland. What was disturbing to the Irish was the perception that they had still not been able to shake the English. In the eyes of the Irish the arena had changed but the formula remained the same. Descendants of Englishmen owned the factories, sons of Ireland worked in them. The English owned the houses and the money, the Irish rented their houses and crowded them with large families.

Both sides prohibited intermarriage, and neither side challenged the status quo or pressed the issue. For a Protestant to date a Catholic was simply not thought of, so the divisions grew.

Recreation consisted of church affairs for the most part, with Protestants meeting in their churches and Catholics meeting in their homes. When sporting events were entered into, lines were drawn by religion. For ten years the situation evolved pretty much as could be expected as the divisions grew, but the two groups learned to be civil to one another if not openly cordial. If there was any consolation at all in the situation the Irish found themselves in, it was that home and business ownership was possible for hard workers who would save and bide their time.

Then the great equalizer came. Shortly after the United States of America elected as its new president a tall, self-educated man whose honesty had endeared him to the electorate, trouble broke out that escalated far more quickly than anyone thought it could.

The November election of 1860 that named Abraham Lincoln as president of the United States was soon followed by one of the bloodiest civil wars the world has ever seen. After the south announced its secession from the Union, the call went out across the north for volunteers to fight the war to preserve the union.

In the factories the Irish may not have been equal, but on the battlefield they were as Americans of English and Irish descent fought side by side with Americans of every other national origin against brother Americans from the south.

The memory of Joshua Bradford's revolutionary war heroics were passed down with great pride throughout the generations that succeeded him in the country he fought to create under the command of America's first president.

By the year 1861, there were 130 of Joshua's descendants scattered throughout New England. When Abraham Lincoln issued the call for volunteers to fight the Civil War, sixteen of these Bradford descendants between the ages of eighteen and thirty answered the call. There were six Bradfords, three Cooleys, two Winns, two Rutherfords, a Smith, a Royce, and a Young.

Rarely had so many men from the same extended family fought with such bravery and tragedy in one campaign. By the end of the first year, nine of the sixteen had lost their lives in various encounters of the Civil War, mostly due to the fact that the brave descendants of Joshua Bradford sought the front lines to fight for freedom for men of all colors and unity for the United States of America. By the summer of 1863, only three of the original sixteen were left alive.

July 3, 1863, was a very hot day as these three stood together near a small clump of trees on Cemetery Ridge at Gettysburg, Pennsylvania. General George Gordon Meade of the Union Army had suspected all day what Leon Royce, Linus Cooley, and Cyril Bradford were about to find out. This day would see the climax of the battle of Gettysburg.

The men talked and checked their weapons and waited for the battle they hoped would not come but that they all knew had to come. Alongside them, Patrick Cunningham of Indian Springs, Connecticut, smiled and joked and talked to his hometown Protestant friends as the camaraderie of wartime slowly melted the divisions between them.

Cyril Bradford remembered Patrick Cunningham's face that day, young, handsome, and proud, and smiling his big Irish smile. It was hard to believe that such a vibrant young man, so full of life and happy about the opportunity to serve his country, in fact had little more than an hour to live.

While the hot summer sun beat down on the two armies that stood across the field from one another, the battle that would ultimately decide whether one nation or two would exist between Canada and the Gulf of Mexico was ready to begin. For an hour, from eleven o'clock until noon, a tense calm hung over the scene as Major General George Pickett prepared his southern troops for the most heart-wrenching charge in American military history.

At noon it began. The southern cannons exploded in a deafening volley that filled the air with smoke and dust and clouded temporarily one of the most incredible scenes in American history. When the smoke cleared, the Union forces could hardly believe their eyes. There, across the open field, was a solid line of Southern soldiers a mile wide and three deep, marching across the field toward them!

The Union soldiers prepared to hold their ground as Pickett's charge continued, and when the Confederate forces were about thirty yards away, Linus Cooley took a musketball directly in the face and died while blindly groping for his musket. As the life drained out of him, only Leon Royce and Cyril Bradford were left alive from the descendants of Joshua Bradford who had answered their country's call to duty.

As the Confederates kept advancing, the sickening sound of men gasping and moaning filled the air, and when the Confederates broke through the Yankee line, Leon Royce found himself face to face with a young southern soldier. His musket spent, he was defenseless as the southerner knelt down in front of him and shot him in the chest from point blank range as he lunged to try and knock the musket away.

Cyril watched both of his cousins fall and reached for the man who had shot Leon. Out of the corner of his eye, he saw Patrick Cunningham wrestling with a tall, blond southerner, and when he heard a loud agonizing yell, he was unable to determine if it was Patrick's or the southerner's death cry.

He did not have time to worry about it though as he felt a blinding pain in his left leg when a musketball tore through the bone of his shin. Dropping his musket and rolling in agony, he heard a shot go off near his ear, and when he looked up he saw Patrick standing over him with his musket. He had just killed the southerner who stood ready to run Cyril through with his bayonet.

Cyril was heartsick as he watched Patrick fall to his knees above him, coughing up blood as he struggled to breathe. With his face twisted in agony, Cyril squinted as Patrick staked his claim on the last bit of earth he would ever defend, the small circle of ground on which his friend, Cyril, lay wounded.

When another southerner ran toward the two men, Patrick picked up Cyril's musket and shot him, and when yet another southerner came in with his bayonet lowered, Patrick braced himself like a rock in front of Cyril and waited until the man was upon him before pulling the Confederate over the top of Cyril, and putting him in a headlock. While still coughing up blood, he held onto the southerner until another Union soldier ran him through with his bayonet.

Cyril was unable to move as the fearsome hand-to-hand battle raged all around him, and then, almost as quickly as it had all happened, it was over, as the Confederates went into retreat.

Sadly Cyril watched helplessly as the young Irish-American who had saved his life lay dying at his feet. Patrick tried to speak, but the color had all drained out of him and he could not form any words as the blood continued to gurgle out of his mouth.

"I'll take care of your parents," was the only thing Cyril could think of to say, and before Patrick Cunningham could acknowledge him at all, his eyes closed and he turned his head to the side at Cyril's feet and died.

Back in Indian Springs, Connecticut, no one of either English or Irish descent could possibly know the ramifications of this incident, but the significant thing about it was that one man, Cyril Joshua Bradford, would never forget that his life had been saved by an Irish-American.

Contemplating the irony of the incident, Cyril realized that although he had long since stopped thinking of himself as anything but an American, he understood the Irish skepticism of any and all things British and found it extraordinary that despite his English ancestry, albeit several generations old, this Irish immigrant had died for him anyway, as an American comrade in arms.

Lying on the bloody battlefield of Gettysburg, Pennsylvania, weakened by the loss of blood from his severe leg wound, Cyril could not imagine why, at that moment, a memory popped into his head of something his brother had said to him when he had been only five years old.

"It's not right to judge people until you have all the facts, Cyril," his brother Elwin had once said to him. "And you can never judge an Indian until you have walked a mile in his moccasins."

Then he turned and looked at the dead body of his friend Patrick.

"I'll take care of your parents," he whispered again across the field of glory where William and Mary Cunningham's son lay dead at his feet.

▲   ▼   ▲

In three days, 43,000 Americans lost their lives at Gettysburg in similar fashion, and only one descendant of Joshua Bradford out of the sixteen that had entered the Union Army was left alive.

The war would drag on for almost two years after the Battle of Gettysburg, but November 19, 1863, occasioned an event that Cyril Bradford would remember for the rest of his life. Just about recuperated from the musket blast that had shattered his leg and left him with a permanent limp, Cyril was still in Gettysburg, Pennsylvania, when he received word that he would be guarding the President of the United States, who was coming there that day to dedicate the Gettysburg National Cemetery.

After orator Edward Everett spoke for over two hours, President Abraham Lincoln stood and walked into the center of the crowd, and Cyril Bradford stood less than ten feet away, his musket at ready, peering over the crowd as President Lincoln began to speak:

"Four score and seven years ago, our fathers brought forth on this continent, a new nation, conceived in liberty and dedicated to the proposition that all men are created equal.

"Now we are engaged in a great civil war, testing whether that nation, or any nation so conceived and so dedicated, can long endure. We are met on a great battlefield of that war. We have come to dedicate a portion of that field as a final resting place for those who here gave their lives that that nation might live. It is altogether fitting and proper that we should do this.

"But in a larger sense, we cannot dedicate, we cannot consecrate, we cannot hallow this ground. The brave men, living and dead, who struggled here have consecrated it far above our poor power to add or detract.

"The world will little note, nor long remember what we say here, but it can never forget what they did here. It is for the living, rather to be dedicated here to the unfinished work which they who fought here have thus far so nobly advanced. It is rather for us to be here dedicated to the great truth remaining before us . . . that from these honored dead we take increased devotion to that cause for which they gave their last full measure of devotion . . . that we here highly resolve that these dead shall not have died in vain . . . that this nation, under God, shall have a new birth of freedom . . . and that the government of the people, by the people, and for the people, shall not perish from the earth."

While many in the crowd were still preparing themselves mentally to hear the rest of Lincoln's speech, he walked away, and the Gettysburg Address was history.

The president himself thought that the speech had been a failure, but Cyril Bradford stood in awe, having never been so moved by anything he had ever heard another human being say. All he could think of as he listened intently to the president's speech was the handsome young American who had died while saving his life.

While the crowd at Gettysburg dispersed, Cyril received notice that he had performed his last official duty, his leg injury being too severe to allow him to continue his enlistment. He was honorably discharged to return to his home in Connecticut.

Two months later, at a supper held in his honor at the Baptist Church in Indian Springs, Cyril was asked to relate to his friends and relatives some of the words of President Lincoln at Gettysburg. Calmly he sat down to try and write the speech as well as he could remember it, and incredibly, he reproduced it almost word for word from memory, having heard it only once.

Upon his return to Indian Springs, Cyril went to work immediately for his brother, Ira, in the office of the factory Ira owned in the center of town. Ira put Cyril in charge of personnel and labor relations, and because of the absolute respect with which he treated every man and woman there, Bradford's Mill soon got the reputation as the best place in town to work.

In time Ira Bradford's ever increasing wealth gained him the chairman of the board position at a prominent local bank, where decisions were made as to who got loans and for what reasons. Then, after his Uncle George had closed his sawmill in Laurel Hill, Ira bought the 200-acre plot that George had turned into a gentleman's farm. This Ira kept as a place at which to retire when George passed away.

That same year construction began on the grey stone church that would become the center of life for the Irish Catholics of Indian Springs. As their dream became a reality, Saint Patrick's Church was built on land directly across the street from the Hanley residence where the first mass had been said, and the dream of their own church had been born. The land upon which Saint Patrick's Church was built had been purchased from a friend of Cyril Bradford's named Lewis Parkess. Soon the real estate transactions that followed had local banks reeling in money as the Irish Catholics started coming in with down payments on houses all around their church for which they had been saving money for fifteen years.

When Patrick Cunningham's parents walked into the bank on Main Street, Indian Springs, to make the first mortgage payment on their thirty-year loan, they were stunned speechless to discover that their mortgage had been paid off by a donor who insisted on anonymity.

"Are you sure there isn't some big mistake?" Patrick's father asked Ira Bradford several times, absolutely amazed that anything like this could possibly have happened.

"Quite sure," Ira said smiling. "I know the gentleman who paid off your loan quite well, as a matter of fact."

No amount of prodding by William and Mary Cunningham could convince the banker who had handled the transaction to divulge the name of the person who had done the deed, but not a day went by when he was not remembered prayerfully at daily mass, which the Cunningham's never missed for the remainder of their lives.

▲   ▼   ▲

In 1873 Saint Patrick's School was opened with seventy-five children and one lay teacher. It would take only two years after that for the school to be staffed by the Sisters of Mercy, who were moved into a convent in town that the parishioners purchased for them.

As time went by in the ever-more crowded mill region of downtown Indian Springs, it became increasingly apparent that something had to be done to improve the services that were necessary in that region of town. Fire protection was needed, as well as trash pickup and a bigger local public school. So in 1873 the process was started to create a borough government that would be separate and distinct from the town government, a government within a government for the special needs of the people in the factory district.

By the time the bylaws of the newly incorporated borough of Indian Springs were published for public inspection, there had already been a great deal of debate over the various provisions and regulations so extensive and all encompassing that it made at least one resident feel like he was in a jail and not a township.

Ira Bradford read the charter with deep consternation, and when he got to section 19, his blood started to boil.

. . . section 19. Animals On Highway. No cattle, horses, mules, asses, sheep, goats, geese or swine, shall roam at large upon any highway, street or common, in said borough, for the purpose of being kept or pastured therein, either with or without a keeper.

. . . section 20. Fast Driving. No person shall drive any horse or horses in any street or highway in said borough, at a rate of speed exceeding eight miles per hour, nor in such a manner to endanger or unreasonably incommode any person passing therein.

. . . section 21. Vehicles On Sidewalks. No person shall drive, wheel, draw, or push any cart, wheelbarrow or other vehicle of burden or pleasure upon or along any sidewalk in said borough, except for the purpose of crossing such sidewalk to go to or out of some adjacent enclosure, provided this section shall not apply to children's carriages drawn by hand.

. . . section 22. Animals Upon Sidewalks. No person shall permit any goat, sheep, swine, horse, mule, or cow under his care to go upon any sidewalk in said borough, except for the purpose of crossing said sidewalk to go to or from some adjoining enclosure.

. . . section 23. Highways and Crosswalks Not To Be Obstructed By Teams. No person shall stand with, or permit any team under his care or control, to stand across any public highway or street in such a manner as to obstruct the travel over the same, and no person shall stop with any team in any public street at the side of or so near to another team as to obstruct public travel, and no person shall stop with any team or carriage upon or across any crosswalks in any street of highway in said borough.

On and on, ad infinitum, it seemed to Ira, the rules and regulations read, discussing fines, penalties, ordinances, taxes, and other such troublesome issues that drew the spirit right out of Ira Bradford and left him more disturbed than anything that had happened to him since losing fifteen cousins in the Civil War.

That night he slept most fitfully and early the next morning he hitched his team and he and his wife headed off of Highland Terrace and down onto Main Street pulling a wagon with his personal belongings loaded into it as he headed out of Indian Springs. He stopped to water his team at the Holt Fountain in Haymarket Square, and a friend of his, Sam Harwood, yelled up at him.

"Where you goin', Ira?"

He answered in his distinct Yankee accent. "Back out to the fa-hm in Laurel Hill where a man can breath free. I don't ba-long he-ah no mo-ah."

"Borough chaht-ah don't agree with you, Ira?"

"Folks are all gone mad he-ah! I'm leavin' this town for-ev-ah!"

"Ira, it ain't all that bad."

"It ain't, huh? Tellin' a man where he can go and where he can't go and puttin' speed limits on a man's hoss ain't bad? Man, that just ain't American! I'm goin' back to the fa-hm, where they ain't no rules!"

With that Ira Bradford whipped his team and headed out, and when his brother Cyril heard the rumor that he had just up and left all of his responsibilities at the factory and the bank, he went out to the farm to see what had gotten into Ira.

Ira met him at the door of the farmhouse holding a set of keys.

"It's all yours, Cyril. Every bit of it. The house on Highland Terrace, the factory, the machines, equipment, and the deeds to all the same. I'll die before I'll live under the kinds of slave rules those donkeys have set for the people in the borough."

"Ira, are you sure you won't reconsider and regret this later on?"

"Look about you, Cyril," Ira said, waving his arm across the vast expanses of Bradford land in Laurel Hill. "How can a man leave this for the pollution and rules of a crowded town gone mad! Before long there'll be ten thousand people in Indian Springs, walkin' around in shackles, carryin' rule books! You live there if you want to, brother. It's not for me."

With that Ira Bradford turned away from his brother and walked back into the house he had bought from their Uncle George at which to retire. Cyril smiled as he closed his hands on the keys to one of the most profitable textile mills in New England.

Ira Bradford was forty-four years old when this incident took place. He lived for fifty-two more years before dying at the age of ninety-six, but despite the fact that his farmhouse in Laurel Hill was a scant nine miles east on the sprawling farmland the Bradford family had held for several generations, he never set foot inside of or missed Indian Springs again.

Ira and his wife, Cora didn't start their family until they arrived in Laurel Hill when he was forty-four and she was thirty-two, but they had four children after that. Like most of the Bradfords of Laurel Hill, Connecticut, Ira raised his four children as Baptists, and like all of the Bradfords, he raised them as Republicans. Because he lived until 1925, he got to vote for John Fremont, Abraham Lincoln, Ulysses Grant, Rutherford Hayes, James Garfield, James Blaine, Benjamin Harrison, William McKinley, Theodore Roosevelt, William Taft, Charles Hughes, Warren Harding, and Calvin Coolidge.

One week after Ira Bradford left Indian Springs for Laurel Hill, the Bradford Woolen Company executives sat nervously and prepared to meet their new owner. Every officer and director of the company sat with bated breath, unaware of who it was to whom Ira had sold out, aware only of the directive he had hung on the company bulletin board calling the meeting of department heads and shift supervisors to hear from the new owner.

When Cyril Bradford shuffled through the door with his hands stuffed down into his pockets, beaming his broad, pleasant smile, cheers erupted in the room, and men rose to their feet to applaud him and pat him on the back.

With friendliness and fairness, Cyril had already made his mark in the textile business, and everyone who knew his methods was immensely relieved and overjoyed at the dawn of what promised to be a new age of prosperity and pleasant working conditions in their chosen field.

The way Cyril Bradford handled himself from that first joyous meeting throughout the remainder of his tenure as mill owner served only to expand and heighten his reputation as the best man in town to work for. Cyril had a natural talent for getting the most out of each of his workers, from department heads to shift supervisors, crew leaders, and floor workers. He did something that no other mill owner before him had ever felt comfortable doing, in fact, that many of them considered at first to be a mistake.

Twice a year, Cyril would invite each of his workers into his office, on the clock, where he would sit and talk with them at length, asking them about their goals, their ambitions, their families, and whatever hobbies and interests occupied their leisure time. Sitting out in the middle of his spacious office on a large easy chair, he offered a like chair to whatever person he was entertaining, and the two people sat together eating snacks and drinking coffee or soft drinks that Cyril would provide, laughing and learning about one another.

Inevitably when a new employee would start at Bradford Woolen, two strangers would meet and two friends would part. Always at some point in the conversation, the person's particular job would be discussed, and Cyril would acquaint each worker with the importance of his or her particular job in the overall operation of the factory.

Before the worker left, he would know two things: Cyril Bradford cared about him, and his job was an important part of the overall success of the mill. The workers responded in kind, giving him a hard day's work for an honest day's wage and including him in their families lives with invitations to weddings, family outings, and various and sundry occasions.

While Cyril could not possibly attend everything he was invited to, he would always acknowledge each invitation with a thank you note and a gift, and in this way he became the unofficial leading citizen of Indian Springs.

Largely because of Cyril Bradford's personal style, the mill soon received applications for employment from the best people at all the other mills in town to the point where other mill owners became worried that Cyril was engaged in a campaign to steal all their best. Cyril soon set all of their fears at rest by agreeing to a two-fold plan which suited all parties concerned. First, an unwritten law was established and agreed to by all the local mill owners that no worker could jump from one mill to another without first passing a year's time away from his previous employer within the industry. This agreement was instituted immediately and when word was let out into the mill community, people universally decided to make the best of the factory they were in.

Secondly, Cyril agreed to meet once a month to address an assembly of other owners to teach them his successful methods, which they all wanted to know because of the impressive production totals he was racking up on a consistent and persistent basis.

Soon mill owners all across New England began to hear about the remarkable work ethic which set Indian Springs workers in a class by themselves in the textile industry of New England.

Many of the Irish Catholics who had found jobs there would move up the ranks within the company and no one was ever heard saying anything derogatory about their fair, honest, and caring employer, Cyril Bradford.

▲　▼　▲

If things were going well for the Irish in Indian Springs, they were getting worse in Ireland. One of the most beautiful counties in Ireland is the large county on the western shore which juts out from the mainland into the Atlantic Ocean. Mayo is its name and its people are hearty, proud, and Irish to the core.

Like most Irishmen in 1883, Mayo countrymen were irritated by the British problem which would not go away. It seemed as though every time you turned around you encountered some form of harassment from the British. If you believed in your heart that Ireland should be ruled by the Irish, British officials in Ireland affected you like mosquitoes.

In the 1640s, when Oliver Cromwell wreaked his havoc on the Irish, forcing them "to hell or Connaught," the Irish were given a choice of banishment to the barren though beautiful province west of the Shannon River, or "a one way ticket to hell" at the end of a Protestant sword. The westernmost county of this beautiful province of Connaught is Mayo, where the Callahan family was driven two centuries before under Cromwell's cruel advance. Here, in the least accessible region of Ireland to outside influences, the Irish have maintained an Irish heritage that in all other provinces has been eroded by foreign influence.

For over two hundred years, the Callahans survived as seafarers, fishermen, and traders, and one young son made a fair living with his fists. The Mayo Irish would gamble on anything. These hearty shoremen were a rough and ready brawling brood who loved dogfights, cockfights, and boxing. If you were good with your fists, you could save a lot of aggravation working on the docks or out at sea by betting on yourself in the boxing ring.

For over seven years, one young gladiator had not lost a fistfight and had made enough money from his battles to support he and his mother both, without a job. His name was Michael Callahan, and he was the toughest brawler you could find in all of Ireland. Since fights were informal and records were not kept, no one could be sure how many wars he had survived—in fact he didn't know himself—but it can be safely assumed that he won well over a hundred fights in succession in the years between 1876 and 1883.

With each victory his confidence grew, as did his stubbornness, and although he was compassionate and fair with his fellow Irishmen, he was short-tempered and antagonistic toward all British. In those years the British had a policy of internment whereby suspected troublemakers could be arrested and held in prison indefinitely without having been convicted, simply as suspects of crime or insurrection.

"BRITS OUT" was the town of Westport, county of Mayo, province of Connaught's slogan, scrawled dozens of times in green paint throughout the octagonal marketplace in the center of town.

With Michael Callahan's temperament and the British policy of internment, trouble for the young Irishman was always only a heartbeat away. The summer of 1883 brought trouble to the streets of Westport, County

Mayo. Situated at the eastern end of Clew Bay, Westport lies nestled in what is truly one of the most beautiful places in the world.

Every year, on the last Sunday of July, fifty thousand or more visiting pilgrims meet at the historic place to climb the infamous Croaghpatrick, or "Patrick's Reek," called simply "the Reek," which is the holy mountain on which Saint Patrick fasted for forty days and forty nights before banishing the snakes from Ireland and ultimately converting the nation to Catholicism.

The holy mountain tapers down into the sea, and hundreds of islands can be seen from the crest. A view of incomparable beauty from high atop the Reek shows you the majesty of the mountains, the clarity of the lakes and rivers, the barren desolation of the boglands, and the dangers of the unforgiving coastline. Many a seafaring adventurer has lost his life when the pounding Atlantic surf crashed his vessel into the rocky coastline.

A fisherman of County Mayo was a risk taker who fished the waters of Clew Bay in a sturdy canoe called a currach. This currach is a light but durable canoe made of tarred fabric over a wooden or wicker frame.

For weeks before the annual pilgrimage to the Reek, the local fishermen would work overtime in the bay making certain that the people on pilgrimage would have enough to eat. As the crowds built, so did the interest in the dock fights, and matches would be made, fights held, and debts paid all in a short period of time. The crowds would then disperse to regroup in another location for another fight. Coming in with the catch, the fishermen would often congregate to an area to bet on the fights, and many an unsuspecting pilgrim was lured into the biggest crowd to fight the bearded warrior, Michael Callahan.

As the dock crowds grew one steamy July night in Westport, bets were coming in on Michael Callahan, and more bets on a tall, muscular pilgrim from Dublin in town for the climb to the Reek. Currach after currach floated up to the dock as the noise grew around the two fighters who stood opposite one another, staring each other down as the bets came in.

When all the bets had been placed, the dock ref brought the two men together and explained the rules: Bare knuckles, no rest period, first man down off his feet loses. The large pilgrim from Dublin slowly peeled his shirt off to reveal a bulging set of muscles as Michael loosened up by throwing punches into the air on his side of the dock.

When the referee yelled "Go!" the two men charged one another and in less than a minute Michael had slipped and ducked every punch thrown by the pilgrim and dropped him with a flurry of punishing body shots that broke several of his ribs before a giant right hand to the face toppled him backward on the dock, where he lay moaning and unattended as bets were collected.

When some British soldiers were seen running toward the crowd, the crowd quickly dispersed and Michael got into his currach and paddled away, stuffing a large roll of money into his pocket. When he got to the center of town, he was surprised to see that all the "BRITS OUT" graffiti had been painted over, and he was not the only one who noticed because the next day they were all painted on again.

Furious at the insolence of the slogans and their wasted effort painting them over, local officials slapped a dusk curfew on the local populace and again painted over the "BRITS OUT" signs. The following afternoon a group of men who had lost a lot of money on the fighter they sent up against Michael Callahan demanded another shot at him with a different fighter, and Michael smiled and gladly obliged.

Just before dusk a large crowd met at the same place and the same scene was repeated. This time the men infuriated the local Irishmen by announcing that they were going to punish them by bringing in the best club fighter in England, Buster McNulty from Liverpool, who was prepared to give Michael Callahan and his cocky Irish followers a humiliating lesson.

The bets were redoubled and the wager accountants beamed with pleasure as they counted their percentages for once in their lives unconcerned with who won, because their percentages alone added up to over a month's pay.

When McNulty charged Callahan across the dock and jumped on him, both fighters hit the deck at the same time, and Buster rolled Michael over onto his back and butted his nose with his forehead. Michael's back was bruised when he hit the deck, and the butt to his nose and bruise to his back angered him. As the two men wrestled on the dock, Michael got right into Buster's ear and whispered, "You'll pay for that, lad."

The men were stood up and separated, and McNulty was warned that another incident like that would result in a forfeit. When the dock ref motioned them together again, Michael circled McNulty with fire in his Irish eyes. As he ducked every punch thrown at him by the Englishman, Michael picked the Brit apart, mercilessly jabbing away at him and opening several cuts all over his face with stinging jabs that were not thrown with a knockout intended.

McNulty became totally frustrated, as he was unable to find the range against the quicker, though smaller, Michael Callahan. Every time another stinging jab would rip a cut open on his face, McNulty would lunge at Michael and Michael would escape, then bore in again to pepper him with more pulled punches, never letting the big one go that would put McNulty out of his misery. Finally, after fifteen punishing minutes, during which time the Englishman had his face permanently rearranged, the loud cheering from the dock crowd attracted the officials and the dock lookout ran up to the center of the crowd to yell at Michael. "Put him away, Mickey, the Brits are about."

With that Michael gritted his teeth and braced himself before driving a crushing right hand into McNulty's face, and as McNulty started to wither and fall, Michael stepped back and watched him fall.

A roar went up, and Michael grabbed a stash of money from the local wager accountant before running down the hill to the dock. On his way, he was stopped in his tracks by a beautiful freckle-faced lass who smiled at him so warmly that he forgot momentarily where he was going.

"You use your fists awfully well, man. Do you live around here or are you a pilgrim?" she smiled.

Michael smiled at her and asked her the same question.

"I'll be here only a week, for to climb St. Patrick's Reek, but I'll bet you can show me more interesting sights than that while I'm here," she said.

"I'm in a whale of a hurry now, lass, but if you'll be back here when the sun goes down, I'll do just that," Michael winked at her as he fled.

People were running in every direction as the British soldiers ran into the crowd, and again Michael jumped into his currach, escaping with another wad.

Later that night Michael saw absolutely no reason to abide by the British curfew as he made his way back to where he had met the girl. Michael Callahan had always walked on the edge as far as the British were concerned, and there were many who wished he would take one step too far someday so they could put the hammer down on him. Probable cause could lock people away for years at a time in those days, and insolence or insubordination of any type could add years to prison time once you were locked in so that the British could effectively control any problem areas by removing undesirables from the streets.

With tempers already frayed by the painting incidents, the British were looking for anyone they could arrest, and that evening the ante was upped as a British soldier was beaten to death on the street. Before the soldier's body was found, Michael came strolling into town three hours late for curfew and smiling about the time he had had with the freckled girl.

Liam O'Doul, a local police officer on duty, saw him and tipped his hat to him as Michael was heading for his home.

"Little late, aren't you, Callahan?" O'Doul called out.

"Freckle-faced smiles give me insomnia," Michael joked, and the officer shook his head in resignation to Michael's disregard of the curfew.

"Get home with you, and I'll not put you in my report," O'Doul said. "But be careful. Another officer might not be as lenient as me."

Michael smiled and headed home. Later that night, the body of the British soldier was found brutally beaten and Lieutenant McCabe flew into an outrage.

"I want the man who did this arrested and put to death! Call in all the extra help we can find and knock on every door in town until you find out something. O'Doul, you were out tonight. Did you see anyone out after curfew?"

O'Doul was afraid to admit that he had not reported Michael Callahan so he stretched the truth in a way that damaged Callahan anyway.

"I chased one man back over the stone bridge that crosses the Carrowbeg River," O'Doul said. "I couldn't tell you who it was, but this much I know. He was powerfully built, like a fighter, and he was running up the hill toward the cabins."

O'Doul knew that Michael Callahan was a boxer. He knew also that Callahan lived across the river. He would leave the deduction of primary suspects to the police work of Lieutenant McCabe.

As McCabe put two and two together, O'Doul ran toward the Callahan hut. At 2:00 A.M.. he pounded on Michael Callahan's door and was met by Michael's mother, Ruthie. The one-room mud cabin the Callahans called home was all the family had to show after 200 years in Westport.

"A British soldier was killed tonight," O'Doul panted, nearly out of breath, to Ruthie Callahan. "Michael was out past curfew. You'd better tell him they'll be looking for him soon. But don't tell anyone I was here to tell you or they'll hang me too!"

The words stung Ruthie Callahan and sent a shiver down her spine. She gasped as O'Doul ran off into the night. Her memory took her back twenty years to when her husband, Kevin, was beaten to death by a crowd of Protestants retaliating for the murder of one of their own by picking out a random Catholic for execution.

Michael had only been three years old when his father had been killed, and all she had told him was that he had slipped and fallen on his way home from the pub. Michael never told her that he had gotten the real story many years later for fear that she'd worry about him running off to seek revenge, and getting caught up in the never ending cycle of violence that had always been Ireland's curse.

As she threw the curtain back that separated Michael's cot from the rest of the cabin, she was shaking. Michael was sitting on his cot, wide awake, and Ruthie hugged him as the tears filled her eyes.

"Where shall I go?" Michael asked her quietly.

"Oh, Michael. If you don't get out of Ireland, they'll kill you, sure," she forced herself to say, her heart breaking in her chest.

"I'll have to say good-bye to my brothers and sisters then," he said, but his mother would have no such thing.

"Go!" she yelled at him, shaking him by the shoulders. "You haven't the time. Their cabins are in the opposite direction from the bay."

As Michael dressed, his mother hurried to the corner of the hut and wrenched the dresser filled with winter clothing away from the wall. Underneath the dresser she lifted the floorboards up and pulled out the stash of money Michael had just given her. As she counted out the bills, Michael came out from behind the curtain. She was crying openly with big salt tears running down her cheeks.

"Don't get caught, Michael. Please don't get caught. Last month they took Brian O'Malley for nothing more than a wise remark to a Brit, and two weeks later he was found hung. Called it suicide, the Brit's did, but everybody knows they killed him. If they'll hang an O'Malley for an insult, there's no tellin' what they'll do to a Callahan for a murder."

Michael embraced his mother and stuffed the cash into his pocket.

"In a few months, write me at Mamie Larkin's address in Clew Bay. Give me an address where I can reach you. But use a fake name, and when it's safe to return, I'll let you know."

Michael hugged his mother tightly.

"I love you," he said to her, and it was the first time he had told anyone that in over twenty years.

"Michael, I'm not going to ask you if you killed the Brit. Whoever did it must have had a good reason."

Michael looked at her by the candlelight of their small mud hut and saw the pain in her eyes. He wanted to tell her that he had not done the killing, but he decided not to say anything.

"I'll write you," he said instead, and he opened the door and ran into the moist Irish night.

When he was gone, Ruthie Callahan sat on her bed and listened to the beating of her heart as she waited for the next knock to come at her door. The closer to dawn it got, the lonelier she became, and the sun never rose through the heavy clouds that set in over Clew Bay that morning.

For Ruthie Callahan, the sunrise was never the same again. The death of a British soldier had taken her son away from her, and she would never see him again. As she contemplated the thought, the agony was almost too much for her to bear. *God, it's a terrible curse to be Irish,* she thought to herself as she sat in her cabin and ached.

Out in the bay, Michael paddled his currach quietly toward the boat slip at Mallarney across the bay from Crough Patrick. At dawn he stood on the dock and waited for the shipping office to open.

"Are there any ships leaving out of Ireland this day for foreign shores?" he asked the morning clerk.

"There's one leaving at 8:00 A.M.. for Sydney, Australia, and one at 10:00 A.M.. for Boston, Massachusetts, in the United States of America," the clerk answered mechanically.

"I'll take the eight o'clock for Australia," Michael said calmly.

The clerk stopped what he was doing and looked over the top of his glasses at Michael.

"That ship's been booked for over four weeks, lad."

"Well, then, are there any openings on the ship for America?" Michael asked.

"In quite a hurry to leave Ireland, aren't you, lad?"

"Is that so unusual these days?" Michael asked him.

"How many bags do you have?" the clerk asked him.

"Just the clothes on my back," Michael answered, looking down at the logbook in front of him. "What else do people leave Ireland with?"

After Michael was through counting his money out to the clerk, he walked a brisk clip up to the dock, where he paid a hefty price for some rapidly drawn up immigration papers for other side of the ocean. Hurrying into a small store, he bought a duffle bag which he filled with a couple of changes of clothes, and a full-length coat.

Back at the dock he kept his head down and avoided eye contact with the many people who were starting to flood the docks to see their friends and relatives off. When the passengers started boarding the ship, Michael was in the first group that walked up the ramp. On board he turned to take a final look at his homeland. For a fleeting moment, he considered walking back down the ramp against the people who were walking up and marching headfirst back into town where he would fight any man who tried to take him, but thinking of his mother and the grief he knew that would cause her, he thought better of it.

For one last time he panned the shore of his fatherland and whispered to himself under his breath, "God bless this wretched country."

With that he turned and disappeared below to his bunk where he lay back with his eyes closed until he felt the giant ship floating away from the dock. When the ship was a good distance away from the pier, he came out of his bunk and walked above, but the hoards of people standing near the edge of the ship prevented him from taking a final look at the shoreline of his homeland, and instead he just sat down in back of the crowd with his back to the wall.

A good distance out into the ocean, after thinking about old memories, he suddenly became aware of the fact that the sun had emerged, and as the hoards of people broke away from the railing, he got up and slowly walked over to the edge. But all he could see where Ireland used to be was the edge of the ocean and a horizon covered with miles of dark clouds.

That night when sleep finally came, the last thing he remembered before dozing off was the dark, full clouds and the endless ocean that never seemed to make it all the way back home.

▲   ▼   ▲

For the first three days at sea, Michael did not say a word to anyone and avoided interaction with everyone on board the ship. Other passengers busied themselves in recreation of various types on deck, and after awhile Michael got to know his shipmates by sight. Whenever groups of even two or three people would assemble, Michael would move on until he found someplace where he could stand apart alone.

On the third night out, the crew sponsored a get acquainted dance which drew the families and individuals on the ship into interaction, and at the dance Michael noticed the commotion that everyone was making over one particular girl. No fewer than six young men Michael's age were congregating around her and following her all over the ship. Many of the young women on board put their heads together to whisper about her, displaying their obvious jealousy, and Michael thought it was amusing the way they talked about her derogatorily when she was being attended by all the gentlemen but smiled openly and warmly at her when she would approach them.

The young woman, he guessed, was no more than four years younger than him, and one thing he did know was that she was very, very attractive. More than once during the course of the evening he saw her glancing his way, and he tried to look the other way when she did, but one time their eyes met, and he found himself staring into her eyes from across the room.

The first night went by uneventfully, and before the dance ended, Michael finished his drink and went back to his bunk.

The next day he stood at the stern of the ship, watching the ripples the ship made as most of the other people went to the bow to see where they were going. As he stood over the railing with his hands clasped in front of him, he felt the presence of someone standing near him and when he turned around, it was her.

"Mornin'," she smiled.

"Mornin'," he grunted, looking at her quickly but then staring out into the ocean.

"Nice day today," she said cheerfully.

"Yup," he answered quietly.

For several seconds she stood next to him, but when he didn't say anything more, she felt very awkward. Trying to make light of the matter, she cranked her head around to look him square in the eyes.

"Been nice talking to you," she smiled. And then she walked away.

With that she made him smile for the first time since leaving Ireland, but after she was gone awhile, he suddenly felt very lonesome, a feeling that had never plagued him before, and then he felt himself becoming angry. All the rest of that day and the next, he stayed in his bunk alone, and at the end of the day he came outside to watch the sun set over the ocean.

From his vantage point behind the crowd of people who stood on deck to watch the sunset, he saw her again, and as usual, she was surrounded by men. When she turned and saw him, she excused herself from her company and drifted over toward him.

"I haven't seen you for awhile," she said to him, still smiling.

"I apologize for the other night, Miss. I didn't mean to be rude."

"That's okay," she said, brushing the incident off. "I could see you were deep in thought."

"Name's Callahan, Michael," he said.

"Maureen Malloy," she said. "I know who you are."

"How do you know me?" he asked her, surprised.

"My brothers made a good deal of money betting on you at the dock fights."

Michael smiled.

"You seem to be quite popular around here, Miss Malloy."

"Single girls are in great demand on this ship, it appears."

"There appears to be a good deal more single men on board than single women," Michael observed.

"The American dream is a very powerful force," she smiled. "Ships like this are full of young Irishmen seeking their fortunes in the new land."

"Is your family with you?" Michael asked her.

"No. I'm alone. But a lot of people from Roscommon are on board, and most of them know me from home."

"It must be nice to travel with friends," Michael observed.

"I never see you talking to anyone," she said.

"Don't know anyone aboard," he answered.

"Well, you know me now, Mr. Callahan."

When she walked away, his eyes stayed glued to her for a long time. *I hope she doesn't end up with some jerk,* he thought to himself. *She could be the best girl in Ireland.*

The next morning she smiled at him across the room at breakfast, and later that afternoon as he was standing in his customary place on back of the ship, he felt a soft hand on his arm, and as he turned she said, "Boo!" and handed him a drink that she had brought him from the cafeteria.

"One for you, and one for me," she said, and he smiled at her warmly.

"I've decided that if you won't come to me, I'll come to you," she said, and the way she smiled warmed his heart.

"Are you going to America to box?"

"Oh, not really," he answered. "Why are you going there?"

"Have you got a couple of hours? It's a long story," she said.

For the next three hours, the young man and the young woman stood together at the railing of the ship watching the wake the ship made in the ocean as it moved steadily on to America. By the time she was finished with her story, the moon was shining brightly in the sky, and the stars filled the warm summer night.

She had been the third daughter of a family of three boys and five girls, and the prospect of staying in Ireland had scared her. Many young men of the county had courted her, but she had not wanted to get serious with any of them. The ones she was at all interested in seemed always to be second and third sons destined for emigration, and the ones she was not interested in had been the firstborns. At age twenty, she began to get restless staying home and finally after long discussions with her parents, she decided to emigrate to America, the land of the free.

"So here I am. Heading for a new country I know nothing about, and I don't mind telling you I'm a little scared."

Michael gazed into her eyes and longed to tell her that he could take all of her fears away, but he could not find the right words, so he said nothing. But there was something in his eyes that told her nevertheless, and soon the two young people gravitated to one another, and as each day passed by, they grew closer and closer together.

Michael would talk to her about everything except the one thing she was most curious about, and after sufficient time had gone by and they knew each other well enough, she asked him.

"So what's your American dream, Mr. Callahan? I've been telling you all of mine."

Michael turned from her and looked out over the ocean.

"I don't really have an American dream, Miss Malloy," Michael said thoughtfully, looking back toward the land he had just left. "Just an Irish nightmare."

Michael took a long breath and told her the story of all the events that led to his being there, and as the evening wound down he found himself standing very close to her on the deck and talking very softly to her, and when his story was finished he looked at her seriously, and locked his eyes deeply into hers.

"But if none of that had happened, I'd never have met you, Miss Malloy."

"Things have a way of working out, don't they, Mr. Callahan."

"I'm glad I met you," Michael said to her softly.

"I can't believe I've known you for such a short time," she said to him. "It seems as though I've known you all my life."

"You know, we must be getting pretty close to America by now," Michael said to her, and for the first time an uneasy feeling gripped them both.

"I heard a crewman say we might reach shore tomorrow," Maureen said.

"I guess we'd better get a good night's sleep tonight, then," Michael said. "I'll walk you to your cabin."

The son and the daughter of Ireland walked together slowly and silently and when they got to her berth, they looked at one another and smiled, and just as they had done every night since they had started seeing each other, he nodded to her and she curtsied to him.

"Good night, Miss Malloy," Michael nodded.

"Good night, Mr. Callahan," Maureen curtsied.

The following afternoon, August 10, 1883, a shipmate sitting in the lookout tower lifted his hand high into the air and yelled, "Land, ho!" and several men went running to all parts of the ship to inform the passengers that their destination had been reached.

As the ship neared the dock in Boston Harbor, a buzz of excitement filtered all through the crowd of passengers nearing their new homeland. Women were fixing their hairdos and their clothing, as men rushed to the deck to stand at the railings and watch the land reaching out to draw them in.

Characteristically Michael Callahan stood back a way to make room for the hoards rushing by him to get the best vantage point they could at the bow of the ship. Standing behind the crowd with his back to the railing, he was scanning the crowd for the girl who had made the trip go by so fast for him.

He saw her before she saw him, and as he looked over the top of the crowd he saw her glancing this way and that, standing on her tiptoes and darting between bodies as she searched the crowd. When she saw him she stopped and looked in his direction, and for the first time he saw a worried look across her face.

God, she's beautiful, even when she's frowning, he thought, and he stood upright and waved to her.

She waved back and walked toward him slowly, attempting to smile through the frown that was drooping her eyes. The drawn look in her deep green eyes saddened him, and his face tightened up in solemnity behind his great full beard.

When she reached him he fixed his eyes on her and a tremendous sadness filled him and rushed through his veins.

"In which direction will you be headed, Mr. Callahan?" Maureen Malloy asked with the anxiety in her voice ill-disguised.

"Inland, until I find a county in America that's at least as beautiful as Ireland," he said somberly and not just a little apprehensively.

She stood very close to him and gazed deeply into his eyes as the bond that had grown between them drew so perilously close to coming to an end.

As he looked at her, he thought of Ireland and its terrible beauty, of its ancient struggles, its tragic present, and its hopeless future. In her eyes he saw those ancient struggles and the character her own personal struggles had built into her. Never in his life could he remember feeling so close to another human being, and as the dock drew closer, something he could not understand made his legs start to feel weak and filled his eyes with tears as he fought his emotions.

I can't let her go, he thought to himself. *I just can't.*

"I don't suppose it would be proper for me to ask you to accompany me, Miss Malloy," he said to her softly, his voice quavering. "Maureen," he added, calling her by her first name for the first time. "But this much I will tell you. It would be a true American dream for a man like me to have a girl like you beside him as he looks for the land of his future."

He spoke the words softly, and as he spoke them, her heart leaped and her eyes began to sparkle.

"Well then, I expect I'll be headed in the same direction as you, Mr. Callahan," she said to him cheerfully. "Michael," she added, as the frown on her face was replaced by a broad, beaming smile.

When she smiled, something in the way her eyes sparkled and the quick lilt of her head caused Michael Callahan, age twenty-four, to do something he had wanted to do several days before when first he had gotten to know Maureen Malloy, age twenty.

Gently he put his arms around her and pulled her up against him, and when she melted into his strong arms and lifted her beautiful Irish smile toward him, he leaned over, and on the deck of the immigrant ship, in close proximity to the shores of Boston Harbor, in the sunlight of their new land, he kissed her for the first time, and the destiny of many generations if Irish-American Callahans was sealed.

▲   ▼   ▲

The decade between 1873 and 1883 marked a period of unprecedented growth within the textile industry of New England. Fortunes were made by the industry leaders, and modest investments were rewarded with staggering sums of money in a time when windfall profits went largely untaxed.

People's lives changed overnight, and as always, money affected different people in different ways. Some men viewed it as a scorecard on how well they were doing and spent it lavishly on homes, luxury, and lifestyle. Others, like Cyril Bradford of Indian Springs, lived by different personal codes and were fueled by different dreams.

It is said that you cannot outgive a giver. For those who understood that principle, the greatest person to have in your debt is a man with much to give. Looking back on his life, there were very few people who had directly affected his life as much as his brother, Ira, and the young Irish-American friend, Patrick Cunningham, who had saved his life at Gettysburg.

Ira he was able to directly thank; Patrick, he was not. But an honest man remembers his word, and Cyril began to imagine myriad ways to do for the elder Cunninghams what he said he would to the man who had saved his life when he was in the most danger.

The first year he had bought their home for them anonymously. The second year, and every year thereafter, he had gone down to the tax office and paid their taxes for them. When huge windfall profits began to come to him, he saw it as a way to benefit a couple immensely, and in 1883 he attempted to set them up with a bankroll by opening up a savings account for them at the local bank.

But this was the year that William Cunningham finally called a stop to it. Embarrassed to the point at which he felt obliged to finally do something about it, he wrote an open letter in the local newspaper that had everyone in town speculating about the writer and the person it was written to.

The letter read as follows. . . .

To Our Dear Anonymous Donor,

For years now, you have been exceedingly generous to us. We have been unable to understand the reason why, or to speculate as to the source of your generosity. All we know is that whatever debt you feel you have owed to us has been more than fully paid.

With deep gratitude, and undying thanks, we must respectfully request you to stop these exceedingly generous gifts, as they are beginning to become an embarrassment to us. No person should be required to donate to any other a sum totalling more than ten years hard labor, and continue to add to that sum each and every year thereafter.

Therefore, any further gifts from you to us will be given away by us, so would you please elect a charity of your choice as our substitute, and benefit them in our stead? Our prayers for you are unceasing, and we remain permanently grateful for your help.

Sincerely,
Only you and the Lord know who

Cyril Bradford knew immediately who had written the letter, and decided to honor the Cunninghams' wishes, turning instead to his brother, Ira, as the newest beneficiary of his philanthropy.

Were it not for Ira, Cyril would not be the owner of the immensely profitable Bradford Woolen Company; Ira would. And although he knew that Ira had achieved unusual happiness and fulfillment on the 200-acre plot of land his grandfather Joshua had worked a sawmill on and his Uncle George had converted to a gentleman's farm, Cyril was aware that with four children after the age of forty-four, and an expanding dairy farm, Ira could never have too much land.

Consequently he set about to find Ira some more acreage, and in a very short time span, he was able to secure for Ira another sixteen hundred acres at a price that, although was not inexpensive, would nevertheless never be any cheaper. One hundred and fifty thousand dollars was, in Cyril's estimation, a reasonable price for sixteen hundred additional acres of prime farmland, and a price Cyril was all too happy to pay for the peace of mind he knew it would buy for Ira.

When Cyril presented Ira with the deed to the land, registered in the tax assessor's office as five hundred plus or minus acres, but drawn out to the full sixteen hundred on the map, Ira sat back and smiled, not surprised in the least by Cyril's generosity.

"Brother, I'll simply repeat to you the same words you said to me ten years ago when I gave you the mill: Are you sure you won't regret this later?" Ira said.

"Did you ever regret leaving the mill?" Cyril asked him.

"Not even once," Ira answered confidently.

"Then I don't suppose I could ever regret rewarding you for a decision that has given me my fortune," Cyril answered him.

The two brothers smiled at one another and shook hands, mindful of the tremendous success both of them had enjoyed in the land of their ancestors.

"Now let me tell you about my newest dream," Cyril said to Ira, sitting back in his lawn chair on Ira's front lawn in Laurel Hill.

"The people in Indian Springs have worked very hard for the success of the Bradford Woolen Company. I should be honored to repay them in the form of an endowment that will benefit their children and their children's children in the years to come."

"What did you have in mind for them, Cyril."

"The town needs a hospital. Every town does. I could buy a nice summer cottage by the shore in Newport, Rhode Island, or a ski slope in Vermont, or I could squander my fortune in any number of decadent ways, but Martha and I don't need any of that. Let other men do that kind of thing, not that I begrudge them, if that's what they want to do. But I'd get just as much pleasure out of seeing my name on a hospital as I would about seeing it on a yacht."

"When would construction begin?" Ira asked him.

"Right away," Cyril answered. "Why wait?"

"Hospitals have to cost a lot of money, Cyril."

"The people will pay their share," Cyril said confidently. "And if they don't, I'll pay for it myself."

"Cyril, you are truly one in a million. I knew that way back when your dog came home through the wilderness in answer to your prayers. Way back then I knew God had his hand on you."

Ira's assessment of his brother continued to be true. Large national and international contracts for fine woolen wear continued to be landed by the Bradford Woolen Company, and vast improvements were made on the mill. With improvements came expansion, and with expansion and bigger orders came the adding on of a second shift, which nearly doubled the work force.

With the rapid expansion of the work force came the increased importance of a good personnel director, and Cyril Bradford had the man he considered to be the best. His name was Roland Aubuchon, the son of a French immigrant who had come to Indian Springs a generation before and gone to work immediately in the mill with the many Polish, German, French, and other European immigrants who came during the years between 1873 and 1883.

All the hiring was done by Roland Aubuchon, whose job it was to determine from employment applications and background checks which applicants were best for which particular jobs at the mill. Attendance and punctuality were the main criteria Aubuchon used, as well as personal recommendations and discussions with previous employers to determine the reliability and attitudes of each applicant.

Only rarely did Aubuchon make a mistake in hiring someone, and bad apples rarely showed up in the Bradford Woolen Mill because he was an excellent judge of character and a man endowed with an abundance of common sense.

Never in ten years had Aubuchon deferred to Cyril Bradford the decision to hire anyone. Then one day, during an interview, Roland Aubuchon realized after only a few questions that he was not interviewing the applicant but that the applicant was interviewing him.

For the first time ever, Roland realized that after talking to the man for over ten minutes he still knew precious little about him except that the man had ascertained that this was indeed the factory owned by Cyril Bradford, and that he would be most obliged for the opportunity to speak with Mr. Bradford himself.

"Yes, well I do all the hiring around here. Now do you want a job here or not?" Roland asked him, growing more and more perturbed as the interview continued.

"I won't know that until I've had the chance to talk to Mr. Bradford myself," the man insisted.

When Cyril heard a knock on his door, he was surprised to see his loyal employee in such an obvious state of chagrin.

"I got a guy out here who's being most difficult. Insists on talking to you before he'll answer any questions. Says he wants a third shift job where he doesn't have to talk to a lot of people. I told him we don't even operate a third shift, but he insists on talking to you anyway."

"What's his name?" Cyril asked Roland.

"I don't know. Some Irish name. The guy got me so frustrated, I can't even remember his name."

Cyril smiled at his loyal friend.

"Well, send him in," he said, and Roland left to summon the most difficult job applicant he had ever interviewed.

When the man stood in Cyril Bradford's door, there was very little light left, for he filled the entire door frame with his body. Cyril got up from behind his great desk and walked around it, extending his hand to the man.

"I understand you're looking for work?"

"For the right man I'll work," the man answered.

"And how will you know when you've met the right man?"

"He's got to be as fair with Irishmen as they say you are, and he can't be British," the man said sternly and solidly. "It's as simple as that."

"What county are you from in Ireland, sir?"

"County Mayo," the man answered. "Clew Bay."

Cyril extended his hand to the man.

"I'm Cyril Bradford."

The man took Cyril's hand and shook it. "Michael Callahan."

"What kind of work do you do, Mr. Callahan?"

"I can do anything anybody does in a factory," Michael answered. "What I cannot do is work with difficult people. I lose my temper too easily and knock too many people down."

Cyril was intrigued by the man and impressed by his obvious honesty and straightforwardness.

"And you can't work with British," Cyril said.

"That's right."

"Can you work with Protestants?"

Michael shrugged. "I wanted to ask you about that," he said. "Do the Catholics and Protestants get along as well as I've heard they do in your mill?"

Cyril Bradford sat back in his chair and looked long and hard at Michael Callahan.

"Mr. Callahan, this is America, not Ireland. In this country we all have to get along because there are so many different kinds of us."

"I'll level with you, Mr. Bradford. I like to level with everybody. I've been in this country for only a few short months, and I've already seen a good deal of injustice. Usually it's the strong against the weak, or the powerful against the defenseless. I don't like that. I hate all kinds of unfairness, but I'm especially sensitive about Brits over Irishmen. I admit I'm quite prejudiced myself against tyranny and injustice. The only way I could work for you is if I felt in my heart that I'd be treated fairly and with respect, despite the fact that I'm Irish. And I won't work for you at all if you're British."

Cyril Bradford was constantly amazed at the undying hatred of anything British that he had encountered from every true-blue Irishman he had ever known. He thought back to Gettysburg and the young man who had saved his life, and he decided for Patrick Cunningham's sake to try and understand this man, despite the bitterness that was obviously eating him alive.

"I have a number of Catholics working for me here at the mill, and an equal number of Protestants. There are many fine Irish-Americans working here. They worship at St. Patrick's Church on High Street, on land a friend of mine sold to them to build their church on."

This fact Michael Callahan seemed interested in, and already Cyril could see the change come over his countenance, as the stern look loosened up considerably.

"I've been to the church on occasion myself, for weddings and funerals of my workers."

"You've been inside the church?" Michael asked incredulously.

"Yes, many times."

"That would never happen in Ireland."

"Yes, well America is quite a different country."

Callahan laughed.

"Brits are Brits wherever you go," he said. "Your name sounds very British to me, as a matter of fact."

Cyril Bradford looked across the floor at Michael Callahan.

"Mr. Callahan, the best friend I ever had was an Irish-American. His name was Patrick Cunningham and he died to save my life in the Civil War. Saved me twice in sixty seconds when I was defenseless. Then he died at my feet."

Michael Callahan looked away from Cyril Bradford. The next thing he said came out with no forethought or malice, but rather as a kneejerk reaction to a lifetime of bitterness.

"Lots of Irishmen have died so Brits can live."

Cyril Bradford bristled, and for the first time in many years, he felt his temper starting to flare. If anyone else had been sitting across the table from Michael Callahan at that moment, the episode would no doubt have taken another course, but Cyril Bradford had spent a lifetime studying people of many diverse backgrounds, and he wanted to get inside this rugged, difficult man.

When you can love the unlovables, you can build an empire, Cyril thought to himself, and he checked his tongue, and considered the source of the remark.

Cyril stood up and started to pace, considering the circumstances under which Michael Callahan had lived the first part of his life and decided not to respond to Michael the way he wanted to.

"I want to tell you something I think you'd like to know, Mr. Callahan. Two and a half centuries ago, my ancestors came to these lands from Great Britain to escape the religious persecution they were suffering there. So I can appreciate the way you feel. My grandfather was Lieutenant Colonel Joshua

Bradford, who served under General George Washington and helped to drive Lord Cornwallis and his British army out of our country."

"Cornwallis?" Michael perked up immediately. "That man did a lot of damage in Ireland. Your grandfather should have killed him."

"My grandfather fought against the British to help create this country, Michael. Will this be your country now?" Cyril asked him poignantly.

"Mr. Bradford, I came to this country because I was suspected of killing an unfair and disrespectful Brit," Michael answered. "My country will be where I and my family are treated with fairness and respect."

Cyril Bradford extended his hand to Michael Callahan.

"I need a night watchman," Cyril said, creating a new job at the mill on the spot. "He has to be strong and fearless and honest. A man like yourself. I'll give that man a fair wage in exchange for his dedication and his loyalty."

Michael Callahan stood across from Cyril Bradford and judged him by his eyes. Then he took his hand and firmly shook it.

"I'll be the best employee you have, Mr. Bradford."

"Can you start tomorrow?"

"Yes."

"Is there a Mrs. Callahan?"

"Yes. Maureen."

"Will you and Maureen dine with Martha and I tonight, then?"

"Why, yes sir. We will." Callahan answered. "Where?"

"In my home."

Michael Callahan was quite surprised to be invited to the home of his employer, the Protestant American of English descent. That evening a lifelong friendship between Cyril and Martha Bradford and Michael and Maureen Callahan was started in the parlor of the Bradford home on Stafford Street in Indian Springs, Connecticut.

Michael Callahan did indeed become Cyril Bradford's most loyal employee, guarding his factory at night like it was his own. Shortly after he went to work for Bradford Woolen, Michael and Maureen started their family, getting a fifty cents an hour raise every time they had a child. They were very happy as the nineteenth century wound down in America.

Two years after reaching the shores of Boston Harbor, Michael received a letter from Mamie Larkin of Westport, County Mayo, informing him of the death of his mother. The letter did not say that she had caught the flu and died alone, shivering in her bed one cold January morning in the mud cabin that Michael had always kept heated while his mother took care of the meals.

It did not tell him that the British had worn her down with interrogation and harassment, stealing and tearing up her mail, and stoning her cabin at night, terrorizing her, and trying all means to wear her down in an effort to find out the whereabouts of her fugitive son, Michael, for whom justice was awaiting the next time he showed up in Mayo.

The letter only said that Ruthie had died and been buried in the family plot alongside her husband, Kevin, in a small funeral attended by a handful of close relatives, with an equal number of British soldiers looking on from the edge of the cemetery.

Only once in all the years of his employment did Michael Callahan have Maureen go directly to Cyril Bradford and request a night off. It was the day he received the letter from Mamie Larkin and that night he sat alone in the large rocking chair that graced the living room of the apartment they rented from Cyril Bradford. He did not move all night and never once got up to go to the liquor cabinet. He simply sat there with his eyes open, rocking back and forth and fighting back the intense emotions that were coursing through his veins. With the early morning light, he hugged his wife closely and led her into their bed.

As the first few years of the twentieth century unfolded in Indian Springs, Connecticut, the textile industry was moving along smoothly and the descendants of Englishmen continued to hold ownership of the major industries, while the descendants of Irishmen contented themselves to work in their employ.

Then early in the twentieth century something happened which would change the whole equation in Indian Springs and send the town careening off in an entirely new direction.

Everything changed in the early part of the twentieth century. That's when the Italians came.

▲　▼　▲

Part 2

The Melting Pot

When nature's forces moved the great ancient glaciers through the exquisitely beautiful Piedmont region of northern Italy, one of the most spectacular landscapes on Earth was created.

The Alps! Tall and majestic they stood with hills, meadows, and lake basins covered by the dainty and beautiful edelweiss, crocus, soldanella, and rhododendra flowers that colored the slopes leading up to the mountains that stood guard over the northernmost expanses of the ancient land of Italy.

The views from the high places were among the most enchanting spectacles on Earth, and the people who lived there were a proud and hearty lot known to all the world for their friendly and unified nature. Few other people in the world were known specifically for their remarkable unity.

The closeness of their family life spilled out into the community where all one needed for mutual acceptance and value was to be Piedmontese.

Symbolic of the Piedmont region was the simple folksy way they built their homes, from the stone and timber of the region and the way they used the climate and the soil to create farms and vineyards from which the full-flavored cheeses and scented and fortifying wines were produced.

In the heart of the Piedmont region stood the ancient city of Biella, where centuries before, the Roman Emperors had recognized the indomitable spirit of these unified and friendly people and granted them the right of self-government.

In Biella, industry lived side-by-side with traditional pastoral and agricultural life, and many of the families of surrounding villages had made their way there through the years to work in the factories and refineries.

In Biella, as in many other cities, towns, and hamlets of the region, the life was slow-paced and happy, and no one was in a great hurry to do anything.

Banks were open for only about two hours each day, and everyone in town took a lunch break in the middle of each day which lasted from one until three o'clock. During those days, it was not uncommon for the people to go down to the wineries, where you could draw from them what you had brought in throughout the year.

Because the people of Biella worked at the constant improvement of their already exceptional family life, the community was the obvious beneficiary, and the entire town was remarkably free of crime, both violent and petty. They respected the land, they respected one another, and they respected the rule of order that the churches, most specifically the holy Roman Catholic Church, had passed down through the generations.

One of the many things Biella was noted for was the way its foreign missionaries had distinguished themselves in all corners of the world. One local family, the Strobinos, had sent several men into the service of the Savior, and a local hero was Archbishop Giovanni Strobino, who had been martyred in the mission fields in Africa. A stalwart son of Biella, he had given his life to bring the good news of the Savior to foreign lands.

Foreign lands were on the minds of many of these children of Biella early in the twentieth century. One of these foreign lands was being talked about more and more as time went by, for despite the comfort of growing up in the town of your birth, there is, and always has been, a kind of intangible allure that draws the most adventurous members of all societies to new frontiers wherever they appear. Early in the twentieth century, such a frontier beckoned to people from all corners of the globe with its promises of freedom and financial independence.

It was a land vast, open, and free, with limitless space and thousands of times more mountains than those in Italy, which had guarded their families for so many centuries. The land was one flowing with milk and honey, in which letters sent home by the brave souls who had left home and family to emigrate there had claimed, with the exaggeration born of excitement that "the streets are paved with gold." The land was one of unlimited opportunities, where hunters and fishermen found paradise in the abundant forests, and where the people governed themselves. There the sons and daughters of immigrants could choose whatever field of endeavor their hearts led them to pursue. They could devote their lives there to success in their chosen field unhampered by government or traditions and encouraged by the free spirit of their fellow citizens.

It was a land rich with promise for far-sighted individuals anywhere in the world, and the young people of more than one foreign land considered it to be the best land in the history of mankind to adopt and then pass on to future generations. Called "The home of the brave, and the land of the free," it was a land to which adventurous young people from all over the world were flooding in record numbers to stake their claims on the future, for if its shores welcomed the tired, poor, wretched refuse of teeming foreign shores, it also called the best and brightest of every foreign land. The land was named for the famous Italian explorer, Amerigo Vespucci, who first discovered a way to determine the circumference of the earth at the equator, missing the actual distance by only fifty miles. Amerigo's maps and letters of the new continents earned for him the honor of having both of the continents north and south of the equator named after him.

In the land of North America there stood a number of free and united states, and one young couple had been caught up heart and soul in the excitement of its promise and the allure of its beckoning call.

He was a handsome, twenty-four-year-old shoemaker, the eldest of four children, who had received formal schooling for only four grades, quitting at age nine to become an apprentice in his trade. Barrel-chested and exceptionally strong, despite his five-foot-five-inch height, his eyes were set deeply into his brow, and his chin was square, giving him the appearance of determination and authority.

She was a lovely twenty-year-old maiden who had already been weaving cloth for seven years in the woolen mills, along with her duties at home helping her parents to raise twelve other children in the family. Lithe and sure of herself, she was blessed with beauty and grace, having long enjoyed the reputation of being the nicest girl from one of the friendliest families in town.

They had been in love it seemed like forever, since he had first met her in Mosso Santa Maria before her family moved to his hometown of Biella. They had talked often of marriage throughout their lengthy courtship. For the better part of two years, they had dreamed together of the impossible but beautiful dream of moving to the United States of America together and starting a family in the home of the brave, the land of the free.

As beautiful as Italy was, they were captured up in the dream of America, and when he thought of the vast expanses of American land that would take centuries to fill, he realized how much Italy suffered by comparison. For his future generations, he wanted nothing less than the best.

His name was Vittorio Bellino, and he was on fire with a vision of promise for his children's children and a hunger to give his lovely fiance, Antoinette Rosato, the very best a man could give his wife.

"An-toin-yet-ta!" The beautiful four syllable name rolled off his tongue with reverence whenever he spoke of her to any of his family or friends. He had smiled proudly the previous Christmas day, 1909, when in a large circle of friends his little sister Gabriella had told his brother Fortunato, "God never made a boy who loves a girl more than Vittorio loves Antoinette."

On one particularly clear and beautiful spring morning in April of 1910, Vittorio took the long walk from his home in Chiavazza on the Biella hillside across town to her home on Via Guglielmo, and she came running out to greet him, embracing him as she always did when they met. Then, holding hands, they walked back to the doorstep of her house. On the doorstep, before entering her home, he held back a little and she hugged him again and kissed him. By his stern look and the tenseness in his mannerisms, she knew right away that he was preoccupied with deeper thoughts.

"What is it, Vittorio," she asked him, smiling up at her longtime boyfriend.

"Antoinette, all week I've been thinking. There's something very important I want to talk to you about. But it's going to take some time. I'm going to ask your father if we can go up into the hills today to Oropa, and then we'll talk."

"I'll ask him," she said cheerfully, but Vittorio held her back.

"No, I'll ask him," Vittorio said, and the resoluteness in his voice made her heart quicken, because she thought for a moment that this was going to be the day she had dreamed about, when Vittorio would ask her father for her hand.

Later that morning, Vittorio and Antoinette took the long walk out of Biella and up into the Alps. Behind them, Antoinette's aunt, three of her sisters, and her grandmother walked and talked about fifty yards back, but always in sight of the young couple. The walk was long and arduous for the aunt and the grandmother, so Vittorio took care to walk slowly, and as he and Antoinette talked to each other about their dreams, the rest of her family sang and laughed and enjoyed the beauty of the day.

Wearing ankle-length black dresses, their shoulders draped with white, hand-woven shawls, and their heads covered with brightly colored scarves, they carefully placed the flowers they picked into their wicker baskets as, talking, laughing, and enjoying themselves they tried to speculate about the topic of conversation taking place up ahead of them.

For the several miles it took for them to get to the rolling hills where they laid out their picnic blanket in sight of the famous sanctuary of Oropa, Vittorio repeated to Antoinette his dreams for their future generations and the stories he had heard of how beautiful America was.

They ate their lunch and waved across the field to her family members, and when they were finished, Vittorio held both of her hands and smiled deeply into her eyes.

"I can't take you with me the first trip," he said. "You know that, I'm sure. But if you'll come as soon as I send for you, I'll set everything up for us and send for you as soon as I can."

With total trust in his judgement, she gazed into his eyes, reassured by his self-confidence, but not yet fully understanding the idea he had just voiced. Then, from out of his pocket, he pulled a small gold band which he held out to her in his powerful hand. It looked so small inside the palm of his strong right hand.

"It's not much, Antoinette. Just a simple gold band. But I had three words engraved on the inside of it which will be constantly on my mind until I see you again."

As she reached for the ring, her knees began to tremble, and then her hands, and when she read the words, her eyes filled with tears.

Oggi, Domani, Sempre, were Vittorio's words to Antoinette. *Today, Tomorrow, Always,* and suddenly the realization hit her that Vittorio was going away. For how long, only the great God Almighty knew.

"Oh, Vittorio," she said slumping into his powerful arms and crying uncontrollably. "I don't want you to go!"

"I know, Antoinette, my love. I know."

He held her very closely and kissed her through her tears.

"But it will not be forever. Only until I become an American, and establish myself and then I'll send for you. By the time you get to America, we'll have a house. We'll have money. I'll be an American. And when you get there, we'll get married. And there, together, we'll raise our family in the land of the free."

"How long will all of this take?" she asked him nervously.

"I don't know. A year. Maybe two. I honestly don't know."

"But, Vittorio, what if it takes five years?" she cried out frantically.

"*Buono Dio,* Antoinette. I don't see how it could possibly take five years. But if it takes five years, then it takes five years, that's all. God will be with us throughout our time apart."

In the quiet warmth of the afternoon sun in the familiar Alps, the young couple sat together in faith, hope, and love, and laid out their plans for the major decision of their lives, which would chart the course of their future generations.

"Antoinette," he said quietly, looking deeply into her eyes. "Will you come as soon as I send for you?"

"You know I will," she whispered through her tears. "But are you absolutely sure you'll wait for me?"

"Antoinette, more than anyone else in the world, I love you. I've always loved you, even more than myself. You know I'll wait for you. And I'll pray every night that God will keep you safe until He brings us together again. And when He does, we'll be together forever."

She totally broke down then and cried longer and harder than she had ever done before, and as he held her close, he closed his eyes and kissed her through her tears.

Across the field, Antoinette's sister started to get up to go over there, but her grandmother held her back and cautioned her to keep her distance as the event unfolded.

For many minutes after she stopped crying, he held her, and the love that flowed between them bonded them together. They had never come close to anything sexual in their long courtship, and this embrace was all they would have throughout their coming separation, but the way they embraced that day was the bond that sealed their loyalty, their promises, and their love.

With the sun illuminating the high Italian mountains, in sight of the Sanctuary of Oropa, Vittorio Bellino took Antoinette Rosato's hand and said the following words.

"Antoinette, no two people who leave one another for any length of time, who love one another as we do, should rely on mere fate to bring them back together. We will call on Almighty God to watch over us and bring us back together again."

There in the Italian mountains, as God watched over them from a distance, Vittorio and Antoinette prepared for their separation.

"Pray with me now," he said to her softly.

She laid her head on his powerful shoulder and closed her eyes as Vittorio put his arms around her and led her in prayer. He closed his eyes, and sought the perfect words from within him as he laid their fate in the hands of their God.

"Almighty Father, look down on Your children now. We consecrate our lives to one another. We place all of our hopes and all of our dreams at Your feet. Be with us, Almighty Father, every minute of our separation from one another. And bring us safely back together, in Your mercy, and in Your perfect timing."

When he opened his eyes, Antoinette still had her eyes closed, and the pain in her face caused him to look away.

"In the name of the Father, and of the Son, and of the Holy Spirit," he said.

"Amen," she said quietly.

She looked up at him respectfully, though her heart was already aching, and although she was heartbroken that they were separating, her love for him was overwhelming. And so, resigned to a lengthy separation and filled with hope for the future and dreams for a better life, the young couple folded up their picnic blanket and started down the mountain into town.

All the way down the mountainside, Vittorio Bellino repeated the dreams he had spelled out so many times for Antoinette Rosato.

"When you get to the shores of America, I'll be standing there waiting for you. From the moment you set foot on the dock of our new land, I'll be with you. Our home will already be built. Our income will already be established. Friends you haven't met yet will be awaiting you with presents to welcome you. I'll be an American, with all the rights and privileges of Americans and the church we will be married in will already have our wedding date on its calendar. Your home will be laid out, your wardrobe of new clothes hanging in the closet. Your kitchen will be set up, and our bedroom neatly arranged. Our flower garden will be planted, and our vegetable garden prepared.

"The entire town will be awaiting your arrival, and the procession to our wedding reception will be lined with new friends. You'll be like a queen arriving in her land. I will already have told all of our neighbors about how beautiful you are, and when your arrival reunites us, paradise will be ours."

On and on he talked, promising his betrothed the world with a fence around it, and as they approached her home, she stopped him and smiled.

"Now it's my turn," she said. "When I get to America, you'd better have our wedding planned immediately. I won't want to spend one night out of your bed. We'll make love every night and have many children. I'll cook meals for you like you've never tasted, and our children will never know the meaning of hunger. Our house will be the center of attention for all of our children's friends, and we'll show the Americans the meaning of community. Your God will be my God, and we'll live happily ever after in our country."

When the couple entered the kitchen of Carlo and Lucinda Rosato, they were beaming. Every eye in the room turned toward Vittorio and Antoinette, and Antoinette walked over and kissed her father on the cheek.

"Father, Vittorio has something he wants to ask you. And he has told me that he wants to ask you in front of our whole family."

Vittorio Bellino took off his hat and bowed to Lucinda Rosato and then to Carlo Rosato.

"Mr. and Mrs. Rosato," he said respectfully, holding his hat in his hand. "The question I am going to ask you will require an answer which, because of the great love you have for your daughter, I know will cause you great pain."

Carlo Rosato sat back sternly and the children looked at one another quizzically, as all the joking and laughter of a few moments before turned, in an instant, to stoic silence in the room.

"Everyone here knows how much I love Antoinette. That is understood," Vittorio said. "But none of you knows the thing we have been discussing for so many months because we did not want to upset anyone prematurely. Of course, we want to be married, but the blessings I am going to ask of you will not be as simple as giving me your daughter's hand in matrimony."

Because Vittorio had always been respectful, Carlo Rosato sat and listened to him, even though he was not sure he wanted to hear what came next.

"Mr. and Mrs. Rosato, if you give your permission, I will be leaving for the United States of America, where I am going to apply for citizenship as an American."

Lucinda Rosato closed her eyes and put her hand to her mouth as she sat back in her chair, and several of Antoinette's brothers and sisters gasped. Christina, the littlest one, started to cry.

"When I have my citizenship, in a year or two, I want Antoinette to join me in America where we will marry and live our lives as Americans."

Tears filled Carlo Rosato's eyes as he exhaled in shock and reached out for his daughter Antoinette, who rushed into her father's arms as he cried in sadness.

"Is this what you want, my beautiful one?" Carlo asked her painfully.

"Oh, Father, I love you and Mother and all of the children so much. But I want to marry Vittorio and to be with him wherever he goes."

Carlo looked at Vittorio painfully but spoke to him as an equal.

"What will you do in America, Vittorio?"

"What I do for money is not important, Carlo. If I have to, I can be a shoemaker, like I am here. What is important is that I'll make your daughter my queen. I'll devote my entire life to making her happy."

Antoinette reached for her mother's arms as Carlo Rosato extended his hand to Vittorio Bellino. When Vittorio took Carlo's hand, Carlo put his arm around Vittorio's shoulder and shook him a little.

"You can be a shoemaker in Italy, Vittorio," Carlo said, although he knew by the tone in Vittorio's voice that the decision had already been made to leave.

"Italy is the land of my birth, Carlo, but the opportunities here are limited. I want to become an American so my children can have a better life."

Carlo Rosato looked deeply into Vittorio Bellino's eyes. Then he stood tall and squared his shoulders in a way that made everyone present fix their eyes and ears on his next words, which he spoke in a voice that quivered with emotion.

"Vittorio, I have only one question for you. Do you love my daughter enough to fight for her?"

Vittorio winced and spoke firmly and clearly. "Carlo, you know I do."

Carlo Rosato looked deeply into Vittorio's eyes and saw clear into his soul and knew that he was telling the truth.

"Then we will enjoy the time we have left with our beloved daughter and keep her safe and warm until she joins you in your country."

Vittorio smiled broadly and stepped forward to embrace Carlo Rosato. "Thank you, Carlo. Thank you. And thank God."

Four-year-old Gabriella Rosato ran around the table and jumped up into Vittorio's arms.

"Why do you have to go?" she cried.

"Now let's not have any tears from you," Vittorio said, touching her nose with his finger. "The sooner I leave, the easier it will be to go. You think it's going to be easy for me to leave your sister?"

"No," Gabriella said, pounding her little hands into his chest. "What do you think, it's gonna be easy for me to see you go?"

Vittorio laughed and hugged Gabriella as all the other children rose up to touch Vittorio as Gabriella had.

"Have you told your parents, Vittorio?" Lucinda Rosato asked him.

"Not officially although I've been talking to them about the possibility for some time. The only thing I did tell them is that when I made the decision, if Antoinette says okay and after I've cleared it with you, I'll be gone very quickly. I know a ship leaves from Genoa on Tuesday, which means I'll have to be leaving tomorrow morning to make it there on time."

"What time will you be leaving?" Lucinda asked.

"At dawn. Which means I have much to do tonight. With your permission, I'd like Antoinette to be with me when I tell my family tonight."

"Of course," Carlo said.

Attilio and Speranza Bellino did only a little bit better at concealing their pain than Carlo and Lucinda Rosato had as Vittorio and Antoinette told them. They were a little bit better off financially than Antoinette's parents and they did not see the emigration with such permanence as Carlo and Lucinda, as they considered the possibility of international travel between Italia and Estati Uniti somewhere down the road.

At dawn the following morning, April 28, 1910, Vittorio threw a backpack across his shoulders and said an emotional farewell to his parents, embracing them firmly and kissing them both on both cheeks. He then took a last walk through the town of his birth, down Via Firenze in Chiavazza, and across the river to the Rosato residence on Via Guglielmo in Biella. There only two people were permitted to come outside to see him off. Antoinette and her father, Carlo, met him at the edge of their property, and as the sun rose over Biella, she had never looked more stunning to him. For over an hour she had stood in front of the mirror, brushing her hair out the way Vittorio liked it and using the expensive perfume her father had given her mother as a Christmas gift two years before.

She wore a violet dress and a flower in her perfumed hair, and Vittorio's heart quickened when he saw her. When the two young people saw each other, they were so full of emotion that they were unable to say anything for a moment. Under the eyes of Carlo Rosato, they embraced one last time, and Vittorio whispered, "Lord God Almighty, bring us together again."

He broke from their embrace and looked deep into her big sad eyes.

"I love you," he whispered to her softly.

With everything that was in her she fought the urge to cry. "I love you," she answered. With the way she looked when she said it burning into his mind, he turned and started walking away. As he reached the bend at the end of the street, he turned one last time and waved to them, and when he rounded the corner, he was gone.

Suddenly feeling like a very little girl, she turned and buried her head into her father's shoulder, crying and refusing to look in the direction Vittorio had gone as she refused to unlock the hold she had on her father. Carlo Rosato listened for Vittorio's footsteps growing fainter on the cobblestones as he headed on foot for the train station in Biella for the ride to Genoa and his emigration by boat to the United States of America.

Carlo Rosato could do nothing but hug the daughter he loved so much, whose heart was breaking as the sun rose warmly over the valley Vittorio Bellino was walking through, out of Carlo Rosato's sight forever, for Carlo would never see him again.

None of the people involved in this human drama was prepared for the times that would follow, and it was probably a good thing that they were not, for it is uncertain if in the course of world events and human affairs it would have been possible for any of them to believe that it would be nine and a half years until Antoinette Rosato saw Vittorio Bellino again!

▲　▼　▲

When Vittorio reached Genoa, he immediately started making new friends. Alone in his emigration, he met some families, many couples, and several single people who, like himself, were all congregated there for their exciting and hope-filled voyage to America. On fire with his dream, he was determined to make the emigration a pleasurable experience.

Armed with a broad smile, he introduced himself to each of his fellow Italians and befriended every one of them. No one making the trip was from

Biella, and the closest anyone came to his hometown was the couple he met from Quaregna, an equally friendly and excited couple named Annibole and Rosa Rinaldi. Representatives of many regions were there. Calabrese, Marchegian, Siciliano, Piedmontese, Napolitan, all of them Vittorio befriended, and as each day passed by, he assumed more and more of an undeclared leadership role.

His greatest contribution to their passage was his absolute determination to master the English language, which rubbed off on his fellow travelers. For several hours each day he would lead the group, a handful at first, then more, and finally all the Italians, in English drills. With a simple textbook which he shared generously with his fellow emigrants, he set up a system of drills in which the group would repeat days of the week, months of the year, numbers, letters, animals, vegetables, nouns, verbs, common phrases, and short sentences.

By rote they learned all the words, aided by picture charts drawn by Rosa Rinaldi. The tedium of drilling was counteracted by the good nature with which Annibole exaggerated the pronunciation of words, waving his hands and saying his numbers as though he were doing a Shakespearian play.

This inevitably drew great laughter from the man who was becoming Annibole's closest friend, Vittorio Bellino, whose infectious laughter soon spread to the rest of the group whenever Annibole went into his antics. Sporadically Annibole would burst into a half-English, half-Italian litany that was always funny and his irreverent antics drew laughter from the whole crowd, making the learning of the language an enjoyable rather than a tedious assignment.

Always when someone seemed to be having difficulty due either to his individual temperament or his general slowness in learning, Vittorio would take the time to approach that person, giving him extra time after the larger group split up. In so doing, he learned the language well himself, and he became noticed by everyone aboard. His generous smile, his willingness to go the extra step in offering his time to help people, and his unabashed methods of hugging and touching all of the new friends he was courting drew them to him in a way that sealed his leadership.

The three weeks it took for the ship to get to America passed by in a flash, and as the ship neared the shores of their chosen country, their excitement grew measurably. Then one beautiful late spring afternoon, the immigrants were met with an awe-inspiring sight.

There, rising high above New York Harbor, stood the most impressive structure any of the immigrants had ever seen. Vittorio himself felt a rush of tremendous excitement when first he laid eyes upon Lady Liberty.

There she stood, tall and erect, her torch held high above the harbor, drawing the eyes of the world to her light. A crew member of the ship who had made the transatlantic voyage many times before stood aloft, and with a large megaphone that he held to his lips he recited to the immigrants the five lines that are inscribed on Liberty's plaque. . . .

"Give me your tired, your poor,
Your huddled masses yearning to breathe free,
The wretched refuse of your teeming shore.
Send these, the homeless, tempest-tossed to me,
I lift my lamp beside the golden door!"

Never could Vittorio Bellino remember having been so moved by any words he had ever heard. Silently and reverently he stood and listened as he gazed at the Statue of Liberty, and felt the thrill he had long dreamt about surging through his bloodstream as he entered the boundaries of the country of his choice!

When the ship touched dock on Ellis Island, Vittorio smiled a broad, beaming smile and joined in the cheer that erupted aboard.

The passengers now walked down the gangplank toward a frightening screening process in which many would-be immigrants were turned around and forced to return to their old country for various reasons, usually involving poor health. But this day, every individual on board made it through, and as they entered New York City, many aboard were met by family and friends.

Those who were not found themselves gravitating toward Vittorio Bellino, as he walked along the dock smiling and taking in all of the sights. Seeing the crowd of about twenty people off the boat, a tall, burly man with a pipe in his mouth yelled at Vittorio. "We need dock workers, man!"

Vittorio smiled at the man. "How many do you need?" he asked him.

"Many as we can get," the man answered.

Vittorio approached the taller man gingerly and the small crowd of passengers from off of the ship followed him.

"We need lodging and fair wages," Vittorio said to him matter-of-factly, and the man stood tall and spoke his words loud enough for everyone in the circle to hear him.

"Best wages in the city, and barracks for the men to live in."

"Many of our men are married," Vittorio said to him. "And they have their wives along."

"Those need to look elsewhere for lodging then, but jobs for them we have."

Vittorio looked around at his friends. A few of them nodded, and Vittorio smiled and shook the man's hand. "Let's talk business," he smiled.

Over at the side of the dock, no one paid any attention to the tall man dressed in a fine woolen suit who stood and watched the events unfolding on the dock.

Within three days, each of the immigrants that congregated together around Vittorio Bellino had found lodging and a job, and for many of them it was this early camaraderie that kept them secure. After a week, the man who had hired the immigrants realized that he had happened upon a fine workforce, but he was not the only one who noticed this. The quiet man in the woolen suit came by every day and stood apart watching the Italians working and growing more and more impressed with what he saw as each day went by.

On Friday afternoon of the first week, when the five o'clock whistle blew across the docks and the Italians started to congregate on the docks for their ritual after-work stop at the pier restaurant, the man in the suit walked up to Vittorio.

"Mr. Bellino?" he asked politely.

"Oh?" Vittorio answered.

"My name is Roland Aubuchon," he said, extending his hand to Vittorio. "I work for a textile manufacturer in Connecticut, and I'd like to talk to you about the possibility of you working in our company."

Vittorio shook the man's hand.

"Thank you, sir. Where can we go to talk?"

"The restaurant at the end of the pier where you and your friends have eaten every night this week is as good a place as any," Aubuchon said.

"You're talking about jobs for my friends as well as myself?" Vittorio asked him.

"That's why I'm approaching you, Mr. Bellino. There are jobs for as many of your friends as you can convince to follow you."

"Why us?" Vittorio asked him, smiling his broad smile and putting his arm around Roland's shoulder.

"Because I've watched you, Mr. Bellino. And your friends. Hardest working bunch of men I've ever seen, and we already have a pretty good labor force. But anyone who works as hard as you men deserves to have a better lifestyle than you can find here in the city."

"Where is your company located, Mr. Aubuchon?"

"Well, it's not my company, Mr. Bellino. Can I call you Victor?"

"Vittorio."

"Vittorio, it's not my company, but I work very closely with the owner, Cyril Bradford, and I'm sure he would take my advice and hire as many of your friends as you can convince to join you. The company is located in Indian Springs, Connecticut, a good hundred miles north of here. It's an absolutely beautiful little town, not at all like the city."

Vittorio and several of his friends were listening intently.

"Let's eat and talk about it," Vittorio said, as the men entered the restaurant at the end of the pier.

For two hours after dinner, Roland Aubuchon sat and told Vittorio Bellino and a dozen other men about the history of the textile industry in Indian Springs, its recent expansions, and the town where the company was located. The last thing he emphasized was the amiability of the factory's owner, Cyril Bradford, and by the time he was finished, many of the men were ready to go right away.

Vittorio thought better of it. When Roland was through, he looked to Vittorio for an answer.

"Well, for one thing, I don't speak for any of my friends. They're all free to do whatever they want to, but this much I will tell you. I personally wouldn't want to throw away what we have here with no guarantee of employment. But if there was a way you could guarantee us all a job, I think a number of us would go with you to Indian Springs."

"I'll go, Vittorio," Annibole Rinaldi broke in. "I don't like dock work anyway, and Rosa is very uncomfortable in New York."

"When will you be returning to Indian Springs, Mr. Aubuchon?" Vittorio asked him.

"Tomorrow. I was here for only a week visiting relatives, but I mix business with pleasure. I've been here before to recruit workers for the company, and no one I've ever recruited has left the factory yet."

"Mr. Aubuchon, Rosa and I will follow you there if you can guarantee me a job, under the conditions that I be allowed to report back to Vittorio after a week to let him know my feelings about the job," Annibole said to the American.

Roland Aubuchon stood and shook Annibole Rinaldi's hand.

"That, sir, is a deal. How does that sound to you, Vittorio?"

Vittorio looked across the room at all the men around him.

"I want each of you to tell me his feelings," Vittorio said to them.

Each one did, and the dozen men there were unanimous in agreement.

So the next day, the last Saturday of April, 1910, Roland and Theresa Aubuchon and Annibole and Rosa Rinaldi left New York City for Indian Springs, Connecticut, and the rest of the Italians in their circle of friends went back to work on the dock.

Two weeks later, as the men were finishing up their day's work, Annibole Rinaldi strode up to Vittorio Bellino, beaming with a smile, and the look on Annibole's face was all Vittorio had to see to know that he was finished with New York City.

For several hours, Annibole described to Vittorio and fifteen other Italians the textile mills, the Irish-Catholic Church, the mill-owned tenements, the Willimantic River, and the vast forested lands surrounding Indian Springs.

He told them how graciously Rosa had been welcomed, how nice the people were, especially the Irish people who took Annibole and Rosa into their church circle with so much warmth and openness. He told them about the mill and the excellent workmanship and clean working conditions there. On the dock in New York Harbor, with the salt smell of the Atlantic Ocean, he painted a picture for them of the town which excited them and set a fire of hope burning in them.

And then Annibole told them the best news of all. He had been commissioned by Cyril Bradford himself, under the recommendation of Roland Aubuchon, to instruct Vittorio Bellino to personally choose twenty men who would be guaranteed jobs upon their arrival in Indian Springs.

Vittorio was mobbed by men wanting to be included, and when Annibole was finished, the sixteen men there present had all agreed to go.

"Fortunately, I have four more to recruit, instead of anyone to eliminate," Vittorio said.

That night Vittorio and Annibole paid a visit to four family men he knew the addresses of, and by noon the next day people were packing their bags for Indian Springs, Connecticut.

On Sunday morning they attended mass and after mass they set out for their destination, the beautiful little town where two rivers met to form one, the Willimantic River in Connecticut.

Never had any group of people approached the small Connecticut town which would become their home with such excitement and anticipation, and never had any representative of any factory in the region happened upon a harder working or more appreciative group.

As they wound their way toward their destination, Vittorio silently prayed for the girl he had left behind, whom he had not told anyone about yet, because the vows he had made to her and the feelings he had for her he held as the most sacred part of his being. He had as yet not deemed it time to tell anyone else he knew about Antoinette, the love of his life.

▲　▼　▲

The first years in Indian Springs were exciting ones for the Italians who came to the town in 1910. They had come in search of America; they had found Indian Springs. And together they had all decided to make this country and this town a much better place in which to live.

It did not take them long to start the ball rolling on decisions that would benefit the lot of them, while adding their special touches to an already special town. In 1911, twenty-eight of these first Italians banded together and founded the Italian Cooperative and Social Club, patterned after consumer-managed grocery stores in Italy.

This cooperative was founded for the purpose of investing money to buy food for their families at cost. On Saturday night they would meet together and pool their orders for their personal needs for the week. The only members of this original club were Italians. They bought a small store and a horse-drawn wagon and shared the duties of going house to house taking orders and making deliveries.

The Italians were treated with a wait and see attitude at first by the long-standing residents of the town, but as the weeks went by, they soon got the reputation as hardworking, honest, and respectable residents, and they were very eager to please their employer, if they were also disturbed by the initial prejudicial attitudes they encountered by some of the townspeople.

Like any group of people who are new to an area, they had to establish themselves and their reputations and earn the respect of the people who were there first. Naturally they stuck together at first, and in February of 1913 they began construction of a recreation hall where they could meet for social events. In July of 1913, the hall was completed and the Italian Benefit Society founded.

It cost a dollar to join, and one hundred and sixteen local people of Italian descent joined the first year of 1913. The others had all been imported into town by an aggressive recruiting campaign waged by the mill owners once the solid work ethic of those first Italians had been determined. For the next two years, the Italian Hall was the center of social events within the Italian community. There they held tournaments in bocce, horseshoes, and cards. They had plays, parties, dances, wedding receptions, and game dinners.

They also united politically and decided that the best way to make progress in the town was to develop a strong political unity which could elect candidates of Italian descent to local offices. The first major challenge to political advancement those early Italians faced was the disturbing reality that so many of them had not yet obtained their citizenship and consequently, could not vote or hold public office. Their idea was right and their numbers in place. The only thing that remained was the task of gaining their citizenship.

At the threshold of major political progress, a challenge occurred which temporarily diverted the Italians from their political goals. This challenge they responded to immediately and effectively in a way that surprised and sobered their antagonists. In 1915 a new wave of Ku Klux Klan activity spread north into Indian Springs. Based on anti-Semitism, anti-Catholicism, and anti-black sentiments, it threatened virtually everyone who did not fit into its standards of Anglo-Saxon purity.

A cross-burning was done on the front lawn of St. Patrick's Church by a group of white-sheeted Klansmen, who, having no blacks or Jews in Indian Springs to vent their prejudice against, turned on the Roman Catholics.

Wop Club Burns Next was painted on the outside wall of the grey stone church building, which would probably have been ignited had it been made of wood.

For the next week, the Italians prepared a welcoming committee for the Klan, and eight days later, as the town slept, the white sheets rode in. Carrying torches and riding on horses, a dozen Klansmen rode up Club Road to the Italian Hall where they were immediately surrounded by forty-five men who had set up a barracks inside the hall.

In an instant, the Klansmen were surrounded, and as two of them tried to break out of the circle, they were pulled down off of their horses, which galloped down the road, riderless. When all twelve sheeted night riders were down off their horses, a short, powerfully built Italian walked out from behind the bocce courts and started pacing up and down in front of them.

"You 'een tr-rouble now, boys," Vittorio Bellino said, shaking his finger at the white sheets.

"Michele!" he summoned, and the rugged boxer from County Mayo, Ireland, stepped out of the shadows to stand beside Vittorio Bellino.

On his night off from the night watchman job he held, Michael kept watch with the Italians hoping the Klansmen would ride in when he was there. They did.

"Go ahead an-a take off dees' a-funny hats," Vittorio said to Michael.

Some of the Italians giggled as Michael Callahan walked into the midst of the Klansmen and began to rip off their hoods, one by one, until all of them stood bare-faced and trembling inside the circle of men.

Vittorio continued to pace in front of them, looking at each of them as he walked by. He did not recognize any of them, which was a relief for him, because he did not want any of them to be local men. Some of the Italians were smiling, but most were dead serious as they waited to see what Vittorio Bellino and Michael Callahan would do with them.

After Vittorio had gotten a really good look at each of them, he walked slowly over to the bocce court and sat down on a stump in the grove of trees. He started to shake his head back and forth as he took off his hat nonchalantly and started to fan himself with it while the suspense of the moment built.

No one dared move, as it became obvious to everyone involved that Vittorio was going to take as long as he wanted to make his point.

"Some of my friends' wives an-a cheeldr-ren were scared when they saw the cross burning on our church lawn," Vittorio said quietly.

He got up slowly and strolled over to the biggest Klansman, staring him right in the eyes.

"I don't like boys who scare women an-a cheeldr-ren."

The Klansmen all looked down and around uneasily.

"Michele!" he said forcefully. "You like-a boys who scare women an-a cheeldr-ren?"

Michael stared through the man sternly.

Vittorio turned and started pacing again. In front of one small Klansman he stopped and stared into his eyes.

"You look-a scared this time," he said, as he continued to pace. "Our priest-a told us to for-rgeeve you!"

Vittorio stopped abruptly in front of one of the men and pointed at Michael Callahan.

"You know-a this guy?" He asked him, pointing at Michael Callahan.

The man looked at Michael and shook his head no.

Vittorio laughed.

"Oh, he beats ever-rybody he fights in-a the ring. You should-a see him. Michele, whadda' you think we should do with these-a boys?"

Michael Callahan shrugged. "Tell them I'll meet 'em one by one in the ring at the fairgrounds on Saturday night," he answered Vittorio matter-of-factly.

"Saturday night?" Vittorio said. "What about tonight?"

Vittorio stepped up to the biggest Klansman.

"You wanna talk to my friend-a Michele tonight?"

The man shook his head and turned away.

"How about you?" he asked another of the Klansmen, pointing his finger inches from his face.

"No," the man answered meekly.

"No?" Vittorio said pacing his slow pace up and down in front of them.

"You know," he said quietly. "We like-a this town. It's a nice-a town. Good jobs. Good hunting. Good fishing. Good place for cheeldr-ren. I think-a we're gonna stay. But you're not gonna stay."

As he paced, each of the Klansmen followed him with his eyes as he walked back and forth in front of them, their fate obviously in his hands.

"I think-a this-a one time, we're-a gonna' listen to the priest. But!" he suddenly yelled loudly startling the Klansmen, a cold look across his face as he shook his finger again in the air. "We don't wanna' see these-a burnin-a crosses-a no more!" he yelled making a sweeping motion with his arm.

"Vittorio," Annibole Rinaldi yelled from the crowd. "I think their clothes smell!"

Vittorio turned and looked at them. He walked up to the biggest one again. "You burn crosses. You must-a have-a matches, no?"

The man reached inside his trousers for a box of wooden matches. Vittorio snatched the box from his hand and tossed it to Annibole.

"Then burn them," he said, tossing the matches to Annibole.

There, under the midnight stars in the summer of 1915, twelve men were assisted in taking off all of their clothes, and a bonfire was lit, burning sheets, shirts, trousers, shoes, socks and underwear.

When the twelve stood there naked, Vittorio and Michael stood between them and the rest of the men, and this time Vittorio spoke to the men of Indian Springs.

"Not one of these men is to be harmed in any way tonight. They are to be freed, unharmed, and left alone. Does everybody agree to that?"

A lone laugh was followed by an outburst of louder laughter as Vittorio turned to the naked men and spoke the final words.

"I don't think-a you boys ought to show yourself in our town again," he said to them quietly. Then he waved his hand in the direction of the road leading out of the club area. "Go," he said, and in less than ten seconds they were all running down the road, their white butts the last the Italians ever saw of any of them as they ran off into the night.

Sporadic Klan activity was heard of in surrounding towns after that, but no more incidents ever took place in Indian Springs again.

Throughout those early years, the Italian community was growing in stature and numbers, and as they moved closer to the day when they would all become citizens, the only thing that was disturbing to them was the slow progress they were making monetarily, for their factory wages were not much higher than necessary to meet their day-to-day expenses.

But if they had a low standard of living, they also had a very high quality of life. The things they deemed important they excelled at. They were happy, they loved their families and friends, and they were exceptionally close-knit in their community affairs, with respect for each other's feelings and mutual progress foremost in their minds.

Men respected other men's wives and were loyal to their own. They cared about other men's children, and one family's tragedy was a community problem whenever anything bad happened to any of the children. The community pulled together, and Indian Springs was really a very excellent place to live.

Throughout all of those early years, Vittorio Bellino was torn by a problem which he had a great deal of trouble resolving. He was trying desperately to save enough money to send to Biella for his fiance, Antoinette. Like many of the Italians of the time, he worked all day on the railroad, laying down tracks from Indian Springs to Monson, Massachusetts, and then he worked second shift in the textile mill. When he was through with his shift, when most men would go home to bed, Vittorio would walk to the Italian Club, where he would clean up the barroom, getting to bed about 1:30 A.M. He would sleep until six then get up to go to work on the railroad again.

Ordinarily it would be easy to put away a good sum of money that way, but people with families to feed would always come to Vittorio with problems, and inevitably he would end up giving them some money. In this way, he was delaying the time when he would be able to send for Antoinette, but he did not have the heart to refuse people in need.

Finally, after the realization that he had not seen Antoinette for over five years began to grate on him, he began to get angry about it, and soon the word went out not to ask him for any more money. Still he grew in stature in the community, though the locals began to joke that he was stingy enough to be a Republican. *That reputation was not the worst one to have,* he thought, and in the spring of 1916 he realized that he finally had enough money saved up for a down payment on a house.

He looked at several houses and settled on a duplex on Brendon Street upon which he made the down payment with every cent he had. With tremendous excitement, he wrote to Antoinette with the good news, and within a week he began to clear out the backyard for the garden he had promised her.

For the next year, he made great progress, working tirelessly on all of his jobs and spending every extra hour painting, repairing, digging, planting, and maintaining his property, and although it was irritating to him how long it was taking him, he kept his hopes alive through prayer and dreamed of the day when Antoinette would join him.

The only recreation Vittorio allowed himself was the Saturday night fights. The fight game had become the biggest attraction in town, with fighters coming in from as far away as Springfield to the north, Boston and Providence from the east, New York to the west, and the Connecticut shoreline to the south.

Weight divisions were established, grudge matches built up over the years, and southern New England championships fought for at the Indian Springs fairgrounds. Every Saturday night the exhibition hall was filled to capacity, and Saturday in Indian Springs was an exciting day for the townsmen.

Fans usually lined up behind fighters from their own national origin, and championship fights in all divisions took on extra excitement when fought between the Irish and the Italians, with assorted Polish, Hispanic, or African-American fighters rising to prominence. Throughout the entire local history of the fight game, every fighter took at least one loss with one notable exception.

One fighter remained undefeated. Standing in a class all by himself, the legendary bearded brawler from County Mayo, Ireland, Michael Callahan simply could not be beaten.

It got to the point that he would not fight anymore until somebody emerged that no one else could beat and then, inevitably, he would be dragged out again to put his undefeated record on the line yet another time. He never lost. While everyone expected him to lose someday, his reputation continued to grow, as did his record, and he won over sixty fights in succession spanning almost three decades. He refused to tell anyone his age, although everyone knew he was at least in his late forties, but younger fighters were no match for him ever.

Try as they might, boxing clubs from all the major cities could not find a fighter who could defeat him, his iron will carrying him through every war he entered. The one thing he absolutely refused to do was fight outside of Indian Springs. If you wanted Michael Callahan, you had to come to him. Many men came, none went home a winner.

While the fairground exhibition hall was always filled to capacity, for Callahan fights it overflowed. Through the years, very few men got to know Michael Callahan, as he continued to isolate himself from contact with anyone, working as a night watchman in Cyril Bradford's factory and spending time with no one but his immediate family.

The only person other than Cyril Bradford who ever went out of his way to get to know him was Vittorio Bellino, who was as extroverted as Michael was introverted. No one else who came to Michael Callahan's door was ever allowed inside except his fight manager, Sugar Desmond, or his employer, Cyril Bradford.

Michael liked Vittorio and would always smile at Vittorio's accent, and for some reason Vittorio felt comfortable enough with Michael to make him the only person with whom he would discuss Antoinette. While other men knew that there was a girl back in Italy for Vittorio, only Michael Callahan knew about the depth of Vittorio's love for her.

One morning at dawn, as Michael was preparing to make his last round around the factory, he looked up and saw Vittorio standing there, somberly.

"You look like you lost your last friend," Michael said.

"I lost one of my best ones," Vittorio said. "And one of your best ones as well. Cyril Bradford died last night."

Michael Callahan's face contorted in sadness.

"God bless his soul," Michael said.

The next day, the wake of Cyril Bradford drew more people than any other wake in the town's history, and when his will was read the townspeople were stunned by the generosity of one of his bequests.

Cyril Bradford had left a staggering sum of over $50,000 in a trust fund for the construction of a hospital, to be named Bradford Memorial Hospital, in his memory, the only stipulation being that the hospital never be moved out of Indian Springs. None of the principal of the endowment was to be spent, thus ensuring that the hospital would serve the townspeople for many generations to come.

On a windswept morning in March of 1917, as over six hundred people watched far and away the biggest funeral the town had ever witnessed, Michael Callahan, Vittorio Bellino, and four other men carried Cyril Bradford's casket to his gravesite, and people from every national origin mourned his death.

No one at the grand old man's funeral that spring morning knew that at that moment, German U-Boats were preparing torpedo attacks on two American ships. This would change the course of events the world over.

After the American ships *Illinois* and *City of Memphis* were attacked, President Woodrow Wilson sent for members of Congress to assemble in special session, and on April 2, 1917, while armed cavalry held angry crowds back outside the U. S. Capitol, the President of the United States prepared to address a joint session of Congress.

"There is one choice we cannot make, we are incapable of making; we will not choose the path of submission."

A tense Congress listened as the president continued.

"The world must be made safe for democracy. It's peace must be founded upon the trusted foundations of political liberty."

As members of Congress sat glued to their seats, the president asked them for a joint resolution declaring war on Germany for the sake of the nation. As he left the rostrum, President Wilson received a thunderous ovation, and four days later, after an 82-6 vote in the Senate and a 373-50 vote in the House, the United States of America was at war.

The selective service began the task of registering every American male between the ages of twenty-one and thirty-one. All across America, millions of young men registered for the draft, and in Indian Springs, Connecticut, things were much the same.

One problem turned into a tremendous opportunity overnight for a large segment of the population of Indian Springs. As non-citizen aliens, immigrants were not required to register with the selective service. By the time 1917 had arrived, better than 95 percent of the Irish-Americans had already become citizens, but only a small percentage, less than 10 percent of the Italians, who had come much later, were citizens.

On the other hand, any alien who volunteered for the service would be accepted for armed service as aliens in the American army, and were guaranteed of U.S. citizenship upon the occasion of their honorable discharge from the service.

The meeting in the Italian Club in late 1917 after the initial drafting of American citizens had fallen more than one hundred and fifty thousand men short of what was called for provided the Italians with a great opportunity.

"We are not required to join," Vittorio Bellino told his friends at a special meeting. "But if we do, citizenship will be ours when we're discharged. The normal five-year waiting period will be waived for volunteers. And those of us who have applied for citizenship and are still waiting to hear from Immigration and Naturalization will have to wait no longer. My friends, it's a great day for us. Once we have served our country, we can really organize, unite, register to vote, run our own representatives for office, and make significant political progress in town."

"I say we all join," Annibole Rinaldi yelled out, raising his fist in a rallying cry, and a cheer went up in the Italian Club.

So shortly after their meeting in 1917, seventy-five Italians from Indian Springs traveled to Rockville, Connecticut, where they offered their services as Italians in the American army and prepared to travel overseas to fight for their adopted country against the Germans.

Vittorio Bellino was thirty years old when he appeared in Rockville, and speaking for all the Italians in the room, he volunteered their services to America. Even the selective service representatives were deeply moved as they registered the men, and in early January of 1918, they were all called back to be inducted.

Vittorio's next letter to Antoinette was the last one he sent to her from America before entering the service. He told her the good news first, that their home had been purchased, their garden dug out, his citizenship assured. Then he told her the bad news. He was going to France to fight with the Americans against Germany. His letter was brief, but full of endearments, and he signed it, "*Oggi, Domani, Sempre.*"

In Biella, Italy, when Antoinette Rosato received his letter, she begged her father to allow her to join the Red Cross as a nurse to volunteer for duty in France.

When Carlo Rosato saw the urgency in her face, he consented, and in early February of 1918, almost eight years since the last time they had seen one another, Antoinette Rosato and Vittorio Bellino converged on the most dangerous place in the world, their love for one another and their desire to be Americans equally strong in their hearts.

What awaited them was tragedy and suffering, the likes of which neither of them had ever experienced before, for while some people take their citizenship in the greatest country mankind has ever seen quite for granted, other Americans have to pay very dearly for it.

▲　▼　▲

In a war zone, every soldier does not face equal danger. For the greater good of the entire army, sometimes it becomes necessary for some to position themselves in harm's way on the front line of resistance to enemy advances, and it is there that many of the most tragic and heartbreaking human losses of any war occur.

When the American armed forces were preparing to meet the Germans in Belleau Wood, just such a situation presented itself. Oftentimes it is not possible for commanding generals to offer up any particular role in armed conflict for volunteer status, but Belleau Wood presented the Allied forces with a number of unique options. Because of its relative strategic unimportance and the flexible nature of the timetable for massive confrontation, the battle for Belleau Wood was neither vital nor even necessarily imminent, although the war itself was.

On occasion, field commanders will meet with their most sterling young officers to discuss available options and ask for input on potential strategies. Just such a meeting took place in the prelude to battle that morning in the French woods. Sitting quietly, mesmerized by every word, was the young American military academy honor graduate, Lieutenant Clyde Bradford of Indian Springs, Connecticut, the only grandson of Cyril and Martha Bradford. Offering no input to the many suggestions that were thrown out, he simply listened and weighed all the suggestions he heard. When the field commander thanked his officers and dismissed them, Lieutenant Bradford walked back to his platoon somberly and called them all together.

Under his charge were the Italian immigrants of Indian Springs, Connecticut. Fighting in the American army, they were men he had come to admire and respect, feelings they shared about him. In one of the most extraordinary of all the unheralded scenes of World War I, Lieutenant Bradford laid out a chilling and extraordinary challenge to the men in his command.

"Gentlemen, we have the opportunity to make history today and to speed up the timetable of our country's victory in this war. But what I am going to suggest to you is a mission so dangerous and so extraordinary that I would not blame any one of you for not wanting to go along. If we volunteer for this mission, and only volunteers will be sent, it is likely that many of us, if not most of us, will not be coming back. And I assure you that I will not volunteer unless each and every one of us is united in our resolve to carry our mission to its completion and do our part in this victory, or die fighting for our country."

"What is it that you want us to do, Lieutenant?" Corporal Vittorio Bellino asked his young friend quietly.

"Vittorio, I'm not asking any of you to do anything," Clyde Bradford said, smiling at his older friend. "All I'm saying is that if we volunteer, we can make a real difference here today. But I want you all to know, that the assignment I'm referring to will cause us to be known as 'the sacrifice line,' and that's exactly what we're apt to become. Just beyond the field out there, in the woods on the other side, the German army waits for us. If we take this mission, we'll be the guys who go out there first to the front lines to engage them with machine guns, grenades, bayonets, or bare hands, whatever is necessary to hold them back before they meet the main forces. They're already calling us 'the Guinea Squad.' If we volunteer for this mission, we have a chance to have our American brothers use that title in a much more reverent manner than they are using it now."

"We'll do it," Annibole Rinaldi blurted out instantly, as proud of his Italian heritage as he was of his impending American citizenship. Vittorio scanned the expressions of all of his friends, humbly aware that whatever he

had said to any of them before had been treated with the utmost consideration. This time he waited for each of them to go before him with their own
input before he suddenly realized that all of their eyes were upon him as the
last man to offer his opinion. He let his eyes rest upon each of them before
gazing back at Lieutenant Bradford. It was not with the same zeal of
Annibole Rinaldi, or the broad smile of Angelo Carocari, with the same
confidence of Enrico Tonoli, the same nonchalance of Attilio Panciera, or
the rugged determination of Serafino Strazza, but ultimately, Vittorio
Bellino did what they all did that day, there in the woods of France. With a
serious look on his face that gave evidence of his understanding of the enor-
mity of the undertaking this handful of friends was embarking upon, he
looked into his lieutenant's eyes, and nodded, and the die was cast for one
of the most heartbreaking encounters of the war.

When Clyde Bradford stood at the entrance to the field commander's
tent, the men inside looked up from their maps and heard his offer to volunteer for the front. The company commander stood up and walked around
to the front of his desk, sitting down on the edge of it to talk to his young
lieutenant. He reiterated the statement he had made earlier. Because of the
nature of its duty, the sacrifice line had to be made up of volunteers. No
company commander coveted the role of assigning men to such a dangerous detail, so Lieutenant Bradford's superior officers were both pleased and
relieved when he told them that the Italians had volunteered.

"All right, then," the company commander said, laying his maps out on
the folding table before them. "With the dawn's early light, your men will
take the hill beyond this field and hold the Germans at bay until reinforcements come. Lieutenant Bradford, I'm not going to lie to you, this is going
to be a very dangerous mission. We'll be able to tell a lot about the enemy
from the way your mission unfolds. Are your men prepared for this?"

"Sir, there's not an American citizen among us except myself. These
men are going out there to earn their citizenship. They're excited, proud,
and ready for battle. We'll take the hill and hold it for America. You can
count on it."

That night the Guinea Squad slept restlessly and the predawn hour
found them strapping grenades to their belts, knives to the inside of their
boots, and ammunition belts around their shoulders. They prepared for battle quietly, each with his own last thoughts, before marching out to meet
themselves in the ultimate challenge of their lives.

Lieutenant Clyde Bradford made his own personal rounds, checking
each man's equipment and making eye contact with each of them, bonding
his will to theirs as they readied themselves for the storm of battle.

As the first light of dawn crept into the eastern skies, the Guinea Squad
started to move forward. Silently and relentlessly they crept up to the field
that led to the hill they were to take. When they confronted the enemy, they
were to do whatever was necessary to hold the Germans back as long as
they could before one of two things would happen. Either the Germans
would advance and meet the Guinea Squad in the first skirmish of daylight,

or the Italians would hold the hill while the Americans moved in behind them for the battle. In any case, Lieutenant Bradford's platoon was cast in a pivotal role in the ensuing battle for Belleau Wood.

While the Guinea Squad held the hill beyond the field they were nearing, the Americans would be busy setting up the second line, a more heavily manned intermediate position, a sort of barrier reef to break down the possible German surge. Well to the rear of this intermediate position was the main line of resistance, full of the heaviest numbers of American troops, which had to hold, if Lieutenant Bradford's line and the intermediate line could not. Not far behind this most heavily manned line was the defending artillery.

"Onward, the Guinea Squad," Annibole Rinaldi joked, laughing at their irreverent title as he walked alongside Vittorio Bellino in front of the group.

Vittorio Bellino laughed quietly as his arm found its way naturally around his friend's shoulder as they marched out to battle. Pushing Annibole away, Vittorio smiled at his closest friend and felt good to be by his side.

"You married men stay behind us," Vittorio whispered to his friends, who fell in quite naturally behind him, just as they had always done.

"Never mind," Annibole Rinaldi said. "There's no preference here. Married or single doesn't matter out there, only that we're Americans fighting for our country and our pride." Then he whispered to Vittorio. "Let's get it done."

Vittorio Bellino and the other Italians in the sacrifice line knew that they were pawns in a chess game, but they also knew that American citizenship was the prize for those of them who would be able to return. With pride and camaraderie, thankful for the opportunity to prove themselves to their fellow countrymen-to-be, they marched forward to the fight.

Perhaps the most amazing thing about Belleau Wood was that there was nothing there of significance for either army to win. The army that won Belleau Wood would win a forest. It was of no tactical significance to either army and of little value to the victor. The Germans could not regroup large forces there from which to launch any meaningful offensive, and the Americans saw no strategic value in it at all.

Belleau Wood was a place like Lexington or the Alamo, an insignificant place fought over savagely by two armies meeting each other's resolve in a do or die struggle for no other reason but that the time had come to fight. The winner of Belleau Wood would win one thing: momentum. It was a ferociously fought battle for trees, rocks, and superiority by determined men of iron will.

When Bradford's platoon reached the end of their short march through the trees to the open field that led up to the hill they were to take, Vittorio Bellino's last thoughts before entering the danger zone were of the girl he had left behind in Italy eight years before. He saw her in his mind's eye, the way she looked that last day he left Biella for the United States of America. She was gorgeous, and her eyes were so beautiful, full of belief in him and hope for the future. He remembered his last days with her, and his prayers for their reunion, and a peace fell over him, as though he knew beyond any doubt that his God would bring them back together again.

At the break in the woods lay a quarter-mile-long buckwheat field into which the Guinea Squad marched with their helmets down to protect their faces and necks from potential enemy fire. Quickly and quietly they stormed into the field and headed for the hill. When they were all in the field, the Germans unleashed a punishing round of machine gun fire, and Angelo Carocari was the first man to fall.

Annibole Rinaldi was beside him, and as the platoon hit the dirt, they heard Annibole's fateful word.

"*Morto!*" he yelled out in Italian. "Dead!"

When the first volley was finished, Attilio Panciera calmly stood and unloaded a machine gun volley of his own in the direction of the German fire, and just as Lieutenant Bradford yelled, "Down!" he took a single shot from a sniper and fell down, also dead.

"Stay down!" the young lieutenant yelled out. "Crawl forward and keep shooting, but for God's sake, keep down! Corporal Bellino!" the young lieutenant shouted.

"Oh!" Vittorio answered.

"We've got to make it to that grove of trees. If we can get to there, we can hold them off forever, until reinforcements come."

"I'll cover you!" Enrico Tonoli yelled out from his position behind a bunker in the middle of the field.

Annibole Rinaldi and Serafino Strazza fell in behind Vittorio Bellino and Clyde Bradford, and the four men began to crawl forward toward the trees as Private Tonoli gave them cover fire. Behind them they did not know how many of the remaining men in the platoon were being picked off, one by one, by sniper fire, and by the time they were within thirty yards of the grove, only a handful of men were still alive.

Suddenly, out of nowhere, a grenade blast exploded in front of them and tore the hearts out of the three men who saw it hit. When it exploded, sending rock and shrapnel flying in all directions and raising a huge cloud of dust and fire where it had hit, everyone knew how close it had come to Lieutenant Bradford. When the dust cleared, the men saw what was left of their young lieutenant's body strewn across the ground in front of them. Steam was rising from the wounds that covered his body, and his face had been torn apart so that what was left of him was unrecognizable.

For a moment, they all froze, but then they heard a loud, angry yell coming from behind them as Private Tonoli stood and ran at the Germans. Cut down on his way to his friends, he never made it to them as he died in a hail of enemy bullets.

The three men at the front used the opportunity to make their final dash into the trees and used their first opportunity to riddle the enemy with gunfire from behind the cover of trees to hold them back while the five remaining men who had been pinned down in the buckwheat field ran up to join them. With these eight now assembled, the first line of American troops had been established, but the charge the Germans mounted immediately thereafter gave them little time to regroup.

There at the edge of the woods, the front line of German troops came at them. Vittorio glanced behind him and saw Annibole Rinaldi kneeling behind a machine gun that he was using to mow down the first Germans that emerged from the woods. Only then realizing that he had received a leg wound that was bleeding profusely, Vittorio ducked behind a rock and started throwing grenades at the charging enemy. One German got through and leaped over the rock at Vittorio. Vittorio stood to meet him head-on, wrestling him down to the ground and snapping his neck with a harsh twisting motion that killed him instantly. As he wrestled with the German, a bullet hit the back of his helmet, knocking it off of his head and dazing him as he fell forward, away from the charging Germans.

Looking up his eyes suddenly and grotesquely fixed on the most horrible and sickening sight of his life. There, in the heart of Belleau Wood, under intense enemy fire, less than ten feet away from him, a dozen bullets ripped into Annibole Rinaldi's chest and face, shaking his dying body like a rag doll, and spewing his flesh and blood all over the tree he sat against. Helplessly, Vittorio watched his friend torn apart by enemy bullets as he knelt in shock and horror before the sight. An aching agony gripped his chest as Annibole Rinaldi died, and for a moment he felt the blood drain out of his face as his eyes stayed riveted on the awful sight.

All around him men were screaming and dying, and suddenly he turned around in a rush of anger and screamed gutturally in the direction from which the Germans had come. All of the original enemy soldiers that had charged the group had by this time been killed, and no more came at them for the moment.

Regrouping his own thoughts, he turned and scanned the area. Clyde Bradford, Annibole Rinaldi, Enrico Tonoli, Attilio Panciera, and Angelo Carocari were all dead, as were about a dozen German soldiers and the rest of the Italians who had not made it through the field to the trees. Serafino Strazza and a young German soldier lay dying a few feet away. For the moment all movement had stopped. The realization hit Vittorio that only he, Strazza, and the young German had survived the initial assault. He ripped a piece of cloth off of his uniform shirt and bandaged his leg wound, then he scurried about on his belly gathering up whatever weapons were left from the sides of the dead American and German soldiers.

Across the field, a dozen United States marines prepared to charge across and reinforce the survivors of Lieutenant Bradford's platoon, but as Vittorio watched them he became aware that they would be sitting ducks once they emerged in the clearing.

No American Marine will die while I am still alive, Vittorio vowed to himself resolutely, buckling down to hold the enemy off by himself.

Just as the Marines started into the field, Vittorio stood and yelled at the top of his lungs, "Go back!" which drew a hail of gunfire in his direction from the Germans.

The Marines wisely retreated, and Corporal Bellino hit the ground behind the tree. A trio of Germans came running at his position, but he shot all three of them and bunkered down in his position.

The standoff was established. Neither the Americans nor the Germans could advance as long as the Germans had their guns aimed at the field, and the Americans held their position in the woods. Little did the Germans know that only one man held them off.

For over eight hours the standoff continued as the Americans brought their army up behind the Marines at the edge of the field.

At dusk the German surge came. Vittorio was frightened when he saw the number of them. He quickly estimated that there were over a hundred of them, and it was then that he knew he was a dead man.

Oh my God, I am heartily sorry for having offended You, he prayed silently. *And I detest all my sins because of Your just punishment. But most of all because they offend You, my God, Who art all good, and deserving of all my love. I firmly resolve, with the help of Your grace, to sin no more, and to avoid the near occasion of sin. Amen.*

Vittorio checked his ammunition one last time and prepared to meet his maker.

Not one American death while I am still alive, he said to himself one last time, and he stood and started firing at the Germans for the last time.

He barely felt the bullets that tore into his arms, legs, and torso. Before he knew what had hit him, he was unconscious, and the German who came upon him aimed his rifle between Vittorio's eyes, but the young soldier's superior officer touched his arm, and said to him in German, "Forget it. He's a dead man."

When Vittorio came to, it was night time, and the rain was pouring down heavily. Severe loss of blood and wounds to his arms, legs, and spinal column had him pinned to the ground as though he were driven in by a stake. Incredibly he lay there all day and throughout the night, unable to move and barely alive. By the next day he was delirious, and God only knows what kept him alive, but the torrential rains continued as he lay there clinging to life.

Late in that June day after the rains stopped, when the 23rd Infantry extended its front to take over the portion of Belleau Wood where Vittorio Bellino lay, they found him, delirious but miraculously alive.

Back in the field hospital, tired Red Cross field nurses did whatever they could to keep the fallen combat troops comfortable. Hundreds of men were cared for by the loving hands of the beautiful Italian nurse named Antoinette Rosato. She worked long hours, tirelessly devoting herself to the comfort and care of the wounded soldiers.

Knowing only that Vittorio Bellino was stationed somewhere in France, she drove herself to the limit of her own personal endurance as she did all she could for the trench warriors, hoping against hope that he would not be one of the men she saw brought in maimed and bleeding from the war zone, and afraid to think of the worst possibility.

On June 14, 1918, she was assisting a doctor in an operation when he was brought in. In the twentieth hour of her shift, she was devoting all of her attention to the man on the operating table and she did not see the two medics who passed only six feet behind her carrying the battered body of Vittorio Bellino.

Vittorio was semiconscious as the doctor turned to his pretty young nurse.

"Miss Rosato, you've put in a very long day."

Vittorio thought he was dreaming, but the doctor's words made him open his eyes and look in her direction.

As the doctor continued, Vittorio Bellino's heart leaped in his chest when he saw her, although he was unable to speak.

"Go home and get some sleep, Antoinette," the doctor said, and Vittorio tried with all his might to cry out to her, but the word would not come.

"An-toin-et-tah," his mind screamed out, but he was pinned to his stretcher and unable to speak. He tried desperately to reach for her, but it was no use.

She tiredly wiped the haze from her eyes before leaving the tent for some much-needed rest but she never looked in his direction.

The absolute thrill of seeing her threw a new surge of life into him, however, and when the doctor turned to the Marine Corp medic who stood over him, Vittorio Bellino was wide awake and straining frantically to say something.

"What do we have here, Corporal?" the doctor asked the marine.

"One tough goddamn American, Sir," the Marine answered, and the doctor who stood over Vittorio was deeply moved that a man so badly wounded could have such an incredible will to live.

▲　▼　▲

Over the course of the next several weeks, something started to happen within the deepest recesses of Antoinette Rosato's mind which she did not realize or understand. The stresses of long hours amid circumstances of traumatic injuries had frightened her more deeply than she realized, and the thought of her beloved Vittorio out in harm's way had terrified her in her deepest subconscious mind. Trying to deny her fears consciously, she was unable to fool her subconscious mind, and each soldier she had seen placed before her in a macabre parade of dismemberment and death had chipped away at her tolerance for danger to the point at which even the slightest possibility of injury terrified her. Loud noises frightened her, as did quick movements, and she started to withdraw within herself, where she began to be ruled by her deepest fears.

Recognizing the toll the war was taking on her, the Red Cross sent her back to Italy. There she became convinced that something terrible had happened to Vittorio when he failed to write to her. She was even afraid to pray for him, afraid that if he was already dead, she would lose the only thing she had left, which was her rapidly diminishing faith.

Alone with her fears, she busied herself with mundane chores back in her hometown of Biella, where she had gone to wait for some word, any word at all, from Vittorio.

Meanwhile, in an army hospital in France, Vittorio was fighting his own particular battle for survival. Many times he was tempted to give up hope, as the spinal wounds he had suffered continued to cause him excruciating pain whenever he tried to move. Ironically the severity of his spinal wounds may have actually helped him to recover from the flesh wounds the other gunshot wounds had inflicted on him. Because he was unable to move, the flesh wounds had all the time they needed to heal.

Bandage changes came every day and were the most discomforting ordeals of his daily routine, which included being rolled over and cared for personally by dedicated Red Cross nurses.

His major organs intact, once the flesh wounds had healed, he then began the long process of recuperating from the spinal cord wounds, which unfortunately led him into the first stages of a degenerative condition called osteoarthritis, a kind of progressive decaying of the backbone which plagued him for the rest of his life.

Throughout his entire recuperation, he was so distraught and he felt so helpless that his pride prevented him from trying to contact Antoinette. He absolutely refused to allow for the possibility that she would seek him out if she knew where he was, where she would see him in his weakened condition. Oftentimes throughout his own ordeal, he contemplated sending her some word, but he was terrified to think of having to rely on her to attend to his basic needs or to allow her to see him as an invalid.

Consequently, while he was in the hospital, a decision which arose out of his subconscious mind began to chart a course within his personal life which very few people could ever understand about him. Mindful of the worry with which his fiance back in Italy must have been beset, he was nevertheless unable to bring himself to contact her while he was not in perfect health. Something told him that it was more important to him that Antoinette thought he was well than just merely alive, and not being well, he was in no frame of mind to contact her while he was recuperating.

So Antoinette sat and waited as the days turned into weeks and the weeks into months of Vittorio's recuperation. He did contact his brother, Fortunato, however, dictating a letter to a Red Cross nurse in which he petitioned his brother not to tell Antoinette anything about his injuries while he was not yet whole, and asking Fortunato to write to him with news of how she was doing.

While Fortunato could not totally understand his brother's feelings, he complied nevertheless, and said nothing to Antoinette about his brother's wounds. The letter Fortunato Bellino received from the hospital his brother was recuperating in came at a very pivotal point in his life.

In Italy Fortunato Bellino had grown up angry and mean. The younger brother of Vittorio Bellino had received the same four grades of education as his brother, but unlike Vittorio, he had not continued to educate himself after his formal schooling was completed.

Slapping his hands together, he said, "That's enough," on the last day of school and went to work immediately in the textile mills of Biella. There he had not been working for long when an argument with another employee got him into a fist fight on the work floor. In front of several co-workers, the ten-year-old boy received a very bad beating, the humiliation of which lasted long after his physical bruises had healed.

It was the worst embarrassment of his life, and he vowed to himself never to lose another fight. Immediately he started working out in private, lifting weights, shadowboxing, and subjecting himself to intense personal discipline in an effort to prepare himself for the inevitable next fight.

It angered him that he should have to go through such punishment because he never looked for fights, but he wanted to be ready for the day the next one found him. He did not have to wait very long. On his eleventh birthday, the same older boy who had beaten him before cornered him in a factory rest room and tried to push his head into a toilet. Emboldened by his first victory over Fortunato, the boy pushed his luck a little too far onto a boy hell-bent for revenge. Within a few seconds, the older boy's arm and nose were broken and Fortunato was being held down by two men who had heard the commotion and broken up the fight. Both Fortunato and the other boy were fired from their jobs, and when Fortunato got home, he was yelled at by his father, Attilio, not for fighting but for doing it on the job, which he needed, instead of waiting until after work.

Sullen and angry, he retreated more and more into himself and quietly continued his grueling regimen of personal training, growing angrier and angrier as he grew stronger and stronger. By the time he had reached his mid-teens, the only person with whom he could converse comfortably was his brother Vittorio, but when Fortunato was sixteen, Vittorio moved to America. This left him alone to sort out all of his problems, a job he did not do well with as the years wore on. By the time he had reached his nineteenth birthday, the year was 1914 and he was already well into his second year of full-blown alcoholism.

Now a construction laborer during the daylight hours, he spent his evenings drinking huge amounts of wine well into the night. Inevitably fist fights would break out, and Fortunato Bellino soon got the reputation as the quietest guy in the world when he was sober, but the worst person to be around when he was drunk. He was a mean and angry young man, turned dangerous by his nightly companion, Piedmont red wine.

Once when a man called him stupid for a comment he had made about a soccer game, he cleaned out a whole barroom, throwing one man completely through the picture window in front of the barroom and injuring four other men who tried to hold him back. When the bartender came around the bar with a club, Fortunato took the club away and cracked the man's kneecap with it before trashing the bar and several hundred dollars worth of bottled liquors that sat on the shelf behind it.

Only the willingness of his father to put the Bellino home up for collateral enabled Fortunato to be bailed out, and the sympathy of a local judge got him off on only a three-month jail term.

When Fortunato got back to Biella after his stint in jail, he talked to no one but family and very close friends. Throughout all of his ordeals one young woman in Biella stood by him. Antoinette Rosato, fiance of Fortunato's brother Vittorio, had always held a kind of calming influence over Fortunato, who she knew missed and needed Vittorio almost as much as she did.

He would visit her often, when his life's troubles began to get the best of him, and in her quiet way she would divert him from the storms of his dangerous paths whenever he would seek her out.

In his own way he loved her very much—as his brother's woman—and he felt very protective of her in his brother's absence. It was in the ninth year of his brother's absence that he received the letter from Vittorio asking him to keep him informed of Antoinette's well-being while hiding from her the injuries from which Vittorio was recuperating.

Vittorio wrote the letter to Fortunato from Paris, where he had been transferred to complete his recuperation until he was well enough to make the transatlantic voyage back to America.

That year, when Fortunato was twenty-four years old, the most serious threat to Vittorio and Antoinette's vows to one another occurred. At the same time that Vittorio was recuperating in France, Antoinette was returning to life as usual in Biella after her stint as a Red Cross nurse in Belleau Woods. Back in Biella, a young Italian named Rico Randazzo had decided that Antoinette Rosato was the girl for him.

With letters and cards he had courted her in France, and when she returned to Biella the letters and cards turned into wine and roses. Rico Randazzo stopped by her home frequently to talk and ask her out. Characteristically she treated him cordially, even though she told him immediately about Vittorio in America and her promises to him and politely declined to go out with him.

Still he was pleasant to her and very good looking, with a strong physique molded by years of stone mason work. And nine years had, after all, been a very long time to be away from Vittorio. It was nice to have a young man paying attention to her, and while she never considered being unfaithful to Vittorio, she felt good to have someone else around, especially one who was trying as hard as Rico Randazzo.

She could not know that Vittorio was very nearly recovered from his wounds in France, and he did not even know how close he was to the time when he would be discharged from the service, at which time he had planned to return to Indian Springs and send for her.

One night while visiting her with wine and roses, Rico Randazzo said something to Antoinette which set in motion a chain of events that changed Fortunato Bellino's life.

"He'll probably meet some American girl, and that will be it for you," Rico told her.

That was his mistake. The next day, she saw Fortunato and told him for the first time about the interest Rico Randazzo had expressed in her and about the seed of doubt he had planted in her mind about Vittorio's loyalty. And after all, she had not heard a word from him for several months. Hearing this Fortunato's blood began to boil.

"What's his name again?" he asked Antoinette calmly, even though he was seething inside.

"Rico Randazzo," Antoinette answered him dutifully. "He's a stone mason out of Biella, and he's very nice to me, except he keeps telling me to forget about Vittorio, which bothers me a little bit."

"Your flower garden is very nice," Fortunato said, smiling at her calmly as he changed the subject. "You give it a lot of time, don't you?"

"Oh yes," Antoinette answered. "I don't want to lose my touch before Vittorio sends for me. In America the soil is very good, and all the Italians on Brandon Heights where Vittorio lives have flowers and vegetable gardens. He told me so in his last letter. I'm practicing on these flowers because I don't want to disappoint him when I get to America."

Fortunato smiled at her warmly. "I can't imagine my brother being the least bit disappointed in anything you do," he said to her softly.

Later that day, as Rico Randazzo was shoring up the wall he had built with a trowel of cement, Fortunato Bellino tapped him on the shoulder. Rico had been joking with his men and he was smiling as he stood to greet the six-foot-two-inch construction laborer that he had seen before on various local jobs.

"Fortunato, what's going on?" Rico smiled, reaching out to shake the hand of Vittorio Bellino's younger brother.

When Fortunato threw the wine bottle aside that he had been drinking from and refused to accept his hand, the men who were working for Rico put their trowels down and stood behind him.

"Antoinette Rosato is my brother's *fidanzata*," Fortunato said firmly.

Rico Randazzo laughed. "Who are you trying to shit?" he said. "He's probably in America right now plowing some American girl while Antoinette sits home and gets older. If he loved her, he never would have left her here for me to find."

Fortunato acted quickly and decisively, and Randazzo never saw the first right cross Fortunato threw that broke his jaw. As Rico's back hit the wall he had been working on, the other men on the crew rushed in. Fortunato lifted his right foot into the first man's groin, broke the second one's nose with his right elbow, and knocked two of the third one's teeth out with a straight left hand.

With Rico's three men sprawled around on the ground, he returned to Randazzo. He threw him onto the ground and sat on him, and then mercilessly pummeled his face to the point where Rico Randazzo was good looking no more.

Rico tried desperately to escape from Fortunato's wrath, but Fortunato was too strong for him and he continued to rearrange Rico's face long after he had already severely beaten him.

"Tell me you'll never see her again, and I'll let you up," Fortunato screamed into what was left of Randazzo's face.

The thought that Fortunato was not finished doing damage terrified him as he lay there stunned by the severity of Fortunato's discipline.

"Bellino!" the man with the broken nose cried out. "Enough is enough!"

"Let him tell me when he's had enough!" Fortunato screamed back at the man as he punched Randazzo's face again.

"I've had enough," Randazzo groaned quickly.

Fortunato grabbed Rico Randazzo's hair and pushed his face in the dirt as he got up off of him.

"You come near Antoinette Rosato again, and I'll kill you." Fortunato sneered. "Mark that in your stone."

That night both Attilio Bellino and Carlo Rosato advised Fortunato to get out of Biella for awhile.

"Go to Mosso Santa Maria and stay at your cousin's house, and we'll send for you when we're sure the Randazzo boy is not going to press charges," Attilio told him.

Fortunato agreed and Antoinette promised to keep in touch with him. He never told her that he had known all along that Vittorio was still alive, though injured, and she never said anything to Fortunato about what she had regarded as far too serious a punishment for something she should have been able to handle herself. Still she was relieved that the way had been cleared for her to avoid having to decide how to handle the Randazzo situation. In Italy many decisions like that are made for women by the actions of Italian men.

▲　▼　▲

Vittorio Bellino's recuperation in Paris, France, was long and arduous, but in May of 1919 he was finally well enough to go home. He was transferred by troop ship back to the United States, and on May 31, 1919, he received his honorable discharge in Camp Upton, New York.

He immediately hopped a train for Hartford, Connecticut, where he decided to walk back to Indian Springs. The walk was therapeutic for the proud new American citizen as he covered the entire twenty-eight miles to Indian Springs in the daylight hours.

His heart was filled with joy as he strode the final miles up through the Willimantic River valley and into the downtown section of his hometown. A young boy on horseback asked him if he wanted a ride back into town, but Vittorio declined, asking the boy instead to ride ahead and announce at the Italian Club that Vittorio Bellino was home and hungry for some home cooking.

In the two hours it took for him to walk back up the river road, word spread fast that Vittorio was on his way home. By the time he got there, the club was full of old friends who stood and cheered for him in a hero's welcome. He smiled and greeted each well-wisher, and when Rosa Rinaldi rushed to embrace him, everyone stood back as he burst into tears in her arms. She had known for several months about Annibole's death and she had been hoping against hope that Vittorio had survived.

"I was with him when he died," Vittorio whispered to her, choking back tears. "I don't think I'm able to talk to you about it now, but someday I will."

She looked at him sadly and he trembled a little as he wiped the tears out of his eyes.

"This much I will tell you," he said, scanning the room and picking out family members of all the boys who were lost in Belleau Wood. He lifted his finger for emphasis, letting his eyes meet everyone's in the crowded hall. "They died as heroes, fighting bravely for our country."

It was the first time he had ever said "our country," and he lost his composure as his eyes filled again with tears.

Rosa touched his lips as he turned away to hide his tears.

"Vittorio, the polenta will be ready in fifteen minutes," Reno Posocco yelled to his friend and Vittorio nodded and excused himself as he walked out of the side door to gain his composure.

Rosa Rinaldi looked out of the window and saw him sitting alone on the old stump near the bocce courts, and she decided at that moment never to ask him to talk about it. No one else asked him either, and for the rest of his life he was unable to bring it up. No one blamed him for that, and the memories Vittorio had of the heartbreaking deaths of his friends in World War I, he carried with him to his own grave.

As far as local politics were concerned, the greatest single result of World War I was the large number of newly registered American citizens that swelled the voting lists when the Italians who had survived the war registered to vote. With unity and commitment, these new American citizens of Italian birth made rapid progress as they started taking over the town, board by board, committee by committee, increasing their foothold on decision-making committees that ruled the town.

First came the interaction at political meetings held apart from the rest of the community at the Italian Club. Political decisions on what the Italians wanted or needed were discussed and agreed upon at the club before being brought up at town meetings so that by the time any issue was brought up before the town, one significant block of votes was already committed to one course of action.

As the Italians piled up victory after victory, they began to grow in confidence. They decided that the best way to secure the advancements they had made was to nominate candidates from both political parties who were Italian to run against each other in the general election.

The major difficulty they encountered in this was in finding numbers who wanted to be Republican. The majority of people in the town were laborers and the labor unions were always heavily Democratic, while the mill owners, the well-to-do, and the people in the town who were of English descent were, for the most part, Republican.

"We need Vittorio to be a Republican," Tony Lanzetta yelled out at a meeting.

"No!" Gazzo Francini protested loudly and emphatically. "Vittorio would win, and we don't wanna no more R-r-republicans in office in this-a town!"

The remark was greeted by a loud chorus of laughter and Vittorio laughed too. He also registered as a Republican. But most of the Italians, in fact the vast majority of them, registered as Democrats. That year a local unit of the Amalgamated Textile Workers Union was formed and wages instantly increased at the mills as collective bargaining talks gave the mill workers the salary boosts they had been unable to secure as aliens working for small wages.

The union was invited to assume responsibility of the growing cooperative grocery business, and a new organization was formed, the Worker's Co-operative Union. One hundred and twenty workers bought one five dollar share each, and the Co-op Food Store became the number one grocery store in town.

Throughout the rapid rise of the Italians' position in Indian Springs, the Irish harbored a jealousy that they could not rectify. The Italians had definitely earned their advancement by hard work and unity, but the Irish were also hard workers, even if they lacked the same sense of unity which had carried the Italians so far forward.

Instead of learning from the Italians, as Sugar Desmond had hoped they would, they put their emphasis on competing with the Italians in other areas, like the sports world. The Irish had a baseball team; the Italians had a baseball team. The teams would pair off in Hyde Park for marathon games of legendary notoriety and stories would be passed down from generation to generation of heroics on the ball field.

The only problem was the Irish and Italians always split. Try as they might, neither faction could gain an upper hand in any sport—any sport, that is, except one. The Irish still had Michael Callahan. When he fought an outsider, Indian Springs had him, but when he fought a local, the Irish had him.

He was getting older now, and to look at him it was hard to believe that he was in his fifties. That he had never lost a fight was almost unbelievable, but he was truly a legend in his own time. He had won his last fight only two months previously, with another stunning first round knockout of a twenty-three-year-old boxer from Providence, Rhode Island, who was eleven and zero, with eleven first round knockouts, before meeting Michael.

Michael Callahan still worked as a night watchman at the Bradford Woolen Mill and despite his fifty-cent per week raise every time his wife, Maureen, had had a child and the new better wage structure that the union had brought in, his family was too large for him ever to save any money, so the Callahan family still lived in a rented tenement on Furnace Avenue. The money he made on each of his fights was soon gone, and it was uncertain how long he could continue to fight, as Father Time marched relentlessly on. In fact he himself had often given thought to the day when he would be able to walk away from the ring for good to do what he had always found most enjoyable, which was just to sit and talk to the people he loved the most in the world, his own wife and children.

Each fight he fought had the chance of being his last, but as the money grew short and another challenger arose, inevitably the call would go out and he would step into the Indian Springs fairgrounds exhibition hall ring one more time, secretly hoping each time that this would be the last time he would have to fight.

As the November elections drew near, Vittorio Bellino was very excited because the Italians had a good chance of winning the first selectman position that year, with the brilliant young politician, Pop Arnetti, who was making great strides in the community. All the attention was drawn to the local election, since it was not a presidential or gubernatorial year for elections.

It is said that politics makes strange bedfellows, and that year an Irish-American who was beginning to turn heads in political circles also burst onto the scene. His name was William Desmond, and his friends called him Sugar. With a likable smile and a confident air, he became known in political circles as a man who was always on the inside of any winning trends, and his willingness to deal with the Italians and support their political efforts soon got him an ear in the growing Italian political block. Sugar Desmond was no fool. Down the road, he would have many political chips to cash in, and he was willing to bide his time and ride the wave of the Italian advancements.

Sugar Desmond had the reputation of picking winners and when he walked in the Italian circles that autumn with his big cigar and his bigger smile, new confidence filled the Italians as the election neared.

For one local Italian man, there was another reason to be excited that fall of 1919. Back in his Brendon Street home one October night that fall, he sat alone adding long columns of figures, over and over again. Each time he looked at all the figures before him, he became more and more excited as he realized that he was only one more paycheck away from realizing his most cherished dream.

Once he cashed his Friday paycheck, he could send the money to Antoinette and with any luck at all, she could be in America by Christmas! Could it be true? He carefully checked all the figures and verified that his calculations were correct. For a moment he just sat there smiling, and then he leaped up out of his chair and let out with a loud yell of excitement.

Then he sat down and wrote this letter to Antoinette.

My love,
With great joy, and thanks to Almighty God, I am sending you the money to join me in our country.

As I have promised you, our home has been purchased and furnished. My income is secure, and my citizenship earned. I have some good friends to introduce you to, and it is time now for us to be married. I am totally healed from minor wounds received in the war, and looking forward to your arrival, and the beginning of our family in America.

I have enclosed the money for your voyage here, and when you write to me confirming your arrival, I will be awaiting you on the shores of our new land. My heart overflows with joy as I await you, my queen. I miss you and I love you with all my heart.

Oggi, Domani, Sempre,
Vittorio

In Biella she was outside hanging a wash load on the clothesline when her little sister, Gabriella, ran up to her and handed her the letter from America. The sun was shining brightly in the Biella morning when she tore open the letter, and she screamed and cried out with joy when she recognized Vittorio's handwriting.

Her mother ran out of the house when she heard Antoinette scream, and as mother and daughter embraced, Gabriella read the letter to Lucinda Rosato.

"I knew he was alive. I knew he would send for me. I knew it all along. I only wish Papa was still alive to share in my joy," Antoinetta rejoiced.

After booking passage on the ship that would take her to her paradise, Antoinette sat down and composed the following short response to her fiance's letter.

My love,
I will be arriving in Boston, on or about Christmas day, excited and thrilled beyond my ability to express in words. I am not altogether certain, but I may be accompanied by someone else I know you will be overjoyed to see, but I have not cleared anything definite with that person yet, so do not get your hopes up on that.

Besides, I want all of your thoughts to be about me. My heart leaps with joy. We'll be together again, at last, and nothing will ever separate us again.

You have fulfilled your promises to me, and now it is my turn to fulfill my promises to you.

All my love,
Antoinette

▲   ▼   ▲

When Vittorio received the letter from Italy that he had long dreamed about, he headed straight for the Italian Club, where he finally told everyone about the girl he had been waiting for and his plans to get married. Soon all of the Italians were excited for him and anxious to meet the mystery girl that Vittorio had kept secret from them.

Approaching his employer with a request for special leave, Vittorio received no opposition to taking a leave of absence to travel to Boston where he would meet his betrothed in Boston Harbor. In fact, on Friday, December 19, he was called into the office of the Bradford Woolen Company, where a fellow Republican from Laurel Hill, Connecticut, who held a large quantity of shares in the mill, greeted him.

"Vittorio, my name is Alden Bradford. My grandfather was Ira, and his brother was Cyril Bradford. You served in France with my cousin Clyde. We heard in Laurel Hill about the coming marriage about to take place between you and your fiance from Italy. At the Bradford Woolen Company, we have known for a long time that a very big reason for the banner years we've had at the factory over the past decade is the remarkable work ethic that you and your fellow Italian-Americans have brought to our operation. I think it is only right that I should reward you.

"I've received authority to give you two weeks off with full pay, and I've got another surprise for you if you'll follow me outside."

Vittorio was beaming as he followed Alden Bradford outside to the back of the Bradford Woolen Company which overlooked the river. There, dressed handsomely in full travel readiness, was a team of horses and a brand new covered wagon made of polished mahogany with lots of leather and velvet seat cushions.

"A loan to you from the company to transport your new wife from Boston to Indian Springs."

Vittorio was beside himself with excitement. He could not restrain himself as he reached out and threw a bear hug onto the surprised and somewhat embarrassed Alden Bradford, whose background was not as accustomed to such outpourings of affection. Still Alden Bradford smiled broadly as Vittorio Bellino reached his hands up in clenched fists, laughing with joyous emotion.

"Antoinette will be so surprised!" he exclaimed.

"When you return to Indian Springs, we'd like to have a welcoming party for Antoinette at the Italian hall. We'll prepare a special welcome for her if you'll trust our women to put it together. It was Pop Arnetti's idea. He said he'd like to work something out for the Italian women and the American women to do together to make Antoinette feel welcome."

"She'll be very pleased, I'm sure," Vittorio beamed.

"Good, then you can consider it done," Alden Bradford said. "When will you be leaving, tonight or tomorrow morning?"

"There's a very special event taking place tomorrow night at the exhibition hall," Vittorio answered. "Michael Callahan's last fight."

"That's right," Alden Bradford answered. "He did announce his retirement from the ring after this fight, didn't he."

"I'll go to the fight, and Sunday morning I'll head for Boston."

That night the exhibition hall was filled to overflowing with the largest crowd in the history of the fight game in Indian Springs, as the bearded warrior from Ireland prepared to meet one of the greatest challenges of his life. The man he was fighting was undefeated in twenty-four fights, and he was the best fighter to come out of New York City in decades.

Callahan was going to be paid the staggering sum of two hundred dollars to face the tall, black slugger, Joe Robinson, who many thought of as a future heavyweight champion of the world.

"May as well go out in style!" Robinson's manager said to Michael Callahan, never expecting for a minute that his fighter could be beaten, especially by anyone as old as Michael Callahan.

Robinson's entourage had already arrived by the time Alden Bradford offered the wagon to Vittorio Bellino. They stepped down off the train man after man, with trainers, managers, doctors, and cornermen all stepping down before the tall boxer himself stepped down, looking over the crowd intently. Several local men were there to greet the Robinson entourage, although Michael Callahan stayed home. They were shown to their rooms at the Springs House, the plush local hotel overlooking the famous mineral springs where the Indians used to meet generations ago.

Robinson was insulted that Michael Callahan did not even have the courtesy to greet him, and on the deck of the train station he vowed "to punish the old fool" for his disrespect.

Michael smiled when he was told this and sent a message back to Joe Robinson. "You better bring a cannon with you into the ring."

At ringside that night, Joe Robinson didn't wait for the customary introductions to get into Michael Callahan's face.

"Saint Patrick wore a dress," Joe Robinson whispered to Michael the first time he saw him.

Michael said nothing, but just stared deep into the young fighter's eyes with the ice coldness he had stared down hundreds of opponents with before.

When the fighters were announced, Michael ignored his opponent as he walked up to the ring announcer and took the megaphone from his hands.

"I want to thank you all for coming here tonight, and for supporting me all these years. As I have said, this will be my last fight here tonight."

"What will you do now?" a fan's voice yelled up into the ring.

Joe Robinson paced irritably in his corner, as all the attention of the moment went to Michael Callahan. The young fighter was not used to having the attention on the other side of the ring.

"If I can answer your question without sounding like the old fool my opponent called me, I started to really like just sitting out on the back lawn with my children, listening to the birds sing and the river flow by, and that's just what I'm going to do from now on after tonight."

Callahan's answer brought a thunderous ovation from the many local men who had made many week's pay betting on him throughout the years, and the longer the ovation took, the more impatient Joe Robinson became.

When the opening bell rang, the impatience of youth overcame the young fighter, and he did something that had not been done to Michael Callahan in over thirty years. He charged across the ring, swinging wildly and lunging at Michael awkwardly. Michael grabbed him and got him in a clinch, but when they broke, Robinson butted him with his head.

Pandemonium erupted and the crowd jeered as the referee attempted to regain order. Michael's memory was jolted back to that day, so many years before in Ireland, when a young Brit had thrown him onto his back on the dock, and the anger that rarely filled him came rushing back in. His words to the young black fighter were the same ones he had said to the Brit ages ago.

"You'll pay for that, laddy!"

When the fighters were signaled together after the break, a fire unlike any the regulars at ringside had seen in Michael Callahan's eyes for many years returned to him. When he started to swat, the sound the bare knuckles made on Joe Robinson's face and skull was loud and scary. Robinson was hit so many times in such rapid succession that he did not have time to launch an assault of his own. No one watching the fight could ever remember Michael Callahan being so brilliant, and when Robinson went down before the bell ending the first round sounded, he was unable to shake the cobwebs out of his brain as the referee counted him out.

Michael had honestly not wanted to knock him out so soon, with every intention of carrying him a few more rounds for punishment, but he just got too carried away.

In a move Michael Callahan could not understand, Joe Robinson's manager rushed over to Michael immediately after the fight and surprised him with the offer he made to him.

"Come on the road with me, man. You and I can make millions together!"

What he did not know about the purity of Michael Callahan's short speech before the fight was that Michael had meant every word of it, and that the most relieved person in the whole auditorium that evening was Callahan himself, finally and totally convinced that his last fight had been fought.

He looked at Robinson's manager, smiled slightly, turned away from him, and walked out of the ring and toward the dressing room. Thunderous applause followed him as the Irish champion walked out of the ring toward his retirement. As he entered the locker room for his shower, Sugar Desmond stood and kept well-wishers at bay, and Michael Callahan felt very good to be unlacing his boxing shoes for the last time.

▲　▼　▲

The next morning, Vittorio Bellino attended mass before starting out for Boston, Massachusetts, in the cold December wind. He thought of the ship that was out at sea at that very moment, bringing the woman of his dreams to America's shore. He bundled up in the scarf that Rosa Rinaldi had woven for him and felt for the shawl that she had created as a welcoming gift for Antoinette.

Out at sea, two people from Biella, Italy, were eagerly awaiting their arrival in Boston Harbor. The woman was fancifully dressed in travel clothing she had stored for nine years in preparation for her arrival on the shores of her country to be. The man, her brother-in-law to be, was traveling the same way his brother had traveled nine and a half years previously, with nothing but the clothes on his back.

The woman had been waiting for nine and a half years to see her fiance. The man never thought he would see his brother again. But circumstances in Italy had made it wise for him to seek a new land and a new start, and no two people in the world could better help him to do that than Fortunato Bellino's brother and future sister-in-law, Vittorio and Antoinette.

With excitement and anticipation, the young people sat aboard the ship that steamed along on its way to America. In only a few days, the captain and crew had made it a point to meet Antoinette Rosato, who was the kind of passenger that attracted a lot of attention. She was beautiful, friendly, and a joy to serve, and they had befriended her almost immediately. As always Fortunato kept his eyes on her and watched her like a bodyguard, and having him alongside of her made Antoinette feel safe and well-protected.

On Christmas Eve, after a five-week transatlantic voyage, the ship's captain invited Antoinette and Fortunato to the head table in the dining area to join him in the captain's dinner, the last big banquet before arriving at their destination.

"We have something special planned for you, Miss Rosato, if you'll agree. We'd like to give the people aboard something to remember their trip by, and with your permission we want to tell them your story before we land," the captain told her.

"How will you do that?" Antoinette asked the captain shyly.

"Have you speak to the people at the end of dinner tonight, tell them a little bit about your story, kind of a human interest story, and then when they're all familiar with your story, prepare a special event where you get to depart the ship first tomorrow morning, to reunite with your husband-to-be. The only thing that could go wrong is that he won't be there."

"He'll be there," Fortunato said loudly.

"Oh, I don't know," Antoinette answered shyly, looking to Fortunato for advice. "Fortunato, do you think anyone will care enough about me to delay their own departure even for a minute?"

"Miss Rosato, it's a human interest story that all people love. Trust me. I know it's a good idea," the captain said.

She looked to Fortunato again.

"It will be something your grandchildren will tell their grandchildren about," Fortunato smiled at her.

"Oh, all right then," Antoinette smiled meekly.

"Good," the captain said. "Then let me introduce you to the people, and you can tell them your remarkable story."

As dinner wound down and the crowd busied itself in after-dinner conversation, the ship's captain stood at the podium and tapped his glass to get the attention of the crowd.

"Ladies and gentlemen, tomorrow is Thursday, December 25, 1919; Christmas Day. I'd like to wish all of you a very Merry Christmas. We will be arriving in Boston Harbor at about noon. Many of you will be arriving back home from foreign travel. Some of you are visiting America on a trip and will be returning home after you visit our country. But there is one passenger aboard whose arrival in America tomorrow will be a very special one, both for her and for the gentleman who is meeting her. She is the beautiful Miss Antoinette Rosato, and I'd like to introduce her to all of you now. Miss Rosato."

Antoinette stood up to a polite and gracious round of applause as she shyly approached the captain's podium.

When the beautiful young woman stood at the podium, her naivete and beauty soon won her fellow passengers over as she greeted them shyly.

"Hello, and Merry Christmas to all of you. It's a little embarrassing for me to presume that any of you would be interested in me. But our gracious captain thought some of you might be interested in sharing with me the joy that is in my heart right now."

It was probably the best way for her to have started, because everyone on board immediately stopped talking and fixed their eyes on the beautiful young Italian girl as she unfolded her remarkable story, in very good English with a touch of an Italian accent.

"Nine and a half years ago, when I was twenty years old, I was very much in love with the man I am going to meet tomorrow. I still love him just as much, probably more. When he left to go to America, he promised me that he would send for me as soon as he could. If either of us had known about the many difficulties and the world war that would have delayed our reunion, I promise you I never would have let him go."

Some of the people laughed; all of them listened intently.

"But the world was a different place then. My fiance joined the allied war effort and fought for his new country in the forests of France. I went there myself, as a Red Cross nurse, hoping to find him there. I treated many men, but I never saw my Vittorio. I prayed for him every night," she said as her voice started to crack. "that he would remember me, and that God would keep him safe."

She had to pause to clear her throat, and people all through the silent dinner crowd were wiping their eyes as she continued.

"I know that God loves us, and that he chose Christmas Day as the day of our reunion because we made him the third partner in our relationship."

"She's a remarkable woman," the captain whispered to his first mate, and the man nodded.

"And tomorrow He will be rewarding our perseverance. I can't wait to see my Vittorio."

When she left the podium to sit down, a round of applause that started quietly soon spread throughout the entire crowd as every person in the room stood and clapped for her. Then the captain stood up again.

"Ladies and gentlemen, with your gracious permission, I would like all of us to share in the joy of Vittorio and Antoinette's reunion. When we dock tomorrow, I will call for him on the ship's loudspeaker, and when he gets to the ramp, I will let Miss Rosato leave the ship first."

The crowd stood as one and broke into a thunderous ovation as Fortunato stood and smiled at her, and Antoinette sat at her table and smiled through her tears.

On shore Vittorio Bellino was preparing to attend midnight mass at the Roman Catholic Church in Boston Harbor. Alone with his God and his thoughts, he was praying that everything would be acceptable to Antoinette, and that God would give him the wisdom and the ability to be a good husband and father of children who loved God and appreciated his loving kindness as much as he did.

Long after the service ended, Vittorio knelt and prayed, and finally, as the young curate was ready to lock the doors of the church, he touched Vittorio's shoulder, and Vittorio made a special request of him.

"Father, I want my soul to be pure when I meet my fiance tomorrow. Will you hear my confession?"

There in the quiet darkness of the church, Vittorio Bellino cleansed his soul in the sacrament of Penance, and that night he slept well, despite the thrill in his heart as he awaited the arrival of his love.

Christmas Day broke clear, and cold, and calm, and quiet. The horses blew warm breath into the cold air that froze in a cloudy mist in the clean morning air. Vittorio was the first person on the dock to await the arrival of the ship from Italy. To keep warm he sang Christmas carols to the horses as he paced back and forth, rubbing his hands together and blowing on them.

For several hours he stood there, pacing the dock and greeting those who approached him to admire his horses and buggy. An old man shared the coffee in his thermos with Vittorio, and as Vittorio was listening to the man elaborating about the Christmas dinner his wife was preparing for his son who was coming home from Italy, the ship rose up out of the sea.

"Land, ho!" a shipmate yelled, and Antoinette took a last look at herself in the mirror of her cabin. She wore a warm fur coat that her father had given to her before he died, with a heavy fur collar and thick sleeves. The coat was long, with fur pockets she could fit her hands into. This she wore over an ankle-length black print gown, with high heeled leather boots, which made her only two inches shorter than Vittorio, who was himself only five-foot-five. Her hat was black velvet, covered with white cloth and a feather in the side. She looked very proper and beautiful as she emerged from her cabin, where Fortunato stood to take her arm and escort her to the captain's quarters.

"Good morning, Mr. Bellino," the captain said shaking Fortunato's hand. "You look lovely, Miss Rosato," he said, bowing to her. "Are you ready to meet your fiance?"

"I'm so excited, I could burst," she said, beaming with pleasure as the ship neared the dock.

On shore the man waited, his eyebrows raised toward the approaching ship as he paced the dock like a caged tiger. He wore a long black coat, full-length, and buttoned down the front, over a white shirt and tie. Clean shaven, a black beret was his head covering over his fresh haircut. He carried his gloves in his pocket, preferring instead to rub his hands together and blow on them as he paced the dock in his new high-topped black shoes.

Looking out the porthole of the captain's quarters, she saw him before he saw her, and tears of happiness filled her eyes and started rolling down her cheeks as she saw him there, pacing across the dock as he watched the ship roll in.

"There he is!" Fortunato beamed, pointing Vittorio out to the captain, who smiled and said, "Splendid!"

The captain turned on the ship's loudspeaker and made the announcement calmly and slowly to the people aboard.

"Ladies and gentlemen, we have spotted Mr. Bellino on shore, and when we get to within hearing distance, I will turn the loudspeaker toward shore to summon him. Please allow Miss Rosato the courtesy of leaving the ship first."

With fifty feet to go, the captain directed the loudspeaker to shore.

And suddenly Vittorio was not in Boston anymore. He was in Biella, before he met Annibole and Rosa Rinaldi, and before he ever saw the golden shores of America; before he ever knew that there was a Statue of Liberty, and before he first laid eyes on the rolling hills and exquisite beauty of the small New England town that he had made his own; before he met the men that had preceded him to America, and the men whose paths he crossed there, men who had contributed, each in his own way, to the greatness of America, men like Cyril and Clyde Bradford, and the selfless martyrs of the Guinea Squad; before he had ever heard the call to arms of World War I, or felt the rush of pride that filled him every time he heard school children recite the Pledge of Allegiance to the flag, or sing along with the National Anthem.

Suddenly he was back in 1910, and the only people there were Carlo and Antoinette Rosato, and he was staring at her in her lovely violet dress and smelling the fragrance of her perfumed hair. He was saying, "I love you," to her, and hearing her say the same words back to him, and it seemed like none of the pain and loneliness of the past nine and a half years even exist-ed. All that mattered was that she was here, and this time he was not going away, but coming toward her, and behind it all were the words he remem-bered whispering into the air at the base of the shrine in Oropa so many years before, "Almighty Father, bring us safely back together again, in Your mercy, and in Your perfect timing."

"Will Mr. Vittorio Bellino please step forward," he heard a strange voice say across the top of the crowd on the dock.

"Here I am!" he yelled at the strange voice that was coming from the ship. The people on the dock separated as Vittorio ran toward the ramp the ship was pulling up to.

"Mr. Bellino, we have a wonderful Christmas present for you, sir," the voice on the ship's loudspeaker said.

Vittorio was straining his eyes to see when he heard the most beautiful sound he had ever heard.

"Vi-tor-r-rio!" she cried over the loudspeaker.

"Oh!" he bellowed, hearing her but not yet seeing her.

"Vi-tor-r-rio!" she yelled again, her voice cracking as his heart leaped with joy. His eyebrows raised with the ultimate anticipation, he stood at the dock as the ship touched shore, and as the door to the captain's quarters opened, she ran out onto the deck and into the bright sunlight of the cold, Christmas day.

And then he saw her.

Suddenly, out of his subconscious, another memory assaulted him of the last time he had seen her, only a few short months before. In the trauma of his injuries and the confusion of his recovery, he had buried deep into his subconscious mind the reality of the day he was brought in out of Belleau Woods. At that moment, it all came back to him vividly, even though he had not thought of it since the day it had happened. He was lying on a cot, car-ried in by United States Marine Corps medics, broken, battered, and deliri-ous from the loss of blood. The Marine Corps doctor was speaking to her, and he heard the doctor say her name.

"Miss Rosato, you've put in a very long day," the doctor had said to her, and Vittorio's heart had leaped in his chest, although he was unable to speak.

"Go home and get some sleep, Antoinette," the doctor had said, and as she turned to leave the tent, unaware that he was there, he had tried with all his might to call out to her, his mind screaming out the word his mouth could not speak.

Surrealistically he felt himself back in the field hospital trying with all his might to call out her name, and the beating of his heart bounced him back and forth from that time to this one, but this time, on the shores of his home-land, the name he had tried so desperately to call out those many months before, came out.

"An-toin-et-ta!" he cried out, the tears pouring out of his eyes. "An-toin-et-ta!" he cried out again, his voice cracking with emotion.

The sound of her name was like music to his ears that cold Christmas morning in 1919, and people all across the dock and on the ship stopped what they were doing momentarily to watch the miraculous human drama unfold.

She ran down the runway into his arms, crying as she ran, letting all the anxiety and pain their long separation had caused her flow out of her as she reached for his arms.

He smiled broadly as he reached out for her and when they embraced, he closed his eyes and felt the tears running down his face. For the briefest of moments, time stood still as every eye in the harbor watched them, and then, in a matter of a few seconds, the other people on board started their way down the ramp, and life moved on.

Vittorio and Antoinette were not aware of any of the other people that filed by them in the bustle and confusion that followed, and it was only after most of them had gone by that Antoinette smiled radiantly up at Vittorio and spoke to him in fluent English.

"I have a very special surprise for you," she beamed. And with that, she looked to her right, and out of the sunlight stepped Vittorio's beaming younger brother, Fortunato.

"O-o-oh!" Vittorio exclaimed as he reached for Fortunato and embraced him.

Fortunato laughed happily and returned Vittorio's bear-hug, patting his brother on the back as they embraced.

"You have brought me a best man," Vittorio said to Antoinette as he looked up at Fortunato.

"And a driver," Fortunato added, nodding to Vittorio's horse and buggy. "Is it yours?"

"It was loaned to me by my employer," Vittorio answered him. "But enough. We will talk all about it on our way home."

"We will only get as far as the first restaurant if I drive," Fortunato answered, but at that moment, Vittorio and Antoinette would have been agreeable to anything.

And so, in the cold of the Christmas Day of 1919, in the back seat of the horse-drawn wagon that headed out of Boston, Massachusetts, toward Indian Springs, Connecticut, the first chapter in the lives of one very remarkable couple came to a close, and the second chapter began.

Every family has in its ancestry somewhere, a couple, or a single individual who, in one fashion or another, forsakes one background in exchange for a new beginning. Some, like Vittorio Bellino and Antoinette Rosato, choose the country they decided could be the greatest one in mankind's history to adopt as their own. And in their case, both the country and the couple would benefit.

▲ ▼ ▲

Back on the Boston to Indian Springs road, the buggy carrying the three young people from Italy rolled steadily along on its way back to a home two of them had never seen. In the back seat the young couple sat and talked, laughing and sharing together the many stories they had missed while they were separated, and in the driver's seat, the single man sat and listened intently, enjoying the young couple's reunion almost as much as they were.

Delivering Antoinette well-protected and unharmed to his brother, Vittorio, had been Fortunato Bellino's focused mission over the past several weeks of his life. Now, his goal accomplished, he sat in the driver's seat, the reins in his hands, and as the sounds of happiness flowed over his shoulder, he became aware of another emotion that crept up on him quite unexpectedly.

The longer they talked and laughed and bonded themselves closer together, the more acutely aware he became of the emptiness in his own life. As the buggy bounced and rattled slowly along on its way to what would become Vittorio and Antoinette's triumphant entry to the hometown she had never seen, the darker side of Fortunato's mind started to cloud his thoughts. His mind drifted back to Italy, where his parents were, and he became aware of the deepest secret of his life, which he had not told anyone, and that he had vowed to himself never to tell anyone else about for fear of looking weak. There in the deepest recesses of his mind, he faced his own personal demon, the only one he had never been able to defeat.

As the brother he loved talked and laughed and enjoyed the closeness of his betrothed, Fortunato felt the bitterness of being alone creeping in on him. His parents were very happy together. His brother had always had Antoinette, as long as Fortunato could remember. But the longer his life wore on, the more afraid of loneliness he became, and the more convinced he became that he would never find the love of a woman he sorely craved.

I'm too ugly, he had told himself countless times. *My hands and feet are too big, I lumber instead of walk, and I don't have the patience or the ability to understand women. I see many women that I am attracted to, but none that have I have ever wanted to marry. It's a good thing anyway,* he thought. *I wouldn't have the slightest idea what to do if a woman ever showed any interest in me. Other men are smooth, I am clumsy. Others are smart, I am dumb. I know I have good character, but I am much too unattractive to ever hope to find a woman to love me, so I better put that idea out of my mind.*

The longer he thought about it, the more lonely and bitter he became, and instinctively, without even realizing he was doing it, he reached into his coat pocket and pulled out one of the bottles of whiskey he had purchased from the ship's bartender. Waiting until Vittorio and Antoinette were preoccupied, he took a long slug down his throat. Several times along the way he did this until the loneliness was displaced once again by the emotion the alcohol had always replaced it with, the anger that was always there waiting to well up inside of him. The anger had become a part of him and it took control of him once again.

Whenever the demon anger had possessed him, he had retreated within himself and avoided contact with other people, afraid of what the results of his actions would be. Vittorio started to become aware of the fact that Fortunato had not spoken in quite some time, and he reached over the seat to tap his brother's shoulder.

"It's so good to see you, brother," Vittorio said to Fortunato in Italian, for Fortunato spoke very halting English. "We have so much to catch up on."

Fortunato turned away from his demon to smile at his brother.

"I can't believe how good you look, Vittorio. America must suit you very well."

"America is a wonderful land, Fortunato. I hope you'll be staying here with us for a very long time."

"Oh, I don't know, brother," Fortunato said to him, shrugging his shoulders. "I don't know anything about your country."

"The country is beautiful. The hunting and fishing are exquisite, and the people are the friendliest in the world."

Fortunato was listening intently to his brother, believing every word that came out of Vittorio's mouth as he had always done, coincidently listening to his brother's description of the friendliness of the American people as they entered a narrow bridge that stretched out over the top of a narrow stream. Almost simultaneously another horse and buggy entered the same bridge from the other direction, and it soon became apparent that the two buggies would not be able to pass one another on the bridge.

"Come on, man, back it off! We're in a hurry over here!" a young man yelled from the other buggy.

Fortunato's attention was immediately directed at the man in the other buggy. For a moment no one moved, and then Fortunato spoke quietly to Vittorio over the seat.

"We came in first," he said quietly.

"It's okay, Fortunato," Antoinette said to Fortunato. "We can back out and let them pass."

"Come on, you crazy bastard, back it off!" a different man yelled, and as he did Fortunato grew very somber as he turned and stared at Antoinette.

"We came in first," he repeated, and Vittorio knew immediately that the men in the other buggy had made a very big mistake. Vittorio had long known that Fortunato was an excellent and loyal friend to have, but that it was far better for you if he were your friend than your enemy, for he was as ruthless an enemy as he was genuine a friend.

He did not wait for the action to develop any further, he created it. Reining in the horses, Fortunato jumped down off the buggy and lumbered toward the other buggy.

"Come on, you arrogant bastard, get it off the bridge," a third man yelled out, apparently thinking there was safety in their numbers as the Italian walked boldly toward them.

When Fortunato reached the buggy, he reached up and grabbed the driver's collar. "You back it off," he said, and his accent gave him away.

"An immigrant!" the burliest of the four young men blurted out. "An arrogant, marble-mouthed immigrant. You're in America now, marble-mouth. You don't tell Americans what to do."

With that something clicked in the back of Fortunato's mind, and he yanked the driver out of the buggy and threw him onto the wooden bridge as he reached for the burly loudmouth.

Antoinette screamed as Vittorio started to run to his brother's aid, but before he got there, Fortunato had two of the men thrown off the bridge and into the stream, and the burly one trying hopelessly to hold off his flailing arms as blows from Fortunato's fists rained down on him. The fourth man was frantically trying to back the buggy off the bridge.

"Enough!" Vittorio yelled tersely, and it was probably the only voice in the world that could have held Fortunato Bellino back at that moment.

As soon as Fortunato held back his huge right hand and pushed the man away, the man ran back to his buggy and quietly helped his friend pull it off the bridge to let the Bellinos through. Vittorio trotted back and took the reins of the buggy as Fortunato stood and watched the men clear their way, and only after the Bellino's buggy was across the bridge did Fortunato leave the proximity of the other men, who looked down and around and any-where but into Fortunato's eyes.

When Fortunato had first made his decision to take a stand against the four young men, he had moved into a new realm that Vittorio had not seen him in before. He had been wound up tighter than a coiled snake, ready at any moment to strike, and the intensity and quickness of his response to the challenge on the bridge had only partially spent his pent up anxieties. That, combined with the empty whiskey bottle Vittorio had stumbled over when he jumped down off their buggy, had put a very big scare into Vittorio Bellino for his brother.

Antoinette grew a bit ashen when she saw the worry on Vittorio's face as he walked Fortunato back to the buggy after he destroyed the men on the bridge. Vittorio had seen the first evidence of what Antoinette had known for many years after Vittorio's departure from Italy. That Fortunato Bellino was a danger to other people was not the worst part of the problem. As long as he stayed so tightly wound up, he was a far greater danger to himself, and Vittorio realized this graphically that day on the bridge.

Fortunato Bellino was a time bomb ready to explode, and Vittorio knew that despite the way he had destroyed the men on the bridge, he had still used restraint, and there was no telling what kind of destruction he was capable of if he ever really went off.

With his arm around Fortunato's shoulder, the only man in the world who had any positive influence left over the lumbering giant led him back to the buggy.

My poor brother, Vittorio thought to himself as they walked back to the buggy in silence. *He needs a lot more love than he's gotten so far in life, that's for certain.*

⋀   ⋁   ⋀

The ride from Boston to Indian Springs had been such a pleasant affair for the three young people, with the exception of the incident on the bridge, that the time went by very fast. Although it had taken the better part of three days, it seemed like only yesterday that the ship had landed in Boston harbor. Nevertheless, on her third day in America, Antoinette started to get a very warm feeling as the buggy entered a very beautiful stretch of land high in the snow- covered mountains of northeastern Connecticut.

"Oh, Vittorio, what a beautiful countryside this is. Are we very close to our home?"

"It's the very next town we'll enter, Antoinette. We're in Laurel Hill, Connecticut, now."

"What are all of these bushes? They're so beautiful."

"Those are mountain laurels. They grow wild in the Nipmuck Forest. Wait until June if you want to see something really beautiful. When these bushes flower, it's the most beautiful sight in America. The hills are covered with brilliant white and pink flowers. I swear heaven can't be more beautiful."

"Why doesn't anyone live right here? It's so incredibly beautiful."

"People do live here, but not right on the road. There are some very big farms out in the hills. As a matter of fact, we're riding in a buggy owned by the owner of one of the biggest farms in Laurel Hill, a man named Alden Bradford. His people were among the first to come to America, centuries ago."

"Why do they call it Nipmuck Forest?"

"A lot of things are named after the Indians who used to live here years ago. The Nipmuck Forest, the Willimantic River, even the state of Connecticut."

"Are there any Indians living here now?"

"Not that I know of. Not in this area anyway. There are some on reservations south of here, but most of the Indians were killed off by plagues or Indian wars about two hundred and fifty years ago. But you can still find arrowheads and other Indian artifacts down on the river road that leads into Indian Springs from the south."

"Can we go there and look for them?"

"We can do everything you want to now. But first you have to meet the people of your new town."

"Oh, Vittorio, do you really think any of them will care about me?"

Vittorio looked at Antoinette and smiled.

"You really don't have any idea what to expect when we start down the next hill into our hometown, do you?"

"I'm a little bit afraid," she blushed.

Suddenly Vittorio got a very warm feeling inside him as he reached over to put his arm around her.

"I have a feeling today will be a day you'll never forget," he said to her with a smile.

In a while the buggy started its descent out of Laurel Hill into the town of Indian Springs. At the border of the two towns, a welcoming party of two couples met the buggy and presented Antoinette with a bouquet of freshly cut flowers from Indian Springs Conservatories and a fruit basket to munch on as the buggy moved on down the hill toward town. The horses rode up ahead to announce their entry, and Antoinette was smiling broadly as the buggy reached the top of East Main Street.

When they rounded the corner, a fifteen-member brass band started to play *Here Comes the Bride*, and Antoinette laughed with surprised pleasure as the band fell in in front of the buggy, which started winding its way up Main Street toward the Italian Club.

"It's the Italian band. They've been practicing for weeks for your arrival," Vittorio told her. Lining the sides of Main Street were dozens of people who ran up to the buggy and threw bouquets of flowers and wrapped Christmas gifts into Antoinette's lap, as the welcome continued to astound and humble her.

Fortunato was beaming broadly as he turned and pointed out to her the first of many signs hung in the windows of the local merchants:

> *"Welcome home, Antoinette."*
> *"Vittorio's Queen is our Queen."*
> *"Indian Springs welcomes Antoinette Bellino."*
> *"Antoinette, we've waited for you a long time."*

On and on they rode past many other signs of similar sentiments, and as the people started out of the pubs, restaurants, and local stores to wave and blow kisses at the town's newest resident, Antoinette began to cry. "Oh, Vittorio, what a marvelous land you have brought me to. It's even more glorious than I had imagined."

"Wait," Vittorio smiled broadly. "The best is yet to come. You haven't met the people yet."

When they finally reached the Italian Club, the buggy was surrounded by the women of the Ladies Auxiliary, each of whom stepped up to introduce themselves and embrace Antoinette. Rosa Rinaldi acted as her personal hostess and walked with her around the grounds as the men prepared the banquet meal upstairs.

When she walked into the banquet hall, she was astonished at the amount of food that covered the head table. Polenta and mostaccioli filled several bowls, with large kilns of tomato sauces with sausage, meatballs, or chicken, depending on individual taste. There was squirrel or rabbit meat available, as well, with large plates of venison steaks, and a huge bagna caoda in the center of the table. Salads of all types covered one whole table, homegrown in one of the local vegetable gardens which all of the Italian-Americans, without exception, had in their yard. For an appetizer, a huge antipasto with every kind of cold cut you could imagine sat in the middle of a table, surrounded by freshly baked Vienna bread from one of the local bakeries, which also supplied the cakes people who had any room left in their stomachs ate for desert.

Orzo soup with chicken livers started the main meal off, and the livers that were not sliced up and put into the soup were saved for the risotto, with cheeses of various types cubed and set out on plates for a snack. One whole table was reserved for the calzones and the cheese-filled or meat-filled ravioli, and Antoinette had a very hard time deciding which table to stop at first.

When the dinner bell sounded, all the people who had walked up to the club from various directions to meet Antoinette and enjoy her welcoming feast started into the banquet hall. When all were seated, Pop Arnetti introduced Father O'Neill, the pastor of Saint Patrick's Church, where Vittorio and Antoinette were to be married four days later.

The only non-Italian at the head table, Father O'Neill was greeted with much respect and welcomed to stay after he said the grace because the Catholic faith is the same the world over and the reverence the people expressed for their parish priests knows no nationality.

After the meal, the good Father excused himself and shook as many hands as he could on his way out, but he left quickly, knowing that soon the homemade grappa would start to flow, and then the bocce, mora, and horseshoe games would begin, and they were often punctuated by language the priest knew would embarrass the men if they knew he overheard it.

Periodically the Italian band would strike up a tune, and the celebration after dinner was filled with much dancing, singing, and hand-clapping as the laughter and merriment continued.

The bocce courts outside were surrounded by spectators as the contestants, their white tank-top tee-shirts covered by woolen sweaters, battled long and hard for the day's bragging rights, every so often throwing their fedoras up into the air to celebrate a win as gold teeth glistened in the sunlight, and men laughed and slapped each other on the back as the wine and grappa continued to flow.

In the auditorium, women sat around in shawls and brightly colored scarves talking and answering all of Antoinette's questions about her new town and her new country.

It was there that she asked Rosa Rinaldi to be her maid of honor, and when Rosa graciously accepted, she then proceeded to excuse both herself and Antoinette, whom she knew must be tired from her long voyage from Italy and her trip into Indian Springs from Boston.

In the late afternoon, Vittorio and Antoinette walked together to Rosa's house, where she was to stay on the night before the wedding, and that night, Antoinette Rosato slept for ten hours and woke up the next day smiling.

The next morning, the very first thing she wanted to do was to go with Vittorio to see their new home, and when she walked up the snow-covered dirt road that led to their home, she was beaming with pleasure. At their front door, she lay her head on Vittorio's shoulder and started to cry, hugging him tightly to assure herself that it was not all just a wonderful dream she would wake up from to find herself back in Biella waiting against hope for his long-awaited letter summoning her.

When she walked inside the door, everything was just as Vittorio had described it to her. Her kitchen was set up with the finest of cookware, and her closet was filled with fine materials for her to create her wardrobe from in the weeks to come.

"Your bedroom is here. Fortunato and I will sleep on the veranda until after the wedding, and then Fortunato will lose a roommate, and you'll gain one."

Antoinette blushed. "I hope we don't keep him awake at night!"

Over her bed, a wooden plaque in the shape of a crescent banner was nailed to the wall. On it, three words were carved: *Oggi, Domani, Sempre.*

Later, when Vittorio offered to have Fortunato live with them, Fortunato flatly refused.

"I won't hear of it," he said. "I'll live in the mill tenements. There are plenty of rooms for rent."

"Fortunato, it's not necessary," Vittorio said. "You can save money if you live with us."

Fortunato smiled. "I don't know much, brother. I'm not as smart as you. But one thing I know. A newly married couple needs privacy. You have to think of yourself for a change, Vittorio. You can't think of other people all of the time. I appreciate your hospitality, but I'll be fine in the mill houses."

"Okay," Vittorio shrugged. "But you'll have your meals with us."

"That's a bargain I'll accept," Fortunato said as he shook his brother's hand. "Now tell me about the boxing matches I've been hearing about all over town."

"The fights are every Saturday night at the fairgrounds. Men from all over the country come here to box. A man can pick up a good bit of change betting on the right fighters."

"I don't want to bet. I want to fight."

"Good thing to stay away from, Fortunato. These are not street fights. There are referees and rules."

Fortunato continued to smile. "When's the last time anybody saw a real good fighter around here?"

"Don't get involved, Fortunato. The fighters make peanuts compared to some of the beatings they take."

Fortunato looked at Vittorio with surprise. "I don't take beatings, brother. I give them."

Vittorio looked nervously at his brother. "You'd have to fight as a heavyweight. And the scramble that's about to take place at the fairgrounds starting Saturday is going to be intense."

"Why's that?" Fortunato asked.

"Our reigning champion just retired, and the bragging has already started about who's going to fill his shoes as the new champion."

"Well I can save everybody a lot of trouble then and close all their mouths tomorrow night."

Suddenly a very relieving thought crossed Vittorio's mind. *It's a good thing Michael Callahan retired before Fortunato got here,* he thought. *No town in America would be big enough for the both of them.*

"You can't go this Saturday night, anyway, Fortunato, my reception will be in full swing."

"Good way for me to avoid the temptation of wine," Fortunato argued.

"Look, Fortunato, if you do fight, I want to be with you in your corner."

"You don't have to see it, brother. You'll hear about it."

"No way. I want to be with you when you fight."

Fortunato laughed. "Then you have a decision to make. It's unfortunate that the fights are Saturday night. You'll have to decide whether you want to spend the evening with me or with Antoinette."

Vittorio laughed. "Why don't you just wait until next week?"

Fortunato reached over and touched his brother's arm. "Vittorio, when I was in Italy, you were never there to hold my hand when I fought. I had my share of them, and I met up with some pretty rough boys. The world is full of them. Then they meet me and find out their limitations. You have a great honeymoon with Antoinette. You'll hear about me the next morning."

The next Saturday, January 3, 1920, Vittorio Bellino and Antoinette Rosato were married in Saint Patrick's Church, nine days after she had arrived in America. To say that their wedding was beautiful would be an understatement.

Schoolgirls lined the aisles with flower petals, as the organ music played, and the all-boys choir, with a vast number of soprano voices, filled the church with beautiful singing, the likes of which she had not even heard in Italy.

When Antoinette Rosato walked down the aisle with Rosa Rinaldi, her attention was drawn to the magnificent carvings of the stations of the cross, donated to St. Patrick's Church by the artist and sculptor Attilio Strobino, who sat in attendance at her wedding, and was just one more friend she had yet to meet.

The smell of freshly cut flowers from the conservatory mingled with the incense that she had always loved, and she felt as beautiful as she looked as she approached the altar to meet her betrothed. When Fortunato led Vittorio out of the sacristy to the altar, where Antoinette met him, Vittorio looked more handsome to her than ever before, and she could not remember ever being so happy. Local dignitaries joined people from all walks of life as Antoinette Rosato became Antoinette Bellino, and when she walked down the aisle she felt like the luckiest woman on the face of the earth.

Outside Alden Bradford's horse and buggy was again waiting to take them to the Italian Club, where the reception was this week's reason for the people to congregate and celebrate. Again the wine flowed freely, as the band played the songs of Italy and America as the people danced and reveled in the excitement of the moment.

The dancing lasted all afternoon, and toward dusk Vittorio started looking more and more in Fortunato's direction. Fortunato had grown strangely quiet and withdrawn over the past hour or so, and when Vittorio got up to dance with Antoinette, Fortunato slipped out of the door.

Vittorio snapped his fingers in the direction of Bruno Donato, beckoning him, and when Bruno came over, Vittorio whispered to him, "Send somebody with him."

Bruno was glad for the opportunity to follow him to the exhibition hall at the fairgrounds—not to play nursemaid to him, as he thought Vittorio had meant, but to watch what unfolded when Fortunato got there.

At the bottom of Club Road, across the dirt oval horseracing track, the fairgrounds exhibition hall was already full of spectators when Fortunato Bellino walked in. Two middleweights were shadowboxing and waiting their turn in the ring when Fortunato strolled in silently and walked right around the ring and into the dressing rooms behind it.

In the fighters' dressing rooms, he stood and looked over the fighters who were dressing for their fight.

"Bruni and Treacy ready?" Teko Lombardi yelled out from the door to the arena.

"Ready!" Fredo Bruni yelled.

"Ready!" Liam Treacy yelled.

"The middleweights are starting now. Be ready in case it's a quick one."

Fortunato watched as the two fighters prepared to enter the ring. Out in the hall, hooting, catcalling, and foot stomping were filling the hall with noise as the trainers did their last bit of preparation to send their fighters into war.

"Scusa me," Fortunato said, holding Teko Lombardi's arm. "How do I get a fight?"

"Who da hell are you?" the irritable fight arranger snapped at Fortunato as he walked around in the room.

"I want to know how I can get a fight," Fortunato answered.

"You can start by having the courtesy to ask me tomorrow after tonight's card is finished," he barked.

"No, no, I want to fight tonight," Fortunato insisted.

Teko Lombardi squinted up into Fortunato's face, his old eyes just now focusing on the young man who stood before him.

"Hey, ain't you Bellino's brother?" the old man asked.

"Yes," Fortunato answered.

"Well you ain't gonna be able to fight tonight, kid. The program's already drawn up. Been set now for over two weeks."

"I just-a got here last-a week," Fortunato argued, raising his shoulders and throwing his hands out in protest.

"Look, why don't you just go out into the auditorium and watch the fights, and we'll set you up with a fight someday down the road."

"Can't make any money that way," Fortunato said.

"You can't make any money in one fight anyway," Lombardi said. "It'll take three or four fights before you can fight for any kind of decent purse."

Fortunato left the training room disappointed and a little bit angry, and outside in the auditorium he sat and listened as the ring announcer, Sugar Desmond, went over the format of the eight-man elimination tournament to be fought over the next six weeks to determine the successor to Michael Callahan as New England Champion.

"Four men fight tonight, four next week, the two winners of tonight in two weeks, the two winners from next week a week later, and the New England Championship fight two weeks after that," the announcer boomed out through his hand held megaphone.

As the first two fighters started toward the ring to be introduced to the crowd, Fortunato walked toward the ring and started to pace back and forth below the ring.

"Down in front!" a number of people in the crowd yelled out impatiently.

"Somebody get that clown to sit down!" another man yelled out loudly.

Fortunato was oblivious to the crowd taunts, and when two of the boxers, Fredo Bruni from Providence and Liam Treacy from Boston, started to climb into the ring, Fortunato climbed in with them.

"I'll save all of you a month!" Fortunato yelled at the top of his lungs to the ring announcer. "I'll beat these four tonight, and the other four next week, and I'll be the new champion."

Bruni and Treacy stared at Fortunato across the ring and Sugar Desmond just stood there, too surprised to know exactly how to react.

"Who is he?" the crowd started to whisper to one another, as everyone looked back and forth to see who was going to make the next move.

"Well, are you all gonna stand there like statues or what? I'm here waiting!" Fortunato yelled.

"Get him out of here!" Bruni's manager yelled at the ring announcer, and when he did, Fortunato walked across the ring and got right into Bruni's face.

"You let him do your talking or do you do your own?" Fortunato said, jabbing his finger into the fighters stomach.

"It's no problem," Bruni said to Sugar Desmond. "If Treacy wants to wait a minute, I'll beat this bum and then fight him."

Fortunato smiled and walked back over to one of the corners. Sugar Desmond followed him.

"I don't know what kind of a stunt you think you're pulling, but you better be ready to get your ass kicked, because you just challenged two of the best fighters in the country, and there's two more right behind them," the announcer sneered at Fortunato.

"I seen a lot of good fighters," Fortunato smiled at Sugar Desmond coolly.

"You know the rules?"

"Yes," Fortunato answered. He didn't.

"Where's your cornermen?"

"It's just-a me," Fortunato answered.

"You got gloves?"

"No."

"Now he does," Liam Treacy said, throwing his gloves over to Fortunato, but when Fortunato was unable to get the gloves on over his huge hands, Fredo Bruni took his gloves off too.

"I'll fight the guinea barehanded!" he yelled, which drew a round of laughter from the crowd. Bruni was Italian too.

"I never liked the new rule about wearing gloves anyway," Bruni said to his trainer.

"Okay, son, what's your name?" Sugar Desmond asked.

"Fortunato Bellino."

Sugar Desmond stood and stared into Fortunato's eyes and as he started to put two and two together in his mind, a broad smile spread across his face. "You're Vittorio's brother?"

"Yes."

"He just got married today."

"You wanna cut the crap and get going? I want to make it to the end of the reception before the wine runs out."

"How much do you weigh," Sugar laughed, amazed at Fortunato's confidence.

"Two-forty."

Desmond walked to the center of the ring, shaking his head in amazement, as Liam Treacy's cornermen took their positions behind Fortunato in his corner.

"In this corner, from Biella, Italy, with an American record of no wins and no defeats, weighing two hundred and forty pounds, For-tu-na-a-a-to-o-o Bell-i-i-i-no-o-o-o-o!"

The local Italians in the audience went wild as they realized who Fortunato was while the rest of the crowd greeted the young challenger with boos and catcalls.

As Sugar Desmond announced Fredo Bruni, Fortunato turned to Bruno Donato and handed him a ten-dollar bill out of his shirt pocket. "Bet it on me," Fortunato said.

When Fortunato peeled off his shirt, Fredo Bruni grew somber as he looked at Fortunato's remarkable physique. For a man of two hundred and forty pounds, there was not an ounce of fat visible on his rock solid body.

When the two fighters faced each other in the center of the ring, Fortunato smiled at Bruni, and Bruni could never remember facing anyone as cool before.

"Shake hands and come out fighting," Sugar Desmond said to the two men, and when the opening bell rang, Fortunato walked into the center of the ring and waited for Fredo Bruni, who danced around flicking jabs which Fortunato easily knocked away. After no more than ten seconds had elapsed, Fortunato walked Fredo into a corner and with two savage body shots, doubled him over. An unbelievable overhand right dropped Bruni to the canvas at eighteen seconds of the first round, and a ten-count later, the fight was over.

The murmurs that went through the crowd told everyone who saw the knockout how stunned the crowd was at Fortunato's power, and as he walked to his corner, he looked for Bruno Donato in the crowd.

Donato lifted two tens into the air and Fortunato said, "Bet it."

Next up was Liam Treacy. Fortunato didn't take quite so long with him. When the bell rang he charged Treacy and one smashing right hand sprawled Treacy on the canvas, out cold in four seconds.

The crowd was in awe, as the buzzing reached a fever pitch after the destruction of Liam Treacy. Once again Fortunato walked to his corner, still without having broken a sweat.

Donato lifted a twenty and two tens into the air and when Fortunato said, "Bet it," one more time, a huge smile crossed Bruno Donato's face as he lit a cigar and turned to look for bets.

"Two to one!" a man yelled at Donato, but Donato would hear nothing of it.

"He's green, I tell ya, the kid's green. Biff Ostrowski ain't no Liam Treacy neither. It's an even money fight."

In a few minutes, Biff Ostrowski, with his 23-2 record, had forty dollars bet on him against the stunning new local hero, Fortunato Bellino, and the crowd noise reached a fever pitch as Biff Ostrowski was introduced.

Ostrowski had fought six times previously at the Indian Springs fairgrounds, and each time he had won his fight in very convincing fashion. The curiosity that surrounded the fight had every fan on his feet as the two men squared off in the center of the ring.

Ostrowski pushed Fortunato before the fight started, and Fortunato pushed him back, and when Sugar Desmond yelled, "Save it for the fight!" the crowd noise increased.

When the bell rang, the exhibition hall went wild, and when the two fighters met in the center of the ring, Ostrowski slipped the first two punches that Fortunato threw. A roar went up as Ostrowski connected with two body shots, but Fortunato only laughed when he was hit.

When Fortunato continued laughing, Ostrowski began to get angry. Fortunato ducked and dodged the next several shots Ostrowski threw, and when Ostrowski finally got one in on Fortunato's chin, Fortunato stood and unleashed a barrage of punches that drew loud gasps from the crowd as the punches ripped into Biff Ostrowski's face and chest. For the next several seconds, Fortunato looked awesome, and it soon became apparent that the fight would never reach the end of the first round as Ostrowski struggled to survive under Fortunato's punishing assault.

The crowd roared as Fortunato Bellino hammered away at Biff Ostrowski, who tried frantically to stave off his relentless charge. At two-eighteen, Fortunato landed a savage flurry that put Ostrowski on the canvas. As he tried to get up, the blood from his nose and mouth made a pool on the canvas and he was counted out as he struggled, unable to rise to his feet.

The Italian section of the crowd went wild as Fortunato stood calmly looking down at his third victim, as he dabbed at his lip which Ostrowski had split a little bit, drawing a little bit of blood.

"Bellino! Bellino! Bellino!" the crowd chanted as Fortunato's fourth scheduled opponent climbed into the ring. When he saw them carrying Biff Ostrowski out of the ring, James Jackson suddenly felt an emotion he had never before experienced before a fight. Looking across the ring at the powerfully built boxer who had just beat three of the toughest heavyweights in New England in the combined time of two minutes and forty seconds, Jackson suddenly felt no desire to be in the ring against this young savage.

When the bell rang to start the fight, Jackson looked very frightened to Fortunato, and Fortunato had to chase him across the ring as Jackson tried to run away from him.

Maybe I can make him tire himself out, Jackson thought to himself, but when Fortunato cornered him against the ropes and started hitting him with head shots, James Jackson started looking for the canvas.

If I stay down, I'll escape with my brains intact, Jackson thought to himself and he was counted out at twenty-three seconds of the first round.

Fortunato walked around the ring, calmly holding his hands upright as the crowd went wild, and when Fortunato located Bruno Donato in the audience, Bruno held out a stash of cash to Fortunato, who scoffed it up as he climbed down out of the ring.

"Next week I'll take the other four," he said to Sugar Desmond as the crowd parted and allowed him access to the shower room, shouting out words of praise to him as he passed by.

Forty-five minutes later, Vittorio Bellino turned away from his wife for a moment at their wedding reception and saw his brother standing there holding an envelope in his hand with Vittorio and Antoinette's names on it.

"I thought you were going to the fights?" Vittorio said to his brother.

"I did."

"You leave them early?"

"No the fights are all done."

"But they just started."

"They had four first-round knockouts."

"You're kidding? That's really unusual."

"Here's your wedding present," Fortunato said to his brother, handing him the envelope full of money. "I'm gonna drink some wine."

Vittorio was glad that Fortunato was there. *I'll be able to keep an eye on him now,* Vittorio thought, *so he won't do anything crazy while he's here.*

▲　▼　▲

The next day the town was ablaze with men rushing around to talk to each other about the incredible spectacle they had witnessed the night before. Men who had seen the fights would walk up to each other with great smiles on their faces and just laugh.

"Can you believe it?"

"I have *ne-e-ever* seen anything like that in my life."

"Where the hell did this guy learn how to fight?"

"I can't believe Vittorio never told us about him!"

Men who had not gone to the fights were treated to repeated blow-by-blow descriptions of the fairgrounds massacre, as dozens of men made the rounds to every bar and haunt in Indian Springs, looking for someone else to talk to about the spectacle.

By the end of the day, there were only two kinds of men in Indian Springs: Those who had seen the fights, and those who realized what they had missed. Both groups had vowed to be there the following weekend.

In the aftermath of the night that had made him an instant celebrity in town, a strange feeling crept slowly into Fortunato Bellino. What would have been an emotional high that would last for a long time for most men actually had an opposite effect on Fortunato. He started by drinking more wine than he should have and awoke the next day with a splitting headache. Lying in his bed in the mill house tenements, he felt more lost and alone than he had ever felt before. Now that Vittorio had married Antoinette, he knew he must stay away from them and let them have the time they needed to catch up on almost ten years of their lives apart, despite the knowledge that Vittorio and Antoinette would have an open-door policy with him.

The fact that they were so overwhelmingly happy made Fortunato happy for them but only served as a constant reminder to him of his own crushing loneliness.

Suddenly he wished he were back in Italy where he belonged, where he could work hard, talk to the men on the job, pull more than his own weight, and get the respect from them that always came when everybody knew that he did more work than anyone else on a common job. He got up quickly to dress and start in motion the procedures that would take him back to Italy.

When he stumbled, he realized that he had drunk far too much wine the night before, and the searing pain that hit him in the middle of his temples sat him right back down on the bed. Then he realized that he needed to get something on his stomach, and he could swear he smelled the soup and home-baked bread drifting down the hill from Antoinette's kitchen.

Slowly he dressed and started out the door for the long walk up the hillside to Vittorio and Antoinette's house and when he was within sight of their house, he berated himself and turned around, realizing that it was the day after their marriage and not the time for visitors.

On his way back down the hill, his head started to clear and he remembered why he had come to America. In Italy he had made a mess of his life and left a litany of bruised and possibly vengeful men in his wake. The only intelligent thing to do was to make a new start in America. Still, the loneliness that haunted him sat heavily upon his heart as he wound his way down the hill to town.

A short distance away from the path Fortunato was taking down out of the hills from Vittorio's house, another family was playing out their lives with a new twist in their routine. Maureen Malloy Callahan was not an old woman, but it was very evident that she had had a long, tough road in her life. Bent over and twisted by a horrible case of arthritis that gnarled her hands and stooped her back, she now had everything she could do just to get comfortable, let alone care for her husband and however many of her ten children and sixteen grandchildren were there at any given time.

Many of the household chores had been assumed by her three youngest daughters, the older ones having married and moved out. One daughter, Katie Elizabeth, would start every day rubbing ointments into her mother's hands and back, dressing her, and cooking breakfast for the hoard that was always around the Callahan house. Then she would bring a breakfast tray out to her father, Michael, who would be sitting by the river, casting his fishing pole out into the gurgling water to bring in some of the supper for the Callahan brood.

Michael Callahan's days were much the same now, waking up at dusk to congregate with his extended family around the mill house tenement that had been his home since he arrived in America thirty-six years before. Talking and laughing with each of his children and grandchildren, giving them all as much personal time as he could was his pleasure now, and by the time most of them were either in bed or preparing themselves for bed, he would be pulling on his old jeans and suspenders, getting ready for the short walk over to the Bradford Woolen Mill, which he had guarded for over thirty years from nighttime intruders.

He would light the kerosene lamp, kiss his wife and daughter Katie Elizabeth goodnight, and head out the door for the factory where he would walk round and round all night long thinking about his family, his God, and sometimes, although not as much now anymore, his mother country.

When he would first arrive at the factory, he would place the kerosene lamp in the window on the third floor, and that would be Katie Elizabeth's signal that he had made it to work okay. She would go to bed then, and the next time he would see her was with his breakfast tray out by the river the next morning.

The only thing that had changed about Michael's routine now was that he no longer had to think about preparing for any more fights. For many years, he had kept secret from his wife and family the huge amounts of money he had bet on himself in the fight ring for fear they would berate him for gambling or worry about losing so much money that the family sorely needed for survival. Fortunately God had blessed him with superior boxing skills, which he had used wisely for his family's benefit and put on the shelf when enough of his children were grown and on their own, no longer making it necessary for him to endure the rigorous training he put himself through to keep in shape for every fight.

Michael got word of Fortunato Bellino's thrilling entry onto the scene from a grandson home from school, where the topic of conversation was the same as it was everywhere else in town. He listened curiously, as had everyone else in town, and when his grandson was finished talking about it he walked out back to the riverside to think about the new development in town.

For many years he had been the only fighter he had ever heard anyone talking about with any kind of excitement. He had been the king of the hill for three decades. Every time a worthy challenger would arise, regardless of where he had come from, Michael would listen as the scuttlebutt would go around and then take the man to his knees at the fairgrounds, picking up another stash and heading home to his family.

He had lived the better part of his life in the same small circle that led from the door of his home to the factory where he worked, and back again, with an occasional jaunt through town to the fairgrounds for a fight, but then right back through town again to his home. He had been a very private man, a devoted family man, a dependable employee, and a good fighter. That had been enough.

Now he stood alone in the evening by the river, thinking about the new young fighter that everyone was talking about. For a minute he looked down at his fists, took a deep breath, and started throwing punches into the air, but when he heard a twig snap and turned to see a young grandson coming down to meet him, he relaxed and reached out to welcome his daughter's boy, erasing the thought that was starting to germinate in his mind.

Still the curiosity plagued him throughout the week, and by Saturday it got the best of him. In the thirty-six years he had lived in America, he had led a very structured and disciplined life. He never varied from his routines, ever. The only time he would ever walk to the fairgrounds was to fight. He was probably the oldest living fighter never to have seen another fight. He had simply not been interested. If he was fighting, he was there. If he was not fighting, he saw no need to be among the crowd of spectators. He was a fighter, not a spectator.

But on that particular Saturday morning, he took Maureen aside, out of the earshot of his children.

"I'll be going out tonight, Maureen."

"Out?" she said quizzically. "Out where? You've never gone out in your life."

"This new fighter the lads are talking about. I want to see him. He's Vittorio Bellino's brother, don't ya know."

"I've heard. Michael, don't you go getting any ideas now. I've been dreaming all my life about having you home for good."

Michael turned away from his wife's stare and looked out the window toward the river.

"I'll be taking the lantern. There's no need to wait up for me."

All day long, people rolled into town from all across New England and headed straight for the Indian Springs Fairgrounds. By five-thirty, every seat in the exhibition hall was filled and people were starting to line up outside, yelling and tossing around suggestions and ideas on how to get into the hall to see the fights. By six-thirty, the largest crowd ever assembled in Indian Springs history was threatening to riot if they couldn't get access to the fights.

Sugar Desmond was begging the local fire marshall to make one exception and allow an overflow crowd because no one was prepared for such a large crowd. Finally the fire marshall agreed, and the doors were opened. Men lined the aisles and filled every doorjamb and empty space, crowding around the ring in a near dangerous manner, and when there was not enough room for even one more spectator, Sugar Desmond, in a black tuxedo, stepped into the ring for the introductions.

It took a full five minutes for the first fighter to wind his way through the crowd to the ring, where he stood menacingly searching the aisles for the entry of the local phenomenon.

Fortunate Bellino was not halfway out of his locker room door when the big man was greeted by an absolutely thunderous ovation as men all through the auditorium pounded their feet and hollered at the top of their lungs in a roar that was heard throughout the otherwise peaceful New England town.

"La-a-die-e-es and gentlemen," Sugar Desmond's voice boomed out, even though there was not one woman in attendance. "Welcome to the most exciting arena in America. Tonight one man will attempt an impossible task. Four of the best fighters in America are waiting to end his reign of terror, which some of us witnessed last week.

"In this corner, weighing 235 pounds, from New York City, with a record of twelve wins and one loss, R-r-r-rip Saint-Geor-r-r-rge!"

The crowd noise was rising as the local fans prepared to welcome their new hero.

"An-n-nd in this corner, weighing 240 pounds, with a record of four wins and no losses, with four stunning first round knockouts, from Biella, Italy, For-r-r-tu-na-a-to-o-o-o Bell-i-i-i-no-o-o-o!"

Sugar Desmond was not halfway through his introduction of Fortunato when the crowd noise reached a fever pitch. Outside, a quiet man with a big full beard pulled the collar up around his neck and shoved his hands deep down into his pockets to ward off the cold as he watched the event from the back of the crowd.

In all of his life, Michael Callahan had never gotten the ovation that he had just heard given to the young Italian, and something inside of him suddenly made him very angry.

The first fight lasted about thirty-five seconds, as Fortunato Bellino, his adrenaline in full flow, tore a big gaping cut over the top of Rip Saint-George's left eye, which blinded him and caused the referee to step in and stop the fight.

The second fight was almost a repeat of one of Fortunato's fights from the week before. An undefeated fighter out of Willimantic, Connecticut, Razor Roldan, went down under a thunderous right hand and the fight ended in five seconds of the first round. Roldan was carried out of the ring and did not wake up for almost twenty minutes.

When Big John Yurkovicz, from Brockton, Massachusetts, wilted under a barrage of combinations and fell face-first on the canvas, only about a half an hour had elapsed since Fortunato first entered the ring. Now, one fight away from becoming a legend, the strong young Italian paced in his corner, shaking out the kinks in his hands as the crowd buzzed in excitement, awaiting the final fight.

As Patrick Foley from Brattleboro, Vermont, climbed into the ring to take the final shot at the Biella Bomber, the attention of the crowd was suddenly and dramatically diverted to the back of the crowd, as a path opened up for the bearded Irishman who walked slowly toward the ring, his piercing glare aimed directly into the eyes of the big young Italian holding center stage.

For a moment, time froze as Michael Callahan and Fortunato Bellino locked into one another's stares.

Then it started, with one loud voice, at first, from somewhere out of the crowd.

"Callahan-Bellino!" the voice yelled.

The cry spread to two or three voices, then twenty or thirty, then two or three hundred, and in a matter of seconds, the auditorium was rocking in a chant that sounded like thunder.

"CALLAHAN-BELLINO! CALLAHAN-BELLINO! CALLAHAN-BELLINO!

From the corner of his brother Fortunato, Vittorio Bellino looked across the crowd at the intense stare his friend Michael Callahan was directing at his brother. When he saw the curious way Fortunato was staring back, he suddenly got a very sick feeling inside of him as he exhaled sadly and lowered his head, shaking it back and forth as he stared into the canvas.

Meanwhile the roar continued. "CALLAHAN-BELLINO! CALLAHAN-BELLINO! CALLAHAN-BELLINO! CALLAHAN-BELLINO!"

On and on they roared, demanding the fight that dreams are made of. Suddenly, for no apparent reason, Michael Callahan turned and walked back through the crowd and out again into the cold night.

The knockout of Pat Foley that occurred thirty-five seconds after the final fight of the night began was almost anticlimactic, and Michael was not even at the edge of the fairgrounds when he heard the "Ooh's" and "Ah's" of the crowd and then the inevitable ovation as Fortunato's final victim of the night hit the canvas.

Instead of looking down at Pat Foley, Fortunato was searching the crowd for the man with a beard who had suddenly captured all of his curiosity. But Michael Callahan was gone, on his way home down the railroad tracks that ran through the heart of downtown Indian Springs.

That night the New England Championship belt hanging on the wall in his bedroom, Fortunato Bellino's last thought before he drifted off to sleep was the intensity of the stare he had encountered when he first saw Michael Callahan. He drifted off to sleep, still mesmerized by that stare.

▲   ▼   ▲

"No!" Vittorio Bellino yelled emphatically at Sugar Desmond, slamming his fist down into his kitchen table. "Absolutely no way in-a hell!"

"But Vittorio, it will be the biggest event in the history of the town! We'll have newspaper reporters from ten states here. We can sell tickets for five dollars apiece! We won't even be able to have it inside the exhibition hall because there'll never be enough room. We'll have to build a platform in the middle of the horse track and temporary bleachers to hold all the people. We'll have to do it in the summer because it has to be outside."

"Sugar, put your head on straight! It'll kill any chance we have of ever uniting the Irish and the Italians in this town."

"Vittorio, I think you're wrong," Sugar said respectfully. "It might be just exactly the thing that will finally bring us together."

"I don't know how the hell you can say that," Vittorio protested. "It'll drive a wedge so deep between us we'll never be able to unite. Not to mention the fact that somebody I love is gonna see his whole world come crashing down around him because in case you've forgotten it, only one man can win a prize fight, and I happen to be pretty doggone fond of both of those guys."

"But, Vittorio, that's just it," Sugar kept on. "It doesn't really matter who wins the fight, what matters is that the two toughest men in North America, who happen to be living in the same town, have agreed to put it all on the line to determine which one is the best. After that day, every man, Irish or

Italian, in the history of the town will be able to say that one day the whole world had their eyes on Indian Springs, Connecticut, where the two toughest men on earth fought the fight of the century."

"Sugar, you're talking like a promoter now, not like somebody who gives a rip about two very beautiful men."

Sugar Desmond regrouped and stood there as Vittorio Bellino paced.

"Michael's retired, Sugar, he doesn't need this. And I'm so mad at Fortunato I could knock him out myself."

"Why?" Sugar giggled.

"Because he should have known better than to create this problem. He's supposed to be behaving himself in America. He's running out of places he can run to."

Sugar Desmond laughed. "Look, Vittorio, they probably both want this thing. Why are you objecting to it?"

"Because I'm probably the only person in the world who can stop it. And I'm gonna stop it. It will never happen!"

"Vittorio, follow along with me for a minute. What's the one thing you and I have been working on for the past ten years around here?"

"Putting the Irish and the Italians together," Vittorio said, stopping to put his finger in Sugar Desmond's chest, "the exact purpose we'll be defeating if we let this fight take place."

"Now wait a minute," Sugar continued. "What's the biggest event every spring at the Italian Club?"

"The game dinner."

"And what's to stop the Italians from inviting the Irish to the game dinner?"

"First of all, the charter isn't open. There are so many diehard Italians who still view the club as their sanctuary that I'd be committing a sacrilege if I invited even one Irishman let alone the whole populace. But what's your point?"

"We have the game dinner the day after the fight. Both fighters agree to attend and sit at the head table, regardless of who wins the fight."

"It would never work," Vittorio said.

"Why?" Sugar protested.

"Because if Michael wins, the Irish will be all over us, and if Fortunato wins the Italians will be all over you, that's why. You talk about a powder keg! First of all, the Irish will sit on one side and the Italians on the other side. One spark will ignite the whole room, and forty or fifty guys could get killed!"

Sugar Desmond was laughing now as he pictured the very possible scenario that Vittorio Bellino had just portrayed.

"Well, unfortunately, we have to make peace between us some way, or it's gonna happen eventually anyway," Sugar said.

"Well I don't want Fortunato and Michael to be a part of the spark that lights the powder keg. We'll just have to think of some other way," Vittorio said.

Sugar Desmond started to bend.

"Old friend, I guess I know what you mean. The only thing that would make me sadder than Michael and Fortunato driving us apart would be to see the Red Sox sell Babe Ruth to the Yankees."

For several minutes the two men sat quietly in the room, and then, as Vittorio drummed his fingers on the table, Sugar's eyes started to light up.

"Wait a minute, I got it," Sugar said, snapping his fingers as he jumped to his feet. "How many Red Sox fans do you know who are Italians?" Sugar asked Vittorio.

"Oh God, there's John Frassinelli, Carlo Panciera, most of the Fontanellas, and all of the Julians, Campos, DaDalts, Piccolis, Tonidandels and Casagrandes."

"Yeah and how many are Yankee fans?"

"I guess all the rest of the town. Marco Rossi, Joe Tocchetti, Mark Introvigne, the Pisciottas, Amprimos, Posoccos, Muzios, Andreolis, Cercenas, and just about everybody else."

"Now of the Irishmen, which ones are Yankee fans."

"Every Larkin in town, plus the Cunninghams, O'Haras, Driscolls, Murrays, and Wards."

"And which ones are Red Sox fans?"

"Everybody else. The Hanleys, Malloys, Moriartys, Foleys, and most of the Desmonds."

"So there you have it," Sugar smiled at Vittorio. "We don't have an Irish-Italian game dinner, we have a Yankee-Red Sox game dinner, where all the Yankees sit on one side of the hall, and all of the Red Sox on the other. That will mix the Irish and the Italians, and we'll put Fortunato and Michael at the head table, regardless of who wins the fight, and that will bring us together! Then if a donnybrook breaks out, it won't be between the Irish and the Italians, it will be between the Yankee fans and the Red Sox fans!"

For a minute, Sugar thought he had Vittorio, as his friend sat thinking about it.

"The Yankee-Red Sox part sounds pretty good, but why do we have to put the fight with it?"

"Because the fight has to happen, Vittorio, you were there last night. You saw what went down. And we may as well make the best of it, because you and I both know that the fight has to happen."

"We might be able to make it work," Vittorio said cautiously. "But we'd have to have everybody's promises that egos and antagonisms must be left at the door or the dinner will never work."

"Then will you do one favor for me?" Sugar Desmond asked his friend.

"What?" Vittorio Bellino asked.

"Will you and Fortunato visit Michael Callahan with me and see if we can put this fight together?"

Vittorio shook his head back and forth, but nodded at Sugar reluctantly.

"I don't know why I listen to you, Sugar. This is against my better judgement, I want you to know that," Vittorio said to him.

"Let's go get Fortunato," Sugar smiled.

When the door opened at Michael Callahan's house, Fortunato Bellino was standing behind Sugar Desmond and Vittorio Bellino. Maureen Callahan answered the door and smiled at Vittorio and Sugar.

"Come in, please," she smiled, and the three men walked into the Callahan kitchen. Michael was sitting at the table peeling a banana. He did not get up when the three men entered his home.

Inside the house, children started to scatter, and Fortunato thought to himself, *The Callahans must have company already.*

"I guess you know why we're here," Sugar said to the stern man who sat at the table.

No sooner had Sugar Desmond started to speak than the most beautiful girl Fortunato Bellino had ever laid eyes upon entered the room.

It is said that once in every Italian boy's life, he is struck by the thunderbolt. When Fortunato Bellino first laid eyes upon Katie Elizabeth Callahan, his thunderbolt struck. The fragrance of her hair caught his nostrils as she drifted past him, smiling at him with her big green eyes. His heart melted as he watched her serve her father a cup of coffee and then turn to offer some to his guests.

Fortunato Bellino thought for certain that he had seen her eyes sparkle as she smiled at him, and he nodded to her politely when she offered him coffee. For the rest of the visit, Fortunato heard nothing of what the other men were saying as he kept his eyes on this most gorgeous creature he had ever seen.

As the other men were talking, making arrangements for the fight, Fortunato just stood there mesmerized by Katie Elizabeth, who sat on the floor in the living room playing with the small children, her nieces and nephews, and Michael's grandchildren.

For some reason, Fortunato assumed that Katie Elizabeth was Michael's only child. As for the small children, they were neighborhood youngsters, perhaps, that she was baby sitting. It was a very slight oversight, and seemingly insignificant, but it would prove to be a very important misunderstanding which would be corrected in a most unusual way.

"Is that all right with you, Fortunato?" he vaguely heard Sugar say at one point.

"Yeah, yeah, that's okay," Fortunato answered, totally oblivious to everything everyone was saying in the room.

"Good," Sugar Desmond said slamming his hand down on the table. "Then it's set. May fifteenth, the third Saturday in May, 1920. To be followed the following Saturday, May twenty-second, by the Yankee-Red Sox game dinner at the Italian Club. No hard feelings by the loser, both fighters to attend the dinner and sit at the head table."

"Shake hands," Sugar said, and Fortunato reached over to shake Michael's hand.

"Katie Elizabeth," Michael called into the next room, and his daughter came quickly into the kitchen. "You've not been properly introduced to our guest. Fortunato Bellino, this is my daughter, Katie Elizabeth."

Fortunato extended his hand to Katie Elizabeth Callahan, and when he took her hand in his own it seemed small and soft inside of his rugged big hand. She curtsied politely, and walked over to put her arm around Michael Callahan's shoulder.

My God, she's a dream, Fortunato thought, and he could not take his eyes off of her.

"Katie's never known me to lose a fight," Michael said coldly to Fortunato. "I'm not going to let her start now."

Fortunato was not intimidated.

"Now there's one more thing I'd like to clear up before the fight," Michael said to Fortunato. "In all my life, I've never fought against a friend. We may be good friends later on, but between now and May fifteenth, I don't want to know you," Michael said to Fortunato.

Fortunato looked away from Katie Elizabeth at her father. They were standing in his home, where he was the most comfortable and in control.

"I think that's probably a very wise suggestion," he agreed. "Because on May fifteenth, I'm gonna crush you."

Fortunato turned to walk out of Michael Callahan's house. At the door he turned around. "But regardless of what happens on the day of the fight, I'll be at your door the very next day. Because there isn't a man in the world I'd like to befriend more than you, and I want to see your daughter again."

With that Fortunato Bellino walked out of the door and into the night, and Michael Callahan followed him out with his eyes.

"Admirably spoken," Michael said to Vittorio. "But I'm gonna tear his head off."

▲   ▼   ▲

For the next two months the most exciting topic of conversation in town was the upcoming Callahan-Bellino fight. In the factories and in the taverns, at the club and in the church, the one and only recurring theme was the fight, and the many possible scenarios, and the outcome. Behind the scenes, there was more money wagered in more different ways on the Callahan-Bellino fight than on any event in Indian Springs history.

For the most part, it was an even money fight. It was impossible to pick a favorite, what with Michael Callahan's incomparable string of victories and the remarkable way he had of finding and exploiting his opponent's weaknesses set against Fortunato Bellino's youth, incredible strength, and absolute confidence. Every time somebody would bring up the age issue, some

Callahan fan would recite a list of about twenty fighters the same argument had been used on who had all fallen under Michael's relentless assaults.

And every time somebody would bring up Fortunato's inexperience, some Bellino fan would remind him of the eight consecutive first-round knockouts Fortunato had piled up against the best fighters in the country.

To add another dimension to the impending war, both fighters were observed training hard for the fight each was obviously taking very seriously. For everybody who claimed to have the one bit of information that everybody else was overlooking, there was somebody else to shoot down that theory or counteract it with a theory of his own. In fact, the two fighters seemed to be about the most evenly matched pair that would ever don gloves together at the fairgrounds. Advance ticket sales, for bleachers that had not yet been built exceeded the total population of the town (eight thousand) by more than a thousand a month before the fight.

For his part, Vittorio Bellino tried very hard not to think about the fight. He secretly saw no way that Michael Callahan could win the fight, provided Fortunato was serious. *The only person who can beat Fortunato is Fortunato*, Vittorio reasoned, and he was very impressed to see Fortunato training so hard and disciplining himself so thoroughly. Fortunato put the alcohol totally away for this fight and ran six to eight miles twice a day, as well as ripping to shreds the heavy bag that hung in the fairgrounds hall.

Sugar Desmond, on the other hand, was absolutely convinced that Michael Callahan was so far and away better than any heavyweight in history that it was no contest, regardless of the hype and glamour of Fortunato's eight thrilling wins. In Sugar Desmond's mind, one of the great tragedies he was ever a witness to was the decision Michael Callahan had made long ago to put his family before certain greatness, for Sugar Desmond was sure that the greatest fighter in history was Michael Callahan.

Added to his certainty about the outcome was the fact that when Sugar visited him one evening before he went to the factory, Michael was doing sit-ups and he told Sugar to wait until he was finished. From seven-thirty until ten o'clock, Sugar sat amazed as Michael continued to strengthen his stomach muscles with thousands of sit-ups, non-stop.

At ten o'clock, Michael stopped, turned to Sugar, and said one thing before going into the house. "Nobody ever threatened me before. Especially in my own home, in front of my daughter. With every sit-up I do, I replay again, over and over in my mind, the final punch of the fight. I'm gonna knock him out, Sugar."

With that Michael turned and walked back into the house, forgetting totally that Sugar had been waiting patiently for over two hours to talk to him. There, in Michael Callahan's backyard, Sugar Desmond just shook his head and walked away.

Reporters from newspapers in Hartford, Boston, New York, Providence, Worcester, Springfield, Norwich, Willimantic, New Haven, and Keene came to town a week before the fight to interview the fighters and the townspeople, and the consensus was evenly divided 50-50 as to the outcome.

Throughout the entire prefight buildup, Katie Elizabeth Callahan immersed herself in newspaper reports about the young Italian, three years older than herself and three decades younger than her father, and strangely she began to grow fond of him, even though he stood ready and willing to tear her father to pieces. The strange thing about this was that her father was the man she had idolized throughout her entire life. Probably the only thing that allowed her even to consider the young fighter romantically was her absolute belief that there was no way he could defeat her father. She saw Fortunato as just a strong young man whose strength her father would neutralize, as he had done with every other fighter he had ever faced.

She could not know the secret fears that Michael Callahan had been living with for the last several years, specifically the last several months, that his skills, his legs, and his stamina would give out on him and desert him when he needed them the most. In fact the best thing that he had to go on, other than a firm commitment to train very hard for the fight, was the script he had been burning into his mind about the last punch. Somehow, someway, if he could weather the certain hurricane Fortunato Bellino would be, he was determined to deliver that shot.

Michael trained hard for this, the fight of his life, and coming into the days before the fight, he was very encouraged and honestly felt better than he had felt in many years.

Sitting alone in his sparsely furnished mill house tenement, Fortunato Bellino felt stronger than he ever had, and he was totally satisfied that there was no more he could possibly do to prepare himself.

May 15, 1920, broke warm and sunny and the whole Irish community dressed in green, the color of the boxing trunks Michael Callahan had always worn.

The fight was to be fought outdoors, under the canvas tent the locals had erected in case of rain. When no rain threatened, the tent came down so everyone in every bleacher seat in the infield of the horse track would have a clear view of the ring.

On the morning of the fifteenth, Maureen Callahan cleared all of the grandchildren out of the house and let Michael have the house to himself to sleep as much as he wanted before his war.

Fortunato Bellino slept late and ate a huge bowl of spaghetti at eleven o'clock and another huge bowl at one o'clock to give him the energy he thought he'd need in case the fight lasted the full fifteen rounds it was scheduled for.

Fifteen rounds, he thought to himself. *God help the poor men who have to go that long. Callahan and I will never see that territory, that's for sure.*

Late in the afternoon, as the sun began to set rapidly in the western sky, the air grew cooler and every man from every factory in Indian Springs was wolfing down his supper so he could get to the fairgrounds and get as good a seat as possible for what many believed would truly be the fight of the century.

By late afternoon, many of the men who had been drinking all day long in the taverns on Main Street had put their money where their mouths were, and staggering sums of money had been bet on the fight.

At four o'clock, Rico Fontanella walked into Duffy's Tavern on Main Street and offered a month's pay on Fortunato Bellino.

"No half-dead Irish bum can beat Fortunato Bellino. My last month's wages back me up," the drunken Rico slurred. His bets were covered in ten minutes.

At four-fifteen, Connor O'Keefe stumbled down the steps that led into the Italian Club and slammed a huge wad of money down on the bar at the club. "I've sold me grandfar's guns. I'll bet it all your young bull gets gored tonight by the master."

Connor's bets were taken up immediately.

All across town, similar scenes took place as men symbolically put everything they had on the line with their favorite, anticipating a war of epoch proportions.

They would not be disappointed.

On horseback and on foot they flooded out of every factory and every home, forming groups that blended into crowds as they poured into the arena. Last minute betting was heavy and pocket flasks plentiful as the crowd swelled under the emerging stars.

From hundreds of miles away they came, and even the most liberal estimates of how many would show up paled in comparison to the crowd that arrived. The bleachers were built to hold eight thousand people. Chairs were set up closer to the ring in the infield to hold two thousand more. When the townsmen ran out of chairs, stumps were dragged in and lined up. There were fully a thousand more people outside the infield area, swelling the grounds with more people than the town had ever seen in its history. Outside the infield, local youths sold sandwiches, popcorn, coffee, and whatever else people seemed likely to buy. The noise the crowd made was deafening, and the air was filled with an electricity that had never been approached in anyone's life in attendance.

At eight o'clock, when Sugar Desmond stepped into the ring to introduce the fighters, a roar went up that woke everybody up within a two mile radius of the fairgrounds. The crowd noise was at a fever pitch as Sugar tried to speak.

"La-a-adies a-and gen-tle-men, welcome to the battle of the undefeateds, where tonight we will witness his-s-story!"

Again Sugar Desmond was drowned out by the incessant roar of the hyped-up crowd, which had reached the moment it had been waiting for for several months.

Several times he attempted to introduce the fighters, but he was drowned out each time. Finally, the crowd started to calm enough for Sugar to continue.

"In-tro-ducing, in this corner, from Indian Springs, Connecticut, weighing in at 206 pounds, with a record of eighty-three wins and no defeats, the undefeated, former heavyweight champion of New England, MI-I-I-I-CHAL CA-A-A-AL-A-HA-A-A-AN!"

Half the crowd roared, in as loud a welcome as anyone there present had ever heard, and the roar that went up triggered a great rush of adrenaline coursing through Michael Callahan's body.

He had needed the approval of the crowd more than even he himself had realized, and the ovation he received that night he judged to be far bigger than the last one he had heard, when his opponent had won the championship.

When the crowd noise finally died down, Sugar Desmond continued.

"And in this corner, from Biella, Italy, weighing in at 228 pounds with a record of eight wins, and no defeats with eight first-round knockouts, the New England heavyweight champion, the Biella Bomber, FOR-TU-NA-A-A-TO-O-O-O BELL-I-I-I-NO-O-O-O-O!"

Fortunato's fans were determined not to be outdone in their cheering, and they pounded their feet and roared at least as hard as the Callahan fans. From that moment forward, as the two fighters approached each other in the center of the ring, not another sound was heard for the rest of the night over the incredible, incessant roar of the crowd, as the decibel level rose to the stars in the clear night.

When the referee, Eddie Weeks from Springfield, brought the two fighters to center ring, they stood nose to nose and stared into each other's faces from inches away.

By the time the opening bell rang, every person in attendance who had come for the excitement of the moment had already gotten his money's worth, for even if the fight lasted only a few seconds, the intensity of the moment was the ultimate thrill any sports fan could hope for.

In the center of the ring the two legends met, and as Fortunato Bellino charged Michael Callahan with determined fire in his eyes, any feeling-out period was quickly waived as the two gladiators threw defense out the window and laid into one another from the opening bell. They stood toe-to-toe in the center of the ring pummeling each other relentlessly, with both fighters dishing out and taking an incredible beating.

For two solid minutes of what any fight fan could tell you was the most savage and brutal two minutes of any fight anyone there present had ever witnessed, each fighter threw over a hundred punches, with no less than seventy-five punches each landing and scoring. At precisely the two-minute mark, both fighters dropped their gloves simultaneously and stood back to regroup and access the damage they had inflicted on one another.

The pace of the first two minutes had been nothing short of furious, and the two giants sneered at one another as they lifted their gloves in front of them, and began circling one another as the clock ticked away. For the next thirty seconds they covered each other's flicking light jabs and waited for an opening. When Michael Callahan dropped his gloves and pretended to hike up his trunks to draw Fortunato Bellino in, Fortunato obliged and walked square into a sharp overhand right that rocked his head back and lifted every Irishman in the audience off of his chair as the concussion of the punch sent a halo of sweat around Fortunato's head.

Fortunato soon recovered, however, and ducking a follow-up left, got inside of Michael to deliver a punishing left-right-left body attack that brought a gasp from Michael Callahan and lifted every Italian in the audience off of his chair.

The final flurry of the round lasted a full fifteen seconds, and what was arguably one of the greatest rounds in heavyweight history ended about as even as any round ever fought.

Both fighters returned to their corners, and while no one knew yet what the outcome would be, there was not a person anywhere in the arena who would have bet a plug nickel that the fight would last the full fifteen rounds at that pace. No fighters in any division, especially the heavyweight division, could be expected to sustain such a fever pitch, and this was one fight that looked like a certain knockout.

When the bell sounded to start the second round, it appeared to everyone present that both fighters had decided to make the second round the last one, because, incredibly, the round went off much the same as the first one, with, as hard as it was for the audience to believe, even more shots thrown and connected this time.

The gasps, groans, and cheers of the crowd rose and fell like waves in an incoming tide as the combatants bore down with all their strength and skills, and the roar the crowd made only intensified as the fight progressed.

"I wouldn't want to be a judge in this fight," Aldo Barbieri said to Joe Shea who was standing next to him as round two came to a close. A strange phenomenon started to take place, unnoticed by anyone present. All throughout the crowd, Callahan fans were growing in respect for Fortunato Bellino, and Bellino fans were growing in respect for Michael Callahan, and gradually, almost unnoticeably, Irish were turning to talk to Italians, and Italians were acknowledging Irish.

Rounds three and four were a mutual rest period, and in round five, the first evidence of a turn of the tide started to emerge. More and more now, as the round wore on, Michael was dropping his hands and he appeared to be breathing very heavily and tiring noticeably.

"He's got him, he's got him, he's got him!" a number of Italians started to yell as Fortunato started to back Michael up. In the fifth round the fight swung Fortunato's way, as he landed the most effective and telling blows. Fortunato won the sixth round as well, and the seventh, and in the eighth round, he backed the Irishman up into the ropes, and with a furious assault pummeled him almost to the point where the referee stepped in to stop it. But as though he were possessed of a sixth sense, just at the moment when the referee had just about decided to stop the fight, Michael caught a second wind. He turned Fortunato around with about fifteen seconds to go in the round, and landed a number of hard punches on the head and shoulders of the now-exhausted Fortunato Bellino.

Whether or not Michael had won the round with his final flurry was up to the judges to decide, but the renewed confidence his second wind had given him encouraged him enough to stay on his feet, and the experts at ringside decided that the turning point of the fight may well be determined by how the fighters started the ninth round.

Michael Callahan appeared very tired as the ninth round began, and no one but him knew if it was only an act or not, and then Fortunato backed him into the ropes and started pummeling him again. Blow after punishing blow landed on Michael Callahan's head, as somehow, someway, he managed to stay on his feet. It did not take as long this time for Fortunato to punch himself out, however, and after only a minute was gone, Michael turned Fortunato completely around and put him into the ropes with a barrage of his own.

The Irish contingent was going wild as Michael Callahan completed his best round of the fight, continually bearing down on a confused and very tired Fortunato. When the ninth round ended, Fortunato staggered to his corner and Michael raised his hands up triumphantly to the rising crescendo of Irish cheers.

In the tenth, Michael's second wind continued to carry him through and he outpointed Fortunato with skill and cunning, making up for whatever power he had lost through fatigue.

As the eleventh round began, the scoring appeared to be about even, and it was now down to a five-round fight. The eleventh round was a confusing one for Fortunato Bellino, as everything he did went wrong. Michael was picking off his punches with his gloves and countering with scoring blows that picked Fortunato apart almost at will. Fortunato appeared awkward and tired as Michael scored heavily and locked away a round in his bank, but in the twelfth, just when the fight seemed to be totally in Michael's control, lightning struck.

Out of nowhere, a giant overhand right caught the aging Irishman flush in the jaw and dropped him like a boulder on the canvas.

Every person in the crowd rose to his feet as Fortunato Bellino rushed to a neutral corner and Eddie Weeks knelt over the fallen warrior and began to count him out. With his head spinning and his world coming apart, Michael Callahan heard the God-awful sound of Eddie Weeks yelling in his ear, "four . . . five . . . six . . . seven . . . "

At eight Michael Callahan reached within himself and found, somewhere in the deep recesses of his pride and heart, the strength to stand to his feet.

As Fortunato Bellino charged toward him, Eddie Weeks wiped Michael's gloves off, and when Fortunato swung wildly at him, the old Irishman ducked and grabbed onto Fortunato, holding him tightly, instinctively trying to survive the round.

Sugar Desmond sat in agony in the front row, his eyes filling with tears as his lifelong friend struggled to stave off certain defeat. Without taking his eyes off of the fighters he yelled to the man sitting next to him, "He's never been knocked down in his entire career. That was the first time!"

Miraculously, Michael Callahan managed to last until the bell ended the twelfth round, a round that all the judges scored 10-8 for Fortunato with the ten-point must system.

Suddenly, strangely, as he walked back to his corner instinctively, Michael Callahan became totally oblivious to the crowd. It was as though he did not hear them anymore, as though there was a silence that settled in over the valley. All around him, people were yelling things into his ear, conflicting instructions which he blocked out, and on his stool in the corner of the arena in which he had lived his life, alone under the New England stars, he met himself.

For some unknown reason, his mind wandered back to County Mayo, Ireland, where he used to climb St. Patrick's Hill as a boy so many years ago. He thought of his forced emigration to America and the way he had met Maureen Malloy on the boat. He saw her tired, scared, and very beautiful eyes looking up at him as the ship neared the shores of Boston Harbor.

Then he saw himself running back down the plank into Ireland and jumping into a boxing ring in the square of his hometown. Suddenly he was twenty-three years old again, strong, cocky, invincible, beckoning his accusers forward, and his vision rose him to his feet.

When the bell rang to start the thirteenth round, Fortunato Bellino walked out confidently to end the fight, but the man he met in the thirteenth was not the same man he had almost crushed in the twelfth.

The look in the eyes of his opponent was distant and cold, and the way Michael stared at Fortunato like he was looking right through him changed Fortunato's mind about boring in. Instead, he danced around Michael and Michael became the aggressor. The first few punches Michael Callahan threw in the opening minute of the thirteenth round were awesome, punishing blows which jolted Fortunato to full attention. His body shots were brutal, and the first one he threw cracked one of Fortunato's ribs. When he went headhunting, Fortunato decided to back up.

He ducked on his way back and escaped the biggest shots that Michael fired, but all he seemed able to do all of a sudden was block the shots Callahan was firing. With his back to the ropes, Fortunato knew he had to get out, but he was too busy blocking the relentless onslaught of blows that

Michael was raining down on him. Frustrated and angry with himself, Fortunato tried helplessly to get off the ropes, but Michael kept pushing him back in and hammering him repeatedly with headshots.

Fortunato was confused and angry, and as he blocked Michael's assault he tried desperately to think of a way to turn things around, but before he could come up with anything the bell rang and the round was over.

Walking back to his corner at the end of the thirteenth round, Fortunato was stunned, more by his own inability to turn things around than by any of the many blows Michael had hammered him with. As he sat down on his stool, he knew he had lost any momentum he had enjoyed and that Michael Callahan had taken control of the fight.

"You're still leading, Fortunato, you're still leading!" his cornerman yelled at his face. "If you can stay even from this point forward, you'll win the fight. Bear down, Fortunato, bear down."

Fortunato was breathing very heavily and the confused look in his face worried his cornermen.

"Fortunato, he's tired!" Bruno Donato yelled at his fighter. "He's real tired, I'm telling you!"

I'm tired too, Fortunato thought. *But if I don't do something now, the last two rounds will be a nightmare. The whole thing will slip away, and I'll look like a clumsy ox, throwing it away on points. I knock him out, and I knock him out now.*

Back up on Brandon Heights, Antoinette Bellino sat with several of her Italian friends in the living room of the Bellino home. The grandfather clock ticked slowly away as the women sat saying the rosary. From several miles away they heard the roar of the crowd through the open screen door, and it frightened them that the noise had lasted for over an hour. Winning or losing did not matter as much to the women as it did to the men. Surviving was what mattered to the women, and they knew that the sheer length of the fight meant that both warriors would never be the same again after tonight.

On Furnace Avenue, Katie Elizabeth Callahan sat and rubbed ointment into Maureen Callahan's back as Michael Callahan's wife cried softly in the night. Every roar of the crowd, every swelling cheer that drifted in across the valley frightened her, and all she kept whispering into her tear-soaked handkerchief was, "Oh, dear Lord . . . .Oh, dear Lord."

Round fourteen was a round of boxing that would be difficult to duplicate again in a thousand fights. From the opening bell, an all-out war erupted.

The first punch of the round was a crushing overhand right that caught Fortunato square in the face as he rushed in and buried him flat on his back. Before Eddie Weeks got to three, Fortunato had bounced back up off the canvas and Eddie was rubbing off his gloves. As Michael Callahan bore in, an angry Fortunato Bellino fired a devastating combination and Michael Callahan fell hard to the canvas for the second time in his career.

This time he was not really as hurt as he had been in the twelfth. He was more surprised and angry than hurt, and at the count of four he was up and ready to go. At the one-minute mark, the fighters were again standing toe-to-toe in the center of the ring, and at one-fifteen, Fortunato again hit the canvas hard after a tremendous left uppercut that Michael threw with a loud grunt, lifting Fortunato completely off his feet before dropping him on his back.

Eddie Weeks had to count to eight before Fortunato got up again, and when he nodded that he was all right, Eddie waved the two fighters together again. With a quick volley of punches, Fortunato again found an opening and caught Michael square, dropping him flat on his face for the second time in the round, and by this time, every voice of every fan in the arena was hoarse.

In the second row, Father Charles Sheehan, parish priest and confessor of both combatants, buried his head in his hands and whispered his prayers for the lives of both men, and when Michael Callahan got up again, the two men squared off again in the center of the ring just in time to hear the bell that ended the fourteenth round.

In awe and consummate respect, the whole crowd stood as one, and the raucous cheering and foot-stomping gave way to a minute long ovation of hand-clapping for both warriors, each of whom had tasted the canvas twice in the fourteenth round.

No one in the crowd was aware that at that moment the judges had the fight scored almost a draw. One judge had it 133-132 for Callahan, another had it 133-131 for Bellino, and the third had it 132-132, a fight that would certainly be decided in the fifteenth round.

With about ten seconds left before the start of the final round, Michael Callahan and Fortunato Bellino walked slowly toward one another in the center of the ring, and as the crowd stood as one in a standing ovation, the bell rang and the two men of courage touched gloves and faced each other for the last three decisive minutes.

The eyes of eleven thousand men were riveted to center ring as two men circled one another looking for the first opening. You could have cut the tension in the arena with a knife as twenty-two thousand shoulders dipped and bobbed, with every man in the audience totally involved in the fight. When the first opening came, both fighters swung simultaneously, setting off another punishing but even exchange.

After the initial flurry, which lasted only about eight seconds, another thirty tension-packed seconds elapsed, and then, grotesquely, almost obscenely, the moment Michael Callahan had long feared deep within himself arrived.

Incredibly and sickeningly, he felt his legs start to give out as they began, for no apparent reason, to turn to rubber. Sensing this Fortunato Bellino backed up the aging warrior, and with one punishing combination after another, he had Michael futilely trying to hold him off, until finally, his relentless assault dropped the old champion in a heap on the canvas.

"This time it's over!" Aldo Lombardi yelled, and Joe Shea bit his lower lip and thought, *Oh no, oh no.*

With Michael Callahan looking very old and very tired, struggling against hope to get up, suddenly a weird, almost respectful silence swept over the crowd as every man in the place stood to his feet and watched to see if the incredible career of Michael Callahan was, indeed, finally over.

But his subconscious mind and his indomitable heart would not let it end yet, and almost miraculously, as Eddie Weeks reached the count of seven, the old champion found the will to stand up.

Staggering forward toward the referee, he held out his gloves to be wiped off as he nodded to Eddie Weeks.

"Michael, are you sure?" Eddie asked him.

Michael was too tired to do anything more than nod, and Eddie reluctantly motioned the two fighters together again. Fortunato knew that he had hit the old man really hard with the last punch, and he was amazed that Michael had gotten up, but he was not about to let it get away at this point.

Again Fortunato bore in, and again he hit the old champion with a devastating right hand, and once again Michael Callahan's body thudded to the canvas.

This time, he almost bounced back up, and again staggered toward Eddie Weeks.

"I can go," Michael pleaded with Eddie Weeks. "I can go."

Eddie turned to Michael's corner.

"If he gets hit just one more time, I'm going to stop the fight!" he yelled almost angrily at Michael Callahan's corner.

In that brief instant, a feeling of absolute respect for the old champion filled Fortunato Bellino as he shook his head in disbelief and walked once again toward the tired old champion, whom he knew now, beyond any doubt, he had beaten.

For the first time since they had first met, months ago in Michael Callahan's kitchen, the two fighters talked to each other as the clock wound down to inside the last thirty seconds of the fight.

"What in God's name keeps you up, old man?" Fortunato asked Michael with a clear tone of respect.

And then a most incredible turn of events took place.

"Can't afford to lose . . . ," Michael smiled up at Fortunato. "I bet my life savings on myself, and I got ten kids to support."

For some reason, that answer caught Fortunato Bellino absolutely and totally off guard, and for a split second, he lost his concentration, and dropped his gloves in total amazement and said, "Ten kids!" in wide-eyed disbelief.

At that precise moment, Michael Callahan instinctively reached all the way within himself for every ounce of strength he had left and let fly with the tremendous, overhand right that he had programmed into his subconscious mind as the knockout punch that would beat Fortunato Bellino.

It came all the way from County Mayo, all the way across a thousand miles of ocean and thirty-six years of time, all the way from the ground of his back yard where he had planted it with thousands of repetitions into his subconscious mind. Just as he had pictured it a thousand times before, it caught Fortunato Bellino clean in the jaw, ripping his head sideways and backward, and knocking him flat on his back, out colder than ice.

Eddie Weeks motioned Michael Callahan to a neutral corner, which the old fighter's legs barely got him to, and as he counted Fortunato Bellino out, the young lion never heard a sound as he lay on the canvas unconscious.

The Irish fans could not believe their eyes. No one could. With no more than five seconds left in what had been the absolute greatest fight of all time, the great Michael Callahan had done the impossible, snatching victory from certain defeat, and in the raucous crowd noise, no one but the two fighters had heard a word of the verbal exchange that had passed between them.

The applause that filled the night after the fight was one of respect and appreciation for both fighters, and as the crowd started to disperse, Vittorio Bellino jumped under the ropes to attend to his fallen brother.

With smelling salts and cold water, Vittorio set about to revive Fortunato while Sugar Desmond announced to a dwindling crowd the official results of the fight. In the pandemonium at ringside, no one noticed the two cornermen of Michael Callahan. He put his arms around them and they carried him away into the shower room.

By the time Fortunato shook the cobwebs out of his brain, Bruno Donato was cutting off his gloves, and Michael Callahan was nowhere to be seen.

"Wha . . . ? Wha . . . ha . . . ? Wha . . . hap . . . ?"

"Shhh!" Vittorio said to Fortunato, cradling his head in his hands. Looking out over the crowd, Vittorio noticed an encouraging sight. All over the arena, Irish and Italians were talking and slapping each other on the back and laughing with one another, and deep down inside, Vittorio prayed that the end result of what these two men had done that night would be of benefit to his country.

In Michael Callahan's dressing room, Sugar Desmond was beaming, but Michael Callahan was flat on his stomach, exhausted.

"It's an absolute miracle I beat that man, Sugar, an absolute miracle. And I'll tell you this. Nobody else in the world could have beaten him tonight, and nobody will ever beat him again."

"Michael, you fought the fight of your life," Sugar Desmond told him proudly.

Michael smiled with his eyes closed.

"Don't even think about asking me to fight again. This time I am absolutely through."

"Mickey, you could have been the greatest of all time, the champion of the world. You know that, don't you?"

"I thought of it many times, Sugar. I honestly did. But I think I made the right decision. My kids are more important to me than any of that. I wanted to live with them, and talk to them, and fight their battles alongside of them, and help them along in life. That's why I stayed in Indian Springs all my life and never sought the big time."

In the quiet of Michael Callahan's locker room, Sugar Desmond put his arm around the old warrior's shoulder.

"You done good, Michael. You done real good."

▲   ▼   ▲

That night Fortunato Bellino went home with his brother Vittorio. When Antoinette met them at the door, she led Fortunato to the couch where she sat him down and brought him ice packs for the bruises on his face and hands.

Antoinette never asked what had happened, only what she could do to ease his pain.

"I just want to lie here," Fortunato said. "I feel like I got run over by a train."

His ribs were so sore that he could not turn over without help, and it was not until he had fallen asleep that she asked Vittorio what had happened.

At Michael Callahan's home, Katie Elizabeth met Sugar Desmond and her father at the door. Michael had absolutely refused to allow his wife ever to meet him after a fight. Pretending to have gone to bed hours before, as she had always done, she lay wide awake in the next room, praying silently that he would not be hurt too badly and that this would be his last fight.

"How long did the fight last?" Katie asked her father.

"Fifteen rounds," Michael answered.

"A decision?" she asked.

"No, honey, a knockout," Michael answered.

"Is he hurt real bad?" she asked, not disguising her concern very well at all.

"No, he's okay. I'm the one who's hurt," Michael answered, depositing his tired old bones in his big living room chair.

Katie lifted her father's right hand and inspected his knuckles.

"Little swelling, that's all," she said. "I don't think it's broken."

Michael looked at Sugar Desmond, and Sugar laughed right out loud. Katie had been the best medicine of the night for Michael Callahan. Sitting in his chair in the living room, he held his ribs together and laughed painfully.

"Come here," he said to her, and she came right over and sat on the arm rest of the chair putting her arms around his neck.

"That young lad gave me the beating of my life before I knocked him out. How did you know I got the win and not him?"

"Because you looked at me when you walked in the door," she said.

Michael looked over at Sugar Desmond and smiled.

"You gonna be okay now, Mick?"

"Yeah, Sugar, thanks. In a minute I'll be going to bed."

"Let me know if he needs anything," Sugar said to Katie as he walked out the door.

"You want some food, Daddy?"

"No, honey, just some water with a straw, please," Michael said.

As he sipped the water, she held his hand and she noticed that it was shaking. When the water was finished, she helped him up out of the chair and led him into his bedroom.

"I'll let you sleep till you wake up, Daddy."

She didn't tell her mother that he had been shaking all the way into their bedroom, or that he had moved a lot slower than he usually did after a fight. She just closed the door behind him as he got into bed next to his wife, and her last thoughts before drifting off to sleep were of the other man in the fight.

Fifteen rounds against Michael Callahan. I hope to God he's all right.

▲　▼　▲

The next day, at eleven o'clock in the morning, Fortunato Bellino knocked at Michael Callahan's door. Maureen Callahan answered the door and winced when she saw the swollen and bruised face of the young man.

"How is he?" Fortunato asked quietly.

"Come in, Fortunato. I'll go and get him."

As Fortunato took a seat at Michael Callahan's kitchen table, several of the grandchildren ran from the living room to the kitchen door but stopped in their tracks and stared when they saw the battered face of Fortunato Bellino.

In a minute, Michael Callahan walked slowly into the kitchen and sat down at the table across from Fortunato.

"I just came by to see if you were all right," Fortunato said softly.

"What do you think?" Michael said, smiling faintly. "You put a major hurtin' on me, you know."

Fortunato smiled. "I don't feel too great myself."

"You know I'll never fight you again," Michael said. "You hammered me right into retirement."

"That's not why I came over," Fortunato said.

"I think I know why you came over," Michael said. "Katie, give us a beer," Michael yelled into the next room.

When Katie Elizabeth Callahan came into the kitchen, she immediately walked over to Fortunato Bellino and touched the bruise on his cheekbone. Her hand felt smooth and soft and was better medicine than all the ice he had used the night before at his brother's house.

"There'll be all kinds of pressure now for a rematch, but I'm not going to give into it," Michael told Fortunato. "I told my wife last night that I'm out of it, and I mean to keep my word to her."

"I understand," Fortunato said.

"You'll have a lot of offers to fight now. And you're the best I've ever seen. You can have a great career."

Fortunato exhaled painfully and sat back in his chair.

"I don't want to make fighting a career," he said to the Callahan family. "In fact I don't even like it. I can't even tell you why I do it, to be honest with you."

Both men lifted their beers to their lips and drank.

"I started the same way you did," Michael said to him quietly. "Drank enough Irish whiskey to get angry and wasted all my early years angry at the world. Then I started knockin' people out, and everybody wanted a shot at me. Every time I won, I got more confidence, and then I just did it out of habit. I loved it for a few years, but then I kept doin' it long after it stopped being fun."

Fortunato Bellino hung on every word of Michael Callahan.

"Toward the end," Michael said somberly and slowly, "I did it to help the money situation on the home front. That was the only reason, toward the end."

Michael lifted his beer glass to his lips and swallowed what was left of it.

"When I retired, I was the happiest man in America. And then I heard about you and I got angry. Don't ask me why, I prob'ly couldn't explain it. But I almost fought one fight too many."

Fortunato Bellino watched Michael Callahan closely, and what he saw scared him. Michael was shaking uncontrollably and seemed unable to make all of his words come out properly.

Fortunato glanced over at Katie Elizabeth, and she seemed very concerned.

"Daddy, do you want another beer?" she asked him.

"No, honey," he said holding up his hand. "But see if Fortunato does."

Fortunato held his hand up to say no.

"I'm not going to fight anymore either, Michael. It's not really what I want to do."

"A lot of times a man does what he has to do, not what he wants to," Michael said quietly. "Sometimes he gets drawn into things he'd rather not do. Like I said, you'll have a lot of offers to fight now."

Fortunato looked at Katie Elizabeth, and he was not smiling.

"I hope I have the strength to stay away from it," he said seriously.

More than anything, Katie Elizabeth wanted to tell him at that moment that she knew she could provide him with that strength, but instead she just smiled at him.

"You know, Michael, back in Biella, when a man wants to court a girl, he asks her parents' permission, out of respect," Fortunato said seriously, looking right at Katie Elizabeth.

When she blushed and looked into the living room at her mother, Fortunato looked at Michael.

"Michael, I'd like your permission to visit your daughter."

Katie Elizabeth had a different reaction than Fortunato expected.

"In America a boy asks a girl if she's interested before he approaches her parents," she said.

Fortunato smiled at her.

"There's a lot I have to learn about America," he said. "And in Biella, I never had a girlfriend, so I'm new at this, an' I'm-a doin' the best I can," he smiled.

Katie smiled back at him.

"Of course, I could never date a boy who's always going to be fighting against my father," she said.

Fortunato laughed and held up his hands. "Oh, no," he said. "One time against this guy is plenty enough!"

But Michael was not smiling.

"You know, Fortunato, to my knowledge there's never been an Italian boy who's dated an Irish girl in this town."

Fortunato leaned over the table and smiled at Michael. Talking with his hands, he pointed at himself with both hands as he spoke. "I got knocked out last night. There's a first time for everything," he said.

His good nature disarmed the sternness of Michael Callahan, who smiled first, then started to chuckle, and then started to laugh. When Katie started to laugh too, so did Fortunato, and soon everyone was laughing, with both men holding their sides in pain.

The comedy of the men laughing while their ribs were so sore from the fight made them all laugh harder as they tried to stop to avoid the pain, but couldn't.

Then Maureen walked over to Michael, who had stood up to get into a more comfortable position, and put her arms around him, as though trying to hold his ribs together.

When Katie saw that, she walked over to Fortunato, and he immediately stood up, and reached out to her. When she embraced him, he stopped laughing and put his arms around her. She was the first girl he had ever put his arms around, and suddenly he felt as though he had been the victor.

"Katie Elizabeth will be attending the Yankee-Red Sox game dinner at the Italian Club with me this weekend," Michael said to Fortunato. "If she sits between us, she can prevent the instigators from inciting a rematch."

Fortunato smiled warmly at Katie Elizabeth and spoke to her.

"Since we are in America, may I ask your permission to sit next to you this weekend?"

She squeezed his hand promisingly. "I'd be delighted," she said.

▲　▼　▲

The next day, Katie Elizabeth Callahan opened the door and a delivery boy from the Indian Springs Conservatories handed her a dozen roses. The card said, "I am looking forward to Saturday. Fortunato."

When Michael awoke late in the afternoon and got up for what was the beginning of his day—when the sun went down—the house was full of several friends of Katie Elizabeth's who were whispering and giggling as they admired Katie's flowers.

Michael walked over, read the card, and went into the living room where he sat in his big old reclining chair, his face buried in a newspaper.

At the factory that night, his mind wandered back, as it had done so many times before in his life, to when he first met Maureen Malloy. He thought about the miserable shape he had been in when he met her and about how living with her had altered his life so dramatically, how boxing was the one thing he could not quit that had bothered her so much, and how patiently she had endured all the training sessions he had put himself through and all the wear and tear his fighting had done to his body without ever complaining to him. He thought about holding her at night, and having ten children with her, and about how she had been such a good mother for them.

Always, now, in his quiet times, he thanked God for the miracle she had brought to his life, and for their children, and for her love. And now, as he saw the first signs of the same thing happening with Fortunato Bellino and his daughter, Katie, it made him feel very old.

Making his rounds at the textile mill, he used his solitary time to pray for the blessings of God on all of his children, and this night his thoughts were mainly with Katie Elizabeth.

▲　▼　▲

Throughout history, many traditions are started with one memorable event. The Yankee-Red Sox dinner at the Italian Club has been the occasion of many memorable evenings, but none was more memorable than the first one held on May 22, 1920. Midway between Boston and New York, Indian Springs was a sort of unofficial dividing line for American league loyalty. Most people to the north and east were Red Sox fans and most to the south and west were Yankee fans. Indian Springs was split 50-50.

With indomitable hope, the peacemakers in the crowd of Irish and Italian baseball fans hoped that this night would be a continuation of the new good feelings between the two nationalities struggling to adapt themselves to their new country as barriers broke down and men of many national origins learned to live together as Americans.

The fact that the room was divided by team loyalty and not national origin was a big help in bringing all the individuals in the room together, and the seating at the head table helped as well.

Sugar Desmond acted as master of ceremonies and sat at the middle of the table to Fortunato Bellino's right. On Sugar's right was Katie Callahan, and on her right was her father, Michael. Vittorio Bellino sat on Fortunato's left, and he could not help but notice that all the while he was trying to converse with his brother, Fortunato was fidgety and preoccupied.

The crowd noise was at a very high level, as conversations popped up all over the room, most of them about one of three topics: the just finished Callahan-Bellino fight; the never-ending Yankee-Red Sox rivalry; and the third topic, which charged the air with electricity. One of the most revolting events in sports history had taken place two months previously. Incredibly the Red Sox had sold Babe Ruth, and even more incredibly, the buyers had been the hated Yankees! Red Sox fans felt stunned and betrayed, Yankee fans elated, and arguments over the ramifications were already starting to sweep across New York, New Jersey, and New England.

A few minutes into the dinner, as the Orzo soup was being served, Fortunato changed places with Sugar Desmond and sat next to Katie Elizabeth.

"Thank you for the roses," she smiled.

She looked so beautiful to him that he could not concentrate on anything else that was happening around him.

"Did I send them to a Yankee fan or a Red Sox fan?" he asked her.

"Oh, God, I don't want to be on the wrong team," she blushed. "Which team do you root for?"

Fortunato laughed. "I haven't been here long enough to develop any team loyalties, but it seems to me that whatever port city these guys landed in is the team they started to root for."

"It's a good thing your favorite team has nothing to do with your nationality," she said.

"I know Vittorio is a Yankee fan," Fortunato said.

"My father's always rooted for the Red Sox," Katie said.

"I think you and me should root for the same team," he said.

She smiled. "Then as soon as you pick one, I'll be on your side."

Salad was the next course brought out; ice-cold, crisp lettuce and tomatoes that had been sitting in oil and vinegar, followed by mostaccioli with grated Parmesan cheese, and then chicken with whole potatoes fried in olive oil. Beer and wine flowed freely and as the dinner progressed the crowd noise grew louder.

Fortunato and Katie were oblivious to the events in the hall, however, as they talked and laughed together. They were too preoccupied to notice the insults that had started to fly across the room about this or that player, or this or that event in recent games of the arch-rivals. In awhile, Michael moved over to talk to Vittorio, and as Sugar Desmond was reading over his notes for the evening's program, the brawl started.

Nobody is sure whether it was a Yankee or a Red Sox fan, an Irishman or an Italian who threw the first punch. But in seconds, all the progress that had been made since the Callahan-Bellino fight evaporated and fists started to fly all over the room.

Fortunato saw it as a chance to slip out of the room with Katie Elizabeth, and on their way to the door, he put his arm up and batted down a chair that came flying across the room. With his other arm he directed Katie out the side door, and when they were outside, he kept his arm around her.

With fists and chairs flying inside the banquet hall, Fortunato Bellino stood outside on the porch and realized how good it felt to have his arm around Katie Elizabeth Callahan.

"Do you think you ought to do something about the fight?" she asked him.

"It's not my fight," he said to her.

"Oh, Fortunato, you can stop it in a minute if you want to."

"I've had my last fight," he said to her, their faces getting closer and closer together. "Of course, there's one sure way to end it right now," he whispered to her.

"What way?" she whispered back, enjoying the closeness to the strong young man who held her.

"We walk right into the middle of the floor and tell everybody that we don't want any more black eyes at our wedding next weekend," he said to her softly.

Her eyes suddenly became more beautiful to him than ever before, and the fragrance of her hair intoxicated him. When he saw the seriousness in her eyes and her expression changed to the same kind of stern resoluteness he had seen in her father, he felt stronger and more sure of himself than ever before.

"It would save the jaws and noses of a great many of our children's uncles and cousins if we did," she said.

With those words, a lifetime of confusion and loneliness ended for Fortunato Bellino. On the side porch of the Italian Club in Indian Springs, Connecticut, Fortunato Bellino took Katie Elizabeth Callahan in his arms and kissed her. When they finally broke their embrace, they gazed into each other's eyes with emotions that were exploding.

"Let's not wait a minute longer to tell them," she said.

He opened the door for her and walked with her into the middle of the floor, where one by one several of the bloody faces in the room turned to her.

Building from somewhere deep inside of her was an Irish resoluteness that always seemed to add a spark of fire to her eyes when it came upon her. From the center of the massive brawl she let out with a huge whistle, and then yelled at the top of her lungs. "I'll personally slap the face of the man, Irish or Italian, who throws the next punch."

With Fortunato Bellino by her side, everyone in the room stopped fighting instantly.

"We want you all to look as presentable as you can for the group photographs when Fortunato and I are married next weekend."

A deafening silence spread across the room as every eye in the room focused on Michael Callahan, who was standing at the side of the room with Vittorio Bellino. Slowly, Michael walked toward the center of the room and for a moment, as the two heavyweights eyed one another, there was silence in the room. Then Michael smiled and reached his hand out to Fortunato's, and a thunderous roar filled the room.

Vittorio smiled at Katie and embraced her, and once again everyone in the room was slapping each other on the back and shaking hands.

Sugar Desmond shrugged his shoulders at Vittorio Bellino, and Vittorio lifted his hands as if to say, Oh well.

"Where else in the country can people be fighting one minute and slapping each other on the back the next?" Vittorio said to Sugar.

"That's Indian Springs," Sugar answered.

▲   ▼   ▲

The wedding of Fortunato Bellino and Katie Elizabeth Callahan on Saturday, April 3, 1920, marked the second large Bellino wedding in less than three months. It also marked the opening of a new kind of floodgate in Indian Springs, the uniting of the Irish and Italian communities in a new way that led to countless intermarriages between Irish and Italians in the years to follow.

None of the weddings that followed could provide a more entertaining group photo, however, as every man in the photo had either a black eye, a swollen lip, or a bandage on his face.

That year, 1920, was a year which marked the ushering in of a new era of communication between the two communities and a breaking down of the barriers that had separated the people of all the European nations. By the end of the decade, intermarriages were common, but it all started with the Bellino-Callahan wedding.

That first summer of their marriage, Fortunato and Katie were a handsome couple who got along so well that many other people were encouraged to date outside the circle of national origin.

It was also the year that a baby-boom began, and in early December, Antoinette Bellino met Vittorio coming home from work in the factory where he was a weaver to give him the news that he had long awaited. She was pregnant, and her doctor told her that she could expect the baby to be born in August of 1921.

Vittorio was beside himself with happiness. He bought two boxes of cigars at the Station Newsroom and Coffee Shop, one that said "It's a boy," and one that said "It's a girl," and began passing them out two at a time to be sure he got it right.

Congratulations were enthusiastic for the thirty-four-year-old Vittorio, who was much older than most first-time fathers of that era. For the next nine months, Vittorio and Antoinette did everything right. Antoinette got plenty of rest and stayed in good physical shape, and the couple rearranged their home to make room for the baby.

The happiness they shared that spring of 1921 as Antoinette approached her thirtieth birthday was unmatched in any year they had spent together to date, and it seemed almost too good to be true. Then, on Monday, July 18, 1921, Antoinette's thirtieth birthday, tragedy struck.

She awoke feeling very nauseous and figured that she had gotten over-tired from her birthday celebration on the weekend. By 8:00 A.M. she was feeling very sick, and she began to worry desperately about her baby. In less than an hour she went from worry to panic, and by nine o'clock she was screaming in agony, as something strange and unusual seemed to be happening to her body. Thinking that she was experiencing premature labor, a neighbor woman stayed with her and did her best to help her, but at nine-thirty, when she began to deliver, the umbilical cord wrapped around her baby's neck and strangled him.

No amount of revival efforts could save the baby and when Vittorio was told to rush home, he found her crying wretchedly in her room. The tragedy hit him as hard as it hit her, and the funeral of their first-born son, Clyde, named after Clyde Bradford, his commanding officer in France, was a very sad event.

Vittorio and Antoinette spent the next several years going to daily mass and communion, as they reflected upon their tragedy and prayed for forgiveness of their sins and an answer to the tragedy that had befallen them.

Although they kept on trying for many years, Antoinette was unable to get pregnant again. But Vittorio refused to admit that God's will would not allow them to have children. Vittorio's favorite Bible story became the story of Abraham, and daily for many years the couple prayed for God's blessings in the form of a child. Finally, in the winter of their eighth year of marriage, Antoinette told Vittorio, then forty years old, that she was pregnant again. At age thirty-six, Antoinette was very worried, especially when spring came and the doctor told her she was going to have twins.

The Bellinos spent the next several months doing everything very carefully, and Antoinette began to have nightmares, imagining another tragedy. Incredibly, tragedy struck them again in July, when she was seven months pregnant. Having gotten overtired while carrying her twins, she lost her equilibrium while coming down the stairs from the apartment where Fortunato and Katie Elizabeth lived above them, and in a spell of dizziness brought on by the summer heat, she fell all the way down the stairs.

That night, Monday the 23rd of July 1928, she prematurely delivered twins whose combined birth weight was less than seven pounds. Three days later, the girl, Esea Serafina, died. That left them with a very small baby boy whom they named Aaron Vittorio.

The summer of 1928 found Antoinette constantly hugging and nursing Aaron, whom she guarded with almost fanatical overprotection. That year she fed him constantly and ate voraciously herself, ballooning up to over eighty pounds more than she had weighed before Aaron was born.

On many occasions, Antoinette had the opportunity to leave Aaron with Katie Elizabeth upstairs to go out with Vittorio, but her concerns for Aaron's life left her paralyzed with fear and she refused to leave the neighborhood or to let Aaron out of her sight. Later, when she found out that she could not have any more children, Vittorio and Antoinette realized that all their dreams for their future generations rested with Aaron, and for that reason, he was very sheltered.

Meanwhile Fortunato and Katie Elizabeth had been in no hurry to start a family. They spent the first several years of their married life getting to know each other and socializing in the community, attending parties and social events with regularity, while Vittorio and Antoinette stayed pretty close to home.

It did not take Katie very long after Antoinette had her baby to develop the maternal instinct, however, and in 1929 she and Fortunato decided it was about time for them to have a baby. They moved out of the Brandon Street duplex and bought a small home on the outskirts of town, far enough away from the neighborhoods so that they had no neighbors in sight.

By autumn she was pregnant and not the least bit worried about having her baby at home. In those days it was not uncommon for women to have their babies at home. Her own mother had had ten of them that way, and so in the summer of 1930, while Fortunato was out building roads, she delivered a son by herself in the middle of the day.

That night Fortunato came home and met his son, whom they named Sean Michael, and they were happier than they had ever been.

For the next several weeks, throughout the summer of 1930, Fortunato and Katie lived a very happy life as she cared for the baby at home while he worked on the road all day. With heightened excitement about the prospects of having a large family, Fortunato decided soon afterward to get a night job in the factory, and by autumn Katie was pregnant again.

Fortunato was elated, and the thought that he could be the father of a family the size of Michael Callahan's thrilled both he and Katie. The springtime of 1931 was one of great excitement and happiness for the both of them. They were an ideal couple, good parents, and totally in love, and it seemed as though nothing could get better for them as the year unfolded.

On Sunday, July 12, 1931, the weather was very hot and muggy. Fortunato slept all evening and prepared to start work at 11:00 P.M., after which he would stop home briefly before heading to work on the road on Monday morning. He did not mind working two jobs for his family. Many men did, and he thought Katie was a good month away from the birth of their second child.

At about midnight, that hot and muggy night, Katie Elizabeth Bellino awoke in terrible pain, and lying in her bed eight months into her pregnancy, she knew something was terribly wrong. The whole thing felt so different from the birth of her son, Sean.

Throughout the long, hot July night she sweated and prayed, "Holy Mary, Mother of God, pray for us sinners, now, and at the hour of our death."

Fortunato was in the factory beaming with joy as he alternately weighed the advantages of having a boy or a girl. He smiled as he dreamed of all the wonderful times he would have with his new child, no matter what sex it would be.

At home everything was topsy-turvy as Katie Elizabeth felt the worst pains she had ever felt in her life.

With little Sean asleep in his crib and his mother struggling against her agony in the next room, refusing to cry out, lest she wake her young son, her prayers soon turned desperate as her agony grew worse. With no way to summon any help, she fought her agony alone all through the night, and toward dawn, she lost her battle.

An hour later, when Fortunato arrived home from work, he was dropped to his knees with the shock of his life when he found the wife he loved and his stillborn son both lying dead in their blood-soaked bed. In horror and disbelief, he lay down next to the body of his wife, whom he had loved so much, and found himself quite unable to move for the better part of an hour.

When a knocking came at the front door simultaneously with his son Sean crying from hunger in the next room, he slowly rose up and made his way first to the crib where Sean lay reaching his hand up to his father, and then to the front door. His ashen look immediately wiped the smile off the face of Katie's friend, Margaret O'Hara, who knew that something dreadful must have transpired during the night.

Fortunato stood aside and pointed toward the bedroom where Margaret rushed in and the gasp he heard her mutter felled him backward into the living room chair.

With tears in her eyes, Margaret rushed into the living room and bundled young Sean into her left arm while hugging the crestfallen Fortunato with her right as he stared ahead blankly.

"Are you all right?" she asked him softly.

"Not really," he said, and his lips started to quiver. "Could you just take Sean with you for now while I get myself together?" he whispered.

"Of course," she said. "I'll send John over to be with you."

In a little while, Margaret's husband, John O'Hara, appeared at Fortunato's door, and Fortunato was already halfway through a bottle of whiskey. Fortunato beckoned John to enter, and John said nothing as he walked over and sat down with Fortunato.

"I had a lot of faults. She overlooked them," Fortunato forced himself to say, though his grief hardly allowed him to speak.

Outside, the flashing lights of an ambulance brought Fortunato up out of his chair, and he walked to the door of his bedroom for a last look at his wife and baby. As the ambulance attendants entered the room, John led Fortunato out of it. Outside the front door on the front lawn of his home, John O'Hara watched as Fortunato lost himself to tears.

When he composed himself a short time later, Fortunato reached into his shirt pocket for a pack of cigarettes, and lighting one, he stared blankly off into space.

As the door opened and the stretcher-bearers carried out the bodies of his wife and son, Fortunato started to walk away from his house and into the heat of the morning.

"Fortunato," John O'Hara, said catching up to him. "Why don't you come to our house and sit for awhile."

But Fortunato just held his hand up and kept on walking alone toward town. That evening he showed up at Vittorio's door very drunk and very quiet, and Vittorio ushered him in and put him to bed in the guest room.

For the next three days, Fortunato did not say a word except to insist on a private wake and funeral. After the burials were completed and the people were back at Vittorio's house eating an afternoon meal, Fortunato stunned his brother with the decision he had made.

"I'm going back to Italy," he said evenly.

Vittorio and Antoinette looked at one another with great surprise, and both of them thought the same thing at once. It was Vittorio who spoke first.

"What about Sean? Will you take him with you at such a young age?"

"We'll be all right," Fortunato said shallowly.

Vittorio knew immediately that his brother's judgement had been clouded by the tragedy so fresh and so sudden in his life, and he reached out and touched his brother's arm.

"Fortunato, don't do that," his brother pleaded. "You know very little about the care of a little baby."

"We'll be all right," Fortunato repeated.

"But Sean is so small," Vittorio said. "And he's been so used to his mother. You're apt to run into challenges with him that you're not prepared to handle."

"Like what?" Fortunato protested.

"Like the changing of diapers, for one thing. Have you ever done that before?"

"How hard can that be?"

Vittorio looked at Antoinette, and she saw the concern deep in his eyes.

"Fortunato, the timing is not right. Stay here at least a while longer until Sean is older."

But Fortunato had already made up his mind. The look in his eyes scared Vittorio, who had seen that look many times before. When Fortunato Bellino decided something, it was cast in concrete.

"Fortunato, it's such a long trip," Antoinette said. "Too long to take back and forth across the ocean."

Fortunato looked strangely at Antoinette. "I don't think you understand. Once I go back, I'll never return to *Estati Uniti*. This is Vittorio's country. Not mine."

Suddenly Vittorio felt very sad. "What are you talking about," Vittorio said hurtfully. "You love this country."

"I loved Katie Elizabeth," Fortunato said. "Now that she's gone, there's nothing left for me here."

"Fortunato, all of Sean's people are here," Vittorio said.

"I'm Sean's people!" Fortunato yelled suddenly, slamming his fist on the table.

"And what about his grandparents, Michael and Maureen?"

"Michael and Maureen have ten children!" Fortunato screamed. "I have one. Sean goes with me!"

Fortunato was beginning to get angry now, and Vittorio decided that it would be best not to provoke him. Instead he got up and walked away from the table and out the door, into the afternoon calm. Antoinette looked across the table at her brother-in-law.

"I don't think you realize how much your brother loves you, Fortunato."

Fortunato looked away. "Love has nothing to do with it. I'm going back to Italy."

"Do the O'Haras know yet?" Antoinette asked him calmly.

"No," Fortunato said. "But as nice as they've been to watch Sean for me for the past couple of days, they'll probably be glad to be rid of him."

"Sean has really attached himself to Margaret O'Hara," Antoinette said. "Would you like me to walk with you over to their house while you tell them?"

Fortunato looked at Antoinette with a slight smile. "Just don't try and change my mind," he said.

"I'll get Aaron."

When Fortunato Bellino showed up at John and Margaret O'Hara's door with Antoinette and Aaron Bellino in tow, Sean Bellino reached out his hands to his father, who lifted him up and hugged him, kissing him liberally.

Sean mouthed a loud sound and pointed in the direction of a toy he had been playing with, and Fortunato picked it up and gave it to him.

"If you could watch him for just a day or so more, I'll take him off your hands soon," Fortunato said to John and Margaret. "I'm taking him with me back to Italy."

Margaret O'Hara put her hands to her face and gasped when she heard it. "Oh, Fortunato, why?" she cried.

"Italy is where I belong. And I don't want to hear any arguments from you, I've already gone through that with Vittorio and Antoinette."

John and Margaret looked at Antoinette, but all she could do was shrug. John walked slowly over to Fortunato.

"Of course we'll watch him, Fortunato," John said. "And we hope you'll change your mind."

"I just want to walk with him for a moment out on the lawn," Fortunato said to John O'Hara.

While the Bellinos and the O'Haras looked on, the big man strolled out into the afternoon sunlight, his large feet cushioned by the softness of the green grass. The man looked large and clumsy cradling the small boy reverently between his head and neck. *There is no greater blessing in a man's life,* he thought, as he awkwardly wrapped his arms around his small son, taking exceptional care not to injure the little one with his awkward strength.

"What is to become of us, my boy?" the man whispered prayerfully into his son's ear as he felt the baby's smooth skin next to his own leathery roughness.

Slowly and carefully, the big Italian chose every step, intently concentrating on the protective care he was taking of his boy while their lives bonded together in this rare and extraordinary moment when they had no one left but each other.

The boy was small and he did not comprehend a word of what his father had said, but he felt the leathery toughness of the big man's face and shoulders and arms, and his subconscious mind was programmed with the strength and love with which his father tenderly held him. Later in life, the boy would not remember the day his mother died or the way his father cushioned him so reverently. But this day, the father was acutely aware of the confidence with which the little one's hands wrapped around his neck, and he could not control himself as the tears flowed out of his eyes and down his cheeks onto his little boy's bunting.

That evening, as Fortunato sat at the Italian Club bar drinking wine, John O'Hara sat and talked to Vittorio Bellino.

"Is there nothing we can do to get him to change his mind?" John asked Vittorio. "Margaret has grown so fond of Sean, and we can keep him for as long as it takes for Fortunato to get over Katie's death. Even if Fortunato wants to go to Italy for awhile and leave Sean here with us."

Vittorio shook his head.

"I know Fortunato too well. He's a very proud and stubborn Italian man. And any Italian man like him will fight against governments, churches, men, women, flesh, blood, and principalities to keep his son with him. It is an absolute impossibility to think otherwise."

Sitting there pondering the situation, Vittorio felt pity and sorrow for his younger brother, to whom life had never yielded much of its sweetness except for the exceptional love he had shared with his wife, who was now gone.

"He's confused," Vittorio said to John. "He's just so confused. Maybe he'll change his mind in a day or so."

That night Fortunato sat for a very long time at the Italian Club bar and drank a very large quantity of wine. Several times during the evening the bartenders would ask him if he hadn't had enough, and they busied themselves doing other things so as not to be near him often where he could order more wine. Toward the end of the night, the bartenders decided that he had had enough and told him he was finished, but that angered him, and he walked around behind the bar and picked up a gallon jug which he carried toward the door.

"Hey, you can't do that," one bartender yelled at Fortunato, but Fortunato just glared at him and walked out.

When the bartender followed him outside, Fortunato pushed the smaller man away and the man fell backwards against the building. Fortunato then cracked open the gallon jug and lifted it up to his lips, drinking several large swallows of wine. Wiping his mouth with his sleeve, he puzzled the bartender with the last words he spoke.

"You're not gonna take-a my son," he said as he turned and headed down the road on foot.

He was not halfway home when he finished the gallon jug. Sweating profusely in the night air, he walked up the street toward the O'Hara residence and when he tossed the jug aside, the breaking glass attracted a local borough police officer on his nightly rounds.

"You there!" the officer yelled, and when Fortunato saw the uniform, he started to run. "Stop!" the officer shouted, but Fortunato just barreled up the hill toward the O'Hara house, and at one-thirty in the morning, John O'Hara heard a loud thud on the front step.

"What was that?" Margaret asked, sitting up in bed with a start.

John slipped into his pants and went to the front door, peeking through the window outside. There, at the bottom of the steps, was the motionless figure of a man. John opened the door and went outside, where he met the police officer, and the two men found Fortunato lying in a pool of blood, a deep gash across the back of his head.

Bending over him, the police officer felt for his pulse, but there was none. Fortunato Bellino was dead.

"What the hell happened?" John O'Hara asked incredulously.

"I heard some glass break and I yelled at him to stop, but he started to run, so I chased him. Just before he got to your house, he turned and yelled at me, 'You'll never take my son!' Then he bounded up the stairs, reached for the doorknob, missed it, and fell backwards, cracking his skull on the steps."

The funeral was held three days later, and two weeks after that, while John and Margaret O'Hara were awaiting word on their attempts to adopt him, Sean Bellino turned one year old.

⋀ ⋁ ⋀

Part 3

The Promised Land

Over the course of the next several years, the barriers that had started to crack between the various nationalities broke completely down as immigrant families from several European countries smoothly blended into one another, and the face of the nation changed. America had become a great melting pot, with so many intermarriages, and so much diverse cross-breeding that people were thinking less and less in terms of their mother countries and more and more in terms of being American.

Throughout the decade of the twenties, the quaint New England town of Indian Springs, Connecticut, continued to be one of the nicest towns in America to live in. One of the largest towns in the state in area, it remained fairly constant in its population, with fewer than ten thousand close-knit people playing out their lives in friendship and harmony.

With little to do during the Depression years except work when you could and help one another get by, the people found a good deal of leisure time to recreate in the local parks and ball fields, and rivalries started to develop by streets, not national origin. Baseball, football, and hockey leagues were formed to ensure year-round competition. Those who were not team-oriented continued to hunt the bountiful game in the wide expanses of forest that still made up the widest area covered by the town or fish the many lakes left centuries before by the glaciers.

Skating parties were held in the winter months, and Christmas was a special time in Indian Springs, as all the local merchants decorated the stores in the Main Street area with elaborate displays of lights, decorations, and nativity scenes for the festive season.

Since few people could afford automobiles during those times, most people would walk to one another's Christmas parties, and caroling became an annual tradition that everyone joined in on. Two other days that became very important to local people were Memorial Day and July Fourth, when elaborate displays of fireworks, parades, and cemetery memorial services were traditional events as the town and the nation honored its war dead.

Patriotism was not in short supply in Indian Springs, a town that was intensely proud of its contribution to all of America's war efforts. At each of the town's Memorial Day and Fourth of July parades, honor guards of the various branches of the service donned old uniforms and marched through Main Street to the cemeteries, where war dead were saluted with volleys of gunfire as residents stood together respectfully, their hands over their hearts, their hats in their hands, honoring the men who had given their lives for America.

Gold Star Mothers, women who had lost sons in the nation's wars, were honored in elaborate fashion, riding through town in automobiles accompanied by honor guards of the various branches of the service. They also sat in the front row at the cemetery services that honored their sons.

As the 1930s unfolded, the traditions grew stronger, the patriotism deeper, and the Democratic Party more powerful. The 1930s also marked the solidification of Sugar Desmond's hold on policy-making decisions with the Democratic Party, which had become the party of vastly superior numbers in town, with better than 90 percent of all the immigrants and mill workers registered as Democrats. Despite the rising star of his political foothold on state politics, Sugar Desmond was a man who was aware of his own limitations, and early on he knew that in order to be really effective, he would have to realize that the role of "king-maker" was more apt to befall him than the role of king, since his name was Desmond, from Ireland, not Arnetti, from Italy.

Understanding the superiority of numbers, which the Italian-Americans still enjoyed in Indian Springs, and the solid unification they had always brought to local politics, Sugar Desmond decided that the best hopes he had for political recognition was in backing the right Italian-American, not trying to beat him.

Very early in the 1930s, the right Italian-American emerged. His name was Pop Arnetti, named "Pop" by Sugar Desmond because, as Sugar once observed, he seemed to pop up wherever the action was in any political event anywhere in town. Early on, his broad smile and easy way with people got him noticed, and he made it a practice to befriend everyone from both political parties and all national origins throughout the town. Pop Arnetti was a born politician.

The knack he had for befriending all types of people and taking a personal interest in each of them was one thing he learned early in his career. A great listener, he heard all sides of every story and mediated more disputes throughout the town than anyone else since Vittorio Bellino had done when the Italians had first come to town.

Vittorio picked him out very early as the man to watch and told Sugar Desmond that he would be the man to latch onto if he wanted to pick a winner. Vittorio knew this because Pop Arnetti had learned very early in life the absolute necessity of respecting all people, especially those older than you, to whom respect meant the most.

When difficult political decisions loomed in any local controversy, Pop Arnetti made it a point to visit all people on both sides of the political issue to try and understand the issue well before attempting to mediate it fairly or sway the opinions of the people he believed were on the wrong side. He was smart enough to use diplomacy, smarter still to recognize when diplomacy would not work, and willing to let political fights happen when no compromise could be reached. He did so while working to maintain a personal friendship with people, even when he was on the opposite side of an issue.

In this way, he became very popular, and by 1938, when he was only thirty years old, he was already recognized as a strong political leader in the town. Of course, there were those who he could never please, as there are with any strong political figure, but Pop Arnetti was accepted and recognized as a leader with moxie, respected by friend and foe alike, and both Vittorio Bellino and Sugar Desmond knew that he was coming into his own as the thirties wound down.

In 1938, a major opportunity arose to gain a solid foothold on the leadership of local affairs when one of the most difficult controversies to emerge in several years started to unfold.

At the Italian Club, long a haven from prejudice and ridicule for the Italian-Americans of town, members were wrestling with the issue of opening the charter to membership from outside the Italian community, and a difficult and complex argument developed.

The older Italians were largely in favor of keeping the charter closed. Many feared that opening the charter would make the club nothing more than just another bar, where Italians would come less and less as outsiders came more and more. Their memory went back to the days when the Italians were looked down upon, untrusted, saddled with the names "guinea," or "wop," and when the stings and stabs of prejudice were felt daily as they strived to earn their place of equality and respect in town. For those older Italians, the club had been a place they had naturally gravitated to on weekends to play music in the band, to dance, drink, party, and compete in the games of bocce, horseshoes, and cards. At the club everyone was equal because everyone was Italian, and no guinea jokes or disrespectful slurs were heard. The older members wanted to keep it that way.

The younger members, on the other hand, many of them second and third generation Italian-Americans, wanted to open the charter so that friends from other national origins could join. Some men wanted to include only foreign immigrants and their families, or sons of half-Italians. Others wanted to exclude candidates whose families could be shown to have been prejudiced against Italians, and still others were campaigning for a kind of blackball system of voting in which any member of the board of directors who wanted to could veto any candidate for membership by secretly dropping a black ball in the voting basket when a candidate's name came up for consideration as a member.

Some men wanted an interview selection process, with a litmus test of anti-Italian prejudice. All in all, the debate boiled down to one overriding and complicated issue: Should the charter be opened or not?

As time went by, the argument grew more and more chaotic, to the point where it almost came to blows. Finally one day in the fall of 1938, Pop Arnetti decided that the best way to reach any kind of agreement at all was to add some semblance of order to the discussions. He asked the board of directors to elect him moderator of the monthly meeting, during which time he would give every person who wanted to say anything at all about the issue ample time to be heard, with respect given to all viewpoints and no time limit on any speaker.

Everyone on the board agreed to let Pop run the meeting, and no one knew that he was personally in favor of opening the charter, although those who suspected it were not offended because of his reputation for fairness and his pledge to let all viewpoints be heard.

The night before the meeting, which was held on Sunday afternoon, September 4, Pop Arnetti knocked on Vittorio Bellino's door. When Vittorio opened it, Pop was smiling broadly with his hand extended. Vittorio shook his hand and invited him in.

"Please join us, we're just about to sit down and eat," Vittorio said.

"Why do you think I came at this time?" Pop smiled. "I'm no fool, you know. I know Antoinette's the best cook in America."

If Pop wasn't right, he was close. Antoinette had spent long hours preparing homemade tortellini soup, to be followed by fresh insalata, veal cutlet milano, and homemade cheese ravioli. Of course the bagna caoda was available for snacking on before the antipasto was presented, and the wine from the coolness of the wine cellar was always available. Pop still remembered the day the grapes had been brought in, a cellar full of crates, to be mushed and blended into the finest homemade wine and grappa in the Connecticut valley.

All the neighbors had brought some in to be drawn off in equal amounts to what they had brought in. Pop had been there at Vittorio's home the day they started the process. Fifty-gallon barrels with open tops were filled half full with water. The grapes were pressed and then added to the barrels with fifty pounds of sugar in each barrel. This mixture was covered and left sitting for thirty days. Every day Vittorio and Antoinette would go down into the wine cellar and mix the barrels, and as the grapes came to the top, they were pressed down again to the bottom of the barrel.

On the thirtieth day, the stills were set up. Large copper tubs with covers that fit tight were set atop of stoves. Out of the tops of the covers came spouts with connections to attach copper coils in thirty-gallon zinc tubs. These zinc tubs had cold water in them surrounding the coils, and once the copper tubs were heated on the stoves, the vapors went through the copper coils. When the vapors hit the cold water, it turned them back into liquid which dripped out of spouts into the jugs that caught it, as "grappa."

This day, Pop decided to stay away from the grappa, electing instead to drink the fresh cold water from the jugs Vittorio carried up the hill himself every morning. It was drawn from the mineral springs behind the public library, the same mineral springs water for which the town had always been famous.

Antoinette's bread was warm and fresh, baked earlier that day and warmed over the gas stove before being buttered with a light garlic butter. Dinner at the Bellino residence was an event which was savored and which lasted far into every evening, a fact that could easily be seen by the waist size of both Vittorio and Antoinette Bellino, as well as their nine-year-old son, Aaron.

"Vittorio," Pop said seriously, "things are getting ugly at the club. You may be the only person who can cool things down."

Vittorio was aware of the influence he carried and not at all egotistical about it.

"Tomorrow is a very important day in club history," Pop said, chewing on some crisp celery dipped in the bagna caoda. "I know you don't spend too much time there anymore, but I also know you've always done everything in your power to bring people together in this town. I want you to come and speak to the members at the general meeting on the opening of the charter tomorrow."

"It'sa not gonna be easy," Vittorio said to Pop. "Feelings run very strong on both sides."

"I know. But the people will listen to you. I figure if we give everybody on both sides of the issue enough time to yell, then you can come in and tie it all together before we ask for a vote."

Vittorio was surprised.

"You're gonna ask for a vote tomorrow?"

"Yes."

"I thought it was just going to be informational, to get the feelings on the floor."

"That's what everybody thinks, but I want to settle it once and for all tomorrow. Hard feelings are hurting a lot of people, and we have to get it done and over with before a lot of friendships are lost."

"Whatta you wanna from me?" Vittorio asked.

"After everyone else speaks, I want to call you to the front of the room. You're one of the only members who speaks fluently in both English and Italian. My idea is this. You speak first to the young people in English. You tell them about the way it was when you and the first group of Italians got here in the early 1900s. Tell them about the prejudices you faced, the way people mistrusted you when you all spoke to each other in Italian in the factories, the way you founded the club and the co-op, and the way you unionized the factories. Tell them about the way you joined both political parties and put candidates up who were Italian to run against each other so an Italian would be sure to win, and talk seriously to them about the kind of sacred reverence the old-timers view the club with.

"Lay it on thick, because there will be several guests there from other nationalities, that I want to understand the feelings these old Italians have. The old Italians don't want the charter opened because they fear the younger guys and the guys from other nationalities won't appreciate what you early guys had to go through.

"Make sure they know the hurt you guys had to endure as you struggled for equal acceptance and the importance the club had as a haven from the prejudices you felt."

Vittorio listened intently, deeply impressed with the understanding this young Italian-American possessed.

"Then, when you've spoken your peace to the young guys, turn to the old guys, the Italians, the guys you came to town with way back when. Speak to them in Italian. Remind them of the dreams you all shared of becoming Americans, of the sacrifices of Annibole Rinaldi, Angelo Carocari, Enrico Tonoli, Attilio Panciera, and Serafino Strazza."

Vittorio put his handkerchief to his eyes as Pop Arnetti recited the names, just revered names to Pop and all the Italians who had come to town later, but close friends of Vittorio's, whom he had fought next to, and loved, in World War I.

"Tell the old guys that it's up to them to make the magnanimous gesture again, to extend their arms in welcome to the young men of other nationalities so that equal membership in the Italian Club can be theirs because all of you are now Americans, born Italians, and living as Americans by choice.

"After you're through speaking, I'll call for a vote immediately afterward. Vittorio, you're the one and only person who can do this. You're the only person I know who has the universal respect of everyone in town."

Vittorio looked across the table at the young politician and lifted a celery stick to his mouth.

"You ought to run for president," Vittorio told Pop, pointing at him with his celery stick, before dipping it into the bagna caoda.

Pop laughed. "Not president. Not yet. Maybe selectman someday down the road."

"Make it soon," Vittorio said. "I only wish you'd have been a Republican."

Again Pop Arnetti laughed. "Vittorio, I want to be elected someday. Republicans are going to have a tough time in this town."

"Going to?" the old Republican laughed. "It's a good thing I never wanted to make politics a career in this town," Vittorio quipped.

"So you'll speak tomorrow?" Pop asked, with his hand on Vittorio's arm.

"Okay," Vittorio agreed. "I only hope I don't offend any of my old friends."

"You're incapable of offending people, Vittorio. I wish I had your gift."

"But I don't want to be there for the fighting. I don't like-a fighting. I'll come in at the end."

▲   ▼   ▲

The next day, the monthly meeting of the Italian Club was as loud and explosive a barn-burner as any the Italians had ever had. Meetings in Indian Springs have always been known for that. Pop Arnetti, with the smoothness of an aged politician, conducted the meeting just as he had planned it, and just when everyone had had his opportunity to speak, all eyes in the room drifted to the door that swung open at the end of the bar. Vittorio Bellino stood as broad and barrel-chested as he was short and stately. He was holding the hand of his nine-year-old son, Aaron, and when the door closed behind them, they walked slowly down the three steps into the hall and directly to the head table where Vittorio stood looking over the entire crowd with the stern confidence that had always been his trademark.

"I've purposely asked Vittorio to speak to us last," Pop Arnetti said to the quieted crowd. "As you all know, he is one of the original founders of this club and the Italian Alliance Clubs of North America. Nobody in this room has done more for the Italians in this town than Vittorio. We all know that. I spoke with him at his home last night, that's why I couldn't eat too much today, because Antoinette cooked for me last night."

Everyone laughed when Pop Arnetti said that.

"But I believe that Vittorio has some important points to make, and I know everyone here respects his opinion."

Pop Arnetti sat down, and before Vittorio Bellino began to speak, a contingent of older Italians started to clap. Seeing the respect with which the older men greeted Vittorio Bellino, all the younger men joined in the applause as well, and when the young men started to clap, the older men stood. One by one, the older men stood, and soon everyone in the room of over two hundred people was on his feet in a prolonged applause for Vittorio Bellino.

"*Rispetto,*" one father explained, whispering to his son.

Throughout it all, Vittorio never lost his dignity or let the applause go to his head. He was as humble a man as he was sure of himself, and he had earned the respect of the men of Indian Springs. When the applause died down, Vittorio smiled and sat down on a chair that was offered to him by a young man in the front row.

Speaking quietly in measured words, Vittorio was the first person to speak all day who did not have to raise his voice. His words carried enough weight to be heard by everyone, who remained silent as he spoke.

Pop Arnetti was the only other person in the room who knew what Vittorio was about to say, but even he was impressed by Vittorio's command of every ear and by his remarkably effective delivery. Just as they had planned, Vittorio spoke first to the younger men and then to the older ones. He spoke to the younger men as equals, not patronizingly or authoritatively, but calmly and reasonably.

To the older men, and the men on the side of keeping the charter closed, he spoke affectionately and respectfully.

In the end, he had pulled it off perfectly, and when he was finished talking, his last words before leaving the room were these, "You boy's-a do whatta you want. But our descendants are going to be Americans of mixed blood, not all Italians. And I, for one, do not want any of my descendants to be excluded from a club that has given me so much-a pleasure. So my vote is to open the charter."

As he walked slowly and painfully toward the door, for his war wounds were continuing to deteriorate his backbone, once again every person in attendance at the meeting rose and applauded, and immediately after the door closed behind Vittorio and Aaron, Pop Arnetti stood and smiled at the roomful of people.

"I say we put it to a vote," Columbo Rinaldi, son of WWI hero Annibole Rinaldi, yelled out. Dozens of voices were heard seconding the motion, and as Pop Arnetti banged the gavel to bring the meeting to order, some semblance of order entered the room.

"The motion has been made, and seconded, to bring the opening of the charter to a vote. Is there any discussion?"

"We been discussin' all day!" Zeb Ricci yelled. "Vote!"

"Hearing none, all in favor of the motion say 'Aye.'"

A loud chorus of "Aye's" filled the room.

"All opposed say 'Nay.'"

Remarkably, not one nay was heard. Not one.

Pop smiled as he called on Tubby Bocchino for a motion.

"If it's okay with everybody else, I'd like to ask my friend Gazzo Francini to present the motion," Tubby Bocchino said, pointing to the huge man at the head of one of the tables of older men.

Everyone knew that one of the most adamantly opposed members to opening the charter in the room was Gazzo Francini. Everyone also knew the respect Gazzo had always had for Vittorio Bellino.

Flattered to have been chosen to present the motion, despite his well-known opposition to the opening of the charter, Gazzo Francini arose. At 6' 5" tall, 385 pounds, Gazzo was the largest man in the room and the town.

"I make a motion we do what Vittorio said," Gazzo said, waving his hand and sitting down.

"You can't say it that way," 5' 1", 100 pound Livio Biardi barked. "You gotta say it right."

"You say it then," Gazzo bellowed, standing up and pointing into the face of the short, bulldog-faced Livio.

The smaller man stood next to Gazzo and, amid several laughs, presented the proper motion.

"I move we vote to open the charter, to allow membership to all persons regardless of national origin," he said oratorically.

"All men!" Gazzo again stood and pointed at Livio.

"All men!" Livio quickly corrected himself.

"Repeat the motion!" Becko Zamichiei yelled.

"I move we vote to open the charter to allow membership to all men, regardless of national origin," Livio Biardi said.

"That's better," Gazzo Francini bellowed as he stood pointing at Livio Biardi.

"Do I hear a second?" Pop Arnetti asked from the front of the room.

Again dozens of people yelled out their seconds to the motion on the floor.

"Write down that I'm the one who seconded the motion," Primo Ceppetelli whispered to the recording secretary, Silvio Beffa-Negrini. "This is gonna be an historic meeting, and I want my great-grandchildren to see my name in the minutes."

"Write my name too," Chi-Chi Sfreddo said, pointing down at the minutes.

Silvio Beffa-Negrini waved his hands around and leaned over to whisper to Chi-Chi Sfreddo. "I don't know if you can write two names down as seconding a motion," he protested.

"'Course you can," Chi-Chi barked disdainfully. "Whatta ya think!"

Silvio waved his hands and shook his head back and forth in disagreement, but he wrote it down in the minutes anyway, "At 1:45 P.M. on Sept 4, 1938, a motion was made by Livio Biardi, with help from Gazzo Francini, and seconded by Primo Ceppetelli and Chi-Chi Sfreddo, to open the charter to all men regardless of national origin."

"All those in favor say 'Aye.'"

"Aye," a loud chorus of voices rang out.

"All those opposed say 'Nay.'"

The scattered few "Nays" were drowned out by applause as Pop Arnetti banged the gavel and drummed in a new era in Indian Springs history. No one knew at the time the way the world would change less than four years later when the winds of war blew across the globe, or the impact the small local meeting would have on all the Italian Alliance Clubs of Eastern North America.

But it was Vittorio Bellino's suggestion and the letter he drafted to President Roosevelt on behalf of the 2,500 Italian-Americans who voted to drop "Italian" from the title of their alliance as a gesture of loyalty to

President Roosevelt and the United States of America, that answered for many other Americans the question of who the Italian-Americans were loyal to.

Their convention, called in December of 1941 after the Japanese bombed Pearl Harbor, was a necessary reaction to Italy's involvement in the war, through Benito Mussolini's loyalty to Adolph Hitler and the Rome-Berlin Axis.

The letter, drafted by Vittorio Bellino, was the subject of front page coverage in the *Hartford Courant* on December 18, 1941, and it mirrored Italian-American disgust with Mussolini and the Italian government's alliance with Germany and Japan. Vittorio's sentiments to President Roosevelt were a "Pledge of Allegiance" to America from former Italians who wanted the world to know that they were now Americans.

Unlike the Japanese-Americans on the west coast who were forced to endure embarrassing and insulting internment, the Italian-Americans on the east coast, largely due to the influence of men like Vittorio Bellino, had satisfied the doubts of powerful men in the Roosevelt administration, further advancing their own Americanization and ingratiating them with other Americans with whom they lived in their own communities.

It was one more evidence of Vittorio's commitment to making the country he would pass on to his future generations the finest place on the globe in which to live.

▲　▼　▲

It was difficult to match the quality of life in Indian Springs, Connecticut, in the late 1930s and early 1940s anywhere in the United States of America. The good feelings that existed among all the townspeople were evident in many ways, not the least of which was the fact that nobody anywhere ever locked his house. It was not necessary, because theft was unheard of in the hard-working mill town, where people of all backgrounds universally respected one another's persons and property.

Little League baseball and midget basketball and football leagues were formed as fathers throughout the town donated whatever time they had for the mutual benefit of all the children. School teachers and the education system were held in the highest regard, both in the public school system and at Saint Patrick's parochial school.

Every neighborhood had its share of chicken coops and rabbit cages, and most families had vegetable gardens and fruit trees. Dandelions, mushrooms, and wild berries of all sort were plentiful, and on any given afternoon in the warm seasons, small groups of women wearing handmade shawls and carrying homemade wicker baskets would congregate together for walks in the woods to gather mushrooms, berries, and greens, as their men hunted the woods for wild game, primarily rabbits and squirrels.

In the Italian neighborhoods, polenta conscia was everybody's favorite meal, and most pots were cooked with recipes written by Antoinette Bellino. A masterful cook, she spent long hours every day cooking for Vittorio and Aaron Bellino, and anyone else who happened by. And happen by they would, often and regularly, to share in some of Antoinette's incredible cooking and free recipes.

By now both Vittorio and Antoinette weighed well over two hundred pounds, a fact Vittorio accepted as unavoidable whenever he heard the inevitable compliment which he knew to be true, that Antoinette was the best cook in America.

Her cooking would start each morning after she got home from daily mass, a ritual she had enjoyed along with hundreds of other local people who lived in the neighborhood of St. Patrick's Church. The lion's share of worshippers at daily mass was from the Irish community, as had always been the case, and every pastor was, of course, of Irish descent, although the nuns that taught at St. Patrick's were from many different backgrounds.

Probably no group of people in town was treated with more reverence and respect than the Sisters of Mercy, dedicated servants of the Lord Jesus and of Holy Mother Church, who had taught hundreds of local people throughout the years in grades one through eight at the parish school.

Dedicated women committed to their vows of poverty, chastity, and obedience, the Sisters of Mercy went wherever they were sent to do the will of God, but the word was out within their order that the choicest of all assignments was St. Patrick's Parish in Indian Springs, Connecticut. Because of the closeness of the townspeople, the respect with which they were treated, and the reverent atmosphere of St. Patrick's parish, it was the best of many good assignments. Each year when assignments were made, nuns at St. Patrick's would hold their breath and pray that they would be able to stay another year, and nuns at other parishes would hope to be assigned there. Transfers came often, as the needs of each parish changed, and rarely would one sister stay in the same parish for over five years.

One exception to that rule began in 1938 when the perfect nun for St. Patrick's School presented herself to Father O'Neill to assume teaching duties at the school. Never had the parish been more blessed than the day this extraordinary young woman appeared at the rectory to meet her new pastor. No one knew the impact she was destined to bring to the town the first day she arrived in the summer of 1938.

This young nun was destined for a long-standing assignment as Mother Superior and her popularity as a teaching nun was enhanced with each class she would graduate.

As a young girl growing up in Worcester, Massachusetts, she had decided very early in life to serve her Lord as a teaching nun. The youngest of twelve children of William and Kathleen O'Roarke, Alba Rose had received her vocation as a result of a life of love and affection from her devout parents, with whom she attended daily mass every single day of her life.

Though many of her older brothers and sisters would frequently over-sleep and miss daily mass, Alba O'Roarke never did. Every day she would make her rounds and try to arouse as many of her siblings as she could, and one day Stephanie O'Roarke turned her head and buried it into her pillow, saying to her sister, Karen, "Here comes Sister Mary Alba." The girls gig-gled and the nickname caught on, and though her sisters thought the nick-name would anger her, all it did was flatter her. When Alba announced one evening at grace before the meal that she was going to become a nun, the entire table except her father and mother laughed.

William O'Roarke quickly silenced his children with a cold stare and a snap of his fingers and lifted his youngest daughter's spirits with a vow he made to her on the spot.

"Alba, if I have to work a hundred hours a week and cut off the allowances of each of your brothers and sisters to pay for your schooling in the convent, I'll do it. You have made your mother and I very happy today by being the first of our children to receive a vocation. It is a gift from God Almighty, and He has blessed our whole family by choosing you."

After he spoke with such sincerity, each of Alba's brothers and sisters lined up to congratulate Alba and she felt very special and committed to making them proud. It was a commitment she would honor completely.

For the next several years, she grew in knowledge and grace, and her entire family attended her ordination with pride and thanksgiving, feeling blessed that one of their own should have been so chosen. On the happy day of her ordination, she willingly accepted the sacredness of her life's commitment to poverty, chastity, and obedience, and her personal, special request to the Lord her God, was that He would bless her with a special role in the great tapestry of His divine plan that would enable her to prepare many people in diverse ways for a life of greater service to their God.

The name she selected did not surprise anyone.

Sister Rose Alba was a nun's nun, absolutely and totally committed to the Lord Jesus and his Blessed Mother, Mary, but so in love with life and people and so effervescent in her mannerisms, that she drew many others to vocations of their own with her smiles and acts of kindness and love.

Immediately after pledging her vows, she was singled out by her superi-ors for advanced education, and while she had been anxious to begin teach-ing, she spent the next six years furthering her education in post-graduate schools where she received her master's degree and her doctorate.

One of the happiest days in her life came when she finally received her first teaching assignment, at age twenty-eight, after what had seemed to her like a century of preparation and schooling. Her only reservations were due to the fact that she was sent by God's will away from the people she loved to a place she had never been before called Indian Springs, Connecticut.

Little did she know at the time, but St. Patrick's Parish and the Indian Springs convent would become her home for over thirty years and an assignment she would deeply love.

Her superiors in the order knew very early that she was a sister who had been blessed by a special talent with young people. The assignment of eighth grade teacher was one that was made with the utmost of care in any parish because the eighth grade nun was the last teacher each of the children would have before being thrust into the Godlessness of the public high school system.

It did not surprise anyone that Sister Rose Alba's first assignment cast her in the role of eighth grade teacher, a role she accepted with prayer and dedication. Possibly the best scorecard on Sister Rose Alba's abilities as a teacher was the attendance record of her students. Nobody wanted to miss even a single day of school in her class.

With strict discipline that provided an atmosphere for learning, she tolerated no breach of her simple but effective rules. And she rarely got one. When she did, the student was quickly disciplined first with a curt verbal warning, and then, if necessary, an even quicker dose of corporal punishment with a whack across the knuckles with her wooden ruler. She rarely had to use this method, but when she did, she invariably got the desired results—strict attention and total compliance with the rules.

The rules were simple to understand and obey: All children sitting upright in their chairs, eyes forward, hands clasped together on top of the desk, with the fingers intertwined, feet flat on the floor. No speaking unless spoken to. Right hand raised when offering an answer to a question. When called upon to give an answer, stand up next to your desk. Give your answer completely and clearly, saying "Sister" before and after your answer. Then sit down quietly.

Students who breached any of the rules automatically missed the next recess, where they were spoken to personally by Sister Rose Alba. She would reinforce the absolute necessity for good behavior in order for the learning process to be enhanced and personal self-discipline in order to be more effective in one's chosen role later in life. Repeated disciplinary problems would result in expulsion from school and reassignment to the public school system, a step that was rarely reached in Sister Rose Alba's tenure at St. Patrick's.

Each lesson was well planned and informative, and there was such a strong emphasis on total class understanding that each student pulled together with Sister to ensure that each student understood every lesson to the fullest of his or her comprehension and retention.

Math was the first subject of every day, followed by English grammar. Reading was third, followed by a fifteen minute recess, outside on nice days and inside with classroom games during inclement weather. After recess came the best part of every day for the students of Sister Rose Alba.

Though she went to great length to make each of her subjects exciting and fun to learn, she excelled in one particular subject matter, which, because of her enthusiasm and melodrama, kept each of her students spellbound with each day's story. The subject was religion, and every day was a different episode from the Old Testament or the life of the Savior, Jesus Christ. Her specialty was the modern application of the lessons from the life of Christ.

No student could sit under Sister Rose Alba's teaching for one full school year and not be thoroughly acquainted with the importance of the personal application in one's own life of the many lessons of Christ's teaching.

Because of the sincerity of her love for the Lord Jesus, her devotion to His teachings, and her commitment to spreading His word, religion became the favorite subject of many of her students. Practicing His teachings in their daily lives became the primary goal of many of her students.

Her vows of poverty, chastity, and obedience she took seriously, and her prayer life was full and faithful; consequently her words were listened to with great credence and she herself was treated with great respect.

By the year 1943, Sister Rose Alba had assumed the duel roles of eighth grade teacher and mother superior of the Indian Springs convent. With repeated high praise by each succeeding St. Patrick's Parish pastor, Sister Rose Alba was continually requested for re-assignment, and every seventh grade student throughout the years was told by parents, teachers, older siblings, and friends to pray that their class would not be the first one to have a different teacher upon the re-assignment of the beloved nun.

Late in March of 1943, a tragic event took place in the life of one of Sister Rose Alba's eighth grade students. For some unexplained reason, Sean O'Hara woke up about an hour earlier than usual that fateful day in March. Not wanting to awaken the parents who had adopted him upon the death of his real parents, Fortunato and Katie Elizabeth Bellino, twelve years previously, Sean dressed quietly, and took the lunch that Margaret O'Hara had made for him the night before, closing the door quietly and leaving for school early.

His little dog, Spotty, upon hearing him leave, came running out after him through the house and out into the yard, whereupon Sean directed him to return to the house. Obediently the dog made his way back, jumping through the hole the O'Haras had cut for him behind the kitchen stove where an old deerskin had been hung to keep out the cold.

When Spotty jumped through the trap door, his long nails caused him to slip across the hardwood floor and his momentum careened him into a chair which hit the leg of the table, turning over the kerosene lamp the O'Haras kept burning on the table as a night lamp.

The lamp fell and flames shot across the tablecloth and spread to the curtains in the kitchen. Before the O'Haras awoke, the house was totally engulfed in flames and Margaret O'Hara was awakened by the crackling sound of the fire burning through the walls in her bedroom.

With a loud scream, she leaped out of bed and ran toward the door of her bedroom and down the burning hall which led to Sean's room. John O'Hara was up in no time, but was quickly overcome by smoke and so disoriented that he ran face first into the doorjamb as he tried to follow his wife and fell backward onto the floor, choking and gasping in the heavy smoke.

Neighbors never heard Margaret's screams and before anyone else knew about it, the entire house was ablaze. By the time the first people got there, the old house was burned almost to the ground and the bodies of John and Margaret O'Hara were burned beyond recognition. Spotty, the dog, also died.

During recess, when word reached Saint Patrick's School that the fire had been at the O'Hara residence, Sean bolted out of the schoolyard and ran toward his house, straining against every part of his body which begged him to stop, and when he caught his first sight of the burned out ruins of his home, he stopped, suddenly too nauseous to run any more.

Still he walked as fast as his endurance allowed him and when his uncle, Vittorio Bellino, saw him coming, he intercepted the boy and threw his arms around him.

"Thank God, you're alive," Vittorio said, hugging the boy who was straining against his uncle's strength to get closer to the house.

"My folks?" he yelled frantically at his uncle.

"Sean, they never had a chance!" Vittorio said mournfully, holding the boy's shoulder and looking him square in the eyes.

"NO-O-O-O-O!" Sean yelled, pushing his rugged uncle aside and running toward the house.

Two burly firemen intercepted the boy before he could plunge into the burning shell of a building and roughly pulled him away for his own safety.

"Sean!" Vittorio yelled. "Stop!"

The strength of his uncle's command froze Sean O'Hara in his tracks, and unable to stand, he dropped to his knees and started crying out, "NO! NO! NO! NO! NO-O-O-O-O-O-O!" at the top of his lungs.

Firemen and onlookers watched in pity as he screamed his grief into the empty spring morning. Vittorio Bellino knelt beside his nephew, and soon Sean O'Hara stood and composed himself and just stared at the smoldering remains of his home. For the better part of a half hour, he said nothing, with Vittorio standing by his side, his arm around Sean's shoulder.

At age thirteen, Sean O'Hara had already lost four parents in tragic accidents. After what seemed like an eternity, during which time all kinds of jumbled thoughts raced through his mind, Sean O'Hara turned to Vittorio Bellino.

"We could make a room out of your old chicken coop, and I'd try not to be any trouble for you," Sean said sadly.

Vittorio's eyes filled up with tears as he threw a big bear hug onto his brother's son.

"Absolutely not," Vittorio replied. "You'll move in with us. Aaron will be happy to have a roommate."

Sean attempted a smile, but it came out as a frown as he buried his head into his uncle's shoulder.

By nightfall, Vittorio and Aaron had moved in a brand new bed and rearranged Aaron's room, and Sean O'Hara had a new home.

When Sister Rose Alba heard of the tragedy, she took special care to converse with Sean at every recess, and she made sure Sean knew that Jesus Christ had spent his entire life having never seen his real Father and every year after age twelve without his foster father, Joseph, whom God had called home early in Jesus' life.

Sean smiled at Sister Rose Alba out of respect. He wanted to say to her, "Yeah, but Jesus was stronger than me," but he said nothing, realizing that her heart was in the right place.

Sean was an easy boy for Sister Rose Alba to talk to because he listened well and he was most respectful, but toward the end of the school year she realized that his mind was often thousands of miles away and his heart was just not into his schoolwork any more.

All that summer, Aaron Bellino and Sean O'Hara were inseparable, hunting and fishing together and playing baseball in the park as well as many of the local games, like fox in the woods, bocce, and duck on the rock.

At supper time, Antoinette made great portions for her men, Vittorio, Aaron, and Sean.

When their freshman year at Indian Springs High School started, the personality differences between Sean and Aaron started to surface and the boys started to drift apart. While Aaron had always been a homebody, Sean soon developed a wanderlust.

Aaron wanted nothing more than to come home right after school and hit the refrigerator, but Sean soon took to riding his bicycle all around town, talking to people, and seeing whatever he could see. He started to realize that he enjoyed the company of girls more than boys and developed a number of infatuations at the same time, learning a little more from each girl he would link up with, and learning very early that there is no pleasure quite as nice as the softness of a girl's lips.

One day when he was fourteen years old, an incident happened which he did not realize at the time would prove to be a major turning point in his life. Although he had never been very excited about hunting or fishing, Sean was appreciative of anyone who took an interest in him, and when one man, Tony DeNardi, offered to take him fishing after school, Sean smiled and said, "Sure."

All day in school, Sean wondered why he had agreed to go fishing when the thought of it did not interest him at all, but he had told Tony DeNardi that he would, and one thing that Sean had always held sacred was his personal word. Sean thought Tony looked goofy with his broad smile and his fishing license hanging off his broad-brimmed hat, but he threw his books into the man's pickup truck and jumped in with him.

"I have to make a quick stop at the club, then we'll go to Crystal Lake," Tony said, and Sean got ready for a boring day of fishing in exchange for a chance to make happy a man who was doing his best to do a good deed.

When the man and the boy walked through the doors of the Italian Club, it was the thousandth time for the man and the first time for the boy. Tony left Sean standing there for a minute as he walked over to the man he had come to talk to, and Sean was left to scan the room for familiar faces.

Many of the men he knew, some he did not, and his attention was drawn to a table where an older man with silver hair and a friendly smile sat alone shuffling a deck of cards. With his back to a wall, Mario Lanzetta looked comfortable and natural, and Sean was drawn to the man with the fast-shuffling hands and the easy smile.

Mario was smiling at the boy as Floriano Tonidandel walked through the front door and down the three steps into the barroom.

"Deal 'em," Floriano hollered across the room at Mario, and Mario slammed the cards down on the table and got up in a mock pantomime of a man furiously dealing cards.

"I got time for a few hands," Mario hollered across the room to the man who knew he would be there all day.

"Maybe this young man would like to play?" Mario said, nodding at Sean.

"No, not me, thanks," Sean answered bashfully. "I'm going fishing."

The next thing Mario Lanzetta said caught Sean totally off guard. It disturbed and intrigued him simultaneously, and it was a phrase that would haunt him throughout his life, one that he would never forget.

"You come follow me," Mario said, smiling, and pointing at his chest. "And I'll make you a fisher of men."

If he had not been smiling so cordially, the sacrilege would no doubt have hit Sean the wrong way, but Mario's smile was so engaging and unoffensive that Sean was deeply drawn to the game they were about to play.

In a few moments there were seven men sitting around the table and the cards were flying out of Mario Lanzetta's fingers as he spoke rapidly and loudly, and dollar bills started jumping into a pile in the middle of the table.

Sean was totally amazed. He had never seen so much money in one pile in his life, and every time Mario gave everybody another card, they threw more money into the middle. Three times in a row, when the cards were all dealt out, Mario lay down his cards, everyone else looked at them, and then Mario stood up and raked in the money, first sweeping it up in front of him at random and then sorting the bills out into piles of different denominations.

Sean heard Mario called more different derogatory Italian and American names in five minutes than he knew existed, but Mario just chuckled and made piles out of his money.

After three hands, Tony DeNardi walked over to where Sean was standing and barked at him angrily.

"Sean!"

Sean snapped his head over at Tony and looked at him with his eyes beaming.

"Get over here," Tony commanded, and Sean knew right away from the tone of Tony's voice that he had been watching something Tony did not approve of.

"You stay away from those men," he said, nudging Sean toward the door, but as Sean and Tony left, Sean glanced over his shoulder at Mario Lanzetta, and when Mario winked at him, Sean felt a rush of excitement that he knew he wanted to feel many more times in his life. In the course of only a few short minutes, Sean O'Hara, age fourteen, had seen Mario Lanzetta, age sixty-six, make more money than Sean had ever seen in a lifetime, and whatever game it was that they had been playing, Sean was determined that he would someday learn it.

Later on that afternoon, swatting mosquitoes while sitting in a pool of water in Tony DeNardi's boat, Sean watched as Tony hooked onto a four-pound bass, yelling excitedly as he pulled the fish into the boat.

"Baby, come home!" Tony yelled, smiling broadly at Sean, but as Sean smiled cordially at Tony, and said, "Nice fish," he was secretly thinking that back at the Italian Club, Mario Lanzetta was at that moment sitting in a comfortable chair in an air-conditioned room, raking in another big pot of money.

▲　▼　▲

Sean O'Hara discovered many things the summer of his fourteenth year. He discovered that there were many games like the one he had seen at the Italian Club going on all over town. In pool halls and bowling alleys and the back rooms of the taverns on Main Street, card games flourished. He learned how beer tasted, and whiskey, and how it made you feel afterward, and he made the decision to postpone any involvement with that vice at least for a few years.

He learned how to drive cars and motorcycles from older friends who made him the wheel man on nights when they would be drinking beer. He also learned from looking into their eyes how to tell when one of the girls they would pick up on endless cruises through town was interested in him. All of these things Sean learned while hanging around downtown while his cousin Aaron stayed at home eating his mother's food and watching television.

One conversation Sean was sorely lacking in was discussions about television shows. Even at age fourteen, Sean knew that television was robbing people of their lives, one night at a time.

One night when Sean was standing by the jukebox at Bill's Pizza Shop, his bicycle parked outside the door, a girl with a low-cut blouse and no bra, who was a good four or five years older than Sean, strolled up to him, stood a few inches away, and asked him if he had a light for her cigarette.

Sean smiled and reached across the counter for a book of matches that was laying there in plain sight, and as he smelled her perfumed fragrance, he struck a match. When she leaned forward, her blouse opened more and Sean looked at her breasts as she held his hands and he lit her cigarette.

She inhaled deeply and blew the smoke out into Sean's chest. She smiled into his eyes before she turned and strolled out of the shop, her short black skirt clinging to her as tightly as a second skin.

Two young girls in Sean's class laughed in the booth they were sitting in, and one of them spoke to Sean.

"Bet you wish you could?" she giggled as Sean pursed his lips and whistled.

"She sells it, you know," the other girl taunted Sean, and Sean thought she was only kidding.

But then he was stunned when the man Sean had seen the girl with earlier shuffled over and engaged him in a private conversation.

"Your girlfriends are right," the man whispered to Sean. "Whenever you want to buy some, you just ask me, and I'll set it up with her."

The man had messy brown hair that hung over his shoulders, a dirty white tee-shirt that smelled of perspiration, and his breath smelled of cigarette smoke.

"Don't think I'll be buying any," Sean smiled.

"Hey, don't get judgmental on me, man. The lady said she was interested, and I'm just passing the word on."

Sean didn't think he had sounded judgmental, and he turned away from the man and said, "No thanks."

"Look, Sport. Some people work with their hands, some people work with their minds, and some people work with their bodies. If you don't want any, you don't want any, but just don't get judgmental."

The two girls in the booth giggled as the smelly tee-shirt walked out, but Sean was not amused.

I'd probably have a bad attitude if I had to live that way, too, he thought as he walked out of the pizza shop and mounted his bicycle, which he aimed in the direction of downtown. He did not want to buy the girl, but he had memorized the way her breasts looked and the way her hands felt on his, and he thought about her just the same.

Already life was beginning to move very fast for Sean O'Hara, who discovered very early a fascination for things that were not good for him.

He picked up a number of part-time jobs after school, mostly clean-up jobs and dishwashing at local bars and restaurants, and at night he set up pins at the bowling alleys. When there were more pin-setters than bowlers on a given night, he got to know a number of local girls, and when the girls weren't out, he played poker.

Poker was a game of discipline, pure and simple. The saying, "Lucky at cards, unlucky at love," was used only by the losers Sean knew, and he knew a lot of them. Sean soon determined that the man who would exercise the most discipline would be a winner on both counts. With patience and discipline, Sean learned how to win both games.

Downtown he heard about the parties the older teens would have in the fields on weekends, and Sean decided that that was where he wanted to be. There he found out what girls who drank too much beer got like, and he had to admit it was fun finding out. Soon he would look for the girls he had met at field parties, and he started staying out later and later into weekday nights as well as on weekends. When Antoinette asked him what he was doing out so late, he said, "Just trying to work things out, that's all," and in that way he knew he was not lying.

At night, in town, with nothing but time and patience on his side, Sean learned that girls like it better if you're not too aggressive and that once a boy acted too jealous or too possessive, it was over for him. Sean learned that life was much smoother when he let the girls come after him. He also learned that the best fun you can have with a girl is when she knows she's competing with another girl for you.

From watching other boys his age who were ruled by their own urges, he realized that patience and self-discipline were rare and elusive virtues that many boys did not have the slightest idea how to control. Time and time again, otherwise intelligent boys would become overly possessive with their girlfriends, and when they alienated them in this way, it was amazing how the girls would gravitate Sean's way afterward.

Sean developed one strict rule which he enforced upon himself instinctively and absolutely. He vowed never to entertain a girl who was coming to him on the immediate rebound from another boy. He had many chances, but he absolutely refused. It would have to be common knowledge for at least a two-week period of time that the girl was unattached before Sean would even think about dating her. In that way, it could never be said that he stole a girl away from anyone. In time, as the years went by, this rule proved to be a good one, as many of the girls he had a chance to be intimate with went back to their old boyfriends, a lot of whom Sean knew personally.

Working in the bars at night, Sean liked to look at the girls when they first walked in. Nothing slipped by Sean O'Hara as he bided his time and watched the way the older boys and girls acted in the bars. He got to where he could tell by the way a girl walked, by the expression on her face, by the way she moved her hair or hands or fidgeted with her pocketbook, how the night was going to end up for her. Sean learned body language before he heard the term, and all of his lessons were fascinating.

Every new girl fascinated him, and he could not believe the way some of them got when the music got louder and the drinks started to flow. Out on the dance floor, as he watched them kissing the boys they were with so passionately in public, his imagination soared over what it would be like with each of them behind closed doors.

Girls became Sean O'Hara's overriding obsession in his mid-teen years. Occasionally, he would find himself slipping into the easy tendency to chase a particular girl, and that was one lesson he had to learn and re-learn not to do. Every time he chased a girl, she got away, and every time he let a girl chase him, he caught her, and nothing in Sean's world, not even a big night in poker, was ever so good.

Sean was mesmerized by the softness of their skin, and the fragrance of their hair. One after another, girls would come into his life in various different ways with the same end results. Every one of them loved to be held and kissed and touched, and once they were aroused, there was no limits to the pleasures they could provide.

Sean also learned a very disturbing thing about girls, which he believed to be a universal truth about them which was yet one more difference between the sexes. He learned that it didn't matter how often a girl said she loved him or how much she pledged her loyalty to him. Not one of them that he had ever met had had the moral character to keep that vow, which Sean felt the majority of men he knew would do, because for a girl, a vow of loyalty meant nothing. As many times as Sean would find a girl he felt comfortable enough to stay with, and whom he would ask to be his steady girl, he would keep his promises to her and she would break hers to him.

More times than Sean wished to think about, a girl he would start to like would just up and leave, no explanations, no forewarning, just a letter, a phone call, or a quick face-to-face, "Sayonara, Jack," and Sean was history for them.

At first he had his heart broken many times, then he did a lot of soul-searching to see if there was something wrong with him. He tried improving his appearance, or his clothes, or his behavior, but it didn't matter. Girls were just fickle creatures whom for Sean O'Hara were here today and gone tomorrow. That was the way it was, and he guessed that that was the way it would always be.

He felt more at ease when he saw the same things happening to other boys around him on as regular a basis as it happened to him, and although it didn't make him feel any better, it at least educated him that he wasn't the only boy in the world to whom heartbreak was an everyday thing. Boys everywhere were getting their hearts broken. Boys everywhere were finding out that their girlfriends had been with somebody else, and boys everywhere were being forced to understand, as Sean did, that that was one of the rules of the game.

In those torrid early years of Sean O'Hara's adolescence, every lesson he was filing away in his memory bank only applied to the girls who frequented the dead-end places he was exposing himself to. The thought never occurred to him that he was looking in the wrong places for the kind of girl he most wanted and needed.

▲　▼　▲

Throughout the next several years, Sean's wanderlust continued. For some unknown reason, he would get onto his motorcycle or into his car, and ride and ride, town to town, back road to back road, searching out every corner of every town around him, developing acquaintances with people of all kinds, and searching incessantly for something he could not quite put his finger on.

An anger began to accompany him and a feeling of abject emptiness, and the only time the feeling would go away was when he had a girl in his arms, but when she would go, the emptiness would return, and soon a loneliness he could not understand, the origin of which he could not begin to trace, began to haunt him.

It moved in with him and followed him everywhere and pounded in his brain. It put an aching in his chest that soon even the soft embrace of a young girl could not take away, and without knowing how it had happened, Sean O'Hara knew that he was in trouble.

Not knowing where to turn for help, he turned in precisely the wrong direction. One night, while out cruising in his convertible car, he stopped at a package store in Monson, Massachusetts, to see if he could buy some liquor, even though he was three years under age.

"Bottle of red wine, please," he asked the woman behind the counter, who should have asked for his ID, but didn't.

"What kind?" she asked.

"Any Guinea red," Sean said, and the woman put a gallon jug of Vino Duva on the counter.

"That's good," Sean said.

Out in his car, Sean cracked open the bottle of wine and took the first sip of hundreds of bottles of red Italian wine that he would drink while driving alone around the back roads of the towns surrounding Indian Springs. He would drive until he couldn't see anymore, then pull over on some back road and go to sleep.

One morning as the sun came up, he awoke in a field with his car on its roof, and as he sat up, his head began to pound.

"Somethin's gotta' give," he heard himself say in a voice that sounded strange to him, and that afternoon he drove to Springfield, Massachusetts, on his motorcycle to an armed services recruiting center. It was Friday, May 28, 1948.

That night, as both Sean and Aaron were preparing to graduate from high school, Sean announced at supper, "I'll be leaving next week."

The three Bellinos looked at him simultaneously, and Vittorio put his fork down and said, "Where are you going?"

"I joined the Navy," Sean said, nonchalantly, and visions of combat flashed through Vittorio's mind.

Very quickly, Vittorio reasoned to himself that it had been almost three years since the bombing of Nagasaki, Japan, which had ended World War II, and that if Sean was going to join, now was probably the best time to get his service out of the way, before another war broke out somewhere.

"If Sean joins the Navy, I do, too!" Aaron smiled confidently.

"No!" Antoinette snapped at the top of her lungs, slamming the frying pan she was holding down on the table.

"No, no, no, no, no!" she screamed again. "You will never join the Navy, or I'll kill you before you walk out the door!"

Vittorio was surprised at his wife's outburst, which was very uncharacteristic of her, and he decided not to interfere, but to see what Aaron would say instead.

"Ma, I'm twenty years old," he argued.

"And Sean is eighteen," she yelled. "Too young to join the Navy. And Sean smokes, and drinks, and gambles, and does a lot of other things he's too young to do. And if he was my son, I'd box his ears, but he's not, and I won't tell him what to do. But you are my son, and if you ever say one thing about joining the Navy, I'll rip your head off and spit down your neck!"

Antoinette was screaming with livid rage, and Aaron couldn't help but chuckle. When Sean and Vittorio looked at one another and saw the smiles on one another's faces, they both started to laugh at once. Soon all three men were laughing uncontrollably, slapping their legs and holding their sides, bellowing out of control to the point where all three had to leave the table to keep their sides from splitting.

None of them had ever heard Antoinette Bellino speak in this manner, and the cold seriousness in her face made it all the funnier.

"You think that's funny?" she raged at Vittorio, holding a long wooden spoon she grabbed up in his direction.

Abruptly the realization hit Sean O'Hara like a hundred-ton anchor, that if it were not for him, Antoinette would never have yelled that way at Vittorio.

This realization hit him harder and faster than any mood change of his life, and the sudden remorse it caused him made him stop laughing and start crying. With giant tears of remorse in his eyes, he threw his arms around Antoinette, and when Vittorio and Aaron realized that Sean was crying, they stopped laughing instantly as their faces grew somber.

"You've been very kind to me," Sean sobbed as he put his hands on top of Antoinette's. "But when I cause you to yell at Vittorio, it's time for me to leave."

Vittorio suddenly felt a deep sadness for the boy, reminiscent of the sadness he had felt for the boy's father so many years before when Sean's mother had died.

Antoinette was suddenly ashamed of herself and hugged Sean O'Hara in remorse.

"Oh, my boy. I'm sorry. I don't have any idea in the world why I spoke the way I did."

"It's okay," Sean said, pushing away from her. "It's okay."

His voice choked with emotion, struggling as he held back his tears, he looked at each of the Bellinos one by one as he spoke.

"You have to be just about the greatest family in the world," he said. "And I'm blessed to know you. But you can't be expected to care for me any longer. I joined the Navy because I wanted to. I'm leaving next week."

There was a quiet that settled over the room as each of the four people looked at one another somberly. And then a slight smile cracked Sean's lips, and he spoke to Aaron. "And when the day comes for you to join the Navy, wait till I'm home, because I want to watch when your mother spits down your neck."

As Aaron started again to laugh, now all four of them joined in, but this time it was Vittorio who changed the mood when he suddenly drew all of them together with his strong arms and voiced the following prayer, "Lord, God Almighty, You who have stood watch over all of us for all of these years, we solemnly pray to You today, to guard Your son, Sean, and to be with him all the days of his life, and to bring him back safely to us here after he walks the road of service to his country. We pray in the name of the Father, and of the Son, and of the Holy Ghost. Amen."

"Thank you, Uncle Vittorio," Sean said respectfully. "I know in my heart, without any doubt, that God will answer your most sincere prayers. Thank you."

The following morning, Aaron Bellino awoke to find a note on Sean O'Hara's pillow.

"Went in early. See you after basic training. Love, Sean."

At breakfast, Aaron lay down the note, and when Antoinette picked it up and read it, she sat down heavily in her chair, buried her head in her hands, and wept.

▲　▼　▲

Maura Hardy was the eldest of four children born to Patrick and Ann Hardy. From the time she was a little girl she had had a crush on Aaron Bellino. She had seen him many times with his mother and father at church where she attended daily mass with her mother. She had even remembered helping Aaron with his schoolwork when Aaron repeated first grade, although when reminded of that fact later on, Aaron could not remember this.

Aaron had spoken only Italian when he first started school and had to repeat first grade because of it. Then the second year, he had been sick most of the year, so when Maura started first grade, Aaron was two years older but in the same class.

He was the biggest boy in his class, and Maura had always thought of him as mature and strong. Now, with high school graduation night around the corner, she was worried that she would not be seeing him as much anymore, and the thought of losing the boy she had always dreamed of marrying terrified her.

That year, 1948, the Indian Springs High School graduating class planned a trip to Washington, D.C. When Maura Hardy found out that Aaron Bellino was going, she was beside herself with relief.

It'll be a piece of cake, she told herself. *I'll hit him with every ploy in the book and before he knows what happened to him, we'll be engaged.*

The trip was scheduled for seven days, and two of Maura's best friends, Mabel Briggs and Glenna James, were cut in on the plot.

With adroitness that was worthy of CIA action, these three girls schemed, plotted, and connived, and every time Aaron Bellino turned around, it seemed that Maura Hardy was standing there. Only one seat was left on the bus, one seat in the restaurants, one seat at the plays, and the right group on all the shuttle buses. Always Aaron Bellino got thrown in with Maura Hardy, and she was so easy to talk to and attentive to all of Aaron's needs that he began to believe that it would be difficult to imagine traveling anywhere else without her.

On the last day before they loaded the bus to come home, Aaron asked Maura to take a walk with him in the garden behind the hotel.

"It's been a great trip," he said to her, and he reached out to hold her hand.

"I've enjoyed every minute of it," she smiled.

"You know, with sports and everything, I never really had much time to spend with girls," Aaron said to her almost apologetically.

"Nothing wrong with that," she said.

"And I'm no big pro at courting, either," he said.

Maura smiled at him. "Who wants a pro in that category?" she asked.

"Do you want to have kids?" he asked her nonchalantly.

"I think we should get married first!" she said, slapping him on the arm.

Aaron broke into a total red-faced blush as he stumbled all over himself to apologize. "Oh, I didn't mean that. I mean I didn't mean anything about now. I m-mean I d-didn't mean . . . ."

She jumped in and rescued him.

"You mean do I want to have kids eventually," she said. "I know that's what you meant. And of course I do. Yes."

Aaron was wiping the perspiration off of his suddenly soaking wet forehead.

"God, I've never been so embarrassed in my life," he intimated to Maura, his voice shaking and his face still beat red.

She felt so sorry for him that she put her arm around his waist and lay her head on his shoulder. When she did that, he put his arms around her and for the longest time they just stood there in each other's arms, his heart pounding a mile a minute in his chest.

"What I should have said is this," he said after a while of feeling how good it felt to be holding her. "Do you think we could be happy together?"

She smiled up at him, put both of her hands behind his head and kissed him, and when she was finished, she said, "You tell me!"

Three weeks later, at a large church wedding in Saint Patrick's Church, Aaron Attilio Bellino and Maura Ann Hardy were joined in holy matrimony, and Vittorio and Antoinette Bellino stood in the front row beaming with happiness.

After a two-week honeymoon in Europe, during which time Aaron and Maura visited Biella, Italy, and Fethered, Ireland, where each of their families had come from, the couple returned to tell Vittorio and Antoinette the decision they had reached while honeymooning in Italy.

"You paid a great price to serve our country, Pop," Aaron said to Vittorio. "And every school child in town knows it's been recorded that Indian Springs, Connecticut, had the highest percentage of men in World War II of any town in the entire country. I'd feel terrible if I didn't do my part. Maura and I have agreed, before we have any children, I'm going to join the Marines."

"The Marines?" Antoinette yelled.

"Mom, don't start. I owe it to my country."

Suddenly, Antoinette was shaking with fear. "Ar-r-on," she pleaded, rolling her r's like the Italians do so it sounded almost like "A-dun."

"You're my only son," her voice quivered.

"I can't live my whole life in a shell, Mom. I'm joining the Marines. My word is final."

That night started the long and slow withdrawal of Antoinette Bellino into a silent fear she never voiced to anyone else. It came out in repeated nightmares, when she would wake up shaking and covered with sweat, and Vittorio would listen, sorry for the pain she was suffering, but unable to take her fears away. During these terrifying nightmares, she would whisper blankly into the darkness.

"*Aar-r-on e un soldato*," she would say, rolling her r mournfully, which means in Italian, "Aaron is a soldier."

No one but Antoinette Bellino could possibly understand the incapacitating fear she was experiencing that these words accompanied.

▲   ▼   ▲

The first time Sean O'Hara heard about the fights, he was cleaning toilets aboard the Mount McKinley as it sat at anchor in the Norfolk, Virginia, naval base.

"You goin' to the fights tonight, O'Hara?" another sailor asked him as he went about his duty.

"What fights?" Sean asked, having heard nothing at all about them before.

"The fights on deck. Navy's having an elimination tournament to pick the best fighter in port to fight against the Army guy."

"Oh, yeah?" Sean asked curiously. "What weight division?"

"All of them. We're sending our best eight against the Army's best eight next month in Washington. It's gonna be televised by armed services networks all over the world."

Sean had never been to Washington, but it was a place he had always wanted to see.

"Really? How do you get into the competition?"

"You want to fight?"

"Sure. Why not? It's a free trip to Washington, right?"

"Sean, there's some pretty rough boys in this man's Navy."

Sean just smiled and shrugged as if to say, "So what?"

"All you gotta do is show up on deck and weigh in. Every time you win, you advance. When one guy's left, he's the man."

Sean O'Hara had never been in a boxing ring in his life. But he had heard all of his life about the legendary fight that had taken place between his father and his grandfather, and he felt somewhat of a oneness with the two men. His father he had never known, but his grandfather he had known right up until his death in 1936 when Sean was five years old.

It had been hard at that time for Sean to envision his grandfather as a boxer, his great white beard laying across his chest as he sat quietly in his same old chair amid the noise of his grandchildren all around him. All day long he sat and smiled at one or another of his little ones, his hands shaking incessantly as they had done, non-stop, since the Callahan-Bellino fight sixteen years before. Sean could only vaguely remember him, and then he could remember only two expressions on his face. He was either smiling at one of his grandchildren or staring out the back window somberly and sullenly as though he were thousands of miles away.

When Michael Callahan died, the only impact it had had on the boy of five who was now preparing to fight for the Navy was that the great old chair in the living room of his home sat empty, and the quiet, white-bearded old man was gone.

The only thing Sean remembered was that his grandmother would shoo anyone and everyone who sat in his chair out of it, saying with reverence for her dead husband, "That was Michael's chair. No one else sits there."

Now, as Sean prepared to step into uncharted waters, he remembered only the legends he had heard about the greatness of Michael Callahan and the one and only loss of the sad and tragic Fortunato Bellino.

As the Navy trainer taped up his hands on board ship, with all the sailors milling around who were waiting to bet on the fights, Sean felt a rush of excitement coursing through him. In a few moments, he would be face to face with an opponent who would be trying to tear his head off, and the thought elated him and filled him with a strange sense of destiny.

Sean O'Hara weighed in at 146 pounds, so he was to fight as a welterweight. Looking across the ring at the man he was ready to meet, he felt nothing in the way of fear, only a rush of excitement and adrenaline coursing through his veins.

When the two fighters stood across from one another in the center of the ring, Sean stared deeply into the center of his opponent's eyes, the way he had seen Michael Callahan stare, and assuming that same look filled him with a sense of power and invincibility.

When the referee was finished giving his instructions, the two fighters returned to their respective corners to await the opening bell. When the bell rang, Sean charged across the mat like a tiger unleashed. In less than fifteen seconds, he knocked his man out, the fight was history, and Sean surprised himself with the power that coursed out of his arms.

Standing over his fallen opponent, he felt a deep guttural yell rising out of him as he turned and fired a dozen more piston-like punches into the air.

No one watching the knockout could help but notice the incredible power and speed that had emanated from Sean O'Hara's gloves after his first knockout, and after three more, he was chosen as the man to beat in the welterweight division. By the time the finals were reached, Sean was six and zero with six knockouts inside of two minutes, and the tall black sailor who stood across the ring from him ready to decide who would fight the Army looked like he would rather not have gotten that far.

The black sailor gave Sean the best opposition he had thus far faced, however, going the full three rounds, and when the decision was announced, Sean was seven and zero with six knockouts.

One month later, in Washington, D.C., the Army beat the Navy, 6-2, with the Navy's only two wins coming in the lightweight and welterweight divisions. The Most Valuable Boxer award was won by the Navy, however, and when Sean O'Hara stepped forward to receive the M.V.B. medal, he felt an elation the likes of which he had never before felt.

"What are you plans now?" a sportscaster asked him under the hot lights of the TV cameras.

"Soon as I get out of the Navy, I'm gonna turn pro," Sean said to over a million people on worldwide television.

"Well, we know you'll make America proud. Congratulations to you."

"Thank you, sir," Sean said, and as he bowed to the TV cameras, a loud cheer went up at every bar and tavern in Indian Springs, Connecticut, hometown of America's newest hero.

The rest of Sean's enlistment period he spent fielding questions from the many fellow sailors who wanted to know all kinds of tips on boxing and where he had learned to fight so well.

"I don't mean to sound cocky, but I think it's a natural gift," Sean would answer, honestly assessing himself and the reasons for his success. Realizing that he had had no formal training, however, he would secretly work out in the gym on his own, doing the kinds of exercises he imagined would be the best ones for strength-building and agility, and all the time he would dream about something he had not even thought about just a couple of months before.

I wonder what it would be like to be the welterweight champion of the world, Sean thought to himself. He continued to work out in the gym and counted the days until his discharge, dreaming all the while about what it would be like to be world champion.

▲   ▼   ▲

One week after Sean O'Hara had won the Army-Navy boxing tournament in Washington, D.C., an event took place several hundred miles north in Boston, Massachusetts. Though he had no knowledge of the event, it would have a profound impact on his life many years later.

The date was April 23, 1950, the thirteenth birthday of Colleen Bradford, third of four beautiful daughters of Alden and Cora Bradford of Laurel Hill, Connecticut, and great-grand-daughter of Ira Bradford, who had left Indian Springs once and for all the day they put a speed limit on his horse.

For a full month leading up to her first day as a teenager, Colleen had looked forward with great anticipation to her birthday present, a trip with her parents and sisters to Boston, Massachusetts, to hear the exciting young evangelist who was drawing crowds of record numbers in his youth crusades across the country.

When her father told her she could have anything she wanted for her birthday, her sisters thought she was crazy not to ask for a new saddle for her pony, Dancer, or a new dress for the after school events, now that she was going to be a teenager.

"I want to hear Billy Graham speak," she asked simply. "That's all I want."

Alden and Cora Bradford were determined that she would have her wish. So on Sunday, April 23, 1950, at an open air rally on Boston Common that drew over 16,000 people, Colleen Bradford sat and listened to the tall, handsome evangelist on the first day of her teenage years.

She was overwhelmed by the massive sea of people who listened as the dedicated servant of Jesus Christ offered his simple and deeply moving answer to the problems of every individual in attendance: acceptance of the Lord, Jesus, and a personal invitation for His guidance in your life.

Never in her life had she been so moved by any other person. She had made a pilgrimage to Boston, the farthest she had ever been away from the farm before, seeking a chance to hear Billy Graham, but she had found much, much more. Throughout the sermon of the remarkable young man, Colleen Bradford listened as though the only person in the crowd was her.

Then, at the end of his quiet, humble, unassuming sermon, when he bowed his head and invited anyone within hearing distance to step forward and accept Christ, Colleen Bradford, age thirteen, exited her seat and walked forward to the base of the temporary platform that had been erected on Monument Hill for Billy Graham's crusade.

There, a short distance away from where her ancestor, Joshua Bradford had fought his first blood-soaked battle against the British 175 years previously as a young American fighting to establish a new country where his children's children would be free to live the way their God led them, Colleen Bradford bowed her head and gave her life to Jesus Christ.

From that day forward, her dedication to Jesus Christ was sincere and complete.

▲　▼　▲

Aaron Bellino's two-year enlistment in the United States Marine Corps was scheduled to come to a close on September 30, 1950. The nearer he came to his discharge, the more fearful Antoinette Bellino became for his life as the Korean War raged on, so it was a good thing that on the night of Thursday, September 14, 1950, as America prepared to go to bed, no one in Indian Springs or anywhere else in America, knew about the impending American invasion of Inchon.

Just after a typhoon swept across the Japan-Korea area, a naval bombardment took place near Inchon. The island of Wolmi-Do was the first objective of the multi-national force led by General Douglas MacArthur. In the early morning hours of September 15, a group of U.S. Marines, including Sergeant Aaron Bellino, arrived on the narrow beach, scaled the sea wall, and within twenty minutes of landing raised the American flag atop the hill dominating Wolmi-Do. The entire area was secured within an hour and a half. Wolmi-Do was taken without a single fatality.

Later that afternoon, more severe fighting was going on in the city of Inchon, and by the morning of September 16 the North Koreans were driven out of Inchon. Only 196 casualties were suffered by the U.N. force, with twenty men killed. The American public awoke the next morning to hear that an incredible victory had taken place at Inchon.

But the victory was not without cost back in America for one family. Hearing about the fierce fighting that had gone on in Korea, Antoinette Bellino, age fifty-eight, suffered a massive heart attack, and though she somehow survived, she suffered severe damage to the arteries surrounding her heart and she was hospitalized at Bradford Memorial Hospital for an extended stay.

In Korea, the initial victory by Aaron's battalion was quickly followed by a swift advance into Seoul itself, which the North Koreans defended fiercely. After heavy fighting in which over one hundred thousand prisoners were taken, the North Koreans evacuated Seoul on September 28, and when General MacArthur held a ceremony in the hall of the South Korean National Assembly, MacArthur restored Seoul as the seat of government.

With tears flowing down his cheeks, a grateful President Rhee said to General MacArthur, "We admire you. We love you as the savior of our race."

One month later, Aaron Bellino returned to a hero's welcome at the Civil War monument in Hyde Park, Indian Springs, Connecticut, but excused himself immediately to visit his mother in the hospital.

When he walked into her private room at Bradford Memorial Hospital, beaming with a broad smile, he tried not to show her how surprised he was at how grey she had become, and walking over to her bedside he shook her arm to wake her up, saying "Mom, it's Aaron."

Never had anything his mother ever said to him shocked or saddened him more than the reply she made, which acquainted Aaron with the brain damage she had suffered in a shock subsequent to her heart attack.

"You not Aar-r-on!" she said, staring at the strange man who stood before her. "*Aar-r-on e un soldato!*"

Aaron recoiled in surprise before leaning over his mother to kiss her. Two minutes later, when Aaron's wife, Maura, walked into the room, she discovered her marine corps husband wiping tears from his eyes as he slumped over in his chair while his mother stared off into space.

▲   ▼   ▲

The fire that swept across the fairgrounds in 1950 burning down the grandstands and the horse barns out back, changed the face of Indian Springs forever. The grandstands were replaced, but the horse barns never were, and shortly afterward the old harness track was banked and turned into an auto racing track.

When Indian Springs Speedway opened, it brought a new wave of excitement into town, as well as a new crowd of drivers who followed the racing circuit up and down the east coast, wherever there was a payday for another win.

Donnie Messeck was the most exciting young driver on the circuit that year because he put his foot on the floor and steered, totally oblivious to the dangers that surrounded him and determined to use the stock cars as a springboard to his dream of winning the Indianapolis 500.

He won everything in sight and picked up a contingent of strong fans and dedicated crewmen who followed him wherever he went, determined to be a part of his fortunes when he hit the big time.

He also picked up a gorgeous little blue-eyed girl who loved his big smile and his devil-may-care attitude. She also liked the fact that he provided her with so much excitement and asked her so few questions while providing her with all her basic needs. This was enough to keep her happy as she tagged alongside of him that summer in her own quest to discover the world.

She was in the pits talking to his crew when the blinding crash drew the crowd to its feet, and she never saw his car go up over the top of another car and fly off the track on the third turn. As the roar of the twenty-three remaining cars in the race diminished to a loud purr, the ambulances and fire trucks sped around the outside of the track. The field ran under yellow while the wreckage on the track was cleared, and Donnie Messeck's body was removed from his car.

That night after the races, she just sat there in the exhibition hall, stunned and confused, and she had absolutely no idea where to turn when Sean O'Hara sat down next to her.

As everyone else paraded by to pay their respects, she reached out and gripped his hand, and in dazed shock, she wouldn't let it go. For hours he sat there with her, listening to her, and when the crowd started to thin, she realized she had no place to go.

Three of the men in Messeck's pit crew were fighting over which one would take Nadia with him, and all the while she sat closer and closer to Sean and gripped his hand tighter and tighter.

"I don't even have any money," she said. "Donnie handled everything."

"It's okay," Sean said. "I know a place you can stay."

She never asked any questions, just followed him out and jumped on the back of his Harley Davidson motorcycle, and he drove her to the Springs House Hotel.

"We've been booked for weeks, sir, you can't get a room on race night."

"I'm sorry to put you through so much trouble," she said.

"It's no trouble," Sean said. "You just need a place to sleep and some privacy."

He drove slowly down the hill into Indian Springs, and took her to his apartment. "I live alone," he said, "but you can sleep in my bed and I'll sleep on the porch."

The next day he bought her breakfast and she told him about the roundabout road that had brought her to his doorstep.

"I lost my parents ten years ago in Europe and came to America with an aunt when I was seven years old. I only spoke Polish when I first got here, but I learned English fast. I didn't like the guy my aunt married, and just took off one day from our beach front home in California. Hitch hiked across the country and met Donnie at Talledega, Alabama. He was exciting, and fun to be with and I just kept tagging along. Now he's dead."

Sean could not believe how much alike they were and how quickly he felt as though he had known her all his life. For several hours they walked through the park and talked, and before he realized it he was kissing her passionately.

"Don't ask me to explain it," she said, "Because I can't. All I know is that I love you so much it hurts."

That night in his apartment, she unpacked her duffle bag.

For such a small duffle bag, it was filled with a surprisingly large assortment of the same kinds of things: sandals, faded blue jean shorts and halter tops, and a large assortment of very short, very thin panties and nighties.

She bundled all of their clothing together, carted it all to the laundromat, took over the top drawer of his bureau, and Sean had a roommate.

For the next six weeks, they made love three and four times a day, in their apartment, in the park, on the beach, everywhere they went.

"You are me, and I am you," she wrote on a card he found on his pillow one night as she was taking a shower, and Sean was head over heels, obsessively in love.

Six weeks after Nadia came to town, Benito Strazza showed up at Sean's door.

"Got you a good one," he smiled at Sean. "A top-ranked contender. Win this one, and the title is just around the corner."

"Who?" Sean asked, glancing at his watch nonchalantly as he wondered how long Straz was going to be there. Nadia had gone out for a pack of cigarettes and would be home soon, and Sean was thinking about bed.

"Johnny Saxton. July Fourth in the Garden."

Sean squinted.

"Oh, Straz. I can't fight on July Fourth. That's the day I'm getting married."

"Married?" Benito barked, almost choking on his cigar. "I'll kill you. You can't get married now. You're about two fights away from the goddamn championship of the world!"

Sean stared at the wall beside Benito Strazza, and never saw Nadia listening to the conversation from outside the door.

The next day, coming home from the post office in the morning, he found a note pinned to his pillow.

"I've never loved anyone as much as you, but I have to leave. I can't marry you now or ever. Someday you'll understand and forgive me. Love always, Nadia."

The engagement ring he had given her was pinned to the note.

His heart started to pound as he jumped up and pulled open the top drawer, which almost came out of the bureau in his hands. It was empty. He ran outside, not knowing where to go, and flying around town on his Harley, he searched for her everywhere, but with each place he went to that he came up empty, his hopes and dreams faded. Finally, he found one of her girlfriends, and she started to run away. Sean caught her, jumped off his bike, and spun her around.

She was crying.

"You know where she went?" Sean asked frantically.

"Florida," the girl said.

"Where in Florida?" Sean screamed painfully.

"She didn't know. She just started hitch hiking and told me not to tell you where she was going. Oh, Sean. I'm so sorry."

Sean leaped onto his Harley and roared down the river road like a cyclone. *It's only been about four hours, I should be able to catch up to her,* he determined. He had on a pair of blue jeans, black boots, a white tee-shirt, and a black leather jacket. In his pocket was seventy-six dollars. Florida was about fourteen hundred miles away, and it was getting close to dusk.

Thinking back he remembered that he had forgotten to close the inside door to his apartment, and he never told anyone where he was going, or how long he thought he would be gone. He didn't know, or care about that, or about anything. He knew only one thing as he tried not to clench his teeth so hard to postpone a headache for as long as he could. No matter how long it took, no matter what price he had to pay, he had only one burning compulsion. He had to find Nadia.

▲   ▼   ▲

On the first night, he stopped at every single truck stop and rest area there was, without exception, and did the same thing the next day, and all the next night, as he worked his way down the coast.

If I can make each stop quick, and keep moving, I can catch up to her whichever one she stops at, he reasoned. Finally, on the second day, he slept under a tree in a rest area, and four hours later, refreshed, though his muscles were aching, he started out again. This time he drove a hundred miles at a time before stopping. Then on the third day he saw the "Welcome to Florida" sign.

In Florida his odyssey continued as he searched for her incessantly for days on end, stopping only to sleep. In bars and taverns, parks and campgrounds, beaches, and small town restaurants, every place he went, he showed her picture to the local people, coming up empty thousands of times.

When he ran out of money, he took a job, as his odyssey stretched out into time. It didn't matter what he had to do—wash a car, fall a tree, collect a debt for somebody, repair a small engine—anything for enough money to get to the next motel, to the next town.

For the first several months, he never worked for more than three days straight in any one place, then the jobs lasted longer, as he learned to rent motel rooms by the week and search for her in the evenings after work, covering several towns in the same small radius while keeping a menial job for as long as it took to fund himself until he moved on. He started down the east coast first, went inland for awhile, then worked his way back up the Gulf coast. When he had made one complete circle around Florida, he started the same round again. Finally, one day toward the end of his second complete loop around the state, he was totally exhausted and he spent his last penny for a hotel room in Pensacola, where he crashed on a Saturday night and slept for almost twenty-four consecutive hours.

He took a job the next morning with a construction crew and he'd been on it for almost two full weeks when one Friday evening finally came.

On this Friday evening, after his construction crew had finished for the week, Sean showered in his beach-front motel room, put on a pair of swimming trunks, lit a cigarette, and stood staring at the bottle of whiskey in the cupboard.

His muscles were tired from carrying building supplies all day long through the sand to the six carpenters he was charged with keeping supplied. *There will be no searching for her tonight,* he reasoned, *I'm just too tired.* So he reached for the bottle of whiskey.

He cracked open the cap as he walked across the floor, slid open the sliding door, and walked out onto the beach.

The sun was sitting low in the afternoon sky, and most of the sunbathers had already gone home. Sean sat on a lawn chair, his muscles tight and his legs very tired. The waves broke hard on the shore as Sean sat back and watched the water coming farther and farther up the beach with each crashing wave. Seagulls dipped to pick up whatever morsels they could find washing up with the rising tide.

It would be Monday now before he could work again if he decided to stay in Pensacola, which would give him two full days to search for her. It was this night, Friday, that he was worried about. It was hell not knowing where she was or who she was with, and especially if the people she was with cared about her or only about themselves. He had long since decided that one for himself in his mind. For a while he wrestled with the possibility that the whole search was only the result of his own selfishness, jealousy, or pride. He had thought deeply about all the angles, and decided that it was love that was driving him, nothing else. He knew they could be happy together because he knew how happy they had been, and that nobody could possibly ever love her any more than he did.

If he could only find her, and find out what had gone wrong, he would try to understand whatever it was that had caused her to leave so he could correct it and make things better than before and never give her any cause to leave again.

He looked at his watch, and saw that it was only six-thirty. The sun wouldn't be down for another hour and a half, and by that time he knew he would be drunk enough to sleep through the night if he just kept on lifting up the bottle. It was not a good way to ensure sleep, and he thought about leaving the bottle on the table, but his arm just kept reaching for it. He was too tired to get up, and the whiskey felt too good to stop drinking.

After several slugs, the long and winding road that had brought him to this solitary motel in Pensacola, Florida, led him right back to where it always did. He stared blankly out into the ocean and drifted back to Indian Springs where Nadia stood on the corner of Main Street, her big blue eyes scanning all of the young men who drove by or stopped to talk to her. She wore sandals and faded blue jean shorts with a violet halter top that left most of her flat stomach exposed. Her light brown hair hung over her eyes until she'd brush it back with her hand, which she did often as she looked for Sean.

Suddenly, she would see him, and he played it over and over again, the way she smiled as she walked toward him quickly, the spring in her steps cutting precious fractions off the time it took for her to reach him. When she threw her arms around him, he melted on the spot, and the warmth of her body against his became the only thing that mattered to him then, and now, as he sat alone on a beach in Florida, fifteen hundred miles and hundreds of painful days from the last time he had seen her.

The stone in his chest grew heavier as he tried to shake himself loose from thinking too much about her, the way she smiled, her fragrance, the softness of her skin and hair, and the taste of her lingering kiss.

He took a deep breath of the fresh salt air and exhaled loudly as he turned and looked out across the windswept beach.

And then he saw her, walking slowly, alone on the beach, her bare feet choosing every step carefully, blessing the sand every time her foot lighted on its softness. She shook her soft brown hair out of her eyes and the ocean breeze blew it back across her shoulders.

His heart quickened as the sight of her lifted him to his feet.

"Nadia," he whispered, focusing his eyes on her as his legs started to carry him to her.

She kept walking slowly away from him, her thin string bikini lighter than the ocean breeze on her suntanned body, and when she heard him calling to her, she turned her head halfway around.

"Nadia!" he cried, desperately and prayerfully, and when she turned all the way around and looked at him, she saw the tears in his eyes and the smile on his face, and she instantly wished that she was her.

When he saw that she was not Nadia, he caught himself up short and dropped his arms down by his sides as the spirit drained out of him.

"I'm sorry," he apologized quietly, looking dejectedly into the sand. "I thought you were someone else."

He turned to walk slowly back up the beach, and after he had taken only a few steps he heard her call out to him.

"Hey," she said lightly.

Sean turned and gazed into her beautiful eyes which stared at him compassionately as the evening sunlight shone in her hair.

"I'll be her."

Sean took one step toward her, and she came to him slowly, unlike the way Nadia used to, but when she melted into his arms, he hugged her passionately and months of pent-up anxiety welled up in his eyes as the dam of his emotions burst, and the roar of the crashing surf drowned out his tears heard only by the girl in his arms who knew nothing about the girl, Nadia, other than the fact that he missed her desperately.

▲ ▼ ▲

When he woke up at midnight, the moonlight was shining in her hair. He ran his hand over the soft skin of her back and she woke up and smiled at him. She touched his lips with her fingers and drew him to her, and they made love again in the coolness of the night. Later, he stood and walked over to the window and looked out at the moonlight shining across the Gulf.

After awhile, she stood behind him with both arms around him, and he turned and drew her to him again.

"I don't know what to say," he said to her softly.

"Then don't say anything," she said.

They stood and ran their hands over each other's bodies as they looked out over the ocean.

"Want to walk with me on the beach?" she asked.

"What's your name?" he asked her.

"Angel," she answered softly.

Sean smiled.

"I should have guessed."

Out on the beach, she held herself close to him and they walked slowly along the beach.

"Who is she?" Angel asked him.

"I lost track of her about a year ago when she moved away," he said somberly. "But I'll find her."

"You know she's here?" Angel asked as they strolled slowly through the sand.

"I know she left for Florida. That's all I know."

"Where are you from?"

"Connecticut."

"How did you come to be in Pensacola?"

"I've searched just about every town in Florida over the past year. Picking up odd jobs and earning enough for food and shelter, then moving on. I have to know what went wrong."

"Will you be here long?" she asked and she hugged him tightly when she did.

"I was going to stay another week," he said, looking out over the ocean. "But it wouldn't be fair to you if I did."

She grew somber after that and they walked together for only a short distance longer, then she stopped and knelt down in the sand.

Sean looked at her affectionately, and knelt down next to her and she was staring out across the ocean.

"I'm sorry," he said.

She smiled at him.

"I wish you'd stop saying you're sorry," she said. "I did it for me."

"We still have the rest of the night," he said.

"That's good," she said. "It's getting chilly out."

They walked together silently back to the room, and when they were in bed it was her turn to cry.

Sean did not know what to say to her, so he didn't say anything, just wrapped his arms around her and she clung to him for the rest of the night.

In the morning she slipped out of bed while he was still asleep, showered, slipped into her bikini, and stood at the door watching him sleep.

When she turned the doorknob, he rolled over and looked up at her and she gazed at him sadly.

"Don't lose tomorrow searching for yesterday," she whispered, and she was gone.

Sean laid his head back on the pillow, and in awhile he showered, dressed, kicked over his Harley, and sped off into the Florida morning, with Nadia ever on his mind.

▲　▼　▲

One year after Aaron Bellino's return from active duty, Maura Bellino gave birth to an eight-pound, ten-ounce boy whom Aaron and Maura named Joseph Aaron. His birthday was October 18, 1951. The first person they called to tell about the happy news was Joey's grandfather, Vittorio, who had turned sixty-four years old just two days before.

Vittorio was beside himself with elation as he lifted Antoinette off of her chair and danced her around their living room in glee.

"It's a boy! It's a boy! It's a boy!" Vittorio chanted as he and Antoinette laughed and cheered in their living room, celebrating the birth of their grandchild.

"Now we have someone to carry on the name," Vittorio said to Antoinette as though he hadn't reminded her of the reason why they wanted the baby to be a boy at least a thousand times.

Antoinette was now almost totally healed from her ordeal, with only minor brain damage to slow her down, and she could appreciate Vittorio's elation at having a grandson.

"What's his name?" the men at the Italian club asked Vittorio when he bounded down the steps and into the hall in excitement.

"Joey," Vittorio answered, and because of his accent, it sounded to everyone like he had said "Jewey."

"Jewey it is," Gazzo Francini repeated, and to all the old Italians Joey Bellino was Jewey Bellino.

Leaving the club, Vittorio was walking toward his car when he spotted the young man sitting on the stump by the bocce court, making some repair to the back of his motorcycle.

"Sean," Vittorio smiled, throwing his arm around his nephew's shoulder. "Where did you go?"

"To hell and back, Uncle. But the important thing is that I'm back. I have to find Straz."

"Benito Strazza's been looking for you for a year. You gonna fight again?"

"If Straz hasn't forgotten me."

"Come on, we'll go home and call him. There's a new little man in town I want you to meet anyhow."

That night, eating dinner with Vittorio and Antoinette, Sean never told them that he almost didn't come back. He never told them about the day he sat on his Harley at the borders of Georgia and Florida and wrestled for a long time with the decision to head back down south to search for yesterday, or to throw in the towel on his dream and turn around to head north to try and salvage something out of a life he had all the potential of throwing away.

He never told them how long the decision took, or how many times he changed his mind while the traffic went by in both directions. And if he wanted to, he couldn't have told them what it was that made him fire up his Harley and head north, because he didn't know himself. All he knew was that somewhere, in the jumbled confusion of his life, the answers to the mystery of his life had to be hidden, and for now he would have to live moment to moment as long as his broken heart could hold out.

▲　▼　▲

Sean O'Hara's first defeat sent him into a very bad tailspin. It came at the hands of Melvin Johnson, a black fighter from Philadelphia who was ranked tenth in the world. Sean had worked very hard to get to the point where he was ranked eighth at the time, and the loss was devastating, not only because it dropped him out of the top ten, but also because it was such a one-sided fight that it caused Sean to do the very thing no fighter can afford to do—question himself.

Nothing he had thrown at Johnson could hurt him, but Johnson had hurt Sean early and often before knocking him out in the fourth round. Sean had been 16-0 as a professional leading into his first top ten fight, and because of his ranking, he was supposed to win the fight. The betting line had Sean favored by two to one, and it bothered Sean, knowing that many people who had believed in him had lost their money when he lost the fight.

After the fight, which was held at Madison Square Garden on March 14, 1953, Sean locked himself in his room, a sparsely furnished hotel room in New York City, where he cracked open a bottle of Italian red wine. Aching and disoriented, he fell back into an old habit; locking out the world, and drinking alone.

With both eyes swollen and his head aching, he put away a very large quantity of wine very fast, and when he awoke in the middle of the night with his head pounding, his mouth dry, and his bladder full, he felt worse than he had ever felt before.

"Who the hell do I think I am?" Sean said out loud to the four walls in his hotel room, as he lay there suffering his defeat alone. Trying to play back what had happened to him in the ring, he searched alone for the answer to his defeat, but the only conclusion he kept reaching was that he just plain wasn't that good.

As a neon light advertising Ruppert Knickerbocker beer flashed on and off outside his hotel window, Sean O'Hara reached the depth of his despair, and the loneliness that had plagued him all of his life came crashing down on him like an avalanche.

Trying to salvage something good out of his defeat, he remembered that he had been paid more for this fight than for any previous fight, and the sum he had received—about two thousand dollars after cornermen cuts and miscellaneous expenses—would at least allow him enough money to exercise "plan B'"he had decided upon as an option in case he lost.

He would return to his hometown and establish a small tavern business for himself where he could be his own boss and lick his wounds in the privacy of his own domain.

One week after he returned home, he bought a tavern in the center of Indian Springs, a building that used to house the old railroad station, and had a large sign painted for the roof that read, "SEAN'S TAVERN."

Before he opened the doors for his first day in business, he decided to take one more fight, reasoning that the best thing a young boy who falls off a bicycle can do is get right back up and ride again so he doesn't start to fear it. But approaching his next fight, he realized that he had never been afraid of fighting, only of losing.

The next fighter he fought took the full force of all of Sean's frustrations, and he knocked his man out in the second round. So, returning to Indian Springs from his rankings-wise inconsequential fight in Hartford, Connecticut, Sean went into the tavern business at age twenty-two, with a professional record of 17-1, with fourteen knockouts.

Within two years, with little self-discipline and no guidance, his record was 22-6, as he split the next ten fights he took and dropped further from sight in the welterweight rankings.

In early March of 1955, as he approached his twenty-fifth birthday, he was at a crisis point in many areas of his life. He had not allowed himself enough time between fights to take any kind of meaningful assessment of his direction in any avenue of life, just fighting and training for the next fight, fighting and training for the next fight, over and over again, and all without any particular goal.

Consequently, every other aspect of his life had suffered, and as he approached his twenty-fifth birthday, he faced the danger of falling through the gaping cracks that were laid out in front of him, before he had really lived his life.

Realizing this one afternoon while sitting alone on a bench in the park, he decided to simply walk away from boxing with no official announcement or press release.

For the next year, from the spring of 1955 to the spring of 1956, he did nothing but work in his tavern, and once again he fell back into the habit of looking for whatever comfort he could find from the many girls who happened into his tavern either by accident or by design. The only difference between his high school years and his mid-twenties was that he had relaxed his standards and his own personal codes when it came to the women he would entertain after hours in his tavern, and one day he woke up in bed with a girl who was one of his regular customers without any idea at all how she had gotten there, or what had happened the night before.

As his head cleared, and with his temples pounding, he slipped into his clothes and walked into his kitchen where he filled a glass with ice, covered it with scotch, lit a cigarette, and waited for the girl to wake up.

During that time, while the rollercoaster of Sean O'Hara's jumbled and confused life carried him along on one continuous drunken card game, on the sidelines of which was an endless parade of faceless women, Aaron Bellino's life had taken exactly the opposite direction.

His son Joey was five years old in 1956, and Aaron divided his time between his duties as an Indian Springs borough police officer, and a devoted community servant and family man. With his wife, Maura, by his side, Aaron Bellino organized and ran all of the local after-supper recreation leagues, from little league baseball in the spring to midget football in the fall and midget basketball in the winter. While still too young to play, Joey Bellino nevertheless got to accompany his father to all the various fields and gymnasiums, with the positive results Aaron had worked for starting to take hold as Joey learned the fundamentals of all the sports at a very early age.

Blending the two roles of paid police officer and volunteer coach was easy for Aaron Bellino, a tireless promoter of good will and community spirit in his town.

▲　▼　▲

While Indian Springs had become just about the kind of town Aaron Bellino's parents had dreamed about before coming to America, and helped to create upon their arrival, a little town ten miles east of Indian Springs was continuing in the same tradition it had developed centuries before.

Since the days when the Indians still roamed the woodlands of Laurel Hill, the Bradford family had lived there, farming the spacious hills and valleys and guarding against the expansion of the town by jealously holding onto all the lands they owned and passing it down from generation to generation only within the family.

To buy land in Laurel Hill, Connecticut, in 1956 was as easy as landing on the moon. It was impossible. On one farm in Laurel Hill lived the family of Alden and Cora Bradford. Their four daughters, Audrey, Brenda, Colleen, and Dora, all were blessed with exceptional beauty, and of the four, Colleen was the quietest and the most beautiful.

On the farm where the four girls had grown up happy and healthy, Colleen Bradford was so quiet that she would only talk if someone talked to her first, and so beautiful that many people only talked about her and not to her. Most of the boys were afraid to talk to her because she was so beautiful she seemed almost unapproachable. And most of the girls were so jealous of her beauty that they did not want to get too close to her for fear of suffering by comparison.

So she went about her way quietly, and not too far along into high school she simply stopped liking school. She really only went because she had to, but the farm was where she would much rather have been. On the farm she had real friends, her horse, Dancer, her father's hunting dogs, and her mother, who was her best friend, and whom she would sit and talk to for hours as her sisters played. Cora Bradford understood her daughter Colleen's dislikes for school and protected her from growing up too fast by assuring her that she could stay on the farm as long as she wanted to.

By the time she was sixteen years old, she was ready to quit school, but the open door her mother left for her at the farm helped her to grit her teeth and endure her last two years at high school, which was an empty and lonesome time for her.

While her sisters stayed after school to take as big a bite out of high school social life as they could, joining drama and ski clubs, cheerleading squads, and dance classes, Colleen wanted only to hear the final bell which meant she could throw her books into her locker and get on the bus for the long ride through the Bradford farmlands to her home.

Except for school, the only place she went was to church, and that was with her mother, but one very big positive in all of her unhappy years at high school was the close relationship she cultivated by a rich, full prayer life with her Lord and Savior, Jesus Christ.

The more she came to trust in Christ, the more a peace settled over her and she was no longer worried about the types of things that used to bother her, like her lack of popularity at school or the lonesome feelings she used to have when wondering if there was a boy anywhere in the world who was made for her. In the quiet recesses of her mind, she would envision him, tall, handsome, and in control of his life, as Billy Graham had been that night years ago when she had seen him in front of thousands of people, leading them to their Lord.

With Jesus as her Lord, the events of her life would happen as He would have them, and she laid all of her trust at His feet. Somewhere out there, God was preparing a perfect mate for her, and she was willing to wait on the Lord, and His timing.

▲   ▼   ▲

The first time Sean O'Hara saw Colleen Bradford, she was walking down the street in front of his tavern and he was washing beer glasses in the sink. He put down his sponge, shut off the faucet, dried his hands with a bar rag, and walked around the bar to the front window. He stood in the window and followed her down the street with his eyes.

"Stop dreaming," an old man on a barstool said.

Sean turned and smiled faintly at the man.

"She's out of your division," the man next to him laughed.

Sean turned away from them and watched Colleen Bradford walk. He loved her long brown hair that hung almost down to her waist. Her breasts were high and pointed, and her high-heeled shoes emphasized the shapeliness of her legs. *God, is she gorgeous,* he thought.

"You ever want to be welterweight champion, you better forget that stuff," the first man laughed.

Sean turned and walked back around the bar. He lit a cigarette and opened up the sports page. *I better forget about everything,* he thought. *My shot is gone, and I wouldn't even know where to begin with a girl like that.*

Later that afternoon, after Sean had had four or five scotches, the three o'clock whistle blew at the mill across the street and dumped the mill rats out, pouring them out onto the hot pavement to head for the taverns and bars. Sean wiped off the counter and lit a cigarette to prepare for the afternoon rush.

Somebody will be in to help me through the night, he thought, *either Marilyn, or Darcy, or Pam, or maybe Michelle.* Always there were girls in Sean's life, until a card game started or until somebody breezed in who wanted to go to the track. Then he would throw the keys to one of the regulars, glad for an evening's pay, and take off with a racing form as his business ran itself and enough money came in over the bar to meet the expenses and keep the doors open.

On more nights than he cared to count, Sean would return to the tavern drunk and broke, as Lincoln Downs or Narragansett Park took all the money from him that he had taken from his friends in card games.

Throughout it all, the aching loneliness that had haunted him for years worsened, the empty chasm in his heart that he could not fill deepened, and he grew more and more desperate for an avenue of escape out of the hell that had imprisoned him.

On Sundays he would wake up when he did, and with his tavern closed, kick over his Harley and head down the river road for Misquamicut State Beach in Rhode Island. Cruising at a breathtaking roar and passing every car he came upon for no reason, he took chance after chance, with the trip to the shore—which should take an hour and a half—taking less than a blistering hour.

Safely there, he would park his Harley and walk to the shore, a case of beer in his cooler, and sit on a blanket on the beach to bake in the sun, drink beer, and converse with whomever happened by. Some days he would meet a girl, some days he wouldn't, and his loneliness would grow either way. On days he wouldn't meet any girls, his loneliness would grow a little. In the hours immediately after any new girl he would meet would leave, his lone-liness would grow a lot.

At the end of the summer of 1956, Sean O'Hara was in very bad shape. Throughout it all, every day at the same time, just before the mills emptied out, the beautiful girl from the insurance company would walk by on her way to the post office with the day's mail.

"There goes O'Hara's girlfriend. You won't get a beer for five minutes now," Ellington Joe complained every time Colleen walked by.

"Colleen Bradford?" a woman at the bar asked Joe one day.

"You know her?" Sean's ears perked up.

"Sure I know her. She's Cora Bradford's daughter from Laurel Hill," the woman said.

"Uh-oh, get another bartender," Ellington Joe laughed. "When Alden Bradford finds out O'Hara's looking at his daughter, he'll come out of the hills with a shotgun."

Sean ignored the men and turned to the woman at the bar.

"I wondered why I hadn't met her before," Sean said. "She just start working in town?"

"Right out of high school. She's only about eighteen years old. Much too young for you, that's for sure. Plus she'd never go anywhere you'd be apt to go. You'd never see her in here, let's put it that way."

"Why?" Sean smiled. "Something wrong with this place?"

The woman laughed.

"There used to be a set of trolley tracks that ran right through the center of this town. You're on the other side of them from where she goes, let's just put it that way."

The woman reached for a cigarette, and Sean lit it for her.

"Where does she go?" Sean asked.

"She does her job and goes home. Has chores to do on the farm. Then I think she goes to church about every other night with Cora."

"Where does she go to church?"

"Laurel Hill Baptist."

Laurel Hill had always seemed like a little paradise to Sean. With its rolling hills and quiet farmlands, it was totally different from the insanity of downtown Indian Springs.

"Did you know that there are more cows on her uncle's farm than there are people in Laurel Hill?" the woman said.

"Is that right?" Sean smiled.

"I'm quite serious. There're only about six hundred people in Laurel Hill, and her uncle's dairy farm has over a thousand cows."

"That the farm she works on?" Sean asked.

"All those Bradfords work together up there. On the dairy farm, in the cornfields, the orchards, the maple syrup house. They really stuck together through the years. You really have to give them credit."

"She wouldn't turn around twice to look at your ugly pug, O'Hara. You better stick to boxing and pouring beer, and while you're at it, you can start right here," Ellington Joe said.

"Yeah, give us all another round," the man next to him yelled, pounding his mug on the wooden tavern counter.

"Sean O'Hara and the farmer's daughter," Ellington Joe laughed. "Alden Bradford gets wind of that, O'Hara's face'll be on all their milk cartons."

"Missing in action!" the man next to him laughed, slapping his leg.

As the men had their fun, Sean walked back around the counter and stuck his hands back down into the dishwater.

"What'd you say her name was?" Sean smiled at the woman at the bar.

"Colleen Bradford."

Sounds almost Irish, Sean thought. *All but the Bradford. But that part can change.*

▲　▼　▲

At eleven o'clock the next morning Sean was sitting at the bar reading the sports page when the door hinges squeaked, and when he lifted his head out of the paper he saw Benito Strazza standing in the doorway smiling.

"You ready for a good one?" Sean's manager beamed, his gold tooth shining in the sunlight.

"I'm all ears," Sean said.

"I got you an undercard fight to a world championship in Syracuse."

"No!" Sean said, standing up out of his chair excitedly. "You kidding?"

Benito danced over to Sean and slapped him five.

"September twelfth. Johnny Saxton is fighting Carmen Basilio at ten o'clock for the welterweight championship, and you're fighting Melvin Johnson at nine in the same ring," Benito beamed.

"Televised?" Sean asked excitedly.

"Televised! Plus, if you knock the guy out, you could get a shot at Basilio. Saxton will never beat him again."

Sean slammed his hand down on the bar and spun around.

"How'd you pull that one off?" he beamed as he hugged Benito Strazza.

"I told you, kid. Leave the trainin' and the managin' to me, you just do the fightin'. We'll end up on top yet."

Sean O'Hara was very excited as he fired a series of punches into the air.

"September twelfth doesn't give me very much time to get ready."

"That's why I told you always to stay in shape. You been workin' out right?"

"Course."

"No smokin', no drinkin', no women, lot of runnin' and weights."

Sean looked the other way.

"Little shapin' up is all you need at this point. If you want it bad enough, you can get a shot. But you gotta' beat Johnson first."

"No problem," Sean said, even though he knew it would be a problem. The last time they had fought, Sean had taken the first and worst beating of his life, and everything in his life had gone into a tailspin after that. But some major questions had been rolling over and over in Sean's mind since the Johnson fight which he was more interested in having answered than anyone. Sean had to know if his tailspin had started with the Johnson fight, or if it had been the result of losing all of his confidence when Nadia left. If he could beat Johnson, he knew he would have a whole new lease on life, as time continued to dissipate the painful loss of the only girl he had ever really loved.

"I'll be by later with some papers for you to sign. Meanwhile keep busy workin' out," Benito Strazza told him.

Benito left and Sean stood alone in his tavern, happy to have a challenge in front of him once again. Moments after Benito left, the morning crowd started to come in, but Sean's mind was not on his tavern.

"Straz just left," Sean said to Dom Antognoni.

"He did? You got a fight?"

"Melvin Johnson in Syracuse, September twelfth. Basilio and Saxton are fighting for the title right after us. The winner of our fight could get a shot at the title against the winner of theirs."

"Whoa," Dom exclaimed, raising his eyebrows. "You ready?"

"Not yet, but I'm gonna' be if you'll run the tavern for me for a couple of weeks."

"Anything you say, kid. I'm not goin' anywhere."

Sean tossed him the keys. "You can start right now. I'll be back at six o'clock."

"Stay out of the club!" Dom yelled at Sean's back as the fighter ran out the door.

He stopped at the bank and the post office to do his morning errands, and walked out the door of the post office thumbing through the mail. When he looked up Colleen was standing there, the sunlight shining in her hair.

"Morning," he smiled at her warmly.

"Hello," she smiled.

"I'm Sean O'Hara. I own the tavern across the street."

"It's nice to meet you," she said, and she kept on walking past him into the post office.

Standing outside in the sunshine of his new hope, he was feeling good and decided to wait for her, and when her business was completed, he held the door for her.

"I hear you live on a farm?" he smiled, holding the door for her.

"So you already know who I am," she said.

"Your family's been here longer than the hills, the way I hear it."

"Just about as long," she said as she started walking up the street.

"Is it okay if I walk with you?" he asked her politely.

"Sure," she smiled.

"What's it like living on a farm?" he asked.

"It's nice," she said quietly. "I like it very much."

"Must be a lot of work to it," Sean said.

"I keep pretty busy," she smiled. "But I don't mind it at all."

"What do you do for excitement?" he asked her.

She smiled up at him. "Riding my horse is about as exciting as it gets."

"You ride a lot?"

"You ask a lot of questions," she said, and Sean caught himself.

"I'm sorry," he said. "I don't mean to be nosey. I see you every day going to the post office, and I just wanted to make friends."

"That's okay," she smiled. "It's just that I just met you, and I don't even know you."

"One sure way to solve that," Sean said. "How about I pick you up for dinner tonight."

Colleen Bradford stopped right in her tracks. Sean was only the third or fourth boy who had ever asked her out, and he had not taken the several years the other boys had to get to the point.

She was more surprised than anything else as she stood and stared at him.

"Did I say something wrong?" Sean asked, looking around a little bewildered.

"No, but I can't believe you just up and asked me out like that."

Sean was puzzled.

"Did I do it wrong?"

She laughed. "No, not at all, just about a hundred miles an hour too fast. I met you eighty yards ago, and now you want me to make a date with you before we walk the length of a football field."

Sean threw his hands up in the air and laughed.

"Ho," he yelled playfully. "You know how long a football field is!"

Colleen smiled at him. "Thank you for asking me to dinner, but I have to say no. Like I said, I don't even know you."

Sean smiled as he turned and walked back across the street, his mind already working overtime to put him in a position where he would meet her again.

The next day a story about his upcoming fight appeared in the local paper, and when the office girls started talking about it, Colleen's ears perked up when she realized who they were talking about.

A boxer, she thought, and she laughed right out loud at her desk in the insurance agency.

"What are you laughing at?" one of her co-workers asked.

"Oh nothing," she replied. "I just thought of something funny."

That evening while she was riding her horse with her sister Audrey out in the back meadows, she told Audrey who she had met in town the day before.

"Did you say you'd go with him?" Audrey asked, very surprised.

"Of course not. I don't even know how old he is," Colleen said.

"God, Colleen, he's got to be ten years older than you, anyway," Audrey said. "If he was that good a find, he'd be married already. Plus he's a boxer. Good guy to stay away from if you ask me."

Colleen hadn't asked her. She had only told her about Sean O'Hara and how polite and cheerful he had seemed, and that was all. The only other thing she had to go on was the negative way the girls in the office had talked about him, but that was par for the course in there.

The next day she turned her head to look at his tavern as she walked by, and when he sauntered out and smiled at her across the street, she slowed down to meet him and they walked together toward the post office.

"I heard all about you," she said as they walked together, and Sean smiled his customary smile at her.

"All lies," he said.

"You don't look like a boxer to me," she said.

"You know many boxers?" he joked.

"No."

Sean laughed. "I didn't think so. What's a boxer supposed to look like."

"Busted face, no teeth, and a lot of scar tissue."

She stopped and inspected his face for a minute. It was not all that worse for the wear, but she winced as though she had seen something grotesque.

"On second thought," she said, mimicking revulsion.

"You think that's cute, wait 'till you see me on the thirteenth," Sean joked, and his easy way drew her in.

"You really going to fight in Syracuse?"

"Yup. Why, you know somebody there?"

"No. It's just that it's a long way away."

"Not that far," he said. "I've been all over the world."

"Where?" she asked.

"Oh, Europe, the South Pacific, the Orient. I was in the Navy."

Colleen was slowly starting to warm to the man who walked her down the street. He was definitely the most different individual she had ever met, full of stories and experiences she had never heard about before.

"Tell you what," Sean said. "Why don't you go to the beach with me this Sunday, and I'll tell you all about it."

It was the second day she had ever talked to him, and the second time he had asked her out. Again, he surprised her and stopped her short in her tracks.

"Do you ask every girl you meet to go to the beach with you?" she said.

"No. Most of the girls I meet don't know how to swim," he said to her so seriously that it made her laugh.

"I don't believe it," she laughed. "You said that with such a straight face."

"I have to go train now," he smiled at her. "I'll see you tomorrow. I'm going to keep on asking you out until you say yes, so don't be surprised next time, okay?"

Sean smiled as he left her standing there, and she felt herself smiling at him.

Absolutely the craziest idea I've ever heard, she thought to herself. *Me with Sean O'Hara. Talk about a mismatch. He'd be bored with me in an instant.*

Little did he realize at the moment he was walking away from the finest looking girl he had ever seen that as he crossed the street to change into his jogging clothes, she was standing there worrying about being too boring to a man who was light years apart from the kind of man she had had in mind as a partner.

Still, he's nice, she thought, *and persistent. I'll give him credit for that.*

▲   ▼   ▲

The next day Sean was busy in the weight room when Colleen went to the post office, and the day after that, and the day after that. By the time she saw him again, almost a week had gone by, and he had put her out of his mind as he concentrated on getting ready for the fight.

"Well, hello," she said, stopping outside the post office when she saw him again a week later. "I haven't seen you for a while."

"Training," Sean said. "The guy I'm fighting beat me pretty bad the last time we fought, and I've got a lot of work to do to get ready. I'll see you again, though," he said, and as he walked away she found herself wishing that they had had longer to talk.

She wants to say yes, Sean thought, *but something's holding her back.*

That afternoon, as Colleen was saddling up her horse, her sisters began to confront her about Sean O'Hara.

"You stay away from him," Brenda Bradford said seriously. "He's absolutely no good."

Colleen winced a little as her sister spoke, unable to understand what it was that made her sister feel that way. Colleen did not know why he had been on her mind so often. Everybody was running him down, and he was not at all like the kind of person she had dreamed about. But still, she found herself thinking about him often and counting the days until his September 12 fight.

The fight business began to trouble her, though, and when she was riding her horse out across the fields in the farmlands of Laurel Hill, her mind would wander to the pictures she had seen of prizefighters who had lost fights. She could not imagine anyone wanting to punch Sean O'Hara, or him wanting to punch anyone else. The fight game seemed so barbaric to her. In fact, much about his lifestyle seemed foreign to her, from his tavern business to his Navy experiences and everything else about him that was different, if it was intriguing.

Still, it was nice to think that someone was showing an interest in her, even if everyone in her world seemed to be against him.

Throughout the next several weeks, she read the sports pages every day and looked for stories about Sean O'Hara. She was surprised to read that he had once been the most valuable fighter in the Army-Navy tournament, but the event had taken place before she had become a teenager and the thought only emphasized the difference in their ages, about nine years. It seemed as though his greatest accomplishments had taken place light years before.

He continued to meet her and walk with her on the street, and she continued to say no to him every time he asked her out. After awhile she lost track of the number of times he asked her out, but she knew it had to be more than twenty times. Still, he never gave up and she almost wished she could shut out all the people and all the reasons that told her going out with him would be wrong, and get up enough courage to hop onto the back of his motorcycle and go to the beach with him, as he had asked her to do.

As she continued to wrestle within her own mind, he continued to train, and one day about two weeks before his fight, as he was doing bench presses in the gym, he looked up and saw a number of people looking down at him. He sat up in a full sweat and seemed very puzzled as he eyed them.

"Mr. O'Hara," one of the men started, "we're relatives of Colleen Bradford."

Sean stood and smiled at the man, extending his hand to him, but the man would not shake his hand.

"I'll get right to the point. We don't want you to think that we're harassing you, or trying to intimidate you in any way. That's not our intention at all. But we want you to know one thing. We all love Colleen, and we're all in agreement that it's probably not a good idea for you to continue to see her."

The smile started to leave Sean's face and it was replaced by a puzzled look as he scanned the faces of the people that stood before him. He started to shake the tightness out of his arms as he began to pace back and forth in front of them.

"You know, I've been wondering what kind of pressure she's been under that's prevented her from agreeing to go out with me. I must have asked her out fifty times, and she keeps on saying no."

"Well, maybe she's trying to tell you something," one of the girls said.

"I think she's trying to find a way to say yes, if you want to know the truth. But she's torn between doing what's good for her, and going against a few of you."

Sean scanned the faces of each of the people who stood before him and made a quick decision that none of them was overly pushy, so he decided not to press the issue.

"Thank you for your visit," he said. "You can mark my words, I'll never forget it. Now if you'll all please excuse me, I've got a lot of work to do."

He turned his back on them and bent over a bar with six twenty-pound weights on it, pushing it over his head ten times while inhaling and exhaling loudly.

The relatives looked at one another, and one of them motioned the rest of them to the door, which they exited through as quickly as they entered.

That afternoon, Sean walked across the street to greet Colleen as he had done so many times before, but this time he was not smiling. He was serious and very polite, and he leveled with her the way he should have weeks before.

"Colleen, I don't know exactly what your family and friends have been saying about me, but I know the pressure you must be under to stay away from me. I also know that I like you very much, and I want to get to know you much better than I do. Talking to you on the street like this every day just isn't cutting it. I know once we have a chance to get to know each other better when we're not in such a rush, you'll see that I'm not as bad as they're all telling you I am."

She looked at Sean, and then down at the ground.

"We don't have to go to the beach, you know. We can go anywhere, out to a movie, or out to eat, or just out for a drive, anything you want to do. But I'll be honest with you, it's getting a little old getting shut down every single day."

She looked at him, and the way she looked made him believe again that she wanted to say yes, and when she started to stammer, he felt sorry for her.

"Oh well, I . . . ah . . . I . . . oh, I better not," she said, and she turned and ran away up the street.

Suddenly, for the first time since he had met her, he was overcome by a terrible feeling of inadequacy and revulsion. As he watched her running up the street, so young and pretty and so very confused, he felt a feeling of disgust descending on him.

Who the hell do you think you are? he thought to himself. *Why don't you leave her alone. You know you're not good enough for her.* As he stood there on the sidewalk less than two weeks away from the most important fight of his life, he decided to throw in the towel on Colleen Bradford.

Turning to walk to the gym he had made up in the back of his barroom, he suddenly felt very weak and very tired. Lifting weights in his gym, he knew that all his motivation had left him, and he fell far short of his maximum weights in every exercise.

No wonder Straz said to lay off girls before a fight, he thought to himself. That night he did something nobody in his right mind in his situation would do. He bought a jug of wine, reasoning that it would not be as bad for him as scotch, and drank the whole thing in the park while huddled in a blanket looking at the stars.

Over and over in his mind he bounced back and forth from one personal tragedy or defeat to another, and the loneliness that had always plagued him came crashing down on him again. For the next two days his depression continued, but then a mental image of the beating Melvin Johnson had given him the last time they had fought began to find its way to the forefront of his mind, until the fear of another humiliation in the ring began to drive him to train harder than ever before. He avoided all places where he might chance to run into Colleen, and before he knew it, it was Monday, September 10.

Benito Strazza met him at his tavern at 9:00 A.M., and the two men left Indian Springs for a hotel in Syracuse. The weather in Syracuse was unseasonably cold for the next two days, and as Sean walked the streets around the boxing arena he pulled the collar of his black leather jacket up and zipped it fully over his white tee-shirt, while keeping his black woolen sock-hat pulled down over his ears. He tried not to think of anything but the fight, but his mind kept drifting back to the moment when Colleen had turned her back and started to run away from him.

I know she wanted to say yes, Sean thought to himself, over and over. As he stood by a telephone pole looking out across the city, he saw a young couple walking arm in arm across the street, and his eyes followed them for a long time. They looked happy together, and they were laughing and talking as they walked.

Sean leaned back against the pole and wondered how long such happiness would elude him, and when Benito Strazza saw him there deep in thought on the cold night, he yelled out to him.

"Hey," Benito yelled. "What the hell are you doing out here in the cold? Get your ass inside and get some sleep."

"I'm all slept out, Straz. I wish the fight was tonight."

"Yeah, well it ain't," Benito yelled at him. "It's Wednesday night, and I don't want you out here tonight."

Sean slowly peeled himself off the pole and started back to the hotel with Benito.

"You okay, man?" Benito Strazza asked him.

"Yeah, yeah, I'm rarin' to go. I feel real good."

"Strong?"

"On top."

"Rested?"

"Yup."

"Then do me a big favor, okay? Don't come out here unless you ask me first from now on, okay? Don't sneeze unless you ask me. Don't fart unless you ask me. Don't do nothin' unless you ask me from now until the fight, okay kid?"

Sean laughed at his friend and trainer, Benito Strazza.

"You're more nervous about this fight than I am," Sean said, pulling Strazza over to him in a headlock and shaking him. "You better go back inside and have a little nip."

"Never mind about me," Benito said, pushing Sean off of him and holding his hands up, palms out between them. "You just get your ass into bed, and I'll pick you up at your door for breakfast in the morning."

That night Sean went to bed before he was tired and did not sleep well all night. For several hours he thought about Colleen Bradford, and about her long brown hair and her naive look; about Laurel Hill, Connecticut, and the farmland she grew up on and about the way she had almost said yes to him when he had asked her out the last time. He did not pay any attention to the warnings he had received from her relatives, because what they thought did not matter to him at all. The only thing he thought about was how good it felt when he was walking with her, and talking to her, and there in the restlessness of his hotel room in Syracuse, New York, he decided that as soon as the Johnson fight was over, he would make dating Colleen Bradford his top priority.

The next morning he overslept, and Benito did not wake him up. When he finally awoke late in the morning, he walked through the fight arena and saw the locker room he would be assigned to, and walked up the aisle from his locker room to the ring so he'd have a feel for the way things would unfold the following night.

In Laurel Hill, Colleen Bradford stayed by the television set and listened for any reports at all from the sports world, but nothing was said about the relatively minor event in Syracuse. The Wednesday morning paper said nothing about Sean's fight, and only had a short article about the importance of the championship bout to Carmen Basilio.

That night the fight was not televised in Connecticut, and the radio was so full of static that no one could hear a word. The late-night sports did not have the results, and when Colleen rushed to the newsstand to buy a paper she asked if anyone had heard anything about Sean's fight, but no one had. The Basilio-Saxton fight results were not even printed because the fight was too late, and it wasn't until she found an afternoon paper several hours later that she was able to read that Carmen Basilio had won the welterweight title from Saxton. She scanned the article and in the last paragraph was the one sentence that said anything at all about Sean.

"In preliminary fights, Jones knocked out Freeman, and O'Hara lost a decision to Johnson."

That was it. No write-up, nothing, just, "O'Hara lost a decision to Johnson."

Images of broken and beaten fighters flashed across her mind, and she felt herself concentrating on little else as she tried to do her work that afternoon. When she walked down the street with the afternoon mail the regulars at Sean's Tavern were surprised when she crossed the street and walked through the door of the tavern.

Every eye in the tavern looked up at the lovely girl who stood looking very nervous and out of place in the door.

"Has anyone seen Sean today?" she asked shyly.

"No, honey," Dom Antognoni answered. "He's not back yet. Shall I tell him you asked about him?"

"Please," she answered, and she was out the door.

Later that evening, when Benito Strazza's car pulled up alongside the tavern, Dom Antognoni was on the sidewalk ready to open Sean's door. He got out slowly and pulled his hat down lower over his forehead, adjusting the dark glasses that covered his battered and swollen eyes.

"Close one?" Dom asked.

"I should have had him," Sean said disappointedly. "Worst feeling in the world is right after the ring announcer calls off the other guy's name and lifts up his hand, leaving you standing there in the middle of the ring."

"Did you think you won?" Dom asked him.

"Jeeze, I thought I did," Sean shrugged, "but it was real close, and I can see how it could have gone either way. But it was unanimous, even though it was close. One judge had it 114-113."

"You okay?" Dom asked.

"Yeah, I'm okay. But I think I got a couple of broken ribs. Just sore, that's all."

In the commotion of all the people who came out of the tavern to great Sean, Dom Antognoni forgot to tell Sean that Colleen had stopped to see him. He stood outside the front door and talked to everyone briefly before excusing himself and walking slowly around the bar to the back room where his bed was set up.

"Hey Dom, close up early tonight, would you please? I want to get some sleep," Sean said as he closed the door and walked over to his bed. He sat on the side of the bed and stared at the floor, and tried to get up enough ambition to bend over and pull his boots off, and as Dom Antognoni was closing the front door, she drove up.

When Dom saw her, he snapped his fingers and apologized to her for forgetting to tell Sean that she had asked about him.

"That's okay," Colleen Bradford said. "Is he alone?"

"Yeah, yeah, he's in the back. I'm gonna lock you in so he'll have to let you out."

Colleen reached over and touched Dom Antognoni's arm. "Is he hurt real bad?"

"Naw, naw, lotta cuts and bruises, that's all. Maybe a couple broken ribs. He's been hurt worse."

Dom Antognoni locked the door and as Sean lay on his bed in the quiet darkness of his room, lit only by the street lights outside his tavern window, she walked around the bar and stood in his door frame.

When he saw her, he attempted to sit up, but winced when a jolt of pain hit him in the ribs.

She rushed across the room and knelt in front of him.

"I was so worried about you," she said honestly, as she rested her hands on his arm.

He smiled at her and put his hand behind her head, feeling the softness of her hair.

"Does anybody know you're here?" he smiled at her.

"Mom does."

"She let you come?"

"I've been driving by all night. I was so worried, I couldn't think of anything else."

"You should have told me that before the fight," he smiled. "If I knew you were in my corner I might have fought a little better."

She reached up and touched the swelling over his eye.

"This one's gonna be black," she said.

"They both are," he said.

"Why do you fight, anyway?"

"Beats pouring beer," he answered.

"Why do you do that, too?" she asked.

"You ask a lot of questions," he smiled, quoting a line she had once said to him.

She sat up on the bed next to him.

"When you didn't see me all those days after the last time I saw you, I had a lot of time to think," she said. "If the offer still stands, I'll go out with you."

Sean attempted to laugh, but it hurt him too much.

"Oh, God, I don't believe it," Sean smiled. "Now that I feel like the football after a super bowl, you decide to go out with me."

"If you don't want to,"

He put his arm around her. "Colleen, are you kidding? You're all I've thought about since the last time I saw you outside. Your relatives won't be too pleased if you go out with me, though."

"Oh, I don't care about them. They don't ride their horse alone every night through the farmlands."

Sean kept his arm around her as he gazed into her eyes.

"Loneliness is no joke, is it?" he said.

"It's not natural," she said.

"Would you like to go out to eat someplace this weekend?" he asked her.

"Why don't you come up to the lake for a picnic this Sunday afternoon?"

"Your lake? With all your relatives there?"

"I told you, I don't care what they think. If they don't like it, tough!"

"Look, Colleen, I don't want to push any of them, either. Why don't we just go to a movie or something, somewhere out of town."

"There's no good movies anywhere."

"Then I'll take you for a ride on my bike."

"I hate motorcycles. I'm afraid of them."

Sean laughed. "We've got a lot in common, don't we."

"We'll find something to do," she said. "We'll talk about it tomorrow. You need a good night's sleep now."

Sean got up and walked her to the door. At the door, he did not touch her, but smiled into her eyes.

"Hey, thanks for stopping by."

In the quiet darkness of Sean's Tavern, Colleen Bradford smiled up at him as he stood there swollen and sore from his loss in the ring.

"Don't let so much time pass before you talk to me again," she said.

"Don't worry," he said.

He walked her to her car, and when he closed the door behind her, he smiled at her and waved.

As she drove off, a huge weight seemed to drop from his shoulders, and inside he smiled as he lay on his bed. There in the quiet of his room, the Melvin Johnson fight and the lost opportunity to fight Carmen Basilio seemed far behind him as he thought of how soft her hair had felt in his hands. As he drifted off to sleep, Colleen Bradford was the only thing on his mind.

▲   ▼   ▲

The next day everyone who came into town approached Sean cautiously as they felt out his mood before deciding whether or not to ask him about the fight. No one could figure out why he was so cheerful as he sat at the end of the bar, his hands and ribs taped and his eyes swollen behind his dark glasses.

Dom Antognoni washed glasses and poured drinks as Sean sat at the bar, unable to bend over yet. He talked quietly and cordially to the tavern patrons, but as soon as he saw Colleen walking to the post office he abruptly stood up and walked across the street.

"Hey," she smiled.

"Hey," he answered.

"Feeling better today?"

"Like a million bucks, all crumpled and wrinkled," he laughed. "I think it will be a good idea for me to come up to the lake on Sunday."

"That's funny, I was starting to think it might not be. But I have another idea. I go to church in the morning. Why don't you go with me."

"Oh, I don't know about that," he backed off. "If you think your relatives are cool to me, wait till you see how a bunch of Baptists take to an Irish-Italian Catholic. Plus you go to church with your mother, right?"

"Yes."

"I think I'll pass on that invitation. What time will you be at the lake?"

"About one. How do you like your hamburgers?"

"Often."

"I'll see you there then, okay?"

"I'll be there."

That Sunday afternoon, the Bradfords stopped and listened as the far off roar of a motorcycle echoed across the fields of Laurel Hill to the Bradford's lake high in the back hills. Colleen walked to the edge of the field, and when Sean saw her, he stopped the bike and she got onto the back of it. He slipped it into gear and drove right into the middle of about eighty relatives who stood around the barbecue pit, and when he shut the bike down, they all started to disappear in different directions.

Friendly group, Sean thought as he got off his bike and walked with Colleen over to meet her father and mother.

When Colleen politely introduced Sean to Alden and Cora Bradford, Alden just stared at Sean as he shook his hand, while Cora was much more receptive. Sean attempted to make small talk, but the visit he had received from some of her relatives was still on his mind, and though he was not deterred from seeing Colleen, he was uneasy because he did not like being anywhere where he felt unwelcome.

Even at Vittorio and Antoinette's house, he had felt out of place, and the thought occurred to him that he had not felt at home anywhere for a very long time.

Suddenly he saw the man who had done the talking when the relatives had visited him.

"Colleen, who's that?"

"That's my cousin's husband."

"He's not a Bradford?"

"No, why?"

Sean was puzzled. Maybe the Bradfords weren't against him after all, and their opposition to him was instigated by this guy.

"I've seen him before, that's all," Sean said, not wanting to draw Colleen into any battles that were not hers. As the afternoon wore on and Sean made it a point to talk to several of the uncles and aunts, his uneasiness gradually dissipated.

They're not a bad sort, he thought. *Individually they're all okay, just a little hard to get to know, I guess.*

Sean determined in his mind that he would get to know each Bradford individually and befriend them all in his own way, in his own time. The one thing he was most impressed with about them as an extended family was the way they all seemed so individualistic, and yet there they all were, together as a family, over eighty of them, from all over Laurel Hill and Indian Springs.

"I'd like to have a family this big," Sean said to Colleen.

"How many are in your family?" she asked him.

"There's just me," he answered, looking away so she said no more.

"How many children are in your father's family?" Sean asked.

"Thirteen," Colleen answered. "And they're all here, too."

"That's remarkable," Sean said.

"What is?"

"That they all stayed so close. It's a tribute to your family."

He was looking away past the grove of trees that shaded the sandy beach of the lake and out into the distance where people sat in rowboats fishing the private lake peacefully in the afternoon sunshine.

"Can you tell that this is a manmade lake?" Colleen smiled at him.

"It is, really?" he questioned her.

"Yes. Man and woman, I should say, because I helped my father lay the dynamite that we exploded to make the craters this side of the dam. We worked on it all summer when I was only twelve."

"Is that so?" he smiled at her in surprise.

"So if you ever want anything demolished, you know who to see about it. I'm a real blast," she joked, slapping him on the leg.

He smiled and gazed out over the lake with her, and she thought about her large family.

"Where are your parents, Sean?"

"My parents?" he said, looking out across the water. "They died when I was a baby. Then my adoptive parents died too. I've been living alone for a very long time. I don't like it much."

"Let's take a walk," Colleen suggested, and for the rest of the afternoon, the couple walked out through Bradford lands around the lake, across the fields, through the meadows and the orchards, and down to the stables in the valley, behind the barn. There they mounted a couple of horses and rode out for miles into the countryside, passing several mailboxes that all said Bradford.

They laughed and talked as Colleen taught Sean how to ride, and as the sun shined down on them riding through the hills, Sean and Colleen both felt good to be together. Every day for the next month, they met after she got out of work and the longer he knew her the more he began to realize what it was that made him feel so comfortable with her and kept him coming back.

Always, throughout their conversations with one another, she would talk to him about her Lord, Jesus. No one had ever done that before.

She did not do it in an overpowering way, in a condescending or patronizing way either, but in a quiet, simple, confident way that made him realize the source of her beauty and strength. She was an exceptional girl, and the more time he spent with her, the more he came to realize it.

Her faith in Christ was total and unwavering, and her belief in His promises was absolute. She was absolutely the most rock-solid individual he had ever met, and he knew after spending several days with her that he wanted and needed to have what she had.

He began to ask her questions about her faith in Jesus and about her prayer life, and one day, a month into their relationship, as they sat on the swinging chair that hung from a huge oak tree on Colleen's back lawn, the pieces of the puzzle all began to fit together.

Rocking back and forth slowly with Colleen by his side, he listened to her intently as she talked calmly and confidently about the foundation she had built her life on, about the day she had heard Billy Graham, and the vision he had planted in her mind of the God-man, Jesus Christ, giving His life for her.

Sean's life of loneliness and frustration passed before him, as he heard this innocent girl telling him about the day she was set free, and he knew beyond any doubt that he needed what she had far more than anything else in the world.

There, in the quiet calm of her homeland in Laurel Hill, Connecticut, Sean O'Hara made the major decision of his life. Colleen Bradford was the most perfectly well-founded individual he had ever met, because she was so totally dedicated to doing the will of the One she had accepted as her Savior and allowed to become her Lord, Jesus Christ.

"He didn't suffer so much because he wanted to, Sean. He suffered because he loved me. If I were the only person in the world, He'd have given His life for me."

Suddenly, under the explanation of Christ's love from Colleen Bradford, Sean O'Hara felt as though Christ were dying for him at that moment. Sean started to feel a debt of gratitude to this brother man of his who had taken onto Himself the suffering and death that could free Sean from all of his confusions.

As he sat there and understood that, all the loneliness he had ever felt seemed to pale before him, as he thought of the loneliness Jesus must have felt as they raised his broken body up on the wooden cross. All the defeats he had ever suffered seemed small compared to the humiliation the Innocent One accepted for him. All the confusion he had grappled with throughout his complicated and twisted life evaporated, and with tears welling up in his eyes, he forced himself to ask her the question that changed his life.

"Colleen," he said quietly and slowly. "Have you ever led anyone to a personal acceptance of Jesus Christ before?"

"No," she answered quietly, swinging slowly back and forth with Sean beside her on the swinging chair. "Not yet."

Under the deep blue sky of Laurel Hill, Connecticut, on the afternoon of October 6, 1956, Sean O'Hara stood up and looked at Colleen Bradford and she looked stunning and beautiful, more radiant than anyone he had ever known.

"Will you lead me?" he asked her quietly.

She stopped the swing and looked deeply into Sean O'Hara's eyes.

"All you have to do is humble yourself before Him and ask Him to come into your life and take control of it, and He'll send His Holy Spirit down to lead you in the right direction in life by guiding you at every crossroad."

Sean was amazed as he gazed into her beautiful, sparkling eyes.

"God, where did you come from?" he whispered to her sincerely.

Sean turned away from her momentarily, embarrassed by his tears, and glanced up at the clouds that floated slowly across the deep blue sky. He was filled with emotion as he envisioned a young man, covered with blood, being lifted up, wincing in agony, on a wooden cross with nails in his hands and feet. He tried to speak without emotion, but his tears betrayed him as he turned away from Colleen.

"Jesus," he whispered, his voice cracking, and then he dropped to his knees, unable to verbally continue, but there, in the sight of the girl who had brought his Lord to his door, Sean O'Hara reached into the deepest recesses of his heart and gave his life to Jesus Christ.

Kneeling there thinking about his Savior offering His life for him, Sean O'Hara contemplated the miracle of One so strong enduring so much for one so weak.

When he stood, Colleen came to him slowly and put her arms around him, and lay her head on his powerful shoulder, hugging him for a very long time. With his arms around this remarkable girl, Sean O'Hara felt that he had finally found what a lonely lifetime of searching in all the wrong places had never revealed to him.

Without speaking, they turned and walked together back to her farmhouse, and after eating supper together with Sean and her family, she walked him to his motorcycle, which he mounted and fired up.

Before he left, he reached for her and pulled her close to him and kissed her for the first time, and when they gazed into each others eyes before he drove away, they felt a oneness that seemed somehow to be sealed by the Savior they each had made their own.

▲   ▼   ▲

At their home in Indian Springs, Vittorio and Antoinette Bellino were beginning to enter their golden years. Now seventy and sixty-six years old, respectively, they had come to terms with their advancing ages and learned to live at a slow, deliberate pace under a comfortable and pleasant routine that identified their personalities.

They got up at dawn, washed, dressed, and walked arm in arm to church where they attended daily mass with the hundreds of other Italian, Irish, French, and Polish immigrants and second and third generation descendants of immigrants from those and other foreign countries who had made daily mass at St. Patrick's Church an integral part of their daily routine.

As always, the Sisters of Mercy sat in their special pew near the side entrance leading up to St. Patrick's School, where, under the direction of Mother Superior Sister Rose Alba, the good sisters taught the children of the parish under the same strict disciplinary codes that their parents had prospered under.

After mass, Vittorio and Antoinette would linger outside, where townspeople would speak to Vittorio, now Indian Springs' borough warden, about the particular things that concerned them—a cracked sidewalk, a pot-hole, an idea to beautify Main Street. As always borough warden Vittorio Bellino heard every idea and weighed them all carefully, throwing out suggestions that the people had a chance to digest, mull over, and present as one of their own at the next Court of Burgesses meeting, where borough decisions affecting their neighborhoods were made.

A good working relationship existed in those years between the Republican, Vittorio Bellino, and the Democrat, Pop Arnetti, who had risen to the position of first selectman of the town of Indian Springs. Together the two men ironed out differences between the town and the borough, which was the smaller mill district within the town, for the benefit of all people concerned. Meanwhile Sugar Desmond, content to stay in the background, continued to rise in prominence in state politics, and his reputation as king-maker in state politics increased.

Outside the church, Antoinette would invariably get into a discussion about children, a neighborhood party, or an upcoming banquet at the club, and as the crowds gradually dispersed and went their separate ways, Vittorio and Antoinette would again be left alone to walk together back up the hill to their hillside home on Brendon Heights.

There, in the early morning light, every clement day of their lives, Vittorio and Antoinette Bellino would raise the American flag on the tall pole sunk in the ground of their front lawn, and when the flag reached the top of the pole and unfurled itself in the morning breeze, the couple would stand back, place their hands over their hearts, and pledge allegiance to the flag of their chosen country.

For the Bellinos, each of the four seasons offered a different opportunity for enjoyment. Winter, with its magnificent white beauty, was a time for enjoying the crispness of the air, and the brisk, cold walk they took every morning made the warmth of their modest home that much more inviting when they returned home from mass. There, in the living room, they sat under the constant tick-tocking of their seven-foot-tall grandfather clock which stood against the wall that led from their bedroom into their living room.

While Antoinette would busy herself in the kitchen, starting her day-long project of cooking everything from scratch, Vittorio would sit in the warmth of the living room and read the newspaper or work in his den on borough concerns, drafting letters, making entries into the borough ledger, or preparing paychecks for those on the borough payroll.

Upstairs, where their son Aaron lived with his wife, Maura, and son, Joey, the noise would not start until a little later in the day, and Joey would invariably run through Antoinette's kitchen before walking out the back door to walk down the hill to St. Patrick's School. Antoinette always stuffed a treat into his lunchbox and told him the menu she would be cooking for Vittorio's supper.

By the time Joey left for school, Aaron was already on the job at the police station downtown. At night, when Joey went to bed, Aaron was usually doing double duty at the station or picking up odd jobs to make ends meet and save for the day when he and Maura could buy a house of their own.

Springtime was Antoinette's favorite season because of the smells in the air. The freshness of the fertile earth was her favorite smell, brought out by the running water of the melting snow or the spring showers that watered her flower and vegetable gardens. She breathed deeply and freely every morning and loved the fragrance of the wild spring flowers that grew abundantly in the hills of Indian Springs. In the spring, the vegetable gardens were planted, and in those years, everyone had a vegetable garden and most families had chicken coops and rabbit cages behind their houses. The life was slow paced, and the people took the time to plant bountiful crops of their own on whatever acreage they had and clean out the root cellars for canning and preserving their vegetables.

Summer was when the richness of life was at its best in Indian Springs, and Vittorio and Antoinette's home always had an open door to anyone of any background who wanted to come in, sit, and make friends. As always in those years, no one in any neighborhood ever locked the doors to his house. It was not necessary. Everyone in Indian Springs respected everyone else's families and properties, and trust was the rule of thumb. In the mill town, where everyone worked hard for their living, people respected the fruits of everyone else's labor, and people as well as property were safe.

In any season, Antoinette always had a soup on the stove at any time during the day. And no matter how much food she cooked, and invariably she'd cook far more than she and her family could eat, the food never went to waste because Vittorio and Antoinette were rarely without guests.

As the years drifted by, people all across town would reinforce Antoinette's reputation as the best cook in America. Looking at Vittorio and Antoinette, it was a fact that was not hard to accept. She was almost as round as she was short, and he had added a very large stomach to his barrel chest.

As Vittorio's degenerative condition of his backbone continued to worsen, he suffered his pain alone, never complaining, but filling the house with a new smell, that of the liniment he used with regularity to ease his increasing pains.

Throughout all of those years, he would often take Aaron aside and renew with him the instructions he had laid out years before. "Remember," he would tell his son, "when we get old, you take care of your mother. She has had many shocks and strokes, and each one leaves her a little bit less alert. She will need your help in her old age. Me, I can always go to the veteran's home if I absolutely have to."

Aaron nodded, although he never considered it for a minute. Vittorio and Antoinette had cared for him when he was young, he would care for them when they were old. That was just the way it was going to be.

For Vittorio Bellino, autumn in Indian Springs was *numero uno.* Nowhere in the world was the fall foliage more breathtakingly beautiful than on the river road that led into Indian Springs. The river road was the long road between Sean O'Hara's tavern at the place where Furnace Brook and Middle River met to form the beginning of the Willimantic River, and Route 84, which took travelers between Boston and New York. Route 32 on the map, it was always known as the river road to the locals. The river road wound through the valley and carried travelers through the old lands where the Nipmucks, the Pequots, the Mohegans, and the other Algonquian tribes used to meet every year for their tribal pow-wows.

Each fall, when Vittorio would walk its length, he would remember the year he returned from the war and walked back home up the river road. The wildlife was still as plentiful in the wide expanses of forest that still existed in 1956 New England, even though the pollution of many years of factory work had taken most of the fish out of the rivers.

Still, several towns insisted on maintaining their fishing rights to the legendary river, and outsiders were often confused as they saw four different town boundaries drawn in the short jaunt from Route 84 into Indian Springs. The towns had simply elongated their town lines to reach into the Willimantic River, so all of their sons and daughters could fish the plentiful stream.

As always autumn was the season when Vittorio felt most alive, and the cool nights and warm days were akin to his liking. When the mosquitoes and muggy days of summer left, the days were warm and wonderful in autumn. Many meals were still made out of the woods, as the men who would walk with Vittorio would shoot the rabbits and squirrels, while the women would gather the wild mushrooms, dandelions, and berries.

Polenta was better with fresh rabbit or squirrel meat, and many bocce debts were paid off in fresh game for the polenta.

In the fall of 1956, two of the funniest things that ever happened in the Bellino household preceded one of the most frightening. The first incident involved a simple misunderstanding that sent Vittorio's grandson, Joey, into a laughing spell that spilled out into the whole family. Watching television one afternoon in his grandparent's living room, Joey Bellino, age six, saw a cartoon of Alvin and the Chipmunks. Innocently enough, he asked Vittorio if he could have a 45 R.P.M. record by Alvin. Looking up from her cheese ravioli, Antoinette said "Who?" and Vittorio barked, "Alvin Presley!" impatiently, having heard of the young entertainer who was electrifying the country.

Joey looked at Vittorio and started to laugh. Joey was "Jewey," Matt Dillon's sidekick on Gunsmoke was "Fustoon," and now, to Vittorio, Elvis was "Alvin." It caught him so off-guard, and Vittorio looked so absolutely disgusted that Antoinette had not heard of "Alvin Presley" that it set him off laughing so hard that his sides began to ache.

Seeing his grandson in such an out of control fit of laughter, Vittorio, too, started to laugh. Soon, he joined his grandson, and the two of them were clutching their sides and rolling on the floor like little children. Antoinette came out of the kitchen when she heard the rumbling of Vittorio and Joey as they rolled playfully on the floor, and she, too, fell to laughing. When Joey's mother, Maura heard the commotion from upstairs, she came downstairs and stood in the door smiling in total surprise as her son and her in-laws rolled from couch to chair to floor, laughing harder than she had ever seen anyone laugh before.

Not even knowing what they were laughing about, she was drawn in nevertheless, laughing at the way they were laughing, and when Joey realized that she was laughing just as hard as them, having not even heard the joke, that became the funniest thing of all.

That night, when Aaron came home, they told him about the funny story and he started to tell them about the funniest thing he had ever seen. It involved his nextdoor neighbor, Floriano, trying unsuccessfully to mount a horse, and try as he might to tell the story, he could not get past the part where Floriano kept falling off, and every time he tried to repeat the story, he burst out in laughter, which itself became funnier than anything he could possibly have told in a story. Soon all the Bellinos were again laughing and slapping their legs.

When bedtime finally came, Vittorio could not remember a day in his life when he had laughed harder or longer.

That night, as the house lay quiet with everyone asleep, he was awakened in the middle of the night by Antoinette tossing and turning as though she were in the middle of a nightmare. When she groaned and hit the floor with her feet, mumbling incoherently, he turned on the light to see her sweating profusely and wild-eyed in terror.

"Antoinette," he called out to her, trying to wake her out of her stupor, but she was wide-eyed with fear and obviously in bad physical trouble. He ran to the stairs and yelled to Aaron, who ran downstairs and called the doctor. In less than fifteen minutes, Dr. Alfred Schiavone drove up in his pajamas and robe and ran into the house with his black bag.

"She's having a stroke," he said. "We've got to get her to the hospital."

The ambulance was called, and when the attendants came in with a stretcher, it took Vittorio, Aaron, Dr. Schiavone, and one of the attendants to pry the wild-eyed Antoinette away from the iron bed rail she had put a vice grip on with her fingers.

She was totally incoherent as the blood stopped flowing sufficiently to her brain, and when the doctor jumped into the ambulance with her and she was whisked away to the hospital, Vittorio knelt on the floor and prayed for her life.

Joey watched from the stairs as his grandfather, who only a few short hours ago was so happy, now knelt in frightened prayer.

The next morning, Dr. Schiavone knocked on Vittorio's door, and Vittorio swung it open anxiously.

"She's resting comfortably," he said immediately, "And she's alive. But I have to tell you, if she has another one like that, she'll never live through it."

Four years later, when she celebrated her seventieth birthday, Dr. Schiavone, one of the last great family physicians who made house calls in Indian Springs, had already been dead for over two years.

By that time the young doctor who had taken his place as local family physician was already aware of "the old Italian woman on Brandon Street with the incredible will to live" who had survived two heart attacks, two strokes, and several incapacitating shocks. Her arteries were her only weakness, he determined, their hardness due to a lifetime of rich foods, with too much cheese, eggs, and red meat.

▲ ▼ ▲

As life progressed and Sean O'Hara continued to date Colleen Bradford, a whole different set of challenges presented themselves to the young couple. Accepting the Lord Jesus was one thing. Choosing a church to worship in was quite another matter. Try as he did, Sean could not bring himself to feel comfortable in the church Colleen had grown up in. There were many reasons for this, not the least of which was the way her current pastor, the Reverend Elrod P. Tinkerton, so regularly and incessantly hammered away at the only church Sean O'Hara had ever known.

For Elrod P. Tinkerton, the issue was simple. There were born-again Christians in the world, and then there was everyone else. And among those who were not yet born-again were the papists who had been deluded into believing in the Holy Roman Catholic Church and not in the Lord Jesus Christ. Of course every opinion he had about the Catholic Church was garnered from anti-Catholic books he had read as a young seminary student, and Sean O'Hara could not, for the life of him, understand the Reverend Tinkerton's thinking, since Jesus Christ was now, and always has been the cornerstone of the Roman Catholic Church.

The fact that a personal surrender to the Lord's will had eluded him throughout his life, until he met Colleen, had nothing to do, in Sean's understanding, with the methods or traditions of the Catholic Church, but only in his walking apart from those teachings in his troubled years.

For Catholics as well as Protestants, Jesus Christ was Lord. Sean felt that he could just as easily have been led to a saving knowledge of Jesus Christ by a Catholic girl as by a Protestant girl, as long as her personal commitment to Jesus was real, and Colleen Bradford just happened to be a Protestant girl.

After all, hadn't Sister Rose Alba talked about Jesus every day in school, many years before Sean had set out on his own path in life, where a series of bad decisions at crucial turning points in his life had taken him farther and farther away from her teachings?

Still, Sean immersed himself in a study of the Protestant Reformation, just in case there was something he had missed that would cause him to want to educate Catholics about their error, if there was one, so as to ensure that everyone would experience the same life-saving certainty of their own salvation that Sean had recently experienced. This he would do in exactly the opposite way in which the irritating Elrod P. Tinkerton did, knowing in his heart that the way to win people to your side was not by downgrading or belittling them, like the Reverend Tinkerton did, but by drawing them in gently, the way Colleen Bradford could do, just by the way she carried herself in life.

Meanwhile, there was the disquieting certainty that he lived with, that every time he entered Colleen's church, there were hoards of believers zeroing in on him like he had a target on his head, constantly trying to bypass his upbringing and save him from his Catholicism. All it did was irritate him, deeply and sorely.

When one girl in Colleen's church, a reporter for a youth group's bulletin, who had heard about Sean's acceptance of Jesus Christ, asked him for an interview as a boxer, Sean agreed.

"What's the interview going to be about?" Sean asked her.

"Just a general interview to let people know a little bit about you," she said. "It'll be good practice for you when you win the championship. Then every sports columnist in the country will be hounding you."

Sean and the girl sat down in a room away from interruptions, and she took out a pencil and paper.

"I've heard that you recently accepted Jesus as your Lord and Savior?" she started out.

"I guess I've always known He was my Savior, but I just recently gave my life to Him, and made Him Lord of my life, yes."

"You used to be a Roman Catholic," the girl said, more as a statement than a question.

"Not a very good one," Sean said.

"When was the date you were born again?"

Sean realized that they hadn't been talking for thirty seconds yet, and already her questions were telling far more about her than any of his answers could tell about him.

"Tell you what," he attempted to smile at her. "Let me ask you a question. What religion are you?"

"Why, I'm a Baptist, of course, but I'm not the subject of this interview, you are. What religion are you?"

"Christian," Sean answered, "And I didn't ask you your denomination, I asked you your religion."

She sloughed off his words and took control of the interview again, asking him the questions she wanted and taking him down the avenues she chose.

"Where do you go to church, now that you're born again?"

"Here, with Colleen, and St. Patrick's, by myself," he said curtly, now starting to get irritated.

"But that's a Catholic church. Isn't that contradictory to your conversion?"

Sean felt a stab and his heart quickened as he stared across the table at the girl.

"I thought this interview was going to be about boxing?" he snapped at her. "And let's get something straight. My acceptance of what Jesus Christ did for me is not an indictment of my Roman Catholicism, it's an indictment of the way I messed up my life without Him."

"So you continue to go to Catholic church?"

"Yes."

"Do they read the Bible there every day?"

"What's that got to do with anything?"

"Why do you keep asking me questions, Sean?"

"Because you're not really asking me the kinds of questions I thought you were going to ask me, you're just trying to pry answers out of me that you want to hear."

"Maybe you didn't really understand what you did when you accepted Christ," she said.

"Maybe you didn't understand what Jesus did when He accepted me," Sean said. "He saved me from the blank alleys and dead-end streets I always chose on my own. Every day I ask Jesus to be with me at the crossroads and show me the right roads that one day. His Spirit tells me when I pick the right roads and when I pick the wrong ones. I used to stumble down every blind alley I ever came upon. Now I have better discernment at the crossroads. I wish I could tell you I was sure I'd always take the right roads from here on in, but at least now I have a Voice directing me in the right way."

"Maybe you'd be more sure of yourself if you were more deeply rooted in your faith," she smiled at him condescendingly. Then she jotted down a few notes before she got up and walked away, leaving him staring at her back incredulously.

He shook his head like he'd just suffered a first round knockout and stood up slowly to walk out of the room.

Later that same day, at the end of the church service, the people were led out to the back of the church to the small river they used for their baptisms. Two people were baptized that day, and when they were being congratulated afterward, a man walked up to Sean, smiling.

"When you gonna get baptized?" he asked Sean.

"I've already been baptized," Sean answered. "When I was a baby."

"Oh, that don't count," the man said, waving his hand in the air, as if to erase Sean's baptism.

"It does to me," Sean said, once again irritated by the insensitivity they all seemed to have to the things he held sacred. Right then and there, Sean vowed never to be baptized again, no matter how much pressure they put him under. To do so would be to wipe out the validity of the baptisms of all those family members who had gone before him in the Catholic tradition. That he would simply never do, not now, not ever.

When the Protestants' infrequent communion service approached at the end of the month, Sean had a very difficult time trying to decide whether or not to participate. All week he thought about it and thumbed through manuscript after manuscript, book after book, catechism after catechism, trying to decide whether taking Communion with them would be right and proper, since they had rejected the doctrine of transubstantiation and opted instead for a kind of memorial service, where everything they did only represented what Christ had done. This was not as real to him as the Catholic ritual of taking on Christ, and becoming one with Him by receiving Communion in the holy sacrament of the Eucharist.

Back and forth he went, wanting to worship God ecumenically but irritated at the Protestants' inflexibility with regard to his personal beliefs, many of which he knew they had absolutely no understanding of or desire to learn. When he ended up receiving Communion with Colleen, he did not feel good about it, as he should have, but traitorous to his Catholic beliefs.

Incredibly something as simple as worshiping God in the method and tradition of the people he was worshiping with, which many would have done as easily as praying before meals in the home of the host whose table you were at in the traditional manner he had always done it, should have been an easily accomplished, over and done with event. For Sean O'Hara, it was not. He worried about what he had done all week, and the following Sunday he began to feel very uneasy when it came time to pick Colleen up for church.

His dilemma was compounded by the understanding that he had somehow been targeted by people he knew were not the best representatives of their particular denomination, while objectively realizing that he was not the best representative of his, either. That fact doubly irritated him, which drove him deeper into his books to try and grow in his faith. Along with several texts of both Protestant and Catholic teachings, he also read the Bible cover to cover and honestly found that to be the best of all his reading.

"Maybe if we go to Bible study an hour before service, you'll feel more comfortable," Colleen suggested.

Sean was really not too excited about Bible study with Elrod P. Tinkerton, but he loved Colleen, so he agreed.

He didn't feel any better when the Reverend Tinkerton eyed him skeptically and started out by telling his class a number of sad stories about foolish Christians who had "yoked themselves with non-believers" in their marriages, only to fall upon numerous hard times that invariably led to the dissolution of their marriages.

When he left that subject for a lesson on salvation by faith, Sean's attitude started to come unraveled. First of all, it grated Sean the wrong way when the reverend looked directly at him as he preached.

After hammering what he called the Catholic Church's "doctrine of salvation by works," which he had very distorted, the reverend continued to harp away at the theme of salvation by faith alone, so obnoxiously that Sean was tempted to interrupt him.

First of all, Sean couldn't understand why the reverend couldn't just talk. Even to this small group of people, he had to be an orator. Sean reasoned that he maintained his air of authority vocally. No one dared question him because his retribution was feared to be venomous. Even at home, especially at home, Sean had heard downtown that he was never questioned or challenged on anything. The word around town was that he had once beaten his wife senseless when she asked him to explain why he had been so hell-fire and brimstone in one of his sermons.

"Don't you know that I've been called to save the rabble from their evil ways, woman!" he admonished her. "And that I'll do so, thank you, without any input from you!"

When she continued to press the issue, to ask if he didn't think there was a gentler way of doing it, she incurred his great wrath and suffered his vengeance physically. The beating he doled out to her caused her to be hospitalized with a broken nose and a fractured cheekbone, and it left a lasting impression on the couple's young daughter, Myra, who despite loving them both, grew to fear her father, questioning his self-proclaiming authority at every turn, albeit silently, and within herself.

When asked if it was true that he had done the beating, the reverend's wife simply said, "I had it coming," declining to tell anyone else about how she had received her injuries, as the attending physician advised her to.

After sitting in the reverend's class and listening to as much of his condemnation of the Catholic Church's supposed doctrine of "salvation by works" as he could stand, Sean started fidgeting in his chair, and Colleen reached over and put her arm on his. He had all he could do to keep quiet, and she knew it by the miffed look on his face as he listened to the monologue from the pulpit.

Colleen knew that if Sean started to talk, the reverend would take his home court advantage and zero in on him like a dog salivating after raw meat.

Sean wanted to challenge him. He wanted to ask him to explain to him why so many of the people in his church appeared to him to be so cocky and smug and not at all penitent like the Catholics he was incessantly running down. He wanted to ask him how long he was going to teach people that it didn't matter what they did after the magical moment of their personal salvation, when they relinquished responsibility for their sins and put it all on Jesus to take the rap for them.

But because of Colleen's arm on his he didn't say anything, he just sat there and listened.

"You need to thank God every night that you understand the lesson that has eluded so many people of weaker faith that continue to this day to try and work their way into heaven," the reverend intoned.

Sean looked at Colleen, and she knew by the look on his face that he had had the last "lesson" he was going to take from her pastor. He got up and walked outside, and she followed him out into the morning sunshine. He was standing by a large oak tree on the front lawn of the church.

"Maybe things just aren't going to work out for you and I," she said, and her words cut him like a knife.

"They'll only work out if we both want them to," he said.

She shook her head and looked off into the morning sky.

"Yeah, well, I need some time alone to think," she said, and she did not look at him when she said it.

"Oh, boy," he said, smoked with frustration, as he started to walk away.

She stood there looking at him with her hair and her skirt blowing gently in the morning breeze, and when he started his motorcycle, the quiet of the Sunday school classes was interrupted as he drove back to Indian Springs, ending his involvement with the Laurel Hill Baptist Church.

The next morning, Colleen asked another girl to take the mail to the post office, but the girl was busy, so Colleen had to take it down herself. When she saw a group of men standing outside Sean's Tavern shaking their heads in disbelief as they peered through the windows, she slowed down in curiosity as she walked by.

"If I wasn't watching it with my own eyes, I wouldn't believe it," Ellington Joe said to Alan Pauquette. "O'Hara's in there ripping out the bar!"

Colleen listened curiously, and when she saw the "CLOSED FOR RENOVATION" sign in the window, she walked across the street out of curiosity.

"What's he doing?" she asked the two men.

"He's ripping the damn bar out right now," Joe said. "Said the bar was out of business. The pool tables and juke boxes are going this afternoon. He says he's gonna open up an exercise room, a kind of school for young boxers."

"How the hell's he gonna make any money doing that?" Alan asked Joe skeptically.

"All I know is what he told me," Ellington Joe said, shaking his head. "He says he's gonna put up a counter at the far side of the room for sandwiches and soft drinks, and send his liquor license back to the state."

"He must be serious, cause the bar's almost gone," Alan said, peering in through the window.

Colleen did not know what to make of it but she decided not to stay around to ask. She walked back across the street and Sean caught a quick glimpse of her, but went right back to work ripping out the bar. He decided not to watch her walking across the street, because it had already been too painful trying not to think of her the night before. But a minute after he saw her, he fired a hammer across the room and the force it hit the wall with broke the hammer and put a huge dent in the wall.

That afternoon Colleen saddled up Dancer before her sisters came over, and lit out into the countryside in a different direction than the girls usually rode together. Riding alone in the wilderness of Laurel Hill, Colleen mulled over and over in her mind the confusing situation she was in. Sean O'Hara definitely did not fit the mold of the kind of stalwart Christian leader she had dreamt about since seeing Billy Graham so many years before. He was very nice until he found himself in church circles, then he became very hot-headed and intense, and he lacked the kind of peaceful disposition the man of her dreams was made of. He was older, with a past she knew little about, except that she knew he had drank a lot and fought a lot and spent many years alone, and he definitely didn't fit in well with the people she knew.

The man of her dreams got along well with everyone, was respected by all her associates, and was a leader in his community. Sean O'Hara didn't fit that mold at all. A loner who avoided other people, his inability to stomach the pastor of her church worried her, and now she was riding alone again in the hills. Still, her mind kept going back to how good it had been before she tried to get him to go to church with her. And she remembered full well the way he had given his life to Christ, but that only added to her confusion. She wanted to be led by her man, not lead him, and something about the whole relationship just didn't add up.

In Sean O'Hara's life, a battle was raging full bore. It was not an easy battle with defined rules and a referee to step in when things got rough, like a boxing ring. It was much more difficult. Deeply in love with a girl with whom he had very little in common, he was determined to change the entire program with which he had lived his life.

The bar was the first thing to go. And the alcohol he gave up cold turkey. Cigarettes followed, then he sold his motorcycle, which he had been too careless with for far too long. He started into a vigorous physical training routine to build his body up to where it had been before he let things slip with cigarettes and booze. He picked up the Bible again, starting on page one of Genesis, and read it cover to cover two more times. And the most marked change of all was that he started doing something he had long since stopped years and years before. He started to pray.

His prayer life was not something this time that was confined to certain hours or times of the day. His prayer was almost constant. From the moment he awoke early in the morning, to the time he went to bed at night, his life was one constant prayer that God would send something into his life that would bring Colleen and him back together again.

Vittorio and Antoinette Bellino, and the priests and nuns of St. Patrick's parish, were surprised to see Sean at the altar railing every morning to receive the sacraments. Those few who lingered after morning mass to say the rosary or walk the stations of the cross saw Sean kneeling alone in back of the church, his head bowed in prayer before his God.

They could not know the battle that was raging in Sean's mind. He was being hit with every temptation he had ever been hit with before, and even as he knelt in church and prayed, flashes of the passing pleasures he had enjoyed in his irresponsible years flew by him. But always, ultimately, his thoughts went back to that day on Colleen Bradford's lawn when he laid his life at the feet of Jesus to do with him what He would, and he prayed alone for the strength to see that commitment through. Whenever his temptations would grow the strongest, he would remember how he felt when he envisioned Jesus Christ being hoisted up, wincing in pain, to take the suffering for Sean's personal weaknesses, and during those times he checked himself and prayed for the strength not to fall back on his weaknesses.

Benito Strazza did not have the slightest idea what had come over Sean O'Hara, but he was going with the flow. In the next five months, Sean fought four times and annihilated every opponent he faced in the ring. Benito, trying to figure out in his own mind what in the world had happened to him, watched from Sean's corner, convinced that Sean could beat anyone now.

"It's a pleasure to watch you fight now, Sean," Benito told him as he wiped him down in his corner after his latest win. "I don't know what turned it around for you, but whatever it was, keep it up."

Sean continued to fight and win and pray for his chances with Colleen, and one day as he stood timing a sparring round with two young fighters he was working with in his gym, he looked up and there she was.

She looked breathtakingly beautiful as she stood there looking at him. He yelled, "Time," and the two young boxers stopped sparring.

"Take a break, boys," Sean yelled, and he walked over to Colleen.

"I have to talk to you," she said nervously.

"Let's go over here," he said, motioning her toward the lunch counter at the far end of the huge room.

They sat together at the counter as Sean poured her a coffee, and she looked at him and checked his face for bruises.

"You're fighting well," she said.

"I feel better than I've ever felt," he answered, referring, of course, to his boxing, because for several months his heart had felt like someone had torn it out and stomped on it.

"I saw the story in the paper that your manager wants to get you a title fight."

"Straz? Yeah, he thinks I can beat anybody in the world right now."

"Is that what you want?" she asked.

Suddenly Sean's emotions betrayed him, and he stared out the window in detached sullenness.

"What I want and what I get always seem to be two different things," he said.

She reached over and touched his arm, and the softness of her touch distracted him.

"I miss you," she whispered.

Her hand felt warm and soft on his arm, and he reached out and put his hand over hers. "I've been praying every day for something to bring us back together," he said.

Her eyes started to moisten as he sat closer to her, and she felt the strength she had been missing.

"Colleen, the stupidest thing in the world is for religion to separate you and me," he said to her seriously. "I love you with every breath I take, and I can't understand why you and I shouldn't be together."

She looked at him, and tears now filled her eyes. He had never seen her crying before.

"Then why don't we try to go to your church?" she said, and he could tell that for her to say that was one of the hardest things she had ever done.

"I never asked you to do that because I knew how hard it would be for you to do," he said. "Don't forget, I heard all the garbage you've been fed about the Catholic Church."

She took a deep breath and looked away, and he wished there was a magic wand he could reach for to wave over the situation and make it go away.

"Colleen, you're the most perfect Christian I've ever met. You don't need to have anything changed about you at all. But I'll tell you this honestly. The Catholic Church is not nearly as bad as the people in your church think it is. For one thing, in all the years I've been going to it, I never once heard a priest say off the altar that Protestants are not going to go to heaven. Once you go with me, you'll see what I mean."

"We can go tomorrow morning," she said.

"It's Thursday," he said.

"You've been going to mass every day, right?"

"Yes."

"Then I'll meet you in front of the church."

The next morning, Colleen Bradford met Sean O'Hara at the front of St. Patrick's Church, and Sean felt a deep measure of respect for her as they got ready to go in.

"Have you ever been inside a Catholic church before?"

"No," she whispered nervously. "I don't have any idea at all what to do."

"Just follow me," Sean said. "When I stand, you stand, and when I kneel, you kneel. And afterwards I'll explain anything to you that you don't understand."

In the early morning crispness of October, Sean and Colleen walked into morning mass. Just as he had told her, she followed everything he did, and when the time came for Communion, she got up out of her seat and followed him to the altar railing.

"*Corpus Domini nostri Jesu Christi custodiat animam tuam in vitam aeternam. Amen,*" the priest said, and Sean opened his mouth and put his tongue out to receive Holy Communion.

"Amen," he said, taking Communion, and behind him, Colleen accepted Communion in the same way.

When mass was finished, Colleen stayed very close to Sean, and because the mass had been said in Latin, she had no idea what had gone on.

"What did the priest say to us just before he gave us Communion?" she whispered to him on their way outside.

"He said, 'The Body of our Lord, Jesus Christ, preserve thy soul unto life everlasting. Amen'."

"Oh, that's so nice," she said, smiling as she put her arm around his waist. Sean leaned over and gave her a quick kiss. It was the first time he had kissed her in months, and he tried not to think about it too much or to give it too much significance. If things didn't last this time, he did not want to think about the loneliness that would follow.

Outside Sean spotted the people he was looking for and led Colleen over to them.

"Colleen, I want you to meet my uncle and aunt, Vittorio and Antoinette Bellino."

"I'm honored," Colleen said, nodding to the Bellinos.

Antoinette smiled and said hello to Colleen.

"The pleasure is mine," Vittorio said. "I've been doing business with your family for many years. Your grandfather is a good Republican."

"Oh, that's for sure," she smiled.

"We fought together many times against these-a Democrats," Vittorio said. "They wanna take everything from the Republicans and give it to themselves," he whispered to Colleen.

She smiled at him. "In Laurel Hill there aren't that many Democrats," she said.

Vittorio laughed. "In Indian Springs there aren't that many R-republicans!" he answered.

Colleen put her arm around Vittorio's waist.

"Well, there's one more now," she whispered to him, and Vittorio beamed with pleasure.

Later Colleen smiled at Sean. "Your aunt and uncle are very nice."

"They're the best people I've ever met," Sean answered. "You can't pick your relatives, but if you could, everybody would pick them."

Sean walked with Colleen down Church Street and onto Main Street, to the door of the insurance company.

"Will I see you later?" she asked him outside.

He smiled at her and held the door open for her. "I'll call you," he said.

They parted company, and Sean walked down the street to his exercise room. He was putting a pot of coffee on when he looked up and saw the pastor of St. Patrick's standing over him sternly.

"Good morning," the priest said evenly.

"Mornin', Father," Sean said, standing in respect.

"Did your girlfriend convert?" the priest asked him immediately.

"Well, no, Father, she didn't, but I've finally gotten her to come to church with me, after many months of praying."

"If she didn't convert, I don't want you to bring her to the Communion railing again then."

Sean was instantly miffed and fell immediately into a defensive mode. "Oh, Father," he said turning his head aside. "Why do you want to do that?"

"Sean, you know I can't give her Communion if she's not a convert."

The priest seemed to be in a hurry to head out the door and Sean tried to think of what he could say to him in a few seconds that would change his mind.

"Father, wait a minute, please. For months I've been telling her that our church is the one that really has open arms. Now you tell me this?"

The priest shrugged, unmoved by Sean's appeal.

"Wait a minute, Father," Sean said, racing him to the door, but not putting a hand on him. "Don't I remember learning when I was a kid that it's not the priest's responsibility to determine the worthiness of a communicant, and that it's on the communicant's soul if he receives unworthily?"

"That's not the issue here," the priest answered adamantly.

"You may be giving Communion a dozen times a day to people who are in mortal sin, Father, you can't tell."

"I can refuse Communion to a person standing in front of me that I know is not a Catholic," the priest said.

Suddenly Sean was very sad.

"She's a better Christian than anyone I've ever known in my life, Father. Better than me. Better than you. Better than any ten Catholic girls I've known put together."

"Well, I'm sorry about that," the priest said. "But I know you don't want to cause her any embarrassment by putting her in a position of being bypassed at the altar rail."

"Then I guess you don't want me to worship in your church any more," Sean said evenly.

"That's your choice," the priest said, and he walked out of the room as quickly as he had walked in.

Sean was caught in a tangle of emotions he felt simultaneously. He was hurt, angry, embarrassed, and very, very sad. As he sat there with the spirit knocked out of him, he realized that the lines had been drawn. He could no longer worship with Colleen Bradford in his church, and he would not worship with her in hers. In Sean's mind, there remained only one other alternative.

"I'll pick you up after work," he said to her on the phone moments later. "Can we ride the horses tonight?"

"Sure," she answered. "I'll see you at five."

That evening Sean and Colleen rode Paint and Dancer out across the fields to a hill that overlooked several acres of wooded Bradford land. They stopped their horses and dismounted, and Sean reached out and held Colleen's hand. They left the horses grazing and walked over to a large maple tree that stood high on a hill from which you could see for many miles.

"If we could resolve our problem with religion in a way that would bring peace and happiness to both of us, would you marry me?" Sean asked her quietly.

She smiled up at him excitedly as he held her hands in the field.

"In a heartbeat," she said. "When I'm not with you, you're all I think about."

He gazed into her eyes, his love for her exploding within him.

"Then here's how it's going to be," he said to her. "I'm sick and tired of being torn in two by people who have no understanding of our situation. And I do not believe that Jesus Christ is going to turn his back on either your people or mine. But I will not be put in a position of choosing between churches or of making you choose either."

She looked at him in confidence.

"So we're going to start our own church," he said resolutely. "Faith Christian Church, with two members, you and me, and I'll be the priest and minister of that church, and Jesus Christ will be our guide. I'll raise our children to know God, and trust Christ, and we won't turn them over to any priest or minister to mess them up with his own rules, regulations, and prejudices. We'll place all of our trust and all of our faith in Christ, and He'll direct our paths."

In the calm breeze of the Bradford lands that her family had lived on for three centuries, Colleen Bradford held out her arms to Sean O'Hara, and when he embraced her she held him tightly.

"Your God is my God," she whispered softly in his ear. "I don't want to have a long engagement," she said to him. "We've both been alone too long. Let's get married soon."

Sean smiled at her and kissed her, and when they walked together to their horses he felt like a new man whose life was only now ready to begin.

▲ ▼ ▲

Kevin O'Hara was born two years later, on July 4, 1960. While firecrackers and Roman candles exploded in Hyde Park and every neighborhood in Indian Springs reveled in celebration of our nation's independence, Colleen O'Hara delivered her son easily and quickly at Bradford Memorial Hospital on Highland Terrace, overlooking the park filled with Americans of all national backgrounds celebrating the birth of a nation.

Honor guards from every branch of the service led the parade up Main Street, followed by convertible cars filled with Gold Star mothers, those who had lost sons in one of our nation's wars.

As always, the cars filled with mothers of men lost in World War II preceded the high school band, which played upbeat John Phillip Sousa songs as the parade wound its way through town to the various cemeteries, where wreaths were laid by gravestones marked with red, white, and blue American flags.

The parade in Indian Springs was marked with fervent displays of patriotism, a fact unsurprising for the small New England town that had sent the largest percentage of servicemen in the entire United States to World War II. The population of the town was less than twelve thousand, but close to eight hundred men had enlisted in the service, giving Indian Springs, Connecticut, that honorable distinction.

For weeks Sean O'Hara had been hoping that his child would be born on the Fourth of July, and when he saw that his baby was a boy, his face burst into a broad grin.

"My God, look at the size of his paws!" Sean exclaimed to the nurse in attendance. He did not immediately comment on the other predominant physical characteristic of his newborn son because he did not know how to put it politely to the nurse.

"Will that correct itself?" he asked the doctor, pointing to his son's enlarged scrotum, filled with fluid that would go down as the days went by. When he was alone with the doctor in the hallway, he laughed as he put his arm around the doctor's shoulder.

"I have to get a picture of this. When he's older, if he ever starts to wimp out on me, I'll pull out his baby picture. 'When you were born, you were all fists and balls,' I'll tell him, and then I'll show him the picture. 'Don't lose your balls now,' I'll tell him."

The doctor laughed.

"It's not uncommon, really, for a scrotum to be swollen like that, but he does have big hands."

"Gonna be a swatter, I guess, like his old man!" Sean said.

Leaving the hospital into the hot summer morning, Sean felt richly blessed as he walked toward his car smiling. In his car, he paused for a moment before putting the keys into the ignition, and the prayer that came to his lips was his first request of his God since the birth of his son.

"Please, dear Lord, whatever else happens, don't ever let me bury this boy. I can't bear the thought of him dying before me."

That night in the park, Sean passed out over two hundred "It's a boy!" cigars, and the next morning he invited Vittorio and Antoinette Bellino to come to the hospital to see his son.

They beamed with pleasure, and when Colleen and her baby came home, they were greeted by Antoinette and several of her old Italian friends, holding enough food to last Sean and Colleen for a week.

Those first few months of Kevin O'Hara's life, Sean was happier than he had ever been. His son added a stability to his life that nothing, not even a good marriage to a girl he deeply loved, could ever have done for him. No longer did he care about doing anything after closing up shop at his gym except coming home to Colleen and Kevin, bouncing Kevin on his knee, and taking long walks through the countryside with his wife and son. He was determined to give his son the kind of love and stability he had always somehow missed, and the idea of many years of pleasure raising his son elated him.

Everything was looking up for Sean and Colleen, and she and Vittorio were not even that upset the following January when Sean O'Hara and Aaron Bellino watched excitedly as their man, John Fitzgerald Kennedy, was sworn in as president of the United States.

Even Vittorio, a lifelong Republican, watched with pleasure as the events of the early '60s unfolded. Aaron and Sean were behind Kennedy, and the only people Vittorio was sure of that had voted for Richard Nixon were he and Colleen. Even Antoinette he was not sure of, and he secretly suspected that her vote had cancelled his in November of 1960, but he decided that he could live with Kennedy, and when the young president stared down Nikita Kruschev in the Cuban missile crisis in 1962, even Vittorio was sure that America had the right man in office.

Nineteen sixty-three was a year that began with such promise and hope that no one in the country could have predicted the tragedies that started that year or the rapid way the face of America changed immediately thereafter. Before the great national tragedy of November in Dallas, there was a painful local tragedy that June in Indian Springs. It was an event which the world took little note of but which changed the course of many people's lives in the small Connecticut community where it happened.

July Fourth fell on a Thursday in 1963, and a gala neighborhood picnic was planned at the Brendon Heights home of Vittorio and Antoinette Bellino. Now seventy-three years old, Antoinette had opted to let the younger women of the neighborhood do most of the cooking for the outdoor celebration, where tables and blankets were set out all over the Bellino's lawn. The neighbors could sit and watch the fireworks thrown into the sky above Hyde Park after the auto races were finished at Indian Springs Speedway.

When Aaron Bellino told his wife, Maura, that he had agreed to work crowd control at the speedway, all the neighbors agreed to wait for Aaron before they would eat, and bocce and croquet games were set up on the lawn to pass time until Aaron arrived home.

When Maura heard the roar of the stock cars beginning the feature race, she dumped the charcoal into the barbecue pit and lit the coals to have the fire ready to cook in a short while. None of the neighbors, including Aaron's twelve-year-old son, Joey, or Sean O'Hara's three-year-old son, Kevin, was aware of the disturbance that broke out in the crowd on the first turn at Indian Springs Speedway a few miles away.

The people on the Bellino's lawn were laughing and enjoying the games and festivities as the problems at the track escalated. When Aaron Bellino and Roland DellaSandro responded to the people beckoning for their assistance, they saw a big, drunken teenager urinating off the top row of bleacher seats as men and women yelled and cursed at him.

As Aaron and Roland started running up the stairs, the burly youth and three of his friends broke into a run, knocking several people over as they ran down the stairs on the other side of their section and out into the parking lot.

Roland and Aaron gave chase, and in the parking lot Aaron saw the four youths duck behind a pickup truck behind the beer stand. Aaron was faster than Roland, with legs that were long and powerful, like tree stumps, and he ate up big chunks of ground as he ran after the fleeing youths. When he rounded the truck and saw the four crowded together near the open door, he caught only a brief glimpse of the burly youth who stood and aimed a handgun at his head.

The youth took aim and fired one obscene blast at point-blank range before jumping into his pickup truck and peeling out of the parking lot, leaving one of his three friends standing there in horror to watch the awful sight in front of him.

Aaron fell like a giant redwood falls, slowly at first and then ominously and heavily, crashing to the ground with a giant thud that caused the dust to raise around him when he hit. Seconds after he hit the ground, a large pool of blood began to form around the part of his head that had been blown away by the blast.

The sight was too much for the friend of the fleeing youths to endure. He turned around and closed his eyes, unable to watch the horror, as Roland DellaSandro tried frantically to stop the bleeding from his partner's head. It was no use, though, and there, in the dusty parking lot behind the speedway, Officer Aaron Bellino died.

Roland stood up and waved frantically for the ambulance in the pits, but the crowd that soon gathered around the dead policeman prevented the ambulance crew from seeing him, and all Roland DellaSandro could do was yell at the top of his lungs in anger at what they had done to his friend and partner, Aaron Bellino.

A short time later, the three youths were apprehended, and one of them, James Whitson, of no certain address, was later tried and convicted of murdering a police officer, and sentenced to life in prison, without parole.

At home Vittorio Bellino was sitting in a lawn chair watching his nephew, Sean, playing catch with his grandson, Joey. Joey watched for the father, and Vittorio for the son, who would never return.

When the three squad cars pulled up to their home, Roland DellaSandro was crying when he got out of the car.

Vittorio knew at once that something terrible had happened and when Roland approached him with tears in his eyes and told him of his son's death, Antoinette, sitting a few feet away, let out with a loud wail. Joey Bellino just stood there as tears welled up in his eyes and rolled down his cheeks.

Vittorio sat down heavily in his lawn chair and slumped forward with his head in his hands only long enough to compose himself from his own shock before reaching out in sympathy for his grandson, Joey, whom he hugged for a long time as both the father and the son of Aaron Bellino cried openly.

Aaron's wife, Maura, had quite a different reaction, one of rage and shock, as she yelled out a pledge of vengeance on the murderer. Shortly, however, she controlled the display of her emotions as she sat in a chair hugging perhaps the most pitiful of all the family members, Antoinette Bellino, who had now outlived all three of her children, and who was suffering an agony all alone that none of the other family members could understand.

There, on the lawn of their simple American home, Antoinette Bellino turned away and shut the world out, and she was not there anymore. After that moment, when whatever it was that happened within her psyche took place, snapping the last string of sanity in a mind frozen with fear for so many years, she was not there again for the rest of her life.

Her face froze in detached pain as she drifted away to a time forty-six years before and thousands of miles away. An endless stream of dead and maimed soldiers was paraded before her, groaning in agony and denial, deep in the Argonne Forest of World War I France.

"Aar-r-ron not dead," she slurred incoherently into the empty summer air. "*Aar-r-ron e un soldato.*"

The funeral of Aaron Bellino was the largest in the history of Indian Springs. Thousands of people from all age groups and every economic and ethnic background filed past the casket as Maura, Vittorio, and Joey Bellino stood, and Antoinette Bellino sat next to the body of the family member they had lost.

St. Patrick's Church could not hold all the mourners but did reserve the first few rows just behind the family for a contingent of local and state police who came to honor their fallen colleague. A representative number of them sat behind the family, while the other eight hundred who attended stood quietly outside, ready to accompany the body of their fallen colleague to his final resting place in St. Patrick's cemetery.

Along with the hundreds of policemen who attended the funeral were hundreds more of Aaron Bellino's friends. Many of them waited in St. Patrick's Hall, located behind the church and next to the school that Aaron had attended as a boy and then coached in for many years as a community volunteer for local basketball leagues.

For twelve-year-old Joey Bellino, the entire ordeal seemed surrealistic as his emotions and fatigue combined to drive him deep within himself for reflection and reminiscence about his father's relationship to him. His anger at the lost years of love and friendship with his father, that seemed finally to have begun after years of seeing him go away to work, was only eased a little bit by the unbelievable show of sympathy and support at his funeral.

He stood stoically and memorized every person who filed past the casket and every sentiment expressed by every mourner, and the entire experience gave him a new perspective of who his father was and what he had meant to the people of the town.

Aaron Bellino had never been elected to political office of any kind, like his father, Vittorio. He had never made any more money than it took to feed his family, and he was not known by many people outside of Indian Springs, except those he had met in the service and at sports events. But he had served his country in the Korean War, he had been a good American, loyal husband, father, and son, and he had left his mark on everyone he touched. In his own way, he had been a role model not unlike the vast majority of other Indian Springs men of his time. He was hard working, loyal, patriotic, honest, and friendly, and he had grown up in a time when those were the virtues of rule, not exception.

When he died in 1963, America was heading into different times.

▲　▼　▲

After Aaron Bellino's death, a very special friendship started to develop between two unlikely people, the old nun who had served St. Patrick's Parish for so many years, Sister Rose Alba, and the young student who had just lost his father, Joey Bellino.

Deeply impressed and fully in admiration of the way he had handled himself after his father's death, Sister Rose Alba began to assign the privilege of special duties to Joey Bellino with regularity, certain that whatever task she assigned to him would be carried out promptly and well. The summer between Joey's seventh and eighth grades marked the time when Sister Rose Alba began to speak daily to Joey Bellino after every morning mass, and Joey would often ask her if there was anything he could do for her at the convent.

As anxious to make an impression on him of the love of God in his life as she was happy to give him the opportunity to improve his self-image by service to others, she accepted each of his offers, giving him many odd jobs around the grounds. When he would work hard at mowing and raking the lawn, she would grab a rake, go outside, and help him. There the two would talk and laugh, and Joey would try to get a head start on the lessons she'd be teaching him in eighth grade.

"I can only tell you that by the end of the year, you'll know full well how much God loves you, how unique you are in the world of men, with your own special calling known only to God at this point, and how great a sacrifice He made for you when He sent you His Son," Sister Rose Alba said to Joey several times throughout the summer. As September approached, Joey Bellino was one boy who was anxious to go back to school. That year of her teaching career, Sister Rose Alba marked as the most memorable of her long and illustrious career. The lessons she had always strived to impress upon all of her students she gave a special effort to present well to that particular class. She wanted very much to do a good job at teaching this boy whom she secretly favored among all the students she had ever had.

There was something special about him that stirred her intuition. She could not put her finger on what it was, but she felt inside of her that there was some kind of special calling that was to be his. With no idea what that calling would be for Joey Bellino, she felt the strong urging of the Holy Spirit to reach him with the clear truth so that when his calling came, he would be sensitive to it and prepared to see it through.

To keep his attention focused, she gave him several high honors throughout the year. Once it was to lead the coronation procession of the Blessed Mother, carrying the statue of Mary in front of a procession of white-dressed girls carrying flowers to lay at the feet of the Virgin before one of them would place a crown on her head, in respect for bringing the Savior into the world. Another time it was to hold up the cross that led the procession of priests and deacons from one station of the cross to the next during Lenten rituals. At funeral masses, she would often choose Joey when asked to send over a couple of altar boys during school hours, and she would always save her religion lessons for when Joey got back.

She admired the way he devoted himself to learning every lesson she set before him and the way he dedicated himself to perfection at each of the various church-related roles she would choose for him in the course of the school year. *Priests are found from among boys like this,* she thought, *and bishops, and even cardinals. And somewhere in the world right now, a boy who will be pope someday is developing himself in just such a way. But even if that is not his calling, parents are being formed in these early years who will, themselves, raise priests and bishops.*

As much fun as it was for her to try and speculate which of her students would end up in which occupation or profession and with which particular other sacred calling, she also realized that it was sometimes the child you least expected to excel who would grow to be the greatest leader and some of the most promising who would surprise and let you down the most.

Nevertheless there was some degree of predictability in human nature, and she had accepted as her calling to bring the best out of all of her students, which sometimes meant giving special attention to the development of those most promising young people.

Try as she might to envision Joey Bellino as some magnificent foreign missionary or some great canon law scholar, she could not help but notice the exceptional athletic prowess he was also developing at the same time as his scholastic lessons were being completed with such skill. Sister Rose Alba believed in each of her students so much that she absolutely expected them to do well in school and to win every one of their games on the athletic field. People have a tendency to live up to your expectations of them, she had decided a long time ago, and the best way to get excellence was to expect perfection.

Joey had to admit that he tried to do better when he knew Sister Rose Alba was going to be in the crowd watching his game.

In basketball he was a power forward; in baseball, an excellent pitcher with exceptional speed and good control; but his best game was football. Scoring no fewer than three and as many as six touchdowns per game, while averaging over 250 yards rushing over a ten game interscholastic schedule, Joey soon turned the heads of private high schools throughout the state, whose scholarship committees were always looking to find that special student athlete who would make their school his alma mater.

While the scouts had their eyes on Joey Bellino, his attention was captured by the person he had come to admire the most in his young world, the sage old nun who had taught so many people before him about the subject he enjoyed the most, the life and times of the Lord Jesus. Joey could never remember a better teacher, and he had loved school and every one of the teachers he had had at St. Patrick's. But there was a certain aura about Sister Rose Alba that made it seem as though she was moving into another dimension whenever she was talking to them about the life of Jesus Christ.

She made the life of Christ seem so real to them that Joey almost felt like one of Christ's chosen twelve when she brought her class through His life from the edge of their seats, and Joey's favorite lesson of all was about the nature of heaven. Heaven, it was explained to them, is a place so good that the mind of man is incapable of comprehending just how good it is. Everything in man's wildest dreams pales in comparison with how good heaven really is.

Learning that, Joey was certain that at the very least he would be able to transport himself back and observe every second of every day of Christ's life as it happened, seeing and hearing every event of Jesus's life. For at least thirty-three years of his time in heaven he would be thrilled to walk the world with his Lord, which was, at the present time, in his mind the wildest and most extravagant dream his thirteen-year-old mind could conjure up.

Sister Rose Alba was so upbeat and inspirational and possessed of such a caring and gentle disposition that by the time the school year neared an end, Joey fully understood what all of his elders had been saying for so long about how good a teacher the old nun really was.

At graduation, in the spring of 1964, Sister Rose Alba did the greatest thing for Joey Bellino that any teacher before, or since, ever did for him. On his final report card, in bold black letters, she wrote a prediction that Joey came to treasure and believe more than any words any person ever spoke to him.

"We'll hear great things of you someday, Joseph," she wrote, and with every fiber of his being, he accepted her words with pleasure and believed them.

He walked over to her and stood before her, unable to think of anything appropriate to say to her, and when he tried to shake her hand, she hugged him, as she did with all of her graduates. As they walked one by one to their families and friends, and away from her, she stood apart and experienced the annual ritual of mixed emotions that all good teachers experience on the last day of school every spring; a lot of satisfaction for a job well done, and a little bit of heartbreak for another happy chapter of her life she knew was sadly over.

▲　▼　▲

On Stafford Street, in their modest home away from the center of town, Sean and Colleen O'Hara were very happy together. As a personal code, he had vowed never to require her to work, no matter how hard it became for him in the unforeseeable days ahead. Other men may ask their wives to share the load, but not Sean O'Hara. What he did for a living had never mattered to him, only that he went the extra mile in whatever he did.

It pleased him to see her happy and free from the stresses of a job, and riding horses with her and Kevin in the hills had been a pleasure beyond description for the man and his family.

So, too, were the walks they took in the woods, and the picnics at the pond. Nothing in life had been more valuable to him than the joy his family life had been.

Just as he had promised her, he had been his son's teacher about God, reading him Bible stories and giving him his first heroes in life, David, Gideon, Moses, Abraham, and Joseph. Sean taught Kevin about Jesus and about the close relationship the O'Haras had with God and His Son.

"What a team!" Sean had said to Kevin one time when asked to name the best basketball team possible. "You, me, Mommy, Jesus, and God! Not even the Celtics could beat us!"

Kevin had laughed, his eyes wide with understanding at the power of the combination, and when Sean had hugged Colleen and Kevin at the time, he had felt like the happiest man on Earth.

Then the bad times had started creeping in, and as is often the case in happy homes, the lack of sufficient income started the whole thing to come unraveled. First the recession had hurt his already meager business, then he had run into a little bit of debt trying to keep it afloat, waiting for the good times to come back. Finally, when they didn't, he had drifted around his old haunting grounds looking for little card games "to pass the time."

Of course he won and staved off the nagging bills. But when times got tougher, he sought out the bigger games, and as usual, he won more money in those. But it was not the same as it used to be. He no longer drank, and he had to endure the slowness of play and the rambling and arguing of the other players as the nights wore on, and he couldn't remember it being such a struggle to win money, or such a bad feeling about taking money from other men.

So he quit the card games, and went back to the worst place he could possibly go, where he never won money before—the horse track. Almost as though it had been the design of the most evil deceiver himself, he hit a big superfecta on his first day back at the track, won big money three days in a row after that, and found himself suddenly leaving his family to gamble at the track every day.

Of course it didn't last. His bills paid, he tried to win more, and when the losing streak started, it was amazing the ridiculous things that happened to keep it going. First he would chase a number relentlessly until he finally got sick of losing, get off of it, and bang, it would come in. Angered, he would get on another number, stay with it until it would come in, and then get off of it, but when he hit it, it would pay peanuts. As soon as he got off of it, it would come right back in and pay a ton. His horses would be ten lengths ahead and break their legs; jockeys would fall off; he would have a winner that would be taken down in an objection; he'd get nipped at the wire; pick first and third in perfectas; first, second and fourth in trifectas; and first, second, third and fifth in supers. He'd bet a horse to win, and it would come in second. He'd bet the next one to win and place, and it would show. He'd bet it across the board, and it would run out of the money. He'd be torn between two horses, bet on one, and the other one would come in. He would get to the track in the second race, and his horse would have won the first; stay away all together for two or three days while his horses came in eight out of nine races, and then go and get hammered as nothing he bet on would get out of the gate. On and on, one amazing thing after another would happen to him relentlessly, until he was at the end of his patience.

When that would happen, he'd go to the bar and drink whiskey, usually far too much, and wake up in his car at dawn, angry and frustrated beyond belief.

Throughout it all, he was concentrating so hard on the racing form, studying with such intensity to try and figure out some system that he never thought about the little boy who sat at home waiting for his daddy to come home.

"Mommy, where's Daddy?" Kevin would ask sadly, pacing the floor in lonely anticipation for his best friend to come home.

"He's out earning money for us, Kev, so we can eat tomorrow."

"But I want to play with him."

"He'll be home soon."

Later, nipped at the wire again, Sean slapped the racing form on his leg as Colleen lifted Kevin off the couch and put the sleeping boy into his bed.

For ten years, Sean O'Hara had avoided the awful scenario that his life had suddenly become, and the frustration of having too little income had exploded in his face like a bad dream.

Then, after mustering up whatever little self-discipline he had left, he did something which totally shot his self-image away. He started reading the help wanted ads in the local paper and interviewing for jobs. Menial jobs that paid nothing would be given to somebody else younger than him. He would be told that he was underqualified for a job that a monkey could do, or overqualified for a job he could live with, but which the interviewer thought he was not cut out for. He was told he was not experienced enough to do a job he could do in his sleep and not educated enough to do a job he could do with his eyes closed.

He was offered an endless string of commission sales jobs, but he did not want to go to work on someone who had just said no to him, when all good salesmen go to work. To Sean, no meant no, and an honest assessment of his personal talents revealed to him that he was a woefully poor salesman and not willing to change himself to become effective in that field. To pay the insurances and put food on the table, he finally settled for a second shift job at the woolen mill, and going back to work for someone else after having supported himself for so long knocked all of the spirit out of him.

Finally, in frustration, he called Benito Strazza on the telephone and asked him to get him some more fights.

"Sean, you're thirty-eight years old. I can't get you any good fights at this point."

"I need a payday, Straz, I'll fight anybody, anywhere."

"I never wanted that for you, Sean," Benito said quietly. "I wanted you to walk away and stay away, when the time came. Too many guys come back and get hurt."

"I can still bang, Straz, you know that. If I have to make the circuit of a bunch of young guy's hometowns so they can pad their records with a bunch of hometown decisions, I'll do it. What does it matter if I get a few more losses? My record as it is will never get me a title shot anyway at this point."

Sean did not see Benito Strazza shaking his head in sadness at the other end of the receiver.

"You'll have to give me a few weeks to see what I can dig up," he said.

"Yeah, well hurry up. I start work tomorrow running a machine in the mill."

Sean's first comeback fight was much easier than he had expected, a first round TKO in Hartford, Connecticut, in which he knocked his man down six times before the ref finally stopped it. For his effort, he was paid eighty dollars.

The second fight was much more difficult, and he had to go six very grueling rounds to earn a split decision in Springfield, Massachusetts. For that fight he again earned eighty dollars. But a strange thing happened to him in that second fight. Standing at center ring with the ref holding the hands of Sean and his opponent while they awaited the judges scoring, he was sure that he had lost the decision because the other fighter was a hometown boy. When the decision was announced and Sean's hand was raised by the referee, he was more thrilled than by any other decision in his career.

I really do still have it in me, he thought, smiling as he hugged his opponent and headed for the shower room. In the shower room, he turned to Benito Strazza. "Straz, I feel absolutely great. Honestly I have never felt better. I want you to get me a contender."

Six weeks later, at Madison Square Garden in New York, a rejuvenated Sean O'Hara electrified the crowd with an inspired performance against a promising young undefeated fighter, winning every round before the fifth when he put together a picture-perfect combination of punches that knocked his opponent out midway through the round.

When his opponent was counted out, Sean's elation at the resurgence of his career caused him to leap into the air with his fists held high, and the broad smile that spread across his face haunted the young fight promoter sitting at ringside who watched the crowd reaction to the popular old fighter's victory.

As Sean hugged his opponent, encouraging him to keep his career alive, and raised his opponent's hand up, pointing at him respectfully to the crowd, James Travis whispered to the man sitting next to him, "Find out who his manager is," and as Sean O'Hara celebrated, James Travis started running numbers through his calculating brain.

Two days later, in Indian Springs, Connecticut, Sean O'Hara, fresh off the most satisfying victory of his career, bet 250 dollars on a football game through a local bookie and lost the bet. In the span of the next three days, he lost seven consecutive doubling bets on sporting events, and walked into the bedroom of his home owing 32,000 dollars to the bookies, twice as much as he owed on his house. In the warm comfort of his bedroom, he sat down on the bed, crushed.

He had told Colleen he was going out to play cards, and still hurting from his most recent fight, he laid back on the bed as Colleen came to him. As she lay there in his arms, the softness of her body a salve for his wounds, it occurred to him that she had not asked him if he had won or lost or how much money he had made or if he had any of it left. All she had done was make everything convenient for him until he had gotten ready for bed, and then stood near him until he came to her. When he reached out to her she had come to him and taken him into her arms, and after they had made love, as she drifted off to sleep, he wondered in the jumble of his thoughts at the almighty miracle his God had rendered to him the day He had sent Colleen into his life.

In the lonely years before he had found her, he had stopped believing she existed and resigned himself to the dull ache his lonely life had become. And then, when he needed her more than he himself had realized, she appeared, and the void she filled had saved him from his misery and his failures.

Now, suddenly, with no forewarning, the cracks that he seemed ready to fall through in life before he met her seemed to be opening up before him wider than ever, beckoning to him, threatening to swallow him up as his old demon, gambling, came storming back grotesquely into his life.

He was more than disgusted with himself; he was distraught over the lack of character that had caused him to seek the quick fix to his financial troubles, only to crash harder and deeper into the hole he saw no way out of. He was sick at his lack of discipline and ashamed of himself for going back to his bad habit like a dog that returns to his own vomit.

He did not want to think about the ridiculous string of bad luck that made so many consecutive wagers go down. Every gambler has streaks like that, but not many lose as much money in a lifetime as Sean had lost in one weekend. What was worse, he didn't have anywhere near enough money to pay the bookies what he owed them.

Colleen did not deserve this. A girl like her deserved luxury and riches, but at the very least comfort and security. What could he offer to her now? Owing more money than many men made in several years, he could only provide her with crumbs, and it pained him deeper than he was able to handle. Not that she had ever required anything more of him than he had provided—his love, his loyalty, his companionship, and the food on their table, as well as the exceptional family life he had engineered with her and their son. But debt? Deep, long-term, prolonged debt? It was tragic and too painful to think about, and yet he had to address it because very soon the collectors would be at his door. And what about Kevin? How could he expect to be any kind of example for the son he loved, when he had been crushed by his demons, beyond redemption?

He was absolutely sick about it as he lay in his bed and worried, his eyes closed and his heart aching. The guilt he felt made him sick to his stomach as he tried hard to think of where he could get the money to pay off the bookies. Adding up the sum he owed them, he knew that immediate payment was impossible.

Somewhere behind it all was a belief in himself, hidden deep within his subconscious mind, which told him that if worse ever came to worse, he could reach deep down within himself and come up with a hard fought string of victories that would put any amount of money on the table that he needed to earn for any possible eventuality in his life.

But he had never planned on running into such a hurricane as eight consecutive paper losses at a time when everything seemed to be looking up for him in life. His remorse was overpowering, but his debt was still there.

If I have to, I'll go on a payment plan with them, agreeing to large interest rates in exchange for time to pay them off. It will cripple my life, he thought, *but it will solve my problem. But Colleen, poor Colleen, who deserves the best the world could offer, what's to become of my dreams for her?*

Lying in his bed, his wife asleep by his side, he thought back to the first time he had seen the old man with a deck of cards in his hands, and he tried to imagine what his life would have been like if he could have gone back and erased just one thing out of it—all the countless hours he had squandered gambling.

He may very well have been the welterweight champion of the world, or owned his own big business, or had the self-image to be a minister to more than just his wife and son, bringing character and stability into the lives of others who had difficulty in one or another avenues of life. Instead he was a second-class fighter, a struggling sole proprietor of a small business, and now, recently, a moonlighting mill rat as well. He was the guy who said the prayers at the house and taught his son about the mercy of God, that was it. And for people like Colleen and Kevin, at least in his mind, that was far from being enough.

In the middle of the night, he got up and walked out onto his back porch and gazed up into the endless heavens, at the thousands of stars that illuminated the night.

"I'm sorry for my failures, Lord," he whispered alone to the heavens. "You, most especially, deserved better from me in my life. I'm placing my fate in your hands, Lord. And I don't have any answers. But You and I both know that Colleen and Kevin deserve more. We both know that."

In the cold chill of the night, Sean O'Hara walked back into the house and went to bed, his fate now in the hands of God.

The next day, as he tightened a turnbuckle on the training ring in his club, Benito Strazza walked in beaming from ear to ear with another man by his side.

"Sean O'Hara, I'd like you to meet James Travis, Homer Jones's manager."

Sean's eyes immediately locked into the tall handsome black man who smiled cordially as he held out his hand to him.

Homer Jones! Sean had been following him since he first burst onto the scene by winning the gold medal in the Olympics. Never had there been a more certain heir to the welterweight crown than him. Eight and zero as a pro, with eight consecutive knockouts, everyone in boxing was waiting for him to get his title shot, and now his manager was standing in Sean O'Hara's business in Indian Springs, Connecticut.

"Homer doesn't want me?" Sean asked James Travis, almost unable to believe that it could be true.

James Travis reached into his pocket and pulled out a type-written contract, spelling out the terms and conditions of the Jones-O'Hara fight to be held as the preliminary to the welterweight championship of the world, in Las Vegas, Nevada, on January 1, 1969. For the fight, Sean would be paid sixty thousand dollars, with a guaranteed title fight on the fourth of July if he won.

Sean looked at Benito Strazza, who was smiling a big proud smile. Immediately Sean did some quick calculating in his mind. *I can pay off the book, pay off my house, give a big bundle to Colleen, and hit the casinos with the rest.*

"Has Homer seen the contract?" Sean asked Travis.

James Travis held the contract out for Sean to see. Homer Jones's signature was already on it.

"Gimme a pen, Straz," Sean said.

Later that day, Sean arranged for Benito Strazza to make all the payments he had thought about, and after examining the details more closely, discovered that he would not have quite as much to give to Colleen after all of his debts were paid as he had first thought. There were travel expenses to consider, handler's cuts, and a bonus to Benito Strazza that he thought about in retrospect.

"Keep the bonus," Benito told Sean. "I'll take my bonus out of your title fight purse."

"Straz, there's just one thing I don't want you to forget," Sean reiterated. "I only want two thousand, no make that five hundred, myself. The rest, after you pay off Costanza and the bank, goes to Colleen. I want to come home from Vegas ahead for the first time in my life, no matter what happens to the five hundred I take into the casino."

▲　▼　▲

The days leading up to Christmas, 1968, were the happiest days of young Kevin O'Hara's life.

"He's a big boy now, Mom," Sean said to Kevin's mother, smiling. "He's ready to go with me to the gym."

Kevin counted it as the greatest privilege of his life to accompany his father to the gym, where the eight-year-old boy watched the thirty-eight-year-old man training for the biggest fight of his life.

"Is Homer Jones as good a boxer as you are, Dad?" Kevin asked his father after watching Sean in a grueling workout with a sparring partner.

"You want the truth?" Sean smiled at Kevin, breathing heavily.

Kevin nodded.

"He's quite possibly the best fighter in the world right now, pound for pound."

Kevin thought about it for a moment, and Sean saw the concern that entered his eyes.

"Do you think he can beat you, Dad?"

Sean wiped his face with a towel and put his hands out for one of his students to unlace his gloves.

"Everybody in the world who knows anything about boxing thinks so, but you remember what happened to Goliath when David came out to meet him."

Kevin nodded again.

"One thing you have to remember about boxing," Sean said to Kevin. "When two men who weigh the same enter the ring, anything can happen. Sometimes it comes down to who has the biggest heart. Don't forget Homer Jones has never been really tested before."

"You're gonna' at least test him then, huh, Dad?"

"Oh, you bet I am," Sean smiled at his son. "Besides, he's young enough to be my son. If I can't beat him with my skills, I can always turn him over my knee and spank him."

Kevin laughed at his father's joke. In eight years, Sean had never had to spank Kevin, and the sight of him spanking Homer Jones made Kevin laugh.

"How old is Homer Jones, Dad?"

"'Bout twenty, twenty-one, I guess. I don't really know for sure."

The truth of the matter was he was nineteen years old, having lied about his age to get a shot at the Olympics. He was still growing and still improving, and boxing experts everywhere figured that after a learning experience with a cagey old fighter who was hard to knock out, he would take the title from the welterweight champion before his teenage years were finished.

For several weeks leading up to the fight, Kevin and Sean O'Hara were inseparable. At first Sean was just glad to be able to give him some of the time he had never taken to be with him but the more he saw the concentration with which Kevin watched him, and the stamina with which he stayed throughout his workouts, the more he began to notice in the eyes of his young son the admiring stare, the hunger to learn, the satisfaction with the progress Sean was making, and one day, without realizing it, Sean began to fight for Kevin, almost more than for himself.

The kid will be brokenhearted when I lose, Sean thought, and then one night, after Sean knocked the headgear off of one of his sparring partners who could not continue after the shot, Kevin surprised his father when he grabbed him by the arm for the first time in his life and looked him right in the eyes.

"You're gonna win, Dad," the boy said seriously, and for a split second, Sean O'Hara believed him.

Sean looked at his young son with wonder and pride, and in his eyes he saw the same confident belief in Kevin's eyes that he had seen in Colleen's, and something made him pull the boy into his arms and hug him tightly for a very long time.

"I don't honestly know if I am, son. But I'm gonna' give it my absolute best shot, I can promise you that."

Two weeks later, as Sean, Colleen, and Kevin O'Hara sat at the supper table in their home eating supper quietly, Kevin put his fork down and walked around the table. He sat in his father's lap, put his arm around his neck, and exhaled fully.

"I want to ask you a question, and it's okay if you don't give me the answer I want to hear," the boy said.

Sean and Colleen looked at one another, and Kevin got very serious. "I want to go with you to Las Vegas, to watch the fight."

Colleen laughed a little bit and answered him before Sean could. "It would be no place for an eight- year-old boy, Honey, and Daddy won't be able to watch you out there."

Kevin nodded at his mother obediently, and walked back around the table where he sat down and stared into his plate somberly.

Sean looked at the boy across the table and then up at the boy's mother.

"He's going with me," Sean said, and Kevin got the brightest grin on his face that either of his parents had ever seen.

"E-e-yes!" the boy shouted, throwing his fist up into the air in elation and jumping up out of his chair.

"How are you going to do that?" Colleen asked Sean, willing to go along with the decision if she just understood the arrangements.

"He's been coming with me to the gym every day anyway. On fight night, Straz can get him a seat near my corner, and after the fight I won't have to be alone in my room."

Kevin was beaming with excitement and anticipation, and Sean was thrilled at the thought of having him along.

"The truth of the matter is that he brings the best out of me," Sean said to Colleen seriously, "And I'd be happy to have him along."

One week later, Benito Strazza and Sean and Kevin O'Hara boarded a plane at Bradley International Airport bound for Las Vegas, Nevada. Sean had five hundred dollars cash in his pocket, Benito had all the tickets and hotel reservations, and Kevin had his father's bags as the three of them boarded the plane.

When they broke through the clouds for the first time and looked down at the tops of the bright fluffy clouds, Kevin looked out the window and smiled.

"Wow, Dad, look! It's just like being in heaven!"

Sean hugged his son and smiled at him.

"I once had a school teacher many years ago who used to talk to us about heaven," Sean said. "Her name was Sister Rose Alba. She was an absolutely excellent teacher. You know what she liked about heaven?"

"What, Dad?"

"She liked where the Bible says that eye has not seen, nor has ear heard, nor has it entered into the heart of man, the wonderful things which God has prepared for those who love Him."

Kevin looked out of the plane's window, and down at the tops of the clouds. "You mean heaven is better than this?"

"Oh, much, much better. Better than your greatest dream. Better than you can imagine in your mind. You know what else she told us?"

"What?" Kevin asked, eager to learn.

"She told us what Jesus said to his disciples in my own most favorite verse out of the whole Bible."

"What's that, Dad?"

"Jesus said, 'In my Father's house, there are many mansions, if it were not so, I would have told you. I'm going there to prepare a place for you. And after I go there and prepare a place for you, I'm coming back to get you and take you there myself so you'll be with me where I am.' More than any other verse of the Bible, I love that one, Kevin."

"I do too," Kevin said.

The father and the son sat and talked like this all the way to Las Vegas, and Kevin O'Hara could never remember feeling so happy, or so good. They talked about many things and all the many places they'd go together, now that Kevin was old enough to accompany his father on his life's journey.

"After the fight, I have something special planned for you and me and Mommy to do," Sean said at one point.

"Tell me," the boy said.

"I'm going to take the two of you with me to Hawaii for two weeks. Out there we're going to go snorkeling in the bays and kayak surfing on the big kahuna waves. We're going to eat in fine restaurants, rent Jeeps to tour the islands in, see all the pineapple plantations, the tropical rain forests, and the volcanoes. We're going to beach parties and luaus, and you and me are going to run on the beach while Mommy gets a suntan. And at night, after you go to sleep, me and Mommy are going to plan out the next chapter of our lives together, because I'm leaving some excess baggage behind me after Las Vegas."

Kevin did not understand what his father had meant by the last statement, but all the fun they'd have in Hawaii excited him.

"Oh, Dad, thank you. Does Mommy know?"

"Not yet. But I have some other surprises for her, too. Mr. Strazza is going to make her very happy with one big present."

"Dad, when we get back to Indian Springs, do you have to go away every day anymore like you used to?"

"Why, do you want me to stay home with you?"

"At first I wanted you to stay home with me so I could play with you, but I'm getting a little old for that. But maybe we could work together, you know, build something for Mom, or something like that."

"We'll do a lot of building together when we get back, son. We'll start by building a new life together. I'm through going away at night from now on."

Looking out the window, Kevin fell asleep momentarily and Sean sat and looked out over the top of the clouds, his arm around his boy, and his thoughts at home with his wife, ever there awaiting him as he fought the battles of his life, giving him the source of his strength, the freedom to follow his dreams, and the love he needed to return to.

▲　▼　▲

In Las Vegas, Sean took Kevin with him into the fight arena where the fight was going to be held. He showed him the locker room in which they'd get ready for the fight, and the corner they'd be fighting out of, near where Kevin would sit.

"After the fight, we'll come back to our room and call Mommy from that phone."

"Will we tell her about Hawaii then, Dad?"

"We'll see."

That night, when they entered the hotel they were staying at, they passed through the lobby overlooking the hotel casino. Bells were ringing and lights flashing on the slot machines. Dealers in tuxedos stood at blackjack tables dealing knockout punches to hoards of people. Beautiful girls carried drinks on trays to men who didn't even see them for the action on the tables. The glamour and allure in the casino was magnetic to Sean, and as he stopped for a moment to pan the room, he felt his old demon beckoning him.

Holding Kevin's hand in the hotel lobby, he suddenly realized who his real opponent was in Las Vegas.

"Dad, what are those people doing?"

Sean picked up his son and hugged him.

"They're chasing dreams none of them is ever going to catch."

"It looks like fun," the little boy said happily.

"At first it is," Sean said. "But it becomes a nightmare you can't wake up from."

The boy was intrigued by the action in the casino, and Sean was riveted to the boy's first impression of the demon that had gripped him all of his life. He flashed back to the day he stood alone watching Mario Lanzetta deal cards, and realized that Kevin O'Hara stood at the crossroads that he himself had made the wrong turn at.

"Satan disguises a lot of bad things by making them look good," Sean said quietly to Kevin. "But I want you to look carefully at something many people miss. Look at the faces of the players."

It was Kevin's turn to pan the room as he went from one gambler to another to try and find victory or happiness in one of the faces.

"What do you see?" Sean asked his son.

"Not too many smiles," Kevin said observantly. "Some look nervous. One man is very angry. They're all thinking very hard."

"That's because most of them are unaware of the time rushing by them or the value of what they're laying out on the table for the dealers to sweep away. They're losing their lives one minute at a time, and their money one dollar at a time, until sooner than any of them realize, both will be gone."

"Let's go, Dad, I don't want to stay here any longer. Let's see what our hotel room looks like."

That night, the night before the fight, Sean and Kevin talked late into the night, planning the next stages of each of their lives. They called Colleen, said their prayers, and Kevin was the first one to fall asleep.

As Sean lay there with his eyes closed, he thought about the action in the casino downstairs and he envisioned himself standing at the dice table rattling the bones. He won six straight passes, doubling his bet every time, and sat there with $32,000 in chips stacked in front of him. Forty-five minutes later he was down to his last dollar, which he was putting into the slot machines, a nickel at a time. Glancing up he saw Kevin standing there looking at him, a puzzled look on his face.

"Dad, what are you doing?" Kevin asked him, and Sean stood there and started to shake.

"It's a character flaw, Kevin, but I've prayed hard that you won't pick it up from me."

"It looks like fun," Kevin said, and Sean woke up sweating profusely, his heart beating rapidly in his chest. He reached for the nightlight by the bed, turned it on, and saw Kevin sleeping next to him, safe from the nightmare that had gripped his father.

He checked his pocket, saw the five hundred dollars still there, and realized it had been a dream. One minute later, the phone rang in Benito Strazza's room.

"Get over here right away," Sean said, and in two minutes, Benito was standing at his bedroom door, breathing heavily.

"Give this to Colleen, too," he said, handing Benito the money.

"You scared the shit out of me at two-thirty in the morning to give me five hundred bucks?" Benito snarled.

"Smile, will you, my nightmare's finally over," Sean said.

▲　▼　▲

He wore a shiny white satin robe trimmed at the collar, sleeves and lapels with bright emerald green. His trunks were shining and emerald green, trimmed with white stripes down the sides. On this night, like all other nights, he aroused the crowd when he first entered the arena and the crescendo of cheers rippled throughout the arena as he approached the ring.

His posture had been set in the locker room, and he took his body to another gear as he prepared to fight. The quickness he had enjoyed as a young fighter was mirrored in his preparations to enter the arena as an old fighter. His many wars had given him a ring savvy that showed out of his eyes as confidence. Even when he was in subconscious doubt about the outcome of a fight, he had managed through the years to leave his doubts in the locker room and come out bobbing, weaving, and confident.

With his hands on Benito Strazza's shoulders and his hood drawn up over his head, he bounced out of the locker room surrounded by handlers and cornermen, and made his way toward the ring. This night, his eight-year-old son followed him, totally enthralled by the entire experience.

He loved the arena into which he entered that night. He loved everything about it, the music, loud, hard and pounding, as he bounced up the steps and into the ring, the rumbling the crowd made as the spirit of anticipation entered them, the electricity of the arena, as men fixed their eyes on the man in the ring and awaited his opponent, and above all, the personal thrill of the challenge before him.

When he broke through the ropes, he dropped his hood and lifted his hands to the approving crowd, dancing and jabbing, forward, backward, and side to side, smiling and confident as he threw punches into the air. His trainer stood beside him, flashing his gold-toothed smile and dancing with him to the upbeat music that accompanied his arrival in the ring.

With all the pre-fight excitement in the arena, no one was aware of the lethal operation that was taking place in the locker room of Sean O'Hara's opponent. James Travis did not want to take any chances with the cagey old pro from Connecticut, not with a title fight and millions of dollars at stake. In the few minutes he had between the time his fighter's gloves were handed to him by the inspection team and the time his fighter entered the ring, he feverishly worked his fighter's gloves over, slitting them open at the seams and pulling out all the woolen stuffing that cushioned his knuckles from his opponent's face.

He worked quickly and professionally, and no one would become aware of his treachery for many months after it was too late.

Presently the attention of the crowd was drawn to the other side of the arena, where the ritual entry into the ring was repeated. Homer Jones wore black from head to toe and his skin was as black as his garments. The only white shone from his teeth and eyes. He did not look at his opponent when he entered the ring, just danced by him almost close enough to brush him, but their eyes never met as they prepared to enter battle, each in his own particular way.

The introductions were made, the referee's commands given, and the bell rung as Sean O'Hara blessed himself and turned from his corner to face the fight of his life.

From the opening bell, it was a war. Early in the first round both fighters threw all their training and all their logic out the window, as something unexplainable entered both of them and tempers flared at center ring. From the opening bell, both fighters gave the crowd occasion to rise to their feet and the roar that rose in the arena was deafening as the concussions of each blow echoed across the ring.

Both fighters threw defense out the window, and for three violent minutes hammered each other mercilessly. At the three minute mark, both sluggers were chastised by their cornermen for stepping out of the game plan, but when the second round began, it became obvious that this fight was going to be a war.

By the fourth round, Sean O'Hara's face was getting unusually red, although no cuts were opened on his brow. In the fifth round, Jones broke his nose, and it angered him more than hurting him. By the end of the eighth round, he began to look like a pumpkin-head as the swelling around his forehead, eyes, and cheekbones added inches to his face. In his corner at the end of the ninth round, Benito Strazza begged his fighter to allow him to stop the fight, but Sean's only thought was of his eight-year-old son who sat at ringside believing in him, and he glared at his trainer and warned him not to stop the fight under any circumstances. Strazza agreed in a decision he would live to view as the worst decision he had ever made in his life.

Eleven of the twelve scheduled grueling rounds were ground out toe to toe. Midway through the eleventh, Father Time caught up to Sean O'Hara. Already beaten nearly senseless, he was fighting on instinct, the belief that he could win with the ultimate effort of his life expended, the only thing left he had to go on.

But suddenly, his second and third winds already expended and the aching numbness in his face and temples so excruciating that he wanted to scream, he felt the tightness in his legs and the burning in his lungs descending on him as Homer Jones sensed the turning point.

Stepping backward into the middle of the ring, Jones drew O'Hara forward, and when the old fighter began to stalk him, the young fighter struck. A savage left-right, left-right combination bounced Sean O'Hara's head back and forth from side to side, and before the referee had time to react, the old warrior was out on his feet. Falling forward, his legs gone and his eyes glassy as his arms dangled limply by his sides, he was on his way to the canvas for the last time when the young fighter made the split second decision that horrified everyone who saw its consequences.

In the excitement of the moment, he decided that he was not satisfied just letting Sean fall forward, and instead he braced himself, bent down, and delivered one last unnecessary but brutal uppercut that sent his beaten opponent's body careening backwards toward his corner. When he fell, already unconscious from the violent assault, his head struck the turnbuckle so hard that it sounded like a watermelon hitting the pavement.

Never bothering to start the count, the referee waved his hands frantically to signal an end to the carnage as though his late reaction were enough to retrieve some of the damaging blows the young fighter had meted out.

Many in the crowd were cheering, some were gasping, as Homer Jones walked around the ring, smiling and alternately holding his hands up and blowing kisses to the crowd on all four sides of the ring. The ring doctor from the Nevada State Boxing Commission bounded up into the ring, and with a stunned Benito Strazza by his side tried desperately to revive the fallen boxer.

At ringside, an eight-year-old boy sat riveted to his chair, the sudden violence of the moment pinning him helplessly to his seat, as the doctor waved impatiently toward the locker area for the stretcher bearers.

When they started running toward the locker room with the lifeless body of his father on the stretcher, he was drawn up out of his chair, but he got blocked out by the huge crowd at ringside. At first no one noticed the young boy who climbed through the ropes and ran to the victorious fighter. The fighter himself was surprised at the audacity of the young boy who lifted both of his hands up and felt his gloves. For only a split second, as he pulled his gloves out of the boy's hands, the fighter's eyes met the boy's. There was a darkness in the boy's eyes and a coldness that Homer Jones would never forget, even though it would be years before he knew who the boy was.

Suddenly the boy was pulling people out of the way and dodging through them frantically, but by the time he got into the locker room, the only thing he saw on the other side of the room, was the doctor pulling a sheet up over his father's head.

Benito Strazza was reduced to tears as he ran from the dimly lit table where his father's body lay, over to the boy who stood stunned at the door. Benito embraced the boy, and all he could say was, "I'm sorry, Kevin. I'm so, so sorry."

The doctor stood by Kevin's side and spoke to him somberly.

"We take every precaution to prevent things like this from happening, but every once in a while, they do. It's the nature of the sport. It's the first death we've had in over eight years. I'm sorry, son."

Kevin was unable to cry for the shock he felt, or the anger. He kept going back in his mind to the last unnecessary blow Homer Jones had delivered, and the way he smiled at the crowd as his father lay dying in the corner. And as long as he lived, he would never forget the awful truth he had discovered when he found the gloves of Homer Jones to be without any padding.

Looking at the white blanket laying over the lifeless body on the locker room bench, Kevin O'Hara was sure that his father had found his mansion, and that his life with Jesus would be better than the one he had had on Earth.

"If there's anything I can do, Kevin, anything at all," Benito Strazza said through his tears.

In the dank heat of the Las Vegas locker room where his life was changing before him, Kevin O'Hara gave Benito Strazza his answer.

"Just one thing," the somber little eight-year-old boy said evenly as he pictured Homer Jones blowing kisses to the crowd. "Teach me how to box."

▲   ▼   ▲

Part 4

The Last Generation

When Annibole Rinaldi died in France in World War I, his wife Rosa never left Indian Springs. She never remarried either, choosing instead to honor his memory by working hard all her life as a weaver in the Bradford Woolen Mill, and saving all of her money so that Annibole's son, Columbo, would be able to be the first Rinaldi in their family to go on to college.

Columbo took his privilege very seriously, having watched his mother walk back home up the hills from the woolen mills every work day for over forty years.

When other college boys played, Columbo Rinaldi studied, and when he received his bachelor's degree in business administration, his mother was beside herself with pride. He took a job as an assistant administrator at Bradford Memorial Hospital, and two years into his employment the top administrative position in the hospital became available. With visits to Pop Arnetti and Vittorio Bellino, a request for their help, and a few well-placed phone calls to the executors of Cyril Bradford's estate by the two local leaders, Columbo Rinaldi soon became the chief executive officer of the Bradford Memorial Hospital.

He took his job very seriously and ran the hospital well, bringing some of the top surgeons in New England to the small town and expanding the hospital's outreach to several surrounding towns.

Columbo and Christina Rinaldi raised three beautiful daughters, Leanne, Maria, and Celia. In the course of his work at the hospital, Columbo came to know many very good doctors and the lifestyle he saw them living gave him what he considered to be the inside track on a very important bit of information he earnestly desired for each of his daughters to learn well.

"If you want to live a better than average lifestyle, marry a doctor," he told them many times as they were growing up. "They're far more apt to have integrity, compassion, and bigger incomes than the boys you're likely to meet in Indian Springs, where most men are destined to work for small wages in the factories."

From the time they were little girls, Columbo had drilled into them that they were to be friendly with all young male suitors, so they would be sought after for their charm as well as their beauty, but that they were not to get serious about anyone other than medical students almost ready to graduate, or young doctors.

When his daughters were through with eight grades at St. Patrick's School, he sent them all to private Catholic all-girls high schools so that they would continue to be influenced by the nuns while postponing their involvement with boys.

In the summers he sent Christina with them, either to his cottage in Old Saybrook, or to his A-frame in Vermont, where they stayed all summer. He would meet them there on weekends. This was so they would not have the opportunity to develop any relationships with local boys, very few of which he observed were able to break out of the blue collar factory mentality that kept them all enslaved.

In Lion's Club and Rotary Club meetings, he had had far too many opportunities to hear the factory owners and corporate lawyers talking about the unequaled work ethic of the Indian Springs worker that kept the factories of Indian Springs here while so many others were moving down south. Once, he heard a rather obnoxious corporate executive at one of the local mills talking freely as the booze flowed liberally, and the things he was saying hit Columbo Rinaldi very hard.

"Gimme a single mother, or a young married guy with two kids and a mortgage, and in six months I own them," he slobbered.

Columbo caught himself before he said anything to the man, thinking of his own mother and the way she gave herself to the factory all of her life to put him through college. He also reinforced in his own mind his determination to get his daughters married outside of town so they would not be trapped in the same net.

For weeks after he had heard these things, he was especially hard on his daughters, explaining to them over and over why they must never be trapped in Indian Springs. The next time he saw his offensive friend, the man was again drinking liberally as he loudly described the closed door agreement the several factory owners had made long ago to leave the employees of the other factories alone for at least a year between the time they ended their employment with one factory and the time they were hired at another one.

"This benefitted all of us," the man explained boisterously. "It allowed each of us to keep our best men and prevented us from getting into bidding wars for their services, which kept wages down and profits up. Without this agreement, we might have lost the wage battle years ago and been forced to move to another state where big business has to go to illegals to keep wages down."

Columbo managed to be standing nearby as the man continued to drink and pontificate.

"In the old days it was the Europeans, you know, the Italians, the Irish, the French, the Germans, the Polish. They were the lifeblood of our system back then. They were hard working people, those immigrants, work for peanuts, and hard at that. Then it was their children, who they raised with the same pride in workmanship and hard work ethic that kept us going. Those people raised their kids to give us a hard day's work and to keep their mouth shut and be happy they had a job when things got tight for them financially.

"Then, as long as we were able to keep the goddamn unions out we worked those poor bastards for crumbs and held our profits. But the ball game is changing now. We've had to bring in a bunch of Asians and Central Americans recently to keep the same level of production up as in years not that long ago. The third generation is not nearly as sacrificial as the first two were, so now you have the Pakistanis, the Laotians, and even a few Mexicans, Salvadorans, and Panamanians to pick up the slack. They work for half the amount of money you'd have to pay an American to keep him, and send all of their money home to wives and kids they haven't seen in years. In ten years, they go back to their countries and live like kings."

Columbo's blood was running hot as he listened to the offensive way this soft-handed drunk was running his mouth in the meetings, but it only served to reinforce his desire to have his daughters marry doctors.

That night he called his daughters all together, swore them to secrecy about what he had heard the executive saying, but told them everything he had said, word for word.

"Don't get me wrong, girls, I have absolutely nothing against any of the boys you all know in town. In fact I like most of them very much. They're all very good boys. But let's face facts. Look at what their fathers do, and you can get a pretty good idea about what they'll do. They go to work, drink beer on their way home, pick up a gym bag or a baseball glove, and head out the door for the local leagues. Afterwards they go home to their small houses spread out around the factories, and kiss their sons and daughters goodnight, and thirty years from now those little kids will be doing the same things two streets down the road. I'm telling you, marry a doctor, and he'll buy your ticket out of here."

Commuting to private high school, the Rinaldi girls rarely picked up a copy of *The Indian Springs Press*. Whenever they did they never read the sports pages because all that was in there was a lot of boring box scores and statistics, which none of them paid enough attention to to understand anyway. Consequently they were unaware of all the Indian Springs High School records that were falling like trees around a beaver dam to one young local boy named Joey Bellino.

He was the first four-sport letterman in the school's history, all-time leading rusher in football, all-time leading scorer in basketball, all-time leading hitter in baseball, and he scored in eleven different events in track and field. In fact, the big story between his junior and senior year at Indian Springs High was the rumor that he wanted to run track as a senior instead of playing baseball, leading to a fist fight between Don Carcia, the baseball coach, and Khalid Amin, the track coach, which almost cost both men their jobs.

"He's got a chance to play in the major leagues!" Don Carcia screamed.

"But he wants to run track!" Khalid Amin countered.

"His family doesn't have any money, and his best chance of getting a scholarship is in baseball."

"But he runs the hundred in ten flat and broad jumps twenty-five feet."

"I've had him with me for three years," Carcia hollered.

"I'm trying to kick off a new sport, and I need him more than you," Amin argued.

Back and forth they argued until fists flew, and when it was all over, Joey apologized liberally to Don Carcia, but did what he wanted and ran track.

At graduation he received the coveted Melnick-Levinthal Sportsmanship award and a full scholarship to St. John's University. None of that meant anything nor was the reason for the Bellino family being invited to the graduation party of Maria Rinaldi. Columbo and Christina Rinaldi just wanted to have Columbo's mother, Rosa's good friends, Vittorio and Antoinette Bellino attend, and they were very fond of Maura Bellino.

Joey really wanted to play baseball that night, but since the whole family had been invited, Joey decided that it was only proper for him to make an appearance, even though he told the guys he would slip out early to come to Olympic Field and play ball. He wore his blue jeans and sneakers and an old tee-shirt that said New York Yankees on it.

When the Bellinos arrived at Columbo Rinaldi's home, the party was already in full swing. The invited guests included many of Columbo and Christina's friends, and while Leanne, Maria, and Celia were being cordial to everyone, there was no one there for any of them to become overly interested in. After all, they had always been each other's best companions. As usual, everyone that came to Columbo's home commented to him on the beauty of each of his daughters.

When Joey Bellino walked through the door, he didn't have to say anything. In fact he was unable to. When he first saw Celia Rinaldi, he was stunned. Could this be the same girl he had known in grammar school, with the skinny legs and braided hair; the girl who stayed in the corner and watched everybody else having fun, always in the background, the consummate wallflower? The last time he had seen her, she had been in a St.

Patrick's School uniform and not in a dress like the one she wore tonight, the kind that showed that she was not at all a little girl any more.

When Leanne and Maria saw the way Joey Bellino looked at Celia, they immediately went to work to fan the fire.

"Why, Joey Bellino," Leanne called out across the room as she and Maria danced across the floor to greet him. "How big you've grown. Now don't be paying all your attention to Celia. It's Maria's party, and I'm here too," she smiled, waving her hand in front of his face.

Joey hugged Leanne and kissed her on the cheek, but across the room his eyes had found Celia's, and they were both unable to look away. He was drawn across the room to her, and when he was near her she reached out both of her hands palms down, and he reached up and held them both. They smiled at one another and all Joey could say was, "You look great."

She blushed and said, "So do you."

For the rest of the party, the two of them stayed close together except for the time when she would be talking to her father's many guests and socializing with everyone, the way she had been taught. Every once in a while, her mother would come by and encourage Celia to mingle more, but Celia always managed to get off in a corner somewhere with Joey to catch up on the lost years between the last time they had seen one another.

The night flew by for both of them, and when the party was breaking up, Columbo walked over to his youngest daughter and hugged her.

"Time to start cleaning up now, honey, tomorrow we have to start packing for the shore."

Celia surprised both Columbo Rinaldi and Joey Bellino when she smiled up at her father and said, "Dad, can Joey come and spend a day at the beach with us?"

"Well sure, I guess so, if he wants to, have you even asked him yet?"

She smiled her radiant smile at him.

"I just did," she beamed.

At that moment, nothing in the world seemed more important to Joey Bellino than finding out exactly when. Outside, she held both of his hands the same way she had when they had started off the night, and when she stood on her tiptoes and kissed him goodnight, it was in the driveway with all the lights on, in front of her two sisters, with several other people around, but the way her lips felt on his for the brief second and the way he felt immediately afterward changed the course of his life forever.

After that moment, all Joey Bellino could think about was Celia Rinaldi. He saw her in his dreams, and when he woke up, on his way to his summer job in the factory, at work, as he punched out after work, in the car, in the bar, and on his way home after the bar. Celia Rinaldi was the only thing on his mind.

It had all happened so fast to him that he had not had time enough to sort it all out. He had dated many girls before, all the way through high school, cheerleaders from Indian Springs High, as well as Ellington, South

Windsor, Granby and Suffield, whom he had met and asked out at sporting events; girls from his class, as well as those a few years younger; and friends of the girls he knew at Indian Springs High from other schools. He had had more than his share of infatuations and relationships, some good, some great, but never had he been hit with such a powerful thunderbolt as when he rediscovered Celia Rinaldi.

For almost two weeks he had to wait to see her at the beach, and by the time the day came, the invitation had been extended to Rosa Rinaldi and all of the Bellinos, who crowded into Columbo Rinaldi's cottage.

On the beach, Leanne and Maria had already agreed to help get Joey and Celia alone, and when the two of them wound up walking the beach alone, it only fanned the fire already burning in Joey Bellino. Already the most attractive girl he had ever seen with her long brown hair blowing in the wind, she was especially alluring in her bathing suit, designed for modesty, but unable to conceal the fact that she had very definitely left her little girl years behind her.

Wherever the young couple walked, Joey could not take his eyes off of her, and the easy way they laughed together and got along made his mind race with anticipation of what else lay ahead for them.

For Celia, however, it was an altogether different thing. He was good-looking enough, there was no question about that. And he was strong and masculine, and she was drawn to him for those reasons as well. She had not dated that many boys and all of her curiosities about them and their bodies and the things boys and girls did when they were together had fascinated her for so long. For all of those reasons she had found thinking about Joey Bellino a very pleasant thing to do. Besides that, he had a sense of humor and an easy going way about him, and it would be nice, she thought, to let things flow, let nature take its course and see what developed.

All day the two young people stayed together on the beach, and that evening when the two families returned from the cottage to the beach for a campfire and a cookout, Celia Rinaldi began to take interest in Joey Bellino for quite different reasons. Not only was she very much attracted to him physically, but she was also starting to realize that he was a lot deeper and more sincere than she had hoped he would be, because he was talking to her about things she had not even begun to think about yet.

He was talking to her about his dreams for the future and laying out for her the things he had decided were important in life, starting with his understanding of his relationship with God and continuing naturally through his dreams for establishing a family unit for himself that would be supportive of his walk with God, and with one another, and then finally, about his love for America and his strong desire to serve his country in the armed services before marriage could ever be undertaken.

It had not taken Joey Bellino long to come to that topic after spending just one magnificent day with Celia Rinaldi. For Celia, there at the campfire, looking into Joey Bellino's eyes as the fire illuminated his face, she suddenly realized the effect she had had on him, and because she was starting to like him very much, she realized that the way she had been thinking about him was all too wrong.

Sitting there on the beach as he talked so quietly and easily to her, she realized that the time had come to make some very important decisions. She was curious about his body but confused because she did not want to be falling in love. She really wanted to like him enough to have sex with him but not enough to fall in love with him. He would never be a doctor. That was obvious with everything he was talking about. He would probably join the service, fall short of a professional sports career, come back to Indian Springs, marry some local girl who loved sex, have a bundle of children, and work in a factory.

She decided that it would not be fair for her to allow him to think that there was any chance whatsoever that they would end up together. And she would not allow herself to do what some of her friends had done to their boyfriends—take advantage of his affection to the point where she would try it with him to see how it felt to have sex with him and then manufacture some reason why they had to break up.

An image flashed across her memory of the look on one of her friend's boyfriend's face when she overheard a conversation they were having.

"Are you breaking up with me?" the boy had asked.

"Not now," her friend had said to him. "I'm not through using you yet."

She had said it as a joke, but the boy looked pained and confused, and she decided not to do that to Joey.

In her mind, her best course of action was just to save herself for marriage, and tell Joey Bellino good-bye.

She wanted to tell him that night about her plans to go away to medical school when her last year of high school was finished, but in the revelry on the beach, she got distracted, and soon it was time for the party and the weekend to end. She did not find the right opportunity to talk to him alone that night, and for that reason, he left the party and the shore, thinking once again about only her.

She found herself thinking about him all week herself, and when he called her on Thursday, she invited him down again the following weekend. This time there were a number of other young people around, and Joey tried to disguise his feelings for Celia by mingling freely with everyone else, but every time he looked at her, his heart ached a little more. For some reason, she could not bring herself to say anything to him about her true feelings, and soon he was coming to Old Saybrook every weekend to see her.

Finally, after the entire summer had gone on like this, Celia made sure that she got the opportunity to see him alone before he left for college.

She was not prepared for what happened to her next. Joey asked her to take a walk with him, and there on the moonlit ocean beach, apart from the campfire, Joey Bellino took Celia Rinaldi in his arms and kissed her. It was a long and ardent kiss that she did nothing to resist, and he would have done more, but she pushed him away and started to walk away from him, and farther away from the campfire.

"What's wrong?" Joey asked, catching up to her and putting his arm around her waist.

"I'm not ready for this," she said. "I mean, I don't want this now."

Joey continued to walk by her side and already the disappointment was starting to creep in.

"What is it?" he asked her calmly. "Am I going too fast for you?"

"No. It's not that at all," she answered, unable to tell him her true feelings.

"Is it that you don't like me enough?" he asked her quietly.

"No, it's that I like you too much," she said, only confusing him more.

He was relieved at that, but he still could not understand her.

"I just don't know if I'm ready to get serious with anybody," she said, looking away.

"It's okay," Joey said. "I know you're only sixteen years old. I can wait."

The first thing he said would have been fine. It was the second thing that bothered her.

"I don't know if you should," she blurted out immediately, before she had time to think things over. "I might not be the right girl for you."

Joey wanted to stop her right there, take her in his arms and kiss her again, and keep on kissing her until she knew that she very definitely was the right girl for him, and many months later, in a jungle halfway around the world, he wished that he had, but instead, he just dropped his arm from around her waist and continued to walk by her side along the beach.

"Why do you say that, Ceil?" he asked her quietly.

"Because I know what's going to happen," she said, suddenly looking very upset. "You're going to fall in love with me, and I'm going to fall in love with you. And then we're going to do everything we can to get to see each other and be alone with each other, and then either we're going to make love and then I'll have to break up with you, or you're going to ask me to marry you first and I'll have to say no, and both of us will get hurt real bad, either way."

The pain in her face was very evident to him, and Joey hugged her and held her close, and while he was trying to stay strong, he felt a helplessness and aching sweeping over him in waves.

"Why will you have to say no, Celia? I don't get it. In fact, to be honest with you, I was going to ask you tonight to marry me so we could walk back and tell everybody before the beach party breaks up. I guess I should have given you more time. I can't help it that I've fallen in love with you so fast. But like I said, I'll wait."

He said it again, she thought, and then she really got upset. It had all happened so fast, and he could not be blamed, because she had done nothing to dissuade him. But she could not blame herself either because she could not have guessed that he would get that serious, so soon.

"It's not that I don't like you. You know how much I like you. But I, I just can't. . . ."

She stopped and started to shake her head, and look away into the stars. "I guess I just don't know how to say it to you without hurting you," she said, sincerely trying to be honest with him.

That hurt bad enough itself, as he felt the end of something that could have been so good dying in front of his eyes.

Neither of them spoke as he tried to look into her eyes, but the hurt in his face caused her to have to turn away. Finally he tried to reason with her, and broke the impasse calmly.

"Look, I'm already hurting, so why don't you just try and be honest with me, and tell me the truth, no matter how hard it is, then at least I'll know your real feelings," he said.

It was a very hard thing for her to do, and she did not do it very well, but she did it the best way she could at the moment.

"It's just that . . . well, it's like your family has never really had all that much, and my family has had, like a little bit more, and I just don't want to live any differently, or rather any worse than I always have."

Her honesty was so stark, even though she probably could have chosen different words, that he empathized with her feelings, even though her words cut him to the marrow of his bones. Her words surprised him so much that he just stood there, unaware of what to say to her, and too hurt to respond. Looking back on it later, he wished that she had just simply told him that she didn't love him and didn't think she could ever love him, because that would almost have been easier to accept. In fact, she had not worded her true feelings at all well, but what she said, she said, and it set the course of the rest of his life all the same.

They walked back to the campfire quietly, and he did not even kiss her when they parted, just waited for her to be looking the other way, and then disappeared into the night.

Three days later, he walked into the Marine Corps recruiting center in Springfield, Massachusetts, and sat down across the table from a pleasant young Marine, who was very surprised when he asked him to contact St. John's University and tell them that he was not coming the following week because he felt as though his country needed him more than their basketball team did, in a place on the other side of the world called Vietnam.

▲   ▼   ▲

When Walt Johnson was drafted, the Chicago Cubs organization was not happy.

"Get on the phone and call the draft board. Call his congressman, his senator, call the goddamn president if you have to. Walter Johnson is not going to go to Vietnam," the general manager shouted.

For three days, the phone rang off the hook at everybody's office that had any remote measure of influence in the selective service process. The Cubs came up empty every time.

The general manager was sitting up in his chair strumming his fingers on the desk, his head aching from trying for three days to think of something, anything he could do to save their most promising pitching prospect in ten years, when the phone rang.

"Hello," the general manager answered gruffly.

"You can forget about trying to keep me out of Vietnam," the voice at the other end of the line said. "I want to go."

"Walter, we're trying very hard to get you reassigned."

"I volunteered for Vietnam," Walt Johnson said.

The G.M. laid his cigar down in the big glass ashtray on his giant mahogany desk.

"Yes, well there are a large number of assignments available to young men of your dedication that don't involve combat roles, and . . . ."

"I said I volunteered. If I make it back, I'll have a lot of good years with the Cubs, but my country needs me right now more than the Chicago Cubs do."

"Walter, the United States needs men in the field, but not any particular men. Let somebody else go."

There was a long silence at the other end of the phone.

"A lot of guys don't believe in this war. I do. Some guys that are in the service are afraid to go over. I'm not. I appreciate you trying to help me out, but I'm going to Vietnam, and I haven't even thought about baseball in several weeks. When I get back, the Cubs will still be in Chicago. I'll call you."

The phone line went dead, and three months later, the six-foot four-inch black All-American from Brooklyn, New York, was sitting next to Joey Bellino on a troop carrier bound for DaNang, Vietnam.

"I don't care how good you are," Joey joked with him, "I'll hit your best pitch so far out of the park, you'll never recover your confidence enough to make it with the Cubs. And if you can't strike me out, you'll never get the chance to face a major leaguer."

Walter Johnson felt the lust for competition that was so much a part of him rising up to take control of him.

"Shee-it, man. I'll strike you out three times before you hit a ball out of the infield against me. I don't care how good you think you are."

The conversation was heard by several men in their platoon, and for the first several weeks in Vietnam, arguments abounded about who each man thought was right. Surprisingly the two men became best of friends, as each found out two identical things about the other. First of all, their exchange on the troop carrier was totally out of character for each of them, both of whom were very modest men. Second, both men were 100 percent sure they were right as well, and their mutual curiosity made a good basis for their friendship to grow.

As their tour in Vietnam continued, they went out on patrol together many times, covering each other's backs and leading the rest of the men in their circles by their example. At night they found themselves seeking each other out when each mission was completed, and their mutual interest in sports of all kinds, especially baseball, made a good springboard for what both of them believed would be a lifelong friendship.

One day, coming in from a thirty-day stint in the jungle, the young Americans' attention was drawn to the several parcels that had come to them from the States. Gifts of various sizes and shapes were pulled out of the packages, and one boy from Omaha, Nebraska, let out with a big yell when he opened his package.

"Whoa, ho, look at this!" he shouted. "Two baseball bats, eight fielder's gloves, a catcher's mitt, and two dozen baseballs!"

Every eye in the circle went to Walt Johnson and Joey Bellino, who stood staring at one another challengingly.

"Ten bucks says Wally strike's the guinea out three straight times," a loud voice yelled out.

"I got twenty that says Bellino gets two hits before the nigger gets one by him!" another voice answered.

In a matter of seconds, there was a riot scene as everybody within earshot was yelling out his opinion and backing it with a bet. The classic confrontation was set for the following day after breakfast, before the recon-naissance missions began. It was as good a diversion as the boys could come up with in the tense atmosphere of the field.

That night, Joey Bellino was lying on his bunk with his hands behind his head when he looked up and saw the tall young New Yorker standing over him.

"Don't get mad at me tomorrow," he smiled.

Joey Bellino laughed. "Don't you get mad at me," he answered.

"I'm kind of glad Henry got that equipment, really. If one of us got killed out there before we found out the score, the other one would think about it for the rest of his life."

The young New Yorker was smiling broadly as he talked to his friend from Connecticut.

"There's a lot of things I need to find out as soon as this war's over," Walter said to Joey.

Joey Bellino smiled up at him.

"Can I tell you a secret?" the big man whispered.

"Sure," Joey smiled.

"You'll never tell a soul?"

"Not one person," Joey said.

"I'm probably the only eighteen-year-old kid in New York whose never gotten laid," Walter Johnson giggled.

Joey Bellino laughed right out loud.

"Shoot," Joey answered. "Half the macho men in this outfit who tell all their big time stories haven't either."

"I was half thinking of hanging around the base in DaNang with the rest of the boys on our next three-day pass and looking up one of these little Vietnamese ladies to see how it is, but I'm too scared somebody'll recognize me and rib me about it for the rest of my tour."

"Since we're on the topic of big secrets, I'll tell you one too," Joey said.

"The only reason I haven't done it yet is that I'm afraid my girlfriend will ask me, and if I say I did, she'll have a reason to do it too, and I don't want anybody else sleeping with her but me."

Walter Johnson slapped his leg and laughed at Joey's honesty, and Joey smiled at Walter's reaction.

"You know, Bellino, all kidding aside, I'm goddamn glad I met you, you know why?"

Joey was still smiling at his tall friend.

"So many of these guys are smoking that wacky-weed that I'm afraid I'd get into it myself if it wasn't for you being around to talk baseball with. And I know myself too well," Walter Johnson said. "I've never done anything half-assed. If I got into that weed, they'd find my ass floating about ten feet off the ground in Hanoi with about a hundred bullet holes in me. 'Cubs Top Draft Pick Floats into Enemy Territory on Weed Smoke!' the headline would read."

Joey laughed.

"Hey!" another voice piped up. "Get back to your bunk, Johnson, no consorting with the enemy. You want to strike this wop out of the box tomorrow, you don't be making friends with him tonight."

The next morning, every man in camp lined up to watch Walter Johnson warming up.

"The guy's awesome!" Henry Miller from Orwigsburg, Pennsylvania, said to Joey. "He's got about ninety-five mile-an-hour heat and a sinker ball that drops out of sight about a foot before the plate."

"Yeah, well, he never faced anybody that could drive him all the way to DaNang before," Joey answered confidently, swinging the heaviest of the company's two bats to loosen up. "Go on out there and throw me a couple of warm-up pitches, and we'll get his attention quick."

On the makeshift playing field, Joey Bellino rocked Henry Miller's first several pitches, sending the boys in the outfield to the edge of the jungle. When both young men were warmed up sufficiently, Henry Miller paced off sixty feet and kicked a pile of dirt up into a mound for Walter Johnson.

"It's not big enough," Joey Bellino said loud enough for everyone around him to hear.

"What ain't big enough?" Henry asked Joey impatiently.

"The field. The field's not big enough."

"You clown, Bellino, I threw you twenty pitches, and you never hit one into the woods. Besides, the jungle's about four hundred and eighty feet away."

Joey shrugged and stepped up to the plate.

"Three times you gotta strike me out, big-leaguer, before I get a hit. And before you throw your first pitch, I got a confession to make. I batted six-hundred in high school and only struck out twice in four years."

Walter Johnson smiled. "That was against Connecticut farm boys. You lookin' at New York thunder, now, boy!"

Every eye in the field was upon the two friends, who smiled each other down until Henry Miller yelled, "Pla-a-ay ba-a-ll!"

Then the two boys got deadly serious as, all of a sudden, months of bragging faced off and quiet spread over the field.

Joey let the first pitch go, and Henry yelled out, "Baw!"

He took the second pitch right down the middle, and it smacked into the catcher's mitt so hard that it echoed in the outfield. He swung and missed at the third and fourth pitches, and it startled him that he had struck out for only the third time in five years in serious competition.

He stepped out of the box and adjusted his sleeves, his crotch, his feet, and his stance, digging in more solidly with his back foot and exhaling loudly before stepping back into the box.

Walter Johnson breezed a fastball by him and then fooled him with a slider and a sinker, and in three pitches, Joey Bellino was down on swinging strikes to his last at bat in the bet.

"Give me the lighter bat," he called over to Punch Garrett from Baker, Florida, and Joey looked embarrassed as he told Garrett quietly, "I can't get around on this guy."

Joey swung and missed at Walter's next pitch, and then took three straight balls low and outside. The 3-1 pitch he hit so hard that the bat shattered in splinters as the ball went foul. He took a few moments to regroup and set himself in the batter's box with the heavy bat.

The next pitch, a 3-2 fast ball, came right into Joey Bellino's wheel house, and the crack it made when his bat hit it startled Walter Johnson, who had never had a ball hit that hard off of him in his young life.

He turned and watched it rising higher and higher into the air as it flew toward the edge of the jungle 480 feet away. When it cleared the trees, it was still forty feet off the ground, and Walter just stood there and laughed.

"Holy shit, man, that's the longest home run anyone's ever hit. Mickey Mantle hit one 565 feet once, and if that one isn't at least as long, my name is Ho Chi Min."

Henry Miller was running out toward the jungle with a tape measure, and Joey Bellino was standing at home plate, smiling.

Walter Johnson looked embarrassed as Joey walked out to him.

"Johnson, you're the greatest pitcher I ever faced, and I mean that sincerely. And just between you and me, I hope I never have to face you again.

Now I can see why the Cubs were all bent out of shape when you came over here."

"Okay, boys, fun's over," Lieutenant Claiborne Emhoff from Birmingham, Alabama yelled out. "Johnson and Bellino, you guys are on the same team now. We're going out in the brush for thirty more days. Bellino, you take the point."

"Yes, sir," Joey said, saluting his commanding officer as Henry Miller ran back in out of the woods.

"Five-hundred and forty freakin' feet!" he exclaimed wide-eyed with disbelief. "I mean to tell you that sucker flew five-hundred and forty freakin' feet! I mean if I hadn't seen it with my own freakin' eyes I wouldn't have freakin' believed it!"

"Shee-it, how you think I feel, sucker?" Walter Johnson slapped him on the back. "First thing I'm gonna do when I get back stateside is tell the Cubs about this mother," he said to Henry, pointing at Joey Bellino.

In the jungle outside of camp, the mood changed fast. The soldiers walked quietly and carefully, inching along in the jungle on their mission. For six hours, they saw nothing and then they heard a loud scream as Trevor Mills from Detroit, Michigan, fell into a hole and impaled himself on the pungi sticks set up below to maim the person who fell on them.

When the men around him went to his aid, they were met by machine gun fire out of the jungle, and before anyone knew it, Walter Johnson had thrown a grenade into the brush where the machine-gun fire was coming from.

The grenade exploded, the shooting stopped, and when Joey and Lieutenant Emhoff parted the trees to see what damage had been done, they saw the body of a small Vietnamese boy still holding onto the machine gun.

"What the hell?" Lieutenant Emhoff exclaimed, surprised. "A kid! He can't be more than twelve years old! What the hell is wrong with these gooks?"

Later on that afternoon, the eleven men left after Trevor Mills died from his fall onto the poison pungi sticks, found themselves waiting for Lieutenant Emhoff to get his orders on the two-way radio he was carrying.

"We're gonna take the hill on the other side of this field," the lieutenant said. "The gooks got it now, but were gonna take it before dawn."

That night, Joey Bellino slept surprisingly well because he was so tired from the heat and the long march the day before. When Lieutenant Emhoff touched his arm to wake him at oh-four-hundred, he got up quickly and prepared for the storm of battle quietly.

The men moved so quickly and so quietly in the night that it seemed almost impossible that anyone on the other side could have heard them, but when one young American walked through a trip wire, the first flare went up and the air immediately filled with an incredible volley of gunfire as the fire fight broke out. Men scrambled in every direction and screams were heard from both sides as the shots continued to ring out. A grenade exploded in the trees, another one in the field, and as the Americans stormed the hill, men fell dying on both sides. The whole battle lasted less than six minutes, and just before the Americans took the hill, they saw the North Vietnamese running away, down off the back side of the hill and into the jungle beyond. Almost simultaneously Joey heard a loud muffled blast going off to his left about forty paces away.

"Oh, God!" Joey heard Henry Miller yell out, and when he ran over to see what had happened, his eyes were assaulted by the most grotesque sight he had ever seen.

He looked at Miller frantically, but the look on the young Marine's face told him that there was nothing that could be done for their friend, who Joey could not identify. Lieutenant Emhoff appeared suddenly, pushing Joey out of the way, and as he knelt down to try and save his man, he saw that there was nothing to save. On the ground in front of him was the mangled body of a man, killed by the explosion of a land mine.

Henry Miller was on his knees, crying.

"Get a hold of yourself, Private Miller," Lieutenant Emhoff yelled.

"A land mine," Miller cried. "A goddamn land mind. He'll never pitch for the Cubs now."

Joey felt a rush of revulsion coursing through him, and in his mind he said, *Oh God, no!*

"Bellino, go back and round up the wounded," Joey's lieutenant commanded.

When the men who had lived through the fire fight came together on the hill, they took a quick inventory. Five dead, three wounded, the hill taken. As the other men sat cleaning their weapons on the hill, Lieutenant Emhoff sat apart, talking to his commanding officer on the radio. After an hour had elapsed, he walked over to the men. It was six-thirty in the morning, Friday, February 14, 1969.

"We're to sit tight and await further orders," he said.

Joey was certain the hill must have been very valuable to have sacrificed five men for it. He could not believe that Walter Johnson was dead. Such a gifted athlete, with so much of his life ahead of him, and in the confusion of his grief, he kept playing over and over in his mind the secret Walter had told him before he died. He had never had any sexual experience at all, and now he never would. Somehow that fact took on a great deal of significance to Joey Bellino in the jungle of Vietnam.

The morning dragged by slowly as the tension of the day kept each man keenly alert. The Viet Cong seemed to be gone, but they were sneaky adversaries, fighting on their own turf, and the Americans could never be too careful.

At eleven-thirty, the call came through from their company commander that started to change the way Joey Bellino thought about the Vietnam war.

"Pack it up, boys, we're dropping back," Lieutenant Emhoff said.

Joey Bellino froze as the other men started to put their gear together. No one noticed the incredulous, pained look on Joey's face as he stared at his lieutenant.

When Lieutenant Emhoff glanced over at him, he was puzzled when he saw the big young man from Indian Springs, Connecticut, sitting on the ground staring at him.

"Why did we take the hill, sir?" he asked his lieutenant measuredly.

The big lieutenant looked him squarely in the eyes. "Pack up your gear and let's go, Bellino."

"I want to know why we took the hill," Joey insisted, with his voice shaking and tears of anger welling up in his eyes.

"I said pack it up," the lieutenant barked, and when he did everyone else stopped for a moment and looked back and forth at Joey and Lieutenant Emhoff. The lieutenant was a big man, not as big as Joey, but about six-foot one and two hundred pounds, and a mature twenty-nine years old to Joey's nineteen.

Joey stood up, now crying, and walked toward his lieutenant, who also stood up to face him.

"No, sir," Joey Bellino answered. "Not until you get on that radio and ask why we took this goddamn hill."

"You take one more step toward me, Bellino, and I'll knock you on your ass."

"I want to know!" Joey cried out. "I want you to tell me why Walter Johnson and the other men are dead, and why we sacrificed their lives to take this goddamn hill, and why now we're walking off of it and dropping back so Charlie can set up here again."

"Stand at attention, Corporal Bellino," the lieutenant yelled out, but Joey just kept walking toward him, crying.

When he reached for the radio, Lieutenant Emhoff slapped him across the face, and when Joey looked at his lieutenant through his tears, he fell to the ground at Lieutenant Emhoff's feet.

"Why?" he cried out, sobbing. He looked at Lieutenant Emhoff, pleadingly, and the big lieutenant stood over him, frowning.

The other men watched solemnly as Lieutenant Emhoff looked down at the young Marine.

"I don't know why we took the hill," he said almost apologetically. "And I don't know why we're dropping back. All I know is that I'm to follow my superior's orders, and you're to follow mine, that's all I know right now."

Joey stood up and walked away from Lieutenant Emhoff, where he looked into the trees beyond and shook his head.

"I'm sorry, sir," he said, loud enough for everyone to hear.

"Just pack it up, Corporal, you don't need to apologize to me."

Joey walked over to his gear and hid his face from the rest of the men as he started to pack it up. When he turned around, Lieutenant Emhoff was standing over him.

"It's okay, Joey, forget it," the good lieutenant said to him.

"It's okay," Henry Miller echoed, and when Joey looked into the faces of his friends, he could tell by the look in all of their eyes that it really was okay, and that life would go on from here. Still, the answer to his question was hidden somewhere in the jungle of Vietnam, as it would be hidden from many young Americans for many months to come.

▲ ▼ ▲

Back in the United States of America, another boy was going through an equally disturbing time in his young life. At his farmhouse in Indian Springs, Kevin O'Hara was waking up several times every night with nightmares of varying degrees of intensity and confusion.

On the one hand, he was being pounded in the head by a faceless opponent in the boxing ring, whom he was afraid of but whom he would not run from. He was ashamed of his fear, determined to face up to it, but not at all sure if it was something he was supposed to be concentrating on.

On the other hand, he was wrestling with a nagging bitterness over losing his father, an intense desire to exact vengeance on the man who had killed him, and an equally strong pull of an inner voice that kept telling him that revenge was wrong and belonged only to the Lord, his God.

It was a difficult and trying time in his life, and the worst part about it was that he did not have anyone he could talk to about it. The only person in the world who he felt could understand his situation and help him was his father, who had been killed, and so he was left to face the confusion and the conflict alone and unguided.

His predicament would have been bad enough by itself, but it was complicated by an incapacitating problem he was forced to deal with at school. Early on, Kevin was diagnosed with a severe attention deficit disorder which made schoolwork extremely difficult for him.

In addition to being hampered by A.D.D., he was also dyslexic, and while schoolwork came easily to his classmates, Kevin was soon hopelessly lost. He decided to compensate for his disability by concentrating on tactical aggressiveness, strength of character, steadfastness of purpose, acceptance of personal responsibility for his own choices, and keeping himself strong and in good health.

He read very poorly but watched a lot of movies, identifying with characters who were strong and single-minded of purpose.

The chronology of the predicament he found himself in soon led to a very unsatisfactory course. He trained hard to learn how to box. He ran for ten or more miles each day to build up endurance. He prayed for the strength not to let his bitterness rule him, and for the wisdom to know if it was the right thing to do to let his bitterness go. The closer he came to believing that vengeance was in fact not his, the more he actually wanted it.

He sincerely wished that he could somehow gather up enough courage to release his bitterness, and subconsciously began to look at it as sinful, but then he was assaulted in his dreams by this faceless opponent who was hammering him, who he became more and more determined to defeat.

All in all, it was a very perplexing situation, and it caused him to withdraw within himself very deeply, and become very much of the same kind of loner that his father had been when he was young. Many times he believed he had the proper answer to his problem figured out. His father was dead. He had been killed by Homer Jones. He wanted to make Homer Jones pay for that, but it was not his duty. The best thing for him to do would be to leave the vengeance up to his Lord and go on with his life. To pine after revenge was sinful, to plan for it dangerous to his own chances at happiness in the future. But in the back of his mind, he knew that everything he was doing was bringing him closer to the time when he would go against his better judgement, and confront Homer Jones.

He planned for it, trained for it, viewed it as sinful, wished he were not so powerfully drawn to it, was remorseful about seeking it, but put every subconscious act that he did in line with events that were leading up to it, and all this at an age when most of his young classmates were concentrating on learning to read, write, and compute numbers.

His mother became very worried about him and the countless hours he spent running, lifting weights, pounding away at his father's punching bags, skipping rope, shadowboxing, and punishing his young body and mind.

She attempted to talk to him, but was greeted only by blank stares and stubbornness. Each time she tried to reason with him or crack into the shell he was building up around him, the only thing that came close to working was to put her arms around him and hold him, but when she looked into his eyes, all she saw was a sullenness that deeply saddened her.

"Kevin, Honey, what are you doing to yourself?" she would ask him time and time again. And she always got the same answer.

"I don't know," he would say. "But I'm getting better at it."

They would walk back into the farmhouse from the barn out back, and somewhere in the night she would awake to hear him wrestling with his own private demons, as he tossed and turned and battled his confusions in the darkness of his bedroom.

Her heart ached for him, and she wished there was something she could do to help him, but as hard as she thought about it, there was nothing she could come up with to help.

"Lord, God Almighty," Colleen O'Hara would pray. "Guard my son, Kevin, and guide him. Put your angels around him, and be merciful to him. I'm putting him in your hands, Lord. I just don't know what to do with him."

▲　▼　▲

After the day in the field when Joey Bellino lost his best friend, Walt Johnson, he also lost the smile that he had worn for most of his life. Without understanding why, he suddenly became very bitter and pessimistic about life. He was edgy, short-tempered, and very angry. He did not want to admit it, but he was not at all satisfied that the United States government knew what they were doing in Vietnam. *Why don't they let us walk in, whale the hell out of the Communists, and go home?* he thought to himself. *They'll be easy to beat. We're bigger, infinitely stronger, better equipped, better armed, and on the right side, morally. So what's the problem? And why in the world are we dragging it out so long? It's not at all necessary.*

He was very sad when he saw so many Americans giving in to the temptations of drugs and alcohol, especially the marijuana that was so easy to get in the field. And every man who came back after a three-day pass came back either stoned, dosed with some venereal disease, or both. In the field, he was starting to see good young American boys committing vile acts of depravity to dead Vietnamese bodies, cutting off the heads and mounting them on their tanks, or hanging them up on trees, run through with pungi sticks.

He was on edge all the time now, quick-triggered in the field, and constantly angry with himself for his sudden, rather constant use of profanity, which he had never done before Vietnam.

Once, in an ambush and violent firefight, he was sure he had lost his mind when he manned a machine gun and screamed profanities as he blazed away at whatever moved in the bushes. Later that night, he awoke in the middle of a peaceful night, crept over to a machine gun, and unloaded a long volley blindly into the jungle at the noise that had awakened him. The next day when the first light of dawn came, he and another man went into the jungle and found a small monkey shot so full of holes that he looked like the target on a firing range.

That morning, Lieutenant Emhoff came over to Joey and gave him permission to go back in on a three-day pass.

"Mail this letter for me, would you please, Corporal? I haven't written to my little son in a long time."

"You have a son, sir?"

"Yeah," the lieutenant smiled. "Shane. He's six years old. In about three more months, I'll be home with him for good."

At camp, Joey found a mailbox before he did anything else. The letter mailed off to Lieutenant Emhoff's son, Joey next found himself hanging around outside the beer tent where half-nude Vietnamese girls were dancing, as the young Americans improvised on popular songs, singing lyrics one of them would make up until the words began to haunt him, as he drank more and more beer.

"Ma-ma-ma-ma-ma-ma, live through the day. Ma-ma-ma-ma-ma-ma, live through the day, and just make it 'til tomorrow, oh-oh-oh ma-ma-ma-ma-ma-ma, live through the day. . . ."

The drunker he got, the angrier he got, and as he saw the face of Walter Johnson telling him that he had thought about getting himself a little Vietnamese lady, he continued to look at the dancers. When a girl came up to him and offered him a hit on her marijuana cigarette, he looked somberly into her smiling eyes.

She's beautiful, he thought. *Beautiful. And she's out here screwing every jackass in America for a few lousy bucks.*

"No thank you," he waved her off, but as the crowd belted out the song he found himself humming along with it as he watched the scantily clad oriental girls working the crowd of drunken Americans. After he waved off several girls, they just kept on coming on as he kept on drinking beer, and finally he took a joint into his hands and put it up to his lips, inhaling it deeply, as the crowd kept on wailing out the song.

"You got to bring me some-a-lovin', bring me some-a-lovin', bring me some-a-lovin', bring me some-a-lovin', all your-a-lovin', bring your-a-lovin', all your-a-lovin', hey, hey, hey, hey. . . . Ma-ma-ma-ma-ma-ma, live through the day, and just make it 'till tomorrow, hey, hey, hey. . . . "

On and on they sang, and things were getting worse for Joey, not better. Suddenly he was assaulted by the memory of Celia Rinaldi, and he felt very lost, and very alone. When he looked up frowning, he saw a young American lifting up a topless Vietnamese girl and sitting her down hard on the back of a truck, and when he saw her breasts jiggle when her backside hit the truck, that was his undoing. He stood and started scanning the crowd for a girl.

The girl he chose was timid looking and very young. She looked frightened and out of place. They did not speak each other's language, but their eyes told each other the only thing they both needed to know, and when he reached out his hand to her, she took it and led him into a small hutch apart from the beer station.

She knew he was very drunk when she led him into her hutch, a six-by-eight foot enclosure with a dirt floor and a small table and wash basin filled with soap and water. He fumbled with his clothes, and when he had them off, she started to soap up a wash cloth, and he lay back on the blanket on the ground and fell asleep.

"Agh!" he heard her exclaim angrily, and he woke up and tried to sit up, but the hutch was so hot that it made his head spin, and he lay back down and closed his eyes. The girl stood up angrily, cursing him in Vietnamese, but when she saw the tears running down his face, she took pity on him and sat down next to him. She began stroking his face and neck, and when she got him to look at her, she was smiling.

She pulled him over on top of her, but he was too drunk to do what she wanted him to do, and she lost her patience with him again, pulling a wad of bills out of his pocket, waving it in front of his face and pushing him back on the blanket to sleep. Later on that night, he awoke and found her next to him, but he was too sick and still too drunk to move.

The last thing he remembered before he dozed off to sleep again was hearing a girl in the next hutch moaning out, "Jackie, Jackie-ie, oh Jackie-ie."

No one paid much attention to him when he walked out into the field the next morning. Someone handed him a mug of hot coffee, and he drank it quickly, shook his head in self-disgust, and walked out into the morning heat. He walked around aimlessly for the rest of the day and fell asleep on a grassy hill that afternoon.

A few days after he got back to his platoon, he was revolted to learn that he had contracted gonorrhea in the hutch, and he told no one but the medic who gave him penicillin what had happened. In the field, he decided that he never wanted to see another drop of alcohol, another joint, or another Vietnamese girl ever again, and he concentrated on staying alive as he was haunted by choruses of "Live Through the Day," which came to him so often in the field that it almost drove him crazy.

Ten days after he was totally rid of the venereal disease, while escorting a small group of Green Berets out past the demilitarized zone, his platoon was ambushed and he watched in horror as Lieutenant Emhoff was shot to death before his eyes.

It is said that a good soldier fights on training and a dead soldier fights on emotion. Joey knew that, but suddenly nothing in the world mattered to him more than killing the man who had shot Lieutenant Emhoff.

At that moment, he lost all fear he had taken with him into the jungle. He lost all thoughts about home. He lost all memories, good or bad, about any other event, recent or ancient in his young life. All that mattered, whether he lived or died, was that the devil who had killed Lieutenant Emhoff must die.

He had a six-year-old at home, Joey thought soberly. *A six-year-old son.*

"You're a dead son-of-a-bitch," Joey whispered into the Vietnam heat, as he snuck alertly from cover to cover. Suddenly he stood face-to-face with the sniper, stood quickly, and fired into the man's face.

He sprawled backward and fell dead on the ground. Joey heard himself breathing rapidly and felt his heart pounding in his chest, and as he stood looking down at the man he had just shot, he saw something coming at him out of the brush.

It's a grenade, he thought as he lifted his left hand up instinctively, to shield his eyes. The grenade fell to the ground, and Joey dove backwards for cover, but before he hit the ground, it exploded, and the deafening explosion ripped into him as he lost consciousness.

▲　▼　▲

Back home in Indian Springs, Connecticut, his mother, Maura Bellino, and his grandparents, Vittorio and Antoinette Bellino, prayed for him every day at morning mass. They picked up the intensity of their prayers when the days went into weeks, and the weeks into months, when they did not hear anything at all from Vietnam. This was unusual and very troubling to them because he had written regularly from basic training and throughout his first several weeks in Vietnam.

Now his letters had suddenly come to a complete stop, as the nightly news in every American living room alternated from the body counts from Vietnam to the ever-expanding anti-war movement that was gripping and sweeping across the nation.

Maura Bellino's daily ritual was to wait at the loading dock of the Indian Springs post office after every daily mass for any word at all from Vietnam. The longest four months of her life were the months that separated the present time from the last time she had heard anything from her only son.

After the mail was cased, her mailman walked out every working day, and shook his head sadly, "Not today, Maura."

The long walk back up the hill got harder and harder for her as each day went by and she continued to cling to hope that Joey was alive. Her in-laws, Vittorio and Antoinette Bellino, would be waiting for her daily, and Vittorio was starting to feel so bad for Maura that it was the only thing he thought about all day long. The long months since the last time they had heard from him were excruciating for all of them, and as each day went by, the last letter he sent to them became more and more precious to them. To his mother he had said, "Pray for me," to his grandmother, "I'm eating good," and to his grandfather, "The weather's great, wish you were here."

The letters had come at least once a week, sometimes twice, and were cordial and brief. On one occasion, the Bellinos received a visit from Celia Rinaldi, who showed them the last letter she had received from Joey in Vietnam. She could not know that he had spent long hours over each of her letters, ripping up tens of sheets and copying several drafts of each of the letters he had sent to her before getting them just right for mailing. On his letters home to his mother and grandparents, the margins had not been so straight or the letters so carefully crafted, but the letters had come more frequently to his family, even though none of them had heard from him in over four months.

With great interest, eighty-three-year-old Vittorio Bellino listened intently as the granddaughter of his dearest World War I comrade-in-arms, Annibole Rinaldi, read them the letter she had received from Joey. The feelings he described to Celia were so much more intense than the ones he shared with his family. He told her stories of the battlefield heroics of the men he hoped it would be possible for her to someday meet. He also mentioned that the hardest part of his whole combat experience was the conflict that raged in his mind over what was right in the eyes of God. He had thought long and hard about that and rationalized that God had had his hand on America from the outset, and that he was too small a cog in the wheel of the overall picture to try and figure any of it out, opting instead to be the best Marine he could be, and let God be the judge of his intentions.

He told her about the tall young baseball player who had been drafted by the Chicago Cubs, and about the hit he had gotten against him during recreation. He also told her about some of the magnanimous things the men he fought beside had done in the field so as to make them bigger than life for Celia, so she would feel that what they were doing was right and overlook some of the faults they all had. He seemed to be preparing her in advance for whatever quirks they developed in Vietnam, which he felt they were entitled to, having put themselves on the line for the freedom of the South Vietnamese people.

He repeated to her several times that the men he fought beside, along with his father, Aaron, and his grandfather, Vittorio, were the greatest heroes in his life, and when she read the next part, she had to fight back the tears that were welling up in her eyes as she read.

"As always," he wrote, " . . . my number one dream is to come back to Indian Springs after we win the war so I can give my grandfather some great-grandchildren to carry on his shoulders and tell stories to the way he always did to me."

He signed his letter to Celia, "Love," but not, "I love you," and the postmark on that letter indicated that it was the last one he had sent home from Vietnam.

They had Celia stay for supper that evening and talked about everything except the possibility that none of them wanted to believe. Celia Rinaldi was very impressed at the way the Bellino's long ordeal had brought them so much closer together. Here, before her, was Vittorio Bellino, a legend in the hearts of the townspeople, whose entire life's dream and the dreams for his future generations were dependant upon the safe return of his grandson from the war he had volunteered for, growing quieter and quieter and, it seemed older and older as the days drifted by, as he sat in his cushioned chair and listened to the ticking of the grandfather clock. And Antoinette, the pained old woman who had waited for her husband for so long so many years before, and then followed him where he had led her, was slowly growing older and older, her heart aching from worry as she sat rocking back and forth in her rocking chair, cocking her head from side to side as she breathed heavily and whispered her prayers and worries aloud. And then there was Maura, Joey's mother and wife of Vittorio and Antoinette's slain son, trying unsuccessfully to mask her worries by talking about positive things that always seemed to betray her real feelings of fear for her son's life. And all of them trying to make small talk about anything but the only thing that was on their minds as Celia sat there and ached for each of them in her own private way.

Somehow she knew, though, that Joey would return. She really did. She simply knew that God would not sweep the dreams of two generations out from under them by taking Joey away. She knew for sure when she started to put her coat on to leave, and Vittorio reached for her hand and the four of them clasped hands. Three of them closed their eyes and bowed their heads as she stared right at the remarkable old man who led them all in prayer.

"Lord God, our Father, protect our boy, Jewey, and bring him-a home safely to us. We praise you for your greatness, and we thank you for the answers to our-a prayers. In the name of the Father, and of the Son, and of the Holy Ghost, Amen."

▲　▼　▲

When Celia Rinaldi entered Yale University as a freshman the following week, she had no idea the shock waves she was sending across the campus. In a university overwhelmingly male in its enrollment, she was far and away the most attractive female. Her natural beauty, which countless women have spent endless hours and untold sums of money to approach, served as her curse at Yale. At the time of their lives when she met the men of Yale University, many of them judged women by one standard and one standard alone. And in that standard, she was without equal. Her beauty and physical charm turned a lot of heads at Yale. She was a perfect sexual magnet, with long sleek legs that put her inches above the majority of females her age. Although she was tall, she was very well proportioned, except for the final curse, her larger than ordinary breasts which stood out straight and firm, accentuated by her excellent posture.

Wherever she walked, she drew the eyes of everyone within range her way. In breezes, her long brown hair blew lightly across her erect shoulders, and when she wore high heels, the sinews in her legs added a bounce to her steps and jiggled her breasts as she walked. Her skin was silky smooth and her lips soft and full. Her eyes were deep brown, her teeth pearly white, and when she smiled at men she melted their hearts.

Anything she wore was alluring because it was impossible to conceal her charms, and she drew crowds of men in every event. How her father had hidden her all these years was a credit to his vigilance in the matter, but he had no idea what he was sending her into at Yale.

Celia Rinaldi had spent her entire life in Catholic schools. She had been shielded and protected, and her only boyfriend had been Joey Bellino, whom she had started to love but sent away in favor of better prospects at medical school.

But her fascination with boys lingered, as did her curiosity. That she could have looked so good and still been so sexually inexperienced was hard for many of the Yale undergraduates to believe, but when rumors to that effect started to circulate, the obvious contest began.

No fewer than twenty men were actively and competitively seeking her attention, and she had to have the telephone in her room taken out within the first month so she could get any sleep at all. She was amazed by all the attention she was getting, and very flattered, and as she became aware of the incredible effect she had on men, she began to dress more, rather than less provocatively, wearing shorter skirts, and opening more of the buttons on her blouses, as well as wearing more makeup and fluffing her hair more.

She had narrowed down to six or eight the male suitors she was encouraging by stopping long enough to talk to them, although she continued to lead everyone on by her dress. After about a month, the game grew dull, and she wanted to act out the feelings that were welling up inside of her with the men she was stringing along.

One Friday afternoon, Charles Anderson, a tall blond medical student in his last year, walked up to her after her psychology class and put his arm around her waist.

"It's Friday night, Celia. There's a keg party at the frat house. I'll pick you up at eight," he smiled at her with a big confident smile.

"Make it eight-thirty," she smiled back, and it was the first date she had accepted at the university.

His heart quickened, and his roommate dropped his books and stood one quarter amazed and three quarters angry that he had not beaten Charles to the punch. All afternoon every member of the fraternity buzzed around telling each other that Charles Anderson was bringing Celia Rinaldi to the keg party that night.

They never showed up. When Charles picked Celia up in his father's Porsche, the first thing he said to her was, "Want to go home and meet my parents?"

"Rushing things a little, aren't you?" she laughed, and the big smile he flashed back at her immediately put her at ease.

"I didn't even ask you if a keg party was all right," he said to her politely as he put the car through its gears and headed out toward the highway.

"I was thinking more along the lines of a quiet dinner," she said, so dinner it was, at a seafood restaurant on Cornfield Point in Old Saybrook where he had grown up and where, coincidentally, the Rinaldis had summered every year for many years at her father's cottage.

She did not tell him later that night when he parked his car near the ocean why she could not bring herself to be at all romantic that night. It had been on that very beach, only a few hundred yards away and a few months before, where she had sent Joey Bellino away because she was afraid he was going to be a factory worker.

At that moment, halfway around the world, Red Cross nurses were changing the dressings on a young Marine's wounds as he remained critically injured and in a coma from the grenade blast that had mangled him beyond recognition. The attending nurses regarded it as a miracle when he finally began to talk, albeit deliriously and incoherently, and when the fever that had long gripped him finally broke, he had realized that he could not see out of his left eye or hear out of his left ear.

For a long time after he regained consciousness, he could do little more than lie there, and he soon realized that one of his eyes was gone. Trying to assess his own injuries, he realized that he had not been wounded in any bodily area vital to his survival, and aside from the painful burns to his left side, nothing seemed to be fatal. But when he tried to move his legs, he was usually wracked with severe pain, at which time he would pass out and go to sleep.

He drifted in and out like this, unable to focus on any thought for any length of time at all, and he had no idea how long he had been this way, or what had happened, or even where in the world he was. Finally, one night in the quiet darkness of his hospital room, he opened his eye and felt the sweat pouring out of his body. He seemed to startle the nurse that walked by him when he called out to her, and in seconds four nurses were standing over him.

"What is it, Marine?" one of them asked him.

"My leg," the Marine said quietly and directly at the nurse.

"Thank God, he's finally starting to talk," he heard one of the nurses say, and he looked at them quizzically.

"So many times we thought we'd lost you," she said, wiping his forehead with a cloth, and her hands felt so good on his head that he reached up and clasped them, and she held his hand in hers as he closed his eye and exhaled loudly.

"How bad am I?" he asked her, but she promptly brushed the question off with a wave of her hand.

"You'll be fine now," she said. "Once we get your leg healed, and some routine skin grafts, you'll be almost as good as new."

"I can't hear you," the Marine interrupted her.

"That we'll have to see about, but rest for now and we'll get to one thing at a time."

"What time is it?" he asked her.

"Nineteen hundred hours," she answered. "And I'll bet you're hungry."

"I am," he said. "I have to remember to send my mother a birthday card. March eighteenth. Could you remind me please?"

Two of the nurses looked back and forth at one another, and it occurred to the young Marine that he had no idea where he was or how long he had been there.

"What day is it, Nurse?" he asked her.

"October tenth. You've been in a coma for seven months. We don't even know your name because your dog tags were missing when they brought you in. You were blown up by a grenade and carried in here barely alive. We don't have any idea who found you or how. All we know is that the day you got hit, a 149 Marines got killed, and only about 7 survived. God only knows what happened out there that day."

The young Marine closed his eye and lay back on the bed. He was too weak to try to piece together anything else.

"If you don't mind now, Nurse, I'd like to get some sleep. I feel weak all of a sudden; I'll talk to you in the morning."

For several moments he just lay there concentrating on the events that had happened to him that last day in the field. It got jumbled in his mind, and after a while, he fell asleep and never ate the supper that was prepared for him that night.

The next day, in New Haven, Connecticut, halfway around the world, Celia Rinaldi spent all day getting her hair and nails done for her date with Charles Anderson. After the concert, they went back to his dormitory room and continued to drink wine as he put a Beatles album on his stereo and sat down next to her on the bed.

When he started to take off her blouse, she protested, but he pushed her back on the bed and pulled her blouse off roughly. She continued to protest, but when he jumped up and turned the stereo up, locking the door, she began to feel trapped. The beady-eyed smile that crossed his face when he approached her startled her, and before she had time to react, he had ripped off her bra, her skirt, and her panties, and he was holding her down on the bed as he ripped off his pants.

When he entered her, she froze, and as he wrestled her down, all of her attempts to push him off of her failed, and in no more than two awful minutes, her life was altered dramatically.

When he stood up and dressed himself as quickly as he had undressed them both, she pulled her clothing on top of her and tried to cover herself from his stares.

He unlocked the door, and walked out, turning to say only two words to her before he stepped outside into the hall. "Get dressed," he said roughly and shut the door hard behind him.

The next day in the cafeteria, Charles Anderson didn't say anything to her. He never said anything to her again, and the shame and anger she carried with her for the next several weeks caused her to lose fifteen pounds and fall far behind in her studies. She stayed in her dormitory room for the better part of the semester, and the only boy she talked to was Robert Franklin, a shy, studious pre-med student who was to be the fourth generation doctor in his family.

Robert was compassionate and hurt when she told him around Christmas time that she was pregnant and needed him to help her to obtain an abortion. He arranged through his father to have the job done and accompanied her to the procedure, which was done in quiet on a Saturday morning in a rented hotel room by a man neither of them had ever seen before. Celia cried for the rest of the day, and Robert stayed with her that night, talking with her until she fell asleep in the hotel bed.

Before the month was over, Robert Franklin was madly in love with Celia Rinaldi, and though he thought about the circumstances of their meeting often, he never talked about it to her on any of the several dates they had after that, and soon it was taken for granted that Celia Rinaldi was Robert Franklin's girlfriend.

He was quiet, and studious, dedicated to being a medical doctor, and even though he was not given to too much partying, he was always kind to Celia and she began to feel really comfortable around him. When he asked her to marry him at semester break, she accepted, and it was only then that he started to change, grilling her about the circumstances of "her affair" with Charles Anderson and probing into her past to try and find anything else he ought to know before he "risked" marrying her.

To uphold him and to assure him that everything was as she said it had been, she decided to sleep with him and do everything only for him, and before long, she was pregnant again.

"I'm not ready to have children," he told her matter-of-factly, when she informed him that she was pregnant.

"Well, ready or not, you're about to," she answered.

"Not necessarily," he said to her coldly, and the way he looked at her chilled her and scared her very deeply.

"What's that supposed to mean?" she asked him, distraught, and he turned away from her and lit a cigarette.

"It means I'll have to see my father, and get the situation taken care of again," he said.

"Robert, I'm not going to have another abortion."

"You most certainly are, my dear," he answered her coldly.

"But it's your child!" she said to him incredulously.

"You're the only one who knows if that's the truth," he said, the words cutting through her like a knife.

"Oh, Robert," she said painfully, putting her hands to her face and turning away.

"I'm at least ten years away from having a child, Celia, at least ten years," he said, and in the next moment she was running down the hallway and out of the ivy league campus forever.

That evening, as doctors monitored the young Marine's progress in the hospital in Vietnam, the girl he loved sat somberly and dejectedly on a train from New Haven to Hartford, where her father awaited her arrival to take her home to their hometown, which was in the middle of the social revolution that swept the United States of America in the dark days near the end of the Vietnam era.

▲　▼　▲

When Columbo Rinaldi's car bounced over the railroad tracks leading into the center of town, he barely beat the train that was slowing down to make the turn that led it down the river road and out of Indian Springs. Neither he, nor his somber young daughter sitting next to him saw the small boy who stood crouched and ready to jump the train as it slowed down behind his father's old tavern.

The boy waited for an empty boxcar, ran alongside of the train the way he had practiced before, and in the darkness of night, leaped aboard the train and rolled over in the empty car. Soon the car picked up speed again, and the boy strained to pull the door shut against the nighttime cold. He crouched in the corner of the train, pulling some old burlap rags up over him and huddling alone in the corner of the car. In forty-eight hours, he'd be in Florida where the weather was warm, and he'd jump off the train and find his way to the convention center in Miami where the Homer Jones fight would take place.

It would not be the first time he'd disappear for a week at a time. Neither his fifth grade teacher this time, nor his fourth grade teacher the times before had noticed anything different about him in the days leading up to his unexplained absences. Nor did anyone know where he went or why—not his mother, his school psychologist, his social worker, or any of the police or school officials who were unable to pry anything out of him when he'd stroll into his house after a week's absence.

He'd simply sit there, stone-faced, and stare at anyone who'd ask him the thousands of questions he'd be grilled with every time he returned. Never once did Benito Strazza remember the chilling words Kevin O'Hara had spoken to him on the night his father had died, and every time Kevin O'Hara would begin an odyssey to a Homer Jones fight, he would lock everything else out and concentrate on the one burning quest that had ruled his life since that fateful night two years before.

In the train yard in Miami, the young boy went unnoticed as he dodged through the nooks and crannies that led him to the fight arena. This time he arrived a day and a half ahead of schedule and found an old abandoned car to sleep in that night.

On fight night, he sneaked into the arena through a delivery door near the concession stand and watched each of the preliminary fights with great interest from seats closer and closer to ringside. By the time Homer Jones entered the ring, he was sitting one row behind the announcer's table at ringside, and when the fight was stopped on a cut midway through the fourth round, Homer Jones got an eerie feeling as his eyes caught the same small boy standing on the floor behind his corner whom he had seen in New York and Philadelphia, the same boy who had been at ringside on each of his films of every fight since the O'Hara fight in Las Vegas two years before.

He started toward the showers but stopped to ask the boy a question he had been wondering about since Philadelphia.

"Who are you?" he asked curiously.

The answer he heard from the stone-faced boy caught him off guard and startled him, as he was suddenly jolted into remembering the first time he'd seen the boy, holding his unpadded gloves for a brief second after he'd knocked out, and in fact killed, Sean O'Hara.

"Name's Kevin O'Hara," the boy said icily. "Get used to me. I'm never goin' away."

A few minutes later, pandemonium broke loose in the ring as Homer Jones's opponent's trainer started screaming at the referee to check Joness' gloves, and when Jones turned around the boy was gone.

The scandal broke in the next day's sports pages all across the country. For two years, the welterweight champion of the world had been using doctored gloves to cut and bruise his opponent's faces and retain his title. He was summarily stripped of his title, and in the ensuing court cases sentenced to eight years in prison for the cruel and underhanded tactics that scarred the sport of boxing severely during that period of its history. His trainer, James Travis, who had done the glove tampering, was banned from boxing for life.

None of the justice meted out to Homer Jones was quite enough to satisfy one young boy, however, who was forced to readjust his plans after the sentencing of Homer Jones to prison, but who continued to practice and hone his skills as he awaited the day, now eight years away, when Jones would be released from federal prison.

▲ ▼ ▲

Alfio Bachiochi stood at his mail case on Wednesday, December 24, 1969, sorting mail on the heaviest first class day of the year. It was snowing outside, and Christmas carols were playing in the post office. Part-time flexibles were pulling on their boots to take a couple of Bucky's streets, easing his load on Christmas Eve. He was sorting mail mechanically, thinking about the parties he'd be attending later on that day, when the letter appeared in his hand. He stopped for a moment to look at it and stepped back from his case quickly.

"Look here," he said solemnly, holding the letter out to the mailman at the next case.

"Mrs. Maura Bellino, from the United States Government," Shany Bruno said.

The two friends looked at one another cautiously as Bucky walked around his case and out toward the back loading dock.

Mail handlers followed Bucky with their eyes as he shuffled toward the back loading dock, unaware if the news was the best or the worst the Bellino family could hear.

He pushed open the swinging doors and walked out into the snow, where he saw her standing there like a Christmas statue, waiting prayerfully the same way she had done for ten months since the last time she had heard from her only son.

"Maura," Bucky said, calling out to her. "I pray to God it's good news."

He handed her the letter, and several faces filled the windows of the back loading dock as she tore it open furiously. She held the letter up to her face and read it quickly, stopping halfway through to scream into the quiet snow.

"He's alive!" she screamed. "He's alive!"

She hugged Alfio Bachiochi and started running up the hill to tell Vittorio and Antoinette, turning to her mailman as she ran.

"I'll let you read it when you get to the house," she yelled as she rounded the corner and disappeared into the snow.

Bucky was holding back his tears as he rounded the mail cases and went back to his station.

"I hurt for her every day," he said. "Now she can have a merry Christmas."

When Vittorio saw her running up the front lawn waving the letter, he knew the news had to be good. She was laughing and crying at the same time, and he fixed his eyes on her as he called into the next room for his wife.

"An-toin-yet-ta!" he called loudly.

"Oh!" she answered from the next room.

"Come on!"

She shuffled out of the living room onto the warm veranda where they stood awaiting their daughter-in-law. He opened the door for her, and when she ran through it and into Antoinette's arms, she handed Vittorio the letter as she cried out.

"He's alive!" she cried, bursting once again into happy tears. "He's alive!"

"Oh, Dio," Antoinette cried, laughing so hard that her great body shook uncontrollably. "Oh, Dio."

In the joyous warmth of their Indian Springs home, eighty-four-year-old Vittorio Bellino walked back into the living room and sat forward on his great old chair, to read the following letter:

MRS. MAURA BELLINO

THIS IS TO CONFIRM THAT YOUR SON CORPORAL JOSEPH AARON BELLINO USMC SUSTAINED INJURIES ON 14 MARCH 1969 IN THE VICINITY OF DANANG REPUBLIC OF VIETNAM FROM A HOSTILE EXPLOSIVE DEVICE WHILE ON PATROL. HE SUFFERED MULTIPLE WOUNDS INCLUDING TRAUMATIC AMPUTATION OF THE LEFT LEG FRAGMENTATION WOUNDS TO THE LEFT ARM LEFT HAND AND FACE AND SHRAPNEL WOUNDS TO ALL EXTREMITIES. HE HAS LOST THE SIGHT IN HIS LEFT EYE. HE WAS UNIDENTIFIABLE FOR EIGHT MONTHS WHILE IN A COMA BUT HAS REGAINED CONSCIOUSNESS AND IS RECOVERING ON SCHEDULE. HE IS PRESENTLY RECEIVING TREATMENT AT THE THIRD MEDICAL BATTALION. CONDITION FAIR. PROGNOSIS GOOD. YOUR ANXIETY IS REALIZED AND YOU ARE ASSURED HE IS RECEIVING THE BEST OF CARE. HIS MAILING ADDRESS REMAINS THE SAME.

WALLACE M. GREENE JR
GENERAL USMC
COMMANDANT OF THE MARINE CORPS

It's okay, Vittorio thought. *It's okay. We'll take whatever he has left and build a good life with it.* But as he sat back in his chair and exhaled long and fully, he closed his eyes and thought about the words.

Traumatic amputation, lost sight, traumatic amputation, lost sight, he kept thinking over and over in his mind. *But he is alive, and that is the most important thing.*

▲   ▼   ▲

As the decade of the seventies started, Columbo Rinaldi kept his daughter, Celia, out of everyone's sight, a virtual prisoner in her own home as she grew bigger and bigger with her child. In her eighth month, she was watching television when the doorbell rang, and she listened from her bedroom as her mother talked with their visitor in her kitchen.

When she recognized his voice, she walked out into the kitchen and stood in front of him, her huge belly protruding in front of her.

"Hello, Robert," she said seriously, and Christina got her coat and went for a ride in the car.

Three days later, in a ceremony attended by Celia's two sisters and both sets of parents, Celia Rinaldi and Robert Franklin were joined in marriage in the living room of the Rinaldi home.

They bought a home in Somers, Connecticut, and Celia went to work as a receptionist for a local doctor to help with Robert's tuition to medical school. Their baby was born three weeks later, and Celia took a week off to recuperate before going back to work. Christina Rinaldi cared for the baby while Celia worked.

In Vietnam, Joey heard about Celia's marriage in a letter from his mother while recuperating from a skin graft to his face. He had been doing fine through several operations, but suddenly lost both his appetite and his good cheer after reading the letter.

He never told the nurses who attended him anything about the wedding in America and went through the motions of doing everything the medical staff told him to while trying to put Celia out of his mind as time went to work on his wounds.

Six months and several operations later, he started, finally, to be anxious to come home. Having learned to keep his emotions locked inside of him, Joey never told anyone in his family how exhilarated he felt when he first saw the shores of America as his plane dipped down to land in his country at last. He never told them how deep his pride went, or how little he thought about the wooden leg he was walking on, or the patch that covered the socket where his left eye used to be.

He never told them, either, about the shock he received when he walked off the plane at Bradley International Airport expecting a hero's welcome, only to be greeted instead by a long-haired man half his size, in an army surplus field jacket with an American flag sewn to the seat of his khaki pants, who, as the first American to greet him when he finally came home from Vietnam, calmly walked up to him and spit in his only eye.

▲   ▼   ▲

As the Vietnam War ended and people's lives got back to normal, America turned the page on one of the most turbulent and troublesome eras in American history. The early seventies saw the beginnings of a readjustment in our lifestyles, and one of the most controversial supreme court decisions in our history.

She first heard about it in early January 1973 at Sunday mass when Father Murphy was leading the congregation in prayer.

"For all the sick and deceased members of our parish," he said.

"We pray to the Lord," they answered.

"For the people of Southeast Asia, for whom the hostilities of war have not yet ended," he said.

"We pray to the Lord," they answered.

"For Pope Paul, Bishop Daniel, and all the other priests and clergy of our church," he said.

"We pray to the Lord," they answered.

"For President Nixon, Vice-President Agnew, and all of our senators and congressmen," he said.

"We pray to the Lord," they answered.

"And for the United States Supreme Court, who this week will be considering a case involving the sanctity of human life," he said.

"We pray to the Lord," they answered.

I wonder what that's all about? she thought. She did not have to wait long to find out. On January 23, 1973, Sister Rose Alba picked up the *Hartford Courant* on her convent doorstep and read about the decision the United States Supreme Court had handed down the day before.

"I can't believe it," she said to the other nuns while sitting at breakfast. "It must be some kind of mistake."

She read the article several times, and each time she read it she became more and more frightened and more and more sad as the reality of what had happened the day before chilled her bones.

"This cannot be happening in the United States of America," she whispered, and as she began to consider the implications and ramifications of the Roe versus Wade decision, she felt like a stone had suddenly landed on her chest.

She thought about all the children who would never be born, about the effect it would have on all the women who would not choose life, now that the choice was given to them, the medical personnel who would assist them in their decision, and the wrongful and utterly tragic error of the highest court in the land.

She thought about it all day, all the next week, month, and into the spring and summer. She began a research project in the summer which startled her and frightened her very deeply when she realized the chilling similarities between this decision and another one which brought the country into the bloodiest and most brutal era of our history, the Civil War.

In the Dred Scott Decision of 1857, slavery was declared legal. In the Roe vs. Wade decision of 1973, abortion was declared legal.

In Dred Scott, a seven-to-two decision of the United States Supreme Court said that a black is essentially a non-person, the property of its owner, who may choose to buy, sell, or kill it, free from interference from abolitionists who would impose their morality on slave owners. In Roe vs. Wade, a seven-to-two decision of the United States Supreme Court said that an unborn child is essentially a non-person, the property of its mother, who may choose to carry it to term, or kill it, free from interference from pro-lifers who would impose their morality on women.

As she sat there staring incredulously at the issue before her, a chilling reality gripped her. There were people alive in those times, and there are people alive today, millions of them, who agreed with and in fact make arguments for both decisions. The Civil War was fought about the first one.

America is still an experiment, she thought to herself. *It's less than two hundred years old. Nothing so morally evil could be tolerated for very long in a country that is to be great. Either the people of the country tolerate it, and the country never achieves greatness, or the people of the country recognize that it is wrong, identify it as a moral evil, eliminate it, and go on to greatness.*

To Sister Rose Alba it was very clear, and very simple. As the sixty-four-year-old nun sat preparing her lessons for the eighth grade class of Saint Patrick's School in the summer of 1973, she was rewriting the curriculum of many of her lessons, preparing to fill her students with the same revulsion and resolve that she had to do everything in her power to fight and in fact overturn this sad and tragic Supreme Court decision, when one of the saddest events of her life occurred.

Sitting in the study, votive candles burning silently in red glass canisters next to her, the warm sunshine changed to brilliant colors by the stained glass window she sat under, the last thing in her mind was the inevitability of the long-dreaded event.

"Sister," a young nun whispered to her quietly. "Father Murphy is here to see you."

Sister Rose Alba quietly closed her books and stood up to follow the young nun downstairs into the convent's living room where the pastor of Saint Patrick's Church sat somberly in the chair under the crucifix.

The priest stood up respectfully and greeted her, and when he sat, she sat on the couch on the other side of the room, and he attempted to smile at the young nun who accompanied Sister Rose Alba into the room.

"Would you like me to leave, Father?" Sister Mary Adrian asked him quietly.

"No, Sister, it won't be necessary. Everyone will hear about it soon enough anyway. You may as well be the first."

He looked across the room at the beloved old nun who sat looking at him, suddenly apprehensive because of his last words, and when he looked into her eyes, he instantly realized that the thing he had to do was not going to be so easy after all.

"Sister, you've had a long illustrious career here at Saint Patrick's," he began, and when he said that she put both of her hands to her face and began to shake.

"For thirty-five years you've served people, taught everyone in our parish under the age of fifty, and influenced the lives of thousands of people."

Her tears were involuntary, filling her eyes and flowing down her cheeks as the inevitability she had long dreaded unfolded.

"There's not going to be any easy way for me to say this," Father Murphy said, turning to Sister Mary Adrian, who was wiping her own tears in the door frame of the room.

He turned again to Sister Rose Alba, took a deep breath, and looked at her compassionately.

"You won't be teaching at Saint Patrick's anymore," he said to her as gently as he could, and when he said it, it was as though a sword had pierced her heart.

She tried not to make a spectacle of herself, but her efforts failed and her tears flowed liberally down her cheeks and into the handkerchief that Sister Mary Adrian handed to her.

"We know your new assignment, but we won't be giving it to you for two weeks. Maura Bellino has agreed to drive you back to Worcester to spend some time with your family, and in two weeks we'll give you your new assignment."

She took a while to get her composure, and Father Murphy waited compassionately for her to stop crying as Sister Mary Adrian sat with her on the sofa.

"Is it anything I've done?" she whispered to the priest sadly.

"Oh no, Sister, not at all, it's simply time for us to make some changes. Your new role is probably more important than this one, in fact," Father Murphy said.

Sitting in the warmth of the convent she had called home for thirty-five years, Sister Rose Alba could not imagine anything more important than educating young people well.

"I don't know how to do anything else but teach, Father," the old nun said.

"Well, if it will be any consolation to you, Sister, your new role will also be in education."

She continued to blow her nose and wipe her eyes.

"I'm sorry, Father. I guess I've always known it wouldn't last forever. But I wouldn't be honest if I didn't admit to you that it hurts. When will I be visiting my family?"

"Be ready in an hour and a half. Mrs. Bellino will be arriving at one o'clock. Your sister Stephanie already knows you're coming to Worcester this afternoon."

The old nun stood and composed herself, even though her heart was breaking.

"Yes, Father," she said obediently, as she knew she would when the inevitable time finally came.

Two weeks later, at four o'clock in the afternoon on August 28, 1973, Sister Rose Alba left for her new assignment—teaching young novices at St. Joseph's Novitiate, preparing them for careers as teaching nuns in a world that was vastly different from the one in which she started teaching in 1938.

Little did she know at that time that she had not seen the last of Indian Springs, Connecticut, or the stunning impact she would have on the town the next time she would enter it over twenty years later.

▲　▼　▲

By the time Homer Jones was scheduled to be released from federal prison in 1977, the whole boxing world had heard of Kevin O'Hara. His picture had appeared on the front cover of *World Boxing* magazine and broadcasters all across the country were familiar with the quest he had internalized since he first started to learn to box, shortly after his father had been killed in the ring several years before.

Fighting awesomely in the Golden Gloves tournament and improving with every bout he had taken since turning professional at age seventeen, he had become one of the most closely watched prospects of his era, and the fight the sports world craved was the one that had to happen: when Homer Jones met Kevin O'Hara.

One week before his scheduled release, while eating dinner in the penitentiary mess hall, Homer Jones reacted violently to a taunt from another inmate.

"Kevin O'Hara's gonna kick your black ass, sucker," an inmate laughed at him, and Jones swept his tray off the table and leaped across the table to attack him. Forty-five tense minutes later, during which the brawl that broke out injured twenty-three inmates and five correction officers, Homer Jones was locked in solitary confinement and the prison was put in a state of lock down.

When the parole board met the following day to consider his release from prison, his sentence was extended for two more years, and the lead sports story in the next day's paper informed the boxing fans of the world that they would have to wait for the Jones-O'Hara match for at least two more years.

In the interim, all the major television networks made Kevin O'Hara their number one item, and sportscasters continued to follow his progress as he fought awesomely and grew in stature in the welterweight ranks.

Homer Jones continued to be haunted by Kevin O'Hara's progress and watched intently as tapes of each of Kevin's fights were sent to him regularly. Kevin's record and skills continued to improve with every fight.

In the meantime, correction officers continued to be amazed at the dedication with which Homer Jones worked on his body, lifting weights for several hours each day, and working feverishly to stay in shape for the day he'd be released to face what was looming as his ultimate challenge.

While Jones lifted weights, O'Hara ran and sparred and sports writers all across the country followed both fighters' progress. No one was more surprised than Kevin O'Hara when he picked up the newspaper two years after Homer Jones's resentencing to find that with only two more days to go before his release from prison, Homer Jones had been implicated in an unsolved murder five years previously while behind bars in which an inmate was found nearly decapitated with his throat slashed and his body dumped in a laundry basket.

As he awaited his murder trial, he was facing twenty years to life in prison, and it became doubtful if the world would ever see the long awaited fight. Still, doubts were raised about the possibility of Jones having committed the murder as stories began to surface indicating that it would have been logistically impossible for Jones to have done the killing because he could not possibly have been in the area where the murder took place at that time. While Homer Jones vehemently denied the charges, his accusers pointed to the fact that more than 90 percent of the prisoners behind bars continue to profess their innocence in the various crimes for which they had been sentenced.

For the next several years, Kevin O'Hara continued to fight, believing that his showdown would someday happen, no matter what lengths he had to go to, to make it happen. Then a new wrinkle developed that no one appeared to have foreseen. As Homer Jones sculpted his body and honed his skills behind bars, Kevin O'Hara continued to grow, up and out of the welterweight ranks and through the light middleweight, middleweight, light heavyweight, and cruiserweight divisions. Before long it became doubtful that the world would ever see a Jones-O'Hara fight for yet another reason. While Homer Jones was stuck behind bars, Kevin O'Hara became a heavyweight.

Still, Kevin clung to hope that he would someday see a fight with Homer Jones, and it took an event of enormous media attention across the ocean to divert his attention from his personal quest. It reached the attention of the world media in March of 1981, and it struck a personal cord in Kevin O'Hara's innermost being.

His name was Bobby Sands. He was a good-looking, passionate Irishman who gripped the world's attention when on March 1, 1981, the twenty-seven-year-old patriot from Belfast, Northern Ireland, refused food on the first day of a new hunger strike campaign for political status for Republican prisoners.

American newspapers followed the story closely, and as the hunger strike continued, daily updates on the young member of Parliament's condition and the plight of the other prisoners who followed him in refusing food were treated with front page headlines. Kevin O'Hara was riveted to the struggle and on May 5, 1981, when Bobby Sands died in the sixty-sixth day of his hunger strike, everyone in the world who followed the drama intensely, including Kevin O'Hara of the United States of America, was affected.

In a matter of days after Bobby Sands's death, Kevin O'Hara had a three-by-two-foot poster of the young hero's picture hanging in his bedroom, alongside a picture of his father in his boxing trunks and a crucifix. The Irish in him was aroused by the martyrdom, and Bobby Sands became his new hero. When nine other Irishmen followed Bobby Sands to their deaths as that awful year unfolded, the world continued its vigil on their progress, and when the hunger strike ended in October of 1981 and the Irish were no closer to ending their plight than they had been when Bobby Sands first started his hunger strike, people of Irish heritage the world over were stung by the tragedy.

Soon after the strike ended, the world turned the page on that awful time in world history, but one young American filed the experience away in his memory in a chilling way, and it did not surface again for well over a decade.

▲   ▼   ▲

As Kevin O'Hara continued to fight and win, another young man from Indian Springs found nothing during that period of his life but defeat. No one took very much notice of the young Vietnam veteran with the wooden leg and the patch over his eye, whose life was played out in the small area of the borough of Indian Springs, Connecticut.

For fifteen years, he lived alone in a small rented apartment in the center of town, sleeping during the day and working all night as a stockhandler in a local factory. He had taken the midnight job to hide from the world, his self-image having been battered by a series of personal losses he had been unable to effectively deal with, and he had drawn so far within himself that very few people ever engaged him in conversation.

Living in an apartment bordered by a woolen mill on one side, Main Street on another side, Furnace Brook on another side, and a barroom on the fourth side, Joey Bellino was satisfied in his isolation. He had no neighbors he would bother or who would bother him.

His life centered around three places within a half-mile radius of each other; his apartment, the Italian restaurant, and his job. He would be at work at eleven o'clock every night, work until seven in the morning, go home and drink wine until ten or eleven, and fall asleep with his record player on, sleeping until dark, when he would wake up and sit in his apartment window and watch the traffic go by on Main Street.

In awhile, he would get up, shower, dress, and walk up the street to the Italian restaurant on Main Street. The Colorado Restaurant was a quiet haven for him where he was treated with good service and respect. Roberto and Theresa Marino had never been able to adjust to the American way of life in the restaurant they started in Colorado.

The homesickness they felt had caused them to change their mind about *Estati Uniti,* and they were on their way back home to their mother country when they stopped to visit relatives in Indian Springs. There they kindled a friendship with Vittorio and Antoinette Bellino, who convinced them to give America one more chance, and the Marinos agreed, opening The Colorado Restaurant, where Joey Bellino ate his meals every day.

There he would eat, drink wine, and sit alone in his booth before walking through the park and back to work at eleven every night. On weekends he would sit alone in his apartment and listen to music, the back door open to the river in the summertime, drinking wine until he was drunk enough to sleep. If he ran out of wine, he would walk down the fire escape that led from his apartment to the barroom next door and drink quietly until someone started talking to him, in which case he would excuse himself and walk back up the fire escape to his apartment.

Later, waking up somewhat more sober, he would make his way to the bathroom where he would urinate and then reach for the medication to kill his headache, downing it with a single swallow of water. He would not look into the mirror because he did not like the face he saw there. He would stumble back into the bedroom and crash onto the mattress, closing his eyes against his failures.

Lord God, he would think, *the world is so perilous. People don't care about one another and I have been a killer in war. Forgive me for my sins and please don't let me hurt anyone else.*

When his depression got really bad, almost to the point of being unbearable, he would subtract his age from the expected lifestyle of the average man and take comfort in the reality that he didn't have that many more years to endure. In those times, he was grateful for the Catholic Church and the nuns who had convinced him beyond a doubt that a merciful Jesus would be there to take away all of his suffering on the day he died.

Then his mind would wander and dream, going over the myriad thoughts that filter through the mind before sleep comes. He would think about when he was young and strong, when he could run fast and hit a baseball a country mile, when he still believed he could do anything he wanted to.

He remembered when he enjoyed going to mass and Communion every day of his life, just after his paper route was finished, and how happy he always felt with the wind in his face riding his bicycle home after mass. He remembered when he would smile a lot, when he had more friends than he could count, and when life was simple and pure.

And always there were thoughts of Celia. Living alone now was not all that bad, until he would realize that Celia was living with someone else. He had lived without her all through the storm of the Vietnam War, and survived the anguish of losing her while preoccupied with his recovery when he came out of his lengthy coma.

At least the storm of war had long since ended for him, as had those long excruciating months of recuperation. The solace of living alone in his hometown was an acceptable alternative to those terrible years.

Still, his failure with Celia still sat there on the edge of his consciousness, always willing to tap him on the shoulder and beat him down a few more pegs. Ending up in a factory carried with it the reminder that Celia had been repulsed by the idea of ending up with someone who worked there. And even if she did, it could no longer be him. Not now when he was only half a man. Besides that, he drank far too much, held little promise of improving his financial status, and had not one chance in a million of ever becoming a doctor so that he would be thought of favorably by a beautiful college girl like Celia.

Many times, on the edge of his drunkenness, he would sit and stare at the telephone, satisfied that he was not foolish enough to pick up the receiver and call her, pleased that he had enough sense not to do that. Still, he thought about her often, and he could feel the frown on his face wrinkling the muscles downward around his mouth as the weight of his failure with Celia bore down on him.

He couldn't count the number of times he found himself in the presence of those he knew were acquainted with her, and listened intently for any conversation that might lead to finding out anything at all about her, from how she was doing, to what events she'd be likely to attend to where she may have been working, even to what town she was living in.

But none ever came. He was careful, ever so intensely careful, never to ask anyone anything at all about her so as not to expose how often he still thought about her, as the months turned into years since he had heard anything at all about her.

He tried not to think about how she had looked on the beach the night he was going to ask her to marry him, because every time he did, he saw how she looked in her bathing suit and began to imagine himself making love to her. Then he thought of Vietnam, and how poorly he had behaved, and he had to fight off the guilt before he could go to sleep.

Burying his head in his pillow, the guilt overwhelmed him, and he tried to close his eyes against his sins, but they were always with him.

God, what have I done? he would berate himself. *How could I have done such terrible things?*

For fifteen years he lived this way, never thinking too much about the future, keeping himself drunk enough not to have to think about too much and sober enough to work, setting his internal clock on the one cycle that was the only thing he paid close attention to. He would drink only long enough to allow himself enough time to make it to work sober, do a good job while he was at work, and start drinking again immediately after work, starting the cycle all over again. On the occasion of an inventory shutdown at the factory, which happened twice a year for a week at a time, he would take his shotgun, hunting knife, fishing rod, and bed roll, and head into the woods where he would live off the land for the week. It was the only time he stayed sober for a week, and it helped him to clear his head. He always went into the woods alone. This he did routinely for fifteen years after returning from Vietnam, more bitter and disillusioned than he at first realized and increasingly more so as the years wore on.

The only time he would break from his routine was holidays, when he would walk up the hills that led out of the Main Street area, to his grandparents' home, where he would attend holiday dinner with his grandparents and his mother, and it never occurred to him that the only time he ever smiled was when he spent time with them.

▲　▼　▲

As the autumn of 1987 neared an end, Joey Bellino heard about the gala party the women of the Ladies Auxiliary of the Italian Club were planning for the one hundredth birthday of the founder of the Italian Club.

"Next month we're going to give Vittorio a party this town will never forget," Connie Costanza told Joey one night in the restaurant. "If Sugar Desmond and Pop Arnetti were still alive, they could use their pull as state legislators to get some kind of proclamation read, or something. But your grandfather outlived them all, and nobody in the governor's mansion knows him anymore. But it's probably better the way we're going to do it anyway. Just Indian Springs people, you know, good friends and neighbors whose folks were close to him."

Joey was happy for his grandfather but disturbed that he'd probably have to socialize with a lot of people. *I'm better off by myself,* he thought, *but the party probably won't last too long, and I can sit with my grandfather and not have to talk to too many people.*

▲　▼　▲

For most of her adult life, Celia Rinaldi Franklin had been painfully unhappy in her marriage, stifled by the arrogance and insensitivity of a husband more obsessed with money and position than he was with her. She had become his trophy to be put on display at social events, to cook his supper, mix his drinks, and have clean underwear for him to wear to the hospital or the golf course.

They had sex infrequently and never made love, and she had become his prisoner in their home. For many years she had lived in a depression glossed over with a certain degree of financial security which masked her feelings of emptiness. There was no happiness in her life, and because of that she wrestled with a sense of melancholy, the roots of which she could not trace.

Throughout the years, she rarely thought of Joey Bellino and never dreamed that he was still thinking about her. When she thought of him, she lumped him in with their grandfathers, Annibole and Vittorio, and his father, Aaron, who had all served their country in war. She thought of strength, compassion, valor, honesty, and honor, but never in her remotest ideas thought of him as a way out of the pristine prison that her marriage had become.

▲   ▼   ▲

On the day of Vittorio's party, Joey woke up very edgy, not knowing just exactly why. When he went to pick Vittorio up, the old man was beaming, always glad to be anywhere in his country where people were celebrating and having fun.

A feast was spread out across the serving tables that reminded Vittorio of the one they had set up for his wedding many years before. The exhibition hall was decorated festively and someone had remembered to flank the head table with American flags, a touch Vittorio always appreciated. The Italian band was playing upbeat songs as the crowd swelled, and when Joey led Vittorio and Antoinetta into the room, he felt a rush of pride in the old people as the crowd rose to their feet and applauded them.

Vittorio waved graciously as Antoinetta laughed in pleasure, and Joey felt a broad smile covering his face. There were hundreds of people there, from all age groups and nationalities, and for the longest time Joey did not see Celia sitting there in the crowd.

He may not have seen her either, were it not for the fact that after the various speeches that had been given, Vittorio was himself called on to make a speech.

As always, whenever Vittorio spoke, the room got deathly quiet, and when he stood to begin, you could hear a pin drop.

Always the gracious one, Vittorio turned the attention away from himself and onto the men he had served with in World War I so many years before, and when he mentioned the name of Annibole Rinaldi, Joey heard someone sniffling. When he looked in her direction, his heart began to pound in his chest.

It was Celia.

She was more beautiful to him than he could stand. She looked elegant and refined, and even wiping tears from her eyes with her delicate hanky, she was the essence of beauty and class. He stared at her with his heart pounding, and time seemed to stand still as he looked at her.

Vittorio spoke for a few moments, drawing both laughter and tears from those in attendance as he had always been able to do, and occasionally Joey and Celia would look in each others direction. Their eyes never met, and neither one approached the other, neither one remotely aware of the feelings they had for each other.

For Joey, all the pain he had felt when he first learned that she had married Dr. Franklin came roaring back to him, and her marriage and the years that had gone by without her had put a chasm between them that made her seem as far away from him as the sun is from the moon.

As he thought about her sitting there and realized that she was probably with her husband, he started to feel incredibly uneasy, and when the discomfort got too intense, he leaned over and whispered into his grandfather's ear.

"I don't like crowds," he said. "I gotta get out of here."

Outside in the cold darkness of the parking lot, Joey wanted more than anything to be drunk. Instead he started the long walk downtown to the solace of his apartment and away from the painful position of looking at Celia and seeing another man's wife.

She gave some consideration to going over to say hello to him but before she realized that he had gone, she decided not to, it having been so long since they'd spoken that she couldn't imagine what she would say to him. The years had made them strangers, she thought, and even if she could have thought of anything to say to him, she had no idea at all how to approach him.

She spent the rest of the time at the party waiting on Dr. Franklin, and never mentioned to anyone how disappointed she was when she looked over to Vittorio Bellino and saw that Joey had gone.

▲　▼　▲

In the factory at night over the next several weeks after the party, Joey continued to take his breaks alone while everyone else sought companionship in the cafeteria. One day in late December, as he drove the forklift through the narrow passageway where the boxes he moved were located, he looked up and saw a new girl working on a machine.

He didn't pay very much attention to her at first, but he noticed right away that she stayed by her machine alone at break time, and for fifteen years he had been the only one to stay in the work area at break time. Neither of them talked to one another for the first week, but one day he noticed her having trouble lifting a crate and walked over to help her.

"Thank you," she said shyly. "You're very kind. I've seen how you help everyone else around here."

In fifteen years, it was the first time anyone had said anything like that to him, other than a quick "Thanks," and he found himself smiling at her.

"Why do you take your breaks alone?" he asked her.

"I don't know," she said. "I guess I'm not very good with people."

Joey looked at her keenly and noticed the shyness in her eyes.

"I know how you feel," he said. "I feel the same way."

"They tell me you were in Vietnam?" she said.

Joey looked away.

"Who's they?" he asked her.

"The others here. I'm too young to remember it, but thanks anyway for serving our country."

Suddenly he noticed how beautiful her eyes were, and as he sat riveted to her eyes, he felt himself smiling at her. It had taken fifteen years to hear any American say that to him, anyone at all. It surprised him to hear her say it. He had thought he would live the rest of his life and never hear the words.

"Your name is Allison?" he asked her politely.

"Yes. My father liked the name."

"I like it too," he smiled at her. "A lot of people don't appreciate the guys who served in Vietnam very much."

"Those people have their heads up their ass," she said.

It was the beginning of the friendship that grew slowly but very steadily between Joey Bellino and Allison Braun that winter of 1987-88.

Every night at break time when all the rest of the people left the work area and headed for the cafeteria, Joey would wander over and sit down next to Allison at her machine. It was small talk at first, but as she warmed up to him, she started talking more and more. Mostly it was questions about him, and she would shy away from talking about herself. All he really knew about her was that she lived alone with a small son, whom her girlfriend watched at night when she was at work.

Gradually, as she warmed up to him, she started to talk more and more about herself. One night she let it all out.

"I grew up in Brooklyn," she started. "Crown Heights. My family is Jewish. Really Jewish. Hasidic. My father went to synagogue more than he came home. He was a clothier, very successful in business, and very rich. My mother was a cosmetologist and heiress to a ton of money. I know they both lost a lot of family in the Holocaust, but they never wanted to talk about it to us.

"I had no problem being Jewish until I entered high school. When I was a sophomore I met a wonderful man. I was fifteen. He was twenty-two. I met him at a party. He was the kindest, most gentle man I had ever known. His name was Carl Braun.

"He was very proud to be German but ashamed of the Holocaust, even though nobody in his family tree had anything to do with it. I chased him so much it was disgusting," she smiled.

"In the summer we made love. He was studying to be a lawyer, but when he met me he quit school so he wouldn't have to go back to college and leave me. He went to work in construction. Then I got pregnant.

"I was so happy. My heart was full of joy—until I told my parents about us. They had the worst possible reaction. They were stunned and deeply hurt that I would fall in love with somebody out of faith . . . especially a German. I told them that we were in love and wanted to get married, but not that I was pregnant.

"They flew into a rage, both of them. Told me that I had disgraced the family and that I had to break up with Carl immediately. I stood my ground and told them that I wouldn't."

She turned away from Joey for a minute to wipe the tears from her eyes.

"Then my father slapped my face," she said, choking up a little bit. "He had never done that before. He told me that I had one day to break up with Carl or that he would kill us both. He looked so serious that he scared me.

"I told Carl, and Carl came to the house to see them. He told them that he loved me and that he wanted to marry me.

"My father glared at my mother and told her that he was going to leave the room before he killed Carl on the spot. She pushed Carl out the door. He was a sensitive man, and he was so hurt. He never got angry, only hurt.

"I told him we needed to elope, and we did. I was sixteen years old. I called my sister three days later from the Poconos and told her. You know what she did? She laughed at me. Laughed! She thanked me for being so stupid, and told me that because of what I'd done, I was being written out of the will, which would make her a millionaire.

"The next day in the synagogue, the rabbi announced to everybody that my parents were going to sit shiva."

She choked up and covered her eyes. Joey frowned as he heard her story.

"Do you know what it means when your parents sit shiva?"

Joey shook his head no.

"It means that in their eyes, you have died. They baked desserts and had a huge family gathering at my house to mourn my death. They sat shiva on me, Joey; a funeral. They walked around in their stocking feet, sat on armless low wooden stools with no backs or arms. The men didn't shave for seven days. All the mirrors were covered and they said prayers of mourning every morning and night.

"I could have ignored it but I could not believe that they were so hardhearted. So I went there. When I walked in, it was as though I were a ghost. They totally ignored me; all of them; my own mother and father, and all the other people we used to ridicule and laugh about together, me and Mom, throughout the years. Some who were close friends and relatives, others that were just casual acquaintances, they were all there. All except me. I had ceased to exist.

"For a minute, I just lost it. I started turning over tables and throwing food around the room and I broke my mother's favorite punch bowl. Smashed it into a million pieces.

"No one moved. I looked at them incredulously but my mother and father just sat there as cold as stone and ignored me.

"I was dead.

"To this day, I cannot understand how anyone, for any reason, can be so hard-hearted and bitter about feelings passed on by their parents that they can kill their own children. It doesn't make sense to me.

"I walked out of the room to go back to Carl. If it had ended there, it would have been bad enough. But it didn't. Three days later, the police found Carl's body burned beyond recognition in a car fire in the Bronx. The medical examiner said that he had been beaten to death before the car was set on fire."

Allison's lips turned white as she began to shake and Joey moved over and sat next to her, putting his arm around her shoulder to calm her.

"I was terrified. I'm terrified now, thinking about it."

She started shaking uncontrollably as she relived her horror to Joey, the first person she had told about it since it happened.

"I was carrying his child and suddenly I realized that they didn't know it yet. I was afraid not so much for my life but for my baby's, and I knew then that I had to move away. I got on a train and headed north. I got out in Hartford because I was hungry.

"I lived in a shelter and started looking for jobs. I had never paid any attention in school because I was going to inherit so much money that it never crossed my mind that I would have to work for a living. I wasn't educated enough to do anything but factory work and I had a baby coming so I started working. I worked in Hartford through the time when Michael was born but I wanted to live in the country. That's when I heard about Indian Springs. I love the town but I really don't like my job. But it's something I can do, and it's a living."

"It's hard work," Joey said. "I give you credit."

A woman should not have to work this way, Joey thought. *Men should work. Women should keep the home and teach the children. Women are not equal to men. They are very different. They belonged on a pedestal, in a position of esteem, shielded from the drudgery of a going out to work every day, shielded from the horrors of war.*

Men like the ones feminists were scrapping against for equality wanted to keep their wives and daughters out of harm's way and stand between them and the evils of the world, safe and warm, and protected under their watch. Liberal feminists who raised their voices so loud in their cry for equality must never have experienced the pedestals that men like me had put them on, Joey thought. *They must want equality because the men they knew had kept them down. If the men in their lives had*

324

regarded them like I regard women, they would not want equality. They would want nothing less than the recognition they all rightfully deserved. They would want to be on the pedestals again, looking down, where the men they were grappling with had had them all along.

A woman should not have to work this way, Joey thought. *Men should work. Women should keep the home and teach the children. But the world is changing.*

As Joey sat there with his arm around her, he looked deeply into her tired, beautiful eyes, listening intently to every word she said to him. When she was through talking, he squeezed her gently, to say I hear you, and I understand.

He did not say anything to her, because he did not have the words, but he knew what he thought. *If I ever married her, I'd teach her the meaning of the word liberation. I'd free her immediately from the slavery she's in right now, and put her up on the pedestal she belongs on.*

He looked up at the clock. Break time was over and the people filed back to their machines.

"I'm sorry to dump it all on you, Joey. I should keep it to myself."

"It's okay," Joey said, touching her arm. "I'm glad you did."

Joey and Allison found themselves looking forward to seeing one another each night at work, and on the rare occasion when either of them didn't make it to work, the other one would worry until the next time they saw one another. One weekend in late January, when a powerful New England blizzard knocked the power out in town, Joey got his boots on and trudged through the snow to see if Allison and her little son were going to be warm enough.

"I have some extra blankets," he said to her as the wind howled outside, and when Allison's little son poked his head out from around the corner of their drafty apartment, Joey smiled and beckoned to him.

"Come here, Mike," Joey said, and when the small boy reached up to him, Joey picked him up and wrapped him in a blanket.

Joey sat and talked to the little boy as Allison put on a pot of coffee.

"You may not believe this," she said to Joey from the kitchen, " . . . because you know how little we actually know about each other, but you're probably the closest friend I have right now. That should give you some idea how many friends I have."

Joey didn't know if it was the alcohol he had drunk earlier or the way she looked up at him, so honestly and friendly, but something made him walk over to her and take her in his arms, and when she held him so closely, he lifted her face to his and kissed her as the snowstorm raged outside the window.

"Do you want to stay?" she asked him.

"I would, but Michael would probably wake up, and he may not understand my being here at night."

Allison hugged him again.

"You never stop thinking of other people do you?" she said to him, and he thought about her for the rest of the night—as he trudged back through the snow, and as he drank an unusually large quantity of wine before finally falling asleep at dawn on Sunday.

Confusing thoughts started to bombard him during the next few weeks and as springtime approached, he started to think about the brief relationship he had had with Celia Rinaldi so many years before, when he thought there was no likelihood at all that he would ever end up in a factory in Indian Springs. But then, almost as though it had been a prediction turned into a curse, the events of his life led him to precisely that place, and he had lived in the shadows of his personal defeats for what was fast becoming the majority of his life.

On a bright Sunday in early spring, 1988, Joey walked up the hill toward his grandparents' home, eager to ask his grandfather a question that had been bothering him subconsciously for many years.

"Are you staying to eat?" Maura Bellino asked her son, who sat with his grandfather in the vine-covered picnic house behind the Bellinos' home.

"Okay," Joey answered her, and Maura went back into the house.

The old man and the young man sat together breaking the freshly baked bread that Maura Bellino had set in front of them to be eaten with their soup. Discussions of World War I or of Vietnam were never entered into by either man, and had not been for many years.

"Grandpa, when you came over from Italy, you worked in the factory for small wages. During the Depression, Grandma did too, walking down the hills to work and back up them at the end of the day. I want to ask you something about that."

The way his lower lip and the skin around his eye tightened made Vittorio Bellino listen carefully to the grandson he loved.

"Don't misunderstand me, Grandpa. Please. But did you ever feel humbled by that or in any way ashamed?"

"Ashamed to work?" Vittorio asked him, looking puzzled by Joey's question.

"Not to work, but to work in the factory, and to have Grandma work with you," Joey said.

Vittorio Bellino could not for the life of him understand why his grandson would feel ashamed to work in a factory. Joey had never told him anything about his short relationship with Celia Rinaldi years before, and Joey himself had never stopped to realize that the short discussion he had had with the young girl so many years before had affected him so deeply and colored the way he thought about his job so powerfully in the ensuing years.

"Honestly, I don't know what to feel about it," Joey said to Vittorio. "I know that you've wanted a better life for me so badly, and sacrificed so much for so long that I don't know what to feel. I'm asking you because I honestly don't know whether to be ashamed of working in the factory or proud of it. I want to know what you think."

Vittorio Bellino placed the spoon he was holding over his soup carefully down on the table next to his plate and leaned forward toward the keeper of his future generations. He lifted the index finger of his right hand upward and shook it to add emphasis to his words.

"There is-a great honor in working for a living in-a your hometown, no matter what it is that you do for work, great or-a small. When you have a wife and cheeldr-ren as your life unfolds, and you go to work for them every day, you will-a find great dignity in it. And happiness.

"An-a when-a your wife has-a to work, it's only when the times get really hard, like the Depression. She's-a supposed to be your helper, that's all. In good times, don't ask her to work. She will help you when she has to, but it's-a your job to work-a for her.

"All what I hope for you, all what I pray for you, is there. Honor. Dignity. And happiness. It is a man's-a greatest achievement. Your confusion does not come from working in a factory. It comes from having no one to work for. What you need is a wife and little cheeldr-ren."

Joey sat forward in his chair and stared deeply at the old man he had always admired so much. When Vittorio returned to his soup, nonchalantly slurping it down as Joey looked at him, Joey felt the strength and wisdom of the man he loved and started wrestling with the deepest secret of his life, which he had kept from everyone since his return from Vietnam.

"Grandpa, I didn't want to tell you this," the young man stammered. "Especially not you, because of your dreams for your future generations."

The Vietnam veteran looked away so that his grandfather would not see the shame and embarrassment in his eyes.

"I can't have any children," the young man said.

The old man stared into his grandson's eyes lovingly.

"The grenade cut my nuts," the grandson whispered.

The old man put his spoon down and sat back in his chair heavily. Suddenly the tragedy of war sat heavily on the old man's heart as he felt a great sadness for the grandson that he loved.

"Jewey," he whispered. "Why you didn't tell me this before?"

"I couldn't tell anybody, Grandpa. It's too embarrassing."

Instantly the old man realized the gravity of the moment. *The way I respond to my grandson's needs will chart the course of the rest of his life,* the old man reasoned. *I have to show him strength, or he may succumb to his feelings of weakness.*

"So that is your cross," Vittorio said to Joey. "Each one carries his own. The Lord our God gives each of us a cross to bear. To the strongest of us, He gives the greatest of burdens."

The young man looked through the old man's eyes and into his soul.

"If you cannot have children of your own, then you can use the strength of your love to help those children who have had their fathers taken away too soon, for whatever the Almighty God's reasons are."

Joey looked away hollowly.

"But it's not the same," he whispered.

Vittorio Bellino reached across the table and placed his hand on Joey Bellino's arm.

"Life doesn't always work out the way we hope it will," he said. "We do the best with what God gives us. Some are given nothing. To those we give whatever we have."

Joey shook his head dejectedly.

"What do I have to give?"

"You are Aaron Bellino's son," Vittorio answered him proudly. "And my grandson. You have great love to give to others. Or will you dash it into the ground and waste it, feeling sorry for yourself? Jewey, you're too good to waste your life. There are a great many people who need whatever strength you have left. Give it to them."

Joey looked across the table at the man he loved and drew strength from him once again, as he always had.

The yard birds sang their songs in the vines as the gentle afternoon breezes rustled the branches in the trees behind his boyhood home, and as Joey Bellino gazed lovingly at his grandfather, he realized once again how strong and powerful the old man still looked to him, and what a blessing he had been to him all of his life.

"Vitto-r-rio," Antoinette suddenly called to him from the back door of their home.

"Oh?" he answered.

"Come on," she beckoned to him across the grassy yard.

He stood up from the table, wiped his mouth off with the cloth napkin she had washed for him, and slowly walked over to her to escort her to her chair. This, after she had spent the entire day working to help her daughter-in-law prepare the meal that was set before them. He went to her, and took her by the arm, and walked her to her chair, which he pulled out for her as she sat.

Joey watched them, and the love he had always felt for them coursed through his body once again.

"Eat," Antoinette instructed her grandson, smiling up at him from her chair. "Eat some more."

▲   ▼   ▲

For the next week, the only thing on Joey Bellino's mind was how he was going to ask Allison Braun out. It had been a very long time since the last time he had dated a girl, and when he had, he had been whole. Now, many years later, he had a wooden leg, one eye, and the self-image of an earthworm. Every night he continued to work in the factory and exchange pleasantries with her, helping her in whatever way he could in her job as a machine operator. But no matter how he tried, he could not gather up enough courage or even imagine the way to break the ice and ask her out.

As each shift ended, he would nod to her and walk out the door and back up the river road to his Main Street apartment. There he would repeat his daily ritual of filling his wine glass, lining up his old forty-five records on the stereo, and lying back on his bed to drink and listen to music.

The blue-collar anthems were always the same, Summer In the City, Chain Gang, Tobacco Road, Hang On Sloopy, Maybe I'm Amazed, She's A Lady, Sloop John B, You Really Got Me, You'll Accomp'ny Me, Solitary Man, Freedom, Five O'Clock World, Like A Rock, and his favorite song of all time, Unchained Melody. Over and over he would play the same songs, occasionally changing to old Frank Sinatra, Elvis, Bob Dylan, Roy Orbison, Beatles, Creedence, America, Tom Jones, Bob Seger or Neil Diamond albums, and drinking large quantities of wine no matter what he was listening to. He could sing along to anything when he had drunk enough wine.

As the days went by, the hunting trip to northern Canada that a couple of his acquaintances from town had suggested to him looked better and better. Both men were hunters and Vietnam vets, used to living off the land, and the trip they had suggested to him was a three-week excursion down an uncharted river in an area north of the tundra line, where guides wouldn't even go.

To get there, you had to go to the northernmost airport in Newfoundland, and then take a private plane 500 miles further north to an Eskimo village called Chimo Bay. There a bush pilot would fly you by pontoon plane another hundred miles north where no humans lived, land on a large lake, and drop you off with a rubber raft in the wilderness before flying back to the village alone.

If you were good in the wilderness, and a little bit lucky as well, you could arrive back at the Eskimo village ten days to two weeks later, provided you made it through what was certain to be severe rapids, harsh weather, and polar bear country.

"I'll have to take two weeks' vacation right before inventory shutdown to give me enough time," Joey told Russ Julian and John Vibberts.

"Then do it," John said. "I'm telling you the fish are bigger, the caribou more plentiful, and the air and water cleaner than any place on Earth up there. It's an absolute paradise."

"John went up last year," Russ told Joey, "and found a river no man has ever traveled down before. It's not even on the map. It's a four-hour hike through the wilderness just to get to the river, and this year he wants to follow it back down to the village. People in the area say that if you can make it through and chart it out with any degree of accuracy, they'll name it whatever you want to call it.

"I'm going to plant a sign in the ground at the head of the river that says, 'Chimo Bay 100 miles, Indian Springs, 1600 miles.'"

"Joey, I'm telling you, every cast gives you a fish bigger than the biggest one you've ever pulled out of the lakes around here. You're going to think

I'm lying to you until your arms get tired from pulling in fish. We're going to name it the Julian River, and put it on the map," John said.

"We'll eat fresh fish and caribou every night and the trip will be something we'll never forget. We might never want to come back," Russ said.

"When you guys leaving again?" Joey asked them as he gave serious consideration to the idea.

"Saturday morning. You got about three more days to decide."

Joey wanted to go, but he was thinking just as seriously about Allison Braun.

"Tell you what, guys. There's this girl at work I've been meaning to ask out. Allison. I'll ask her out on Friday, and if she says no, I'll go," Joey told them. "On Saturday morning, if I'm going, I'll meet you at the Station Newsroom at four in the morning. Either I'm going to be going home to get some sleep for a Saturday night date with Allison, or I'll jump in the car and head to Canada with you guys. Either way I'll let you know Saturday morning."

Russ and John didn't want to wait.

"He'll ask her out like you'll ask Pia Zadora out," Russ laughed at John. "Let's settle this thing once and for all."

That day Russ and John knocked at Allison Braun's door.

"Hi, Allison, we're here to do a friend of ours a favor," Russ Julian said. "You probably wouldn't believe that a thirty-seven year old man could be so socially crippled, but our friend Joey Bellino thinks you're the cutest girl in America and he's afraid to ask you out, did you know that?"

Allison blushed as the two men smiled at her on her doorstep.

"He not only lost his leg in 'Nam, he lost his nerve too," John laughed. "You can't believe how nervous he is about asking you out."

"He's like a junior with the prom coming up," Russ laughed.

Allison was flattered, but didn't know how she could make things any easier for him.

"Look, all we want to know is one thing: Are you at all interested in him? Cause if you are, we can pull the cat off his tongue, but if you're not, we can tell him you got a boyfriend or something, and be on our way to Canada with him."

"Canada?" she asked them, surprised.

They told her the whole story about Canada, and the only thing she heard was "polar bears."

"Look, Joey's a big boy. If he wants to ask me out I'm sure he doesn't need any help from you guys. So thanks, but no thanks."

Russ and John left, and when Allison closed the door she felt happy, like she was in high school again.

"She is cute," Russ said to John.

"As a button," John said. "You think he'll ask her out?"

"Call the guide and tell him there's one more guy coming," Russ laughed. "If he asks her out, I'll clean every fish we catch for the whole trip."

John laughed. "I think you're right. How does a guy get that shy?"

"Thirty-seven years of rejection can do a number on anybody," Russ quipped.

As Friday rolled around, Allison tried to be as friendly as she could to the quiet man with the lowest self-image she had ever known. Halfway through the night, after break time had come and gone with nothing out of Joey Bellino's mouth but a muffled, "Ho," she saw another man driving the forklift past her machine.

"Scott!" she called out to the man over the roar of her machine, "Where's Joey?"

"He had to leave early," Scott yelled loud enough for her to hear him. "He starts his vacation this week. Goin' huntin' in Canada."

Allison nodded and turned back to her machine. She looked at the clock on the wall. Three-thirty. *The sky will start to get light in another hour, and Joey will be gone for at least three weeks.* As the night wore on, it was not the "three weeks" that bothered her as much as the "at least." Working on her machine, she did not remember much about what Joey's two friends had told her a few days before. All she remembered were two words, "polar bears."

Joey had already been on the road for over three hours when Allison showed up at Maura Bellino's doorstep.

"What's the name of the Eskimo village they're leaving out of?" Allison asked Maura.

"Chimo Bay," Joey's mother answered. "Why?"

"I'm driving there tonight."

"Oh, Honey, you can't drive there. There are no roads into Chimo Bay. The only way into the village is by airplane."

Maura was puzzled until Allison told her the entire story of their brief friendship and finished it after awhile by confiding in Maura a feeling she had that took Maura back to her high school years and the class trip she took to Washington with Joey's father.

"He's so shy that I'm afraid if I don't make the first move, we'll never get it together," Allison said. "I'm a little afraid to go, but I'm more afraid not to. All I need is a few phone numbers and a little time and I can put together enough information to be on my way. Michael will be at my girlfriend's, and I'll see you when we get back."

Maura said goodbye to her and later on that morning, after several phone calls to Canadian airports and information centers, Allison left alone for Chimo Bay.

She missed them by a few hours at every juncture, and when the private aircraft she boarded in Newfoundland landed at the Eskimo village, she was told that the bush pilot had left for northern Canada two hours before with the three Americans aboard.

"It'll be at least ten days now before we see any signs of them at all," a young man told her, and Allison walked to a little restaurant on the dock of the Eskimo village.

"I'll work for ten days for meals and a room," she told the woman in the restaurant, and fifteen minutes later, Allison was waiting on tables in Chimo Bay.

The people she met at the Eskimo village were the friendliest people she had met anywhere, and in a matter of only a couple of days, she had befriended everyone who came in. One French-Canadian trapper took a special interest in her, and spent long hours having her repeat her story to him several times while he tried to comprehend what would make her follow this American, Bellino, so far into Canada.

"Have you ever been so afraid to lose someone that nothing in the world mattered more than getting to them?" Allison asked him.

"Not yet," the Frenchman said in his deep voice, "But I hope someday I feel that way about someone. For the rest of your life you'll be glad you took this trip."

Ten days later, as she carried two cups of coffee to a young couple at the counter, the Frenchman came in.

"Ell-oh," he bellowed, smiling at Allison across the room. "Today's the day you gonna be happy."

She stopped in her tracks and looked into his eyes.

"Dey's tree American coming downriver in a raft. Dey fishing."

"Oh, George, do you think it could be him?"

"It's him."

"How do you know?"

"Because I ask him. I say, 'You Bellino?' And he say, 'Yes.' He look surprised. He say, 'How you know that?' I say, 'Somebody wants to know.' He say, 'Must be the pilot.' I smile. He say, 'Tell him we'll be in in an hour.'"

Allison dropped her apron on the counter and ran into the ladies room to check her face and her clothes. She put her makeup on and brushed her hair, and her heart was leaping with joy. In the restaurant, she hugged the woman who had given her the job, and told her she'd write to her from America.

Upstream, Russ Julian and John Vibberts were laughing and packing up the gear as Joey Bellino smiled and paddled the raft toward the dock. The closer they got, the more aware they became of the girl standing on the dock with her hair blowing in the wind.

"Oo-wee, will you look at that!" Russ whistled.

"You don't think she's the pilot, do you?" John said, as Joey tried to focus on the girl on the dock.

Slowly he paddled closer, and when he realized it was her, his heart started pounding in his chest. Russ and John pulled the raft up closer, and when Joey stood up and stepped out onto the dock, she ran to him and buried her head into his shoulder, holding him tighter than she had ever held anyone before. He was too stunned to say anything, and then she put her hands behind his head and kissed him hard and full.

Russ and John just stood there in amazement, hanging their gear by their side and watching the reunion in awe.

"How in God's name did you get here?" Joey smiled at her.

"It doesn't matter," she said. "What matters is I'm never leaving your side again."

Suddenly, in the windswept wilderness of the Eskimo village, Joey Bellino realized that he wanted to believe that more than he had ever wanted to believe anything.

"I guess we have a lot to talk about," he smiled at her.

"Forget about talk," she said, pulling his arms around her again. "Just kiss me again."

At dinner that night, in the restaurant overlooking Chimo Bay, John and Russ started teasing her.

"Do you have any sisters?" John asked her.

"Are you sure you got the right guy out of the raft?" Russ said, and for the first time in many years, Joey Bellino laughed.

They ate fish and drank wine, and told Allison stories of their adventures on the trip, and at about nine-thirty, Russ started to yawn and kick John under the table.

"We're gonna hit the sack," Russ said to Joey, and they pulled their chairs out and stood up to leave. "These rooms warm in this inn?"

"Gotta be warmer than you had it out there," she said, pointing north.

Outside, John shook his head in amazement.

"I hope she's not hooking up with him for his conversation," he said.

"I know it," Russ laughed. "He's a good man with a rod and a gun but I bet he didn't say ten words the whole trip."

"They're very nice," Allison said to Joey when they were gone.

"They're both good guys," Joey said. "But they talk constantly. I guess there's nothing wrong with that. It's just that I'm used to peace and quiet. They're okay, though. Came back from Nam about the same time as me."

"I won't ask you about Vietnam," she said. "When you feel like talking about it, I'll listen. But I'll never ask."

Joey looked away.

"That's good, because I'll probably not want to talk about it too much."

She was looking at him in the moonlight over the bay, and she did not see any of his scars.

"Why did you come here?" he asked her quietly.

"Should I have waited in Indian Springs forever, not knowing if you'd ever be back?" she answered.

"I'd have been back in three weeks," he said.

"I wanted us to start out somewhere else. And I didn't want to wait like everybody says a lady is supposed to. I'm tired of being alone, and I know you are too. And besides," she said, "I love you."

He did not say anything, but just looked at her, her beautiful face outlined by the moonlit bay, and suddenly he became aware of the table between them. He got up and walked around the table, sat next to her, and put his arm around her. He stroked her hair and felt her softness in his arms as the moon cast its shining light across the water.

Sitting that way with her head on his shoulder and his arm around her comfortably, she felt safer than she had ever felt in her life. In awhile, she started to get fidgety and he sensed something on her mind that was bothering her.

"What is it?" he asked her.

"I have to ask you something," she said. "About Michael."

"He's a great kid," Joey said.

"He's never had a man around the house."

"You want to know if I can fill the void?" Joey asked her.

"Something like that," she said.

"Honestly, I don't think I could ever take his father's place, and I didn't even know the man. But I don't think anybody could take the place of a person's dad. A boy's dad is his dad, that's it, period. But I can give him a lot of time, and a lot of love, and he can call me Joey, and we can be great friends."

"Would you let him call you Dad?"

Joey thought about that one for a long time.

"I don't know. I'd have to think about that. If I ever had any children, I don't know if I'd want them calling anyone else Dad except me."

"I wish I'd met you first," she said to him, moving as close to him as she could get.

"It doesn't matter," he said to her. "All that matters to me is that we're together now."

"Can we take a walk out on the dock?" she asked him.

Outside, the couple held each other warmly against the cold Canadian wind.

"We're going to be very happy together, aren't we?" she said.

He stopped and turned her around and gazed into her sparkling eyes.

"As long as I live, I don't think it would be possible for me to be any happier than I am right now," he said.

On the cold Canadian night in Chimo Bay, Joey Bellino held Allison Braun close and kissed her as the moonlight danced in the water.

"Of course you know there's only one thing for us to do now," he said to her.

She smiled up at him happily.

"If I can't find a justice of the peace at ten-thirty at night, I'm no Marine."

She started to ask him if they shouldn't just wait until morning, but he was pulling her by the hand and walking as fast as one good leg and one wooden leg could go, and he was so excited that his excitement infected her. She ran alongside of him, her hair blowing in the wind as they walked into the bar at the inn, and Joey asked the bartender where at ten-thirty at night they could find a man who could marry them.

Providence was with them, because a tall heavy man in a business suit reached over and touched Joey's arm.

"If you're serious, boy, we can do business, but if you're not, I'd like to start my drinking."

"You a justice of the peace?" Joey asked him.

"I'm Judge Rioux. Are you sober?"

Joey talked to the judge while Allison went to the ladies room, and when she got back Joey and the judge were smiling and making arrangements.

"You only have one problem that I can see," the judge told them. "In this province, you need to get your marriage license one day before you're married."

"Can you get it for us?" Joey asked him.

"I already told you I can get it, but you still have to wait until tomorrow to get married."

"So we'll get it now, and get married at 12:01, that's tomorrow isn't it?" Joey asked him.

When the judge smiled at the bartender, Joey knew he had a deal.

"I'd like to call Marilyn, the lady I worked for here, to stand up for me," Allison said.

"Then I'll meet you back here at midnight," Joey said, and he kissed her.

Eleven o'clock saw Russ Julian and John Vibberts flipping a coin to see who would be Joey's best man, and one hour later, several patrons of the Chimo Bay Inn had set up the dock for the midnight wedding of Joey Bellino and Allison Braun.

At 12:02, Joey said, "I do," at 12:03, Allison said, "I do," and at 12:04 Judge Rioux said, "I now pronounce you man and wife."

When dawn broke over the dock at Chimo Bay, John Vibberts and Russ Julian were lying against a pier on the dock drunker than they had ever been, and in a rented room in the Chimo Bay Inn, Joey and Allison Bellino were sleeping in a warm room after their first night of lovemaking as man and wife.

A few months later, their baby son was adopted, and Michael Braun had a little brother. There was joy on Brandon Street in Indian Springs when the phone rang, and Vittorio Bellino picked up the receiver before the first ring was completed.

"It's a boy!" Joey shouted through the receiver to his grandfather.

"It's a boy?" Vittorio shouted into the receiver. "Jewey, you said it's a boy?"

"Yes, Grandpa, a boy."

"Ever-ry ting is alright?"

"Yes, Grandpa,"

"It's official?"

"He's all ours."

"What's he like?"

"Healthy and strong."

"It's a boy!" Vittorio said thrusting his fist upward into the air.

"Jewey!" Vittorio hollered. "Whats-a the boy's-a name?"

"David," Joey said, "so he'll never fear a Goliath. And Vittorio, so he'll live a life of honor and integrity and tell his future generations about you."

Vittorio Bellino hung on every word, and smiled broadly and victoriously as he held the phone to his ear.

"David Vittorio Bellino," Vittorio said.

"Yes," Joey answered.

Vittorio Bellino hung up the phone and smiled broadly at his wife of sixty-five years.

"The adoption is official, and David Vittorio Bellino is his name," he said to her. "What a great American name!"

That night, before he lifted his tired legs up into bed, Vittorio Bellino dropped to his knees in his bedroom and prayed. "Almighty God, You are great and powerful, and You have treated me with such goodness. From my knees I praise Your Holy Name, and I thank You for Your loving-kindness. In my thankfulness and praise, I ask You to grant me this desire. Make David Vittorio strong. Make him courageous. Make him a good American. Give him a role in your great panorama. And when his life is over, bring him home to me in heaven, him and all of his future generations, and mine. In the name of the Father, and of the Son and of the Holy Spirit. Amen."

The next morning, while Joey Bellino was standing over the crib looking down at his new little son, a knock came at the front door of his and Allison's apartment. When he answered the door his mother was standing there, wiping the tears from her eyes.

"Joey," she said, her voice shaking, "the Lord gives and the Lord takes away."

"What, Mom?" Joey said somberly.

"Your grandfather died last night in his sleep!"

Joey sat down heavily in his kitchen chair.

"Does Grandma know?" he asked his mother.

"No. She was still asleep when I went in to wake them for mass. I sat there until the funeral director removed his body and she slept right through it. Christina Rinaldi is with her now. We thought we'd tell her that he went into the hospital and just never tell her that he died."

Joey just shook his head, unable to say anything for the pain of the loss he felt.

"He was over a hundred years old, Joey. He lived a long, full life."

Three days later, at the funeral mass of Vittorio Bellino, Joey came out of his shell. When the priest said his usual comforting words, he turned to Joey Bellino and nodded. Joey got up out of his seat, reverently placing his hand on the flag-draped coffin as he walked past it to the lectern, from which he delivered a heartfelt eulogy to the crowded church.

"He was an extraordinary man," Joey began. He painted a canvas of the old man's life, reminding the people in attendance of the very special love the old man had always exhibited which had been his crowning glory.

He told them the story of Vittorio and Antoinette, of the commitment they had made to one another decades before in Italy, and of the influence they had had in the shaping of the town he would now be buried in. He told them that Vittorio had been born an Italian, but that he had died an American, by choice.

Before he was finished, every eye in the congregation was moist, and he finished with the following words: "He gave us four beautiful gifts . . . gifts that no one will ever take away from us . . . gifts that we will pass on to our future generations . . . and to his. He gave us his name. He gave us his faith. He gave us his love. And he gave us his dreams. Our Father in heaven, we thank You for Vittorio Bellino, and now we give him back to You."

When the organist played the Star Spangled Banner at the conclusion of the mass, it seemed entirely appropriate.

Nine days later, at the funeral mass of Antoinette Bellino, Joey Bellino did not speak. No one did, except the priest. But there, sitting in the small Catholic church, he felt a strong sense of peace and closure as the funeral mass progressed.

He felt that just as Vittorio had prepared the way for her for almost ten years in America, he had done the same for her for almost ten days in heaven. He was as sure of that truth as of anything else he had ever believed.

▲　▼　▲

When Sherry Lynn was born her hair was golden blond and her eyes were deep blue. As far back as she could remember, everyone in her family told her how blessed she had been to have been born with such exceptional beauty. Her early years were filled with love and affection from her mother and all of her aunts and uncles, and her father always smiled at her with pride.

In the school yard in grammar school, she was always the center of attention, even before she understood what all the fuss was about. The older boys always smiled at her and talked to her, and the younger boys picked on her and played games with her to get her attention.

When she was eleven years old, her mother and stepfather's volatile marriage finally exploded in a violent argument while she lay in her bedroom and cried, and the last thing she remembered before the door slammed and her stepfather stormed out was the way her mother was screaming and crying, and the loud banging the furniture made as her stepfather propelled everything he could get his hands onto through the windows and off the walls.

When she tiptoed downstairs several minutes after she was sure her stepfather had gone, her mother was sobbing on the couch, her eyelids swollen and her nose bloodied.

She stood in the doorway of the living room, frowning, with tears welling up in her eyes, and when her mother saw her there, she turned her face away from Sherry and buried it into the pillow on the couch. Sherry went to her and hugged her, and when her mother felt Sherry's arms around her she again burst into tears and hugged her without saying anything.

In awhile, her mother sent her out on an errand, and when she got back, the ambulance was parked in her driveway with its lights flashing.

"What happened?" she asked one of the Boston fireman who was standing in her driveway smoking a cigarette.

"Woman who lives here hung herself," he replied nonchalantly, and Sherry Lynn gasped in anguish and shock.

Two years later, while sitting in the back seat of a car on a sunny day in the springtime, the boy she was with put his hand into her blouse and underneath her bra, and before she had time to react, he was kissing her hard and pulling up her skirt. Her panties were off, and the boy was on top of her, and when he entered her, he hurt her, and her first sexual experience was over before she knew what was happening.

Later, thinking about it, she was angry at the way everything had happened, and she began to think about boys in a much more cautious and critical way than she had ever done so before. She didn't like the way they leered at her, and she found herself unable to trust any of them, as it seemed as though every one of them who took an interest in her only led her in one direction in their various relationships; to talk of physical or sexual things.

She lived alone with her stepfather, and one day, when she pulled the curtain back after a shower, her heart nearly stopped when she looked up and saw him standing there naked, smiling at her strangely. He must have taken pity on her when she gasped because he just turned around and walked out of the bathroom, and she locked the door, covered herself with a towel, sat down on the floor, and trembled for over an hour.

Later that night when her stepfather came home, he never said a word to her about the incident and went about his business as though nothing had ever happened. But then, in the middle of the night, she awoke with a start as he was climbing into bed with her, and she closed her eyes in shame and whimpered when he forced himself upon her. When he was finished, he just got up and walked out, back into his own bedroom, where she heard him snoring a few minutes later.

She lay awake in bed long into the night, and when she was unable to sleep, she sneaked out of her bedroom and out into the night. On the street walking through Boston to one of her aunt's houses, she was deciding how to ask her aunt if she could move in with her when a car pulled up along-side of her and four boys who reeked of alcohol all started talking to her at once.

She tried to ignore them, and when she started running away, they chased her in the car, and one of them got out and wrestled her to the ground. She wasn't sure how many times they raped her. All she knew is that all four of them took turns, and some did it to her more than others.

When they were finished, they all laughed, and the last one shook her shoulders, yelling into her face.

"You ever tell anyone about this, and we'll come back and kill you," he said. "And just so you know I mean what I say, here's a little sample."

He kicked her in the stomach and she rolled over on the ground naked and aching. Lying on the cold ground in pain and chagrin, her distress turned to anger and thoughts of revenge, and by the time the sympathetic police officer who spotted her there on his rounds picked her up, her face was frozen in determination.

The boys were arrested, brought to trial, and put through a grueling public spectacle as the whole city became engrossed in the rape trial. At the last minute, Sherry changed her mind in the courtroom and decided that she could not positively identify any of her attackers. She decided instead to say she wasn't sure and added great relief to all the accused boys and their families.

In the courtroom, after the case was dismissed, she sat there strongly and made some other determinations in her mind.

There's more than one way to skin a cat, she thought, and two years later in a strip bar in Boston's combat zone, on her sixteenth birthday, she started her dancing career. Boys and men of all ages stashed one and five dollar bills into her g-strings and she walked back and forth in front of them, her high heels standing her high above the crowd of men whose eyes followed her nearly naked body all across the stages she danced on.

"From now on, I control men, men don't control me," she vowed to her fellow dancers, and all of the other girls were inspired by the way she took charge of all the men she paraded herself before, showing them what she wanted to, when she wanted to, and picking out the men she wanted to entertain, who would pay her the most for her favors.

Afterwards, her jobs were quick and expensive, and the bouncers who guarded her were always nearby in case any of her customers decided to get out of hand. In a very short period of time, she learned everything she need-ed to know about the people she had decided to work with, what each one wanted, and what she wanted from each one, and for once in her life, she exercised some sort of control over the circumstances of her life.

With the money she made at night, she bought the most expensive wardrobes and went to great lengths to keep herself beautiful in the beauty parlors and exercise clubs, and when she worked, men threw a lot of money her way.

After awhile she bought herself a nice home in the suburbs, paid cash for it, and when she was twenty- four years old, after spending eight years in the life, she decided to walk away from it and change the course of her life.

She leased a commercial building, hired four beautiful girls to work for her, and hung out a shingle.

"Sherry's Boutique" became one of the most popular specialty shops in Boston, and Sherry started to attend symphonies, travel on cruises and foreign tours, and follow professional sports, dating many men casually, but none seriously. She became comfortable in all social settings and was very much in control of her life and her own finances.

Along about the summer of 1979, she became aware of the young fighter who was in all the sportscasters reports and his lifelong quest to avenge his father's death in the ring, and she became enthralled with the whole story. She attended one of his fights in the Boston Garden, and midway through the fourth round, she leaned over to the gentleman who had escorted her and spoke to him.

"I want to meet him," she said to the man, and after the fight, Kevin O'Hara turned around, and when he caught her eye, they stared at one another for a moment and the attraction was mutual and instant.

▲　▼　▲

They started dating immediately after that, and the affair they had lasted for several years. She was always physically attracted to him, but it was the words he spoke to her before their first sexual experience that sealed her loyalty to him. She had long since told him of her torrid past, insisting on leveling with him before it came back to haunt her later on.

She could not understand at first why he was so reluctant to start a physical relationship with her, and when he finally told her why, it caught her off guard and bonded her to him emotionally as well.

"So what you're telling me is this," he said to her one day, quite matter-of-factly. "You've had sex with a number of men, but never made love to any of them, is that right?"

"Yes," she answered truthfully.

"Well, I want to be the first," he smiled at her as he held her close.

She cried as they made love and clung to him tightly in the aftermath. Their affair was strong and very passionate, and the fact that they lived so far apart—her in Boston, where she continued to run her specialty shop, and him in Indian Springs, where he tended the horses and trained for his fights—made the times they had together so much more valuable for both of them, and they were absolutely loyal and devoted to one another since the time they first met.

She would meet him many times and always after any of his fights. She sat at ringside, and then left immediately after the final bell to wait for him in their shared hotel room, where she would meet him at the door, pull him in by his belt, and kneel before him while unbuckling his belt before shutting the door and the world, out of their lives for the next twenty-four hours of love making and room service.

Months dragged into years this way, with one thing after another postponing Kevin's quest for a fight against Homer Jones, and the longest time the two lovers spent apart was when President Bush announced the beginning of Operation Desert Storm. Kevin's Marine Corps reserve unit was called on to serve the country in the Persian Gulf, and Private Kevin O'Hara answered the call.

On the night Defense Secretary Dick Cheney announced a blackout of all media coverage as the United States went into battle, the night passed much more quickly and easily for Kevin in the desert than for his cousin Joey Bellino in the United States.

With the media-pumped prospects of chemical warfare being launched against the American troops and Secretary Cheney's promise to the American people that the ground war they were now blocking out all coverage of would be "very brief, and very violent," Joey Bellino lay awake in his bed in front of the CNN television reports, shivering nervously in fear for the men in arms across the world.

The prospects of many young American men, and now, this time, even women being shattered, burned, and broken by warfare, terrified the Vietnam veteran and he shivered and prayed in deep fear.

"Lord, God in heaven, look down with mercy on the boys and girls from our side and theirs, and send Your angels down around them in this hour. End this war and all wars, Lord. It's not the reason You created us for."

The relief Joey Bellino felt when General Schwarzkopf came on the next day to tell the American public how quick the victory had come was so overwhelming that he prayed in thanksgiving all day long and told everyone he came into contact with the truth about the previous night. He had been more afraid for the American troops that night than at any time in the entire span of the Vietnam War. When the American-led victory came so swiftly and so suddenly, he said that the country ought to have waived the requirement for a presidential election for 1992 and just extended George Bush's presidency another four more years.

That President Bush would lose the ensuing election was a notion you couldn't have sold for a nickel in the immediate aftermath of Desert Storm that year but American politics is a strange thing.

The parade for the returning veterans of Desert Storm was the kind of event that turned out huge crowds in the blue collar Connecticut town that had sent so many men off to America's wars. Residents lined the streets by the hundreds as parade marchers lined up behind the Indian Springs High School Marching Band.

From his apartment window overlooking Haymarket Square, Joey Bellino had an ideal vantage point to participate in the parade the only way he had ever known how to. His ritual had been the same on every Fourth of July and Memorial Day since he returned from Vietnam. He had gotten up, showered, shaved, visited his father's grave to make sure they had not forgotten the flag that belonged there, and then returned to his second-floor apartment above the street where he could watch the parade from the corner window behind the curtains, where he could see out and nobody else could see in.

It was better for him that way. He could share in the festivities and look out over Main Street where dozens of flags lined the streets at each parking meter along the way. And he could do it alone, the way he liked it. He had never wanted any accolades since Vietnam, and he had never gotten any. There were only two things he had ever sought since Vietnam, alcohol and solace. There, sitting in his apartment away from the crowds, he had found both.

"You coming to the parade?" Allison asked him on her way out the door.

"No, Honey. You go on without me," Joey answered his new wife. "I've watched every parade since Vietnam from right here."

Looking up at the clock tower on the Main Street church, he was wondering why it was taking so long for the parade to start when he heard a knock on the door. He thought Allison had forgotten her keys, and when he opened the door, Kevin O'Hara was standing there in full dress uniform grinning from ear to ear.

Joey looked at his watch and then back up at Kevin.

"What are you doing, man?" Joey said. "Get out there. They can't start the parade without you."

Kevin reached over and put his cousin into a playful headlock.

"Or without you," Kevin said through his broad grin.

"What are you talking about, Kevin? The parade's for you, not me," Joey said.

"Then the people are going to wait a long time, because they don't get me without you."

"Oh, Kevin. Don't do that," Joey said very seriously. "Please don't do that."

"You never had a parade," Kevin said resolutely.

"I never wanted one."

"I don't want one either. But the parade's not for us, it's for them," Kevin said, pointing out at the people standing on the sidewalks between the flags on Main Street. "And they need to applaud you more than they need to applaud me."

"Kevin," Joey said, embarrassed by his appearance. "My wooden leg. I'm too slow. I'd screw up the parade."

"Then we walk slower," Kevin said. "But there ain't gonna be a parade if you don't walk in it with me."

Joey looked away at the wall in his modest apartment.

"Can't you get Julian and Vibberts to march instead of me?"

"I already did, and Buzzy Griffin and Barry Molitoris as well. They want you to march with them, and none of us is going anywhere until you come down there with us."

"Why, Kevin? Just tell me why."

"Because you guys gave more than us, Joey. That's why. Now come on, will you? Indian Springs is waiting to pay homage to its servicemen."

All the way up Main Street, Kevin O'Hara and the other returning Desert Storm vets smiled and waved at the crowd cordially, walking over to shake little children's hands and slap five to their friends on the sidewalks.

Behind them, the Vietnam vets walked along quietly and tentatively, unused to the experience, with more age and dignity, careful not to walk too fast for the vet who walked in their midst.

There, Joey Bellino limped along in the middle of the pack, trying unsuccessfully to hold back the tears that he kept on reaching up to wipe away as he heard the cheers of the crowd on the sidewalks.

Every time he felt the tears coming into his eye, he disguised it as a cough, and pretending to have a cold, he wiped his eye often as he heard the crowds cheering for him. He tried unsuccessfully to stop his tears from flowing, but he failed, as old people clapped, middle-aged people smiled and cheered, and children waved flags. There wasn't one person anywhere with an American flag sewn to the seat of his pants.

Walking up Main Street toward the American Legion Home, it occurred to Joey Bellino that none of the people on the sidewalks under twenty years old had been alive when he had been welcomed home from Vietnam by a man who spit in his only eye. None of them could possibly understand how much the applause meant to him in the first parade he'd marched in since Vietnam.

▲　▼　▲

A few weeks after the parade, Kevin O'Hara picked up the *Hartford Courant* at the Station Newsroom and opened it up to a stunning headline.

"Homer Jones to Be Freed," the headline read. The column told the story of another inmate confessing to the prison murder that Jones had been accused of, and his release was scheduled for the following day.

A quick check of his weight after losing so many pounds in the desert, plus the impending release of Homer Jones from prison, made the fight he had been training for all of his life once again a possibility. While Kevin trained, Benito Strazza worked out the details and finally the fight was set.

It was to take place in six weeks at the new Foxwoods Casino on the Mashantucket Pequot Indian Reservation in Ledyard, Connecticut, where American boxing rules need not apply. The reservation was recognized as a sovereign nation, and the fight could be sanctioned there alone because of Homer Jones's prison record.

The day he signed to fight Homer Jones, Kevin drove to Boston, bought a bottle of champagne, and rang the buzzer at Sherry Lynn's apartment. She ran downstairs and leaped into his arms, and five hours later they were making love in a Boston hotel.

"This is the last time we're going to do this until after the fight," Kevin told her. "It's the fight of my life, and I don't want to think of anything else for three months."

"Then we better do it right tonight," she teased him, and when dawn broke they were still making love.

That day he kissed her goodbye and jumped back into his truck for his ride back to Indian Springs with one thing alone on his mind. It was time for Homer Jones to pay the piper.

The fight was set for October 12, 1992, Columbus Day, the five-hundredth year after Christopher Columbus discovered America. That it was to be held at Foxwoods Casino did not bode well for the gamblers who flooded into the casino that day.

"Man, you gotta have rocks in your head to come to an Indian reservation on Columbus Day to gamble," a very loud man yelled out at one of the blackjack tables. "They'll be out for revenge today."

Joey Bellino should have heard the man before he walked in, excited at the prospect of winning a lot of money in his first trip to the new casino. He came down with Nello Costanza to watch the fight between his cousin, Kevin O'Hara, and the former welterweight champion of the world, Homer Jones. Inside of an hour and a half, Joey had lost the nine hundred dollars he had come with plus all twenty-five hundred dollars he had left on his credit card.

"Hey, Nello, how long until the fight?" Joey asked remorsefully after all of his money was gone.

"It's only six-thirty," the bookie answered. "There's three and a half hours to go. You wanna borrow some money, Joey?"

"No way," Joey answered. "I feel like the guy that got arrow-killed and scalped in *Dances with Wolves*. I'll just take a walk around and wait for Kevin and Straz to pull in."

The ride down through the rural countryside of eastern Connecticut was a quiet one for Kevin O'Hara and Benito Strazza.

"I been waitin for this day for a long time, Straz," was the first thing Kevin said when he got into the car.

"I know," Benito said, "and I know you're gonna win big tonight."

It was warm and sunny, and the fall colors were a brilliant mixture of reds, oranges, and yellows, as the white Fleetwood Brougham made its way toward the ring that was set up in the casino.

Homer Jones was already there, secluded in his dressing room, when Kevin's car pulled in. Joey Bellino met him somberly at the entrance, and crowds of people started buzzing with excitement as the three men made their way through the casino to Kevin's dressing room. Cameras had been set up throughout the casino so national audiences could watch the non-title fight live on pay-per-view television. When the pre-fight hype was being broadcast, the cameras panned Homer Jones's locker room where the aging ex-champion sat placidly, his shoulders stooped, as his manager taped his hands.

The cameras quickly changed to Kevin O'Hara's locker room, where the young warrior was pacing like a caged tiger smelling blood. Kevin was dancing and pacing back and forth anxiously, his eyes widely alert, and his body already pumping adrenaline.

As soon as Homer Jones saw the contrast with his own eyes on the television that was set up in his locker room, the reporters and cameramen were barred from the room and ten minutes later his manager appeared to call a press conference.

"Ladies and gentlemen," Jones's manager said in a brief statement, "due to personal reasons, my fighter has decided not to continue his career, and as of this moment, Homer Jones is officially and formally retired from boxing. The fight has been called off, and Homer Jones is going home."

A loud chorus of boo's was heard from the Ledyard auditorium, as angry people paraded out of the arena to their cars. Some people hung on, demanding refunds, but because an undercard had been presented, none were given, and in time the crowd dispersed, leaving only the gamblers left in the casino, whose attention was soon drawn to the table games and away from the ring.

Joey Bellino made his way into the casino locker room, and there he met Nello Costanza, who was livid with rage at the retirement announcement because of the volume of bets he was covering on the fight.

"Let me talk to Kevin without all these reporters around," Costanza asked Benito Strazza, and Benito asked everyone but Joey Bellino, Kevin, and Costanza to leave the room.

"It's a shame, Kevin, I tell you it's a goddamn shame. A disgrace to the sport, he is, like he's always been. All the effort you put in to get your weight down to where you could fight him as a middleweight, and all the years you waited for this fight," Costanza raved. "I tell you, you'd have killed his chicken ass and I think it's a goddamn disgrace."

Kevin shrugged it off quietly.

"It's okay," he said softly and resolutely. "It's a long way to his car."

An eerie silence fell over the room as Nello Costanza, Joey Bellino, and Benito Strazza eyed Kevin O'Hara quizzically.

"Nobody said I had to fight him in the ring," Kevin said quietly.

Costanza looked at Benito Strazza, whose eyes were wide and questioning.

"Look, he's not stupid, right?" Kevin asked Costanza. "He's not going to come out of his locker room with all these people so mad at him. He'll just wait until the crowd clears out and then walk out to his car."

There was a long pause as all eyes were on Kevin, who sat there with his hands folded behind his head looking at Nello Costanza.

"When he gets there, I'll be waiting for him," Kevin whispered icily.

"No!" Benito Strazza yelled emphatically, pounding his fist on the dressing table. "No, no, no, no, no! You'll kill your career, and any chance you have of having a sanctioned fight for the title."

Kevin glared at Strazza stoically.

"I don't give a damn about the title, Benito. I never did. There's only one fight I've ever wanted, all my life, and it happens tonight."

"Kevin, don't be stupid. You'll blow ten million bucks. It's a ploy, I tell you, nothing more than a ploy. He'll come out of retirement in six months and you'll make twice as much as you could have made tonight."

Kevin stood up and walked over to his manager slowly. He looked him straight in the eyes and put both of his hands on Benito's shoulders.

"He's the one who blew the money, Straz. It's not about money for me, or the title, or anything else. It's about one thing and one thing alone. The man has to pay for what he did, and I'm the only man alive who can make him do it. You're a good trainer, Benito, and a good friend, and you can stay with me or leave, but I fight Homer Jones tonight, with you or without you."

"Well it ain't gonna be with me, kid," Benito said, pushing Kevin's hands off of his shoulders. "Your father or your mother, either one, would kill me if I played any part at all in this. Kevin, I love you, kid, I really do, but I'm beggin' you, don't do it. Please don't do it."

Kevin walked away from him and stared at the blank locker room wall. "You better leave then, Straz. No hard feelin's. But I'm doing it tonight."

Benito Strazza looked helplessly at Nello Costanza, and then at Joey Bellino.

"You boys got any influence on this kid at all, you better talk some sense into him, because I'm walkin' out of here right now, and I'm getting into my car and going home. And you're both witnesses that I'm totally against this. Totally."

Benito Strazza walked over to Kevin, who would not look at him, and then slammed the door on his way out of the room.

A quiet hung over the room as Nello Costanza and Joey Bellino stared at one another absolutely without a clue as to what to do next.

Then Kevin turned to Costanza.

"You want to help me?" he asked.

"How, kid?" Costanza answered.

"Just find out where his car will be picking him up, and I'll walk over there myself."

Costanza glanced over at Joey.

"Go ahead," Joey said. "I'll stay with Kevin."

A short time later, Nello Costanza appeared in Kevin's locker room.

"Half an hour. The south entrance. Won't be anybody there but Jones, his manager, and two bodyguards."

Kevin nodded. "Okay," he said. "We'll be there waiting for them."

"Kevin," Nello said, "you sure you want to do this?"

"It's already been done a thousand times in my mind," Kevin whispered.

"Okay, kid. We'll be there with heat in case his goons try to step in on you."

"Don't shoot anybody, Nello, just let me do my own job."

Nello Costanza embraced Kevin and patted him on the shoulders.

Joey Bellino stood next to Kevin O'Hara. "I won't let it get to guns and knives, Kevin," Joey said. "I won't let it get that far."

Half an hour later, all was quiet in the Ledyard wilderness at the heart of the Indian reservation. A long black Cadillac limousine drove up quietly to the south gate of the arena, and Homer Jones, flanked by two burly black bodyguards, stepped out of the building. He didn't get ten steps out of the building when Kevin O'Hara stepped out from the shadows and stood between him and his limo.

"What the hell?" Homer said, stopping in his tracks.

"I told you a long time ago I was never going away," Kevin whispered. "Why are you so surprised?"

"What do you want?" Homer asked him gruffly.

"Come on, Jones, you know what I want," Kevin said quietly. "You made a big mistake not fighting me in the ring tonight, because you blew an awful lot of money, and now you have to fight me anyway."

"Are you crazy?" Homer said. "I ain't fightin' you now or ever. Maybe you didn't hear what I said before. I'm retired, man, retired."

Kevin's face was set in a steely eyed stare.

"You have to answer to me for my father," Kevin whispered to Homer Jones. "You have to answer to me now."

One of Jones's bodyguards pulled a knife out of his jacket, but he stopped when he heard a gun clicking in the shadows.

"Put the shiv away, son," Nello Costanza said, stepping out of the shadows with Joey Bellino standing next to him. Costanza's gun glistened under the street light.

"You white bastards," one of Jones's bodyguards said angrily.

"Don't make this a racial thing," Costanza answered quickly. "It ain't. It's between Kevin and Homer, and that's it. The rest of us are gonna stay out of it."

The first punch thrown was a looping overhand right that caught Homer Jones off guard and snapped his head sideways.

"I ain't gonna lay down for you, kid," Homer said, assuming a defensive position.

Kevin bore in on him and hit him again, hard, in the face. Homer countered with a combination that caught Kevin squarely in the face and the fight was on.

The four other men who watched moved out of the way as the two combatants stalked each other feinting, bobbing, and weaving and throwing scores of punches that landed with varying degrees of effectiveness. Neither man gained any advantage in the early going, although Kevin was the aggressor, backing Homer up with a relentless charge, and the fact that the two men were fighting bare-fisted soon caused both of their faces to welt up and start to bleed. With no bell to end any rounds, it was apparent when the boxers went past three minutes that it would be a short fight because both men were starting to get winded.

At about the four minute mark, Kevin missed with a looping right, and Homer caught him with a hard uppercut which sprawled him back onto the pavement. Before he could get up, Homer surprised everyone by lifting Kevin up with a hard kick to the face which rocked his head back and broke his nose.

Blood started pouring out of Kevin's nose, which enraged him, and he ran at Homer wrestling him to the ground, and slamming his head onto the pavement. Kevin got up and as Homer tried, Kevin hit him in the back of the head, driving his face into the concrete. Kevin kicked him in the face, and as Homer rolled over and over, Kevin kept on kicking him. Homer tried to get up, but Kevin was all over him, and suddenly one of Homer's bodyguards realized that his man was in serious trouble.

"Stop it! Stop it!" the man yelled. "You can't use your feet."

The man tried to stand in between Kevin and the fallen Homer Jones like a referee stopping a bout, but he suddenly felt a strong arm holding him back and he looked up into the cold eye of Joey Bellino, who stood there holding him in an iron grip.

"That's not for you and me to decide, Bro'," Joey said to him sternly, and as Kevin sprawled the old champion backward on the pavement again, Homer groaned. Kevin sat on his chest and pummeled him in the face, and Homer's man pleaded with Joey Bellino.

"You can't let him kill the man," Homer's bodyguard yelled, and something made Kevin O'Hara hold his punches.

"You never even said anything to my mother," Kevin screamed into Homer Jones's swollen-closed eyes. "It was like he didn't even matter!"

"I'm . . . sorry . . . I . . . ," Homer whispered.

But Kevin was not through with him.

"You fought him with unpadded gloves!" Kevin screamed, punching Homer in the face as his own blood trickled down his face and onto Homer's face.

"I'm sorry," Homer whispered. "I had nightmares about it for years."

Homer Jones's other bodyguard piped up.

"Kevin, he told me for years that he was jealous of the love you and your daddy had. His daddy got killed in the Korean War when he was just a baby. He never knew him."

Suddenly Joey Bellino felt a wave of compassion flowing over him for the badly beaten man who lay at Kevin O'Hara's mercy. Kevin felt a strong hand on his shoulder.

"Come on, Kevin, let's go home," Joey Bellino said to him sternly. "I can't let you kill him."

If it had been anyone else other than Joey Bellino who had said that to him, Kevin might not have listened, but he dropped Homer Jones's head out of his left hand and pushed himself off of him, leaving the broken man lying on his back, barely alive.

"You never even said you were sorry to my mother," Kevin said to Homer again, more hurt this time than angry.

"I didn't know how," Homer whispered up at him, and Kevin turned away from him and walked away.

▲   ▼   ▲

Sherry Lynn never told Kevin O'Hara when she became pregnant. She found out a few weeks after his last visit to her, but she was not at all sure she wanted to have the baby, and she did not want to distract Kevin in any way from his life's quest to beat Homer Jones. When fight night arrived she was already three months into her pregnancy, but she hadn't told anyone yet, and she was still undecided what to do about it.

Kevin never imagined that she was pregnant, and it was the farthest thing from his mind as he recuperated from his fight with Homer Jones. He had soundly thrashed the old champion, bruising his face and his head and injuring both of his hands in the process, and he was feeling profound sadness and deep remorse after the fight.

He had always imagined himself feeling elation after his life's quest was completed, but instead he felt nothing but shame and guilt. In his subconscious mind he had long felt that seeking vengeance in such a harsh manner was wrong, and now that he had exacted his severe punishment on Homer Jones, he felt the heavy weight of his selfish sin on his conscience.

I beat the old man senseless, he thought to himself, *and he'll never look the same again.*

Out in the barn, saddling up the horses seemed to take longer, and the joy with which he usually tended to his horses had left him. At midday he walked out toward the pasture with his horses, and after turning them loose to graze, lay back in the grass, chewing a blade of grass as he gazed up into the clouds.

I was wrong, he whispered silently into the heavens. *I should have let You take Your own revenge. I never want to sin against You ever again. It hurts too much afterward.* For a long time he lay there and felt the weight of his sin on his heart. *I want to do right, but I'm unable to,* he lamented.

"Lord, God," Kevin said out loud in hearing distance of no one but his horses, "let me put this part of my life behind me. I don't want the bitterness any more."

That afternoon, after the horses were watered and fed, Kevin walked over to the punching bags that his father had used so many years before.

They were the same ones he had trained on for the better part of his young life. He walked over to the tool chest, pulled out a large knife, and cut down all the bags, tossing them in a heap in the corner.

He walked back up to the farmhouse, showered, shaved, dressed and started his pickup truck, throwing a night bag in alongside of him.

"Goin' to Boston, Ma!" he yelled out the window to Colleen O'Hara, and on the highway into Boston he made some very solid decisions.

No more re-enlistments in the reserves, he said to himself. *When this hitch is over I'll tell the brass that I'm finished and I'm a civilian again.*

In Boston, outside her apartment, Kevin leaned up against his pickup truck, and when Sherry spotted him while walking along the sidewalk with some friends, she left them and ran into Kevin's arms.

"Let's eat in that restaurant in the sky that revolves around and shows you the whole city," Kevin said to her.

She laughed.

"You always liked that restaurant," she said, kissing him and holding his arm in hers.

In the restaurant, as the evening twilight illuminated the Boston skyline, Kevin slid over close to Sherry Lynn and reached into his pocket. He pulled out a small box and handed it to her.

"A question and a pledge," he said to her.

She opened it and the diamond glittered in the light.

"If you'll marry me and move in with me at the farm, I'll love you forever. I'll quit boxing, build up the old farm to what it used to be years ago, and you and I can raise a bunch of happy kids."

Sherry Lynn was caught totally off guard by Kevin's proposal. Somehow she had just never imagined that he would ever do that. She had never thought about marrying him, or anyone, for that matter, and unlike most girls she didn't ever want to get married.

"Oh, Kevin, I don't know what to say."

"You don't have to answer me right away," he smiled. "I'll give you a couple of minutes to think about it."

"I must be dreaming," she said, as she lay her head on his shoulder.

"I got four more months in the reserves, and when this hitch is over I'm packin' it in. This seeing you sporadically is getting really old," he said. "And the only time I feel really happy is when I'm with you."

Sherry felt the same way but she was having a hard time visualizing life on the farm.

"I only have one question," she said.

He held her close to him and she looked deeply into his eyes. "Is it absolutely imperative that we live on the farm?" she asked him hesitatingly. He did not realize at the moment how important the question was, and in the romance of the moment he did the very thing he should never have done. He ignored the question. If he had weighed the importance of the question and handled it accordingly, the entire course of their lives could have changed, but he missed his window of opportunity and passed over her question lightly.

"You'll love it on the farm," he smiled at her. "It'll be a whole new way of life for you."

Sherry Lynn was so in love with Kevin O'Hara, far beyond the physical attraction she had always felt for him, that in the heat of the moment, she set aside the fact that she was not at all excited about living on a farm. She wanted to say yes but held back as she gazed into his eyes lovingly.

"Move in with me now," he said, holding her in his arms. "Tonight. We can get married any time, but I want to sleep with you on the farm tonight."

That night under the full October moon, Kevin O'Hara made love all night long to Sherry Lynn. For the next three days, the couple ran and played like little children in the fields behind the barns and Kevin could never remember being so happy. Out in the fields they were laughing and playing when suddenly she turned to him abruptly and held his arms.

"Hey, are you sure you're not going to get shipped back to Iraq? Saddam Hussein has been pretty quiet since we kicked his ass but we may not be finished with him if he acts up again."

"Are you kidding? Saddam will never challenge George Bush again. And unless the country goes completely haywire, a man like Bill Clinton could never beat a man like George Bush in a presidential election. I really think I've seen the last of my foreign service," he answered.

He hugged her and held her close.

"If I get called up again, you can always live here until I get back if you want to," he said.

She didn't answer him, just hugged him tightly, feeling good in the strength of his arms.

Kevin never pushed Sherry to make a decision, just reminded her every time they talked that he really wanted to marry her, and that he was certain they would be very happy together. The days passed into weeks, and just as his enlistment time was running out, he received a letter in the mail.

"I thought my foreign service was over with Desert Storm," he told her. "But there are some more people in trouble in another part of the world, and we're going in to save them."

"Oh, Kevin, no. Not another war."

"I don't think this one will be near as bad as the last one. We're just going to guard supply lines for food distribution in Africa."

"Africa?" she cried out.

"Place called Somalia. People are starving to death by the thousands, and nobody else in the world can mobilize as fast as us. We're the United States of America, Sherry. We have to go."

Sherry Lynn knew that the United States of America didn't have to do anything. But she also knew that as long as there were men like Kevin O'Hara in uniform, the United States of America always would go in for the rescue.

"Regular Marines are the only ones who will be required to go, aren't they?" Sherry asked him. "Not reserves."

Kevin smiled at her.

"Yes, but I volunteered. I really think you need some time away from me, so you know how much you'll miss me. Then you won't want to be away from me any more when I get back, and then I'm sure you'll want to get married."

The next day at the airport, Sherry Lynn did something she had not done for many years. In the arms of the only man she had ever loved, who was now leaving her for a destination across the world for an unknown length of time, she held him tightly and began to cry.

"Is it too late for you to stay here?" she asked him.

"Why?" he smiled into her moist eyes as he held her in his arms.

She wanted to tell him that she was pregnant with his child, but she didn't know how to do it at that particular time.

"Because I want to marry you," she said through her tears instead.

"You picked a helluva time to say that!" Kevin smiled down at her. "Are you sure?" he asked her.

"Yes," she said, standing on her tiptoes and kissing him liberally. "Yes, yes, yes, yes, yes."

The troop carrier was leaving and there was no time to do anything about their situation at the moment, and shortly afterward, after Kevin left for Somalia, Sherry Lynn left for Boston. When she arrived, she immediately told her roommate, Alanna, how relieved she was to be in Boston for a long while and away from the farm Kevin loved so much.

"I'll enjoy the city for a little while longer and when Kevin gets back, I'll be moving onto the farm with him."

One week later, as Kevin sat atop a Jeep in Mogadishu, Somalia, Sherry stood in front of a mirror in Boston and looked at her bulging belly. *It's too late to hide any longer*, she thought, and when Alanna came in, she eyed Sherry curiously, standing in front of the mirror.

"Don't tell anyone about this, Alanna. Not Kevin, not your boyfriend, not anyone, do you understand?" Sherry said.

"Kevin doesn't know?" Alanna asked Sherry incredulously.

"You didn't know either until just now."

"How far along are you," Alanna asked her.

"About four months, I guess. Kevin hasn't got any idea. I'd have told him, but I still don't know what I want to do."

In Somalia, Kevin never imagined that back in the States, his fiance, Sherry Lynn, was pregnant with his child. He thought about how great it was going to be when they were married and had children, but most of his concentration was directed at feeding the starving people of Somalia. More than he had ever been, he was proud and thankful to be an American.

Back in Boston, Sherry Lynn was fighting her own kind of war, which was far worse than any she had had for a very long time. She was in love with a boy whose child she was carrying, but he was on the other side of the world, and nobody but her, her doctor, and her roommate knew that she was pregnant.

She loved him and wanted to marry him, but the longer he was away, the more she dreaded the thought of giving up the city life that had been the only one she had known in favor of life on a farm. She just could not get used to the idea of living on a farm, and she was having second thoughts about marrying Kevin O'Hara at all.

He's the only man I've ever loved, she thought, *but I don't know why we have to be married. Things were okay the way they were before, and now all this is happening to me all so suddenly.*

But Kevin was in Somalia, and with Alanna sworn to secrecy she stayed locked away in her room in the city as her stomach and her dilemma grew bigger and bigger with each passing week.

On New Year's Eve, the last day of 1992, Kevin was stationed at a private hospital, school, and food distribution center about eighteen miles outside of Mogadishu, Somalia, when a huge crowd moved outside to cheer in a helicopter carrying the president of the United States.

The center, which the Somalis called the "Place of Bones," had become a safe haven for sick and starving people, and when the crowd chanted "Welcome Mr. Bush, Welcome Mr. Bush," Kevin smiled in pride as his president stepped down and walked among the people.

Kevin felt a rush of excitement as President Bush passed by him and smiled a broad smile as he greeted Somali refugees and their U.S. Marine rescuers. Watching George Bush pass by, Kevin felt very happy that his country could elect such men as their leaders. When the president had passed by, Kevin looked down at the white-toothed smile of a young Somali who looked up at him and said, "We Somalis never forget George Bush."

Shortly afterward, the president toured the center's hospital, passing by scores of sick and dying Somali children, some of whom were too near death for the Americans to be able to save.

Outside, the president spoke to reporters about the American troops.

"It's just too emotional for me to see this. I thought I had the most respect possible before now, and now it's even greater. It's the best of America."

Back in the States, Sherry Lynn was in the second trimester of her pregnancy as Bill Clinton took the oath of office as President of the United States. Kevin read every newspaper report of Clinton's inauguration with disbelief, unable to understand how George Bush could possibly have lost to him.

Two days after taking his oath of office, on the twentieth anniversary of the Roe vs. Wade decision legalizing abortion, President Clinton signed an executive order lifting restrictions that had been imposed on abortions by pro-life Presidents Ronald Reagan and George Bush. With one sweep of the pen he turned back twelve years of progress by pro-life forces in the country on what proved to be a very dark day for people who believed in the constitutionality of the right to life.

Sherry Lynn thought about abortion many times during the ensuing weeks, but something kept holding her back. *Kevin will be home soon, and then I'll decide,* she thought.

▲ ▼ ▲

"Sister Rose Alba, your cancer is back," the young doctor said to her slowly in measured tones. "And this time, I'm afraid it is inoperable."

It's what I had expected, she thought.

"It's what my mother died of, and my father, and the only question is how painful will it be, and how long will I have to live?"

"Six weeks, maybe ten," the doctor said, "but with the proper medication, we ought to be able to control the pain."

"Fine," the old nun answered, "Then tell me how to administer it to myself, because my work is far from finished."

"You can't do any more work, Sister. You've reached the time in your life when making yourself as comfortable as possible is your only work."

The magnificent old lady smiled up at the young doctor cordially. "That was never my lot in life, Doctor. Now tell me how to administer the pain medication to myself. I haven't a moment to spare."

The following day, three very young nuns and one very old one drove into Indian Springs, Connecticut, from Worcester, Massachusetts, and at the top of Main Street, the old nun said, "Here."

"You're sure you want to do this, Sister?" one of the young nuns implored her.

"Sister, I've watched a lot of people die in my life, an awful lot of them. Some die with dignity, others with a lot of yakking and complaining, and the results are always the same. When I meet the Lord, I don't want Him to say, 'Okay, Sister, come on,' I want Him to say 'Well done, thou good and faithful servant.' You can drop me off here as I have requested."

The young novices let her out of the car with a prayer and drove out of town as quickly as they had driven in.

With untold joy she started her slow walk down Main Street. The town was very much the same as she had remembered it from two decades earlier, the only exception being the reduction in the number of bars and taverns, which had moved out when the factories started to close. The only difference from the way she walked this day and the way she used to walk before was that she walked a lot slower this time. She was bent over with pain and age, but her smile was the same, if not broader and happier than ever before.

At the Colorado Restaurant bar, Ellington Joe turned white as he put his hand over the top of his glass, which the bartender was attempting to fill up.

"I'm shuttin' myself off, Alfie, I've finally had enough."

"This some kind of a joke, Ellington?" the bartender asked him, but he knew by the somber look on Ellington Joe's face that his longest standing customer was serious and was stopping on his own for the first time in his life.

"Nope, I'm serious," Ellington Joe said. "I know it's time to quit when I see a saint walking by the window!"

Sister Rose Alba walked into the Station Newsroom and a half a dozen regulars recognized her right away.

"Sister Rose Alba, is it really you?" Alfredo Bosco, said beaming.

"Could you direct me to the Bellino residence?" the old nun asked them cordially. "I'd like to speak to one of my old students."

That evening, and the following morning as well, Joey, Allison, and Maura Bellino accompanied Sister Rose Alba to church at Saint Patrick's, and in no time the word had spread like wildfire throughout the town that the grand old lady would have something to say to everyone in the parish at the end of the last mass on Sunday noon.

The church hall was jam-packed with old friends and students, well-wishers and curiosity seekers, as a microphone was set up to reach the ears of those who could not fit into the crowded auditorium.

Broad, beaming smiles met the old teacher as she beckoned for Joey Bellino to bring the microphone to her, as standing made her very uncomfortable.

"It's so very nice to see all of you here today," she started, speaking very slowly and deliberately softly into the microphone so everyone would have to be quiet to hear her every word.

"There was a time when I thought I would never see any of you ever again, but the Lord has a way of doing things His way, in His own perfect timing. There may not have been enough of us before today to accomplish the task I'm going to ask you all to help me with this week."

The swelling crowd was silent in anticipation as the gallant old lady continued.

"As you know, a very momentous occasion is taking place this week in our beloved town," she said quietly and matter-of-factly. "It is something that has saddened me very deeply, and I know none of you had anything to do with it. Of course I'm talking about the abortion clinic that is scheduled to open this Wednesday adjacent to the hospital many of you were born in.

"How did I know this, you want to know? A little birdy told me."

Some of her old students beamed with pleasure as she reverted back to the signature phrase she always used to explain how she knew everything that seemed to be going on behind her back.

"It doesn't matter how I know," she said. "I know. And I'm very saddened by it. Very saddened, indeed. And it isn't right, of course, that a town that has been so blessed by all of God's blessings should be so callous, and let such an abomination take place within its borders. It should not happen, and it will not, while I'm alive."

The room started buzzing, and she held the microphone away from her mouth and asked Joey Bellino to quiet the crowd.

"Please, Sister Rose Alba would like to continue!" Joey bellowed out into the auditorium, and in a few seconds order was restored.

"It really doesn't matter, of course, whether you would call yourself pro-choice or pro-life, there isn't one of us who is free to take the life of an unborn child."

The crowd started buzzing again, and once again Joey Bellino held up his hand to quiet them.

"Of course we were all created by God with a choice. It's very clear to all of us that we have free will. But it is equally clear that we are at no time to choose sin, and the destruction of a human life is, of course, sin."

"What do you mean it doesn't matter if you are pro-choice or pro-life, Sister?" one young girl yelled out.

"I'll prove my point," the wise old sage said, holding her microphone to her aged face. "Will all of you please stand up."

Everyone in attendance stood to their feet.

"Now will everyone who believes that God created us with the right to life, liberty, and the pursuit of happiness please remain standing."

As everyone in attendance continued to stand, she let her eyes pan the room.

"And furthermore, will all of you who are glad that you live in a country that recognizes your free will to choose things like who your mate will be and where you will live, and what you will do for a living, please remain standing, and everyone else sit down."

No one in the room sat down.

"Answered like true Americans, I'm sure," she smiled out at them. "So you see you are all really quite pro-choice, on your freedom to choose.

"Now, will all of you remain standing who would choose life under the following circumstances."

A great hush fell over the standing crowd, as the old nun continued.

"You are an unborn baby, about to be aborted, and through some miracle of God, you are given the choice to live or to die. Regardless of the circumstances of your mother's impregnation, or her physical or emotional state at the time you are given the choice, or the economic status of your parents or your country, or any other extenuating circumstances, all those of you who would choose life for yourselves remain standing."

Not a person in the auditorium or outside of it moved a muscle.

"So you see, if the choice were given to the right person, there would be no abortions done in this country or any other. Survival is the strongest instinct any of us feels, and it is clear that we are all quite pro-life when it is our own life we are concerned with. The trouble, my children, is that the choice is left to the wrong people to make in our society. The innocent unborn life has no choice, and that is his or her God-given right, not any of ours."

The crowd started humming and talking back and forth, and a loud noise spread out across the assembly hall.

After a few moments, Sister Rose Alba looked to Joey Bellino, who held his hand out over the crowd to quiet them, and once again she continued.

"The gospel of John begins with the following statement of fact; 'In the beginning was the Word, and the Word was with God, and the Word was God. The same was in the beginning with God. All things were made by Him, and without Him was not anything made that was made. In Him was life, and the life was the light of men. And the light shineth in darkness; and the darkness comprehended it not.'

"If the Bible is true, then it is true that Jesus is God. It is also true that God is now, always was, and always will be. If Jesus is God, and God always was, and always will be, then at no time can Jesus ever be potentially alive. God has never been potentially alive, He has always been alive.

"Our pro-abortion friends, who prefer us to call them pro-choice, would like us to believe that there is a period in time in the development of a fetus when no life exists, only potential life. That is their justification for ending the development of this 'potential life' through abortion.

"If Jesus is God, who has always been alive, then at no time would He ever be in a period when He was 'potentially alive.' Does it not follow that throughout His period in His mother's womb He was always alive? And if that in fact is the case, does it not follow that every other creature of God that is in its gestation period is alive, and not merely 'potentially alive?'

"When you take that life, then, you do not end a 'potential' life, you kill a life! Therein lies the answer to what abortion is. It is not the cessation of a process during which time life is merely 'potential,' it is the murder of unborn life! This, of course, is something no one may choose to do without violating the commandment of God not to kill.

"As science progresses, and viability is assured earlier and earlier in the gestation period, the moment when life is sustainable outside the womb draws closer and closer to conception. Who are we, who is anyone, to draw that line any further away than that magical moment when God creates life? Our church teaches us, and the infallible words of our Holy Father remind us, that life begins at conception. Death results at any time after that moment when the process of life is interrupted. Abortion is murder, and it cannot be allowed to take place in our town. Not in our town."

"Now I understand what you've been trying to say to me for all these years," Joey Bellino heard one woman say to her husband loudly in the front row as the crowd noise reached a high level. Standing there in the light of the old teacher's wisdom, Joey again felt the rush of excitement that he used to experience daily under her teaching many years ago when he was a child.

Once again Sister Rose Alba looked to Joey Bellino, and once again he spread his hands out over the crowd, who quieted to let the old woman continue.

"I'm going to ask you all to join me on Wednesday for a very important task. I want to stop any and all abortions from taking place at our new clinic. If enough of us join together that day to protest, there will be no business done in our new abortion clinic. It may be difficult, and we may be misunderstood. There is a chance that some of us may be arrested, but there are young innocents there that day who will die if we do not act.

"Many of you have jobs, or go to school, or have some other reason why it will be difficult for you to attend, but I'm calling a meeting for tomorrow evening at seven-thirty, right here in this auditorium for all those of you who wish to accompany me on this important mission. Our goal and our motto will be simply this," she said. "Not in our town!"

Debates raged in homes throughout the town that night, and many decisions were reached, in much the same way as decisions are reached on any given election day in the history of a country. Ultimately it boiled down to the same question in the recesses of most people's minds who contemplated answering Sister Rose Alba's call. "What are the benefits and liabilities to me, personally, if I join her?" the majority of townspeople asked themselves.

In one home, the stakes were much higher than in many of the others.

"I'm joining Sister Rose Alba the day after tomorrow," Celia Rinaldi Franklin told the two men seated at her kitchen table. The men were her father, Columbo Rinaldi, the administrator of the hospital and the abortion clinic, and her husband, Robert Franklin, head surgeon and abortioner at the hospital.

"You do that, and our marriage is over!" Dr. Franklin screamed at her in front of her father, who sat there frowning.

"It ended a long time ago, in a closed-door meeting at the hospital, when the two of you decided that it didn't matter what I thought, and that you were going to perform abortions anyway," she whispered to him coldly, and when she walked out of the room, she shut the door solidly.

Myra Tinkerton heard the news from a Catholic friend of hers, and decided that this would be the day she would stand against her father, Reverend Elrod P. Tinkerton, whose anti-Catholic venom had embarrassed her for so many years of her life in their Laurel Hill Baptist Church. The reverend had remained so distrustful of anything Catholic all of his life that when the church came out against abortion, he took a stand in favor of it, and as the Vatican toughened its pro-life stand through the years, Reverend Tinkerton toughened his pro-choice position. That had embarrassed his daughter, Myra, and she decided to stand with Sister Rose Alba.

Another who heard the news of the stand against the clinic was the young African-American track coach, Khalid Amin, whose father had walked with Dr. Martin Luther King in the civil rights movement of the 1960s, and who had carried a life-long passion for victims of other people's choices. In the quiet of his bachelor apartment, the young Muslim decided to stand firmly with Sister Rose Alba, even if it meant losing his job.

All the next day, Sister Rose Alba rested at Maura Bellino's home, and at seven o'clock that evening she knelt at the front of the auditorium, where several hundred chairs had been set up for the numbers she expected to join her at the clinic.

She thought of all the words of the Holy Fathers she had lived under in her lifetime, whose commands in matters of morality she had always held to be infallible. They were all against abortion.

She examined the action she was about to take in the crossfire of anyone whose words she had ever given any weight to throughout her life, of her parents who had raised twelve children, one of whom before the child's birth doctors told them would be deformed. This child had gone on to be the most delightful sister of all of her siblings.

She thought of the words of Mother Teresa of Calcutta, India, one of the poorest regions of the world, who said that any country that would permit abortion is a very poor country. And she listened to the inner voice that she had come to recognize as the Holy Spirit, telling her that if Godly men and women do not act, ungodly people will fill the void and make the laws we all live under. She was sure she was right and determined to move ahead with her plan not to allow an abortion clinic to function in Indian Springs.

The Roe versus Wade decision may be a greater error by the United States Supreme Court than the Dred Scott decision calling slavery legal, she thought. She was right, she was certain of it, and she knelt before the auditorium and prayed for the strength to carry the noble protest to its completion.

At 7:35, she turned around and the sadness in her face was deeply evident to the handful of people in attendance. She looked out over the empty auditorium, and saw only five people: Joey and Allison Bellino, Khalid Amin, Myra Tinkerton, and Celia Rinaldi Franklin.

All right then, she thought to herself, closing her eyes and bowing her head in sadness. *It will be us six.*

"Come closer to me, my friends," the old nun smiled out over the small group of people. "I'm old, and my voice doesn't travel as far as it used to."

When the small group of people assembled themselves in front of the auditorium, which seemed cavernous to the few who showed up, there was an immediate sense of camaraderie within the group, partially because of the small number of those who answered the good sister's call.

"First of all, don't let the numbers scare you," the old nun said. "The important people are here. I'm reminded of an old phrase I went back to many times in my religious life, when the going got tough. 'You have not chosen Me, but I have chosen you,' the Lord said. Each of you has been selected by our Lord for our mission."

The small group looked at one another seriously, with mutual respect and not a little bit of apprehension.

"Let me reiterate a few things before we get too far into this meeting here tonight. The ways of the Lord are strange, beyond comprehension for many of us, but with faith in Him, I will not question Him, only follow where He leads me.

"I do not question why any of you are here, only thank God for leading you here, and praise Him for his choice of each of you. We will be doing a very important thing the day after tomorrow, much more important than any of us may know at the present moment, and it is vital that we all act with the utmost of restraint and love for everyone with whom we come in contact.

"Let's consider first all of the people who will be in disagreement with us, and you can all count on it, there will be many of them. They will treat us with contempt and ridicule, as they treated the Lord upon his crucifixion. We must not cater to them, or lose our dignity in their midst, only ignore their taunts, and go about our business.

"Then let us take the staff of the clinic we will be closing down, and we will close it down. They are misguided people whose jobs we are going to cost, and they will not be happy to see us. They do not answer to us, and we will not confront them in any way, only ignore them, and do what we came to do.

"There will, of course, be law enforcement officials who will probably come to arrest us. When they do, we will not resist in any way, just take on the limpness of an unborn baby, allowing them to do with us what they will, in symbolic solidarity with the unborn life we seek to protect.

"Finally, and most importantly, are the young mothers whose lives we will most directly impact with our presence. These, more than any others we come in contact with, we must show the utmost of love and compassion for, drawing them into agreement with us by the love we share for them.

"If you hear nothing more of what I say tonight, hear this. Where there is hate, let us show love. Where there are laws which allow the destruction of the lives they carry within them, we must go to the young ladies and offer them love. We must show them real love, not the false love of the great deceiver, Satan, who disguises himself as their helper in the clothes of Planned Parenthood members, and a government policy allowing easy access to medical destruction of God-given life.

"We must talk to them kindly, and nonthreateningly, smiling at them, and beckoning to them with love and understanding, not condemnation or animosity. It is the great deceiver who has already won them over with a clouded view of what is right for them.

"They are sewing the seeds of bitterness and remorse with the destruction of their own unborn babies, getting ready to commit the most heinous form of child abuse, and yet what they will be doing is legal, by the most misguided of all rulings our supreme court has ever handed down. They are as tragic a victim of that terrible mistake as their unborn children, and we must love them back into the fold of those who have chosen life, not death.

"Each of us must at all times remember that the vast majority of the mothers we will be saving from the biggest mistake of their lives have only been treated with kindness by one side in this issue, the doctors, nurses, counselors and advisors for death, not life, and we are their last and only hope. It is a monumental task which we will pray about before we leave here tonight.

"And let's not kid ourselves, there will be some young ladies who will have nothing but disdain for us, those who feel very strongly about what they firmly believe is their own right to choose the fate of the life that lies within them. They will be madder at us than at anyone else they've ever come into contact with, as though we are their worst enemies. They will look at us with absolute hatred in their eyes, and we must not respond in kind.

"Do any of you have any questions at this time?" Sister Rose Alba asked.

In the quiet of the large room, Myra Tinkerton raised her hand tentatively. "Sister, we'll be breaking the law," Myra said meekly, her voice cracking. "I've never broken the law before."

The old teacher smiled sympathetically and tilted her head to the side in understanding.

"Well, you know, it doesn't even really matter if abortion is declared legal or illegal by local or state governments, or even by the supreme court of our land. There is, of course, a higher power to answer to if you do choose to do so. Now I am an old lady, a very old lady. I weigh seventy-eight pounds. I have no strength. Any one of you can walk right up to me now and kill me. But you may not, because it is written that thou shalt not kill.

"The United States Supreme Court has, of course, been misguided at some times in its history. A war was fought in this country not too long ago by many of our ancestors over slavery, while the United States Supreme Court called black people three-fifths of a human being. Our country was dealt with very severely by the higher power for that indiscretion.

"The frightening thing is that we've actually regressed in our times, not recognizing unborn babies as any percent human, with no right to the protection of their lives. Our country will be dealt with very severely if we do not again correct the mistake of our highest court.

"As far as this issue is concerned, our country was going in the right direction under Presidents Reagan and Bush, but now with the election of President Clinton, we are off track once again. It ought to shock all of us to attention. We must be vigilant and do all that we can to change the tone of moral awareness in our country or we will be dealt with again.

"We can start by making sure that there are no abortions in our little town, whether or not they are called legal by the supreme court of our country."

Myra Tinkerton listened to Sister Rose Alba intently and nodded in agreement when she was finished.

"We'll meet right here, the day after tomorrow, just after seven-thirty mass. We'll drive to the clinic and be there to greet the ladies who are going in, and God willing we'll be able to turn some of them around. Before we leave here tonight, we must do one last thing. Let's all join hands and ask the blessings of the Lord our God on our efforts."

In the cavernous echoes of the huge auditorium, the sparsely attended meeting came to a close with a prayer by Sister Rose Alba as another scene, which would have explosive consequences in Indian Springs less than forty-eight hours later, was unfolding several miles east in Boston, Massachusetts.

▲ ▼ ▲

On his way home from Somalia, Kevin O'Hara realized that he had not felt as good since he was a small boy in the comfort and security of his three-person family when his whole world consisted of his father, Sean; his mother, Colleen; and himself. In the transport plane, he had smiled the whole time on his way home from the very satisfying and rewarding mission he and his fellow Americans had completed, saving the lives of thousands of Somalian people.

Listening to the laughter and happiness of his fellow Americans on the way home, he suddenly realized that the only thing that made any sense to him at the present moment was to go home and establish the same kind of home for his family that his father had created for him so many years before, before the unfortunate circumstances that led to his father's death.

Arriving in America, he secured a flight to Bradley International Airport in Windsor, Connecticut, and took a cab to Indian Springs. He spent only a minute with his mother, and hopped into his pickup truck to head toward Boston.

"Does she know you're home?" Colleen O'Hara asked her son as he ran toward his truck.

"No. I'm going to surprise her."

Within hours of his arrival in his country, he stepped out of his pickup and bounded up the front steps of his fiance's apartment.

Upstairs, Sherry was sitting in front of the TV set, cloistered from the rest of the world as she wrestled with her pregnancy dilemma, when the lobby buzzer rang.

"Who is it," Alanna asked through the speakers, and when Kevin answered, Sherry Lynn gasped in surprise.

"I'm not ready for this," she said frantically to Alanna as she got up and threw on her coat.

"Tell him you don't know where I am and haven't seen me for several days," Sherry said to Alanna as she threw together a bag of clothes that she could escape with.

When Kevin saw Alanna's face as she opened the door to him, he knew immediately that something was wrong. She looked very nervous, like she was hiding something, and his joy turned quickly to apprehension.

"It's me, Alanna, not a ghost. What's the matter?"

362

"Oh, Kevin, it's nothing. Come on in, it's good to see you. Do you want a cup of coffee?"

"Just want to know where Sherry is. I've been thinking about nothing else for days."

Alanna looked out of the apartment window at the grey skyline of Boston.

"I can't tell you where she is, Kevin. I don't know."

"Well, she's still living here, isn't she?" he asked.

"Yes, but I haven't seen her for a couple of days. Of course, I've been away myself," she lied.

"Lanna, there's nothing wrong, is there?" Kevin asked her, and she hugged him so she wouldn't have to look into his eyes.

"She's probably out taking a ride. She's got a new Lexus."

The next several hours were anxious ones for Kevin. He rode around to all the places he and Sherry used to go together and saw her face in every setting. He was smiling as he thought about how good it would be for both of them when they were married and living together on the farm, but nervous and uneasy about not being able to find her.

Meanwhile, Sherry was in the depths of her dilemma. For months she had put off her decision and carried the baby she did not know whether or not she wanted to have. She headed out of Boston immediately, and instinctively drove toward Indian Springs.

She was heading back to Indian Springs crying while Kevin was in Boston looking for her and anticipating their reunion. It did not make sense to her that she should be so confused. She knew she loved Kevin, and wanted to spend the rest of her life loving him. She knew he wanted children and to build up the old farm to where it used to be before he had been born, and she wanted very much to be able to make him happy. But she also knew that living on a farm seemed terribly lonely to her, almost a prison sentence, and she was not at all sure she was ready, or even willing, to have a child.

Then she looked back on her own childhood, which had been a constant war in her home. She thought about the wretched way her mother looked at her on the last day of her life, and the sickening smell of her stepfather the awful day that he had forced himself on her a few years later.

As she pulled onto the road that led up to Kevin's farm, she was crying very hard. A sick feeling crept over her as she drove past the farm, and she found herself driving to the hospital. A few moments later, she was sitting across the table from a frizzy-haired nurse in the counseling room of the new Indian Springs abortion clinic.

"I'll be with you in a minute, Honey," the middle-aged woman with the blown-out frizzy hairdo said to Sherry before she walked into the adjoining room. The nurse left the door open, by carelessness or design, and Sherry sat, dabbing her eyes with her handkerchief and listening to the conversation in the next room.

"It's a little bit late, but if you're bothered to the point where your mental health will be affected, then we can get it done. Do you have any other questions?" the nurse asked.

"I do," a young man's voice said quietly. "I don't really want her to have · this abortion," he said.

There was a silence in the clinic, and Sherry could not see the two women looking at one another as the man sat there uncomfortable and outnumbered.

"How do you feel about it, Honey?" the nurse asked.

"I want the abortion," the young girl said, very softly.

"You're sure?" the woman asked.

Sherry could not see the girl as she cocked her head and glanced over at the young man, and then over at the nurse, and nodded her head hesitatingly.

"Well, you know, of course, that it's her choice and not yours," the nurse said authoritatively to the young man.

Sherry was listening closely, but she did not hear any other sound from the room. A few moments later, the young couple walked out of the room, looking very nervous and a little bit scared.

A few moments later, she was sitting in the office of Dr. Mohammed Patel, across the table from the man who could make one of her dilemmas go away. After consulting with him for a few moments, she nodded, and he said one final thing to her as she headed out the door.

"Just make sure you get here tomorrow morning at six-thirty, no later. We've heard that there is going to be a protest march done on the clinic tomorrow morning, and we want to have you all taken care of before that happens."

She registered at the Springs House Hotel for one night and cried herself to sleep.

Back in Boston, Kevin was getting very frustrated. He searched the city all day and late into the night, and after the last nightclub closed he went back again to Sherry's apartment. Alanna let him in, and he asked her if he could sleep on the couch to wait for Sherry. As Alanna went back to bed, her heart was aching for the both of them. It seemed as though she had just dozed off to sleep when the phone rang in her bedroom. She looked at her alarm clock, and it said 5:15.

Sherry was crying when Alanna answered the phone.

"Have you seen him again?" Sherry wanted to know.

"He's here, Sherry, sleeping on the couch, waiting for you."

"Well, keep him there. Tell him I'll be home this afternoon. I'm going to have an abortion this morning."

"Honey, are you all right?" Alanna whispered into the phone, and Sherry was crying when she hung up.

As she lay back on the pillow, she saw Kevin standing in her doorway.

"What's the matter, Lanna. Tell me," he said with deep concern in his eyes.

Then it was Alanna's turn to cry. She turned over in her bed and sobbed into her pillow. Kevin sat on the side of her bed and touched her shoulder.

"Please, Alanna, tell me what's wrong."

"Oh, Kevin," she said, rolling over and looking up into his deep brown eyes. "I told her I wouldn't say anything to you, but I love you both too much to keep quiet. She's so, so confused, and she's about to do something I know she'll regret for the rest of her life if she goes through with it."

Kevin didn't have a clue what was coming next, but Alanna's words hit him like a bolt of lightning.

"She wanted to tell you before you left for Somalia, but she didn't know how. She found out she was going to have your baby several weeks before you fought Homer Jones."

With his heart quickening in his chest, Kevin did some quick calculating in his mind to determine how long ago that was, because it seemed like ancient history to him now.

"She never told you because she wasn't sure she was going to carry it to term. Some days she wants it, and some days she doesn't."

Suddenly, the rush of the impending tragedy started sweeping over him as he grabbed Alanna's shoulders and demanded with his eyes to know the rest.

"She's in Indian Springs, getting ready to go to the clinic to have an abortion."

The look of fear and anxiety that swept across Kevin O'Hara's face seared into Alanna's memory as he leaped up and ran out of the room, knocking over a nightstand in his rush.

She jumped out of bed, ran to the door, and yelled at Kevin's back. "Please don't tell her that I told you, Kevin."

He was out on the street before she finished, and she heard the tires of his pickup burning rubber as he slammed the truck into gear and raced out toward the highway. He drove up over curbs, around traffic and through red lights as he tore out of the city in breathtaking speed. On the highway, the needle on his speedometer was buried as he dangerously weaved in and out of traffic.

Back in Indian Springs, Joey Bellino and Khalid Amin each took one of Sister Rose Alba's arms as they escorted her into church for what was to be the last daily mass she would ever attend in her life. They walked slowly and deliberately, one small, slow step at a time, as the organist played soft slow music and the small congregation of worshippers knelt and prepared for daily mass.

Out on the highway, Kevin O'Hara flew toward Indian Springs in a whir, and at that precise moment, in a well-lit sanitary room in the abortion clinic, the ultimate human tragedy visited itself upon four small human lives.

∧　∨　∧

Everything in its world was warm, soft, and pliable. Safety and comfort was the rule of order. And then its world was shattered. Suddenly, and without warning, the most unimaginable horror pierced its life. Hard, cold, and relentlessly painful, the intruder penetrated its universe. It recoiled in pain and abject terror as the limbs on its lower body were torn away. It opened its eyes and mouth wide and reached down to try and hold onto what was already gone, only to feel the intruder returning to rip away its arms as well.

Its heart pounded thunderously as it sensed there was to be no escaping the fatal assault. Where else could it go? It was already in the safest place in the universe, where sanctity did not permit such an obscene intrusion.

The final thrust tore through its heart and entered its brain, and consciousness was forever lost.

On the operating table, the alert, calculating doctor assembled the parts of the aborted fetus as its mother stared into the wall impassively.

"You'll be fine now, Jennifer." The frizzy-haired nurse smiled at the woman whose inconvenience had been cut away. "You're not pregnant anymore."

▲   ▼   ▲

As mass ended and a small crowd of onlookers started to gather at the front entrance to the abortion clinic, a small group of people assembled at the door of Saint Patrick's Church.

"Where's Celia?" Sister Rose Alba asked, looking around. At her home on Highland Terrace, Celia Rinaldi Franklin lay in her bed and wept into her pillow, unable to tear herself away from her father's or her husband's commands, and opting, instead, to abandon her alliance with the small band of protesters who prepared themselves for their attempts to head off the abortions that had been scheduled for opening day of the new abortion clinic.

"Many are called, but few are chosen," Sister Rose Alba whispered to Joey Bellino, who helped her into the car that would take them to the clinic.

Burying her head into her pillow, Celia Franklin felt traitorously empty, like she imagined the apostle Peter to have felt the morning he denied Christ.

▲   ▼   ▲

Patel reached into the birth canal and pulled the baby's legs out first. It was a perfectly formed little girl, and he pulled everything out except the baby's head. The nurse looked away as soon as she handed him the scissor-like instrument, because she knew she would get sick if she watched the rest of it.

He calmly inserted the scissors up through the back of the baby's neck into her brain, and opened them when they were inside. Then her brains were sucked out, her cranial cavity emptied of all matter, and she went limp in his hands.

Thus executed, the small girl was pulled the rest of the way out, and discarded into the plastic lined wastebasket at his feet.

▲ ▼ ▲

A few minutes later, the car pulled up to the abortion clinic, and five people stepped out: Myra Tinkerton, Khalid Amin, Joey and Allison Bellino, and a very pale and drawn Sister Rose Alba. As they walked slowly and carefully toward the entrance, Joey and Khalid held Sister Rose Alba's arms as Allison and Myra followed. The small crowd of about forty other people spread apart silently as the old nun was escorted to the steps that led into the clinic.

▲ ▼ ▲

It was asleep, quietly developing in warmth and comfort, when something went wrong. There was an alarm sent through its sense of balance, a pulling sensation that was foreign to its experiences, a downward suctioning of its universe, drawing it within itself, and enveloping it in the downward spiral, painfully crushing it until it lost consciousness from the crushing pressure and pain.

"That it?" the young woman asked from her prone position on the killing table.

"Dat's all dere is do id, Ms. Smith," Mohammed Patel answered clinically, the third of his four scheduled procedures now completed.

▲ ▼ ▲

Outside, a pickup truck sped up the driveway and squealed to a screeching halt in front of the building.

▲ ▼ ▲

She lay on the table frowning and fighting back tears, surprised at her own reaction to the impending procedure. She had considered herself much stronger than this.

"Will it hurt?" she asked the dark-eyed doctor.

"Id will feel a liddle bid uncomfordable, dad's all," the Indian doctor answered her.

"Not me," she sobbed, "the baby."

"Don'd wordy," Doctor Patel answered. "Id will be over in no dime."

▲ ▼ ▲

He slammed shut the door of his pickup truck and ran headlong through the crowd of people. He recognized no one and crashed through the doors of the clinic with one sole thought on his tormented mind.

▲　▼　▲

The pain was excruciating as the outside layer of its skin burned off first, and when it gasped in agony, it inhaled the saline solution parching its lungs. Its breaths came in short frantic gulps as it panicked and thrashed against hope in a horror from which there was no escape. Suddenly it was thrust out into a new universe where the air accentuated the burning agony. The lights closed its eyes against its new universe, and it was twisted, crushed, and then thrown downward until its fall was abruptly halted by the cold plastic it landed against. Its back broke with the impact.

At that moment, the doors to the extermination chamber burst open, and Sherry Lynn looked up with a start into the wide, terrified eyes of Kevin O'Hara.

"Am I too late?" he screamed frantically, rushing across the room.

Mohammed Patel and the frizzy-haired nurse stood between Kevin and Sherry, and the nurse put her hands up onto Kevin's chest.

"Hey, you can't . . . ."

He never let her finish. He tossed them both aside like rag dolls, the doctor slamming against his table of lethal instruments, which sent them clanging in various directions across the room. The nurse tumbled through the swinging doors head over heels into the wall on the other side of the hallway.

He screamed at her again, his face drawn up in frenetic anxiety, "Sherry, for God's sake, answer me! Am I in time or too late?"

He looked at her in agonizing shock, his powerfully conditioned legs growing weak underneath him as his mind raced through the emotions of denial, hurt, and revulsion.

She cocked her head sideways, covering her eyes sorrowfully, tears welling up in her eyes.

"Oh, Sherry, no," he whispered, the blood draining out of his face as he weakened from the weight of his sadness, and she turned away from his eyes.

And then it happened. Shockingly. Unexpectedly. Horrifyingly. It sounded so near, and yet so distant, the small, desperately pleading cry coming from somewhere near the bottom of the table. They all heard it at once, Sherry from her table, Patel from the corner of the room, and Kevin from where he stood, inches away from the source.

He looked instinctively toward the source of the cry–the green plastic wastebasket at the foot of the table. Looking in, he gasped in abject horror and saw the most inexplicably horrible sight. There, in the waste heap of the garbage bag, was a little baby–*his* little baby–looking up at him, reaching for him prayerfully while crying in agony and fear, its skin reddened by the burning saline solution, its eyes wide with horror, its mouth wide open in a desperate scream for help.

As tenderly as he could, propelled into action by the plight of his only begotten child, he reached into the waste heap and pulled his baby out, off the top of another baby lying dead and covered with blood below his, but when he did, his hands hurt the little one, who reacted to push them off, and before he could do anything, the baby thrashed and gasped a couple of times, and then went limp in his hands, its eyes locked open in ignominious horror.

Mohammed Patel stared at the helplessly empty man who held his dead child in his hands, and Sherry Lynn rushed out of the room covering her face against the shame.

Involuntarily, Kevin O'Hara fell to his knees on the floor, unable to move, his heart pounding rapidly in his chest, beads of sweat dripping off of his forehead, his breaths coming in short bursts, his horrified eyes fixed on the blank wall across the room and away from the remnants of the human life he clutched to his chest. The baby was the child he had begotten and sought futilely to defend, and then save, whose death sentence he had neither the ability nor legal standing to protest or overrule by the law of the land of his birth.

▲　▼　▲

Outside the front door of the clinic, Joey Bellino glanced down at his wristwatch, and saw that it was only eight-thirty, a half an hour before the scheduled opening time of the new abortion clinic. Crowds of spectators were starting to form, as people from both sides of the raging national issue displayed placards and posters with various competing slogans and pictures.

On the top step of the clinic, Sister Rose Alba sat down, looking very weak and very pale.

"If we're going to lock arms and block the entrance, I'll be on the end," Joey Bellino whispered to the old nun.

"No, Joseph. We'll not impede anyone. As I have already told you, we must love the young mothers into our fold, not hamper them or block them in any way. Our whole approach must be totally non-threatening and absolutely non-violent."

She looked very old and very sickly all of a sudden, and Allison Bellino and Myra Tinkerton sat down next to her, each of them holding one of her arms. She had never told any of them that she was dying of cancer. They never knew.

Inside, the frizzy-haired nurse called the police after she was thrown through the doors by Kevin O'Hara, and no one on the outside knew that the morning's abortions had already been done. Far off in the distance, sirens wailed as several police cruisers from the state police barracks in Indian Springs screamed up Main Street toward the clinic.

As the sirens got closer and closer, the crowd of people turned their heads toward the driveway, and when a dozen cruisers surrounded the entrance, the people backed off leaving only the five protesters assembled at the entrance.

Fifteen policemen approached the five, and when they got to them, they were met at the front door by Doctor Patel and the frizzy-haired nurse. Patel whispered something into the police lieutenant's ear and he nodded and yelled out his orders to his men.

"Ask these people to leave, and if they don't, take them away by force," he said, and he followed Doctor Patel into the clinic.

When Joey Bellino looked up, he saw Roland DellaSandro, his father's old partner on the force.

"You gonna throw us in the paddy-wagon, Roland?" Joey asked his friend.

"Not if I can help it, Joe. Please don't make me. Why don't you all just get up and go away."

"Can't do it, Roland," Joey answered, sitting down on the stoop next to Sister Rose Alba.

"Okay, boys, take these two ladies away," Sergeant DellaSandro said, and eight troopers lifted Myra Tinkerton and Allison Bellino up, one on each limb, and carted them off to the paddy wagon. The ladies went limp, in symbolic solidarity with the way an unborn baby goes to his death—helplessly and without a chance.

"Joey, please. Don't break my heart," Roland begged Joey. "If I have to arrest you it will be the saddest day of my life."

"If I don't let you, it will be a much sadder day for the little innocents who lose their lives here today, Roland. Do what you have to do."

Roland DellaSandro shook his head in sorrow and pointed to the two men flanking Sister Rose Alba on the steps. The eight officers lifted Joey Bellino and Khalid Amin up and carried them off to the paddy wagons as well, leaving only Sister Rose Alba sitting on the stoop.

She was bent over in prayer, and she looked small, frail, and sickly as Roland DellaSandro knelt down beside her.

"Sister, I'm so sorry, Sister, but we have to arrest you too," Sergeant DellaSandro said.

Fifteen Connecticut State Police troopers stood around Sister Rose Alba as a crowd of over a hundred people stood and watched the spectacle unfolding before their eyes. The troopers just stood there, waiting for a moment to see if the old nun would give up her stance, and no one noticed the man who walked around the side of the building or the macabre bundle he held clutched to his chest protectively.

Sergeant DellaSandro nodded to his men, and just as they reached down to lift up Sister Rose Alba, the scene was disturbed by a voice from the side of the building.

"Take your hands off that nun," Kevin O'Hara commanded gutturally.

The troopers turned and saw Kevin O'Hara standing there.

"I have to show you something," Kevin said, distraught.

"Dere he is!" Mohammed Patel shouted out to the lieutenant who had followed him into the clinic, and the lieutenant put his hand on his service revolver.

"We can take you peacefully or by force," the lieutenant said to Kevin O'Hara, loud enough for everyone to hear.

Kevin had a hollow look in his eyes as he slowly walked toward the policemen. Mohammed Patel stood by the policemen's side as Kevin held the bundle in his hands out to the lieutenant.

"He killed my baby," Kevin said painfully, choking back the tears that were welling up in his eyes as he attempted to show the lieutenant his dead child.

"I don't know what kind of a sick prank you're trying to pull, son, but you can put that thing down and surrender or we'll throw the cuffs on you."

Kevin's expression turned to dismayed puzzlement as he looked at the lieutenant. The abortioner stamped his foot down as he got right into the lieutenant's ear.

"Dad's da man who azzaulded me in da clinic!" Doctor Patel insisted. "Addest him ad once!"

The abortioner reached out and tried to grab the dead child out of Kevin's hands, knocking it to the ground. When Kevin dove to try and catch it, he was converged upon by several state troopers who attempted to wrestle him to the ground. When he started to resist, to try and get to the body of his dead baby, the rage that suddenly swept over him infused him with a rush of strength and he instinctively fought back. He swung at several police officers, knocking more than one of them to the ground with his superior strength. In the struggle one of the officer's service revolvers went off, the bullet entering the ground harmlessly.

A collective gasp spread through the crowd, which dispersed as the troopers roughly threw Kevin to the ground, cuffing his hands behind his back and kneeling on his neck. Then they put a straight-jacket around him and picked him up to carry him away to a cruiser.

In the excitement and confusion, no one noticed as the abortioner, Mohammed Patel, picked up the dead child and ran back into the clinic, unhampered by any of the police officers who were directing all of their attention at Kevin O'Hara.

Immediately after Kevin was whisked away in the cruiser, the troopers returned their attention to Sister Rose Alba. Clutching her rosary beads, she was wiping tears from her eyes as they lifted her up and carried her away.

At the police barracks in Indian Springs, the lieutenant was told that there was no room at any of the prisons in Enfield, Suffield, or Somers, and that the six protesters would have to be held in the two prison cells in the barracks overnight.

All six protesters were booked for trespassing and interfering with the civil rights of women. In addition to those charges, Kevin O'Hara was charged with creating a public disturbance, resisting arrest, and seven counts of assaulting a peace officer.

They were placed in two adjoining cells, the women in one cell and the men in the other, and Kevin O'Hara was left in leg irons. As the hours passed by, it became apparent, because of the overcrowding in other correction facilities in the area, that the cells they were in were going to be their homes for awhile, at least until they could be tried on charges brought against them that day.

That afternoon, when the prisoners were being told that their meals would soon be served to them, they turned to arouse Sister Rose Alba, whom they thought had gone to sleep, but it soon became apparent that she had passed out and could not be revived.

"The old nun needs medical care!" a young trooper yelled out to a fellow officer, and twenty minutes later, Dr. Franklin entered her cell.

As the three men in the adjoining cell looked on, Kevin O'Hara made a startling announcement to his two cell mates.

"If she dies, I take her place," he said quietly, and neither man understood what he meant at that moment.

Doctor Franklin knelt over her, to check her vital signs, but he soon looked up at the other people in the room with the startling announcement.

"She's dead," he said blankly, and Joey Bellino closed his eyes and lay his head up against the cell bars.

Twenty minutes later, after her body had been removed, the evening meals were served to the five remaining prisoners, and at first no one noticed when Kevin O'Hara sat staring at his meal blankly while everyone else started to eat.

Soon, they were all looking at him quizzically. He looked up at them somberly. "I'll eat when the abortion clinic is closed," he said, and as the four others looked at him, he pushed his tray away.

He refused breakfast the next morning, and lunch and dinner as well, and Joey Bellino sat down next to him and stared at him. "What are you doing, man?" Joey asked him, putting his arm around his shoulder.

"I told you last night what I'm doing. That's all I'm going to say about it. I'll leave it up to you to tell the proper people about it."

Joey Bellino stared at Kevin O'Hara nervously. None of the other prisoners had yet grasped the seriousness of the situation.

"Kevin, you don't have to do that," Joey said to him, attempting a smile. "It's probably the worst thing in the world you can do for a whole slew of reasons, not the least of which is that the administrators of the clinic might hold you to it and not close down."

Kevin lay back on his cot, his hands folded behind his head calmly, and looked up, deep into his cousin's eye.

"Then I'll die," Kevin said to Joey matter-of-factly, and then Joey started to shake.

"Guard!" Joey Bellino yelled out loudly, and an officer came into the cell area.

"Listen to me carefully. You have to let the world know what is happening in here. My cousin is on a hunger strike and he won't eat until the abortion clinic is closed down."

The young officer stared back at Joey Bellino sarcastically.

"Ri-i-ght," the officer said. "And he wants Roe versus Wade overturned too, right? Okay, Hoss, I'll get right on it."

"Please, officer," Joey Bellino begged passionately. "I don't think you know my cousin Kevin. He doesn't say things he doesn't mean."

The young officer walked back to his desk and lifted up the newspaper he was reading, leaning back in his chair and putting his feet up on the desk as he reached for his donut.

Joey walked back and stared down at Kevin O'Hara with tears welling up in his eye. Kevin looked back at him coolly, not the least bit nervous or concerned.

The next day, the prisoners told everyone they came into contact with during visiting hours about Kevin's hunger strike, and the only people on the outside who exhibited any real concern were Celia Franklin and Kevin's mother, Colleen.

Celia started a massive campaign to get the word out what Kevin was doing and started calling senators and congressmen, as well as state legislators, representatives, and news media people from newspapers, radio, and television.

It was three weeks before anyone would take her seriously. Everyone fully expected Kevin to end his hunger strike as soon as the agony became too intense. Prosecutors postponed the trials of the prisoners to give themselves more ammunition when Kevin ended his strike, readying themselves to attack the level of commitment they had to their conscientious objection to abortion as soon as Kevin ate something.

For two more weeks, the standoff continued and no one seemed to be taking Kevin's strike seriously until, on the thirty-ninth day of his strike, he announced that he would be making a statement at suppertime the following night.

Press reporters gathered to write the story of Kevin O'Hara's abandonment of his hunger strike after forty days, and his simple statement startled them with its directness and determination.

"I never expected my hunger strike to overturn Roe versus Wade. But I made it clear on the first day that I would not eat until the abortion clinic in

Indian Springs is closed down. Over fifty people have been murdered in the clinic since the last time I ate any food. Fifty people with no voice. I am the voice of the unborn. I will say it to you one more time, and then never again. Until the abortion clinic in Indian Springs is closed down, I will not eat. That is my final public statement."

The next day hundreds of people lined up outside the abortion clinic, and people from all across the country started this time to converge on the clinic. In respect for Sister Rose Alba's approach, no one was prevented from entering the clinic, and every time law enforcement officials asked protesters to leave the grounds, they walked just outside the perimeter of the grounds and took up their protests there.

Kevin was visited by many people, prominent and common, right up until the fifty-third day of his strike, when he became very sick and started to hallucinate.

Over and over again in his mind, a jumble of thoughts assaulted him, from being pinned to his chair as his father was killed in the ring to being held back in slow motion as he struggled against immovable objects trying to get to his child before doctors and nurses killed it. He was moaning incoherently as his fellow strikers called for help.

"He needs to be moved to a hospital," medical officials told state police officials, who had long since removed his leg irons after his weight dropped down to under ninety pounds from the two hundred pounds he had weighed before starting his strike.

The room they assigned to him on the third floor of Bradford Memorial Hospital overlooked the abortion clinic that was the object of his protest. All day, he lay quietly, staring out the window at the brick building as though forcing his will upon the inanimate structure.

Every day of his strike, he was permitted only one visitor, his mother, and the jokes that were circulated about him were just as sick as the ones that had followed Bobby Sands to his grave a decade previously.

"Did you hear that they won't let Kevin O'Hara's mother visit him any more?" the joke started. "They caught her breast feeding him."

While some people in the country laughed and others prayed amid the feeding frenzy of newspaper reporters, Kevin O'Hara fought bed sores and fever as he remained locked in his irrevocable decision. In the sixty-fifth day of his strike, while he lay dangerously near death, his mother knew that if it was always only a matter of time, her son's time was very, very near.

▲　▼　▲

When the sun began to set over the Caribbean horizon, the band started pumping up the volume. People flooded out of their seats onto the dance floor and the lines got longer at the bars on either end of the cruise ship's dance floor.

The breezes were softer and much more pleasant than they'd been in the heat of the tropical day as Sherry and Alanna sat with two younger men, soccer players from South America, Sherry thought they said in their broken English.

The more aggressive of the two men was with Alanna, one of his hands down the back of her skirt while the other rubbed the inside of her thighs.

"Not so hard," she grinned and blushed. "I have a sunburn."

She was flirting with him with her eyes and mouth as she brushed her hair back off her face and wrapped her tongue around the straw in her tropical drink, huddling closer to him and the heady scent of his cologne.

Sherry felt sorry for the other man. He was much nicer than the gold-chained gigolo hanging all over Alanna. He was trying just as hard with Sherry but in a less aggressive way, and she was very close to deciding to reward his efforts when Alanna got up and waved at Sherry quickly, giggling and waving her hand like a fan across her reddened face.

Sherry smiled as the two of them rushed away.

"I'm going to use our cabin," Alanna shouted back over her shoulder. "You'll have to use his."

Sherry glanced at the other man, who was staring at her hungrily, and she smiled as he slid closer to her.

He's not a bad looking guy, she thought. *And much nicer than Alanna's. If I don't sleep with him, it'll ruin his vacation, and then the other guy will talk his ear off about Alanna.*

The air smelled like salt water and seaweed, a smell Sherry loved, as the young man touched her hand and nodded toward the sleeping quarters.

"Not yet," she said. "Let's have another drink first."

▲　▼　▲

In the quiet sunlight of his hospital room, Colleen held Kevin's hand and looked into his determined eyes. He looked so frail to her in his emaciated condition. This was the boy she had watched with an admiration bordering on awe as he banged away at the punching bags his father had left to him as his legacy. Now, at little more than seventy barely life-sustaining pounds, he looked small to her, and weak, even though she knew he was the strongest person she had ever known.

A noise in the hallway distracted both of them momentarily, and a young nurse walked over to the bed.

"Mr. O'Hara, Mrs. O'Hara, you have a visitor who absolutely insists upon visiting you both," the young nurse said.

Colleen and Kevin looked over at the door, and a powerfully built black man with dark glasses walked in carrying a bouquet of flowers in one hand and something rolled up in the other.

"Mom, I'd like you to meet Homer Jones," Kevin said weakly as Colleen O'Hara stood up to face her husband's killer.

"Mrs. O'Hara, these flowers are for you," he said, his voice quivering.

She reached out and took them, unable to smile at the man yet.

"I know that an awful lot of time has passed since that night in Las Vegas when I met your husband."

He stood erectly, neatly dressed in a black suit, his voice continuing to quiver as he failed to hide his attempts to conceal his nervousness.

"I was a very young man then. I was confused and only one thing in the world mattered to me at the time. I wanted to be champion of the world because I wasn't champion of anything at all in my personal life. I didn't know Sean O'Hara from Adam, or anything about his personal or family life. I didn't know he had such a lovely wife, or such a remarkable son who he loved so much. If I had known, I would never have killed him."

He turned away from her and looked out the window at the abortion clinic.

"I hope you can find it in your heart to forgive me," he said, quietly and somberly, unable to look directly into Colleen O'Hara's eyes.

Colleen O'Hara laid her flowers down on her son's bed and walked over to the old champion, holding both of his hands in hers. He looked down at her, and she took off his dark glasses so she could look into his eyes.

"Only one man was perfect," she whispered to him compassionately, the crucifix she wore around her neck glistening in the light of the sun. "He'll be back someday."

With those words, Colleen O'Hara freed Homer Jones from the guilt that had tormented him in the inner recesses of his mind since that fateful day in Las Vegas so many years before.

"Yes'm," he answered her, taking her hands in his.

Kevin O'Hara watched this from his bed, and Homer's sincerity satisfied him. Next, Homer unrolled the other thing he had with him. It was his world championship belt.

"For what it's worth, this belongs to you," Homer said to him. "I'll be praying for you in the fight you're in now."

Homer laid the belt across Kevin's midsection, and walked out of the room. When the echoes of his footsteps were gone in the corridor, Colleen again turned to Kevin.

Looking down at what was left of his once-powerful body, Colleen's heart felt like a stone in her chest and the worry lined her face. Kevin felt compassion for her, knowing it had to be hard for her to see him like this.

"I think you probably better stop coming to see me, Mom. You knew it had to come to this."

Kevin's mother reached out and took his hand and searched for something that she could say to him.

"I just wish you weren't so damn stubborn," she whimpered.

"It's not a question of stubbornness. For me to quit now would be a coward's way out, not to mention the fact that it would set the anti-abortion movement back ten years. I won't do that to the millions of unborn people who will die if I give up now."

She wanted to argue with him, to tell him that living is never cowardly because of all the challenges that have to be dealt with each day, but she knew his resolve too well. To argue with him now would only make him more determined, so all she could do was sit and hold his hand and deal with her own broken heart. Still, she searched her soul for something, anything, that she could say to make him alter his course.

He attempted to smile at her with his mouth, but his brow was drooped in a frown.

"I don't know whether to hug you or punch you in the face," she said, and then she was crying. "You have so much to live for, Kevin," she said to him, her voice weak and strained.

Outside, the sky was dark and grey, and the chill in the air caused the young couple that Kevin saw walking together on the sidewalk across the street to huddle up closer together. He thought of his shattered dreams and the way his heart broke as he held his dead child, who would never laugh or love, and he did not feel that he had all that much to live for.

"I just want my life to count for something, Mom. Whatever is left of it. That's all."

"Look at you, all skin and bones. Do you know what they're saying about you? They're saying you're crazy and that you need psychiatric help. A lot of people are not taking you at all seriously. They're saying that to starve yourself to death is not something anyone would do who was pro-life."

"I'm not starving myself to death, Mom, they're doing it to me. They're treating me with as much disregard as they do the hundreds of people they kill every day in their clinics. All they have to do is close the clinic and I'll eat. That's all. The ball is in their court, not mine."

"Kevin, the authorities are not going to give you what you're asking for. They're calling you a religious fanatic, and their official stance is, 'We will not deal with terrorists.' They're even talking about applying some anti-racketeering law to your protest, linking you to organized crime and making you eligible for prosecution. Kevin, I want you to end your hunger strike. Please."

"I can't do it, Mom. When they killed my baby, they killed the last generation of our family. Millions of family trees are ending the same way. If we don't defeat abortion the whole country will pay a terrible price. Every great nation that ever existed had its Achilles' heel that brought it to its ruin. Slavery was Dixie's. Abortion is America's. There can be no compromise, Mom. Too many people have already died because pro-life people have been willing to let a bad Supreme Court decision stand.

"I can't overturn Roe versus Wade in a few short weeks. But I can keep an abortion clinic out of my own hometown. And we have to start somewhere. Besides, maybe a martyr is just what the cause needs."

"Kevin, you're my only son. Don't you have some other way?" his mother pleaded with him.

Kevin glanced over at the picture of Bobby Sands hanging on his wall.

"He didn't," Kevin said, nodding at the picture. And then, directing his mother's attention to the body of Christ, hanging on the crucifix next to it, "and neither did He."

With those words, Colleen knew that the die had been cast, and that there was nothing more that she could do. Her son's words were cast in concrete, along with his decision, and he was only hours away from being a dead man.

He had always been a no-compromise kind of person. That much Colleen knew about her son. That he had not attached himself to the abortion debate before now was probably only because it had not touched him directly until now. But with his strength of commitment, it was the worst possible issue for him to have become involved in if longevity of life was important to him.

"Kevin . . . ." She started to say something, but all she could do was fall across his chest and cry.

He hugged her, and ran his weakening hands across the top of her head, and suddenly he felt very weak and very tired.

The nurse in attendance dried her eyes and walked over to Colleen, touching her on the shoulder gently. Colleen looked up at the nurse, and then at the hollow eyes of her son, and for the final time, she leaned over and kissed him on the cheek.

At ten-thirty that evening, in the quiet of his hospital room, Kevin O'Hara inhaled the last breath his seventy-pound body could take, and when he exhaled and breathed no more, the nurse who was sitting with him shuddered and ran out of the room.

Ten minutes later, a doctor walked into the midst of the small group of reporters and curiosity seekers outside the front entrance and shook his head somberly. "He's gone," was all the doctor said, and as reporters threw questions at him, he just stood there trying to deal with his own personal thoughts.

"What was the exact time of death?"

"About ten-thirty," the tired doctor answered hollowly.

"Did he suffer much in the end?"

"I don't think he felt a thing."

"What were his last words?"

The doctor stood there and scanned the crowd, choking up momentarily when he saw two young college-age girls hugging each other and crying, and when he saw a sober-faced old man shaking his head back and forth with his hands stuffed down into his pockets, he suddenly did not want to be standing there any longer.

"I have no further statement," the old doctor said, and when he walked back into the hospital the crowd gradually dispersed as reporters ran for telephones and the others on their vigil walked slowly away.

▲　▼　▲

The four remaining protesters heard about Kevin's death on the eleven o'clock news, and Joey Bellino sat down heavily on his cell cot, covering his face with his hands.

Prosecutors were already scrambling to get to the trials of the other four, but they were not prepared for the remarkable response they heard about on the radio the next morning.

In their dank jail cells, Khalid Amin, Myra Tinkerton, and Joey and Allison Bellino were infused with new conviction when they heard of their comrade's martyrdom.

They talked long into the night, and by two o'clock their decision had been made.

Through the bars of their adjoining jail cells, Allison looked at Joey somberly, her expression a mixture of fear, determination, and conviction, the trust and belief she had always had in him ever in her eyes.

"If I don't follow him, who will?" Joey whispered to her.

"It's okay," she whispered back. "If you die, I'll follow you."

"And the boys?" Joey asked her.

"Michael and David will be fine," she answered him. "If living with you has taught me anything, it's that God takes care of his own. They're as good for your mother as she is for them, anyway."

In the background, Khalid Amin was listening intently, and he interrupted her. "No," he said to her, touching her arm softly. "You follow me. I'll die after Joey."

"And then I'll go," Myra Tinkerton said to Allison. "I'll die after Khalid. If it's still necessary, you can follow me. But you shouldn't go before us with two children at home. Maybe by the time we all die, you won't have to."

"This can't be smoke," Joey said to them softly, letting his eye make contact with each of theirs. "From any of us. It will require great courage, increasingly more so for each person who takes up the cause. The temptations to quit will be enormous."

"We were all chosen for a purpose," Allison Bellino said. "We won't give up the commitment."

So the extraordinary pact was made.

The next morning when the prison guards placed Joey Bellino's meal in front of him, Joey stared back at them quietly.

"Not in our town," he said simply, sliding it back across the table and refusing food for the first time.

"Not in our town," Allison Bellino, Myra Tinkerton, and Khalid Amin all repeated, raising their clenched fists together in solidarity with Joey Bellino as the guards stood there in stunned amazement.

When the word hit the streets that the disabled Vietnam veteran had taken up the hunger strike, the news spread through the media like wildfire. This time Celia Franklin did not cower. She organized a protest movement in a door to door campaign which had over three hundred people chanting and carrying signs outside the abortion clinic on the first night. The crowd swelled to over eight hundred by the third day into Joey Bellino's strike.

If the people were sad when Sister Rose Alba died, and stunned when Kevin O'Hara died, they were angered and aroused when Joey Bellino took up the cause.

On her quiet farmland north of town, Colleen Bradford O'Hara sat alone in her living room for the first three days of Joey Bellino's hunger strike, staring somberly at the wall across the room, as an idea began to germinate in her mind.

I can't believe it all happened this way, she thought sadly. *I just can't believe that Kevin is gone. But I can't let anyone else die, and I will not let him die for nothing. Bradford ancestors built this hospital before the abortion clinic was added on,* she thought. *Bradford descendants ought to be able to lop off the killing wing and leave it to do what it was originally intended to do. Both Kevin and his baby are dead because of it. There's just no reason for anyone else to die.*

Late on the third night of Joey Bellino's strike, she gave every detail of the idea quick, decisive approval, and decided to go through with it before time would change her mind.

At 10:15 she called Celia Franklin, who was living alone in an apartment in town, and told her to be ready in a half an hour. At 10:20 she put on some warm clothing and walked out to the barn. Her horse, Dancer's Prince, bobbed his head up and down, and followed her with his eyes as she loaded three large saddlebags with the heavy cargo for her horse to carry. She saddled up two other horses, and at 10:45 she patted their necks and talked to them quietly as she led them out into the moonlit night and faced them in the direction of Indian Springs.

Later that night, when Maura Bellino heard a knock on her door, Colleen O'Hara was more determined than ever to do what she had planned when she saw the absolutely terrified and helpless way Maura Bellino looked when she opened the door.

"You want to save your son?" Colleen asked Maura stoically as Maura stared frantically at Colleen and Celia.

"Yes," Maura Bellino answered meekly.

"Then get your coat and come with us," Colleen commanded, and the three women rushed out to the horses.

No one saw the three women riding by moonlight through the woods to the abortion clinic. When the horses and riders stopped at the top of a hill overlooking the back of the new clinic adjacent to the hospital, the horses were relieved when the riders dismounted and pulled the heavy saddlebags off of them.

Colleen tied the horses to trees at the edge of the woods, and at midnight, under the quiet moonlit sky, the women walked boldly down the hill toward the empty building. The horses took no more notice of them for the next few hours, as they busied themselves about their work.

The women stopped at several intervals around the building, on top of it, and finally inside of it, through a window they broke as quietly as they could in the night. They dispersed the heavy load in the saddlebags, chipping away at walls, and running lines from interval to interval in the night.

Four hours after they began, their night's work was finished and they walked quickly up the hill where Colleen again quietly patted the horses on their necks and headed them back up through the woods for home.

When they were a safe distance away, Colleen dismounted momentarily and turned the switch on something she held in her hands, and the deafening roar that followed startled Dancer's Prince, who jumped away before she mounted him again and led them back through the woods to her home.

"What in God's name was that?" the state trooper at the desk of the police barracks exclaimed, slamming all four legs of the chair he was resting on back onto the floor.

Outside, a massive explosion ripped through the night air, and the abortion clinic was blown into a million small pieces by the tremendous rippling explosion. Echoes from the deafening blast rolled down through the Willimantic River valley like thunder in the hills, waking up scores of people within several miles in every direction.

When the dust and smoke cleared, only an eight-foot-deep hole was left where the clinic used to be.

▲　▼　▲

"Turn them loose, I said," the voice at the other end of the receiver yelled at him. "We're dropping all the charges against them. Don't ask why, just let them out, and don't wait another minute. I don't want to hear any arguments about it either, do you understand?"

"Yes, sir," the lieutenant responded, and as dawn broke over the valley, he told the protesters what had happened, turned the key on their jail cells, and set them free.

They had been behind bars for so long that the dawn's early light caused them to squint. Khalid Amin put his arm around Myra Tinkerton and they walked away, leaving Joey and Allison Bellino standing on the steps of the town hall.

Out in the chill of the morning, the only sound was the water of the Willimantic River that rushed under the bridge behind the old Sean's Tavern that now served as an historical society.

Joey put his arm around Allison's waist as they looked out across the Main Street area, out past the river to the park.

"I'm hungry," Joey said to her. "Let's walk over to the Station Newsroom and get something to eat."

"This really is a very pretty little town, isn't it," Allison commented as they crossed the street and started walking up the sidewalk to the coffee shop.

"Always has been," he answered her. "Quiet and very nice. We'll give it to our children the way our generation leaves it. How that is, is in our hands."

Joey and Allison walked together arm in arm listening to the same river that had given the Indians so much pleasure for centuries before the first settlers had found the place so many years before.

"You know it's not over yet," she said to him, laying her head against him as they walked.

"I know it," Joey answered her. "We can't let Kevin die for nothing."

"What are we going to do now?" she asked him quietly, determined to fight side by side with him for the rest of their lives together, in anything he decided.

A gentle breeze blew a puff of sand across their path from the street, as they shuffled along the sidewalk. She was looking up at him confidently, feeling safe in the strength of his arm. He looked ahead somberly as he focused on the thought of small babies struggling alone against any hope for survival.

"I don't know, Allison," he answered her thoughtfully. "I don't know the answers to anything. I just know we gotta do something."

▲　▼　▲

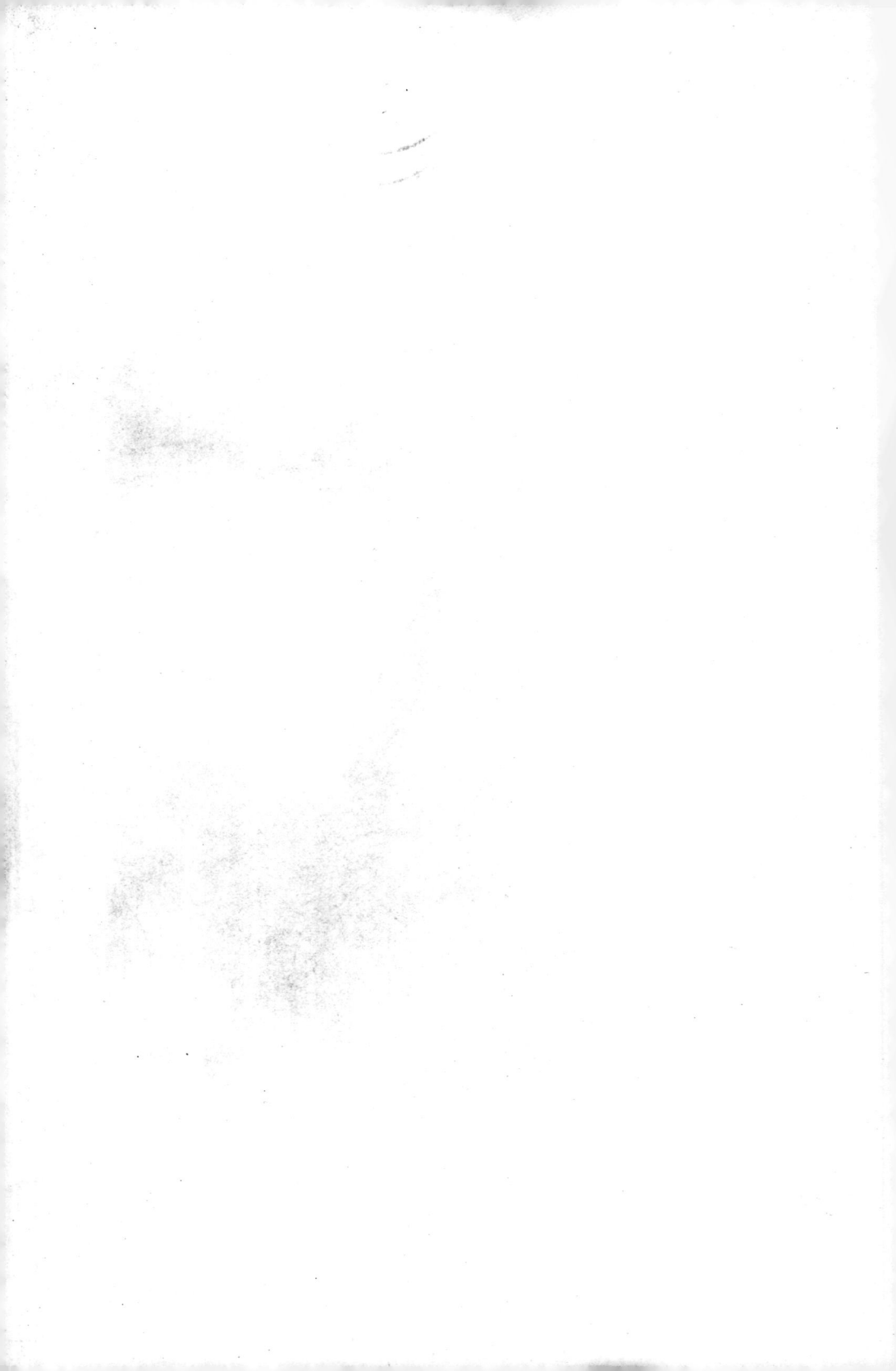